FIRE & NIGHT

FIRE & NIGHT

Book One of Warriors & Mages

V.K. Dixon

XHP
xenia house press

To my very own JD

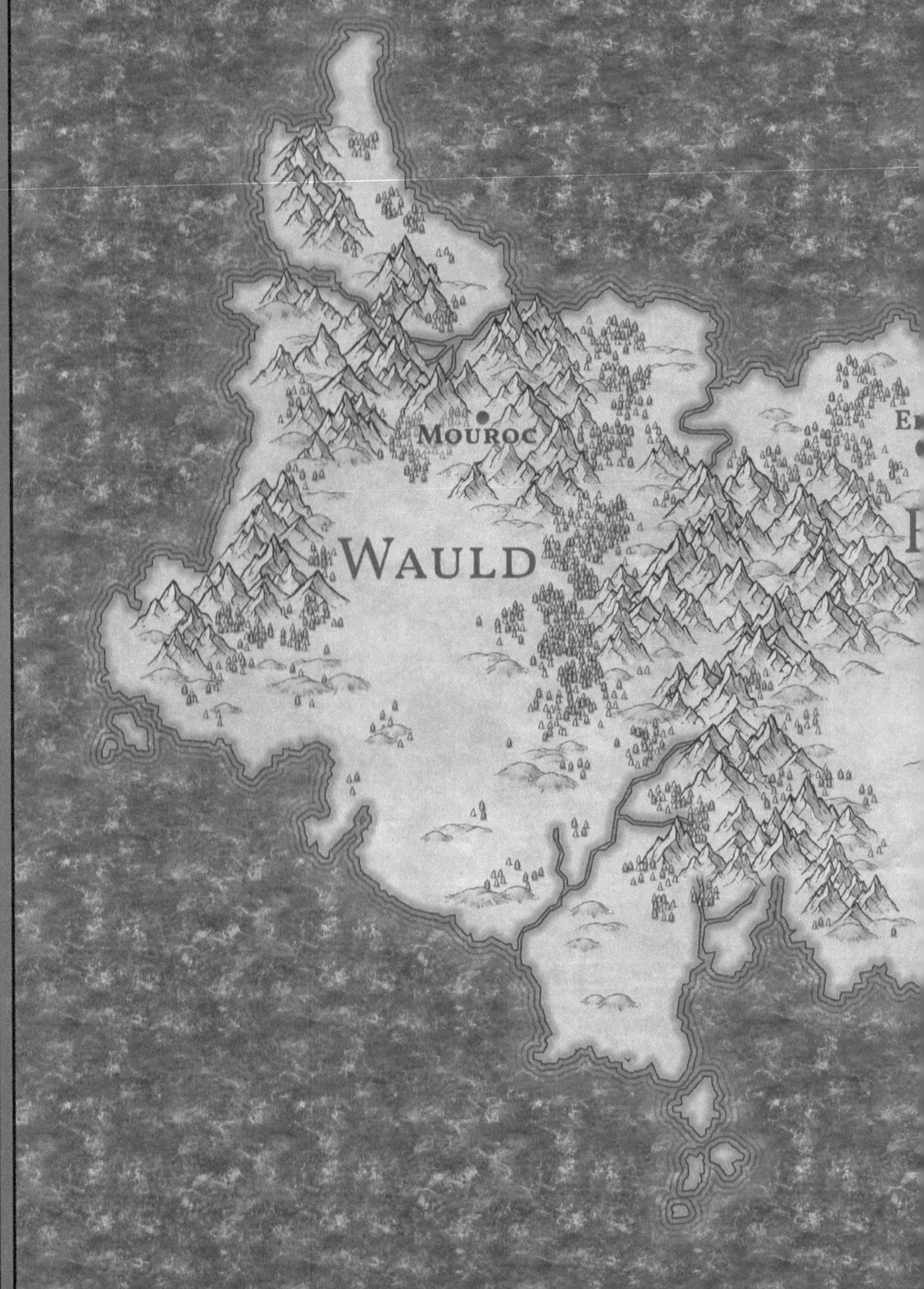

MOUROC
WAULD

HRIA
KEVES ISLAND
ISLE OF
ALLUND

Part I: Whickam Village

He rose with honor from the ivy
to smite the unjust heretics who practiced wicked arts,
to free the oppressed from their tyranny,
to vanquish evil at its core.
Our great and merciful Shepherd King.
Song of the Shepherd, v. 3

NETTERSHIRE
LEEDBURY
BERKELEY
TROLLESTON
WHICKAM VILLAGE
ESTSHIRE
HOUSFORT
BYLAND

CHAPTER ONE

10TH OF TERRAEN, 1573

Gripping the wooden seat of the cart, Evylin scanned the distant edge of Whickam Village. A cool breeze brushed across the valley over the rolling emerald grass, ivory patches of sheep dotting the landscape. With its weathered cottages tucked into the hillocks of southern Ephria, the sun cast a rosy hue onto the pale stone, morning and evening. Lush greenery bordered the buildings, and ivy climbed the walls and fences as though Terraeus itself was giving the village a warm hug.

Or as though it was trying to drag it down beneath the dirt.

Evylin never could quite decide the planet's intentions toward her home.

But as she scanned the edge of the quaint village in the pale afternoon light, tents, horse pens, campfires, and hundreds of men in uniform marred the picturesque view.

Seeing soldiers surrounding their village always sparked a conflict within Evylin. Her instinct was excitement, eyes darting about as the men practiced swordplay, huddled around campfires, and lined up by the kitchen tent. She envied their chance to travel and explore the whole of Ephria. Then her anticipation and intrigue dropped into concern.

Every time the Ephrian Army came to Whickam Village, it either took half the population or the majority of the food stores with it—sometimes both. The army marked trouble for the village, no matter the visit.

"They can't be drafting again," Evylin said, looking over to her uncle on the cart beside her. "We hardly had enough men for them the last time."

Hewitt's gray eyes flickered from the campsite, but he gave no response. Reins held loosely in one hand, he raised the other to scratch at his disheveled beard, singed from the forge and unkempt from bachelorhood. Hewitt bore every hallmark of a small-town blacksmith. As broad as two men, he carried so much muscle and height that he could frighten a bear.

The cart clattered down the dirt road, jarring Evylin's back. After hours on the road, she wished once more that she could ride one of the horses. It'd make the trips to and from Trollenston so much nicer. But the wares they took to sell at the market each season demanded a cart even as small and rickety as this.

"Can our army be so bad off that they need another draft?" Evylin whispered as though the soldiers might hear her from the half-mile distance.

The brown mare hitched on the right pulled at the reins in anticipation of home, and Hewitt tightened his grip. "It's not a draft," he said, his tone almost bored.

The wind cut through Evylin's coat, and she wrapped her arms across her chest. "How do you know?"

"You see those soldiers over there? The ones clustered around the fire." He nudged his head toward the group. "They're enjoying themselves. They're eating, talking, and laughing. That lot near the road is even playing pins."

Evylin watched the group cheer as the wooden ball knocked down all nine pins at once.

Hewitt kept his gaze on the road before them. "No, if this were a draft, these men would not be happy to be here."

"So why *are* they here?" Evylin asked.

Hewitt encouraged the horses with a flick of the reins. "I suppose we'll find out."

The rapid trot of the horses increased the cart's bumpy nature, but Evylin didn't mind, knowing they'd arrive home sooner. Then she could relieve her aching back with the short walk home and find out the truth behind the army's presence in her village.

A few short minutes brought them upon the encampment. Several soldiers glanced up as they passed through. Only a few were diligent enough to pay attention and assess if the newcomers' arrival required action. The rest continued with their prior engagement—whether merriment or work—oblivious to their arrival.

Evylin watched, wary of her uncle's assurances. She wasn't foolish enough to think the army would come this far into the Shires for no reason. Down here at the southeastern edge of Ephria, their province was a mere footnote to the king. Their farms and ports made their small settlements more valuable than some cities, but their distance from the capital made them easy to forget.

If King Ephren sent his men down to Estshire, it was for a reason of great significance.

Deeper into the camp, Evylin noticed a small group of soldiers sparring. Two officers coached them through their paces. Many of the men clutched their swords with clumsy grips. One dropped his altogether after his opponent swung, made contact, and then pitched forward from his momentum.

Evylin couldn't help laughing. "They're new," she whispered to her uncle.

Hewitt grunted.

Of course, he'd noticed. No doubt he'd observed more than she had in half the time.

The cart rumbled on, passing the buildings at the edge of the village. Due to the narrowness of the street, the horses slowed to a walk. To Evylin's right, Mrs. Lyvingston swept her porch, pausing to smile and wave at them. Evylin returned the greeting while Hewitt stared at the road ahead. This late in the day, many of the shopkeepers were busy closing up. Only the tavern kept its doors open past dusk, and even that closed earlier than any in Trollenston, shutting down after dinner.

A small group of soldiers walked past their cart. The men talked among themselves, their voices a blend of depths and tones. Their matching black-brown hair, richly pigmented skin of brown and bronze, and short stature marked them as deep Shire men. The farther south in Ephria, the better the odds of dark complexions and colorings. Even in Estshire, the average citizen bore a vibrant tan compared to the Northerners.

Evylin felt all these new southern recruits were evidence to prove a draft. Yet Hewitt's thick brows took on a decidedly disappointed tilt at the suggestion.

"Then why are there so many recruits?" she demanded.

"How should I know?" he replied, indifference in his gravelly monotone. "The Ephrian officers stopped informing me twenty years ago."

"Uncle."

"Evie."

"You were a general."

"*Were*, which means I'm not anymore. I'm not privy to the army's management these days."

"But you *were*, which means you know why they *might* be here."

"At best, it'd be speculation."

"Then speculate."

Hewitt let out a growl. His foul temper scared all four of Evylin's sisters—and most of the villagers, for that matter. But she'd always found it endearing.

"They're volunteers," he grumbled. "The army must be looking to bolster their numbers, and they've decided to come into the Shires for recruits."

The idea seemed ridiculous to Evylin. "Who do they expect to find? They took all our men five years ago."

Hewitt didn't respond.

The street widened as they entered the village center. To the left, another road led toward Berkley, a two-day journey north. Along that route lay most of the homes and farms within Whickam Village's boundaries. Evylin never spent much time out there. Though her father was the magistrate now, he'd once been the village smith, raising his family in the square, making it her home.

Straight ahead, the village hall welcomed them back. Despite the repairs made more than a decade prior, soot marks still stained its peppery stone exterior. Evylin turned away from the building. All the important meetings and holiday parties took place within its walls. Her father, Magistrate Lawton Glaas, also used it to preside over his cases, no matter how few a year. But Evylin did her best to avoid the building, as did Hewitt, unwilling to relive the memories the building carried.

Despite its dwindling size and lack of need for a magistrate, her father managed Whickam Village under the authority of King Ephren. Over thirty years ago, the settlement was large enough to require such a lawful presence. But the Ephrian Army had drafted almost half the population since that time, and there wasn't much need for law and order anymore. The draft took their prior magistrate as well, the man being one year shy of the cutoff. They hadn't seen Magistrate Caarlton since and had only heard from him a handful of times. The village gossips said how fortunate he was, only leaving behind his widowed mother. Frequent were the remarks on the luck of the bachelor, saying what an absolute shame it would have been if he'd left behind a wife and children.

Despite the earlier magistrate's so-called luck, the draft had not dealt most villagers such a favorable hand.

With all the men between the ages of seventeen and forty-five drafted five years ago, the few who remained were either sons too young or grandfathers too old to be of much use. It had left many of the women in Whickam Village either widowed, married but alone, or single. The few men who returned, discharged from the army, experienced so much trauma or injury that they were of little good to the women during their first years back.

Thankfully, Lawton Glaas was there to step up those five years ago, helping the village stay alive and thriving. Or, at least, that's what Evylin's father promised the populace when he'd nominated himself for the vacant magistrate's position. Once a soldier himself, he knew how to run the perfect regime. He'd been a captain, having many companies to look after. Though not half as many as his younger brother, Hewitt, and with far less success. Yet under Lawton Glaas's steady—if heavy—hand, Whickam Village did thrive more than most other small settlements in Estshire.

The horses stopped in front of the conjoined stables and smithy. While Hewitt unhitched them, Evylin unloaded the small bundle of swords left in the cart. Her thoughts drifted back to the men camped outside their village. Draft or not, they were here for more when they'd already taken too much. The Centurial War between Ephria and Wauld was a cause of justice no Ephrian would dare to deny. But that didn't change the fact that no men were left to recruit.

Stepping inside the smithy, Evylin continued her task. Her late grandfather had once owned the business, sharing the building with his brother, the farrier. While Lawton had once run the shop, he'd given that position over to Hewitt upon his retirement from the army.

The recurring drafts had made both Glaas men soldiers in their day. Evylin's father had returned from the war after six years of service, having sustained an injury and received an honorable discharge. The injury was no graver than a stab wound that needed long-term rest and resulted in a scar on his abdomen, but he reminded the village folk of his bravery in battle every chance he got.

Hewitt, however, served for twice the time. He'd risen through the ranks at a speed unlike anyone the Ephrian Army had ever seen. And he'd only retired when events at home demanded it.

Evylin had always been in awe of her uncle. Whenever he came home on leave, she followed him around like a kitten toddling after its mother. Upon his discharge, she'd clung to his side and never left it, soaking up all the stories and wisdom of his time in the service. Through the aid of Hewitt's rhetoric, the influence of her many fantasy novels, and her childlike reasoning, young Evylin formed the opinion that there were a great many flaws in the running of the war. Principle among them: After fighting a war for nearly two hundred years, something in your battle plan ought to change.

Yet it never did.

Hewitt returned from stabling the horses, and Evylin helped him pull the cart off to the side of the smithy. He grunted his approval of their work before heading inside the small wood and stone structure. "Give me a minute, and I'll have your share," he said.

Stepping into Hewitt's office behind him, Evylin watched as he counted the money. Having made all the weapons and trinkets, he got the larger cut of the two piles, but only by a marginal sum. She'd tried to argue with him once about paying her more than she'd earned. Instead of replying to her rational appeal, he'd swept the entirety of their earnings in the bag and thrust it into her hands. She'd kept her objections to herself ever since.

"Here." He tossed her a leather pouch that clinked as it hit her hand. "Don't spend it all in one place."

Evylin grinned. "Oh, but there's this lovely pink dress back in Trollenston," she let out an exaggerated sigh, "and I simply must have it."

Hewitt grunted. "If only you were serious, you might catch one of those town boys your mother always hints about."

"She doesn't hint," Evylin said, tucking the bag into her coat pocket. "She insists."

His gray eyes swept over her in a sarcastic examination. "You *are* getting old."

"Thank you for noticing," she said with a mock curtsy. She grabbed her canvas pack from the workbench and began backing away to the door. "See you at dinner?"

"Do I ever have a choice?"

"None at all."

Evylin left the smithy and crossed the square. A soft breeze pulled at her already windswept hair. Few people milled about at this time of day. The residents were too busy finishing their chores or returning to their farms. A handful of gray-uniformed soldiers paraded around, no doubt disappointed by the lack of entertainment the village offered.

Aside from the tavern, the small, close-set cottages surrounding the square housed the few tradespeople who didn't make their living through farming. People such as Mrs. Lyvingston, the town healer and midwife. Or old Father Dover, the parson of their tiny kirk. They had a cobbler, a butcher, and a chandler—all women now—but with so few people in their village, whatever trades didn't require specialties, the citizens managed to do for themselves.

Nearing the ivy-covered, two-story residence of the Glaas family, Evylin had two seconds to prepare herself when the darkly stained door burst open.

"Evie!"

A body collided with Evylin's, and the air burst from her lungs as thin arms wrapped fiercely around her waist. "How was the market?" Dolia asked. "Did you see lots of beautiful things?"

Evylin returned her sister's hug. "As always. And, of course, I have a letter for you."

Dolia pulled back, brushing dark brown curls away from her face. Despite having watched her grow up, Evylin still couldn't fathom how her youngest sister had turned from a girl into a woman. With her high cheekbones, lithe figure, and cheery disposition, Dolia caught the attention of every young man in the village and the nearby town. No matter how few suitors there were these days, the youngest Glaas daughter had the luck of her male peers missing the draft five years prior. And the charming, twenty-year-old Devaan MacKenna from Trollenston had caught the girl's heart. Upon his request of Dolia's hand, Magistrate Glaas feigned reluctance at the idea of his youngest leaving him. However, Evylin knew his pleasure rivaled that of their mother's.

Light pink spread across Dolia's cheeks as Evylin held out the letter. "Thank you!" she exclaimed, squirreling it away into the folds of her dress. She leaned in close as though her next words were the greatest of secrets. "We have a guest staying with us."

"Do we?" Evylin asked, amused by her sister's excitement.

"A soldier." Her curls bobbed around her face as she nodded. "And not just any soldier. A captain!"

Evylin patted her sister's cheek, amused. No matter Dolia's love for Mr. MacKenna, her girlish sensibilities sought out romance in everything. "Is that so?" She headed for the door. "And would I be correct in guessing that this captain is at least moderately handsome?"

"How did you know?"

"Because you wouldn't be excited if he weren't."

"Are you talking about Captain Deckard?" Calyn asked as they stepped into the house. She stamped her foot in exasperation. "I knew you wouldn't wait for me to tell her, Doli. You're such a child."

Dolia turned on their sister. "If I'm a child, how come I have a fiancé and you don't?" she asked, waving her letter from Devaan under Calyn's nose.

Calyn turned tomato red.

Heaving a sigh, Evylin pushed between her younger sisters. "Both of you are children, fiancé or not. Now, are you going to tell me about this handsome captain of yours?"

Calyn and Dolia shared a glance, then hurried to follow Evylin up the stairs.

"We can't talk about it out here," Calyn insisted. "He could show up at any moment." Her brown eyes flickered about as though her words might bring him around the corner.

With seven years between them, Evylin didn't dismiss Calyn's dramatics. Though their personalities were often like night and day, Evylin remembered the seriousness of being nineteen. Life and death existed in every action taken in those days. And while she might consider such theatrics ridiculous now, she could not forget her own youthful foolishness.

Once they were all in Evylin's room, Dolia shut the door behind them as though they were entering a sacred meeting.

"Well?" Evylin prompted.

Calyn sighed as she fell onto the bed next to Evylin's pack. "He's perfect."

Evylin huffed doubtfully, and Dolia doubled over with mirth.

"Perfect?" Evylin repeated dramatically. "Sounds as though I need to meet him for myself."

Calyn sat up at once. "I know you're joking. But you wouldn't like him. You'd say he's old and boring."

Evylin turned to Dolia, scrunching her nose. "Is he old and boring?"

The youngest girl continued to giggle.

Evylin brushed a hand in Calyn's direction. "You can have him then."

Calyn was indignant. "He's not, but *you'd* think so. And even if you didn't, you couldn't have him anyway."

"Oh? Why not?"

Calyn straightened her shoulders and lifted her chin. "Because I saw him first."

Evylin and Dolia exchanged pained expressions.

Evylin bit her tongue to hold back a sharp retort. Then she set a hand on Calyn's shoulder. "My dear sister, I would never presume to take a man from you. But tell me . . ." she held her gaze seriously, "has this captain in any way suggested his interest in you?"

Dolia's laughter burst through the room as Calyn's blush deepened to beet red.

Evylin doubted the success of her compassionate expression. "I'll take that as a no."

Calyn sighed, melancholy. "It isn't like he's had a chance, really. The army only arrived this morning."

That caused Evylin to start. "Are you telling me you're so in love with this man after one meeting that you've decided to marry him?"

"Mother always says, 'When you know, you know,'" Calyn defended.

"Tell me then: How do you know?" Evylin pressed. "Why are you so enamored with this man?"

Calyn looked off into the distance, a wistful smile tugging at her lips. "Captain Deckard is a gentleman of the finest quality. He's charming, gallant, and kind. He's the sort of man every woman dreams of."

Evylin looked at Dolia, seeking some sanity.

The youngest Glaas daughter beamed. "He's got a good sense of humor too."

Skeptical, Evylin eyed the pair of them. "Doesn't sound like much of a soldier to me."

Calyn huffed. "That's just because you haven't met him yet." She let out a dreamy sigh. "He's the noblest soldier I've ever seen."

"Mm." Evylin resolved then that her seasonal trips to Trollenston left her sisters alone together for too long. With the eldest two Glaas daughters married with children and Evylin the only levelheaded one among the lot, Calyn and Dolia would have little chance to grow into anything but silly women without her at their side.

"I'm sorry, Caly, but that is ridiculous," Evylin said belligerently. "You can't fall in love with a man you just met. It doesn't matter if he's the most eligible bachelor on Terraeus. A handful of hours is not enough to know. Love is not easy, and it's not fast. Ever."

"So you're telling me my feelings aren't real?" Calyn punctuated her words as though to prove a point.

"Not at all," Evylin said with a smirk. "I'm telling you they're not trustworthy. Attraction and love are two vastly different things."

"And how would you know?" Calyn demanded. "You've never been in love."

"No. But I have read about it. And, honestly, isn't that the same thing?"

A knock on the door halted Calyn's rebuttal as their mother appeared. "I've been looking everywhere for you two," she said to her youngest daughters. "There's a certain captain who would appreciate having dinner before midnight, I'm sure."

At that, the two young girls rushed past their mother with cursory shouts of, "Welcome home, Evie," as they hurried to the kitchen.

Letting the girls pass, their mother turned to Evylin. "Welcome home, dear," she said, crossing the room to hug her. "Did you have a good time in town?"

"It was nice, as usual." Evylin pulled back to kiss her mother's cheek. "I hope the army's encampment hasn't been taxing."

Lady Laurisa Glaas's deep brown eyes twinkled. Though they wrinkled at the edges, no other mark blemished her mother's features. Once the beauty of Trollenston, Laurisa Pinnette married the then-dashing Lawton Glaas at a young age and moved to his home in Whickam Village. When the draft conscripted him into the Ephrian Army, he left his young wife alone for long stints, only returning on the rare leaves granted by his officers. During that time, Laurisa raised the first three Glaas daughters alone. Yet time graced her with the retention of her beauty.

Evylin's elder sisters, Euna and Albina, often remarked on what good fortune it suggested for the rest of them. They'd all inherited their mother's youthful looks, trim frame, richly tanned complexion, and delicate features. And though she hated to admit her vanity, Evylin couldn't help the relief it brought her to think she was half as beautiful as her mother.

Laurisa smiled at her middle daughter. "It's brought excitement, to be sure," she confirmed. "But at least it isn't a draft."

Evylin's eyebrows rose at the confirmation of Hewitt's speculation. "It isn't?"

"Not according to Captain Deckard," she said, then winked. "Speaking of, your sisters are quite enjoying the encampment. And I must say, it's significantly improved my life as well. It keeps me from having to listen to them complain."

"A true blessing, if there ever was one," Evylin agreed.

Her mother squeezed her arm. "Hurry and get yourself cleaned up. We should all enjoy our peaceful household while it lasts."

CHAPTER TWO

Left alone, Evylin set to work. She'd shared a room with her sisters most of her life, but once Euna and Albina each married, Evylin was given a space of her own. A privacy that helped her keep all the money she earned working with Hewitt a secret. While her family knew he gave her some compensation, they didn't know how much. Nor did they know her purpose in saving it.

Splitting the coins between the various hiding places throughout her room, Evylin mentally tallied her savings. Though a measly sum to most, every little bit helped. And after the past decade of work, she had enough to get out of Estshire.

If she could ever find a *way* out of Estshire.

Ephria was a staunchly patriarchal society. A woman was under the headship of her father until marriage, at which time she came under her husband's care. The law was intended to provide women with protection. And for the average woman, like her sisters, Evylin thought it reasonable. It ensured no father or husband could abandon their daughters or wives without severe consequences.

But for women like Evylin, the law was an insurmountable obstacle. The modest and reserved society of Ephria didn't have a place for a woman like her. One who preferred adventure novels over romance, spending her time outdoors rather than in a dance hall, and who could wield a sword better than the average soldier.

Regardless of Evylin's desire to leave Whickam Village for a life of exploration and adventure, should she try, her father could recall her whenever he liked with lawful support. And her father *would* recall her.

Lawton Glaas was the height of respectability. He upheld the Ephrian standards with the authority of their king on his side. And he would never allow his daughter to traipse across the country like a vagabond.

But that didn't stop Evylin from dreaming. Nor did it stop her from working with Hewitt to scheme up her escape. Even though none of those plans had yet to come to anything, she was determined to find a way.

After washing off the grime of her journey, Evylin donned a modest but well-tailored gray dress. Though she and her mother were much alike in personality—lighthearted and even-tempered—there was one way in which they differed greatly: Evylin couldn't understand why a woman should work around the home in a frilly dress with soft silk slippers and hair curled to flow down her back. She found it impractical. Her mother called it necessary.

"A woman should be beautiful at all times. Even when she's working."

That favorite proverb of Laurisa Glaas rang in Evylin's ears as she fastened the laces on her boots. She didn't suppose it hurt to care for one's appearance even in the most mundane circumstances, but she couldn't help questioning if their work would be easier without their multi-layered skirts and hair falling in their faces all day.

Despite her mother's scruples, Evylin's hair was in a state from the early winter winds sweeping autumn away. She brushed it out before tying the top layer back with one of her old satin ribbons.

Knowing she'd taken long enough to meet Laurisa's standards, Evylin went down to the kitchen. "What can I do to help?" she asked as her mother walked by with a meat pie.

Calyn stood over the fire, dumping potatoes into the pot while Dolia stuffed chickens.

Eyeing the large meal, Evylin raised her brow. "Do we really need so much food? He's one captain."

Laurisa didn't slow as she said, "He's bringing Lieutenant Peery with him at your father's request."

"Lieutenant Peery?"

"He came with Captain Deckard to the meeting this morning, and they got on quite well."

Dolia leaned across the workbench to whisper not so quietly, "He's old and stuffy."

"He's your father's age," Laurisa chided.

Dolia pursed her lips as though her point was proven.

"Father's age and only a lieutenant?" Evylin asked.

Laurisa shrugged indifferently. "Perhaps the last draft caught him," she suggested.

"How'd he escape the previous drafts then?"

"I'm sure I don't know. And as it's none of your business, I wouldn't go asking." Her mother pointed to the bench. "Get to work."

The finality in Laurisa's tone kept Evylin silent as she picked up the knife and began chopping the purple carrots and ivory turnips before her. There was a definitive change to the Glaas daughters in the kitchen. Their mother ran it like the officers ran the army: no arguments, no complaints, and no dissension. And though Evylin couldn't claim to enjoy the cooking itself, she did enjoy the company. While their mother ran the kitchen like a squadron, laughter abounded as they did their duty.

The sun dipped to the horizon, turning the world copper. Dolia, working by the window, gasped. "They're back!" she called.

Calyn abandoned her work and ran to the window. Evylin turned to their mother.

Laurisa gave a knowing smile. "Go see for yourself."

Squeezing between her sisters, Evylin peered out the small window. Built into the terrae, the kitchen's narrow, horizontal window sat a mere handful of inches above the ground. The girls stood on their toes to see through the bubbled glass as two men approached the front door. In uniform, they wore formal coats of dark green rather than the usual charcoal gray. Through the dust and furtive view, Evylin worked to identify their houseguest. The officer on the right bore height and a graceful manner in his stride, but the other, with his dark hair and broad-shouldered build, better fit her sisters' descriptions.

"Which one is your captain?" Evylin asked.

Calyn leaned forward, fingers gripping the windowsill as she stared out the panes. "Isn't it obvious? He looks so handsome in green, doesn't he?"

"I couldn't tell even if you had answered my question."

Dolia giggled by her side. "Captain Deckard is on the right."

Furrowing her brow, Evylin narrowed her gaze on the man. Him? Surely not. She couldn't see his features clearly from their distance, but she couldn't fathom her sisters preferring this ruddy, trim man to the strong and mysterious one at his side. "You're sure?"

Dolia snickered. "You fancy the lieutenant, then?"

Calyn shook her head. "You have no taste, Evylin."

The low rumble of Hewitt's voice broke through their bickering. "What could be so fascinating at that window that you've all stopped working on my dinner?" he asked, standing in the doorway.

Laurisa gave him a wry smile in greeting. "You know very well that you are far from the guest of honor at this meal, Hew."

"What a damn unpleasant thing to hear," he said dryly.

A towel hit him in the chest. "If you're going to use language in my kitchen, then you'll be put to work," Laurisa commanded, despite her grin. "Get the birds."

Hewitt lifted the ceramic tray off the kitchen bench obediently. Though they were the most prestigious family in the village, even they didn't use fancy crocks or silver platters like the magistrate of Trollenston. They were, after all, a meager village.

"I'd ask if we are feeding an army with this much food," Hewitt sniped. "But I suppose we are."

Evylin sent him a reproachful smirk. "Your jokes are getting as bad as Father's."

Their father's voice reverberated through the halls, greeting their guests in the foyer. Calyn hurried to wipe her hands and smooth her dress. "Do I look all right?" she whispered to Evylin.

Not wanting to encourage her sister but also not having the heart to disappoint her, Evylin managed a smile and a nod.

"Hurry up," Laurisa ordered. "I don't need the officers thinking my daughters are an unruly brood of cackling hens."

Dolia grinned as she carried a basket of fresh bread out of the room. "They've already met Calyn, Mother."

Calyn's gasp of offense was short-lived as Laurisa quickly ordered her to bring the meat pie.

They'd spread the feast across the table and filled the glasses with wine just as Magistrate Glaas approached down the hall. "I'm sure a home-cooked meal will rectify all the ails of travel," he was saying magnanimously. "When I was a captain, I know I appreciated any break from the road."

Hewitt leaned down to whisper to Evylin. "And he took any break he could get."

Evylin bit her lip to keep from snickering as Lawton Glaas entered with the soldiers behind him. Her father was dressed in a stately tailcoat, its double-breasted buttons and high collar nearly military-esque. Like his daughters, he had dark hair, but his complexion was a truer tan, and his eyes were a crisp blue. Despite his aging features, there were times when Evylin thought she saw what made people call him handsome, though she thought Hewitt was the more striking of the Glaas brothers.

"Officers," Lawton said, gesturing across the room, "may I introduce you to more of my family? This is my brother, Hewitt Glaas, our smith. And this is my middle daughter, Evylin."

As her father explained their return from Trollenston's market, Evylin studied the soldiers. While the lieutenant carried the traditional appeal, being dark and handsome, his age was plain in the gray of his temples and the lines on his face. And there was something of an important air in the tilt of his chin that Evylin recognized in her father's bearing.

In contrast, while the captain was not as impossibly handsome as her sisters suggested, he was agreeable enough. Not striking, no. But he had a steady confidence in his posture, an easy smile, and a young to middling age that compensated for whatever else he lacked. After all, a man in the prime of his early thirties was a rare commodity.

Continuing the introductions, Lawton motioned to the officers. "Hewitt, Evylin, these fine gentlemen are Captain Deckard and Lieutenant Peery."

The captain and lieutenant bowed graciously at the introduction. Hewitt merely dipped his chin in a half-hearted nod, but Evylin curtsied as her mother taught her.

When the captain looked up, he addressed the family as a whole. "It's an absolute pleasure," he said, his voice as warm as his words.

Evylin returned his smile, intrigued.

Hewitt stared back, disinterested.

"Shall we have a seat?" Lawton said. "Captain, of course, you'll have the place of honor."

The dip of Captain Deckard's head offered the perfect amount of humble thanks.

Evylin bit back a grin as she sat between Hewitt and her mother. Her uncle would be chagrined to sit next to their guest.

Lawton let out a dramatic sigh as he surveyed the table. "What a beautiful meal you've made for us, my dear!" He winked at his wife. "I knew I was wise to marry you."

All three daughters ignored the nightly jest, and Laurisa took it in stride, graciously patting her husband's hand. Hewitt let out a "harumph," and the soldiers chuckled politely.

From across the table, Captain Deckard said, "It all looks excellent. I'm sure you went to far too much trouble for our sake."

Evylin did her best to inspect the man without staring. She supposed she understood the appeal. Though not the classic imitation of a hero, his smile might be the very definition of friendliness. And his reddish-brown hair did have a pleasant curl to it. Beyond that, he appeared to have an amiable, if overly complimentary, personality. But she couldn't see any real reason for the uproar beyond novelty.

Lieutenant Peery raised his glass in accord. "Indeed," he said mildly.

With a pleased expression, Lawton suggested, "Shall we give thanks?"

As the family bowed their heads, Evylin glanced at the captain and caught the reverent dip of his chin. Lawton said a simple and rote prayer before adding a special ending about their gratitude to have "these noble guests" at their table.

Evylin noted how Captain Deckard said his "by your grace" at the end of the prayer with more heart than the rest of them. She grinned to herself. Calyn had found herself a pious man, which didn't bode well for her sister's frivolous and dramatic tendencies.

"So, Captain Deckard," Lawton began, "where have you journeyed to us from? We were unaware the army was this far south."

The captain halted in filling his plate. "We were in Basingstoke the past few days. It's quite a lovely area."

"Basingstoke, you say?" Lawton pursed his lips and punctured a carrot from the tray.

"Yes, a quaint village, to be sure. I've only been a few times. You're journeying through all Estshire, then?"

"All the Shires, actually," Captain Deckard confirmed.

Evylin decided he had a pleasant enough voice. There was a refined gentleness to his deep timbre. Much more pleasant than the average man's, at least. And far less pandering than her father's.

"All of them?" Lawton's eyes went wide at the idea. "What brings you down so far?"

"Usual business, I suppose. As the war continues, so must our efforts. And King Ephren has requested that we see what aid our people can give us. City, town, and village."

Hewitt scoffed into his glass, the candlelight catching in the notches of its pattern.

The captain's eyes flickered to Hewitt, but his grin didn't waver. "As you've just taken a trip to Trollenston, Mr. Glaas," he said, drawing the man's steely glare, "you might assist me. The town is our next stop. Would you have any advice for us there?"

Hewitt swallowed down his wine. "It's a town. There's not much I could recommend. Magistrate Steevensun will fawn over you as my brother does, so I wouldn't worry much about your reception."

Evylin smirked at her plate, peering over slyly to catch Captain Deckard's reaction to her uncle's gruff reply. She was pleasantly surprised when the captain's expression grew amused.

However, Lawton did not share his humor. "Really now, Hewitt," he lamented. "You know the respect a captain deserves."

"Oh, yes," Hewitt replied, his tone markedly bored. "I know exactly the respect a captain deserves. Even more, what kind of respect an actual high-ranking officer deserves."

Lawton's fingers went white on his fork.

Glancing at the captain over the rim of her glass, Evylin tried to hide her amusement.

To his credit, Captain Deckard either took no notice of the offensive comment or chose to ignore it. "That's how I remember your name," he said with a note of awe. "You're *General* Glaas. It's a great honor, sir."

Lieutenant Peery froze, looking at Hewitt with renewed interest.

Lawton and Hewitt exchanged bitter looks before the younger Glaas brother turned back to the captain. "I gave up that title when I left the army," he said flatly.

Captain Deckard gave him a respectful nod. "Forgive me, sir, but the lack of your title doesn't remove the impact you left behind. I've heard stories of your work since I was a recruit." He raised his glass in a toast to Hewitt. "Thank you for your service."

"My service," Hewitt growled, "is not a topic I like to discuss."

Taking the rebuff in stride, Captain Deckard gave Hewitt a polite nod, then turned his gaze up the table. "And how about you, Miss Glaas? Did you have a good trip to town?"

A heartbeat passed before Evylin realized the captain was addressing her.

"Oh." Evylin looked around the table, searching for words.

Calyn glared daggers at her while Dolia held back her laughter.

"Uh . . ." She fumbled, glancing back at the captain. "Not particularly."

Captain Deckard's grin quirked to the side. "No?"

"Oh, no!" she exclaimed, realizing her mistake. "No, I'm sorry, I—I meant, it was fine."

"Ah, well, I'm glad to hear that," the captain said, his steady gaze making Evylin uneasy. "Do you often go to Trollenston?"

Evylin took a deep breath before replying this time. "Yes, I join Hewitt once a season to help at the market."

"So you know the town well?"

"Not as well as some." Evylin couldn't help but return his engaging smile. "But yes, I've been there often enough to know it well."

Captain Deckard leaned forward, his direct stare not quite so intimidating anymore. "Do you enjoy your time there?" he asked.

"I've been there so many times, I hardly know," Evylin replied casually. "Though Whickam Village is small and impossibly dull, Trollenston, despite being twice our size, isn't any more interesting. They might have size, but that's hardly enough to entertain me."

Even as the captain's light eyes shone amusedly in the candlelight, the clearing of Lawton's throat told her that she'd chosen the wrong time to share her opinion. "I suppose that's a rather nice endorsement for our village," her father suggested. "Their town may be larger, but we've got more spirit here."

Captain Deckard's eyes flickered away from Evylin. "Even being here for a day, I can tell your village is one of the finest in all Estshire."

Chewing on her vegetables, Evylin glanced sidelong at the captain. She couldn't tell whether his praise was sincere or not. The inflection of his tone suggested that he *was*, but no one found Whickam Village that special. Not unless they had no sense of adventure. And he was a soldier. Surely, he craved excitement as much as she did.

Though Evylin did suppose the draft was likely the cause of his commission. He was old enough that the last draft would have caught him and young enough to escape the one prior. But he was a captain, and anyone drafted in the past five years had little chance of rising through the ranks so fast.

At least, anyone other than Hewitt.

"And having two such impressive veterans in residence recommends your home even more," Deckard continued, though Evylin knew the compliment would only fall on one man's good side. "It's always a pleasure to dine with fellow soldiers."

"And ones of such reputation too," Peery added, turning to Hewitt. "I heard you got into some real scrapes in your day. Stories that put our current men to shame."

"Yes, it was a hell of a time," Hewitt muttered.

Evylin bit the inside of her lip as Laurisa scolded him for his language.

"Do you ever miss being in the service?" Deckard asked Lawton.

Hewitt set down his fork with a sigh. "Should we?"

Lieutenant Peery frowned, but Deckard didn't acknowledge his anger or care that the wrong man had answered him. "I suppose not," he replied. "I know most of our soldiers come through a draft these days. Therefore, I can't blame any man for being thankful to retire. Most of my fellow officers are looking forward to their retirement as we speak."

"Were you drafted into the army, Captain?" Dolia asked sweetly.

Deckard grinned. "No, Miss Glaas, I joined on my own. It was my dream to serve Ephria."

Pushing the vegetables around her plate, Evylin felt smug at finding that she was right. The captain chose his career, which meant he had at least some interest in adventure.

"Really?" Lawton spoke up again. "A career soldier, then? That's not common these days."

Peery let out a rich laugh. "Well, Deckard isn't one I'd call common. It's rare enough to have a career soldier but even rarer to have an officer universally liked by his troops."

"Is that so?"

Deckard let out a thin, embarrassed chuckle. "Hardly."

"He's being modest," Peery contradicted. "I've been in the same company as Deckard for the past four years, and I couldn't have been more honored when he selected me to come on this mission with him."

With evident discomfort, Deckard busied himself with his wine.

"He must be a splendid officer, then," Calyn surmised, a pink flush on her cheeks.

Peery clapped Deckard on the shoulder, jolting him a fraction in his seat. "Most career soldiers are in it for the money or the steady work. Or even the thrill of the fight. But not Deckard. King and country for this one." He patted him twice more. "A servant, through and through."

"That is wonderful," Laurisa said wistfully. "If only we had more men with such conviction in this world."

"Indeed," Lawton agreed as the captain's discomfort grew. "Perhaps then all my daughters would have husbands."

Evylin scoffed dramatically at the outrageous declarations of her family.

An awkward silence passed through the room as everyone's attention was drawn to her outburst. Lawton glared at her while her mother and sisters blushed furiously. Hewitt wore an amused grin, though Lieutenant Peery scanned her disapprovingly. The captain eyed her with something like astonishment.

Face heating, Evylin reached for her wine, muttering, "Apologies. I swallowed incorrectly."

Taking pity on her—and perhaps distracting attention from himself—the captain struck up a new conversation, asking about the village. Evylin sipped her wine and stared at the linen tablecloth. She listened as her father gave a meandering history of Whickam Village, detailing its founding almost a thousand years ago and its progression as the most fertile land in Estshire. There was, of course, mention of the Shepherd King's homeland being only a few miles away. That was the village's greatest claim: They were the birthplace of the first Ephrian king, the shepherd who led an uprising against the vile tyrants who defied the Creator Divine, Allore, and deified themselves, professing to be masters of dark magics, known as Mages.

There was, in actuality, no such thing as Mages. The old rulers of the nation, once known as Auld, had been nothing but charlatans, using cheap tricks to prove their might and secure their thrones. The shepherd, Tavish Ephren, rose up with thousands of other Shiremen to sweep through the eastern half of the continent, driving out the heretics and their false religion. Thus, Ephria was established.

Under the rule of their beloved Shepherd King, the country became a wholesome land dedicated to the true faith, the Allorian faith. They served the Creator Divine through their respectability, hard work, and tender care of the land. They worshipped him through the weekly kirk meetings, living with gratitude for their every breath, and praying devoutly whether they needed something or not.

Evylin wasn't particularly religious. It wasn't that she didn't believe. She simply didn't see the point in pious theatrics when life was a bitter monotony filled with disappointment and loss. Why spend hours praying when it wouldn't change the course of your day? She could honor Allore just fine by being herself.

Though the motherhood of Whickam Village would take exception to that.

Evylin wasn't known for her respectability or tenderness. However, she did work quite hard.

The conversation shifted again as the men discussed the war and politics in polite, pandering statements that could not anger anyone. Yes, the war was just. Yes, His Majesty was noble. Yes, the Wauldeners were thoroughly vicious blackguards. If only the war could end so that they could have their men back home where they belonged.

Those were the sort of comments Evylin could hardly abide by. If they wanted the war to end, surely they should stop sending men to die at the border and start using some logic. A simple assassination of the Waulden king would do wonders in disrupting their aggressive assault to reclaim the Ephrian land. She'd just finished a novel with that very same plan put into action. It worked splendidly for the characters; why shouldn't it work for Ephria?

As the gentlemen continued to converse, the women excused themselves to clean up. Evylin was grateful for the freedom from the tedious dialogue. They gathered the emptied plates and meal's remnants, leaving behind a decanter of wine for the men while they talked. Then Laurisa dismissed Calyn and Dolia so that she could interrogate Evylin while they cleaned.

It was a ritual the mother and daughter acted out whenever she returned from town. Evylin shared the news, and her mother would find a way to make it about marriage.

"How is my sister?" Laurisa asked, beginning the tradition.

Evylin kept her eyes on her scrubbing. "Serene is as ridiculous as ever," she said fondly. "She sends her love."

Her mother let out a forlorn sigh. "I do miss her. I should visit soon."

"She'd be thrilled if you did. You know how she enjoys company."

"Yes." She chuckled, and her dark eyes drifted to glance Evylin's way. "In fact, if I remember, she had more company than usual this time, didn't she?"

Evylin tried to keep her tone from turning sour. "If you're referring to Nixon's visiting cousin, then yes, I suppose. Though he was staying with him and Nelle."

"Ah, yes . . . Aberon, wasn't it?" Laurisa said as though she ever would have forgotten.

"That's the one," Evylin said flatly.

"Did you like him?"

"I didn't meet him."

"Why not?"

Evylin scoffed. "Mother, he's eighteen. I'm not marrying a man nearly ten years my junior."

Laurisa pursed her lips but moved on. "And the market? You sold all Hewitt's wares?"

"Not quite," she said, scrubbing another plate. "The market was full, but we returned with a few swords. The daggers went fast, though. As did the kitchen goods. Much to his dismay, of course."

Laurisa laughed. "He always hated selling pots and pans."

"The price you pay for being a village smith."

The laughter stopped. Laurisa's eyes crinkled in agitation. "And what's so wrong about being a village smith? Or a village anything, for that matter?"

Evylin frowned. "Nothing."

"You embarrassed your father at dinner, Evie."

Evylin wanted to remark that her father had embarrassed himself but kept quiet as her mother continued.

"Sometimes, I regret letting you spend so much time with your uncle. He's done nothing to curb your tongue."

"Mother—"

"Did you ever stop to think that your dislike of our little village might be hurtful?" Laurisa dropped the soap-filled pot back into the washbasin. "Not just to your family's feelings, but also to our potential?"

"What are you talking about?"

"These men could bring us a future."

"A future?" Evylin shook her head incredulously. "What does that even mean?"

"They could send our men home," Laurisa proclaimed. "And they could bring even more men to us."

"Oh, Mother—"

"No, I'm serious. If they like it enough, they could move here when their commission is up. And suggest that others do the same."

Evylin had patience with her mother most days. But she could not abide by this sort of idealism. "They are a captain and a lieutenant," she reminded her. "They are low in the chain of command. And we are at war. Do you really think they'll be able to send our men home? They aren't even in charge of what happens to their own company."

Laurisa's eyes darkened. "Don't you want to get married?"

Evylin blanched. The fact was, she *did* want to be married. But she failed to see what that had to do with the conversation they'd been having.

"If they send men back," Laurisa continued, "you could marry one of them."

Evylin crossed her arms. "So you don't care about our men coming home so they can be with their families? You care so they can marry your daughters."

"Yes."

Evylin's mouth dropped open. "Euna and Albina have been without their husbands for five years. Shouldn't you focus on *them* coming home?"

"Of course, I want them home," Laurisa said effusively. "But I am also perfectly aware that they aren't likely to."

"Mother!"

"No, listen to me." She took hold of Evylin's hand. "I have watched for over fifty years as men have left for war and not come back. Albina hears from Maac every month. But Euna hasn't heard from Druan since back in Chronos. A five-month silence is never good. That's more than half a year."

Evylin cast her eyes down to the sink.

"As much as it hurts, Euna is almost certainly a widow."

"She's given up on him?" Evylin asked somberly. She'd always liked her brother-in-law, Druan, even if he was a bit simpleminded.

"No, of course not." Laurisa looked out the window toward the kirk. "She still prays for him every day. And she always tells the girls he'll be back. But I've seen her as she watches the other widows. It's like she knows she's one of them."

Evylin didn't know what to say.

Laurisa picked her work back up, beginning her drying with renewed vigor. "But this is why we need the men to return. If you don't marry soon, you will be too old."

With a sigh, Evylin continued scrubbing. She didn't bother responding or telling her mother just how little hope she held of ever finding someone worth marrying.

Five years ago, at the prime of Evylin's marrying age, the draft took all the eligible single men within a hundred miles. The only ones left behind were either children, elderly, or invalids. The youth were fine enough for Calyn and Dolia. And while Evylin did want a husband, she couldn't accept a loveless marriage as a nursemaid or an early widow. She couldn't relegate herself to the average wifedom of an Estshire woman either.

Evylin had dreams. She longed to travel and have an adventure. Perhaps she could sail across the sea. Or maybe journeying through Ephria would be enough. She just knew she'd never be content living a small life in her small village until she became a doddering old woman with nothing but novels for excitement.

But her mother was right. At twenty-six, Evylin was getting old, and she didn't want to remain in her parents' house while all the rest of her sisters had lives and families of their own.

Graciously, Laurisa changed the subject, asking more about her family in Trollenston. Evylin struggled to speak around the tightness in her throat. She managed to keep up the conversation just long enough to finish their work, tears building in her chest.

Those thoughts and conversations always scared Evylin. Every single one of them. But she refused to cry over something that she couldn't change.

No matter how many times Evylin tried to puzzle through her predicament, she always came to the same conclusion: It wouldn't matter if there were a hundred eligible men her age within Whickam Village; none of them would want her. They never had. Not even in her youth when she'd been as carefree and pretty as Dolia. The young men of the village refused to pursue Evylin Glaas. Why? Because she made them feel inferior.

Hewitt taught her that. He told her it wasn't her fault the boys were afraid of her. They were cowards, unwilling to recognize value and strength when they saw it. And she was better off without them.

But it didn't help Evylin feel any less unwanted and alone in her youth. And it didn't make her feel any more confident about her fate now.

Evylin couldn't leave Estshire despite the money she'd saved from working with Hewitt. Even if her father didn't contact the authorities to bring her home, a woman traveling alone was dangerous. Tradition alone wouldn't have stopped her, but Hewitt's cautions did. He'd seen the country. He knew what was out there. And even with all his training, she knew better than to test the bounds of the world's goodness.

When she was younger, Evylin had asked Hewitt to go with her. Her youthful innocence was sure that her father wouldn't turn them down if his brother were there to protect her. But it was the first and only time Hewitt had ever denied her. When she pressed harder, he'd given the only reply she'd needed: "I can't leave them."

She never asked again.

So there she was; no hope if she stayed but also with no hope of getting out.

Evylin saw the light underneath her father's office door as she reached the steps. Curiosity drew her to a halt as she heard Captain Deckard's polished voice on the other side. She paused, gripping the railing as her father spoke. "Is it that bad, then?" he asked.

"I'm afraid so," Captain Deckard replied.

"I can't believe we're losing so many men so fast."

"The Waulden Army is getting stronger each day, it seems. Again," Deckard's voice dipped with caution, "we're not spreading this news. We don't want the country to panic. But as a fellow captain, I know you'll understand our position."

Evylin could imagine her father nodding with vehemence at the stroking of his ego. "Of course. I'll be discreet," he said, haughty pride inflecting his voice. "And we'll gather whatever supplies you need. I only wish we could do more."

"Let's just hope my speech proves successful," Deckard replied.

Evylin continued up the stairs. Hewitt was right; the captain was looking for recruits. It was a pity. Here she was, wishing for a way out of Whickam Village, and Captain Deckard was looking for volunteers to join him.

In a perfect world, she could volunteer to be one of Captain Deckard's soldiers. But the world was far from perfect. Even if she managed to lay out a faultless case in her favor, the law prohibited such a notion.

Evylin shut her bedroom door behind her, leaning against it as it clicked into place. Her eyes found the bookshelf where she hid some of her earnings. She'd saved for years, listening to her family's constant pleas that she settle down at last. There was a chance she could continue like that for a few more years. But sooner or later, time would catch up with her, and she wouldn't be able to wait any longer.

Heavy footfalls reached her ears from the hall beyond her door. She glanced over her shoulder as if she might see through the wood at her back. It was almost certainly Captain Deckard making his way down the hall. The door to the guest room creaked slightly as it opened and shut. When his door latched, Evylin's thoughts snapped into place with it.

Perhaps, she thought, *I don't need to be a soldier to leave.* Something about the captain's good nature clung to Evylin's mind. Her thoughts churned as she looked at her bookshelf again.

No, she couldn't volunteer. But the honorable Captain Deckard—the career soldier with a heart for adventure and service—might be the key to her escape after all.

CHAPTER THREE

11TH OF TERRAEN, 1573

Evylin rose late, grimacing at how high the sun had already risen. Her tardiness would irritate Hewitt. She'd stayed up to recount the money stashed away over the years. It was no fortune, but she felt confident the sum would be enough to tempt any man. Even one so devout as Captain Deckard.

She rushed through her morning routine, throwing on the first blouse she found and tucking it into her trousers. A woman wearing pants was the bane of Laurisa Glaas's existence. She begged Evylin to change every time she put them on. The winter months eased the complaints as her long coat provided cover, but Evylin didn't relent even when her mother tried to bribe her in the summer. Skirts in a smithy wouldn't do.

Evylin tied off the end of her braid and bent to slip on her boots. She tucked a small knife into the right one, next to her ankle, a habit Hewitt had taught her.

"A hidden blade has saved more lives than any visible one ever has," he insisted.

Even as she hurried, Evylin ran through her plan once more. Given his piety during the prayer and Lieutenant Peery's praises, she'd plotted how best to convince the captain. If the man was as kindhearted and altruistic as lauded, she could use that to her advantage. Such an honorable man couldn't refuse the sweet village girl who longed for the same adventure as he. Not if she gave a convincing enough speech. Not if she got him to like her.

That was something Evylin had never struggled with. People always liked her. They might disapprove of her hobbies, but they liked *her*. And after Captain Deckard's attentive conversation during dinner, she held no doubt that they would be friends in no time.

No, friendly regard was not her primary concern.

Evylin knew the flaws in her plan were plentiful. For starters, there was little incentive for a captain to accept a position as someone's guard. The Ephrian officers were well paid, according to what Hewitt had told her. Unless the captain managed his money poorly—a doubtful supposition for a pious man—he wouldn't need the funds. But she hoped that playing on that sense of servitude the lieutenant had gone on about might convince him that her cause was a good one.

The biggest hurdle to her plan was convincing her father, but she thought Captain Deckard might be the key to her father's consent too.

Lawton Glaas was as smitten as Calyn. Granted, he wanted the man's praise, while the girl wanted his love. But that worked to Evylin's advantage.

If she could win Deckard's aid, she could let *him* do the cajoling. Her father would never refuse the man if he thought there was any chance of the captain's disapproval.

However, one trouble she hadn't managed to work out before her night's rest was how she'd secure time alone with Captain Deckard. Even if she did earn his friendship during the meals with her family, she had little means of obtaining an opportunity to make her proposal. And what was more, she didn't think she should ask it right off. She needed the captain to like her, yes. But more than that, she needed him to understand her predicament and desire to help her change it. Only then could she make her offer to hire him. Otherwise, she was sure to shock a "no" out of him before she ever got the chance to hear a "yes."

But a single young woman asking to speak with an eligible bachelor like the captain was tantamount to suggesting she wanted to marry him. And while the idea wasn't altogether repulsive, she had no interest in piquing the captain's romantic attentions.

Evylin was looking for an escape from Whickam Village, not an attachment.

Pulling on her coat, Evylin caught a glimpse of movement at the edge of her window. Situated on the second story of the house, her room overlooked the back of the farrier's stables and Hewitt's smithy. As a child, she would sometimes watch the horses as they ambled and grazed in the paddock. When Hewitt returned from the army, she'd come to know that trampled patch of land on a far more personal level.

She'd begged for weeks, and finally, Hewitt relented, agreeing to train the then-thirteen-year-old Evylin. Growing up, she'd played with the toy swords he bought for her and Ryen. The two of them would spend hours upon hours in the woods, practicing the basic binds and feints he'd taught them. They came home every day, covered head to toe in dirt and sweat from the adventures their wild imaginations took them on.

Evylin bit her lip fiercely enough to send a throb of pain that pushed away the memory. She angled her head, the view of the paddock mostly obscured from her doorway, and caught another flicker of movement.

Stepping closer, Evylin expected to find a horse cantering about the fenced yard. Instead, the trampled and browning grass held two pacing soldiers, swords at the ready.

Evylin watched with interest. Her eyes narrowed to make out what details she could of the men. She readily marked one as Captain Deckard. The sun beamed off his coppery-brown hair, making him easy to spot. But the other man she didn't recognize.

Evylin wondered how the captain had discovered the paddock for practice. The farrier must have approved their use of his grounds, though it offered no explanation as to why they were there in the first place. Either way, Hewitt wouldn't like it.

The paddock was where Evylin and Hewitt trained each day. When they finished their work, they'd run through drills before sparring to keep in practice. Hewitt had set up an exercise routine for Evylin in her early days to get her strength up. It wasn't until she was fourteen that he allowed her to use a real sword—dull edge or not.

Everyone in the village knew they trained back there. It had been the local gossips' favorite subject early in her youth. There was a chance the captain had heard it was a good, open space for private practice. But she couldn't figure out why he wasn't training in his camp with the rest of his soldiers.

Evylin watched as Captain Deckard and the unknown soldier sidestepped one another. A moment later, Deckard charged.

Their swords hit in three successive clashes before his opponent pushed in closer, driving his blade down Deckard's and toward his neck. Both men froze as Evylin's eyes went wide. It was over as soon as it began.

A heartbeat passed before the men parted. Evylin could just make out the smile on Captain Deckard's face as the other man spoke. They were too far away for her to see the details of either man. She might have thought the soldier to be Lieutenant Peery, given his dark hair, but this man was broader and far more youthful in his movements.

Deckard reset his feet and gave his reply.

His opponent laughed.

Then they started again.

Evylin watched for several minutes as they sparred. Sometimes, Deckard would begin the round; others, his comrade would. But every time, it ended the same way: The dark-headed soldier would either disarm, overpower, or outskill the captain and come out the victor.

Evylin frowned. Continual losses didn't concern her in normal circumstances. She lost to Hewitt every single time. She could hardly fault a man for losing to his better.

But that was the problem. While his opponent was a good swordsman, little about the dark-haired man's skills matched hers. There was obvious strength and training in his movement, and his strikes were quick and thoughtful, but they lacked finesse. He bore the basic qualities any soldier should, but little more.

So how could it be that a captain was unable to match his soldier?

Evylin backed away from the window. Her plan was growing less sure by the second. Not only would the captain be missing from breakfast—removing an important opportunity for her to develop a friendship with him—she worried that her plan didn't hold any ground at all.

If the man couldn't fight, how could she hire him as a guard?

Though Evylin supposed that was more of a technicality than an actual job. She didn't exactly need a guard, so much as a guide. She could protect herself just fine with the training Hewitt had given her. The position she planned to propose to Deckard wasn't so much about physical protection anyway. It was to prevent the attention she'd attract as a woman traveling alone. A man—no, an entire army at her side, in this case—would solve that problem.

And while it wasn't her preferred method, Evylin wondered if this insight into the captain's swordsmanship—or lack thereof—could be a benefit.

The paddock was the perfect hiding spot. If you wanted a view of it, you had to go out around the main buildings or through the stables and smithy themselves. Or up to Evylin's room. She had no doubt Captain Deckard chose to practice there because he didn't want anyone watching.

Because he was secretly training.

If Deckard wanted to be a better swordsman, she could offer to train him. And, alongside the funds she'd saved, that might be enough to sway whatever qualms he held.

With her developing plans expanding, Evylin descended the stairs to retrieve her breakfast. Her sisters were busy talking about the dance Aunt Serene had invited them to the following month, while their father read his correspondence. Laurisa never stayed long at breakfast, preferring to eat and hurry to her daily tasks. In general, Evylin didn't understand her mother's desire to rush the meal. But today, she felt much the same.

Taking the last bite of her toasted rye bread, Evylin rushed out the front door. It shut behind her with a light *click* as she stepped onto the dirt street and crossed to the smithy. The hem of her coat brushed around the ankles of her boots as the cold morning air burned in her lungs.

Though all her sisters worked around the house, Hewitt had convinced Lawton and Laurisa to allow Evylin to work with him. It had taken months of coaxing, but they won out. Whether that was by sheer force of will or presenting a convincing argument, she didn't care. Working as Hewitt's assistant was far preferable to listening to her sisters' twittering all day.

Tethered to the wagon out front, the horses awaited their day of work. Evylin patted the dappled mare on the shoulder as she passed. The heat of the forge radiated several feet into the square. Its heavy stench of smoke, metal, and leather wafted through the wooden planks of the walls.

Evylin walked in to see Hewitt bundling a set of pots together. "'Bout time," he said when he spotted her. "I've got three orders ready to go, and I'll have Arnie Redd's plow shortly. Get these things loaded while I finish up here."

Ignoring his crotchety mood, Evylin stepped to his side and rolled onto her toes to kiss his cheek. "You're always such a ray of sunshine in the morning, Uncle."

He scowled at her, though she could see an amused twinkle in his eyes. "You're no better."

"I didn't claim to be."

As she loaded the wares into the cart, the low rumble of the forge and Hewitt's tools melded with the whinnies from the stable. But the absence of the familiar sharp hits and grinding slashes of a sword fight caught Evylin's attention the most.

Realizing the soldiers departed while she was eating breakfast, Evylin loaded the final deliveries. The captain was doing an expert job of avoiding her. She refused to let her disappointment show as Hewitt helped her heft the plow into the cart bed and gave her the delivery sheets for each item.

"Should be a full day of travel for you, but when you return, we can train," he promised.

"Are you sure your orders won't overrun you? I do believe your stack is twice its usual size since we left." She gestured toward his office. With each return from their week at the market, the village residents inevitably wound up with broken items or the need for something new. While Hewitt was primarily a smith, he was also the only one people relied on to fix everything, whether that was metal, leather, clay, or wood.

"We'll have plenty for tomorrow," Hewitt grumbled. "And I'm not prioritizing Missy Felming's desire for new handles on that knife set of hers."

Evylin cut her laugh short as Hewitt turned to head inside the smithy. "What are the requirements of becoming a captain in the Ephrian Army?" she called abruptly.

Hewitt glanced over his shoulder with a knowing grin. "You saw that twit practicing, didn't you?"

Evylin smirked. "You only dislike him because he's nice."

"No," he growled. "I dislike him because he's a sycophant."

Rather than challenge his prejudice, Evylin climbed onto the wagon and took her seat. "You saw him train as well?" she prompted.

"I did."

"And . . . what did you think?"

Hewitt raised his brow. "I think he's a shit swordsman."

Evylin chuckled.

"His brother wasn't half bad, though."

"His brother?" she asked, surprised.

"They came in asking if they could train in the back. I told them to talk to ol' Ned as they're not my stables." Hewitt crossed his thick arms over his massive chest. "Anyway, I'd say our Captain Deckard is what soldiers call an 'Officer of Means.' There was almost always one in your chain of command. Got their promotions from their money, not their skills. It's not the nicest thing to call them, but it's often true."

Evylin frowned. "You think he bought his way into being a captain?"

If Deckard had enough money to buy his rank, there was no chance her petty sum would rouse his interest.

"The only other way I know to become a captain is to prove your skill as a soldier," Hewitt said, then hesitated. "Though his brother was decent, and he's only a lieutenant. Could be luck that the captain earned his rank. Or the younger Deckard has more scruples than the elder."

A scoff slipped out of Evylin. "Did you hear the captain last night? He said 'by your grace' like he was in a kirk. If his brother is a more virtuous man, I'd venture to say he's the most boring person on the face of Terraeus."

That earned a slight grin from Hewitt.

"He did look good, though," she added. "The brother. I'd say he'd give us both a fun, if easy, go of it. If nothing else, he'd be someone new."

"Mm." Hewitt drew his hand along his scraggly jaw. "Perhaps I'll see if he'd like a challenge. Can't say I've had one in a while."

"Thanks for the compliment."

Hewitt chuckled. "I taught you everything you know. Don't expect to be a threat to me for quite some time."

At that, he turned and left.

Evylin looked down at the delivery sheets in her hand. Hewitt wasn't making light of the day's travel. Redd's farm was two hours outside of the village. Beyond that, she had to stop at Lorna Twigg's farm to deliver a repaired hatchet, the Baartably farm with their many repaired tools, and Mrs. Lyvinston's with those pots.

Picking up the reins, Evylin began her deliveries. While she didn't care to socialize with the farmers, she enjoyed the travel. Seeing the countryside, no matter how familiar, made her feel a bit freer, like the village might not have quite the grip on her as the ivy did on its buildings.

The sun climbed higher between dropping off the pots and traveling to each of the farms. This late in autumn, the warmth never removed the need for her coat, not with the frigid breeze that swept through the air. Winters were always biting in Ephria, even this far south, just as the summers were blistering.

Evylin finished her last delivery a little after noon. Arnie Redd, a veteran who'd returned home two years back after losing most of his right arm, offered to let her join him and his daughters for lunch. Despite the price her stomach was paying, she felt the pain of hunger would be nothing compared to getting back late.

Her daily sword practice with Hewitt only happened so long as she returned early enough. Any lack of punctuality faced the inevitable delegation of either Calyn or Dolia to collect her to help with dinner. After enough mismanaged days in the past, Evylin worked fast and with purpose to get back to the smithy in time for their training. Usually, she would have brought lunch with her, but in her haste to catch the captain, she now suffered an empty stomach.

When Evylin pulled the cart to a halt two hours later, Hewitt greeted her at the door. "I'll take care of Tansy and Pearl," he said, gesturing inside. "You get those payments and receipts entered."

Evylin hopped down as he unhitched the horses. "I think Tansy picked something up in her shoe on the journey back."

He grunted in response, focused on his task.

Evylin settled at the desk near the back of the building. Hewitt hated doing the bookkeeping, so he'd trained her to take over the second she was old enough. It was a job she never minded; balancing the books was satisfying. Seeing the numbers grow and equal. Matching up orders to deliveries. It felt like closure for each task, and it gave her a sense of accomplishment when she inked in the last figure, filed the receipts, and closed the ledger.

Hearing footsteps, Evylin returned the book to its cabinet. "Did you find anything in her shoe?" she asked without looking over her shoulder.

"I'm uncertain of whom you're referring to," a man said, "but I assure you I have not been looking in any woman's shoe."

Evylin bumped into the desk as she whirled to find the captain and another soldier in the smithy. Her face grew warm under Captain Deckard's friendly gaze. "I apologize," she said, hurrying out of the office. "I thought you were my uncle. He must still be working with the horses."

"Ah." Deckard laughed, and the man at his side smiled as well. Seeing them side by side, there was no question in her mind: This was the captain's brother. Though he had dark brown hair and a more angular shape to his face, they looked remarkably alike.

Captain Deckard's good humor grew. "I do hope he's successful in his search."

"I was," Hewitt said, walking through the smithy's entry.

Both soldiers turned as he passed, drawing their shoulders back as though their commanding officer had stepped into the room.

Evylin raised a hand to cover her uncontrollable grin.

"Excellent," Captain Deckard said, his smile never faltering though his brother's disappeared altogether. "I hope she's received a clean bill of health."

Hewitt glared at him. "The horse is fine. Can I help you men with something?"

"Yes, it's rather ironic," Deckard replied. "Our supply of horseshoes has run low, and I was hoping to purchase some from you."

Hewitt narrowed his eyes. "How many do you think a one-man-operated forge can manage in a couple of days?"

Neither man responded.

"You'll have better luck in Trollenston."

Deckard exchanged a look with his brother before turning back to Hewitt. "I was hoping I could have you do it."

Evylin wanted to warn him that he was pressing his luck.

Hewitt began clearing a workbench roughly. "Why?"

Deckard didn't answer again, but his brother raised his dark eyebrows at Hewitt's gruff tone.

"Because I used to be an officer?"

The silence was confirmation.

"As I said last night," Hewitt dropped a hammer onto the bench with an echoing *thunk*, "my past is my past, and I want it left that way. Now, if your horse had thrown a shoe, I'd be happy to fix it. But I don't need your patronage as a display of gratitude."

Deckard maintained steady eye contact with the growling man. "I completely understand," he said calmly. "My apologies for any offense." He gestured to the soldier at his side. "As a matter of fact, my brother's horse *has* thrown a shoe. It's what gave me the idea of purchasing from you in the first place. Perhaps you'd assist us with that and recommend a smithy in Trollenston to replenish our stores?"

Evylin studied the captain, impressed by his backbone. Few men were brave enough to remain in the same room when Hewitt was in a rage, let alone continue to converse with him. He might be an "Officer of Means," but he also had enough courage to stand his ground. Or maybe it was just enough stupidity.

Hewitt gave a sharp nod but said nothing further.

"Wonderful," Deckard replied. "Thom, I'll leave you to schedule an appointment." His brother gave Deckard a withering look, but the captain grinned and turned to Evylin. "It was a pleasure seeing you again, Miss Glaas."

Returning his infectious mood, Evylin dipped her head in a mock bow. "The pleasure is all mine, Captain."

Deckard held her gaze, his blue eyes shining in the shafts of light from the windows as he returned her bow but lower and with a regal sort of flourish that made her laugh. "Until next time, then," he said, straightening to his full height. He patted his brother's arm, nodded to Hewitt, and gave Evylin one last glance before leaving.

Evylin watched as he disappeared beyond the smithy doors. Something in the inflection of his words struck her. There was a warmth and almost an affection in his tone that made her uneasy. Was he attempting to charm her the same way he'd done to her father? The intensity of his gaze and the gentle tilt of his smile gave her an odd sense of attentiveness, as though he were truly seeing her, truly listening to her.

She rather liked it.

The forge seemed to roar, drawing Evylin's attention. She turned away from the door to catch the captain's brother staring at her with his brow furrowed and mouth the tiniest bit agape. Uncomfortable with his inspection of her, she looked at Hewitt, who still glared after Deckard.

Clearing her throat, Evylin took the awkward silence into her own hands. "So," she said, adopting a cordial expression, "you're the captain's brother?"

He blinked a couple of times. "Oh. Yes," he stumbled over the words, then scoffed at himself and shook his head. He renewed his smile, and Evylin saw the resemblance to the captain again in its warmth and sincerity. "Yes, I am. Lieutenant Thom Deckard, at your service, ma'am."

Hewitt turned upon his address, gray eyes narrowed. It wasn't the same stare he'd given Deckard. That one was positively scathing. Now, he tilted his head, studying the lieutenant with a far more curious expression.

Seeing that she'd have to carry the conversation, Evylin leaned against the workbench. "Why don't you bring your horse by tomorrow morning? It shouldn't take more than fifteen minutes."

Lieutenant Deckard nodded, some of his dark hair dipping onto his forehead. He brushed it back, and Evylin couldn't help noticing that, while the captain was handsome enough, this Deckard was what she'd expected from her sisters' descriptions: muscular and broad-chested, with striking blue eyes and sharp, mysterious features.

Calyn would have a fit if she met him.

"If that works best for you," he replied, uncertainty in his tone.

"Actually," Hewitt said, stepping around the bench. "I have a proposition for you."

The lieutenant straightened like a soldier receiving his orders.

"I saw you and the captain practicing this morning. You were good."

Thom glanced at Evylin again.

"Would you have any interest in sparring with me tomorrow?" Hewitt asked.

His bright eyes grew wide. "Really?" he asked, then frowned. "Why?"

"Because the only person I can fight with in this blasted village is Evylin. And I'd like to test my skills against someone new."

Thom Deckard stood dumbfounded. He looked from Hewitt to Evylin and back several times as though uncertain of whether Hewitt was having a laugh at his expense. She had no doubt the idea of a woman training in swordplay sounded like a joke to him, and his hesitation marked a healthy skepticism toward her uncle.

"Deckard told me about you," he said, caution lining his deep voice.

"Did he?" Hewitt replied dryly.

"You were a legendary general, but you don't like to talk about it."

"Right enough."

"But you want to have a go anyway?"

Hewitt raised a bushy eyebrow. "Swordplay and conversation are two entirely different things."

Lieutenant Deckard hesitated, then grinned. "All right."

Hewitt didn't display the slightest bit of enthusiasm but nodded. "Bring your horse in a little after noon tomorrow, and we'll get it patched up before we begin."

The lieutenant gave them a polite bow. "It was nice to meet you both," he said, though he looked mostly at Evylin while he spoke.

They both returned his farewell as he left.

Evylin waited until he was out of earshot before turning on her uncle. "So I take it we won't be practicing tomorrow?"

Hewitt glanced over at her. "What? Oh." He paused and considered it. "I suppose not."

Evylin tapped the workbench in mock agitation. "I appreciate that you asked if I was all right with that. Shows a great deal of respect and consideration."

"You can come and watch," Hewitt offered as he headed to the paddock. "You'll probably learn more from observation than you can from me anymore."

Evylin followed him out into the sunshine, beginning to unbutton her coat. "That's not the point."

"What is the point?"

She caught the sword he tossed to her. "Nothing," she said with a dramatic sigh. "But maybe ask before you decide to change our plans."

CHAPTER FOUR

Hewitt won, as he always did. But the exercise left Evylin's body buzzing with pleasing adrenaline.

"See you at dinner," Evylin said, grabbing her coat on the way to the door.

A grunt came from behind her. "I'm not coming."

Evylin paused, then turned around to face him. "You know that's not an acceptable answer."

Hewitt locked his office door without replying.

She surveyed his sullen mood with amusement. "Does this have anything to do with a certain houseguest of ours?" she said.

Hewitt ignored her, but she waited patiently. After shuffling around and organizing the tools and projects they'd already put away earlier, he pulled on his coat and fixed her with one of his glares. "I refuse to be part of that charade again. Lawton and Captain Deckard can compliment each other until they're blue in the face. I'll be fine in my own home, thank you."

Evylin raised her brow. "I think you made your feelings perfectly clear to Captain Deckard. He won't bother you again."

Hewitt stared her down. "He's nosy."

"Nosy?" Evylin laughed. "Uncle, he obviously asks questions because he assumes everyone wants to talk about themselves. Which I guarantee works for him every other time."

"As I told you, he's a bloody suck-up," Hewitt said bitterly. "Either way, I don't like him."

Evylin crossed her arms. "I think you're biased."

Hewitt scowled. "And I think you're as wooed by his charms as your sisters."

Evylin couldn't help the humor she found in her uncle's irritation. She could only see a child pouting about a lost toy. "Are you truly so upset by his questions last night that you've determined to hate the man? He was trying to be courteous. You're acting as though he accosted you."

Hewitt fidgeted with the rag he used to wipe down the worktable.

With a sigh, Evylin stepped up to the table and met his eyes. "He doesn't know you. He doesn't know why his questions were rude."

Hewitt hesitated. Her words were true; he just didn't want to admit it. So she wouldn't make him.

"Come to dinner," Evylin insisted, backing toward the door. "Ignore the captain if you must, but you know Mother and Father will have your head if you're not there."

He didn't reply.

Hand on the door, Evylin called over her shoulder, "See you soon, Uncle."

Pulling the large smithy door shut behind her, Evylin braced herself against the icy wind. They never got snow in Estshire, but that didn't stop the evening chill from permeating the bones. Winter hit fast and hard on the Allundan Isle, Ephria's continent, and the Shires weren't immune to it. Turning to walk home, Evylin pulled her coat tighter just as a hand landed on her arm.

"Miss Glaas," someone said as she jerked around, startled by their sudden arrival.

Evylin puffed out an embarrassed sigh as she looked up at her uncle's newfound nemesis. "Oh, hello again, Captain." Her hand dropped away from the collar of her coat. "I thought you'd gone back to camp."

Deckard nodded, his friendly demeanor present as always. "My apologies for surprising you like that. You're right, I did, but I was returning to your home to pick up a few things. Might I join you?"

Evylin looked at her house, a mere twenty yards away. "Are you sure you can stand my company for that long?"

His laugh had a breathy, carefree quality to it. "I imagine I can endure it," he replied, and they began their short walk back, a respectful distance between them. "Actually, I was rather hoping for a chance to speak with you alone."

Drawing her shoulders back, Evylin braced herself. She couldn't fathom what he might want to say to her. Had he taken offense at Hewitt's behavior? His lighthearted smile didn't suggest any irritation, but he could be good at hiding it.

After Hewitt's suggestion moments ago, a far more unwelcome thought crossed her mind. Evylin swallowed past the rising tightness in her throat, afraid the captain might have mistaken her friendliness for an interest.

Glancing up at him, she adopted his jovial demeanor as a defense. "I'm honored. Though I admit, I'm unsure how I've gained such favor."

Deckard's posture relaxed. "In the pursuit of honesty, I have a confession myself. In all the settlements I enter, whether a small village like this or a large town, I try to find someone from whom I can get advice. I find it beneficial to learn about the area so I don't offend or cause any trouble." He turned to give her a meaningful look. "And you seem to have just the sort of knowledge and pleasurable company for which I search."

Stopping in her tracks, Evylin stared up at the captain. The fading sun caught in his eyes, revealing a curious blend of blue and green. The more he was around, the more she understood Calyn's infatuation. And why Hewitt disliked him so much.

"My uncle's right about you," she said lightly.

Deckard's ruddy eyebrows quirked up. "How so?"

"You are a sycophant."

There was that laugh again. This time, it bled into the first of his words. "At least now I know why he hates me. I thought it might be something I said." His eyes crinkled at the edges. "I suppose I was right."

Despite his friendliness, Evylin tried to decipher the truth about this man. She couldn't quite tell if his good nature was an act. He did seem to appreciate her candor despite the sarcasm accompanying it. But a man as well-traveled and experienced as a captain would never value the opinion of a village girl. Especially when he knew nothing about her.

"How can I help you, Captain?" she asked, determined to puzzle him out.

Deckard resumed their walk as he began. "As our conversation last night was cut short, I was hoping you might provide more information about Trollenston."

It was an innocent enough request. "I see," she said. "What would you like to know?"

"Would you have any insight into the town's feelings toward the war?"

Taking a quick breath in, Evylin considered how to give a full report without being too callous. "We share the same views from everything I've heard. Of course, we all support the war. Nearly two centuries of attacking our country for the sake of land have not borne any compassion for Wauld. No one in Trollenston, Whickam Village, or anywhere else in the province thinks the war to be wrong, to my knowledge. We are defending our country and its safety.

"However . . ." Evylin continued with a sigh, "the war has taken almost every young, healthy man in the whole of Estshire. Some families can barely survive. We all understand the war, but we would really like to see it end."

Taking in her words, Deckard looked over the square. In his short time in the village, he had to have seen that aside from the soldiers he'd brought with him, nearly all its occupants were female. Aside from the farrier, her father, and Hewitt, all the men left in the village were on the farms and in the fields, scrambling to keep the settlement functioning.

"Thank you for that assessment," Captain Deckard said, turning back to her. After a breath, he continued, "Do you think that would reflect poorly upon the acquisition of volunteers? If we want the war to end, we'll need the men to do it."

Evylin gave him an apologetic smile. "I'm afraid your search for volunteers will only disappoint," she said softly, "here or in Trollenston."

The way the captain's eyebrows pinched together, she worried she'd been too blunt. She shifted from foot to foot as his silence stretched. Had she already ruined the chances for her plan? Would he want anything to do with her now?

But then Deckard gave her that charming smile. "Thank you for your honesty, Miss Glaas," he said warmly. "It is greatly appreciated."

Evylin nodded, looking away toward her home. They stood only a few feet from the door now. She ought to excuse herself from his presence. But she didn't quite know how.

Following her gaze, Deckard rubbed his bare hands against the cold wind. "I do—" He hesitated, then began again. "I do have another question, if I might ask it?"

At Evylin's nod, he continued, "Can you tell me . . ." His eyes turned from the door at last as he continued to wring his hands, "is your sister . . . ?"

Taken aback, Evylin blinked in response. Then the corner of her mouth lifted. "I would ask if you were referring to Calyn or Dolia," she said knowingly, "but the fact is they are both madly in love with you. Though I warn you, Dolia does have a fiancé whose heart would break if you stole her away."

It took a moment, but a weak laugh puffed out of Deckard. And for the first time, his smile did not hold its usual heartfelt quality. "I'm sure you're overstating to tease me. But I warn that you shouldn't lie to a man about that sort of thing."

Evylin couldn't help her amusement at his nervousness. "Oh, no," she insisted. "Everything I've said is true. Dolia is engaged, and they are both quite overcome. Indeed, the very first thing either one said upon my return from town was that we had a handsome, charming, and impressive captain staying with us."

She was brave enough to admit that however much her sisters' infatuation colored their opinions, they weren't completely wrong. Deckard was handsome, if not striking; he had a charm in his easy humor and friendly personality, and he carried himself well, which did impress Evylin.

Deckard's gaze drifted again to the door leading into the Glaas home. He clasped his hands behind his back now, like a soldier receiving a rebuke. "They are too kind," he muttered.

Noting his discomfort, Evylin worried she'd misinterpreted his question. "Any particular reason you ask?" she prompted uneasily.

Deckard's eyes, more blue than green in the early evening light, met hers with solemnity. "I travel a lot of places, Miss Glaas," he said, his voice deeper than before. "And it isn't abnormal for young ladies to . . . take a liking to me or my soldiers, as men are scarce in most settlements and, particularly so, in villages."

Deckard took a steadying breath before concluding, "I don't like encouraging those feelings when I know I cannot return them. In an effort to mitigate any hurt I may cause, I try to find out which of the ladies I need to be wary of early in my stay."

Evylin studied this version of the captain, questioning if this might be the true Deckard. He seemed pleasant and joyful, but Hewitt's assessment appeared correct. Deckard presented himself with an impeccable temperament to get on people's good side and survive the drudgery of his task.

Only equipped to handle awkward moments one way, Evylin wore a sly grin. "I do sympathize with you, my dear Captain," she said. "But I fear the damage has already been done."

Deckard furrowed his brow in confusion.

"Though my sisters may have overstated your finer qualities," she continued, "they didn't lie. You are pleasant enough to look at, and you do make delightful company. As a bachelor, your presence itself is an offer of marriage to every unattached woman in sight." Evylin let out a dramatic sigh. "I'm afraid you must resign yourself to the fact that you will leave a string of broken hearts wherever you go."

A second ticked by in utter stillness, causing Evylin to wonder if she'd gone too far with her jest. Her confidence began to slip. But to her relief, Deckard let out a scoff that turned into a hearty laugh.

"Thank you," he said. "It isn't often that people sympathize with me. Or make me laugh in the process."

Evylin gave him her best curtsy. "I would say I live to serve, but according to Lieutenant Peery, that's your job."

An embarrassed chuckle slipped out of the captain. "Peery talks too much."

Evylin smirked. "If memory serves, *you* did most of the talking last night, Captain."

"I asked questions," he defended, "as any houseguest should to keep the conversation going."

"That's right. You did the asking, and my father did the answering. Two peas in a pod, I suppose."

Deckard's expression grew more and more amused. "Are you suggesting I talk too much?"

"Not at all," she laughed. "Though Hewitt would absolutely say so."

"Absolutely."

She shook her head, her laughter trailing off. "No, you don't talk too much, Captain. Not for me, anyway."

A twitch pulled the corner of his mouth down.

Evylin froze, realizing the connotation of her words. She cleared her throat, grasping for a recovery. "Your pleasant conversation is a boon to me, you see," she scrambled to add. "It keeps my father's attention off me and my unladylike behavior."

Deckard's smile returned, still a hint sheepish as he tugged at the bottom of his dark gray coat. Evylin decided that Calyn was right; he did look better in green.

"A service for a service, I suppose," he said, meeting her eyes once more. "I thank you for your help, Miss Glaas. It's been most enlightening."

"And rather disappointing, I'm sure," Evylin noted. "I wish I could give you better news. As I wish I could tell you that my sisters aren't foolish enough to fall in love with a stranger. But I can't."

Deckard shook his head, his eyes earnest. "Please, don't feel you've disappointed me. Though I don't deny that I'd hoped for different answers, I couldn't be more pleased to know you've told me the truth. Few people I've met are willing to do that."

Unsure how to respond, Evylin only managed a slight nod.

This was the perfect moment to enact her plan, she knew. She should say something. Perhaps start a conversation about the captain's life as a soldier. Or possibly ask what adventures he'd experienced. Anything to lead to a discussion of her predicament.

But she couldn't form the words. Not while he stared at her so attentively.

The silence between them stretched longer than comfort allowed, and at last, Deckard reached for the door. "Thank you again for your time," he said as the latch clicked free. The door swung wide behind her.

"Captain Deckard," she heard herself say in a rush.

His brow rose in anticipation. "Yes, Miss Glaas?"

The words caught in her throat.

He waited.

"Uh . . ." She faltered, glancing toward the village square for help. A few soldiers clustered near the tavern. She turned back to meet his expectant gaze. "You should bring your brother to dinner."

His head tilted to the side. "Oh?"

Propelled by her panic, Evylin nodded enthusiastically. "My mother would be appalled to learn you have a brother, and she never got to play hostess to both of you."

To her surprise, he looked disappointed. "Of course."

"Good."

Another beat of silence stretched before Deckard gestured toward the entrance. "Until dinner, Miss Glaas," he said, dipping his head.

Infinitely disappointed in herself, Evylin stepped through the door. She should have said something. That was her one chance to be alone with the captain. If she wanted to earn his aid, she needed that moment to plant the seed of compassion that would produce her opportunity for escape. Any suggestion toward her interest in leaving would have ensured a better outcome than that.

Mortified and unsure of what else to do, Evylin hurried up the stairs as Captain Deckard walked slowly behind her, their shared path awkward after their goodbye. The second she shut her bedroom door behind her, she heaved the annoyed breath she'd been holding. She paced to the center of her room and gripped the footboard of her bed.

Stupid. Cowardly. Embarrassing.

She'd failed herself.

A second door shut in the hall, and Evylin turned as she imagined the captain entering his quarters. Her hand drifted to her mouth as a slow realization sparked in her thoughts. For all her disappointment, he was the one who'd sought her out, wasn't he?

Here she was, plotting ways to befriend him, and *he'd* come to her. What's more, he'd responded well to everything she said, which was a shock considering how most men responded to her sarcastic candor.

Evylin couldn't help smiling as she remembered his laughter and smiles. Despite her presumed failure, the truth was plain: She didn't need to scheme up a way to win Captain Deckard's friendship.

She already had it.

CHAPTER FIVE

Before dinner that evening, Lawton made it clear that there would be no working in the smithy the next day. "Captain Deckard is giving his speech tomorrow," he said moments before their guests arrived. He fixed Hewitt with a pointed glare. "Everyone in the village is missing a day of work. Your customers will understand if you do too."

Despite his earlier protests, Hewitt had arrived on time for the meal. It pleased Evylin to have him at her side. But her father risked riling an already testy man. Hewitt valued two things in life: his shop and his independence. And now, his brother had managed to take them both away in seconds.

As Hewitt's hands curled into fists, Evylin gripped his wrist with enough force to draw his glare. She tipped her left eyebrow up to insist that he play nice. It took several seconds before his hands relaxed, and his snarl turned to the floorboards.

Captain Deckard and his brother arrived promptly, as expected, both wearing their green coats. The captain was as charming as ever, while the lieutenant displayed a hint of reluctance at meeting the family. He did smile at Evylin, though, upon seeing her again, and he responded as a gentleman should when Laurisa welcomed him.

However, his character was truly tested when Calyn entered the room. The girl almost dropped the bowl of roasted potatoes in her hands at the sight of him, and an audible gasp of awe escaped her.

"Ah," Lawton said, gesturing toward her. "Here is my other daughter, Calyn."

Calyn stared at the lieutenant in wide-eyed wonder, confirming Evylin's suspicions. Whatever infatuation her little sister felt for the captain, it held little depth and relied solely on novelty. Thom Deckard's striking blue eyes, dark hair, and muscular physique were all Calyn needed to forget the man she'd sworn to marry only the day prior.

The lieutenant glanced at Deckard as if looking for help while Calyn gaped at him. Receiving no aid beyond an amused glance, the younger man sighed. "It's a pleasure to meet you, Miss Glaas," he said politely.

Calyn's cheeks flushed pink. "Absolutely," she muttered, then gasped at her faux pas. "I mean, no, it's—it's a pleasure to meet you. I—well, any friend—I mean, family of the captain's, is our friend, or . . . family?"

Pressing her lips together, Evylin struggled to hold in her amusement. She glanced the captain's way to find Deckard wearing a contained smile as his eyes flickered between his brother, Calyn, and Evylin.

When her father suggested they take their seats, Calyn rushed to set the potatoes down. She dropped them onto the table with a *thunk* as the bowl slipped through her fingers in her hurry to steal Dolia's usual seat so she could sit next to Thom.

As expected, Captain Deckard and her father carried most of the conversation. But Deckard found ways to draw Evylin and his brother in as well. Though Lieutenant Deckard didn't bear the same easy and sociable disposition as his brother, Evylin found that his sense of humor matched hers. Witty with a hint of cynicism that she couldn't help laughing along to.

Hewitt remained silent, no matter how many times Lawton asked the Deckard brothers questions about the war or military life. He didn't even glare at them. Instead, he listened in, even nodding a few times while Deckard and his brother spoke of their experiences. It was a pleasant, if boring, surprise.

And Evylin took care not to let the whole evening pass without making up ground on her plans. When Calyn had finally worked up the courage to distract the lieutenant with questions, Evylin checked the other end of the table where Dolia kept their parents' attention with her wishes to visit Devaan in Trollenston.

Taking her opportunity, Evylin reached for her wine glass, angling inconspicuously toward Deckard in the process. She caught his eye and whispered past Hewitt. "I think I found the solution to that problem of yours."

Her uncle narrowed his eyes while Deckard furrowed his brow, leaning in as she had. "Which problem would that be?" he asked, keeping his voice low.

Evylin tipped her head toward their siblings. "Your overly attentive friend."

Following her direction, Deckard surveyed the pair. "I think you might be right," he replied wryly.

They shared a knowing grin and sat back. Evylin applauded herself for sharing a conspiratorial joke. That was something only friends did, wasn't it? And she'd done it quite successfully too.

Evylin had never had many friends. While she got on well enough with Euna and Albina, they'd never had much in common. And Calyn and Dolia were so much her juniors that, alongside being so dissimilar, they'd never had the chance to be truly close. Yet she'd not felt the need for others with Ryen at her side. It hadn't bothered her being separated from her sisters. She'd had no reason to feel alone.

While her sisters were busy pining after boys and admiring pretty dresses, Evylin spent her time in the woods, reenacting legendary tales with Ryen. And when they grew tired of their own company, he would talk the village boys into letting her join them. As she could throw a punch and climb a tree as well, if not better, than any of them, it all seemed ideal.

But that was before the fire.

And before Evylin found herself unbearably alone.

Sipping her wine, Evylin allowed the oaky tannins to tingle along her tongue, pulling her back to the present. She focused on making the dinner a success, interacting with the captain and lieutenant as much as possible to distract herself from the unwelcome memories.

But even with all the laughter and lively conversation, when she returned to her room, the heavy pressure of memories strained against her chest. She moved through her nightly routine in a lazy and unfocused haze, leaving her skirts and blouse in a pile by the wardrobe. The pressure rose through her sternum and into her throat, raising heat with it.

As her nightdress fell to settle around her calves, Evylin pressed her lips together in resolve.

That was why she needed to leave. Whatever course she chose, Whickam Village offered her one thing: pain. The pain of her past and her inevitable future, the pain of isolation and monotony.

Evylin dropped onto her bed, staring at the cream plaster ceiling. Her eyes scanned its smooth, aged surface. She'd made a promise to herself and to Ryen. She had to make this work. She *had* to convince Deckard to take her with him. And she was running out of time.

Captain Deckard had announced at dinner that the army would leave the morning after his speech, giving her only a little more than twenty-four hours to gain his services. Yet even should he accept her request, she had no assurance that he could convince her father to let her go. And she feared that no matter his answer, she'd be stuck in Whickam Village for the rest of her life.

A soft knock startled Evylin, and Calyn opened her door.

"Can I come in?" she asked, half inside already.

Glad for the distraction, Evylin patted the space next to her. Calyn shut the door, then bounded over. The mattress bowed as she threw herself under the blankets at Evylin's side.

"Oh, Evie," she sighed, brown eyes wide, "he's so handsome, isn't he?"

Evylin brushed some hair out of her sister's eyes. "Yes, they both are. Quite a lucky family, the Deckards."

"Did you notice the little scar on his brow?"

"On Captain Deckard?"

"No, no." Calyn shook her head. "On *Lieutenant* Deckard."

"Can't say that I did."

Calyn heaved a wistful sigh. "It sort of puckers when he smiles. It's very endearing. And his eyes. They're the most beautiful shade of blue. They look gray at times. Almost silver. You had to notice that, surely?"

"It's hard not to notice that, yes," she admitted.

In fact, it was hard not to notice either of the Deckard brothers' eye color. The lieutenant's gray-blue gaze was as remarkable as the captain's green-blue eyes were fascinating. *A lucky family, indeed.*

Calyn dropped her head onto Evylin's shoulder as they lay side by side. "I don't know what to do."

"About what?"

"About Lieutenant Deckard."

Evylin took her sister's hand. "And what exactly are you hoping to do?"

"I . . ." Her whisper broke before she tried again. "I'd like to marry him."

Having heard such a similar declaration the day before, Evylin didn't put much stock in it. Still, after twenty-six years of life with four sisters, she knew not to make fun of their more delicate emotions.

"I'm not sure why you've come to me," Evylin said. "I understand your attraction, but what makes you so sure you'd like to marry him?"

Calyn drew back to rest on her arm and stared down at her. "What do you mean? Why wouldn't I want to marry him?"

"You don't know him."

"That doesn't matter."

"Doesn't it?"

"Not if you're in love."

Evylin took a deep breath. She knew her sister too well to think she could change her mind, but she was determined to check her fanciful ideas anyway. "Caly," she moved to sit up, too, "please don't take this the wrong way, but you're not in love."

Calyn's mouth gaped, but Evylin hurried on. "You met him a handful of hours ago. And you have no means of knowing if Lieutenant Deckard has any interest in you either. It isn't wise for you to set your hopes on his affections. Not until you've had more than one conversation with him."

"I'm not stupid, Evie." Calyn glared at her. "I know that I said I liked Captain Deckard yesterday, but . . . well, I didn't know then."

"And what makes you think you know now?"

Calyn frowned.

Scooting closer, Evylin took her sister's hand once more. "I'm not saying that you shouldn't take an interest. I'm not even saying I think it's a bad idea," she conceded. "All I'm saying is that you should give it time."

"I don't have much time."

Evylin blinked, hearing the same words she'd thought to herself earlier. She was running out of time. And while she managed to soothe Calyn's romantic anxieties after another hour of discussion, her own worries plagued her mind throughout the night.

With Calyn asleep beside her, Evylin snuggled deeper into the warmth of her blankets. What would she do if her plans failed—if she never managed to leave Whickam Village? Could she live fifty or more years like this? Would she relegate herself to marrying an old man just so she wasn't alone? Was it possible for her to find a younger bachelor in town who would be willing to marry a woman so much his senior? Would she want to?

Or would her inaction trap her here within the walls of her childhood, with only Hewitt and the pain of their past for company?

12TH OF TERRAEN, 1573

Fastening the gray skirt around her waist, Evylin glanced in the mirror to ensure a respectable appearance. The morning light made her hair appear golden around the edges rather than its usual deep brown. She'd taken care to do it the way her mother would most approve, its wavy edges dropping below her shoulders.

Driven by her increasing nerves and need for help, Evylin hurried through her breakfast and off to the smithy. Lawton's orders might keep the shop closed, but she knew Hewitt would be there anyway. The only time he spent in his small apartment was when he needed sleep, and the rest of the time, he lived at work.

Sure enough, he stood there tinkering with Missy Felming's knives when Evylin entered. "Morning," he muttered.

"Good morning." She leaned on the edge of the workbench across from him. "Sneaking in a bit of work, I see."

Hewitt spared her a glance. "We've still got time before the captain gives his speech. I may as well make some use of my morning."

"You're a pillar of the community."

He scoffed and went back to work.

Evylin chewed on her bottom lip as he tested a variety of woods against the original handle.

"What is it?" he asked without looking up.

Crossing her arms, Evylin didn't need to ask how he knew she was up to something. He always knew. "I was hoping to run something by you," she explained. "I need your advice."

Hewitt's gray eyes flashed to her face like the light glinting off the blade he held. "On what?" he asked as though he already knew the answer.

"I've had an idea. One that I think . . ."

He stared at her as she hesitated to speak it out loud. Despite Hewitt's support of her desire to leave Whickam Village, she'd never actually produced a plan that didn't include his leaving with her. No matter how assured she was that he would always stay in the village, she'd never been able to imagine parting from him. And she worried he'd take this new plan to mean she didn't love him enough to stay at his side.

Taking a deep breath, Evylin forced herself to say it anyway. "One that I think will get me out of here."

The knife clunked onto the bench as Hewitt let it go. "Really?"

"Yes, but . . . well, I'm worried that I don't have enough time."

Hewitt's eyes narrowed. "Enough time for what?"

"I thought to ask Captain Deckard to take me with him."

His shoulders tensed.

Forcing her next words out quickly, Evylin worked to explain. "I've saved every penny you've ever given me, and it's a rather large sum now. I intend to offer him payment for being my guide through Ephria. I know that alone may not be enough, but I think if he got to know me—got to know my situation . . . He's a kind, religious man, and I thought he might feel compelled to help me as an act of service."

Hewitt was as silent as he was still.

"I figure that with him at my side," she continued, "I'll have no reason to fear traveling. I can see the country and have an adventure, just as we always dreamed. No one would dare question an officer in the army. And I'd be more than capable of keeping us safe should we run into any trouble."

An unusual quiet fell over the room as she proffered her case. Without the forge crackling or Hewitt's tools clanging, it felt eerie.

Evylin took a deep breath. "What do you think?"

"That's it?" Hewitt asked, his voice a low rumble. "That's your plan? Hire him as a guide?"

The inflection of his words told Evylin all she needed to know. "You think it's a bad plan?"

"I think it's a stupid plan."

She sighed, used to his blunt delivery. "Why?"

"Because it's childish. You're smarter than that, Evie. You know it would never work."

"I'm making a perfectly sound offer." She set her hands on the bench to lean closer. "Over a hundred crowns to act as an escort should tempt anyone."

"Not him."

"Because he's pious? You don't think the money will tempt him?"

"He's a captain, not a tour guide," Hewitt said sharply. "It wouldn't matter if the money tempted him; he cannot accept it. It's his job to travel with the army and gather volunteers. Bringing you along for the ride is not an option."

Evylin stepped away from the bench, shoulders drooping.

"If his commanding officers discovered that he'd taken money to be your little chaperone, it would result in a censure. It's unprofessional and completely unheard of."

"It's not like I'd be asking him to leave his post," she argued. "I'm simply asking for an escort. Surely there are contingencies for emergency situations."

"This isn't an emergency."

"Isn't it?" she demanded.

Hewitt's sharp glare softened at the rise in her voice.

Setting a hand to her head, Evylin sucked in a deep breath. "I can't stay here anymore!" The words came out like a plea of desperation. "You know that."

"I do."

"This is as dire as it gets," she whispered in panic. "Every day, my chances are slipping farther and farther away. I settle and marry one of these idle and idiotic men, or I resign myself to being alone for the rest of my life. Either way, our dream goes unfulfilled. I'm not running out of time, Uncle. My time is already gone."

He held her fierce stare with his own.

"This is my last chance," she insisted. "I have to do something. And if I make a fool out of myself in the process, then so be it. At least I'll have tried."

Hewitt scratched his singed beard, lips pressed together. His breath drew still, the air around them falling silent. She knew this statuesque calm of his. Hewitt worked through his more challenging projects and problems in this way, with a tranquility that gave him focus.

He shifted his weight as his hand fell away. "You're right," he said, his tone gentle. "But this is not the way."

Evylin shook her head, at a loss.

"Listen to me." Hewitt reached across the workbench and grabbed her shoulder. "The captain cannot take on travelers. This is not the way."

"It could be."

"No. And even if he agreed, you know Lawton would recall you the second you stepped foot outside Whickam Village's boundaries."

Evylin wilted but offered her optimistic solution in a meek whisper. "Father likes him. He respects him. The captain might be able to convince him."

The way Hewitt's left eyebrow tipped up said her hope was futile.

Dropping her eyes to the work-worn wood on the bench top, Evylin let her plans crumble into despair. Her uncle was right. She'd been far too wishful and idealistic in her planning. And her dreams—*their* dreams—were at an end.

Hewitt's calloused palm cupped Evylin's cheek, tipping her head up to look at him. His soft, steady gaze cut through her fears. "We'll find another way. I promise."

"How?" she whispered in disbelief.

Hewitt drew away. "I'm . . . working on it."

"We've been working on it for the past thirteen years."

"Just . . ." He held up his hand, begging her patience. "Just trust me, Evie. I'll get you out of here. No matter what."

The conviction of his words and his tender expression lightened the pressure in Evylin's chest. She wanted to trust him, but it was as she'd said: They'd worked on her escape for half her lifetime, and still, they had nothing. She wanted to believe that Hewitt would find a solution. But she couldn't see how anything would change.

"Do you trust me?" Hewitt asked, his confidence evident in each word.

Evylin let out a stuttering breath, eyes falling to the dirt beneath her feet. Did she trust him?

"Always," she said, then met his gaze once more. She didn't see how his plan would be any different than hers—wishful and faulty. But if there was anyone in this world who could be relied upon, it was Hewitt.

"Then act like you mean it," he ordered.

A thin laugh escaped Evylin at the charge. "Your plan better be good," she returned. "It better work."

"It will," he promised, then stepped around the workbench. "Now, come on. Our noble captain should be starting his speech. And it'd be a pity to miss that, now, wouldn't it?"

"Uncle." Evylin caught his arm before he walked past her.

"What?"

Try as she might, Evylin couldn't stop her voice from trembling. "You don't think there's any chance . . . ?"

"It wouldn't work, Evie. Not by any means."

Though she supposed she should have been relieved to let go of her faulty plan, Evylin only felt more anxious. She'd thought she had her answer. She'd thought she was going to escape. And now, she had to start all over again with no more direction than before.

But, Evylin reminded herself as she followed her uncle out into the sunshine of the village square, *Hewitt has a plan.* And she would take comfort in that.

CHAPTER SIX

Evylin followed Hewitt through the crowd in the square. His brown coat blended with his dark hair even in the bright morning light. With shoulders back and head held high, he still carried himself like an officer. One of the things that had drawn Evylin to him as a child was his strength and calm, his gravitas and openness. He never altered himself for company. He was—for good or ill—Hewitt Glaas, and there was no changing him.

Weaving her way through the crowd, Evylin kept her eyes on Hewitt's back, taking comfort in his familiarity. The village's residents stood in the square to listen to Captain Deckard. With so many men taken over the years, the crowd was sparse compared to the populace of Trollenston. But there were still enough men who hadn't met the draft requirements five years prior, along with the women and children, to make the small village center feel like a sheep pen.

"I'm surprised you care enough to be here," Evylin remarked as they halted near the middle of the crowd. "I half expected you to ignore Father's request."

Hewitt glanced down at her. "I'm interested to hear what the captain has to say."

"You think he might have an opportunity for you?" Evylin teased.

Hewitt didn't reply but crossed his arms. His eyes lifted to the smoke-stained hall. Four soldiers stood on the steps, their posture upright and expressions relaxed, a display of grandeur rather than crowd control.

Evylin chewed on her lip as she scanned the hall's scarred façade. "Have you come to like our captain's friendship?" she jested, wanting to forget the building. "You were far more civil last night. Could you be changing your mind?"

"My feelings are as they were."

"A pity. I, for one, find him quite entertaining."

"I noticed," Hewitt grumbled.

Evylin was about to retort when the hall's wooden doors opened. The crowd's chatter died down as Lawton walked out with Captain Deckard. Only occasional murmurs and the not-so-hushed whispers of children broke the silence as the men approached the edge of the steps.

"Good citizens of Whickam Village," Lawton called. "For the past two days, I've had the great honor to host Captain Deckard of the Ephrian Army in my home. He is one of His Majesty's most noble soldiers and the very picture of what a man ought to be."

Evylin thought of rolling her eyes or whispering a biting remark to Hewitt, yet she couldn't disagree with her father's assessment. Captain Deckard did seem to be an exemplary gentleman, though an underwhelming soldier. He was respectful, good-humored, and honorable. The only trait he lacked was skill with a sword.

Lawton continued his verbose introduction. "Captain Deckard requested I bring you all here today so that he might speak with you on behalf of our benevolent king."

Hewitt scoffed at that.

"I thank you for leaving your farms and businesses to come and hear him. I know his words will prove as welcome as his presence." Lawton stepped to the side and gestured to Deckard. "You may proceed, Captain."

Deckard bowed to Lawton, then took the magistrate's vacated spot on the steps. Every compliment her father paid the captain matched his appearance. In his dress uniform, any man or woman would be hard-pressed to think him anything but noble. He looked finer than she'd seen him yet. The white cravat, tied with the perfect drape, was an elegant contrast against his emerald coat. Silver buttons gleamed in the sunlight, polished like new. Even his black trousers, tucked into his boots, showed no seam or wrinkle.

The soldiers on the stairs didn't come near the captain's superior regalia. Though they all wore green coats, the wool was a much lower quality than the rich velvet of the captain's. Lieutenant Peery stood to the far right of the hall, chin held high and hands clasped behind his back.

Out of curiosity, Evylin searched for Lieutenant Deckard in the crowd, surprised not to see him next to his brother. She didn't find him, but she did spot Calyn. She didn't appear to have received the same invitation as everyone else in the village. While they were all dressed in their usual workwear, the rosy-pink collar of Calyn's best dress peeked out from under her dark blue coat. She'd even taken the time to curl her usually wavy hair.

"Ladies and gentlemen," Deckard's smooth but commanding voice drew Evylin back to the present, "it is my privilege and duty to extend the gratitude of our sovereign King

Ephren for your diligence and fortitude. Our king knows that you are the backbone of this country, the very lifeblood that keeps it running. Without you . . ." He let his words hang as he looked from person to person in the crowd. "Our kingdom would fall."

Taking one step down the stairs, Deckard continued as he smiled at the crowd. "My speech will be short, I assure you. Our king sent me to you for one important purpose: to *ask* for your help once more."

Tension settled over the village square. His words were nothing but confirmation of the villagers' fears. Regardless of how Deckard phrased it, no one would hear the request, but instead, the truth: The king wanted their men again.

"Our king feels your hesitation and concern. He has not sent me here to *take* from you." Deckard's words were swift, as if to soothe their fears.

Evylin doubted the feat was possible.

"Why has he sent us, then?" Deckard said, one hand on the pommel of the sword at his hip. "Because he needs you. You know our war and our cause; I won't waste your time with the age-old story. We've fought this war for almost two centuries—that is not a fact any of us can forget.

"I came in the name of the king, forcing you out of your fields and businesses for a speech's sake. I know and feel the demand of this sacrifice as you do," he set a hand to his chest, "because I am one of you. I was born in a village much like this in Nettershire. My father is a farmer, and we worked hard day and night to live. Just as you work hard, day and night."

Evylin met Hewitt's quizzical gaze. Captain Deckard wasn't an "Officer of Means" after all. So what kind of officer was he?

Deckard began to pace on the stairs. "Instead of telling you what you already know, I wish to share a story. When I was a boy, each night after dinner, my father would pick up his book of legends—the one his father once read to him—and he'd read to my siblings and me. I swear, I heard those stories so many times I could recite any of them to you now. 'The Tricks of Nikleby Draaw.' 'Iona the Worthy' and all her acts of mercy. 'The Humble Shepherd & Vainglorious Mages.'" Deckard chuckled, as did many in the crowd at the last one.

A low hum rose as people mentioned their favorite tales. Every parent in Ephria told those same stories to their children. Evylin remembered *The Traveler and the Rook*, a collection of legends, from her childhood as well. It had sparked Evylin and Ryen's imagination and love of adventure early on.

A far-off look came to Deckard's expression. "But the one I remember best is 'The King's Knight.'"

Another rumble of approval came from the crowd.

"The story of Euon Sergus always stuck with me," Deckard said. "You all know it, of course. Sergus saved towns and villages all over Allund. He won hundreds of battles, fed the hungry, and adopted an orphan as his own son. He laid down his life at the end, taking the bolt meant for his king. And even in his dying breath, he didn't take any credit for his actions; he simply said that he'd done his duty, and the men who aided him were the only thing that made his actions possible."

Deckard fell silent along with the crowd as the details of Euon Sergus's story flitted through Evylin's memories. Albeit a legend for over a millennium past, Sergus had captured children's fascination for generations. Boys dreamed of becoming such a brave hero; girls dreamed of marrying such a gallant knight. Evylin couldn't deny that the story of Sergus had played its role in her life too.

She bit back a sharp memory of Ryen pretending to be Sergus, claiming Evylin as his right hand as they cut down the imaginary Mages in the woods.

"Sergus's story, legend or not, taught me a valuable lesson," Deckard continued, his gentle voice cutting through the quiet like a sword. "One man can make the difference. Sergus knew he was nothing without the men who stood by his side. He could do nothing without them. And while I can never be Sergus, I can be one of those men who makes the difference."

Deckard rested his hand back on the pommel of his sword. "I am a soldier born not out of a draft or a debt that demands payment. I chose my lot. A fact few of my fellow soldiers can lay claim to." He stepped back up to the top step. "Often, I'm asked why I made my choice. I always tell the story I just told you. I tell them that while I may never lay claim to glory, I may be able to make the difference between Ephria's victory and defeat.

"Why did the king send us?" Deckard asked again. "Because we need the men who can make the difference. This war has raged since long before any of us were born. Help us be the generation who ends it. Help us make the difference."

Deckard's eyes roved across the crowd. His speech fell upon ears that could not respond to its call; he had to see that. Evylin wondered idly if he'd noticed her standing in their midst.

"I will be here at the meeting hall until sundown," he said. "I'd love nothing more than to speak with any of you and answer whatever questions you may have." With that, he gave a bow and turned to Magistrate Glaas.

Lawton hurried forward, not missing the moment to *ooh* and *ahh* about the captain's speech.

Hewitt turned the second Deckard stepped back. "Shall we go meet with the lieutenant?"

"I suppose we should," Evylin agreed. "I was rather surprised not to see him standing with his brother."

"I'm sure the captain freed up his schedule so he could meet with me," Hewitt said as they moved back through the crowd. "After all, he does so want to be a boon to me."

Evylin laughed, waving as she saw her eldest sister, Euna, and her five daughters across the crowd. "But who can blame him for wanting to be on the good side of the famous General Glaas?"

"Who, indeed?" Hewitt muttered, opening the smithy doors as Lieutenant Deckard approached from the main street, a large brown stallion at his side.

Upon their greetings, he said, "I hope you enjoyed Deckard's speech."

"It was very informative," Hewitt said, scanning the horse at a distance. "Which hoof is it?"

The lieutenant gave them an apologetic shrug. "Deckard said to have them all redone."

With a grunt, Hewitt turned. "Right, then. Suppose we ought to get to it."

An hour later, the horse had all new shoes, and the lieutenant handed the small fee to Evylin while Hewitt stabled the horse.

Once he returned, Hewitt gestured for the soldier to follow. Thom watched with seeming surprise as Evylin walked alongside her uncle. "Are you joining us, Miss Glaas?"

"Would you rather I not, Lieutenant?" she asked, crossing through the paddock to the other side of the fence.

He scratched the back of his head. "Of course, you're welcome. It's just—most women don't have an interest in watching men practice."

Evylin leaned against the fence with a sly grin. "I'm not most women."

His brow quirked. "I don't doubt that at all."

Hewitt took his favorite blade from the rack hung on the back wall. "I don't have many training swords, but you're welcome to pick whichever you prefer."

Thom shook his head. "Thank you, but I've brought my own."

"Ah." Hewitt passed Evylin an amused look. "Yes, I suppose a company of recruits should have one or two. Shall we?"

The lieutenant began unbuttoning his gray coat as he stepped near Evylin. "How worried should I be?" he asked, humor lighting up his eyes.

Evylin pretended to frown. "You have no hope."

"Very well." He draped his coat over the fence next to her. "Don't ridicule me too much when it's over, then. I'm only a lieutenant."

"And he's only a smith."

"Mm." He chuckled, drawing the dulled broadsword at his waist. He paced back to the center of the paddock and gave Hewitt a nod.

They took a few moments to size each other up before it began.

Thom stepped forward, one long stride before a shuffle to close the distance. It would have been easy to miss how his sword swept from his shoulder to meet Hewitt's within the blink of an eye.

A sharp *clink* preceded the barrage of a dozen more.

Evylin watched as the men parried back and forth. She could see that Thom's movements were slower than Hewitt's, but he was quick enough not to reveal his every move as he wound up to strike.

Still, it was clear in only moments that whatever natural talent he owned, he did not have much technique beyond his basic training. Always landing sharp blows to the center of the blade, forgetting that the tip was the key to outmaneuvering your opponent. The swords crashed against each other as Thom tried to win through sheer strength.

Evylin couldn't help her disappointment. Although he had the foundation, he lacked the skill to be a truly great swordsman.

It was due to this unfinished training that Hewitt managed to sneak his blade underneath Thom's and, with a deft twist, knocked the lieutenant's arms out of the way while pressing the tip of the blade into his stomach.

A puff of air burst from Thom as he froze.

"Well done," Hewitt said, stepping back to release a controlled breath. "You have some reasonable skill."

Thom looked over to Evylin, brow raised. "Some," he agreed as he worked to steady his breathing, "but not enough."

Resting against the fence, Evylin smirked. "I did warn you."

"That you did."

"When did you first learn swordplay?" Hewitt asked.

"Goodness, I dunno." Thom rubbed a hand against his forehead at the unexpected question. "I was . . . eight or nine when I first held a sword. From there, Deckard and I just knocked about as kids. But I didn't have any real training until I joined the army."

"And when was that?"

"Five years back. When the draft came to Stocburrough."

"Five years? That's fast to become a lieutenant."

A proud, though bashful, grin came to his face. "I'm a fast learner. And my officers liked me." He hesitated. "Deckard always recommended me too."

"And how long ago did he join up?"

Thom glanced at Evylin, recognizing the interrogation for what it was. She shrugged playfully to encourage him. Hewitt wasn't the subtle sort. When he wanted information, he asked for it. And while she was surprised at his interest, she was also curious.

The lieutenant brushed back some of his dark hair. "It's been about twelve years, I think."

"He said he'd heard about me. Have you?"

Thom nodded. "You left quite a legacy."

Hewitt's jaw tightened, but he didn't reply.

Taking his silence as an opportunity, Thom cocked his head as he continued, "According to those who knew you, there hasn't been a soldier of your caliber since you left."

Hewitt glared at the edge of the paddock. But still, no reply came.

"Deckard didn't mean to offend you, you know?" Thom offered. "He—*and I*—we're both used to stories about you. It's somewhat of a shock to meet a living legend. Especially out here in the Shires."

That, Evylin was sure, was the wrong thing to say.

Yet, Hewitt's steel-gray stare turned to the lieutenant with a look of curiosity rather than anger. "Why do you call him 'Deckard'? He's your brother."

"Oh, well . . . that's a formality," Thom explained. "A professional courtesy, if you will. Deckard has all his officers call him by his last name rather than his rank. Says it fosters loyalty and camaraderie. Since I joined the army, it's become a bit of a habit. I call him 'Deckard,' and he calls me 'Lieutenant.' However, we do slip up from time to time. Him more than me."

"Have you always worked under his command?"

"No," he said with a scoff. "No, I only joined his company at the start of this mission. It's the first time we've worked together."

"How did you get lucky enough to have yourself assigned to family?" Evylin asked.

Thom hesitated. "When Deckard got this assignment, he was given permission to build a small team to join him."

"That's nice."

"I suppose so."

Hewitt lifted his sword as though he was bored of the conversation. "Should we give it another go?"

Appearing relieved to have reached an end to the inquisition, Thom nodded.

The second bout went similarly to the first. But while Hewitt won again, Thom was more watchful. They tried again and again for the next hour, Thom growing wiser to Hewitt's ways with each round. A sure sign that he was, indeed, a fast learner.

Despite having lost all the bouts, Thom thanked Hewitt for the time. "It was an honor, sir."

"Thank you for indulging an old man," Hewitt said placidly. "It isn't often I find worthy combatants coming through this village."

The lieutenant smiled at Evylin one last time, gave a gracious farewell to them both, and then left with his newly shod horse.

Hewitt stood by the smithy doors, his eyes locked on the soldier's back. "How'd you like to try your hand against him, Evie?" he asked.

Evylin looked up at him. "I've never fought anyone but you."

"You could beat him."

She took a final glance at the retreating lieutenant. "Maybe. I do think it'd be fun either way."

"You saw how he fights," Hewitt said, looking down at her. "You can beat him."

There was something to the glint in his eyes—something Evylin rarely saw and couldn't quite name. "Why would it matter if I won?" she asked.

Hewitt's mouth turned up cunningly. "I figured it out."

A shiver ran down Evylin's spine, hope and fear mixing inside her. "What?"

"I have a plan. A plan that will work."

Evylin stared up at him in awe.

"All you have to do is beat Lieutenant Deckard in a duel."

CHAPTER SEVEN

Dinner was a never-ending affair.

Or, at least, that was how it felt to Evylin.

Thom had arrived just before dinner to deliver the captain's regrets as he was unable to attend the meal. Although Laurisa invited the lieutenant to stay, he declined, intending to join his brother at the hall instead. Still in her pretty pink dress and prepared to win the soldier's heart, Calyn's devastation was palpable.

This returned the Glaas family to their usual routine. With the two extra chairs removed from the table, Hewitt sat across from Lawton. While Calyn sulked, the rest of them struggled to find conversation. It seemed now that Captain Deckard was the only reason they'd managed to converse so easily the past two nights. The silence stretched as Evylin watched the sideboard clock as the night waned.

She found herself saying internal prayers to Allore, begging that Hewitt's plan—whatever it was—would work. Instead of giving her answers, her uncle had simply said, *"I'll tell you after dinner."* That was of no comfort to her racing mind. And it did nothing to calm her concerns.

Waiting to hear his plan plagued her. Was it really possible? Could she truly leave this place? Hope burgeoned inside of her, filling her lungs with anticipation. Dinner couldn't pass fast enough.

Yet, she also feared the ticking clock. On the other side of the meal awaited change and the potential of a duel she might not win. Could she face the opportunity of dreams fulfilled at last, only to have them taken away?

Abruptly, Lawton broke the silence. "It's been a pleasure to have officers like Captain and Lieutenant Deckard in our midst," he said mildly.

Evylin couldn't decide whether she was thankful for the reprieve from the utensils clinking against bowls and plates or if her father's platitude was an unwelcome interruption.

Calyn sighed, a deep, forlorn sound. "I fear we will never see their like again," she lamented, eyes watery.

"Don't be ridiculous, Calyn," Hewitt said between bites of his stew. "Neither the captain nor his brother could be desperate enough to choose *you*."

"Hewitt!" Laurisa gave him a scathing look before turning with compassion to her daughter. "Ignore your uncle. He doesn't know what he's talking about."

Hewitt pierced his sister-in-law with a stolid glare. "Filling her head with dreams of men who are far too ambitious and intelligent for her doesn't help anyone."

Caught between sympathy for her sister and amusement at her uncle's quips, Evylin found herself confused. His good opinion of the younger Deckard didn't surprise her. But the inclusion of the elder brother did.

Lawton's brow lifted with the same realization. "I thought you didn't like the captain," he remarked.

"I don't like him," Hewitt said sharply. "But that doesn't mean I think he's an idiot."

Calyn glowered. "You think I'm only good enough for an idiot?" she demanded.

Hewitt's gaze darted up to the ceiling. "I think you deserve a man like Dolia's MacKenna. Courteous, caring, and amenable with absolutely no sense of adventure. You'll find an excellent match in Trollenston. Or, with a lot of luck, here in the village. But you've set your sights too high with both the captain *and* his brother: the younger, a true soldier, and the elder, a man who chose to leave the comforts of home to become a legend."

Lawton almost choked on his wine. "Really, Hew." He patted his chin with his napkin. "You act as though you've known the man for years."

"Did you not listen to his speech?" Hewitt growled. "That man has dreamed of becoming Sergus since his childhood."

"No different from any other boy."

"You're wrong!" Hewitt's elbow hit the table with a *thud* as he pointed his finger at his brother. "Any other boy forgets those dreams. The captain never forgot his. He holds Euon Sergus next to Allore. A man who values a legend that much dreams of becoming one himself."

The table went silent while the Glaas brothers stared each other down.

Evylin looked between them, wondering if her uncle was right.

"In his speech," Dolia said, her melodic voice softening the atmosphere, "Captain Deckard said he could never be Euon Sergus. He said his only hope was to be like the men who supported him."

Hewitt shook his head. "You don't understand. That's the lie he tells himself to ease his disappointment when reality proves he can't become the man he wants to be. It's the same lie we all tell ourselves when our dreams can't come true, and we need to make the disappointment easier to bear."

The silence returned, heavier this time.

Evylin couldn't ignore Hewitt's words. She, too, harbored lies she told herself. When leaving Whickam Village looked bleak, she reminded herself that she liked the independence she had here. Traveling to Trollenston was farther than most women in the village journeyed. No one could force her to marry a man with no ambition or wit. At the end of the day, if she got stuck in the village, it was on her own terms. And if nothing else, she had Hewitt. She had Ryen.

Evylin glanced out the window in the direction of the kirk. Sometimes, the lies worked. Most of the time, they made her feel worse.

Dinner no longer passed in amicable silence. Quiet hung over them like a blanket of fog, not a comfortable conversation in sight.

After the clock chimed the late hour, Hewitt put down his freshly emptied glass and turned to Evylin. "I promised the captain the rest of the swords we didn't sell at the market. I could use your help wrapping them up."

Evylin rose with him. "I'll grab my coat."

No one argued, but Laurisa told her not to stay out too late.

"I'll meet you at the stables," Hewitt whispered as they walked through the hall.

Hurrying up the stairs to change, Evylin ran through Hewitt's fight with the lieutenant for the hundredth time. Thom knew how to handle a blade well, but he could never be as fast as her. She needed to focus on speed. She also needed to stay away from direct hits as much as possible. He relied on his strength, and he would overpower her in seconds. She couldn't absorb any blow head-on.

Evylin stepped out of her skirts and into her trousers. In her rush, she lost her balance standing on one leg, forcing her to hop as she shimmied on the pants. Once they were buttoned, she took a deep breath and forced herself to slow her pace. She tied the laces on her boots and braided back her hair carefully. It wouldn't do for her to trip or lose focus due to sloppy dressing. She tucked the small knife back into her boot, then pulled on her dark gray coat, not bothering to fasten it.

After rushing down the stairs, Evylin peered out the front window. She saw Hewitt leading the Deckard brothers toward the smithy. Still in his finery, Deckard looked out of place next to the other two. Hewitt wore his old trousers and winter coat, while Thom wore the usual Ephrian uniform in all gray and black.

Glancing down at herself, Evylin realized she wore an outfit like the lieutenant: black trousers and gray coat. The comparison bolstered her confidence, and she opened the door before it could dissipate.

The men didn't notice her as she shut the door without a sound. Moving with long strides across the square, she fisted her shaking hands at her side, reminding herself of the importance of staying calm. She ran Hewitt's favorite sayings over and over in her mind: *"A level head always wins the fight. Focus is a swordsman's best weapon."*

Hewitt, Deckard, and Thom disappeared behind the stables. She stepped up to the gate and allowed herself one second of hesitation at the threshold to steady her breathing. Then she plowed on into the paddock.

When she rounded the corner, Hewitt nodded to her, the captain and lieutenant turning at the signal.

"Miss Glaas," Captain Deckard greeted. His friendly smile was less cheerful than usual. "What a pleasant surprise."

Coming to a stop at Hewitt's side, she noticed how both brothers scanned her unusual attire. "It's nice to see you, too, Captain," she replied, keeping her voice clear and confident. "You gave quite the speech. Very eloquent. I would volunteer in a second if I were a man."

Deckard chuckled, adjusting the bottom of his velvet coat. "Thank you very much. It's only too bad it worked on you alone."

Evylin fought disappointment for him. "No recruits, then?"

"No recruits," Deckard confirmed, "as you said."

"I'm sorry to hear that."

Thom leaned forward conspiratorially. "I keep telling him that his speech is too boring." He gave his brother's shoulder a slap. "No one's as public-spirited as he. Men need a call to adventure, not to servanthood to trade their lives away."

"He was speaking to a crowd of women," Evylin teased. "Perhaps he knows his audience."

Thom raised a finger at Deckard. "She's got a point."

"I'm not sure the king would agree," Deckard said, a more genuine smile back in place.

Hewitt cleared his throat, sobering them up. "Back to the matter at hand, I believe you said you had an interest in relieving me of some weapons."

Resuming his stoic and officer-like manner, Deckard drew his shoulders back and addressed Hewitt head-on. "Yes, I'd be more than happy to take them off your hands.

We're low on arms as it is. With luck, we'll be adding more men to the ranks in the next settlement. I could use whatever weapons you've got."

"And what about trainers?" Hewitt asked. "Do you have enough men to teach these volunteers how to use my weapons?"

Deckard hesitated, glancing at Evylin with uncertainty. "I didn't think you had any interest in the army, Mr. Glaas," he said, turning back to the bear-like man.

"I didn't. Now I do."

Thom's brow lifted when Deckard looked over at him.

"Our trainers are, of course, excellent," Deckard said curiously.

"But are there enough of them?" Hewitt pressed.

"Are there ever?"

Hewitt crossed his arms. "Would you like more?"

"Of course." Deckard's eyes narrowed. "Do you know of any?"

Hewitt's right shoulder lifted in a bored shrug. "I might. The question is how badly you need one."

Deckard and Hewitt stared at each other.

Feeling as lost as the captain and lieutenant must have felt, Evylin could only conclude that this had something to do with Hewitt's plan. But it didn't make sense. Evylin didn't have the skill to be a trainer. She was a good swordsman but wasn't much of a teacher.

Her stomach roiled with a sneaking suspicion that Hewitt had tricked her into something she wasn't sure she wanted to be a part of.

Deckard sighed, his voice dropping to a low and serious pitch. "Training is not going well," he admitted. "It takes too long to train men for a never-ending war. We don't have enough majors for half our troops, and the ones we do have barely had enough training themselves. If you have a recommendation for a good—and I mean *truly* impressive trainer—please tell me. We need him."

Hewitt grinned at that, his look that of a cat having trapped a mouse. "Excellent," he said slyly. "Then I have a proposition for you."

His hand dropped on Evylin's shoulder like a weight.

"I am the trainer," Hewitt said. "And Evylin is my resume."

Evylin's muscles tensed as the soldiers stared between her and her uncle.

Hewitt didn't wait for any of them to reply. "Here's the proposition," he said, copying Deckard's earlier, officer-like stance—shoulders back, chin up, hands clasped behind his back. "Evylin will fight the lieutenant, supplying an adequate picture of my skills as a trainer. If she wins, I will be your new trainer, and *you* will owe me a favor."

Evylin fought not to gasp. It made no sense. Hewitt had sworn he would never leave Whickam Village again. She was smart enough to know he meant the favor for her escape, but she couldn't understand his change of heart. Thirteen years ago, he'd made his vow. Why would he abandon it for her freedom alone?

Captain Deckard drew a hand along his jaw. "That sounds more like a bet, Mr. Glaas."

"Proposition or bet, it doesn't matter."

"But it does," Deckard countered, his good humor returned. "If this is a proposition, you're offering me something, and I decide whether I want it or not. If this is a bet, we both lay something on the table, and only one of us wins."

Hewitt considered the captain. "Seems you're not as dull as I thought. Make it a bet, then. But I'm afraid your assessment is wrong."

"How so?"

"You win in either case," Hewitt said. "If Evylin beats your lieutenant, I become your new major, and you owe me that favor. If your lieutenant beats Evylin, I become your trainer—plain and simple."

He'd hooked the captain.

But he'd also lost Evylin.

"Uncle," she said, grabbing his sleeve. He turned to her as the next words came out somewhere between a whisper and a hiss. "I'm the one who's supposed to be leaving. Not *you*."

"You will," he assured her quietly. "Just be sure you win."

"I can't promise that."

"Yes, you can." Hewitt turned back to Deckard. "Do we have a deal?" he asked at a normal volume.

Thom and Deckard were in their own heated whisper exchange, but they fell silent at his words.

"What favor do you want?" Deckard asked suspiciously.

Hewitt shook his head. "That's not how this works."

The nickering of horses and chirping of crickets filled the silence as Deckard hesitated. But while he was thinking it through, his brother spoke up for him.

"It doesn't matter," Thom said fiercely. "I won't fight her."

Hewitt frowned. "Don't be daft, man. You won't hurt her."

Thom set his jaw, but Deckard took hold of his brother's arm. "I'm not sure it's your choice alone." He turned to Evylin. "Do you want to do this, Miss Glaas?"

Looking up to scan Hewitt's face, Evylin questioned his revealed plan. If she didn't win, not only would she lose her chance of leaving, but she would also lose Hewitt. Living in Whickam Village was hard enough as it was; it would be impossible without him. A lost dream, she might manage. Losing him was too much.

But what if she won?

The confidence in Hewitt's steady gray stare emboldened her thoughts. His words from earlier rang in her ears. *"Do you trust me?"*

Always.

Meeting Captain Deckard's gaze, now dark blue in the night, Evylin smiled confidently. "Yes," she said.

Hewitt nodded while Thom grimaced.

"Very well," Deckard said, then faced his brother. "You don't have to fight her. But I am asking you: Please, do this. We need him. *I* need him."

Working his jaw back and forth, Thom stared at his brother. Their differences struck Evylin in their silence. Deckard's frame was lean, while Thom's was brawny. The elder carried a few extra inches while the younger had more breadth. The captain appeared distinguished and composed. The lieutenant was masculine and mysterious.

Yet their brows carried the same arch, the angles of their facial structure bearing the same sharp lines. And the blue of their deep-set eyes had the same shifting quality. Their coloring and build differed, but there was no doubt that the Deckard blood ran strong.

Finally, Thom dipped his chin in agreement.

"Wonderful," Hewitt said flatly. He marched over to the sword rack. "Winner is the first to strike a blow that would incapacitate the other."

With tense nods, Deckard and Thom assented.

Stepping over to the fence, Evylin began to slip off her coat.

Thom appeared at her side. "Miss Glaas," he said, keeping his voice low as he worked off his own coat. "I hope you don't take offense, but surely you see how ridiculous this is?"

"Which part?" she asked, draping her coat over the fence post. "The bet or my fighting?"

"Both."

"Don't worry." She patted his arm. "It'll be fun."

As they turned around, Hewitt tossed each of them a sword. Evylin caught hers steadily while Thom fumbled, surprised by the toss and her retort.

Evylin swung the sword out in front of her with a flick of her wrist before settling her right hand below the cross guard and her left at the end by the pommel. She sank into her stance, feet a bit wider than her hips, knees bent, and blade angled across her chest. She couldn't help enjoying how the Deckard brothers stared at her in shock. Whether it was due to her comfort with a blade, her trousers, or the very idea of a female fighter, she reveled in their awe.

Thom shook off his surprise to settle himself, placing his left foot forward, sword primed over the right shoulder to swing down in a heavy blow. She knew he wouldn't come after her with his full strength at first. But he'd learn soon enough to abandon caution.

Evylin pulled in one final, steadying breath to center herself. Her skin tingled in the cool autumnal night as her body grew excited at the anticipation of a fight. *Speed,* she reminded herself. That was her greatest weapon against his muscle.

As Thom stood stock-still, eyeing her nervously, Evylin knew it would take too long for him to work up the courage to charge. So she did it for him.

Lunging forward, she nicked the edge of his sword and spun out of the way as he tried to press in. Thom huffed as his swing took him farther forward than he'd expected. But his recovery was quick, and he charged her this time.

Their swords met in three *snaps* before Evylin ducked under his fourth swing and drove her shoulder into his chest.

While Thom staggered back, Evylin swept far out of his reach. She could hear a small chuckle from the sidelines. Captain Deckard.

After taking a deep breath, the hint of a smile pulled at one corner of Thom's mouth. "You're fast," he noted.

Evylin smiled back at him. "I have to be."

Chancing a look at their audience, Evylin found all the encouragement she needed. Hewitt watched with arms crossed and pride in his gaze. Deckard held up a hand to cover most of the intrigued grin on his lips, his eyes locked on her.

Hewitt gave her a single nod.

It was time to win.

Evylin took a deep breath, realigning her focus back on the fight. Her fingers prickled with excitement. Her muscles flexed, ready for use.

She charged again.

Prepared this time, Thom knew better than to underestimate her skills. The next few blows came harder as their swords met.

Too hard for her to sustain.

Their swords connected, the vibration of the metal tingling through Evylin's arms.

With all her speed and strength, Evylin twisted her sword up and over his, pushing it back and away before releasing the weapon to fall into the dirt.

Dropping to a low squat, Evylin ducked under Thom's blade. She shifted all her weight into her left foot, kicking out with the right. It connected with Thom's knee, driving him down to kneel.

Evylin spun as she rose, grabbing the hilt of the knife in her boot. Before Thom could regain control, she wrapped her arm around his chest and pressed the blade to his neck.

The only sounds in the paddock were the crickets, the horses, and the heavy breaths of Evylin and Lieutenant Deckard. She could feel his chest rising and falling under her hand as her own heart pounded behind her rib cage.

A slow, courteous clap echoed in the night, drawing Evylin to turn toward it. Deckard's eyes shone in the torchlight around the paddock as he studied Evylin a second longer. "Highly impressive," he said, turning to Hewitt. "Congratulations, Major Glaas. You've won, fair and square."

Evylin released her grip on Thom and backed away. She slid the knife into her boot, body buzzing with feeling.

She'd done it.

She'd won.

And now she and Hewitt would leave Whickam Village together. It was a dream come true.

Thom stood, rubbing his neck. While the blade had only grazed him, little could negate the discomfort of metal on flesh. "I don't know if I'd say 'fair,'" he remarked, eyeing her as though seeing her for the first time. "But she did beat me."

"I can teach you how she did it. And how not to lose again," Hewitt said, then faced the captain. "Now, about my winnings?"

"Of course," Deckard said. "You'll be the newest major in the Third Volunteer Company of King Ephren. While your original rank may be much higher than the typical trainer, we'll let the officers in Loclight sort out the paperwork when we return."

"And the favor you owe me?" Hewitt asked.

"I won't lie," Deckard said hesitantly. "I'm a bit worried about what you'll ask of me, but I did agree to your terms. Whenever you have need of something, you can count on me to answer your call."

"You can answer it now." Hewitt summoned Evylin, and she came to stand at his side. "I'm calling on my favor at this moment, Captain. Be sure you understand that if you refuse my terms, the whole bet is null and void with it. You refuse this, and I walk away. Do you understand that?"

Deckard exchanged a worried look with his brother. Thom's jaw was like iron as he shook his head in disapproval.

Deckard rested his chin in his hand. "I do hope you won't ask something dishonorable of me, Major."

The cat-like smile returned to Hewitt's face. "Oh, never, Captain."

Their staring contest continued for a moment more. Then Deckard hefted a sigh. "I made a deal with you. Let us hope I don't prove a fool for it."

Thom grumbled, but Deckard showed no signs of hearing it.

Hewitt winked at Evylin before turning back to the captain. "This is the favor you'll grant me," he said, his voice proud and strong. "Evylin will be joining us on our journey."

Evylin's heart soared. This was the moment she'd hoped for. Their dream would come true at last. She would travel the world and experience all life had to offer, just as they'd always planned.

Then Hewitt added the deal's damning condition: "As your wife."

CHAPTER EIGHT

It took the space of two heartbeats for Hewitt's words to sink in.

"What?" Evylin and Deckard said together. They looked at each other in shock. Evylin wondered if she wore the same expression as him: eyes widened, forehead creased, cheeks reddened, and mouth ajar.

Coming to, she forced her jaw shut and whirled on Hewitt. "Uncle, you cannot be serious."

Hewitt remained as unmoved as ever. "Of course, I am. How did you think you were going to get out of here?"

"Not through marriage!" Evylin exclaimed. However, she realized that wasn't exactly true. She had considered that marriage might take her away from the village. She just hadn't expected it to be this marriage, especially not this soon.

"Sir," Deckard interjected, "I don't think this is a sensible choice for any of us."

"Damn right, it's not," Thom added.

Evylin found little persuasion in their arguments, so she took up her own. "How is this a better plan than mine? Marriage to a stranger? I can hire him. I don't have to marry him."

"Hire him?" Thom asked incredulously.

"Yes." Evylin paused, realizing the oddity of her words. She turned to the captain apologetically, her cheeks growing hot under his gaze. "Yes, I wanted to hire you. To have you act as a guide of sorts. While I can defend myself, a woman can't travel alone without attracting unwanted attention. I thought to hire you—to pay you to take me with you as a traveler with the army."

The Deckard brothers exchanged concerned glances.

"Unfortunately," the captain said kindly, "that's not something the army allows."

Hewitt's steely glare turned on Evylin. "As you seem to have forgotten your situation, allow me to remind you. The law is clear: Unwed, you are under the authority of your father. Unless he approves, you cannot leave the village."

"This cannot be the way to earn his approval," Deckard interrupted.

Hewitt turned to him. "It is the *only* way to earn it, Captain."

"You would have her marry a man she doesn't know?" he demanded. "For what? What could be reason enough for that?"

Shoving a thick finger Deckard's way, Hewitt leaned in. "Evylin *needs* to go. As her uncle and the only one who understands her desire to leave this parasitic village, I found the answer to her problem.

"Marriage is the only means out of her father's authority . . ." He paused to let his words settle in. "Through marriage to you, Captain, she can leave Whickam Village, have no financial worry, and travel under the army's protective banner. Her father will have no say in her future; he will not be able to recall her home. Nor would he want to, grateful that his daughter married Ephria's most *noble* captain. Much as I dislike you, somehow, *you* are her best shot. And I will come along to ensure you're making her happy."

Hewitt glared down at Deckard. While there was only an inch between them in height, her uncle made the difference seem like miles. "This is the price of my commission with the Ephrian Army. Take it or leave it."

Deckard held his gaze for several moments more before stepping back. He set a hand to his clean-shaven jaw, eyes dropping to the dirt as he reflected.

Biting the inside of her lip, Evylin joined him in the introspection. She couldn't deny Hewitt's reasoning. She'd ignored the facts for too long. Marriage was her only means out of the drudgery of life in the village. But up until the past two days, it seemed there wasn't a worthy, eligible bachelor in the whole of Estshire.

Glancing at Captain Deckard, Evylin was surprised to find she considered *this* man worthy.

Thom cleared his throat to gain their attention. "Pardon my confusion, but I fail to see why my brother should sell his life for your service in the army," he said bluntly. "I hate to sound callous, Miss Glaas, but he is not indebted to you in any way. Why should he do this for you?"

"That's not the most altruistic thing to say, Thom," Deckard muttered, eyes still on the dirt. Regardless of the captain's moral compass, it was clear his thoughts ran the same course as his brother's. Benevolent nature or not, this was asking quite a lot of anyone.

Hewitt scoffed. "Altruism has nothing to do with it. He'll agree because he needs this just as much as she does."

Deckard's eyes flashed to the smith.

Thom snarled. "In what possible way does this benefit him?" He hesitated, glancing at Evylin. "Aside from obtaining a rather impressive wife."

"You're too kind," Evylin quipped.

"I know how the army works," Hewitt said, ignoring their banter. "This may not be a draft, but that doesn't mean your commanding officer didn't give you a specific and *very* daunting number of volunteers to bring back. If you don't meet that number, you'll face a world of disapproval. The Shires are low on men. Meeting that number is unlikely. But bringing back a veteran general—a legend, I believe you called me, Lieutenant—who can train your company of volunteers to fight like the soldiers from twenty years past? That might gain you enough favor to bypass their disappointment."

Neither of the soldiers replied.

Evylin, fighting between her dream and her sanity, shook her head. "You're asking both Captain Deckard and me to . . . bind our futures in exchange for—for what?"

"In exchange for your happiness and his success," Hewitt insisted.

Deckard met Evylin's eyes again. In the stretch of silence between them, he appeared as incapable of finding words as her. Hewitt had caught them both off guard with his proposition. And there seemed to be no way around his reasoning.

If Evylin didn't agree, she would be stuck in Whickam Village, hoping—possibly forever—that another man would magically arrive to take her away.

If Deckard didn't agree, he'd leave the village without a single volunteer while the censure of his officers loomed in the future.

The cold night air tore through Evylin's tunic. She wrapped her arms around herself, rubbing her hands over the cotton sleeves of her blouse to stave off her shivers. Could she agree to this? Leave home with a man she barely knew only to see the world? Wasn't Deckard right? This wasn't sensible.

But as Hewitt said, it was the only way.

Suddenly, Deckard walked past them, scooped Evylin's coat off the fence, and returned it to her. "Might I speak with you in private, Miss Glaas? Just over here?" He tipped his head toward the other side of the paddock.

Evylin allowed him to lead her over, sliding her arms through the sleeves of her coat. He didn't look at her for a moment, the silence saying what he couldn't seem to voice. This was an awkward, unnerving, and ridiculous situation.

Deckard turned to her, his eyes soft with concern. "Miss Glaas, please be honest with me. Is this really what you want?"

Wrapping her coat around her, Evylin considered the question. "If everything you've tried hasn't worked," she whispered, "then something in your plan has to change, right?"

The captain scanned her. "I'm not sure I understand what you mean."

Not willing to be completely truthful with him, Evylin gave him only a version of it instead. "I have dreamed of leaving Whickam Village since I can remember," she explained. "Every day, that dream has drifted farther and farther away."

He was patient as she sighed, looking toward the dirt. Her eyes stung, but she held back the tears determinedly. She couldn't remember a day it hadn't been her goal to explore the world. The thing was, that dream had started with Ryen. And when he died, it felt as though that dream had died with him. Obtaining that goal—following through with their childish, idealistic plans—was the one way she could keep him alive.

Evylin met Deckard's gaze again. "I've grown desperate recently," she said with a weak smile. "Grasping at any straw I could find. You heard me before; I've ignored the obvious truth, and Hewitt is right. Marriage is my only chance. And this is the only marriage ever offered to me."

Deckard's head tipped with uncertainty. "Now that the chance is before you, will you take it?"

Words failed Evylin once more. She looked at the far side of the paddock where Hewitt and Thom stood. The lieutenant's arms remained crossed over his thick chest while he watched them. However, Hewitt leaned against the fence in calm contemplation as he waited. He looked so much like his son: dark, wavy hair, steely gray eyes under those bushy brows, richly tanned skin, the strong slope of his nose. It caused her heart to pinch.

Evylin turned back to the captain. His silken cravat glowed in the dim light, as did the silver buttons and stitching on his coat. No one in Whickam Village owned anything that could compare to the luxurious fabric of his dress uniform. Evylin had only seen similar textiles in Trollenston when traders from above the Shires came around. Hewitt told her once that a soldier only obtained a uniform like this once they'd earned the office of captain. It was such a fine outfit for a Shireman, yet he wore it as though it were his everyday wear.

"You said you grew up in the Shire," Evylin muttered. "In a small village like this. Why did you leave it?"

Deckard blinked, surprised by the question. His eyes darted toward Thom, but then he said, "I wanted to serve my country. That was more important than anything."

A nervous chuckle escaped her. "Please tell me it was more than that. You can't be so boring as to be wholly selfless."

It took a second, but Deckard finally smiled as well. "I'm not," he admitted. "I wanted to serve but also the chance to be more. I wanted to be part of something bigger than my village."

"You wanted more?" she asked, surprised to hear her own hopes spoken by someone else.

He nodded.

"Adventure?"

"I suppose so."

"Did you find it?"

He hesitated. "Less than I expected. But far more than if I'd stayed in Stocburrough."

Evylin took a deep, steadying breath. "I want that. However small or inconsequential it might be. I can't be a soldier. I can't fight in a war to become a hero or a legend. But that doesn't mean I can't live a life worth more than *this*."

The captain's expression pinched again. "But is that chance of adventure worth marriage to a stranger?"

"I believe so," Evylin said. The corner of her lips tweaked up then. "And while I may not know you as well as one should, we have had enough conversation for me to know that you're not dull, weak-minded, or old. You're pleasant company, and you understand my desire to see the world. That's more than I can say of any other man I've met."

Deckard's bashful smile told her that he appreciated her approval. "You are strangely easy to talk to for a woman."

"I'm flattered."

Still, he seemed reluctant. "Are you absolutely convinced?"

"I am."

Captain Deckard gave a slow nod, then began to turn toward the waiting men.

Evylin caught his arm. "Wait—" he turned back to her, "are you sure this is what *you* want?"

He met her gaze but said nothing.

"Is marriage to a stranger worth obtaining a volunteer for your army?"

After a long pause, Deckard's smile returned. "Miss Glaas, I wouldn't enter marriage for my personal gain. I believe that's the key to failure rather than success. Marrying you is not about obtaining your uncle. It's about obtaining your happiness." He lifted his brow with a good-humored tilt. "Your uncle is only a bonus."

Evylin smirked shyly. "Hewitt will make a wonderful in-law."

He huffed amusedly. "Somehow, I doubt I'll ever win his favor."

"But it will be awfully fun to see you try."

A soft laugh escaped him. "Miss Glaas," he said, offering his arm.

She took it.

"If nothing else," he set his hand on hers where it rested in the crook of his elbow, a surprising warmth to his touch, "I do believe we'll have quite the entertaining marriage."

Evylin held his gaze as a strange tingle spread from her hand up her arm. "What more could a girl ask for?"

He raised his brow as though considering one or two ideas but stayed silent as he led her back to the men. "Major Glaas, I heartily accept your conditions."

"Deckard," Thom challenged but got no further.

"Congratulations to you both," Hewitt said flatly. "Lawton will accept your offer, but if this is to seem legitimate, you'll need to ask his permission in the morning and propose to Evylin after."

Releasing her, Deckard stepped to his brother's side. "Whatever you recommend."

"Well then, I recommend you come to breakfast tomorrow as well," Hewitt said. "Ask to speak with my brother and tell him I've volunteered. It'll soften the blow of letting Evylin go, knowing I'll be there to take care of her." Hewitt's directive sounded like his training. "Do not mention this arrangement. He won't like that we went behind his back."

Deckard shrugged casually. "He's as proud as every other magistrate I've met," he remarked. His eyes flashed to Evylin regretfully. "Forgive me. I—"

Evylin brushed the comment away. "My father is prouder of himself and his minimal achievements than any man alive."

Hewitt ignored them. "Whatever way you want to tell him you decided on marriage is fine with me. Say it was love at first sight, destiny, or you're simply tired of being a bachelor. He's not likely to believe that Evylin will agree to the marriage, but he will be in favor of it.

"Once he's made sure it's what Evylin wants, too, Lawton will suggest waiting until they can arrange a proper wedding. Captain, you'll have to request she come with us, and Evylin, you'll have to insist you don't want to wait," Hewitt ordered.

The finality of his words unsettled Evylin. "That will be abrupt, won't it? They'll find it suspicious."

Hewitt shook his head. "Not if you convince them you're in love."

Deckard shifted awkwardly, Thom grimaced, and Evylin forgot to breathe.

"We've known each other for two days," she reminded her uncle. "My sisters will never believe it."

"They will if you sell it," Hewitt said. "Dolia sees romance in everything. And Calyn will be too devastated that it's not her to pay attention to how you're feeling."

Thom shook his head. "Doesn't this charade make any of you uncomfortable?"

Hewitt made no response, Evylin chewed on her lip, and Deckard dropped his gaze again.

"It's for the best, Thom," he said, the words lacking his usual sincerity.

"We're in agreement, then?" Hewitt pressed.

Evylin turned to Deckard, waiting for his final word.

The captain and lieutenant exchanged a look. Thom's glare said more than a thousand words, but Deckard turned to Evylin with a polite smile, although it was not as genuine as she'd grown used to.

Evylin's throat tightened. She feared his sense of altruism wasn't strong enough, and he'd change his mind. Somehow, the thought stirred both a sense of worry and hope inside her.

Deckard held his hand out to Hewitt. "We're in agreement," he said as they shook. "In the morning, Miss Glaas and I will marry."

CHAPTER NINE

The soldiers left minutes later. Captain Deckard said a stilted goodnight to Evylin, resting a hand affectionately on her arm while his brother glowered at his side. She couldn't decide whether she found the captain's special attention charming or frightening. She settled on the former, reminding herself that in a matter of hours, he would be her husband.

That thought only served to frighten her more.

The second they were gone, Hewitt put away the swords before snuffing the oil lamps. Evylin waited for him to speak, expecting an explanation for his conniving plan. It didn't matter that he'd secured their dream. She wanted the truth.

Hewitt didn't speak, not even when he began to walk out of the paddock.

Evylin hurried to catch up with him as he rounded the corner into the stables. "You need to explain yourself," she demanded, her strides doubling to match his.

"I thought I explained it all well enough."

"No," she insisted. "You need to tell me exactly how it is that all of a sudden, you're fine leaving with me. You told me time and time again you wouldn't go—that you'd never leave. What changed?"

"It doesn't matter." He picked up his pace. "I've watched you waste too much of your life here. Be happy, and don't ask any more questions."

Evylin grabbed his wrist as he reached for the gate. "You said you'd never leave them."

Hewitt froze, staring out into the village square. The full ivory moon kept the night bright, while the shadow moon's dull quarter added minimal radiance. The night remained crisp, frigid, and still.

Tightening her grip, Evylin angled forward to face him. "Of all people," she whispered, feeling the tension in her own words, "I understood your vow. I nearly made the same one, if you'll remember."

A terse grunt escaped him.

"But you wouldn't let me," Evylin reminded him. "Despite how much I loved him, too, you refused to let me stay even while you swore you wouldn't leave their sides."

Steel-gray eyes met hers. "My family is gone, Evylin," he whispered, a subtle threat in his growl. "After thirteen years, it's time I accepted that."

Evylin's chest constricted at the memory of their shared loss. Thirteen years of dedication to his family, and he was willing to give them up to make her happy. It wasn't fair.

"Uncle," she began, but he wrenched open the gate and cut her off.

"Go home and get to bed," he ordered. "Tomorrow will be a long day."

Staring up at him, Evylin fought with herself. It was his decision. If he'd made up his mind, there would be no changing it. And she had always hoped he'd come with her, even when she thought it impossible.

But she would never forgive herself if she pulled him away from what he truly wanted.

As she opened her mouth to protest, Hewitt turned and walked away. "Goodnight, Evie."

Evylin watched as his broad-shouldered figure disappeared down the back path toward his apartment above the smithy. It was really nothing more than an attic stuffed with a small cot, a wood stove, and minimal furnishings. It wasn't even as large as Evylin's bedroom. But as he spent his days by the forge and evenings at her side, his nights didn't require much more than a bed.

Alone and shivering in the cold, Evylin pulled her coat tighter. She turned to leave but took the back path past her home and toward the distant kirk. Two small buildings lay shadowed in the moonlight: the tiny cottage of Father Dover and the stone-faced chapel with its stubby bell tower.

Evylin diverted from the path to walk through the kirkyard. A short, white fence lined the well-kept grass to differentiate it from the pastureland and keep any scavenging animals out. Weathered stones freckled the turf. Everbloom ivy curled across their curved edges, the creamy four-petaled flowers like little sheep dotting a knoll. Evylin didn't need to look at the engraved names to find her destination. She walked directly to the plot she'd come to visit.

Sinking to her knees beside the light gray quartz embedded into the terrae, Evylin hesitated. What could she say? How was she supposed to feel? Her life had suddenly become an impossible dream.

Their impossible dream.

Gently, Evylin drew her fingers across the engraving on the cold stone. She pushed back some of the pointed ivy leaves, the everbloom flowers tickling her skin. "Hello, Ryen," she whispered into the night. "I have news."

There was no answer.

"I'm leaving. Can you believe that?" She quirked her mouth to the side, holding in the emotion that rose in her chest. "I can't," she admitted, then frowned. "And maybe I won't. Maybe the captain will go back on his word. Maybe that's good."

A sudden, swift breeze caused the kirkyard gate to rattle slightly.

"Hm, no, you're right." Evylin smiled at the grave. "I have to believe. After all, I made you a promise." She traced the curve of his name. "I remember all our plans. First, explore the Shires, specifically the shores. We must see the sea." She chuckled lightly at their childhood joke.

"Then," she continued, "consider piracy. If that doesn't suit us, travel the rest of Ephria. Win dozens of duels, rescue a princess, fight a dragon—we'd have better luck finding Mages—and become legends worthy of five hundred tales."

The breeze grew gentler, tugging at the hair that had fallen loose from her braid.

Evylin smiled despite the way her shoulders shook in the cold. "In other words," she whispered, "have the greatest adventure known to man."

The ridges of the engraving were rough against the pads of her fingers. Her good humor fell away as she stared into the stillness of the night. The rolling hills of Estshire were bare, shrouded in darkness. Thousands of stars sprinkled the amethyst-purple sky of night, the grandest jewels in Terraeus. The vastness of the Heavens spread above Evylin, making her feel unfathomably small as she confessed her greatest secret in a near-silent whisper.

"I don't want to do it without you."

A single tear slipped free, tracing a frigid line down her cheek. She didn't know how long she sat there, the nails of her fingers gripping his name engraved in stone as though she could pull him back to life if only she held tight enough.

"But I have to," she murmured at last. "This is it. If I don't go with him, I will never go. And our adventure will die here in Whickam Village with us both."

Evylin's vision blurred, but she refused to let another tear fall. She sniffled, holding the emotion in, and pressed her lips into a smirk as she looked down at the gravestone. *"Ryen Glaas, beloved son,"* it read.

The simple engraving left out the most important parts about the life of Hewitt's only child, Evylin's cousin. Beloved, yes, but so much more. Daring, clever, good, and full of life. He'd turned rainy days stuck inside into escapades of stealth, sneaking into the kitchen to nab treats or seeking hidden treasures in the attic. His imagination altered reality, making the impossible seem so logical. His hugs were like sunshine, warming one all the way to the core. And his laugh had filled her with the greatest joy.

How did you engrave that into stone? How could you ever sum up someone so unfathomably monumental? How did you memorialize someone so profound?

"I won't let our dream die," Evylin whispered for the thousandth time. She plucked free one of the ivory everbloom flowers. "That I promise you."

She leaned down, kissed the cold stone, and rose.

Evylin walked to the kirkyard gate, the everbloom stem gently clenched in her fingers. After she unhooked the latch, she looked up to find Hewitt waiting on the other side. Neither of them said a word. He gently brushed back the wisps of hair the wind had pulled across her face and gave her the tenderest smile.

Heartbroken yet hopeful, Evylin leaned into his touch for only a moment. Then she left him to say his own goodbyes.

She walked back down the path, the cold night breeze now swirling around her, the everbloom flower protectively cradled in her hand. Her vow filled her chest, locked tight in her soul. She would find adventure for herself and for Ryen, no matter the cost.

CHAPTER TEN

The night lingered too long, much like dinner.

Evylin couldn't decide whether she wanted time to move faster or cease altogether. Thought after thought kept her awake. Sleep drifted in and out, making the night a hazy fog of questions and worry. Unable to discern whether she'd slept or lain awake in that daze of restlessness, Evylin jumped at the sound of a door clicking shut. Heavy but courteous footsteps passed through the hall.

The captain was awake.

Morning light peeked into Evylin's room behind the drapes of her window. She listened as Captain Deckard descended the stairs. It was too early for breakfast by how faintly the autumn sun cast its orange glow on her ceiling. She wondered what he was doing up already.

Had he lain awake most of the night too? Or was he an early riser naturally?

Those thoughts soon devolved into other questions about more intimate sleeping arrangements that Evylin would rather not consider at the moment. She tossed back her covers, determined to find some distraction. Though she would help prepare breakfast, she had more than an hour before she'd be required in the kitchen. So she pulled on her trousers and blouse from the previous night and snuck out the back to run through her exercises. The movement helped to calm her racing mind. In the cold morning air, she didn't sweat even as she pushed her body harder than usual. But her skin tingled, and her heart raced as she slipped back inside and up to her room.

Working off her dirty clothes, she stared into her wardrobe. Her sense of calm was chipping away again as she struggled to make a choice. She ran her fingers over the navy satin dress in the back. It was the nicest piece she owned. And it was her wedding day—a thought that made her breath hitch.

But then she heard Hewitt's advice ringing in her head.

If her father got so much as a whiff of deception, there was a chance he'd refuse Deckard to spite her and Hewitt's plan. Nothing could seem out of the ordinary in her appearance. Not if she wanted to ensure the success of their scheme.

However, she also had to convince her family that she loved Captain Deckard.

With a bemused huff, Evylin selected the light blue wool skirt she most often wore to mass or dinner parties. It was a middle ground of utility and finery. She chose a simple white blouse, tucking it in with care to ensure it lay flat in the mirror. Then she slipped on her boots—no need to take things too far—and secured the knife by her ankle.

She brushed free the knots from her wavy hair, fumbling with it for several minutes before she gave up on making it drape with any elegance. Instead, she grabbed a well-worn ribbon to tie back the top layer.

Chewing on her bottom lip, she stared at her reflection in the long mirror inside her wardrobe. Though pleased with her overall appearance, she felt something was missing. If this were to be her wedding day, she wanted it to feel somewhat special.

Evylin reached for the small jewelry box on the shelf. Her sisters all had matching ones. A gift from their father for their fifteenth birthdays, meant to house all the jewels and trinkets a young suitor-turned-husband might give them. Neither Calyn nor Evylin had found much use for theirs. But Evylin's box held one addition that Calyn's didn't.

Knowing the tradition, Hewitt had made a necklace for Evylin alone. Simple but sweet, he'd engraved the silver pendant with a rosette on the face. A symbol of her middle name.

Clasping it around her neck, Evylin felt it was the finishing touch she needed. Not lavish, but special. Even if no one noticed, she was proud of her effort.

"You're up early, dear," Laurisa said as Evylin entered the kitchen.

Evylin shrugged casually. "I couldn't sleep. Where should I start?"

Laurisa gave her orders, and Evylin got to work. To her great disappointment, chopping apples and slicing sausages only took so much focus, leaving ample room for old thoughts to resurface and new ones to form. Her mind bounced around her decision, plaguing her with fear after fear. Was this the right choice? What if she hated travel? Could she really leave Ryen? And what about the captain? Would he come to resent her? Would he even follow through with the bargain at all?

Calyn bounced into the kitchen, bringing a welcome distraction. She wore a soft yellow dress with lace along the collar. Her hair was delicately arranged across her shoulders. Evylin compared her appearance to Calyn's and felt she'd done an adequate job. She owned nothing so flowery as Calyn or Dolia, but her blue skirt and dainty necklace were sufficient.

"Morning, Mother," Calyn said, kissing Laurisa's cheek. "How can I help?"

After Laurisa set the girl to work on the porridge, she hurried off to prepare the dining room. As Calyn pumped water into a pot for boiling, she peered around the corner, watching their mother disappear. Then she turned around. "Evie?" she called, her voice a fraction above a whisper.

"Yes?"

"How is it . . . How do you know what you want?"

Evylin stopped chopping to stare at her sister. "What are you talking about?"

"You," she replied. "I'm talking about *you*. You've always known exactly what you wanted. Ever since I can remember, it's always been 'adventure'—seeing the world and all that. You've always known. And I never have."

A raw burn rose in Evylin's throat. "Well . . ." She tried swallowing against the tension, which only made it worse. Calyn had hardly known Ryen, being only six at the time of his death. She hadn't understood what their cousin had meant to Evylin. She didn't know of their plans.

"I guess—" Evylin struggled to find words. "I don't know. I guess it's just all I've ever wanted. I wouldn't know what else to want."

Calyn pursed her lips and hummed.

"Why do you ask?"

Settling the pot on the stove, Calyn fiddled with the handle. "It's only what Uncle said last night—about me setting my sights too high. Do you think he's right?"

"Oh, Caly—"

"I don't mind," she insisted. "Really, I don't. He's never liked me much, I know. But it made me think . . . Is he right? Am I looking for the wrong sort of husband?"

Evylin didn't have an answer for that.

"I thought about that all night," Calyn admitted. "It hurt at first, feeling like I wasn't good enough. But then I realized he might be right. I don't know if I could be happy as a soldier's wife."

A fond smile lightened her sister's whole demeanor as she continued, "I'm not like you, Evie. I've never thought about traveling. If I married a soldier, I'd have to go wherever he went or remain here without him. I don't know if I'd like that. Leaving home would mean leaving Dolia, and I don't know if I can live without her. But staying here would mean life without the man I love." Her eyes cast themselves down to the simmering water. "To be honest, I don't know what I want. And I think I should figure that out *before* I marry."

Stilled knife in hand, Evylin watched her sister with awe. How had Calyn suddenly become so wise? While Evylin debated the suitability of her decision, here Calyn proved it to be the right choice. Calyn might not know what she wanted, but Evylin did: the adventure she and Ryen had planned. A life that only a soldier could provide for her.

"You know, Caly," she said with a wry grin, "you're rather smart at times."

With a haughty scoff, Calyn dumped a portion of oats into the heating water. "Of course," she said. "Being a romantic doesn't make a person stupid."

"I suppose you're right," Evylin replied, brushing some hair over her shoulder before returning to her task.

Calyn set the sack of oats on the workbench, eyes narrowing. "Why are you wearing that?"

Evylin's grip on the knife slipped, and she missed her finger by a fraction. "This is what I normally wear," she said weakly.

"You never wear jewelry," Calyn crossed her arms, "or color. Why are you all dressed up?"

Evylin grabbed another apple to slice. "It felt like the right thing to do." The words came out more strangled than she'd hoped. "The army leaves this morning, so we ought to show the proper regard to our departing guest."

A sly grin spread across Calyn's face. "Our guest?"

"Yes," Evylin squeaked uncharacteristically.

"I knew it!" Calyn whispered excitedly, then she squealed with joy. "Oh, I saw you talking to Captain Deckard the other day. I was quite jealous at first. It was obvious you were flirting with him."

Evylin gaped at her sister. "I was *not* flirting."

Calyn's dark eyes twinkled knowingly. "You love him," she said as though she'd discovered a grand secret.

Evylin's stomach plummeted. Of course, her sister was wrong; she didn't love Captain Deckard. And while this *was* what they'd hoped for, she couldn't help feeling guilty for her impending lies.

Unable to hold her sister's bright-eyed gaze, Evylin returned to her work. "That's ridiculous," she muttered.

"I don't think it is," Calyn exclaimed. "You want to travel, and he's a captain. He's also handsome and kind, and we know officers make enough per year. You'll be so happy together!"

Evylin froze mid-chop. "Calyn, you're taking this too far. You don't even know that he likes me."

Calyn squealed once more. "You *do* love him!" She clapped her hands. "Oh, this is perfect. Are you going to ask him to write to you?"

Evylin realized she was somehow caught between a lie and the truth. Her voice was stuck, unable to move past her lips. She stood there, mouth ajar, as her mother returned to the kitchen.

"What merry occasion have I stumbled upon?" Laurisa asked, having overheard Calyn's outburst.

Before Evylin could form a glare fierce enough to silence her sister, Calyn blurted, "Evie's in love with Captain Deckard!"

Laurisa turned to Evylin with wry amusement. When she saw her elder daughter's anxious expression, her smile dropped. "Evylin?" she gasped.

So much hope sprang into her mother's gaze that Evylin felt crushed under the weight of her expectations.

"I'm not in love with him," she insisted, knowing they wouldn't believe her.

And sure enough, they cheered.

"I never thought this would happen!" Laurisa hurried over to embrace her. "Is there an attachment? Will he write to you?"

Evylin grimaced internally. It didn't matter what she said anymore. Her mother and sister were convinced of her love for the captain. And by the end of the morning, they'd have no reason to doubt it for the rest of their lives.

Yet, Evylin ached at tricking her family this way. Assured of her happiness, they would champion her while she lied and abandoned them. It would likely be several years before she would see them again—if ever.

Meeting her mother's dark eyes, Evylin found the strength to mutter, "No, he hasn't said anything."

Laurisa and Calyn wore furrowed brows. "He hasn't made any suggestion of his attraction to you?" her mother asked.

Evylin considered this. She couldn't remember Deckard commenting on her appearance. He'd complimented her honesty and sense of humor. But along with assenting to their marriage, he hadn't mentioned any attraction.

"I can't say that he has," Evylin admitted with disappointment.

"Oh, Evie!" Calyn hurried to her side. "That's miserable!"

Somehow, Evylin's impetuous sister was right. Knowing her husband-to-be might not desire her made her quite miserable indeed.

Dolia bounded into the kitchen. "The charming Captain and lovely Lieutenant Deckard have arrived for breakfast," she announced.

Laurisa gave a final compassionate pat to Evylin's cheek before hurrying to correct her youngest. "If you don't want them to think you the silliest girl in Estshire, you'll keep your voice down. Now here," she said, setting the platter of cured meat into Dolia's arms, "take this to the dining room."

As the youngest Glaas daughter grumbled out of the kitchen, Laurisa picked up another tray. Her expression softened once more as she turned back to Evylin and Calyn. "Bring the rest as quickly as you can, dears," she said and hurried off.

Evylin reached for the fruit bowl, but Calyn caught her shoulders. "Evie," she said with a failed attempt at an encouraging grin, "I'm sure the captain is just worried you'll turn him down. Trust me, I've been jealously watching as he's constantly smiled and stared at you. He might not have said it yet, but he feels the same. I know it!"

A second too late, Evylin realized she should have pulled her sister in for a hug. Her time with her family was now limited, and she wanted to soak up every last second. But Calyn was already back at the porridge, ladling it into a crock. And too soon, they walked into the dining room, carrying the final dishes to the place she would spend her last meal with her family.

Lawton entered with the soldiers as the women placed the dishes on the sideboard. As she caught a glimpse of the captain out of the corner of her eye, the tray slipped from Evylin's fingers with a *thunk*. Dolia wrinkled her nose at the uncharacteristic accident, but Laurisa hurried over to distract the men.

Evylin kept her gaze on the floor. She didn't have to try to act embarrassed in the captain's presence; she felt the emotion thoroughly.

Laurisa greeted the men with a curtsy. "We're so pleased you've come to join us this morning. Shall I prepare a plate for you both?"

Deckard would, of course, give her the kindest smile Terraeus had ever seen. "I thank you for your generosity, Lady Glaas, but I'm afraid I have a small stomach in the morning. May I have a cup of black tea and a bowl of porridge?"

"Of course. Lieutenant?"

"Thank you, ma'am," Thom said, his deep voice groggier than usual. "But I don't mind getting it myself."

"Nonsense. You're our guest."

While Laurisa took Thom's order, Dolia reached for a teacup. Faster than a street cat who'd spotted a mouse, Calyn scooped the cup out of her hand. "Let Evylin," she hissed. "Go prepare Father's plate."

Dolia scowled but did as told.

Offering the cup to Evylin, Calyn winked like a conspirator. "Here. You take care of your captain, and I'll take care of the lieutenant."

Reluctantly, Evylin accepted the cup and began to prepare the tea. Her hands shook as she set the strainer over the cup. Annoyed with herself for letting her emotions get the best of her, she curved her fingers into fists.

Pulling in a deep breath, Evylin stared at the wallpaper. The thick, monochromatic ridges reminded her that these were her last few hours within the walls of the Glaas residence. A frightful and hopeful thing, all at once.

Laurisa appeared at her side, scooping some porridge into a bowl. "He won't leave any later for your delay, dear," she whispered tenderly.

Evylin forced out a self-deprecating scoff. She needed to calm down. If her family thought she was nervous from infatuation, all would be well. But if they began to see through the act, they wouldn't believe her when it came time to prove her "love" for the captain.

"Sorry," she whispered back. "I'm not sure what's wrong with me."

"Oh, I have a good idea," her mother teased, then patted her arm. "Hurry up while I get this bowl to your captain before it grows cold."

Her captain.

Evylin turned back to the wallpaper resolutely. She poured Deckard's tea and turned in time to see her mother set the porridge before the captain, who thanked her. When Laurisa walked behind the captain's chair, she caught Evylin's eyes, jerking her head in his direction.

Everything within Evylin urged her to roll her eyes at the obvious order. Instead, she summoned her manners and began the walk across the room. The porcelain teacup rattled on its saucer, and the men turned to regard her.

Tipping her chin higher, Evylin refused to lose focus even as the captain caught her eye. There was a second of hesitation before the corner of his mouth tipped up. Not the polite, friendly smile she'd seen him giving her mother a moment ago, but a sympathetic one that said he felt every ounce of the nerves coursing through her too.

Setting the tea next to his bowl, Evylin noticed the shadows under his eyes. "Good morning, Miss Glaas," Deckard said warmly.

"Good morning, Captain. I trust you slept well?" she returned with a hint of sarcasm.

He gave her a knowing nod. "Thank you, I did."

Ready to escape the scrutiny that she knew Laurisa and Calyn would be giving them, Evylin excused herself. She caught Thom watching as she headed for the sideboard. Her stride slowed at his glare, but she moved with purpose. Was it disapproval she saw in his eyes? Anger? Disappointment? Or could it be a warning? Had he convinced his brother to change his mind and was now trying to prepare her for the disappointment?

Suddenly, her stomach grew tight, and she filled her plate a little less than normal.

"Will your brother not be joining us, Your Honor?" Deckard asked politely.

"Oh, no," Lawton said, his spoon *clinking* as he stirred cream into his tea. "Hewitt likes to spend his mornings in solitude. As we supposed you did up until this morning."

"I do apologize for not joining you sooner," Deckard said. "I prefer to get an early start on the day. But as we couldn't join you last night, my brother and I wanted to offer our thanks for your generous hospitality. I must say, I'm sorry that this is our final chance to dine with your lovely family."

Laurisa made a sound akin to swooning while Calyn and Dolia both giggled. Lawton began to praise Deckard for his respectability and kindness, which then launched him into a full-fledged monologue on the merits of military officers and their impact on society.

Evylin ground her teeth at the melodrama, then returned to her seat, keeping her expression placid. She risked one glance at Deckard. He nodded with encouragement as he listened to her father's speech, but she wondered if he, too, was thinking of his real purpose for joining their meal. When she caught Thom staring before he returned his eyes to his plate, she determined not to look in their direction again.

However, she struggled to forget that the man she intended to marry was only one seat down the table or that, in a matter of minutes, he'd be asking to speak with her father. She could feel Thom's recurring glare like the sun on a blazing summer day. A tremor shook her hands, but she took a deep breath each time to regain her composure.

Evylin wished that Hewitt had joined them. She knew he'd stayed away to keep up appearances, but it would have calmed her nerves.

When they finished their meal, Lawton patted the small paunch of his stomach. "What a splendid breakfast, my dears," he said, looking over his family. "I daresay your finest yet."

Laurisa squeezed his hand before gathering the plates. Calyn and Dolia rose to help, and Evylin couldn't stop herself from glancing at Deckard. Their eyes caught just as he stood as well, wiping his hands on his napkin.

He looked away and cleared his throat. "Your Honor, I am more grateful to your family than I can say. My stay in your village was far more pleasant than I could ever have imagined."

Lawton's chest puffed out under the praise. "It was a true honor for us to be your host, Captain."

"Thank you, sir," Deckard replied, and in the silence that followed, Evylin's heart skipped a beat. Was that it? Had his brother succeeded in talking him out of the whole arrangement? Had he changed his mind?

Then Captain Deckard added, "Might I request to speak with you privately before I go?"

CHAPTER ELEVEN

The walk down the hall was arduous. Deckard had to remind himself over and over to relax his hands, or else Magistrate Glaas might see the white-knuckled fists at his side. Following the man to his office was like following a commanding officer before a reprimand—the anticipation far more punishing than any outcome possible.

The porridge sat in Deckard's stomach like a rock. Even if he ate breakfast regularly, he was sure his body would rebel against his impending fate. From the moment he lay down last night, he'd lost all control of his senses. His thoughts raced, his body felt hollow, his limbs quit listening as they should, and the tea at breakfast held no flavor.

Lawton opened the study door and ushered Deckard inside. The dark paneled walls matched the foyer, though several bookcases filled the walls here. A grand desk awaited the magistrate's broad frame in the chair behind it. "How can I help you, Captain?" he asked.

Deckard forced his muscles to relax as he sat across from the man. "First, allow me to say I will never forget your kindness and hospitality. Beyond that, your cooperation with my mission was paramount," he said, the routine flowing as smoothly as with every magistrate in the settlements he visited.

"I only wish I could have ensured men for you," Lawton lamented. "I regret no one in my village volunteered."

Deckard paused carefully. "I will admit to wishing for a more fruitful outcome, but I wasn't altogether unsuccessful."

"You weren't?" he asked, openly shocked by the idea. While the magistrate had been cooperative, it was clear he'd never expected a single volunteer to come forward.

"I did have one man come to me last night." Deckard clasped his hands. "Your brother has decided to renew his contract as a major."

Lawton's dark eyes narrowed immediately. "He has?" he asked, surprise and agitation in his tone. "Did he say why?"

Through his fitful night, Deckard had prepared for this exact moment. He hesitated thoughtfully, then replied, "Not in so many words. Of course, I was skeptical after his coolness toward me. But I saw no reason to deny him."

"Mm." A cynical tilt tugged on the magistrate's tense mouth.

"I apologize if it's forward of me," Deckard began, "but do you have any idea why he'd volunteer? He seemed against the army a mere day ago."

Lawton stared at his desk, two fingers resting on his lips in thought. When he looked back up, the tension had returned to his face. "I'm afraid my brother is an enigma even to me," he admitted bitterly.

Deckard wondered about the bad blood that seemed to exist between the brothers. He knew the difficulty siblings could have, but this didn't seem like a petty argument gone too far. And he didn't think he should push for more information.

Deckard moved on. "Do you see any reason I shouldn't accept his recommission?"

Another several seconds passed before Lawton said, "My brother is a difficult man, Captain. For his entire life, he never had many good qualities to recommend him. But just shy of thirty years ago, he was drafted, and for the first time in his life, Hewitt excelled at something. My brother wasn't just a good soldier. He was a great one. He rose through the ranks faster than any man should. I never thought he'd retire."

"Why did he?" Deckard asked, drawn in. He'd heard his officers speak of General Hewitt Glaas since his first day in the service, even though his name was becoming less and less familiar. Thirteen years was a long time for people to remember a man who'd disappeared, even if he'd accomplished the impossible.

Lawton cleared his throat. "There was an accident. He felt the need to come home after that."

The finality in his tone kept Deckard from pursuing the topic. "At the risk of self-flattery," he adopted a humble expression, "perhaps my speech reminded him of days gone by, and he wants a chance at that happiness again."

"Perhaps," the magistrate said doubtfully.

"So you don't have any reason I should decline him?"

"I don't."

"Thank you for your help." Deckard's breath caught in his throat. Now was the time for the second part of the plan. Yet he couldn't speak. He wasn't sure he could move either.

"Was there something else?" Lawton asked.

Deckard met the man's gaze, noticing for the first time how similar his eyes were to Evylin's. They carried the same rounded shape that turned down at the edges. It gave the Glaas family a distinctive, brooding look. Only Lady Glaas and their youngest daughter differed with close-set, almond-shaped eyes.

Deckard finally got a breath out. "Yes, actually." He glanced down at his hands, white with tension. "I was wondering. . . ." The words stopped themselves, catching in his throat.

"Which one?"

Deckard's gaze snapped back up. "Sir?"

The magistrate wore a knowing grin. "Which one of my daughters has caught your attention?"

When Deckard didn't reply, Lawton continued. "I'll make it easier for you. I'd heartily consent to your attachment to any of them. However, I've already promised Dolia to Mr. MacKenna from Trollenston, and I won't go back on my word even if she would. You may have either Evylin or Calyn. It makes little difference to me."

A war began in Deckard's chest, a mix of relief and irritation. The man spoke as though his daughters held no opinions of their own. "I am impressed by your insight, Your Honor, but I must ask: What if neither of them would have me?"

Lawton laughed derisively. "Am I to suppose you're dense, Captain? From the moment Calyn saw you, she fell in love. Granted, those affections seem to have transferred to your brother, but I have little doubt she'd shift back if presented with your affection."

Deckard squirmed at the thought.

"And as far as Evylin goes . . ." Lawton hesitated. "I can't pretend to know her heart or her mind. Hewitt's got her ear, but I'm no fool. There's a plan in place between the two of them."

Deckard flinched.

The magistrate's keen eyes peered at him. "Hewitt volunteering at this time isn't a coincidence. Evylin may be mine, but he sees her as his own. If he's leaving, it's for a reason. And the only reason I can divine is that he hopes to marry Evylin to you."

Unsure if the man had figured out their plan, Deckard asked the question that plagued him most. "Why would he want her to marry a man he despises?"

"Isn't that quite a quandary?" Lawton replied. "A man wouldn't want his most precious treasure given away to a man he doesn't respect. Unless . . ." he held up a finger, "his treasure was in love with said man."

The thought had crossed Deckard's mind. But he'd brushed it off, remembering Evylin's reaction to the idea of their marriage. Either she hadn't known of her uncle's schemes, or she was a bloody brilliant actress.

"You don't think that's true, do you?" Deckard asked uncertainly.

The magistrate's eyes grew wide. "So, it *is* Evylin who's caught your eye? How interesting."

Waiting for an answer to the question, Deckard stayed silent.

Lawton waved his hand as though brushing away his last comment. "As I said, I won't pretend to know my daughter that well. However, I will say this: Evylin is highly selective of whom she gives her time and attention. And I would be lying if I said I hadn't noticed that she's been more friendly with you than with any man in . . . well, ever."

Though hardly an endorsement of love, Deckard couldn't deny that her friendly disposition was encouraging. Growing up in the Shires, he knew the laid-back banter of the locals. But after more than a decade in the service, he didn't trust his ability to discern between a woman being sociable and when she was flirting with him.

Lawton leaned back smugly. "What will it be, Captain? Are you asking my permission to write to her?"

Here it was—the moment Deckard had feared all night. His conversation with Thom haunted him even now in the light of day.

Last night, his brother pleaded with him, begging him not to go through with the marriage. "You'll be throwing your future away, and for what? Some unknown woman's happiness?" he'd proclaimed in Deckard's tent.

"It's more than that," Deckard had argued.

"What could possibly be worth marrying someone you don't love?"

Any other time, Thom's words might have convinced him. But the looming threat awaiting in Loclight terrified Deckard. "You say I'm throwing away my future. But I'll have no future if I don't return with enough men. General Rand has had it out for me since I arrived in Loclight."

"Oh, he's just a vain old snake who's sour all his officers like you better than him."

"It doesn't change the facts," Deckard countered. "Rand has been looking for an excuse to ruin my career for years. If I fail, he gets that chance, and that's it for me. No more promotions, no good assignments, and no chance I'll make any difference in this world."

Thom stared at him with a familiar glare, one Deckard understood without question. His brother was angry with him; worse, he resented him.

"One man won't make up for the two hundred we still haven't obtained," Thom spat. "And Rand will find a way to punish you regardless."

With a sigh, Deckard paced around his tent.

Thom continued in his silence. "Your only hope is to bring back all the men. All five hundred. Rand won't care about training. He won't give a damn about the return of General Hewitt Glaas. He only cares about his orders being followed."

"Exactly," Deckard exclaimed desperately. "And we've only got Nettershire to go before we're done. We won't find two hundred men there. We'll be lucky to get a hundred. One man might not make up the numbers, but he might impress the other officers enough to save me from being one step away from demotion."

A scowl marred Thom's face. "And what about your happiness? Is the success of your career more important than that?"

That caused Deckard to pause. He loved his brother—as he always had—but the feeling wasn't mutual. And this demand to see his happiness obtained made Deckard doubt the sincerity of his brother's objections.

Unable to ponder past the headache that had grown over the past hour of arguing, Deckard didn't try to understand his brother's motives. "You're right," he conceded. "I can't know if we'll be happy together. But I do know this: I will not be happy if I lose my career. I want to do something with my life. And if I have to marry a woman I've known for three days to do it, then, by Allore, I'll marry her."

His brother hadn't taken kindly to that answer. But no matter his arguments, Hewitt was right: Deckard needed this as badly as Evylin. And as fearful as he was of making the wrong choice, he was far more fearful of rejecting something that might save him.

In the fresh morning light of the magistrate's office, Deckard drew back his shoulders and committed himself. He met Lawton's gaze and said, "I was thinking of something more permanent."

Lawton's brow wrinkled.

"If what you say is true," Deckard continued, "if your daughter really does . . . love me, then I don't think I can take any chances. I'm not as young as I once was. I have watched many friends marry and begin the family I want. And I have finally found a woman with whom I could see myself sharing a future."

The magistrate stared at him. "Are you asking for her hand in marriage?"

"I am."

Lawton's chest rose and fell with his breath twice before he spoke. "I will warn you; it may be too soon. Evylin has an aversion to all forms of romance. If I were you, I would write to her. Take a few months to soften her and ensure she loves you too much to say no."

"I don't want to convince her." Deckard was surprised he felt that lie as though it were the truth. "If she says no, I will take it as a sign it wasn't meant to be."

After a reluctant nod, Lawton replied, "Then you have my consent. Will you ask her now?"

Deckard couldn't decide whether he felt relief or terror. "If I may."

"Very well. I will retrieve her."

The magistrate left Deckard for what felt like an eternity. And in that infinity, he dropped his head into his hands, running through his worries another dozen times. When the door finally opened again, Deckard jumped up from his seat. He bumped into the desk, setting a small bust teetering, and reached out to steady it on instinct.

Evylin stepped into the room, her father waiting in the doorway. Her eyes met Deckard's before flying to the floor. Her nervousness was evident at breakfast, but the subtle flush to her cheeks revealed that her discomfort remained.

"I'll be right outside if you need me," Lawton said, then shut the door behind him with a *click*.

Deckard stared at Evylin, noting the difference in her appearance. In the three days he'd known her, she'd only ever worn gray and black. Now, the white blouse and blue skirt softened her every detail. She was rather beautiful, a fact he'd recognized early in their minimal acquaintance.

Deckard stepped away from the chair. "Please, have a seat."

Evylin looked at the jacquard chair, then met his gaze. She pointed to the door and tapped her ear.

Deckard pressed his lips together and nodded. He'd hoped to ease the discomfort of the moment with some open conversation about their choice. But with Magistrate Glaas on the other side of the door listening in, they had to keep up the ruse.

"Thank you, Captain," Evylin said and took the seat.

Taking a deep breath, Deckard prepared himself for the humiliation of their performance. He turned to face her, noticing how her cool brown hair lit up in the sunlight. "Thank you for seeing me, Miss Glaas," he began. "I didn't feel I could leave without speaking to you."

"You flatter me, Captain Deckard," she said, playing her part. "Though I can't imagine why you'd single me out." Though she hadn't spoken with sarcasm, he knew it was there.

Deckard grinned dryly. "I hope that's not true," he said, maintaining his role as the doting admirer. "I must say, I thought it obvious."

Evylin scanned him thoughtfully as she mocked confusion. "I'm sorry, I don't know what you mean."

Deckard took a step toward her. "This isn't the first time I've sought to speak with you since my arrival. And while I wasn't brave enough to be honest then, I had hoped you would sense my regard."

Evylin crossed her arms and leaned back in the chair. A twinkle sparked in her brown eyes. "In what way were you dishonest, Captain?"

Running a hand along his jaw, Deckard considered his next words. The trouble with lying was how quickly it could leap from likelihood into melodrama with one overwrought line. He couldn't blurt out undying love for her nor jump into an instant proposal. Lawton Glaas might be a narcissist like most magistrates in the country, but already, he'd proven himself more cunning than his brother, daughter, or even Deckard had given him credit for.

Deckard looked down at Evylin, her father's eyes staring back at him. Eyes that saw through whatever faultless façade you thought you'd constructed. The two might think themselves unalike, but the truth was plain for Deckard to see: They were far more similar than they realized. And he'd gotten himself into a game he could only win if he made every move with the utmost care.

Deckard set a hand on the desk, placing himself closer to Evylin. "I'm still not sure I'm brave enough to say it."

Evylin bit her bottom lip around a teasing grin. "Is there anything I can do to help?"

"Promise not to laugh at me."

She grimaced, and Deckard knew she was biting back a smart retort. "I would never laugh at you," she promised falsely.

Deckard made the bold move this game demanded. "Miss Glaas, when I met you, I couldn't understand what had happened. One moment, I was walking into your family's home, and the next, I'd met a woman unlike any other."

She rolled her eyes at that.

"You were and are the most singular of women," he insisted, finding himself truthful in that confession. "I have never known a woman so sure or confident. You're intelligent and articulate. You're beautiful, to be sure, but that's a meager start to your merits."

His compliments were a stretch too far, and Evylin blushed. He was surprised to find he liked embarrassing her with his praise.

Deckard knelt by her chair, and she eyed him suspiciously. "Please, don't think I'm being presumptuous." He held back a chuckle, entertained by her nervousness. "My life before you has only been loneliness."

A mostly true statement.

"To think of returning to that life is too much."

Slightly less true.

"I don't want to live without you, Miss Glaas."

Even further from the truth.

"I don't think I can."

A flat-out lie.

Reaching out to take her hand, Deckard gave her a sarcastic grin. "Tell me you feel the same."

A bewildered expression crossed Evylin's face before the corners of her lips lifted. "You're a bloody tease," she whispered in a tone so quiet even he strained to hear it. The look of delight in her smile prompted him to dip his head in thanks as she continued speaking.

"Captain, I don't know what to say." Evylin's words were soft, though back to their usual volume. "I had hope, but only that. And to hear you confirm my hope . . . It is too much. Can you possibly mean that you . . . ?" Her voice trailed off, and she raised her brow, throwing the act back to him.

Deckard accepted her challenge. "That I love you?" he asked, the words sitting uncomfortably on his tongue. "I do. That I want to marry you? I mean that too."

Evylin frowned suddenly, the humor gone from her eyes.

Caught off guard, Deckard loosened his grip on her fingers. Had she changed her mind? Did she want to call it off? He found himself unexpectedly disappointed at the thought.

"Miss Glaas," Deckard began, then shook his head. "Evylin," he started again, infusing his words with far more sincerity, "I know it's fast, and it seems too soon. But my heart asks: What is time to love?"

With an uncertain expression, she stared back at him.

He held her gaze in silent question: Should he continue?

She gave a single nod.

"If you'll have me," Deckard said, the words coming more easily now, "I would spend the rest of my life loving you." He dropped his voice and added, "Even under these circumstances."

They stared at each other, his offer hanging clearly between them. He would choose to love her even as their marriage was the result of a bet lost. And Deckard knew he could uphold that promise.

Evylin's hand was warm in his, soft but calloused from the training and work she did with her uncle. Their chests rose and fell faster than usual, expectation and uncertainty heightening their pulses. The wood floor grew hard under his knee.

Then Evylin's smile grew, and the sparkle of humor returned to her gaze.

Taking his cue, Deckard asked, "Will you marry me, Evylin Glaas?"

"Yes," she breathed.

Instantly, Deckard's body tensed. What had he done? He'd asked a woman he'd known for only three days to marry him, knowing neither loved the other. Had he lost his mind?

Evylin's muffled laughter drew his attention. She pressed a hand to her mouth, but it couldn't hide the joy in her eyes. "Thank you," she whispered between her fingers.

Deckard felt his own smile return.

That was why he'd done it, he realized. No matter his lack of romantic affection for this woman, the damning truth was: He liked making her happy. He relished the sound of her unaffected laugh—light like the summertime air sweeping over the lake. He basked in the fullness of her smiles, the same that brought those small dimples to her cheeks. And if this ridiculous plan of theirs brought him a chance at redemption in the form of Hewitt Glaas while he got to experience the pleasure of this woman's company, who was he to complain?

CHAPTER TWELVE

Lawton waited politely for them to emerge, surprise marking his face when they opened the door. However, he did a reasonable job pretending he hadn't been listening in until after Deckard announced their engagement.

"I couldn't be a prouder father," he exclaimed. "You've found a man of great worth, Evie. You'll be happy, I'm sure."

Evylin didn't do quite as good a job of acting, but the smile never left her face.

When Deckard thanked the magistrate for his blessing, the man waved his hand. "Of course, of course. I couldn't ask for a better son-in-law. When do you think you'll be able to return for the wedding?"

Deckard and Evylin's gazes flew to each other's. So caught up in their plan, they'd both forgotten the need to request an immediate marriage. Their uneasy shock did well to suggest a fear of separation. And Deckard supposed they did have reason to fear. If he left without their marriage finalized, Hewitt wouldn't come with him, and there would be no point to any of this.

"Your Honor," Deckard said worriedly, "if it would be all right with Evylin and you, I don't want to wait. I've no idea when the army will grant me leave, and I've seen too many fellow soldiers with engagements that lasted far too long."

Lawton's eyes narrowed. "You and your company leave today, Captain. And you don't want to wait?"

"No. I know it isn't the way things are usually done," he glanced at Evylin, then spontaneously took her hand, "but I have to ask."

Lawton scanned his daughter as though waiting for an excuse. "Is this what you want, Evylin?"

She paused, looking between the men, her mouth hanging ajar. She glanced down at his fingers wrapped around hers. Then she met his gaze. "You don't have any hope of coming back soon?"

"I'm sorry, I don't," Deckard said, and he meant it. He sincerely wished they had time to become accustomed to their new relationship. "My commanding officers are stalwart in their efforts to win this war, and I expect they'll give me another assignment upon my return. It may be a year or more before I earn leave."

Evylin chewed on her bottom lip. "Then I don't want to wait either."

Lawton didn't seem convinced but said, "If you're both sure, we *can* do it now."

They both nodded resolutely.

"Very well." Lawton stepped farther into the room. "Captain, if you're going to arrive at Trollenston before dark, you'll need to depart within the hour. Evylin, go tell your mother the news and pack your things. The captain and I need to draw up the marriage contract."

Evylin began to pull away, but Deckard held onto her hand. If he were to be the doting fiancé, he'd play the part. He dipped down and kissed the back of her hand. Her breath hitched sharply. When he looked up, she managed to fix her expression into demure embarrassment rather than shock. He let her go, and she disappeared.

Lawton shut the door behind her and turned to face Deckard. His jovial demeanor disappeared. "I don't know what they've promised you, but it isn't enough."

Deckard stared at Magistrate Glaas. His heart pounded against his chest. "I don't know what you mean," he managed.

The magistrate sat behind his desk once more and pulled out a sheet of paper. "My daughter is not a romantic," he said flatly, eyes on the page. "She may read novels, but she's complained many times about the love stories within them. She doesn't believe in love at first sight or fated lovers."

Deckard struggled to salvage whatever he could. "I didn't believe in love at first sight either," he replied. "But then I met Evylin."

"You don't have to lie to me." Lawton dipped his pen into an inkwell. "I don't mind that they think they've fooled me," he began to write as he spoke, "because whatever Evylin and Hewitt get out of this exchange, I get what I've wanted for the last decade too: a husband for my daughter."

"Your Honor, I don't understand you," Deckard said, struggling to maintain the act. "I love Evylin."

Pausing, Lawton studied him. Then he returned to his work. "No, you don't. Now, what's your birth name?"

Deckard stared at the paper on the desk and the pen in the magistrate's hand. Hewitt had been wrong. Magistrate Lawton Glaas didn't care about the attempt at tricking him. Why should he? His daughter, so particular about her life, had agreed to marry a man with reasonable wealth, good standing, and a noble profession. The only reason to object was if the man was disagreeable. And this magistrate, who could see through his brother's tricks and his daughter's lies, could see through Deckard too.

Deckard's entire life revolved around making himself the model of respectability. He worked hard to ensure there could be no objection to him from anyone. No matter the reason for their marriage, he would care for his wife well.

And Lawton Glaas knew that.

Deckard resigned himself to his fate. He sat and replied defeatedly, "Jonn."

Lawton shook his head. "Full name, including titles."

"Captain Jonn Marc Deckard."

The pen scribbled across the page. "Date of birth?"

"The seventh of Pyra, 1541."

"Just the one brother?"

"Just Thom."

Lawton glanced up. "And he's younger, yes?"

"Yes."

The pen resumed. "Parents' names? Full, with titles, please."

Deckard provided the rest of the information the magistrate requested, then permitted himself to ask, "How did you know?"

Lawton's pen didn't falter as he spoke. "My daughter is not a very good actress. She can fool some people, but she's never been able to lie to me." He dipped the pen in ink again. "I was already suspicious; then you both confirmed it."

They *both* did.

Not only was Evylin a bad liar, but so was Deckard, evidently. He didn't know whether to find comfort in that or not. "What gave it away?" he asked.

Lawton reached for another paper to create a copy of the contract. "When I suggested she and Hewitt had a plan, you weren't surprised by the idea. You were surprised I guessed it. Beyond that, *you* were convincing. You may not love my daughter, but you'll be a good husband, no doubt. It was the kiss that gave you away. One so innocent should thrill a bride desperately in love with her groom. It terrified Evylin."

Deckard barely held in his scoff. "Indeed."

Placing his pen back in its holder, Lawton settled a fatherly eye on Deckard. "Might I advise you regarding my brother and daughter?"

"Of course." Deckard scooted to the edge of his seat eagerly.

"Never forget that you've entered into an agreement with two people who think they're smarter than everyone else," Lawton said. Though the words were harsh, there was no malice in his tone. "The most important thing to know about Hewitt is that his wife and son died thirteen years ago, while he was still in the army. When he came back, he was a broken man. Evylin was only a month younger than his son, and they were inseparable. She was as devastated by his death as Hewitt. Upon his return, Hewitt chose Evylin as his son's replacement. In all respects, Evylin is his son now. Don't try to separate them. Don't try to get between them. Hewitt will not allow it."

Deckard considered this sad revelation as Lawton continued, "And don't think you can rely on Hewitt for help either. You've dug yourself a nice hole in the past three days, and he won't respect you for some time."

The magistrate let out a dramatic sigh. "As far as Evylin is concerned, you'll have to do all the work in the relationship," he warned. "She's too afraid of people in general to trust a stranger like you. My best advice? Don't fall in love with her before she falls in love with you. You'll be in for years of heartache if you do."

The suggestion baffled Deckard. "Sir, are you advising me not to love your daughter?"

Lawton shook his head vehemently. "I'm advising you not to fall *in love* with her. The differences between love and being in love are very distinct. You'd know that if you were in love," he said, then glanced at his papers. "In fact, I'm surprised you don't know that. You're old enough to have married years ago. Have you never been in love?"

Taken aback, Deckard was immediately relieved by the knock on the door. Lawton called the visitor in, and Hewitt stepped into the room.

"I came by to tell you my news," the smith said, then sent a meaningful look to Deckard. "I suppose you told him?"

Deckard stood, about to reply, when Lawton spoke before he could. "He did. And I'm glad you'll be going." He smiled at his brother. "Turns out so will Evylin."

Hewitt's brow creased in feigned confusion. "Evie's coming?"

"Captain Deckard deserves your congratulations, Hewitt. He's proposed, and Evylin's accepted. You are standing next to your soon-to-be nephew-in-law." Lawton waved the marriage contract in the air. "The ceremony will take place in a matter of moments."

Deckard wasn't sure he'd ever seen a frown so fierce as the one Hewitt gave him. "Evie said yes to you?" he growled. "Why?"

Looking over at Lawton, Deckard hoped the magistrate would end the charade. Unfortunately, the man simply grinned.

With an internal sigh, Deckard turned back to Hewitt. "I'm in shock, myself," he said. "I never dreamed she'd return my love so soon."

Hewitt grimaced, and Lawton chuckled. "Oh, to be young again. It's easy to forget how quickly we fell in and out of love in those days."

"Nobody had better fall out of love once married," Hewitt threatened.

Lawton stood, ignoring his brother. "The paperwork is complete, so I'll check to be sure the bride is ready." Stopping in the doorway, he turned back. "Hewitt, do try to be polite while I'm gone. It is the poor man's wedding day."

As soon as he disappeared, Hewitt shut the door. His steely gaze met Deckard's as he said, "Your brother is pacing out front like a fox by a hen house."

Deckard pinched the bridge of his nose. "I forgot." He moved for the door. "I'd better go get him."

"Not to worry," Hewitt said, setting a hand on Deckard's chest. Somehow, the simple touch was the most hostile act he'd ever experienced. "My silly niece will be sure he's here to plant the idea of their own marriage in his head."

Hewitt held out a small canvas pouch. "I brought you something."

"Oh," Deckard said dully, accepting the bag. "Thank you."

"It's not for you, you bloody idiot."

Deckard ignored the insult and dumped a thin silver ring onto his palm. Delicate etchings of everbloom ivy covered the band. He wondered at the flower of mourning but decided not to remark on the choice. "It's beautiful," he said, amazed that the giant man could do such intricate work. "She'll love it."

Hewitt nodded firmly as though he'd already been aware of that.

Deckard hadn't even thought to provide a ring. Although he hadn't exactly had time to procure one. And from his limited knowledge, Whickam Village didn't have a jeweler or a finery shop. Still, he felt guilty for not offering his new wife a wedding gift.

Hewitt crossed his arms. "Seems as though you two pulled it off. I suppose that bodes well."

Sure that confessing the truth would provoke a rather loud and unpleasant conversation, Deckard merely nodded.

The door burst open, pushing both men back. Thom appeared, a look of irritation clear in his eyes. "Miss Glaas told me to come in here," he said.

Deckard stepped aside to create more room as Hewitt snorted. "Caly drop any hints while she was at it?"

Thom glowered at the bear-like man. "I'm not as easy to persuade as my brother."

Footsteps on the staircase reached them then, the giggles of Calyn and Dolia echoing through the hall. Hewitt grumbled as they neared the door. He moved to the far end of the room.

The youngest Glaas daughters stepped in, raining wildflower petals over Thom and Deckard. The parade drove them into the corner behind the chair.

"It was the best we could do in a rush," Calyn apologized as she sailed past.

Next came Lady Glaas, eyes damp with unshed tears as she beamed at Deckard. And finally, Lawton escorted Evylin back into the room.

Somehow, in the past half hour, her mother and sisters had taken the time to transform her into a fully-fledged bride. Those charming dimples framed her shy smile as her gaze averted. Her deep blue satin dress shone in the morning light, accentuating her tan skin with a radiant glow. They'd draped her hair over her shoulders in soft waves. The silver necklace still graced her collarbone. He attempted to discern the floral etching on its pendant, thinking it likely made by the same man who'd made the ring clutched in his hand.

To Deckard's shame, his attraction to her had deeply influenced his decision. No, Evylin wasn't a great, stunning beauty. The allure of her features was more gentle, more playful. Yet, if he allowed himself to be duped into a marriage, he was rather thankful he was so drawn to her.

"If you would join hands," Lawton said, offering Evylin's hand to Deckard, "I'll begin the ceremony."

Deckard was surprised to find her hand ice-cold but brushed his thumb over her knuckles reassuringly. "You look lovely," he said.

Evylin's smile betrayed her nerves. "Thank you," she muttered, then nodded to his green wool coat. "You look nice as well."

He knew she only meant to be polite, but he had dressed intentionally that morning. On a normal travel day, he'd wear his gray coat and consider going without a shave. But he felt that marriage deserved more special attention, even if it didn't include his ceremonial uniform.

Lawton cleared his throat and held up a small booklet. "Dearly beloved," he read, "we are here today to witness the union between this man and this woman." He gestured to each of them in turn. "As magistrate of Whickam Village, and with authority granted by King Ephren himself, it is incumbent upon me to lead you in the everlasting vows of Ephrian marriage. It is the holy charge of Allore that we enter the divine union of matrimony, reflecting his love for us. Therefore, let us pray as we begin this sacred ceremony."

In his peripheral vision, Deckard caught a brief hesitation from Hewitt and Evylin before they both bowed their heads rotely. In the winding, expressive discourse of Lawton's prayer, a slight worry niggled Deckard that she might be unbelieving, as was the growing fashion in the cities. But as she'd shown no signs of being openly antithetical toward Allorians, he took her soft "by your grace" as a sign that perhaps she was simply reserved.

With the prayer's end, Lawton's chin rose piously. He gave the routine matrimonial speech, proclaiming the rich promises of the institution and the importance of their vow to stand by each other's side through joy or sorrow, sickness or health, poverty or riches, triumph or failure. He ended the speech by saying, "It is a never-ending promise to prize and serve one another. Is this your intent today?"

Deckard thought Evylin's fingers trembled in his, but she readily said, "It is."

So Deckard echoed, "It is."

"With your declaration of intent, we may proceed to the charge," Lawton said and turned the page. "The adjure of Allore above charges the husband thus: When a man takes a woman to wife, she passes from the headship of her father and becomes under his own. He is to prize and serve her with all his heart and body. This is for her protection and care. A husband is never to abuse this sacred vow. If it is seen that he has, the marriage is to dissolve, and the couple shall part."

Lawton adjusted, facing Evylin. "The adjure of Allore above charges the wife thus: When a woman takes a man to husband, he takes her under his headship and becomes her shield and guardian. She is to prize and serve him with all her heart and body. This is for his protection and care. A wife is never to abuse this sacred vow. If it is seen that she has, the marriage is to dissolve, and the couple shall part. Will you both answer your charges with diligence and grace?"

"I will," Deckard said.

"I will," Evylin whispered.

Lawton turned to Deckard. "I know this was short notice, but did you think to provide a ring?"

With one glance over at Hewitt—his head held high in pride—Deckard proffered the small band.

"Mm." Lawton gave it a dismissive glance. "It was good of you to think of her, but you'll need to get one yourself. A husband with no ring doesn't inspire the faith of a wife. You may place the ring on her finger."

Deckard took Evylin's left hand and slid the band to rest on her ring finger. She looked from it to him and then over to Hewitt. The uncle and niece shared a fond grin.

"Now, with your vows and charges in mind, we will bind the union." Lawton set the booklet down and turned to his wife. She handed him a vibrant emerald ribbon. He held it out before them. "As Allore bound the love of the Ateris, his first children, I now bind together your love." The magistrate wrapped the ribbon around their wrists tightly. The tension of the ribbon dug into the back of Deckard's hand.

Lawton placed his hands over theirs and said the benediction. "May Allore's grace be upon this union." Then he opened his eyes and added in a rote tone, "By the power vested in me, I pronounce you man and wife."

The magistrate untied the ribbon, but Deckard felt suddenly numb. Man and wife. How had he gone from a longtime bachelor to a wedded man in a matter of an hour?

"Now, you'll each sign the certificate," Lawton said. "Evylin first."

As Evylin took her hand from Deckard's, he looked at his brother. Thom pressed a fist to his mouth as he watched Evylin sign. His sharp eyes were hard, his agitation palpable.

Deckard bristled internally.

"Captain, if you please," Lawton called.

Leaning over the page, Deckard confirmed the information above his signature line. Written as given earlier, his name, date of birth, and family marked the page. And across from it lay Evylin's information. With the opportunity to learn something about his wife, he took the time to read:

Evylin Rosette Glaas
born the fifteenth day of Chronos in the year 1547
third daughter of Magistrate Lawton Glaas
& Lady Laurisa Pinnette-Glaas

Deckard brushed the metal pen tip against the glass jar to remove the excess ink before signing. He found himself amused by her name. Evylin Rosette was far too feminine for a woman who could best his brother in a sword fight.

Finishing his signature with its usual flourish, he stood and offered Evylin his arm.

Lawton signed the page as officiant before calling on Laurisa and Thom. "A witness from each family," he said merrily.

Thom gritted his teeth but completed his task without a word. Deckard would need to handle that later.

"Is that all, then?" Hewitt demanded as Lawton dusted the contract to dry the ink. "It's practically midday."

"Nearly, nearly." Lawton folded the page, sealed it, and turned to Deckard. "You may now kiss your bride, Captain."

Evylin's fingers dug into his arm, and Deckard gulped.

He'd forgotten about that bit.

In the corner, Dolia and Calyn giggled. Laurisa wove her hand through Lawton's. Hewitt glared, and Thom turned to the wall. If there was ever to be an awkward first kiss, this would be it.

Deckard looked down at Evylin, and she stared up at him. Her cheeks flushed with the lightest pink against her slightly tawny complexion. Her warm brown eyes darted between his. His heart dropped, finding a spark of fear in her gaze. Not only had she forgotten the marital kiss, too, she didn't want it.

It didn't bode well for their wedding night.

But there was no way around it and no more time to hesitate. If they waited much longer, no one would believe their love story. Although that hardly seemed to matter anymore.

When Deckard gently tipped up her chin, she flinched subtly. Her face felt like fire compared to her cold hands. Slowly, so as not to startle her, he dipped across the short gap. Still, she tensed as he drew near.

Disappointment muddled with shame in his gut. She didn't want his physical attention; that hurt, but even more so, it bothered him to force it on her. Yet, he couldn't exactly refuse to perform the obligatory wedding kiss.

Taking pity on her, Deckard dropped his voice so only she could hear as he whispered, "Close your eyes."

Evylin's eyes snapped shut.

He kept his touch light as he pressed his lips to hers for only a mere second. Then he pulled away. It had hardly been a kiss at all.

The Glaas women cheered, but Deckard doubted Evylin would cherish this memory. Turning back to their witnesses, Deckard smiled, not feeling its joy.

Lawton extended the marriage contract to him. "Congratulations, Captain Deckard. And welcome to the family."

"Thank you, Your Honor." Deckard held the magistrate's eyes as he accepted the contract. He could hear the unspoken reminder as he felt Evylin's hand like a death grip on his arm. He could not fall in love with her.

Not yet.

Part II: The Ephrian Army

Vileness festers in dark places, yet I will seek it out. It is my charge, my burden, my office as the king's knight to be justice where there is none.
Quote attributed to Euon Sergus, circa 615

Burning light filled the sky, Fire emblazoned upon it like a crown of glory. Ninety thousand men trembled under its blaze. The wrath of the Mages would not be cooled by all the steel of Men for they sought glory on the western plains. They sought power.
Excerpt from The Mages of Auld

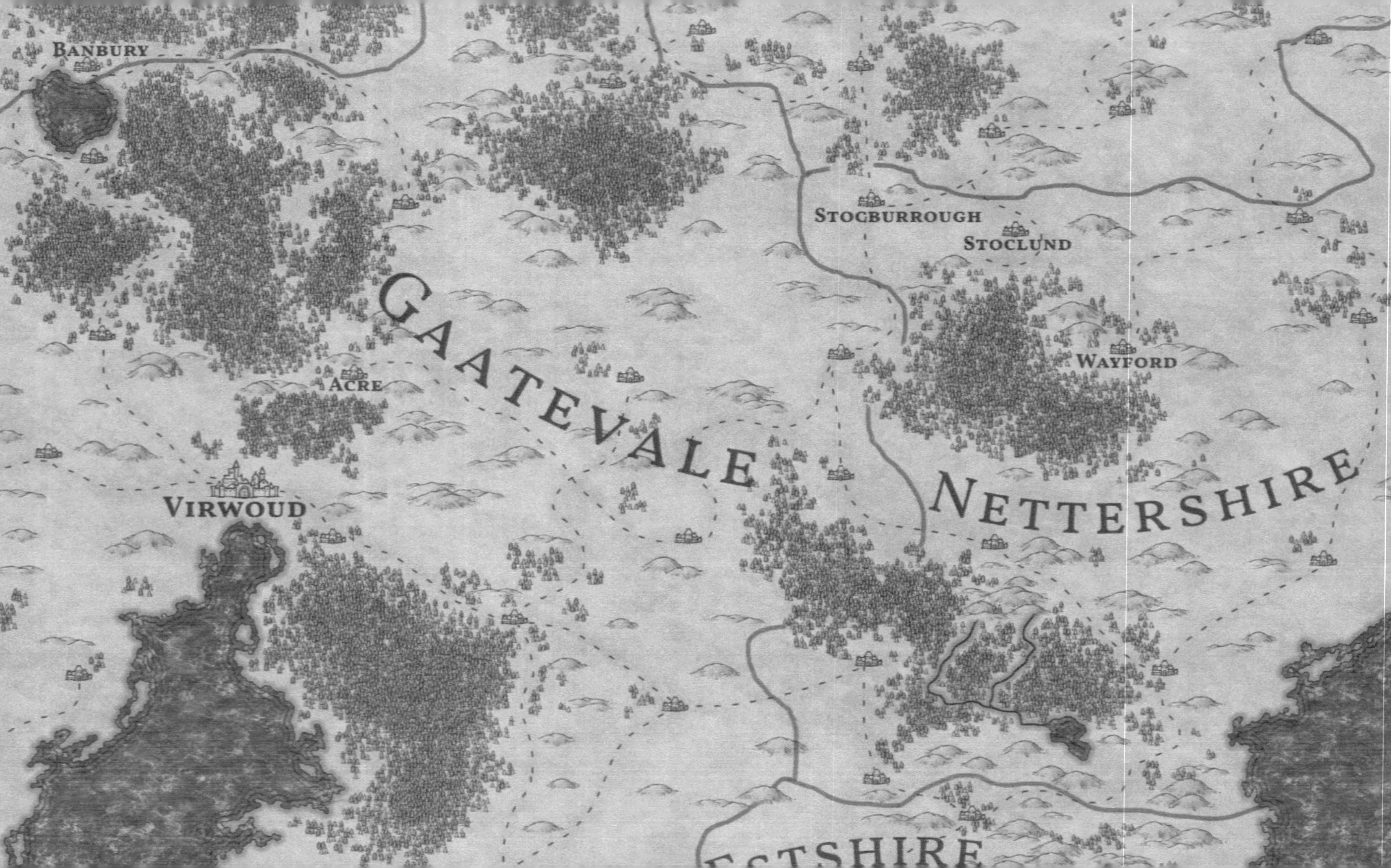

BANBURY
STOCBURROUGH
STOCLUND
WAYFORD
ACRE
GAATEVALE
VIRWOUD
NETTERSHIRE
ETSHIRE

CHAPTER THIRTEEN

None of it felt real to Evylin. Even as her mother pulled away from their embrace, tears in her eyes, Evylin couldn't quite comprehend the finality of their goodbye.

A cold wind cut through, causing Evylin's eyes to water. She thought it would reassure her mother—and all the rest of them—that she regretted leaving. She hadn't even said goodbye to her elder two sisters or nieces. Yet, she couldn't feel the sorrow or guilt she thought she should.

It wasn't that she didn't care to say goodbye. It had nothing to do with a lack of feeling for her family. But it all felt so surreal and dreamlike that Evylin had trouble taking it seriously.

She was leaving at last, going off on the adventure she and Ryen had promised to share all those years ago. And it felt no more important than her typical trip to Trollenston with Hewitt.

"Be safe and write often," Laurisa charged, holding Evylin's face in her frigid hands.

"I will." Evylin mustered a forlorn smile, knowing she'd likely forget.

Laurisa let out another sob and pulled her back in. It was Lawton's interference that convinced the woman to let go. "They must leave, dear." He stroked his wife's arms as he passed her off to their youngest daughters for comfort.

With an apologetic glance at her mother and sisters, Evylin turned to the men. Hewitt had said his hasty goodbyes long before and sat on the cart that carried their trunks. Thom stood at the far end with his arms crossed as he surveyed the farewell. His dark brows hung low over his eyes in what she imagined to be disapproval.

Deckard stepped up to Evylin's side, expression gentle with compassion. "Are you ready?"

Struggling to believe she was actually about to leave with him, she gave him a steady smile. "As I'll ever be," she replied.

He offered his arm to her then, and they took their first steps away from her family's home. Evylin kept her eyes on the horizon. That was her destination. Out there lay the adventure and future they'd longed for. And she was *finally* on her way.

Lawton proffered his hand to help Evylin onto the cart, but she shook her head. "I'd like to walk," she told him, feeling that the physical activity might keep her focused on the moment. Maybe she'd believe it more if she experienced the tangible act of leaving.

Lawton climbed onto the cart next to his brother as Thom fell in line with Deckard and Evylin. They kept back to avoid any dirt or rocks kicked up by the wheels.

Hand tucked in the crook of Deckard's elbow, Evylin let him escort her. The thick wool of his coat and the leather of her gloves should have kept the touch from feeling intimate or uncomfortable. It was less physical contact than a dance. Yet, the knowledge that this man was her husband clung to the back of her thoughts, and her hand instinctively loosened.

Evylin cast one final glance back at her family home, studying the stone façade and climbing ivy, the wide windows and dark oak door, the black shutters and slated roof. She scanned the stables and smithy, which had been her home away from home for years. Then she sent one final look over her shoulder toward the kirkyard, whispering an internal farewell to the boy she'd always carry with her through the pressed everbloom flower tucked in her trunk.

The walk from the square to camp wasn't far, but each step felt important, carrying her closer to their adventure.

Suddenly, an irritable grumble came from Thom, disrupting her internal reverie. "This is a mistake," he whispered fiercely to his brother.

Jaw tightening, Deckard turned to him. "If you can't manage to be pleasant," he said, voice low, "then do us the favor of being useful. Go ahead and make sure the men are ready to leave."

Thom looked prepared to fight him, but Deckard added, "That's an order, Lieutenant."

A flare of anger flashed in Thom's gray-blue eyes. Then he tipped his head in a mocking bow. "As you say, Captain," he muttered, then doubled his stride to push past the cart.

Deckard pinched the bridge of his nose. "I'm sorry," he muttered. "My brother . . . He can be difficult."

Evylin gave him an absolving grin. "I have four sisters," she reminded him. "Little is as difficult as that."

His chuckle sounded a bit too close to a scoff. "You don't know Thom," he said bitterly, then continued, reverting to his usual politeness. "Please forgive him. He tends to say things he doesn't mean when he's upset."

"Doesn't everyone?"

Deckard shrugged. "Thom has a special gift for making it hurt."

"I see." Evylin looked ahead, seeing that the man in question was almost past the buildings and out of the village. "So you don't think he's truly mad at me for ruining your life?"

"He's mad at the moment," he admitted. "But he'll get over it."

"Well, that's something to look forward to."

He granted her jest a laugh, then turned to face forward once more.

The edge of the campsite came into view before them. Evylin studied what she could see of the field ahead, its fixtures diminishing rapidly. Folded and bound according to army regulations, the soldiers had already loaded most of the tents and other supplies into the wagons. A faint smell of smoke still hung in the air from recently doused campfires.

Evylin's heart quickened as she took in the scene. The army camp would be her home for the next several weeks. Or even months. She didn't know how long it would take to get . . . well, she didn't even know where they were going.

"For the record," Deckard said, interrupting her thoughts, "you didn't ruin my life."

Evylin passed him a sly grin. "There's still time."

He laughed again, reminding her of his good sense of humor. With their lives forever intertwined, she was grateful to know they could enjoy one another's company at the very least.

The cart rumbled ahead, the trunks jostling and drawing her gaze. She hoped she hadn't forgotten anything of importance. She'd only had seconds to stow her savings before her mother pulled her away to dress her up while Calyn and Dolia finished the packing. Dressing in her finest for the ceremony seemed frivolous at the time, and now she felt even more ridiculous. Their rush pushed them out the door the second their vows were through, and she still wore her satin dress under her dark gray coat. Its tight bodice would make for a miserable journey to Trollenston on foot, horseback, or wagon.

Despite the heavy coat, Evylin shivered as the wind cut through the corridor of houses and businesses along the street. Though she didn't know their ultimate destination, she did know they were headed north, and this gave her pause. If all her winter clothing was hardly enough for Whickam Village on its coldest days, it would never be enough farther north.

"Here," Deckard said, evidently feeling her shiver. He pulled her closer and wrapped his bare hand around her gloved one.

Taking in the rest of him, Evylin frowned. Though his coat was wool, his trousers were of a thick cotton weave, and he wore no scarf or gloves—nor any other sort of protection from the weather.

"Is it terribly cold in . . . wherever you live?" she asked.

"Terribly?" Deckard repeated with amusement. "No. But it is colder than here."

"And where *do* you live?"

"In Loclight."

She sucked in an awe-filled gasp. "The capital?"

He nodded as though it was nothing.

"How long have you lived there?"

"Almost twelve years. I moved into the barracks right after joining the army, though I was stationed elsewhere for a while. When I became a lieutenant, I could afford my own home in the Military District. Thom shares it with me now. Though neither of us is there much."

"Oh." Evylin wondered if Thom would continue to live at the house once they arrived but wasn't so sure she should ask.

"If you don't like it," Deckard said as they neared the camp, "we can live somewhere else."

"If I don't like the house, or if I don't like Loclight."

"The house," he clarified. "Unfortunately, I'm not given a choice on where I'm assigned. Before this, my assignment was as a colonel's aide both in Loclight and when he traveled, but they could send us elsewhere upon our return."

Evylin didn't know whether that was happy news or not. Moving around the country sounded like an adventure. But then, seeing Loclight, the seaside capital city, was an adventure all of its own. What if she loved it and was forced to leave? Or, worse, what if Deckard was stationed in a small settlement like Whickam Village?

The cart rolled to a stop while Lieutenant Peery brought a couple of soldiers to meet them. The lieutenant ordered his men to gather the trunks, and the soldiers moved quickly—though clumsily—to obey. Looking around, Evylin watched as soldiers ran to and fro carrying crates, bags, and other larger objects. Horses pawed their hooves and shook their heads, impatient to move out.

Deckard slowed their pace and dropped his voice. "I think it'd be best if you called me 'Jonn' from here on," he suggested. "Some might find it suspicious if my wife calls me 'Captain.'"

"I suppose that would sound odd," she agreed, though it felt strangely personal for a man she'd only met three days prior. Peery shook hands with Hewitt, and Evylin nodded over to them. "But your officers call you 'Deckard,' don't they? Shouldn't I do the same?"

He raised his brow, green-blue eyes twinkling. "Our relationship is quite different than the one I have with my officers, I assure you."

She rolled her eyes at his sarcasm. "And what about your brother? He calls you 'Deckard,' and he's family."

"A brother is not a wife."

She pressed her lips together, still uneasy. She didn't know why. Jonn was a perfectly normal, if overused, name. Perhaps she felt it didn't suit him, being too common, whereas he was unusually charming.

Deckard surveyed her, a curious gleam in his gaze. "Do you have a problem with my name, Evylin?"

Prepared to offer him a smart rebuttal, Evylin never got the chance. Her father, Hewitt, and Peery joined them.

The lieutenant gave her a curious glance before turning to his captain to report. "The men are loading the final supplies as we speak, Deckard. We should be ready to leave in half an hour. Sooner, if we can get the men moving faster."

Deckard gave him a sharp nod, his demeanor growing serious. She could feel the muscles of his bicep tighten under her fingers. "Tell them if they get us out of here within a quarter, I'll let them have tomorrow to see the town. If not, they'll spend the day practicing the routine of tearing down and setting up the camp from dawn till dusk to refine their skills." He then glanced at Evylin. "I'll be there momentarily with Major Glaas."

Peery bowed before hurrying off. He barked orders at each soldier that he passed, and they all quickened their paces.

Deckard offered his hand to Lawton. "Your Honor, I'll never be able to thank you enough."

"Not at all, Captain," Lawton said, his expression far too pleased for Evylin's tastes. "You've done more for my family than you know."

Turning to his brother, Lawton managed to keep his happy demeanor. "Good luck, Hewitt. I know Evylin will be safe with you to look after her."

Hewitt grunted a farewell.

Lawton faced Evylin. "Walk me to the cart?"

As Deckard immediately released her, Evylin had no choice but to follow.

"Well, now," her father said as they reached the seat, "you're off on that adventure you always wanted. I hope it's what you dreamed it would be."

Evylin doubted it.

"I really do, Evie," he continued, somehow sounding like he meant it. "Please don't forget your mother and sisters. They need to hear from you."

She nodded.

He tipped his head toward the men. "Remember to take care of him."

"I will," Evylin promised, looking back at her uncle.

"I meant your husband, Evylin," he charged. "Take care of him before anyone else."

Unsure of what to say, Evylin swallowed past the tightness in her throat. "All right."

A heavy sigh left him before he pulled her into a hug. "You will always be my daughter, Evie," he whispered to her, "no matter where you go."

An embrace from her father was rare for Evylin. The last time she remembered hugging him was on her sixteenth birthday. Whether that was due to her own avoidance of him or his of her, she couldn't say. They'd never been close. She hardly knew him for the first six years of her life while he was in the army. When he returned, their opposing demeanors clashed too often to foster closeness. But now, feeling the rough edge of his coat against her cheek and smelling his scent of ink and paper, she leaned into his warmth.

This was her final piece of home.

Her final moment as Evylin Glaas.

"Be safe." Lawton pulled back and jumped up onto the cart. Evylin could have sworn she saw a glimmer in his eyes, but before she could get a clear look, he snapped the reins, turning the horses in a flash, and the cart rumbled back into the shadows of the ivy-riddled buildings.

The weight of a hand on her upper back caused Evylin to suck in a rush of icy air. She looked up to see Deckard at her side, wearing that compassionate expression of his. "We need to prepare to leave."

Evylin bore herself up. "Of course. What can I do?"

Hewitt walked next to them as Deckard led her toward a ragged ring of blankets around a cold firepit. "Actually," he began, "I'm afraid there isn't anything you can do. I need to introduce your uncle to his fellow officers and then oversee the rest of the work."

"All right, so . . . what?" She furrowed her brow. "Should I just follow you around until we leave?"

Deckard glanced at Hewitt, who held up a hand as if volunteering to take over. "Stay here, Evie," he ordered.

"Here?" Evylin gaped at him, heart falling into her stomach. "By myself?"

"It won't take long," Deckard promised. "I'll be back soon."

In her blend of confusion and disappointment, Evylin thought to tell him that she didn't care if he came back; he didn't have a role to play in her and Ryen's dream. But he *did* have a role in her escape. That thought killed what little bitterness had arisen inside of her.

She summoned a smile. "Of course, I understand. Do what you must."

"I am sorry," Deckard promised again.

She waved a hand to dismiss the apology. "No need."

He eyed her cautiously, unconvinced, but he nodded—first to her and then to Hewitt—and the two men hurried away from her into the fray of soldiers.

Alone and with nothing to do, Evylin wrapped her arms around her waist and stared after them. Was this what it would be like? Moments into the adventure, she was already being left behind.

Not far away, a small group of soldiers loaded some canvas tents into a wagon. She watched as they worked together with little success. Instead of sliding the tents in evenly, they bumped the sides of the wagon and snagged on the other tents, already loaded. One soldier had to hop in to help pull the packs the rest of the way.

Evylin chewed on her lip. She could have handled the task with twice as much speed and efficiency after her work with Hewitt. He'd taught her to analyze jobs like that before jumping in and mucking it up as these volunteer soldiers had. But they wouldn't accept her help even if she offered it.

Across the field, more soldiers were hoisting the final crates of what was once their training ground. They carried away the final targets and weapons, clearing the field of any sign of the army's presence beyond the tamped, dying grass.

The few things left unloaded disappeared around Evylin as she waited. So many occasions throughout her life, she'd watched the same process from the village. She remembered one time when Ryen was at her side. The wind had tousled his curly, dark hair just as it tugged strands of her mousy-brown waves across her face now. They'd sat on the low stone fence of Mrs. Cohle's yard, watching the soldiers at work. Ryen had snuck some jerky from his mother's kitchen, and they munched on it while discussing their future travels.

And forever after—even once Ryen was gone—any time Evylin watched the army pass through the village, she would imagine all the places she might go and all the things she hoped to experience.

This time, she was going with them.

So why didn't she feel any different?

"Excuse me," a reedy voice said behind her.

Evylin whirled to face a young man. He appeared colorless, with skin as pale as his white-blond hair and light gray eyes that matched the cloudy sky. His dark gray travel uniform hung loosely on his thin frame, doing little to help him look less like a ghost from one of her novels.

"You're standing on my blanket," the soldier said, pointing at the ground.

Looking down at the red and black wool under her feet, Evylin gasped and began to back away. "I'm so sorry," she said.

The soldier's grin grew as he swiped it from the ground. "Not to worry," he said, rolling it into a ball. "I wouldn't dream of bothering the captain's new wife under normal circumstances, but I'm rather hoping to get tomorrow off so. . . ."

Smiling back at him, Evylin determined against her first characterization. He was less like a ghost and more like a weasel with his long face, prominent forehead, small eyes, and narrow nose.

"What makes you think I'm the captain's wife?" she asked.

"I have my sources."

Evylin began to inquire after such sources when the appearance of Lieutenant Deckard at her side cut her reply short.

"Do get moving, Rafferty," he ordered casually. "We've got places to be, and it's not your job to entertain the captain's wife."

The weasel hefted the blanket in Thom's direction. "I was just packing my things, Lieutenant," he promised. "Ask your lovely sister if you don't believe me."

Thom spared a single glance at Evylin before raising his brow at Rafferty. "Do you want a day off or not?"

Rafferty wiggled his snowy brows. "Turn that frown upside down, Thommy," he said, breaking away from them. "We're gonna spend the day discovering Trollenston's finest!"

Watching the soldier rush off, Thom shook his head. "He's a bloody idiot," he said. Then he smirked, facing Evylin again. "But he makes for good company, and that's lacking around here, so I can't complain."

Evylin stared at him, mouth ajar.

"What?" Thom asked, a look of genuine concern crossing his face.

"Oh, I'm sorry." She set a hand to her chest in feigned surprise. "I was under the impression you didn't want anything to do with me."

Thom grimaced, pushing a hand through his dark hair. "Yeah, uh—I'm sorry about that. It isn't that I'm—well, I'm not really upset with *you*. It's just . . ."

"Just what?"

His gray-blue eyes grew wide like a child caught breaking a family heirloom. "He's my brother," he muttered.

"I'm aware of that."

He nodded.

"I didn't plan this," she assured him. "I didn't even ask for it. I had no more designs on your brother than he had on me. And while I understand your concern for his happiness,

I mean it when I say I have no intentions of making him unhappy." A scoff worked out of her. "I'd rather like to be happy, myself."

Rubbing a hand along the back of his neck, Thom frowned. "Miss Glaas . . ." He grimaced again. "Almighty, I can't call you that now, can I?"

The revelation hit Evylin with an odd blend of discomfort and indifference. "I guess not."

"Well, I can tell you right now, I've got no interest in calling you 'Mrs. Deckard.'"

A nervous laugh puffed out with the understanding that she was now, in fact, Mrs. Deckard. "No," she agreed. "I don't think that will do either."

"What do I call you, then? Evylin?"

"That or Evie will be just fine."

"In that case . . ." He gave her a true apologetic smile. "Evylin, please forgive me for my temper. I have no interest in being at odds with you. I—I rather like you."

Evylin cocked her head, unsure she'd heard him correctly.

"I know that's not the easiest thing to believe after my behavior, but it's true." He dropped his gaze, scratching his temple. "You're clever, amusing, and . . . well, it's not every day you find a woman who can actually wield a sword."

They both smirked at that.

Thom tossed his hands to the side. "I guess what I'm trying to say is that . . . I look forward to getting to know you better. And I guess I'm glad—or I don't mind . . . bloody hell, this is awful."

He straightened his shoulders. "What I mean—"

"Please." Evylin held up her hand to stop him, equal parts amused by and appreciative of his apology. "I understand. And I look forward to getting to know you as well."

Thom's grin was uneasy but grateful.

Evylin took a step back. "Don't let me keep you."

He looked around as if realizing where they stood. "Right." He gave her an awkward bow. "Until later, Miss Gla—Evylin."

Pacing about the charred remains of the firepit, Evylin wondered at the strange apology as Thom left her. The Deckard brothers were a rapidly developing paradox. The captain was personable and courteous. The lieutenant was quiet and temperamental. It was a wonder he'd worked up the spirit to apologize at all. Due to the way Deckard had spoken of him, she'd expected his anger to last for at least a few days.

But from the little she knew about Captain Deckard, she couldn't help wondering if he had something to do with the apology. No doubt, he'd spoken to his brother, insisting that Thom make nice with her. It was the exact sort of considerate behavior to which he seemed so prone.

The soldiers moved with speed at the promise of their day off, and they were, in fact, ready to move out in the fifteen minutes Deckard demanded. As the wagons began to roll past her and the soldiers moved to follow, the captain reappeared. He still carried that contrite smile as he approached her. "We're all ready to go," he said, then motioned back in the direction he'd come. "I made sure one of the wagons saved room for you."

"That's very thoughtful," Evylin said, gathering a handful of her skirt to lift its hem.

He dipped his head. "As beautiful as your dress is, I didn't think it was intended for several hours astride a horse."

"You're in a class of your own, Captain. Few men pay that much attention to what a woman wears."

"That's their loss, I say. It's a privilege to have someone dress so nice for your sake. I'd do you a disservice *not* to notice."

Evylin tossed him a withering look, unsure whether or not he was teasing her.

When they arrived at the wagon, another surprise awaited her. Hewitt sat atop the bench, reins in one hand while the other arm lay across the back.

"I thought you had to ride with your fellow officers," she said, doubling her speed.

Hewitt grunted. "The captain suggested I ride with you instead. Said something about your comfort being more important than army business."

Deckard kept to Evylin's side with ease despite her hurried pace. "You'll have the next two months to get to know the officers," he said. "For now, you can ensure Evylin doesn't have to spend hours next to an old soldier she doesn't know."

"You're the picture of a gentleman," Hewitt grumbled.

"I attempt to be."

Turning back, Evylin couldn't figure out his kindness. Whether he intended to get on her good side or acted out of genuine thoughtfulness, she was finding it hard to ascertain his motivation. "Thank you," she whispered. "I know you didn't have to do this."

"I was happy to. Now, here," he offered his hand, "let me help you up."

Though Evylin's instinct was to deny the help, she knew her skirts wouldn't grant her the independence needed for the task. She took hold of his hand, set one foot on the spoke of the wheel, and climbed the rest of the way with reasonable enough grace, thanks to his support. For such a trim man, he was surprisingly strong and stable.

Once assured she was comfortable and they were ready to leave, Deckard stepped aside and mounted up. His mare's shiny black coat and mane were as pristine as his boots and silver buttons. She wondered if he took the time to tend to the horse himself. No other horses were so perfect in their appearance or demeanor. Or was a splendid horse one of the perks of being the captain?

Hewitt snapped the reins, and Deckard led them off to join the rest of the marching soldiers.

Evylin allowed herself one last look over her shoulder toward the low stone fence she and Ryen had once sat on, dreaming of this exact moment. Her chest constricted. It felt wrong to leave him behind while she went off to live out their dreams.

But she forced herself to turn away, setting her eyes on the dirt road ahead of her. It was no time to wallow in the pain of the past. Not when she was finally on the way to the adventures of the future.

CHAPTER FOURTEEN

The hours passed at a slow, meandering pace as they made their way to Trollenston. Sitting on the wagon next to Hewitt, it felt like every other trip they'd made to the town. Evylin settled in for a quiet journey, studying the sea of soldiers before her.

Deckard had excused himself within the first thirty minutes of their ride. Even when he'd ridden at their side, his eyes had never stopped roving over the soldiers. Used to the silence of her uncle, Evylin hadn't minded his instant shift from friend to officer. They weren't on a holiday, she knew. It was his work. And he had more important things to do than to keep her entertained.

However, Deckard returned later in the day and started a light conversation. He kept it simple and unobtrusive, asking questions with easy answers. What was her favorite thing about Trollenston? Did she have many friends there? How often did her family visit her aunt and uncle? Did she have any cousins?

Evylin didn't mind answering them, and Hewitt even chipped in with gruff one-liners from time to time. It made their journey quite pleasant. But as the sun disappeared behind the encroaching clouds, the distant crack of thunder reached their ears.

The impending rain took Deckard away to patrol the troops and ensure they reached the town before the rain. For the remaining hour and a half of their trip, they saw him only from a distance as he went about his work.

The sun made its hidden descent before they arrived on the outskirts of Trollenston, mixing with the charcoal gray clouds to create a strange fade of brown and orange on the horizon. The soldiers began to set up the camp hurriedly, fighting against the oncoming darkness, the chilling winds, and the drizzle beginning to fall.

Hewitt pulled their wagon to a halt as Deckard appeared with Thom at his side. They dismounted in near unison before Deckard rushed over to help Evylin down. He offered her a nervous smile.

"I have to go see the magistrate," he explained. "Hopefully, he'll be welcoming and offer us lodging. I'd rather not make you spend your first night away from home in a tent."

Hewitt dropped down at Evylin's side. "Don't worry about that," he said. "Serene will raise hell if you don't stay with her."

"Serene?" Thom asked, nose wrinkled in confusion.

"My aunt," Evylin offered.

Deckard pursed his lips, looking up at the cloudy sky. Raindrops landed on his face. He moved to the back of the wagon, where several soldiers were already unloading its contents. They all stepped aside for him to climb in. "Are you sure they won't take offense at our unexpected arrival?" he called, crouching next to one of the trunks.

"Serene takes offense at everything," Hewitt said flatly. "And then she gets over it two seconds later. Jorge won't give a damn either way."

Lightning flashed.

"It looks as if we'd better hurry," Deckard said, still rummaging through the trunk. "Peery and I will go speak with the magistrate if for no other reason than to assure him our encampment is peaceful."

He shut the trunk lid and jumped back down from the wagon. "Evylin," he said, stepping to her side and unfurling a cloak. He wrapped the thick wool around her shoulders, fastening the clasp before settling the hood over her head. "Thom will escort you to your family's home, and I'll join you as soon as I can. Is that all right?"

Surprised yet again by his thoughtfulness, Evylin hesitated, her fingers wrapping around the cloak's edge. "Yes, that's fine."

Deckard donned his own cloak and turned to Hewitt. "Major Glaas, I'm afraid you'll have to stay with the troops. I can't give you preferential treatment."

Unbothered, Hewitt settled his hand on Evylin's shoulder. Deckard took a step back as she turned to her uncle. "Tell Jorge and Serene I'll stop by tomorrow." His eyes flickered to the captain for a second. "And enjoy your evening, if you can."

"I'm sure Serene will ask me a thousand questions, but I'll try," she promised, patting his arm.

Hewitt cocked his head, eyes shifting to Deckard once more. Then he squeezed her shoulder and hurried off.

Thunder rumbled, and the rain increased. The soldiers sped up their work. There were moments of chaos among the recruits as they tried to raise the camp in the rain. But the officers gave their orders, smoothing the process, and dozens of tents went up around them.

Deckard's eyes were back on his men, his feet shifting as though he wanted to rush off and get to work. "Lieutenant," Deckard turned to his brother, "find Peery, would you? And tell Lieutenant Cormier he's in charge until you get back."

"Yes, sir," Thom said, then jogged toward the thickest group of soldiers.

Evylin brushed some hair behind her shoulder under the cloak. "Is it always this hectic? Setting up camp?"

Deckard looked down at her. "No, not always. And not if you're in a company of trained men."

Another flash split the sky.

"I take it that having a company of recruits is rather a handful?"

He grinned dryly. "You could say that."

"Your commanding officers must have quite a lot of faith in you, then."

"How so?"

"If they believe you to be capable of commanding such a unit, they have to trust you to do the job well," she surmised. "I wouldn't put someone I thought incompetent in charge of my new recruits. Especially not when the job is particularly difficult."

The air shook with more thunder, and Deckard stared at her with a curious smile. "You know," his voice was light, "I do believe you're smarter than any officer I've met."

She smirked. "In that case, maybe they ought to put me in charge."

"Maybe they should."

Thom and Peery arrived, ready for their orders.

Turning to the soldiers, Deckard drew his shoulders back, and Evylin could see his shift into the role of captain. "Lieutenant Peery, you and I are going into Trollenston to meet with the magistrate. Hopefully, we won't interrupt his evening meal. Once we finish up there, we'll return to ensure the camp is ready for the night. I'll be staying in the town with my wife's family."

Peery gave Evylin an inquisitive glance before bowing his head to Deckard. "Of course, sir. I'm ready whenever."

"Thank you." Deckard turned to Thom. "Take Evylin to her family, then come back here and send Sergeant Stewert along with a couple of privates to deliver our things. The camp is under your charge while I'm gone."

Thom nodded, a proud glint in his steely blue eyes. "Yes, sir."

Taking hold of her hand, Deckard faced Evylin again. He opened his mouth to speak but seemed to think better of it with the two men standing nearby. The soldiers caught his hesitation and backed away to converse with one another.

As alone as they could be in the open camp, Deckard started over. "I wish I could come with you," he said, voice hushed.

Evylin shrugged, unsure why it should bother him. "That's all right. My aunt will have plenty to say to entertain me, I promise."

He gave a half-hearted chuckle. "I'm glad you won't be alone."

"I managed when you left me alone earlier, didn't I?"

He flinched, and she realized how callous her words might have sounded.

She hurried to correct the blunder. "I mean, I don't mind," she said hastily. "I'm not the sort who has to have company to be happy."

Deckard eyed her doubtfully. "I'm sorry about before," he whispered.

"Truly, I don't care," she assured him. However, the words came out more tersely than she'd intended. Shaking her head, Evylin set a hand on his arm. His cloak was already damp with the rain. "I'm not bothered by it, I swear."

Glancing down, Deckard considered her words. Then he squeezed the hand still in his, her wedding ring biting into her fingers beneath her gloves. "I'll be there as soon as I can," he promised again.

Evylin hoped that her smile assuaged whatever worries he held.

And with that, Deckard disappeared with Peery, leaving Thom to await Evylin's directions to her aunt and uncle's home. With her new brother-in-law in tow, she headed for the town. Trollenston was twice the size of Whickam Village, though its population was a meager thousand or so men and women. However, with its somewhat prime location at the top of Estshire, merchants regularly traveled there to sell their wares. And unlike the village, Trollenston's revenue came mostly from handmade and specialized goods, butchers and bakers, smiths and crafters.

The houses in Trollenston were of a different design too. They weren't as wide or with as much property as in the village. The town was a hub for trade. Most of the buildings in the settlement butted up against each other, creating squat rows of intermixed houses and businesses. Though a few were more spread out the farther out of town you got.

Evylin and Thom moved past the first row of stone buildings. The rain had turned the dirt into mud puddles. She lifted her skirts, not wanting to dirty her satin dress. Their trek was short, even through the town's winding streets, but rain pelted them with every step. They kept their hoods up and heads down, preventing any conversation between them.

The home of Jorge and Serene Loore came into view quickly. Its ironwork windows and maple flower boxes gave it a quaint, welcoming air. Evylin hurried up the steps to ring the bell. Thom waited on the bottom step like a shadow. She could hear the call of her aunt from deep inside the house, then a beat of silence before the pounding of feet grew louder, nearing the other side of the door.

The lock clicked, the handle turned, and Serene was before them, wild brown curls barely contained by her bun.

"Evie!" she exclaimed. "What on Terraeus are you doing back in town already? Did you forget something? I could have sworn I didn't see a thing left in your room."

Evylin took hold of her aunt's arms to focus the woman's attention. "No, nothing like that. I need to stay a few days. I know it's short notice, and I understand if you can't—"

"Nonsense, we're thrilled to have you anytime. Not that notice wouldn't have been nice, but we'll make do." She paused, eyes flittering down to the bottom of the steps before going wide. "Who's this handsome fellow, then?"

Glancing back at Thom, whose face had gone white, Evylin tugged at the clasp on her cloak. "Oh, uh, this is Lieutenant Deckard," she flinched before adding the most important part, "my brother-in-law."

"Brother-in-law?"

"There's . . . yes, there's something I need to tell you."

Serene crossed her arms. "Oh, is that so? You introduce me to your brother-in-law and act like I should expect him when I've never heard heads or tails of a Deckard in the region, let alone in relation to you or any of your sisters. Of course, you've got things to tell me. And neither of you is getting out of this rain until I'm satisfied."

"Uh, Evylin," Thom muttered, stepping back. "I need to. . . ."

Evylin waved him off. "You can go."

"I'll send your things."

"It was a pleasure to meet you, Lieutenant," Serene called.

He gave a nervous glance over his shoulder, then rushed off.

"Humph." Serene leaned against the doorframe. "He's not very polite, is he? Doesn't speak well of the Deckard family."

"Aunt." Evylin softened her expression, knowing not to take her aunt's frustrations seriously. "Might I come in? It's awfully cold out here."

Serene hummed with irritation but moved out of the way for Evylin to enter. "Give me your things, then," she ordered, gesturing for the wet cloak. "Your uncle and I just sat down for dinner, and there's no use in you drenching the floors while we eat."

After Evylin passed off the cloak and removed her coat, Serene let out another dissatisfied hum. "You look nice," she grumbled. "Had a special occasion, did you?"

Evylin peeled off her gloves, careful to hide her left hand. "Yes," she admitted. "But we'd better take a seat. I don't want your meal to grow cold."

Though Serene huffed and puffed, she led Evylin into the dining room off the parlor.

Uncle Jorge greeted Evylin with no sign that he noticed his wife's bluster. "What brings you back so soon?" he asked, filling his fork. "Hewitt with you?"

"Yes, but he won't be able to stay with us."

Serene let out a haughty "humph" as she filled a plate for Evylin. "And where has he found better lodging than here?"

"With the army."

"The army?"

Jorge set his ale down, his brow furrowed but far calmer than his wife. "The Ephrian Army is here?"

Evylin picked up her fork as her aunt placed the plate in front of her. "They're going through all the Shires searching for volunteers. Hewitt joined back up as a major."

"You're joking." Jorge laughed as though he suspected he should.

"I'm not."

Serene crossed her arms again. "And why on Allore's green Terraeus would he do something like that?"

"I assume to come with me."

With a grunt, Jorge returned to his sniggering. "Now, I know you're joking. They don't let women into the army. What really brings you two here?"

Evylin grinned at her uncle. She'd always liked Jorge. He appreciated her humor and never got upset at anyone or anything. The trait that enabled him to put up with Serene, she suspected.

"I promise, I'm telling the truth." Evylin pushed some vegetables around her plate. "And while, no, I'm not a soldier, I am traveling with the army."

Serene's eyes narrowed. "Does this have anything to do with that lieutenant I met outside?"

Evylin took a deep breath. "In a way, yes," she said, picking up the roll on her plate with her left hand. She knew Serene's searching gaze would spot the ring in an instant. "His brother is the captain of the company . . . and my husband."

"Husband?" Serene demanded, eyebrows nearly escaping her forehead. "Well, on behalf of the whole family, I thank you for the invitation to your wedding."

Jorge met Evylin's eyes from across the table. "When'd you get married?"

Cheeks hot as a forge, Evylin tried to keep her confident composure. "This morning."

Serene gasped, but before she could protest, Evylin gave her a firm glare. "It wasn't planned," she promised. "You know we would have invited you otherwise. But there was no time for a proper engagement."

"And what emergency could constitute such a rush?"

"Well . . ." The words tasted bitter before she'd even said them. "We fell in love."

"That's normally why people marry."

She shook her head. "I'm not explaining this right. As I said, he's a captain in the

Ephrian Army, and his assignment is to recruit from the Shires. He came to Whickam Village and . . . we—we fell in love. He had to leave today, and we didn't want to part, so . . . we married."

Hearing herself explain it like that, Evylin realized how absurd it sounded. What sort of fool fell in love and married within days? Anyone who heard the story would think them both mad.

"Oh, my dear!" Serene scooted her chair closer to Evylin's and wrapped both hands around hers. "That's positively romantic. I'm so pleased for you."

Jorge called over, "Cheers!" Then he took a swig of ale and loaded his fork with pork.

Evylin's thoughts froze. "Thank you," she muttered.

"Tell us all about him, then—this captain of yours," Serene insisted, returning to her dinner. "He must be quite something to have caught your heart."

Words still failed Evylin. "You'll meet him soon, Aunt," she said weakly.

"Come now," Serene beckoned with her fork of potatoes, "I want to hear it from you. First, tell us his name."

Evylin's face flushed. She hoped they thought it was from being helplessly in love rather than mortification. "Capt—Jonn. His name is Jonn."

Her aunt beamed in expectation. "Tell us more."

"I don't know what to say." Evylin laughed nervously.

"What's he like, what's he like?"

Evylin opened her mouth to reply, but nothing came out.

"Is he handsome?" Serene prompted.

"Of course, he's handsome," Jorge cut in. "A woman wouldn't fall in love with a man she'd just met if he wasn't handsome."

Evylin supposed her uncle was right. If she hadn't thought Deckard handsome, she wouldn't have considered Hewitt's scheme at all.

"Oh!" Serene gasped and pointed toward the door. "Your brother-in-law! He was handsome." She nodded to her husband as though she held insider knowledge. "Quite so. I take it your captain looks much the same?"

"Yes, they do favor one another," Evylin confirmed, then clarified, "though Thom is a bit more rugged and dark while Jonn is refined and. . . ."

"And . . . ?"

Evylin hesitated. What *was* he?

Thinking back to Deckard in his green coat as he held her hand and proposed to her that morning, Evylin couldn't help but smile. "He's different from most men. He has this . . . this way about him. It's as though you can tell he's listening—really listening when you speak. And he has a good sense of humor. He makes me laugh, and I make him laugh."

Glancing up, Evylin saw she'd lost Serene. Those were all fine things, but it wasn't the information her aunt hoped for. She was the same as Calyn and Dolia when it came to men—handsome features and idealized personas.

Evylin bit her bottom lip and tried to think like Calyn. What would her little sister say about Deckard? What would a woman in love say?

"He is handsome," she confirmed. "He's tall, and he's . . . well, he's unexpectedly strong. And he looks quite good in his uniform. Green is a good color for him."

She thought of how his green coat amplified the shift in his eyes and smiled. "His eyes are the most interesting color I've ever seen. They're not blue, but they're not green either. Somehow, they change back and forth, and I don't understand it." She'd intended to stop there but found the next words tumbling out. "And when he smiles . . . you can feel it."

With a sigh, Serene plastered a giant grin on her face. "He sounds lovely, my dear. Your parents must be so happy to have you settled. And with a captain, no less. What a match!"

Evylin nodded, remembering how her mother wept with joy and her father gushed over Deckard during his entire stay. "Yes, they are both thrilled. The whole family adores him."

"That's as it should be. It's as I told my Nelle: Be sure the family approves, or you'll have hell to pay for years to come." Serene plowed another potato into her mouth. "And, of course, her Nixon is a good example of a clever match. They hadn't known each other for three months before he asked for Jorge's blessing. But we could see straight away that he was the right sort for our sweet girl."

Serene went on about the family for a while after that as Evylin joined their meal. Jorge sat and listened, only offering a thought when it amused him. Something about her aunt's report made Evylin forget why she was there in the first place. The routine made it feel like every other visit. She stayed in the Loore home each season, hearing those same stories from her aunt time and time again. It was a third home for her, making it easy to forget the army waited outside, prepared to take her away on a grand adventure, only at the cost of her marriage.

"But what's kept your dear captain from accompanying you here rather than his brother?" Serene asked suddenly. "Surely, he must stay with us too!"

Glancing at the door as though her aunt had summoned him, Evylin wondered at Deckard's long absence. Between the walk and their meal, an hour had passed since their separation. "He had to meet with the magistrate about the army's presence," she explained.

"Ah!" Jorge chuckled. "There's your answer. Magistrate Steevensun can talk anyone's ear off. Sometimes, I think they only gave him the position in sheer desperation to shut him up."

Serene chortled. "I'm sure he'll be back in a jiffy." She patted Evylin's hand, then stood. "Now, I'd better get your room together. What was that your darling brother-in-law said about sending things?"

Remembering Deckard's order earlier, Evylin explained.

"Mm, well then, when they arrive, Jorge dear, would you send them up? In the meantime, Evie, come with me, and we'll get your room ready."

It took only minutes to freshen up Evylin's usual room. As Serene had no expectations of her arrival, the room was cold, the bed bare, and the oil lamps needed refilling. The soldiers arrived, carried their deliveries to the room, and disappeared within ten minutes.

Looking around at the freshly prepared room, Evylin's stomach dropped.

In the excitement of leaving, the worry of their plan failing, and the whirlwind of the wedding, she'd forgotten the most daunting consequence of all: She was now a married woman. And that meant sharing a room with her husband.

Worse, Evylin realized, staring at the thin mattress, they'd have to share a bed.

Serene finished fluffing the pillows and turned back to her. "There," she said. "All done. Would you like a cup of tea while you wait, dear?"

Shaken by her revelation and the accompanying thunder outside, Evylin forced a smile, hoping it looked more tired than panicked. "Thank you, but no. It's been a long day. I'd like to wash up and rest."

Serene's head bobbed. "Of course. Soaked to the bone as you were, I imagine a respite is exactly what you need. Don't worry; you get yourself freshened up, and I'll fix a plate for your captain. Then I'll send him up to you in a hurry." Her aunt winked at her with the final words before dashing out and closing the door.

Left alone, Evylin sighed heavily and set a hand atop her head.

The bed glared at her from across the room.

She scowled at the yellow patchwork quilt. "Don't look at me like that."

Deckard's trunk loomed in the corner, a marker of his impending arrival. She worried she'd made the wrong choice, staying out of her aunt and uncle's company. Instead of securing a distraction from her thoughts, she'd locked herself into a prison of reminders.

She almost returned downstairs, claiming she'd reconsidered the tea. But they were an old married couple. They knew precisely what she had to fear from this room, even if they didn't know why her case was particularly worrisome.

With no means of escape, Evylin determined to get comfortable and use her time to think through her predicament.

After pulling off the navy dress, Evylin searched her trunk for the thickest nightdress she owned. Though far more comfortable, the white cotton shift wasn't as modest as she required. For one thing, years of use had caused the gown to thin, and the dim light of the lamps revealed more of her frame than she liked. Another downfall was the scoop of its neckline. Though not low enough to suggest romance under normal circumstances, this was no normal circumstance.

Rummaging in her trunk again, Evylin sought out her old, snagged cardigan. Albina had knitted it for her birthday years ago when she'd only started learning. Far too large, the hem asymmetrical, and the wool spotted with tea and ink stains, it was the perfect covering for a woman who wished to discourage physical affection from a man.

Evylin bit her lip as she held the sweater in her hands. Why was she so averse to the idea? It was a normal thing for a husband and wife to . . . No. She wouldn't let herself think about it.

It didn't matter if she'd married Captain Deckard. She'd known him for three days, and there was no chance she'd let him that close, that fast.

There was only one course of action left. Evylin pulled on her sweater, fastened a few choice buttons, and plopped onto the bed. Then she set about planning exactly how she'd talk Deckard out of consummating their marriage.

CHAPTER FIFTEEN

The sky turned deep black, the rain pelting the windows as Evylin waited. In the past hour, she'd paced the room, running through dozens of arguments and counterarguments that would support her case. But even with all her plans and ideas, she was sure no argument would be strong enough to convince Deckard. And, though she refused to resign herself to the fate of a newlywed just yet, she'd grown tired of the thoughts spinning around and around in her head.

Determined to distract herself, Evylin grabbed one of the novels from her trunk and slipped underneath the blankets. She thought about sitting in the middle of the bed as if to mark her territory, but then she worried Deckard might read it as an invitation to be near her. So she scooted as close to the edge as possible and opened the novel.

She didn't read a word in the half hour that followed.

A muted knock caused Evylin to jump. She clutched her book tighter as the front door creaked open, and a pair of voices echoed from downstairs. She couldn't make out their words, but she could tell from the sound of the rich, male voice and Serene's earnest excitement that Deckard had arrived.

Evylin stared at the bedroom door, a wry grin coming to her lips. She could well imagine how Deckard would respond to each offered drink, every random story, and all the attention Serene and Jorge would give him. Head bowed and smile wide, he'd behave as the perfect gentleman. He would completely win Serene's heart, and Jorge would call him a pleasant chap.

After about five minutes of conversation, Evylin heard footsteps starting up the stairs. Serene was still talking, though her voice came no closer. Deckard's, however, reverberated through the hall with increasing volume. "Thank you, ma'am," he said, nearing the door. "I hope you do the same."

The doorknob jiggled, and Evylin froze. She should have turned out the lamps and pretended to be asleep. She could have avoided his arrival and any conversation altogether. The gentleman he was wouldn't allow him to wake her, would it? Or was that honorable persona just an act to get the job done?

The door opened, and Evylin snapped her attention back to the book in her hands. She hoped a seeming immersion in her novel would convince him to leave her alone. But she couldn't help peeking over the pages as the door shut behind her husband.

He stood inside the threshold as if unsure whether she would allow him to remain. Droplets of water clung to his boots, and dark patches ringed the cuffs of his coat sleeves. His hair was damp at the curling edges, but he otherwise appeared unscathed by the rain.

Deckard scanned her, a timid expression on his face. "Good evening," he said with reserve.

Shifting to sit upright, Evylin held the book like a shield. "Good evening."

"I'm sorry for taking so long." His head dipped in penitence. "I intended to be back hours ago, but—"

"Don't worry," Evylin interrupted with a vindicating smile. "My uncle told me about Magistrate Steevensun's ability to converse with a wall. I'm surprised you made it back this early."

Deckard scoffed in humor, and his shoulders relaxed. "Yes, he is a particularly verbose man."

"Is he interesting, at least?"

"Not in the slightest."

Evylin raised her book to hide her laughter. "I bet my aunt could give him a run for his money."

He chuckled. "No, she's far too interesting for that."

"By whose standards? All Aunt Serene talks about is town and family gossip."

"All the magistrate talks about is the many fine establishments within his town," he countered. "And I must admit I'd be happy to hear all the stories your aunt would like to tell me about you."

Evylin gasped in amused surprise. "Well, I wouldn't get my hopes up if I were you. The best gossip Serene has about me is that I've got a sharp tongue and won't settle for the men in town. Though now it will delight her to tell everyone her unruly niece has lost her mind and married a man she only met three days ago."

Deckard took his first step away from the door. "Yes, she was rather enthusiastic at my arrival."

"Don't take it personally," she teased. "Serene's as shocked by my marriage as the rest of my family."

He worked on the shiny silver buttons of his coat. "Because you only knew me for three days? Or because you married at all?"

Hearing the concealed question within, Evylin tipped her eyebrows up at him. "Let's just say I'm not like my sisters, and I never wasted time daydreaming about weddings, dresses, children, or furnishings."

Although it was truthful that Evylin didn't daydream about those things, she *had* imagined finding someone to love someday. It would happen in the midst of her adventures, she'd thought. Perhaps they'd meet on the field of battle. Perhaps he'd save her or her him. But regardless of how it came about, she had dreamed of love and marriage, just in a different way than her sisters.

Deckard worked off his coat, studying her thoughtfully. "I suppose they'll all think I've some special power, then, to be able to convince you to give up your independence."

"Of that, I have no doubt."

Deckard pointed to the far side of the room. "Might I use the closet?"

The domestic question startled Evylin. "Oh, uh . . . yes, of course."

"Thank you." He stepped over to hang his coat next to her drying dress. He took his time, adjusting the seams along the shoulders to ensure they lined up with the hanger, then moving on to the folds in the hem, collar, and sleeves.

Evylin watched as he crossed the room and knelt to open his trunk. "I take it your aunt and uncle pestered you with hundreds of questions?" he inquired, carefully removing a tunic.

Recognizing this as the beginning stages of his preparations for bed, Evylin pressed the book to her chest. "Not as many as you might think." She angled closer to the edge of the bed. "Serene never stays on one subject for long. But they did ask me a couple of dozen about you."

"I hope they weren't too difficult to answer," he replied as he stood.

Tugging at the collar of her sweater to draw it closer shut, Evylin hoped she wasn't blushing at the memory of describing him to her aunt and uncle. "They were easy enough."

"Good." Deckard looked down at the still-folded tunic in his hands.

A hesitant tension seeped into the room as the rain tapped against the window.

This is it, Evylin thought. Her chest constricted, and her lungs refused to take in any more air. He was going to ask. Or, more likely, to insist.

Deckard opened his mouth to speak, but Evylin cut him off in her panic. "I just realized something." The words tumbled out far more desperate and nervous than she'd intended.

He blinked at her outburst. He adjusted his weight and took a step back. "What's that?"

Evylin forced herself to hold his gaze. "We have to share this bed, don't we?"

Deckard's lips parted, but not to speak so much as in surprise. His eyes, blue in the dim light, took a slow journey over her whole form. Covered in thick blankets, her cardigan, and the book shoved against her chest, there wasn't much to see. She caught the vague flash of his tongue darting out to wet his lips before he pressed them back together and dropped his eyes to the floor.

"Yes, we do," he replied with calm gentleness.

Evylin remained silent. There wasn't much to say that her appearance and direct gaze hadn't already expressed.

Sighing, Deckard looked back at her. "How long have you been up here?"

"An hour or so."

His left eyebrow lifted as if in a challenge. "So it didn't *just* occur to you."

"What do you mean?" she asked, uncomfortable with the knowing grin that tugged on his lips.

"Evylin," he said, his tone and gaze far more serious than she liked. "You're sitting on the very thing you claimed to have remembered a second ago."

A handful of seconds ticked by as he waited for her response.

Evylin returned his stoic expression with a smirk. "It's not polite to call a woman's bluff, you know."

Deckard cocked his head at her lighthearted reply.

Now, it was her turn to wait for an answer.

He scoffed. "Do you always combat awkward situations with jokes?"

"Typically."

"Good to know." His eyes locked with hers again. "Are you worried?"

Evylin didn't know what to say to that. She drew her legs closer to her chest, chewing on her bottom lip. It had grown tender after the long day of so much change and worry.

Deckard let out a long, deep breath. "You needn't be."

Scrunching her nose, Evylin stared back at him. "I needn't?"

"I didn't assume you'd considered this part."

The sentence confirmed what Evylin already suspected. She hadn't considered it, but he had.

"What are we to do about it?" she asked.

"What are we—" His humorless laugh cut through the rest of the sentence. "You make it sound as though we're in some alarming situation."

"Aren't we?"

"I don't see how."

"We're married."

"Yes, I *am* aware of that fact," Deckard said, each word slow and thoughtful. "Why is that alarming? Beyond the unexpected nature of it."

"I'm your wife," she said as though that clarified it.

"And I'm your husband. What of it?"

Unsure if he was dense or attempting to embarrass her by making her say it, Evylin glared at him. "It means we have to . . ." Her mouth hung open as the rest of the words refused to come out.

"Share the bed?" he concluded for her. He shrugged. "I wouldn't worry about that. We'll share it for now. That's all."

Evylin's hand dropped from the collar of her sweater. "That's all?"

"For now."

Watching as he dropped the tunic onto the dresser, then sat down on his trunk to remove his boots, Evylin fought between gratitude and irritation. Gratitude for his offer and irritation at the condition he'd attached to it. She didn't need to worry, he'd said, *for now*.

"What about later?" Evylin asked.

Deckard set both boots next to the trunk, removed his socks, and stood. He met her gaze, his strong brow raised. "Well, we'll have to deal with that later, won't we?"

She pressed her lips together, unsure if she should push back.

"Now," he picked up the tunic waiting on the dresser, "I need to change, and as you've made your concerns clear, I'm assuming you aren't comfortable with that happening while you watch."

Evylin blinked. "Do you want me to leave the room?"

Deckard shook his head. "There's no need for that. Just turn away a moment."

She did as instructed, tucking her chin down as she stared at the far corner. Holding the book even tighter against her chest, she stared at the corner of her pillow, trying not to think about the activity on the other side of the room. However, the rustling of fabric and steady footfalls reached her ears, alerting her to the strange and shocking realization that he'd removed his trousers.

Evylin couldn't help the nervous laugh that burst out of her. She tried to muffle it, making it sound like a whimper, and Deckard's movement ceased.

"Are you all right?" he asked, concern filling his voice.

Evylin shook from her barely contained laughter. "I'm fine," she said, but her words came out strangled, and she was sure she didn't sound fine.

"What . . . Why are you laughing?"

Evylin waved a hand in his direction, still facing the wall. "Nothing," she insisted. "It's nothing."

"Ah," he muttered in understanding. The rustling sound resumed for a few more moments, then he said, "I've changed. You can turn around now."

Evylin had to smash her lips together to regain her sobriety. When she felt sure she wouldn't lapse into another fit, she turned as he stepped closer to the bed. The low lamplight cast shadows over most of the room. But the oil lamp sat on the nightstand by his side, giving him a warm, well-lit glow. She worked to keep her eyes on his face to forget the fact that he wore a long sleep shirt and, surely, nothing else.

"May I join you?" he asked gently.

Unable to speak, Evylin let out a hum of approval.

Deckard pulled back the blankets on his side, careful not to lift them off her. The bed shifted under his weight, and she eyed him as he slid his legs under the layers. He kept his distance—as much as one could in a bed of its size—but their shoulders were mere inches from one another as he leaned against the headboard.

Turning just a fraction to look at her, Deckard motioned to the book still pressed against her chest. "Did you want to keep reading?"

"Hm? Oh." Evylin closed the book with a *snap*. "No, I wasn't really—I couldn't focus."

He nodded as she set the book on the nightstand next to her.

"We can go to sleep if you like," she suggested, hopeful of diffusing the awkwardness with the oblivion of slumber.

Again, he nodded. "Are you terribly cold?" he asked. When she furrowed her brow, he gestured to her sweater. "I saw another blanket in the closet if you'd like—"

Evylin held up her hand. "I'm fine. I'm not . . . It wasn't for warmth."

"Right."

Unable to hold his gaze, Evylin turned to stare across the dark room. Neither moved to lie down, nor did Deckard reach for the light. Their discomfort was palpable as the silence stretched for several seconds.

Evylin dropped her face into her hands with another bout of uncomfortable laughter. "I'm sorry," she muttered into her palms.

Their shoulders bumped as Deckard moved to rub his forehead. "No need to apologize," he assured her. "It's an odd predicament we're in, isn't it?"

"Yes."

"I'm not sure how to move forward."

Evylin struggled to ignore their arms rubbing against one another when she shrugged. "Well, we did suggest giving sleep a try."

"That we did."

"Should we attempt it then?"

"Might as well." His smile softened. "I have a feeling, though, that if we both try to lie down at the same time, things might get even more awkward."

"More awkward than this? Impossible."

He chuckled. "I'd rather not test what's possible."

"Well, shall you go first, then, or shall I?"

"After you."

Evylin sat up to begin the process, then paused. "First . . ." She picked at the wooden buttons on her sweater, "I'd like to take this off, but. . . ."

"Oh." Deckard turned his head without any further prompting.

Feeling foolish for asking him not to watch, Evylin removed the sweater as fast as possible. In her rush to pull her arm free, she drove her elbow into his shoulder. "Sorry," she gasped.

"It's fine," he promised, still turned away.

Evylin flung the sweater across the room, satisfied by her aim when she heard the *clack* of the buttons hitting her trunk. She lifted the blankets and scooted down, tugging at the hem of her nightdress. She tucked the blankets under her arms and pulled them to her chin. "Your turn."

Deckard gave her a cautious glance, then laughed.

"What?"

His left eyebrow tipped up. "I can't figure out if your modesty or lack of trust in me is making you cover up like that."

Rolling her eyes, Evylin looked up at the ceiling. "Neither."

"What, then?"

She hesitated, unsure herself. "I guess . . . well, it's just that I've never been alone with a man before. Not like this."

A soft, relieved-sounding hum of understanding came from his side of the bed. "Is there anything I can do to make you more comfortable?" he asked kindly.

Looking up at him, Evylin bit the inside of her cheek. It was a strange sensation, staring up at a man's face as she lay there. She found that she liked it. "Maybe you should lie down, too, and ask me again."

Deckard turned down the lamp, extinguishing the flame, before doing as she suggested. The bed was wide enough for two, but only just. His head hit the pillow, and their arms met. She tried to slide away to give them both more space but met the edge of the mattress. Evylin lost her balance as the blankets shifted off her shoulders. Deckard grabbed her arm to keep her from falling off the bed, sending a jolt of tingles across her skin and a spike of adrenaline at the shock of his touch. He pulled her back, released her, and tugged the blankets back into place. Their arms were touching once more.

They stared at the ceiling, breathing rapidly.

"I feel I should warn you," Deckard whispered, and Evylin tensed. "It's a rare luxury to stay in a home like this."

Her muscles relaxed at the innocent warning. "Oh?"

"And the cot in my tent is not as big as a bed."

"Oh."

They listened to the rain, the steady pounding on the roof less soothing than usual.

"I'm an idiot, aren't I?" she whispered.

Fabric rustled as Deckard turned to look at her. "Why would you say that?"

"I'm not a child," she replied in exasperation. "I know what marriage is. How did I forget I'd have to sleep next to my husband?"

"It is a rather widely known fact."

"I don't know how to do this."

"Do what?"

She turned to face him in the darkness. "*This.*"

Even in the shadows, she could see the subtle outline of his face. "This being?"

"Being a wife," she explained. "Sleeping next to a man."

Turning to lay on his side, Deckard slid an arm under his pillow. "I understand that. It's new to me as well."

"Is it?" Evylin found herself asking. With a busybody for an aunt and a general for an uncle, she'd learned to be skeptical of people's pristine exteriors. And no matter how much Deckard acted as a gentleman, she wasn't naive enough to believe soldiers didn't have their vices.

Deckard stared back at her, and she caught the hint of a wry grin tugging at the side of his mouth. "I'm rather offended, Mrs. Deckard. To think I married a woman who believes so little in my character."

Though she returned his playful tone, she wasn't convinced. "I don't claim to know your character. But I do know what Hewitt has told me. And while he prided himself on fidelity to his wife, few of his soldiers held those same vows or convictions. I carry no expectations that any man—soldier or not—is as virtuous as the world likes to pretend."

The smile abandoned Deckard's face. "Whatever your expectations of men," he said more harshly than she'd expected, "understand that I'm not like that."

With the intensity of his gaze, Evylin turned away under the blankets. Their feet touched in the process, ice on ice. They both gasped as they pulled away from each other.

The movement put them both on their backs again, their arms touching once more.

Evylin pressed one hand to her stomach, the other clutching her wrist like a vise. "I'm sorry," she whispered. "I didn't mean to insinuate. . . ."

It took a second, but Deckard gave a soft, absolving sigh. "It's all right," he promised. "You were right; you don't know my character. Nor do I know yours. But, after tonight, I'm certain my judgment was correct."

Curious, Evylin looked back at him. "Is that so?"

Deckard nodded, the faint moonlight that slipped through the curtains catching a spark of blue in his eyes. "You're an honorable and admirable lady," he whispered. "Even if you do have a sharp tongue sometimes."

They laughed together, and Evylin felt her body ease into the bed. "I don't think anyone has ever called me a lady before."

"Really?"

"I can't remember a time. It's not very ladylike to fight."

Deckard scanned her face. "Well then," he said, his voice warm and soothing in the darkness, "Whickam Village didn't deserve you."

Smiling, Evylin nodded. "That's what Hewitt always says."

"He and I finally have something in common."

Drawing the pillow farther under her head, Evylin closed her eyes. "He'll be devastated."

She heard him chuckle, and silence fell between them. They lay there for some time, the rain and their breathing the only sounds. She wondered if it would take her longer than usual to fall asleep with him beside her. But her breath became even, and her mind grew hazy within a few short minutes.

"Evylin," Deckard whispered.

"Yes?" she murmured.

There was a hesitation, then the soft sound of a sigh before Deckard replied, "Good night."

CHAPTER SIXTEEN

14TH OF TERRAEN, 1573

In the night, Evylin startled awake when attempting to shift to her other side, only to find a person beside her. She'd shared a bed with one of her sisters for much of her life. Only after both Euna and Albina married did she have her room to herself. Even then, Calyn or Dolia—or sometimes both—would occasionally spend the night with her. Sharing the bed wasn't a bother. It was the masculine nature of the bedmate that caused the real alarm.

Even more disconcerting was discovering they'd nestled close, pressing their backs against each other. Warmth radiated from him, seeping through their thin nightclothes like a furnace, an unnerving yet beneficial revelation. If the cot in Deckard's tent was as small as he'd suggested, Evylin knew this would be a minor infringement compared to what would come.

Despite the initial shock, none of those moments kept her awake for longer than a few bleary-eyed seconds.

The sun woke Evylin, piercing through the curtains. She looked around to find Deckard's side of the bed empty. The blankets lay flat, tucked under his fluffed pillow. His boots were gone, his trunk in perfect order, and the room held no other trace of his presence.

Surprised he'd managed to slip out without waking her, Evylin listened. If he left hours ago, the house would be silent—or, at least, as silent as Serene's home ever could be. If he were still here, her aunt would no doubt be in a state of frantic entertainment with food, drink, and effusive chatter.

As Evylin had to strain to hear the subtle hum of conversation from the floor beneath her, she concluded that Deckard was gone.

Evylin rose to prepare for the day. Tucking her blouse into a dark gray skirt, she wasn't sure how she felt about his absence. She didn't mind admitting she liked his company. He was clever and a skilled conversationalist, far superior to most men she'd met. And after their awkward yet reassuring exchange last night, she was more comfortable with the idea of his companionship than she'd expected.

It'd been so long since she'd had a friend other than Hewitt, someone she could trust and confide in. Evylin hesitated, uncertain of the idea that she could trust Deckard in that way. It didn't seem right, accepting him so readily after knowing him for so short a time. Still, she liked him well enough. Perhaps over time, she could come to accept him as a confidant.

Evylin laced her boots, checked the knife's security, and hurried downstairs to find Hewitt sitting at the table. "Good morning, Uncle," she said, stepping over to kiss the top of his head.

Hewitt growled at his ham and eggs. "Morning." He tossed a hand toward a slip of paper. "Your husband left you a note."

Taking the seat across from him, Evylin reached for the teapot. She checked to be sure neither Serene nor Jorge was within earshot as she poured herself a cup. "You sound upset by that."

"I am."

She exchanged the teapot for the folded paper. "Do you have something against husbands leaving their wives notes?"

"No," he grumbled. "I have a problem with them leaving their wives alone the morning after their wedding night."

Evylin furrowed her brow at the insinuation but read the note instead of informing him that such considerations were unnecessary.

Written with an angular, elegant hand, Deckard's message was short and to the point: *"I've gone to meet with Magistrate Steevensun. I hope to be back soon."* As direct as his words were, something about his signature made it feel personal. She thought it might be due to the use of his given name. Or his choice of the closing salutation, *"Yours."*

Hewitt narrowed his eyes. "What did it say?"

Slipping the note into her pocket, Evylin reached for the biscuits and recounted the message.

Hewitt quirked his brow. "Sounds as though you have the day off as well."

Serene walked in with a bowl of freshly scrambled eggs and set them on the table. "Morning, dear," her aunt said and sat beside her. "I trust you slept well. Your captain was down early this morning. I was still in my dressing gown and hadn't even begun breakfast before he arrived to see about a cup of tea. It's a pity he couldn't join us this morning. Did you see his note?"

"Yes, thank you," Evylin said, buttering a biscuit. "He's just gone to a meeting."

Hewitt's chair scraped against the wooden floor as he stood. "We ought to be going too. I need Evylin's help preparing for the journey ahead."

"But we were going to meet with Nelle and hear all about Evie's wedding," Serene objected.

"Sorry." Hewitt sounded anything but apologetic as he pulled on his new, dark green officer's coat. "There's too much to do."

Hewitt strode from the room, and Evylin jumped up, grabbing a second biscuit for the demands of her empty stomach. "We'll be back as soon as we can," she falsely promised Serene. Then she hurried after her uncle.

He awaited her in the entryway, holding her coat ready for her. Stuffing one biscuit in her mouth, Evylin slipped an arm through the armhole, then tossed the second biscuit to that hand before shoving the other through the remaining sleeve.

Once the coat was secure on her shoulders, Hewitt opened the door and stepped out onto Trollenston's main street. A messenger with a full satchel bouncing at his side jogged past two female peddlers as they marched along, calling out their wares. Housewives hurried around the tradeswomen, focused on their morning tasks. While the town was by no means bustling, it was far more active than Whickam Village.

The rain from the night was gone, but the air remained cold from the dampness left in its wake. Evylin shivered, pulling her scarf around her neck for a second loop. Holding both biscuits in one hand, she started after Hewitt. "And what exactly is forcing us to leave a perfectly good breakfast?" she asked.

Hewitt shoved his hands deep into his pockets. "I couldn't stand any more of Serene's chattering." He nodded toward the local smithy as they neared the corner of the block. "Shall we go inspect their wares?"

As a fellow smith and wanting to keep on his good side, Hewitt regularly visited with Vernon Loxley, though Evylin disliked the man. He had an inflated sense of superiority, even worse than her father's. He kept his face clean-shaven, his thick black hair slicked back, and his mouth twisted in a perpetual sneer. He marked up his rates as though he were a specialist and criticized Hewitt's low prices during the market, undercutting his business. It probably didn't help that he eyed Evylin with disdain anytime she tried to join the conversation.

Whatever the case, Evylin always thought Vernon was a sanctimonious blighter masquerading as a pious man of Allore. And when they stepped into the smithy to catch him brandishing a hot poker at his brawny young assistant, she liked him even less.

"Put that down before you poke your eye out," Hewitt growled at the man.

"Ah, Hewitt," Vernon said scornfully, abandoning his harassment of the young man. He threw the poker back into the burning coals of the forge. "What're you doing back so soon? Come to steal more of my sales?" He smiled as though it were a good-natured joke.

"No," Hewitt said flatly. "In fact, you won't have to worry about my thievery anymore. I've rejoined the army."

Vernon eyed him with interest. "That so? That's good for me." He sent a dismissive glance toward Evylin. "I heard the army was traveling through. Not sure how we're supposed to provide them with any men. We're short on supply as it is."

Evylin turned away, leaving the men to discuss the army's presence. Vernon's smithy was far larger than Hewitt's, and it opened onto the street to keep the smoke from filling up the building. The young assistant stood with his back to them, his shaggy-haired head down as he worked on something at one of the workbenches. Vernon's son—who'd missed the last draft by a year—usually worked with him, but Evylin had never seen *this* assistant before.

She couldn't perceive much about him from her angle, but he looked quite strong, as a good smith should be. He wore a well-worn leather vest over his tan tunic. He kept his eyes on his task and worked quietly. But she saw a flush of red creeping up from his soot-stained collar.

Hewitt nudged Evylin's arm, distracting her from her inspection. "Let's go," he said, then bid Vernon farewell—for good.

Over the next couple of hours, they visited their usual haunts, saying goodbye to the acquaintances they'd made through the years. Each season, they checked in at all their favorite shops and businesses, hunting for anything new and interesting. As they'd never revisited Trollenston so soon, it was all the same.

However, the gray coats of the soldiers made for a change to the otherwise familiar sights. More and more of the men appeared as the morning wore on. Hewitt took the time to break down the structure of Deckard's Volunteer Company. Most of the soldiers— somewhere around two hundred and thirty—were privates, being new volunteers. Then there were two corporals, handpicked to help in whatever manner the officers needed. There were eleven officers within the regiment, including Captain Deckard and the newly recommissioned Major Glaas.

Hewitt explained that Deckard had chosen the remaining nine officers for the recruitment mission. Five of them were lieutenants—including Thom—charged with aiding the captain and managing the growing platoons of volunteers. Two were the other majors who trained the men. Two were sergeants who helped the lieutenants and kept the soldiers in line.

Hewitt had little good to say about these officers. "Most are haughty pricks or inexperienced tenderfoots who've never seen combat. Can't say your captain's friends are my sort of people."

Watching a band of recruits amble down the street ahead, Evylin wondered if anyone was Hewitt's sort of person. She loosened her coat in the warming sunshine. "Do you think they're his friends or just the men he trusts to do the job?" she asked.

"Could be both."

"Could be."

He studied her. "You don't think so, do you?"

"He doesn't strike me as the sort to approve of arrogance or ignorance."

"Humph." Hewitt grabbed her arm, guiding her around the next turn. "I'd say you're not altogether wrong."

"Why, thank you."

"Come on," he started across the street, "I'm starving."

CHAPTER SEVENTEEN

"Such a pleasure," the magistrate said. "Such a *pleasure*."

Deckard didn't think he'd ever regain control of his arm as the man pumped it up and down.

"Be assured, my good captain," Magistrate Steevensun continued, "all my citizens will be present at your speech tomorrow. What's more, you'll have too many volunteers to count, I'll wager." The man chuckled like a barnyard chicken. "Truly—*truly*, it's such a pleasure to have you in our town."

"Thank you, Your Honor," Deckard said, a glimpse of freedom bolstering him as Steevensun's emphatic grasp died down. "It will be *my* pleasure to speak to your citizens tomorrow."

Steevensun laughed again, renewing his gusto in shaking Deckard's hand. "I've never met a more exemplary officer, Captain. You are a credit to our army."

"You're too kind." Deckard bowed his head as his hand went numb. He wished he'd brought Thom with him. His brother would have no problem breaking up the meeting. But now, the task fell to Deckard. "I do apologize, Your Honor, but I must leave. I need to check on my men before returning to my wife."

"Yes, yes." The magistrate's nod was as ferocious as the way he continued to shake Deckard's hand. "I'm sure you have much to do. But I do hope you'll have time to enjoy the town while you're here. We may be small, but we have some wonderful establishments. Your wife would enjoy a jaunt around the shops, I'm sure. Do let me know if you need any recommendations. Collun Reid has a quaint little oddities shop down the way, and it's always full of the most unique bits and bobs that the ladies like."

Doing his best not to betray the tingling beginning to spread through his arm, Deckard smiled. "That sounds most intriguing. I'll be sure to take her by if I get the chance," he said with little intention of following through. While Evylin might enjoy such a shop, this was the one town she'd grown up frequenting. The idea he could take her anywhere within Trollenston she didn't already know was slim.

However, the thought of his wife—a term that still struck him with awe—did remind him of an important task he *could* use the magistrate's knowledge on. "There is one thing you might help me with."

The magistrate's dark eyes lit up in an instant.

"Could you recommend a jeweler? Or somewhere I might buy a ring? And a gift, as well."

"Ah, yes—yes, of course!" Steevensun finally released Deckard's hand as he reached to tap his chin in thought.

Deckard slipped the hand behind his back, clasping his wrist loosely in a stance of "at ease" so the man wouldn't try to capture it again.

"Hm." The magistrate nodded as he considered the request. "There are a few spots that might fit the bill. Now, what kind of ring are you searching for? One for you or one for her? Ralph Maason has a nice little shop that might have the ticket. He collects the pretty things from the merchants who don't sell all their wares when they come through for the market. He may not have many options, but the pieces are quite eye-catching. The town ladies often go to him when they're looking to bedazzle themselves." He chuckled again, his broad and rounded frame shaking with mirth.

"Now," he continued, "if you're just looking to get a band for yourself, you could always go to Vernon Loxley. He's a smith and would cut you a fine ring for a fair price. Might even add some pretty engraving for the lady if you're willing to pay a bit more."

Deckard gave him a polite smile but no further response.

The magistrate touched the side of his nose and then pointed to Deckard with a knowing gleam in his eyes. "Something more special, then? Mm-hm. Now, you'll pay the difference for the quality, but you'll want to visit Mr. Townsend's shop about three blocks over. He's a clockmaker by trade, but his son has taken up all sorts of fine crafts, and he does unparalleled work with jewelry. Granted, the average housewife wouldn't know the difference between young Townsend's work and Ralph's pieces. But I'd guess this wife of yours isn't the average housewife, now, is she?"

"No, Your Honor, she most certainly is not." While Deckard doubted that Evylin would take exception to a simpler gift, the magistrate was quite right. She was no average woman, and she required no average piece.

"Then tell Townsend I sent you, and he'll be sure to give you a fair price on whatever you select."

"You have my thanks, Your Honor." Deckard bowed with his hands held tight behind his back. "You've been more helpful than I can say."

Magistrate Steevensun's laugh followed Deckard to the door as the man waved him off. "My pleasure, my pleasure. Now, hurry back to your bride, good captain. She's sure to be missing you."

Deckard dipped his chin. "As I miss her, Your Honor," he said, surprised that he was not altogether lying. "I look forward to meeting with you again."

"Yes, yes, go on, son," the magistrate called as Deckard backed out of the room. "I remember my newly wedded days. Love's light is far too precious to miss out on. You know, Balter." He turned to his steward as Deckard gave a final bow and took his leave. "I think I ought to take a cue from our captain's book and go see my wife. She's always saying I spend too much time working and talking to be with her as I should. I ought to surprise her and enjoy love's light for myself. Do tell Mr. Morten I'll have to cancel our meeting. I'm spending the day with my wife, Balter. Should I take her out on the town, do you think? I think Mariana would like that."

The magistrate's voice echoed down the hall after Deckard. The man might be tedious with his never-ending chatter, but he was a sweet old man who had proven to have a better head on his shoulders than even Magistrate Glaas. And while love was not the foundation of Deckard's marriage to Evylin, he couldn't help thinking it should be. A conclusion he'd come to in the late hours of the night as he lay awake listening to the steady pulse of Evylin's breathing.

Exiting the magistrate's large home, Deckard walked onto the packed dirt streets of Trollenston. With the sun at its peak, he felt his hunger rising. But he had one last task to complete before he could satiate his stomach.

With the first night of marriage done and gone, Deckard found his brother's admonishments circling his thoughts. Was the success of his career more important than his happiness? For Deckard, he knew having one without the other was impossible. But the pit in his stomach didn't come from concern for himself; it was for Evylin.

Her anxieties last night were understandable. He wouldn't deny he'd had his own misgivings about the event. But her fears were far more significant than he'd expected. Evylin carried herself with a confidence and poise that defied such trivial worries. And to get a peek through that veneer of indifference altered Deckard's image of her.

While Evylin chose to marry him for the chance to live out her dreams, he couldn't help wondering if the fulfillment of such dreams would really make her happy. And that led him to the question that plagued his morning: Was the adventure she dreamed of more important than her happiness? He didn't think so.

In the dark of night, Deckard had stared at her silhouette, pondering the risk she'd taken in marrying him. His eyes grew used to the nonexistent light as he studied her. The thick blankets covered most of her form, but her hair draped back to display the curve of her sculpted shoulders and graceful neck as she lay on her side.

It didn't seem fair. She'd won the bet. Yet, it appeared to Deckard that *he* had come out the victor.

A chance at redemption *and* a beautiful wife? That wasn't the bet Hewitt had laid out for him. And yet, it was what he'd lucked into anyway.

The guilt clung to the back of his skull, eating away at his conscience. His stomach rolled with every movement that brought him out of his light sleep. In her slumber, she'd pressed her back against his, and he'd felt his whole body tense in shock. He thought he should shift away out of respect for her modesty. But he couldn't convince himself to move. What if she needed the warmth? And what was the harm? It was she who drew near. And soon, she'd have to sleep with him in his tent. There'd be no avoiding one another then.

That thought drove the pit in his stomach to collapse even deeper.

When Deckard rose that morning, he'd finally come to the only conclusion that could ease his guilt: He wouldn't let Evylin's risk be in vain. Whatever he could do to ensure her happiness, he'd do it. And after thirty years of watching other people's marriages—both the good and the bad—he'd learned there was no chance of happiness in a marriage without love.

Magistrate Glaas's warning rang in his head like a kirk bell, but Deckard chose to ignore the advice. It didn't matter what sort of heartache he was inviting. A marriage without love was no marriage at all. And though it might take a while, he would love Evylin as a husband should.

The clockmaker's shop looked like every other building in Trollenston. The narrow façade of stone and wood squeezed between two buildings. Bubbled glass windows covered most of its street front, and next to the front door was an ironwork sign that read, *"Townsend's Clocks & Fine Pieces."*

Deckard looked both ways before crossing the dirt street, took the short staircase in two strides, and twisted the brass doorknob. A gentle chime alerted the clerk behind the counter to his arrival. The shop interior sparkled from the light streaming through the windows. Sunbeams reflected off every glass clockface, shining metalwork, and low jewelry case.

"Welcome, officer," the clerk greeted as he set his pen next to a large ledger. "What can I help you with?"

Deckard bowed his head. "Good morning. I'm looking for a ring and a gift, and Magistrate Steevensun told me you might be able to help."

The gentleman took in Deckard's uniform and insignia, though he showed no other sign of interest at the drop of the magistrate's name. He was an older man, in his late fifties with dark, peppered hair and richly bronzed skin like most lower Shire residents.

He pushed the ledger to the side, revealing a better view of the pieces in the case before him. "Of course, sir. I'm Philip Townsend, owner of this shop and maker of most of these clocks. What sort of pieces are you looking for?"

Deckard folded his hands on top of the case. "Well, you see, I got married yesterday."

"Congratulations."

"Thank you. It was rather spur of the moment, and I'm afraid there wasn't a chance to purchase a ring for myself or a gift for my wife."

Townsend nodded. "The demand for fine work isn't as high for the man's ring, so we keep our collection small. However, I do have a handful in stock if you'd like to see them."

"Yes, thank you."

As Townsend stepped to another case on the far side of the room, he gestured for Deckard to join him. "Do you know what sort of gift you'd like to present to your wife, Captain?"

That was another question that Deckard had wrestled with all morning. He wanted to present her with something fine: a gift to show his dedication to their marriage, no matter its origin. But Evylin wasn't an ostentatious woman. She didn't wear frilly dresses or sparkling jewels like some women. Even the ribbons she used to tie her hair back bore no embellishment.

What interests he knew she held were reading and, amazingly, swordplay. But a book didn't carry the significance he aimed for, and a weapon wasn't a suitable token of affection, even if that affection was born out of a less romantic design than a dutiful one.

"That is something I may defer to you on, sir," Deckard admitted as Townsend settled the small display of rings on the case between them. "I'm afraid I'm not sure what would be fitting."

"Hm. Well, I'll help in whatever way I can. First," Townsend gestured to the cushion of shining metal bands, "let's tackle your ring, shall we? As I said, we only offer these few. If none of them will do, I can recommend a smith for something less fine."

Deckard looked down at the rings as Townsend described them. They were all simple: three of polished gold, one of etched bronze, and the last of shining platinum. All were of equal quality and craftsmanship, but the bronze didn't suit Deckard's taste, and the gold ones were either a fraction too small or too large for a comfortable fit.

"The platinum will do just fine," Deckard said when he'd confirmed the fit.

"Very good, sir." Townsend marked it down on the receipt. "Now, for your wife?"

"Yes, I'm afraid I'm not sure what to give her."

"Does she already have a ring of her own?"

"She does."

"Mm." Townsend brushed down his mustache in thought. "And you're settled on jewelry, are you?"

"No, but I would like to present her with something special. And I'm not sure what else to get her."

Townsend then ran through the options he had in the shop. While there were all manner of clocks, Deckard decided against them, being too large and difficult to ensure their safety during travel. There were some lovely wristlets he considered but decided against as they were likely to interfere with her training. A concern he'd never thought to contemplate when buying jewelry for a woman, and one he didn't share with Townsend.

The necklaces in the shop were all too glittering for everyday wear, and Deckard didn't think she'd appreciate such an impractical gift. There were other trinkets and baubles within the shop, but they all faced the same complication: None of them would be of any use to Evylin.

"You say she's a practical sort?" Townsend asked.

"Yes," Deckard began, then realized that wasn't altogether true. She was reasonable, but he wasn't sure practicality played much into her logic. A realistic woman didn't make her life decisions based on the daydreams of her youth. "Well, no," he corrected, "not practical. She's not an embellished sort of woman, but I do believe she appreciates a certain level of extravagance."

"Unembellished extravagance, you say?" Townsend replied with amusement.

Deckard scoffed at the ridiculous description. "Is that possible, do you think?"

The clockmaker shrugged. "If I know anything about women, it's that they make the impossible possible many times a day." He crossed his arms and scanned his wares. "You said you didn't have time to buy a ring for yourself. May I assume your wedding was a rush?"

"My assignment made it such."

"But you *did* provide her with a ring?"

"Well, her uncle did. He's a smith, and they are quite close."

"A smith?" Townsend raised his brow. "I'd venture it's a simple ring then."

"Well, he added some fine engraving to the band."

"I think you have your answer."

"I do?"

Townsend smiled. "She may have *a* ring, Captain, but she doesn't have *your* ring."

Deckard hesitated, brow pinching together. "No, I don't think that would—I'm not sure she would appreciate it. As I said, she and her uncle are very close. Her ring may be of a simpler design, but she would never want to replace it."

"I'm not suggesting a replacement," he countered, "but that you give her one to go *alongside* it."

As Townsend swept his hand above the jewelry case between them, Deckard's gaze passed over the glittering rings inside.

"One that represents the love that *you two* share."

Though the sentiment was missing context, Deckard couldn't deny its insight. Evylin's ring was from Hewitt, a symbol of her uncle's love and loyalty. A relationship that Deckard had no place within, and one he knew not to come against.

But Townsend was right. Her wedding ring should reflect Evylin's relationship with Deckard himself and the promises they'd made to each other. He wanted a gift to show his dedication to her. What better way than with his own ring? A symbol of *their* future. A sign of what *he* would give her. An expression of extravagance that would prove how seriously he took the vow he made to care for her, even if there was no love between them.

Smiling, Deckard nodded to the counter. "Show me what you've got."

After finding the size based on Deckard's memory of the small band she currently wore, Townsend pulled out the range of rings that would fit. Half a dozen sparkling diamonds, a glowing ruby, two emeralds, and several varieties of sapphire rings sat on the cushions. But Deckard's eyes passed over them all to settle on the ring at the far corner.

The thin platinum band shone in the sunlight. Tiny, dotted millegrain along the edge embraced eight minuscule onyx gemstones that refracted the beams. It bore no other scrollwork or extra embellishments—just the inlaid stones set to contrast with the white-silver metal. It was elegant and mysterious.

Deckard knew without a doubt the ring belonged to Evylin.

Drawing his finger along the ridges of the band, a tingle of significance swept through Deckard's hand. "This one," he said. "This is the one."

"That one?" Townsend asked in surprise. "Are you sure? It's meant to commemorate a lost loved one."

Deckard thought of the everbloom ivy Hewitt etched on her other ring and smiled at the fitting nature of the pair. "That's the one, Mr. Townsend. I'm quite sure of it."

"Very well," he said, placing the ring inside a small velvet bag. "Would you like to wear your ring out?"

Thinking that it would be a nice surprise to show her both rings together, Deckard shook his head. "I'll wait, thank you."

With the exchange of money and rings made, Deckard left the shop and started back toward the edge of town. The camp and the Loore residence lay in the same direction, and he wasn't entirely certain which was his intended destination. Several soldiers stopped to salute as he passed, calling their greetings. He nodded to them all. With the men on their day off, there wouldn't be many left in the camp. But there was always work to do.

He thought to find Thom for some sparring. He'd never been good with a sword, but he knew the only hope of improvement was to practice. Watching Evylin fight his brother was an experience unlike any he'd ever beheld. Thom never stood a chance against someone like her. She was so fast, so agile, so incredible. The way she moved as one with the sword—like it weighed nothing in her hand—was awe-inspiring. It was artful. It was beautiful.

And he knew it was a deliberate display on behalf of her uncle to show off all her magnificence and merits. Hewitt was no fool. He'd surely noticed Deckard's attraction to Evylin early on. And the man had used it to his advantage.

A fact that made Deckard feel equally ashamed and indifferent.

Slipping his hand into his pocket to take hold of the velvet bag, Deckard considered his predicament. He liked Evylin, that much he knew. His attraction to her was undeniable. It was a stroke of luck that he'd managed to keep her around—granted, in closer proximity than he'd expected. But the early stages of romance were a rocky field to navigate without the complications of their unusual arrangement.

Deckard wondered if it was wrong of him to harbor these inconclusive feelings for Evylin. Should he tell her he already hoped they might someday form an attachment? He found the strange circumstances of their marriage to be an obstacle easily overcome. And he was eager to explore what a future together might look like.

After her discomfort last night, he thought not.

Deckard's dawning attraction and interest suggested a good start toward their ultimate happiness, but only if Evylin shared the same regard. She'd made it clear her favor was not as positive as his. Her actions suggested she liked him well enough, but she didn't seem smitten by any standard.

Deckard hoped his gift might soften her unromantic nature. If he could show her how serious he was about being a good husband to her—about providing her with her long-held dreams—then there was a chance they might find themselves in a happy marriage after all.

Taking the next right turn, Deckard decided his captain's duties could wait as he headed for the Loore home. If he was going to prioritize his wife and her happiness, why not start now?

Standing on the stone steps, Deckard knocked on the oak door.

"Captain," the lady of the house chided upon her appearance, "you needn't have knocked. You're family now. You're welcome to run right in like any other."

Deckard stepped inside, thanking her for her hospitality, and followed Serene into the parlor. He scanned the vacant furnishings and cold hearth. Though disappointed he didn't find Evylin readily there, he imagined she'd spent the morning captive to her aunt's whims. He couldn't blame her for seeking refuge in their room upstairs.

A small pang of guilt welled at realizing how long he'd left her. Well after lunchtime, he worried that she might take his absence as a slight, as though he had no interest in befriending her, let alone being a husband to her.

"Have you eaten?" Serene asked, continuing through the dining room and to the kitchen off the side, not waiting for his reply. "Have a seat at the table, and I'll bring you a plate."

Deckard did as told, settling into one of the tan and green cushioned chairs.

Serene kept up her chatter as she bustled about the kitchen out of his view. "I'm surprised you're back so soon," she called above the clattering of utensils and dishes. "When Evie told me you'd gone to see the magistrate again, I assumed you'd be there all day. He's quite the chatterbox, Steevensun. Don't know that he's ever had a conversation that lasted less than three hours."

Though Deckard thought the pot was calling the kettle black, he kept his amusement to himself. "Yes, he is long-winded, isn't he?" he replied. He forced himself not to look toward the entryway in anticipation of Evylin's arrival. "Though I'll admit, I'm not sure I've met a more pleasant magistrate."

"I'll grant you that," Serene said, then clucked her tongue. "I doubt he'd have half the townsfolk's loyalty if he were only half as amiable. And while he's not the sharpest knife in the block, he's no fool either."

The woman made her return, a plate in one hand and a tea tray in the other. She set the plate down in front of Deckard before resting the tray on the opposite side. "If I remember from this morning, you take it black, yes?" she asked as she poured.

"Yes, thank you."

Deckard accepted the steaming cup of rich brown tea, its strong floral and herbaceous scent the standard of Ephrian society. Deckard himself preferred the softer notes of thistleberry, a more common variety in the north, but this full-bodied and hearty blend came from the olifera bush that pervaded the lower Shires.

"Now then," Serene continued, "what took your fine company from us this morning?" She settled the teapot back on the tray, taking her seat and a teacup of her own. "I thought to get the answer from Evie, but she was gone before we could have a proper breakfast. Although I suppose she may not have been privy to your meeting's purpose. Goodness, your orders may keep you bound to secrecy!"

"No, it isn't a secret," Deckard said, quelling his curiosity at Evylin's absence. "I'm here to recruit new soldiers, and I needed the magistrate to issue an invitation to my speech tomorrow."

"Oh, is that it?" Serene looked disappointed. "Yes, Evie did mention something about volunteers." The woman's deep brown gaze dropped to Deckard's untouched plate. "What are you waiting for? Tuck in."

Deckard tilted his chin toward the entryway. "I'm afraid my mother's training won't allow me, ma'am. Not until both you and Evylin join me."

"Oh, tosh." Serene waved her hand at him. "I ate my own meal half an hour back when Jorge stopped in on his break. And as far as Evie goes, Heavens knows when that girl will be back."

Deckard furrowed his brow. "Evylin isn't at home?"

Her almond-shaped eyes widened. "You didn't know? Well, I suppose you wouldn't have. Yes, yes, Hewitt swept in here this morning and took her off with him." She let out a huff. "That man's a right hurricane."

Quite certain Trollenston had never seen a hurricane in all their days, Deckard grinned. "Is that so?"

"Surely you noticed," she said, then motioned to his plate again. "Do eat, dear. They might be hours, and I won't have you grow faint waiting on the girl."

After dipping his head in a silent prayer, Deckard took up his fork. "Do you know what they're doing that would take them so long?"

"Oh, those two are always gallivanting around the town. I believe Hewitt managed to talk the farrier into letting them train in the paddock just up the way. I never thought it was proper for him to be teaching her such masculine pursuits, but her mother didn't listen to me. I'm sure it was the cause of her spinsterhood. But you're here now, so I suppose there's no real bother in the end."

Serene gestured absently toward the window. "The two of them spend most of their time there or at the various smithies, shops, and stalls when the market is in town. The rest of their time is spent at the Shepherd's Rest, a tavern just up the way."

She gave him a pity-filled smile as she lifted her delicate teacup. "You know how they are—wherever Hewitt goes, our Evie follows. And the other way around. I'm certain it's why he rejoined your army. No doubt he couldn't bear to be without her."

Unable to consider his words too carefully lest the woman continue, Deckard swallowed the remains of his bite. "I came to the same conclusion myself," he admitted. "I have yet to form much of a relationship with Major Glaas, but it's obvious how fond Evylin is of him. I don't know if I've ever met an uncle and niece so close before."

Serene snorted. "Nor has the rest of Ephria." She set her cup back down with a sigh. "I shouldn't speak poorly of the man," she said apologetically. "He's been good for our Evie, I know. And she's been good for him. After everything that happened, they both deserve some happiness in this life."

She beamed at Deckard. "Which is why I'm so glad Evie found you. She's been lonely for so long. And to see Hewitt return to the army . . . well, you've brought happiness to them both."

Picking at the food on his plate, Deckard was too engaged in the conversation to keep eating. "You think he'll be happy back with the army?"

"Oh, yes," Serene insisted. "It was the only place he ever *was* happy. If he hadn't hated Whickam Village so much, he never would have stayed."

Forcing himself not to abandon the meal for fear of insulting his host, Deckard clutched the fork more tightly. "I'm afraid I don't understand."

Serene frowned at him. Then her lips parted in a gasp. "You don't know?"

"Know what?"

With an incredulous scoff, Serene crossed her arms. "I suppose it shouldn't surprise me, Evylin taking his side. She needs to learn that a woman's loyalties shift upon marriage. If you ask me, she should have told you instantly."

"Told me what?"

Glancing at the front door, Serene cleared her throat. She scooted her chair closer to the table, her voice dipping low in a conspiratorial whisper. "Now, don't go telling her that I told you, but . . ."

Deckard braced himself.

"Nearly fourteen years ago now, while Hewitt was still in the service, there was a fire in Whickam Village," she explained. "And his wife and child . . . the poor dears didn't make it out. Due to his grief, the army allowed him early release from his commission. They were generous after all the great things he'd done for them. And he returned to the village a broken man.

"Hewitt was understandably distraught. Irena and Ryen were everything to him. And in his anger, he blamed his brother for their deaths, insisting that Lawton wasn't there for his family when they'd needed him. But we all know the truth—he blames himself. It was his form of penance to live in Whickam Village for the rest of his days, never to leave their sides again."

Though this retelling offered a great deal more than Lawton's, Deckard still felt he was missing vital information. His sympathy for Hewitt grew, certainly, as did his curiosity as to why the man would give up his vow and leave the village. But more than anything, he wondered at the absence of Evylin within this side of the story.

Magistrate Glaas had said his daughter and Hewitt's son were inseparable. She'd been just as brokenhearted by the boy's loss as his own father. Yet, Serene hadn't uttered a word about her in the tale.

Surely encouraged by his drawn out silence, Serene continued, "It shocked both Jorge and me to hear of his recommission. But then, as I said, I'm sure he couldn't bear to be without Evylin. We all know how much he relies on her."

"Yes," Deckard agreed. "Yes, they do mean a lot to one another."

"That they do. I'm not sure I've ever heard a cross word uttered between the two of them. Can you imagine—that gruff old grizzly turned into a gentle giant whenever she's around? I think it was a gift from Allore, their friendship. He knew they needed one another."

Serene's eyes began to twinkle. "And then he brought you to them. I always say timing is everything. We all think we know when love will strike, but only the Heavens know our true destiny. Are you a religious man, Captain? What am I saying? Of course, you are. I saw how you prayed just moments ago. Our Evie couldn't be luckier than to find a man like you. Now, my Nelle, she was always worried she wouldn't find a man of good faith, but I told her it's all in good time. . . ."

As the woman chattered, Deckard ate his meal. He didn't have to worry about disruption from the woman. She was more than happy to talk at him, providing small tidbits about Evylin and Hewitt as she gossiped. And he was more than happy to let her.

Finishing up the hearty potatoes, dried and salted pork, and well-seasoned root vegetables, Deckard took the first break in her speech to stand. "I apologize for cutting my time short, but I should get back to camp."

Serene rose as well. "Ah, yes, duty calls. You will be back for dinner, won't you?"

Deckard bowed his head. "I wouldn't miss it."

Serene let out a coo of approval before shooing him off.

Back on the streets, Deckard unhooked the top button of his coat. The midday sun was high enough to cut through the chill of the morning, and he welcomed the reprieve. He passed dozens of other soldiers on his way to camp, but he hardly noticed as they greeted him. Away from the constant chatter of Serene Loore, his thoughts drifted.

What was it Lawton had said? Hewitt's son, Ryen, was only a month older than Evylin. The two of them were as close as she was with Hewitt now, and, at his death, Evylin was inconsolable. He struggled to remember the boy's age. Had the magistrate told him? It had been almost fourteen years since his death, Serene had said. That would put Evylin and the boy around the age of thirteen at the most.

Deckard's gut twisted at the thought. Thirteen was too young to die. Thirteen was too young to lose someone. How had the young Evylin managed her sorrow? Deckard couldn't ask. She hadn't said a word about her lost cousin. And he had little right to press for such sacred information so soon in their relationship.

Lawton had said that Evylin and Hewitt turned to one another in their grief. He'd taken her on as his own, and the loyalty between them was a line that Deckard shouldn't try to cross. A bond that could never dissolve. One that only a fool would try to join or destroy.

Passing the first rows of canvas tents, Deckard came to his conclusions. It was clear—whatever relationship had formed between Hewitt and Evylin all those years ago, it was over their shared love for his son. And whatever damage the loss had done to such a young girl and a war-hardened general, the two of them hadn't recovered. Not if they were still clinging to each other with such desperation. Not if he was willing to leave his family's graves to stay at her side.

Deckard paused as he neared his tent, turning to look back at the town in the distance. Something about the whole situation didn't sit right. By Lawton and Serene's accounts, it was Hewitt who hadn't managed to move on with his life. The man was still the grieving widower and father. So why had he given up his vow of penance to join Evylin on her travels? What had changed to convince him to leave them?

And what about Evylin? Her father said she was devastated by her cousin's death. Had she made the same vow as the older man? He couldn't imagine she had, considering the way she'd spoken of her dreams to leave the village.

But if she'd grieved with just as much pain as her uncle, how was it that she didn't cling to the past with the same iron grip? Had she managed to heal from those wounds, unlike the bitter old general? She did seem to have the resilient disposition to manage such a feat.

With a sigh, Deckard pushed down the thoughts. He accepted the distraction of his work, doing his best to forget about the complications of his marriage. There was no use in expecting himself to figure it out in one day. And he couldn't expect her to divert her allegiance either. She didn't know Deckard from any other man in Ephria. It would take time to build the trust needed for that level of devotion.

Deckard decided then that until Evylin asked otherwise, he would behave as the same dutiful captain and prove his faithfulness to his wife later.

CHAPTER EIGHTEEN

The Shepherd's Rest was one of only two taverns in town. Named for the most common occupation within Estshire's vast county, the quaint tavern doubled as an inn. As it was only a short walk from the Loore home, Evylin and Hewitt often visited it on their market trips. But unlike most of their visits, it was now crawling with soldiers.

Packed wall to wall, most of the patrons wore a dark gray uniform with emerald patches emblazoned with the crook and sword, marking their rank. Even Lieutenant Peery sat in the corner, laughing with two other officers, neither of whom Evylin had met. It surprised her to see Peery since she expected him to have gone to the meeting with Deckard. Then she spotted an even more familiar face in the crowd.

Seated at the bar, Thom chuckled into a mug of ale while the weasel-like Private Rafferty talked to the barkeep.

"Not possible," the man said.

"Why not?" Rafferty asked, a twinkle in his gray eyes. "I promise you it'd be easy."

"If you could get a cask of Schonese wine, you wouldn't be selling it to me." The barkeep shook his head. "Try tricking someone else."

Rafferty took a swig out of his mug, undisturbed by the dismissal. His sharp eyes roved around the room, landing on Evylin. Instantly, he set his tankard on the counter with a *plunk*, whacked Thom's arm, and leaped off his barstool.

"Mrs. Deckard," Rafferty said, dropping into a bow. A few soldiers looked in their direction. "A pleasure to see you again, ma'am."

Hewitt eyed the small, willowy man as Thom rose awkwardly.

"Hello again," Evylin said, then met her brother-in-law's bright stare. "I'm surprised to see you here."

Thom glanced at Hewitt before giving his reply. "We all have the day off. As much as an officer can have a day off, that is. Deckard told us to enjoy ourselves so long as we keep an eye on the men."

"But the captain doesn't get a day off?" she asked.

"He's the captain, so no."

Evylin started unbuttoning her coat in the heat of the crowded room. "What an unfortunate lot. You'd think rank would provide some benefits."

Thom tapped a finger on the rim of his mug. "The only benefit of rank is the respect and coin that comes with it. Everything else is just more responsibility."

"Sounds like a miserable way to spend your life," Rafferty said, leaning against the bar.

"You're a soldier now too," Thom noted.

"I'm a private. And I intend to stay that way."

"Good luck."

Rafferty gave him a sly grin. "I don't need luck, friend."

"Evylin and I were about to have lunch," Hewitt interjected, then turned to Thom. "Would you and your friend like to join us, Lieutenant?"

The soldiers exchanged a singular, surprised look before turning back and nodding in unison.

"Not sure we'll manage a table in all this, though," Rafferty warned.

Hewitt scanned the room, packed to the brim with men. He held up a hand to tell them to remain before turning to the nearest booth. He set both hands on the tabletop with a resounding *thump*, and all four privates jumped as they shrank back at his presence. "I'd suggest you all move your party to the bar," he growled.

Three of the four looked to the young man on Hewitt's immediate right. He had a black mop of hair and deep tan skin—likely from Setshire. "My—my apologies, sir, but . . ." He swallowed as his eyes caught the emblem on Hewitt's lapel and the bronze braid on his right shoulder. His next words came out as a squeak. "We were here first, Major."

"What's your name, Private?"

The soldier was smart enough not to hesitate. "Haalston. Markus Haalston."

"Private Haalston, do you know who that woman there is?" He gestured toward Evylin. She frowned at her uncle's use of her new status.

Haalston's face blanched as he first took in Evylin and then Thom right behind her. He blinked rapidly as he turned back to Hewitt. "Captain Deckard's wife, sir."

"That's right. And do you want the captain to know you refused his wife a seat?"

"Uncle," Evylin called, "leave the poor man alone. I'll eat at the bar."

"No!" Haalston called. He scrambled out of the booth and motioned for his comrades to do the same. "No, ma'am, the—the major is right. Allow us to serve you."

The four privates hastened out of the way, ales in hand, as they barreled around Evylin, Thom, and Rafferty for the bar.

Hewitt turned back and gestured to the table. "Mrs. Deckard."

Rolling her eyes at his display, Evylin scooted to the back of the booth. "You're absurd," she told him. "Those men didn't deserve to be kicked out."

"They're soldiers, Evie," he said as Rafferty, then Thom, slid across from them. "If they're not used to taking orders yet, they'd better learn now."

Thom eyed her uncle warily. "Deckard won't like it if he hears you used his name to threaten his men."

Hewitt glared at him. "It was in aid of his wife."

Thom's arched brow said he didn't think that attachment meant much. "He doesn't like to run his company through fear. He wants his men to respect him. And suggesting he'll become angered by his wife's lack of a table isn't exactly morale boosting."

"Oh, come on, Thommy," the weasel elbowed his friend, "lighten up. We've got a meal to eat and the company of a beautiful woman to enjoy."

"She's not available, Raff."

"Doesn't mean I can't look."

Thom frowned at the soldier, and Hewitt summoned a nearby barmaid. Once they'd all ordered, Rafferty leaned forward, gray eyes twinkling. "So tell me, Mrs. Deckard: How does a pretty thing like you beat my friend Thommy in a sword fight?"

Hewitt's arm draped across the back of the booth as Evylin smiled. "Lots of practice," she said.

"Sounds boring."

"Only if you're doing it wrong," Hewitt argued. "Why don't you answer a question for me, Private?"

"Sure thing, Major."

"How long have you been friends with the lieutenant here?"

Rafferty and Thom passed a look to each other.

"About a fortnight," Rafferty replied.

"Two weeks?" Evylin exclaimed. "That's all?"

The barmaid dropped off their drinks and Thom pushed Rafferty's down the table. "How long did you think we'd known each other?" he asked.

"I don't know," she said. "But I didn't expect a volunteer and an officer to become that chummy within a fortnight."

Thom smirked. "I told you. Good company's lacking at camp."

"That it is," Hewitt grumbled, turning back to Rafferty. "A fortnight back puts you as an Estshire man. Whereabouts are you from?"

"Rasnaack," Rafferty said, eyes shining madly. "The gem of Estshire, as it's most widely known."

Evylin and Hewitt shared a grin. Near the bottom of Estshire, Rasnaack was the waypoint between the port towns of Bridgewater and Beaminster. The towns were once large enough to supply a large portion of the Shire's sea imports. But after the drafts, they'd lost enough men and workers to shrink from large towns to barely surviving villages. As the middle ground between these two failing settlements, Rasnaack became a hub of illegal trade and suspect merchandise.

"I can't blame you for wanting to leave the place," Hewitt said, lifting his tankard.

The young soldier's flighty gaze flew about the room as he spoke, constantly searching but never settling. "I didn't want to leave. Sure, it's small. But we had plenty of traffic to keep things interesting, and I enjoyed my life there."

"Small?" Hewitt spat the word. "It's a speck on the map."

Rafferty's left shoulder lifted in a half-assed shrug as the barmaid returned with the food. "I had a rather pleasant setup."

Thom thanked the barmaid before she left, then added, "'Pleasant' is one way to describe it."

"Look, I had it made, Thommy." Rafferty shoved a finger in his friend's face. "If not for that blighter, Winchester, I'd still be living like a king."

"A king, eh?" Evylin asked, increasingly intrigued by the strange young man. She filled her fork with the well-roasted venison that fell apart with the lightest touch. "And what sort of state was under your rule, Your Majesty?"

"Let's just say I had a lot of people who depended on me, and I liked to help them out."

"With the proper compensation," Thom noted.

"And yet you left?" Evylin asked.

Rafferty smiled as he scooped up his own bite. "What can I say? Your darling captain showed up, and here I am."

"I suppose his speech made its impact, then?"

Thom and Rafferty laughed as though it was the most outrageous impossibility.

"I mean no offense to your husband, ma'am," the private said. "But his speech had nothing to do with it."

"Then what inspired you to join?"

His silver eyes met hers with a mischievous glint. "The promise of a pardon."

Hewitt stroked his thick beard. "You're a criminal?"

"I'm an entrepreneur," Rafferty corrected, lifting a finger to punctuate his words. His eyes rested on Hewitt only a moment before returning to the room. "People reached out to me when they wanted or needed something, and I'd get it for them. The legality of the items or how I obtained them is debatable. But I, for one, don't see the problem. I supplied a service, and people were happy to pay. What's the harm in that?"

A wry grin crossed Hewitt's face. "How long did you manage this *business* of yours?"

Rafferty's roving eyes paused in thought, then continued their journey. "About six years on my own. I worked with a few . . . mentors, I guess you could call them, for a few years prior."

Evylin tried to do the math, guessing his age somewhere around twenty-three. That meant he'd had to begin his "entrepreneurial" enterprises no later than fourteen.

"I take it you got an early start?" Hewitt remarked, clearly thinking the same.

"I always had a knack for it," Rafferty supplied.

"And how many times have you gotten caught?"

"Once is all it takes, isn't it?" He chuckled. "My own fault, I suppose. Never should've trusted Freddie. Knew he didn't have what it takes to keep his mouth shut. Yet, I gave him a chance. Someone caught wind of me pinching the casks and told the magistrate. I tried to talk my way out of it, but Winchester squealed the moment he spotted trouble. Worst night of my life."

Rafferty lounged lazily in his seat. "When I heard about the army's arrival the next morning, I convinced the magistrate it'd be more worth his while to offer me to the captain rather than hold me until someone from Olbury could come and take me off his hands."

Evylin considered his story. "So you only joined the army to get out of prison?"

"Wouldn't you?"

"I suppose I would," she admitted.

"It isn't that the captain's speech wasn't rousing," Rafferty said. "I quite enjoyed hearing the reference to Nikleby Draaw. That was my favorite as a kid."

"Is he what inspired you to become a smuggler?" Evylin asked.

"Draaw wasn't a smuggler," Rafferty argued as he frowned. "He was a liberator."

Hewitt scoffed. "He liberated people of their things and gave them to other people."

"He was a hero," Rafferty insisted. "He never stole or smuggled anything unless someone needed it to survive. He took care of people."

"And that's what you did? Took care of people?"

"I suppose I did."

"As long as there was money in it for you," Thom retorted.

"Hey, it's a prestigious line of work. You don't get something for nothing, and pinching high-priced or unsanctioned goods isn't an easy task."

"You're a saint, Raff."

"I do what I can." The private turned back to Evylin. "But enough about my glorious deeds. I want to hear about the lovely Mrs. Deckard. I take it the captain's speech left its impact on you."

Evylin grinned. "It was an inspiring speech, to be sure. But I wasn't exactly its intended target."

"Despite your impressive skills, I didn't expect you'd want to join our ranks, ma'am." Rafferty's smile grew impish. "What I meant was that it must have played some role in your inevitable descent into madness and matrimony."

"I see," she muttered. She looked at Hewitt, who grunted, then at Thom, who scraped at a nick in the handle of his tankard.

"Was I wrong?" Rafferty prodded.

Meeting the man's silver stare, Evylin wondered if he was sincere or simply playing a game to get her to tell him the truth. Clearly, Thom had told him about the sword fight, but had he said anything more? It was impossible to read this weasel's dry expression.

"Wrong about what exactly?" she asked. "My madness or the captain's speech affecting it?"

"The speech, Mrs. Deckard."

"Call me Evie." She leaned back and crossed her arms. "In that case, yes, you're wrong. I was mad well before then."

Hewitt snorted while Thom furrowed his brow, and Rafferty beamed.

"Is that so?" His white-blond eyebrows shot up. "Love at first sight?"

"Why do you want to know? You don't strike me as a romantic, Private."

"Please," he waved his hand at her, "we're friends now. Call me Raff."

"Why do you want to know, Raff?" she restated.

"Because you're a confusing woman, Evie." The man lifted a finger, tracing the shape of her face in the air before him. "You're pretty, funny, and friendly. But you're also a swordsman, smart, and, at twenty-six, you clearly didn't feel the need to marry before now. How does a woman like you get swept head over heels in love with a man like the captain?"

Though she supposed she could have pretended offense at his questions, Evylin found herself too amused by his blunt remarks. "How do you know my age?"

"I have it on good authority." Rafferty tipped his head in Thom's direction.

Evylin raised her brow at him, and Thom's jaw went slack. "Uh . . . it was a guess," he muttered.

"Your brother would be appalled," she teased.

Thom huffed. "It was my brother who made the guess."

Astonished to hear that the gentlemanly captain would speculate on a woman's age, Evylin leaned against the tabletop. "He did?"

Thom shrugged. "When he recounted his dinner with your family that first night, I asked about yours and your sisters' ages, and he guessed. He told me last night he'd found out he was right."

Rafferty whispered a rapid string of words to his friend, but Evylin only caught, ". . . last night."

Thom grimaced, making Evylin sure she was glad not to hear the comment.

"Tell me, Eve," Rafferty said, still sniggering at whatever joke he'd made. "What was it about our captain that drove you to madness?"

"In what world does a soldier want to hear about a woman's romantic notions?" she countered.

Rafferty propped his arms on the table. "A world where he's amazingly bored."

"This will only make it worse, I assure you."

"Come now, Evie. Explain to Thommy, me, and your dear ol' uncle how the immaculate and tiresome Captain Deckard won your heart."

"Tiresome?"

"And immaculate."

Evylin turned to Thom. "Does he usually insult your brother?"

"Only when it's accurate," he replied, his blue eyes glowing in the window's light.

She cocked her head in surprise. "You think your brother is boring?"

"You don't?"

"I think he's rather clever, actually."

Thom huffed. "Then you must be easily entertained. It's too bad. I had hoped to like you."

"More's the pity," she returned. "I had hoped to like you."

A smile broke over Thom's face, warm and full like his brother's. Given their different coloring, it was easy to tell them apart. But in moments like that, she realized just how similar their features were.

"Was that it, then?" Rafferty interjected. "The captain's quick wit caught your fancy, and you decided he was the one?" He shook his head, skeptical. "Doesn't add up."

Now convinced Thom hadn't shared the full truth, Evylin felt confident in keeping the secret. "You really want to know?" she asked.

"I really do."

"Fine." Evylin smiled playfully. "I liked him the moment I met him. I thought he was charming and smart, and he actually paid attention to what I had to say. When he gave his speech, his charisma and eloquence impressed me. He's kind, honorable, and has all the other requirements for a good husband. Beyond that . . ." She shrugged, knowing this was the part that would amuse Rafferty the most. "What can I say? He's a pleasant man to look at."

Rafferty didn't disappoint. He howled riotously and elbowed Thom. "Well now, Thommy, that's not such a bad report for you either. You and the captain are a near spitting image."

Lifting her clay tankard, Evylin shook her head. "I'm partial to redheads."

"Partial to flattery is more like it," Thom countered, a dare in his gaze.

"Is that jealousy I hear?" she replied. "Don't worry—I know a lovely young woman dying for a marriage proposal back in Whickam Village."

Thom snarled.

"But no, I have no need for flattery," Evylin teased. "I get so much from Hewitt, I don't think I could stand anymore."

Her uncle snorted beside her, the left side of his mouth tipping up as he finished clearing his plate.

"Tell us, Eve," Rafferty said, balancing his fork on the tip of his spindly finger. "Do you share your husband's love for legends?"

"I enjoy them as much as the next person. Though I prefer the newer tales and novels if I'm honest."

"What's your favorite, then?"

"Legend or novel?"

"Both."

After a second of consideration, Evylin said, "*The Abject of Arund* is one of my favorite novels. Lots of sword fighting. And not so much politics as others, although the romance wasn't quite believable. But my favorite legend?" She didn't even need to think. "*The Mages of Auld.*"

Rafferty's snowy brow rose, bringing his deep-set eyes out of the shadows. "Really?" He clicked his tongue off the roof of his mouth. "Who would've thought—our captain's wife, a heretic?"

Evylin laughed. "I didn't take you for the devout type."

Thom scoffed into his ale.

Rafferty snickered. "Certainly not. The kings have changed the rhetoric of our faith one too many times for it to be genuine anymore. But that doesn't mean I approve of Mages."

Evylin shared a glance with Hewitt. "You sound as though you believe that Mages exist," she said, scanning him with increasing interest.

Rafferty's grin deepened. "Of course, I do."

Looking to Thom to suss out whether the weasel was leading them on, Evylin raised her brow.

Thom lifted his pint in a mock toast. "I told you. He's fun to keep around."

"They're just stories," Evylin said, though she couldn't deny she preferred his theology. Although the Allorian priests taught that Mages were evil, self-serving pagans, she'd always felt adventures with magic beat every other tale without a doubt.

"No," Rafferty contradicted, "they're legends. And legends are based on truth. I'd grant there's some fabrication and exaggeration in them, but they came from historical events."

Hewitt narrowed his gaze. "I traveled this country for two decades. I've been through the Shires, up to Loclight, and over the border between our country and Wauld. I've fought countless battles against Waulden men. Yet, during all that, I've never seen anything resembling magic. Not once."

Thom's mouth lifted in a smirk as he took a bite of his meal, but Hewitt's logic didn't faze Rafferty. "Perhaps you're right," he said, sitting back in his seat. "But perhaps you weren't looking hard enough."

"You think there are Mages out there?" Hewitt asked gruffly.

"I do."

They stared at each other.

"You're a fool," Hewitt said.

"Probably," Rafferty admitted. "But to tell the truth, I hope Mages are real. Then this damn war might make sense."

Hewitt's bushy brows lowered over his steel eyes curiously. "You don't believe in our war efforts?"

Rafferty tipped his head back and forth. "Can't say one way or the other. Wauld has been the most aggressive—raiding and pillaging and the like across our borders. But we *did* technically start it when the ol' shepherd, Ephren, decided to start his little uprising those hundred eighty-some years ago. Wauld has a reason to be angry with us. We *did* take half of their land. But who can blame us? They were oppressing us when we were all one country. And they're only angry because they'd like to keep oppressing us now."

He raised his white-blond eyebrows and continued, "But that's not really a strong enough case for generations of Waulden and Ephrian kings to keep a war going, now, is it? Nearly two centuries of fighting with no frontrunner and no sign of peace? That suggests both sides believe they're fighting for more than land alone."

Evylin had never heard anyone other than Hewitt speak so plainly of their opinion on the war. And he only lamented the running of the war rather than questioning its legitimacy.

But as Evylin listened to Rafferty, she couldn't help but agree with his sentiment. The lack of effort from either King Ephren or King Blount of Wauld to reach peace was beyond pure stubbornness. If Rafferty wasn't right—if there wasn't something more going on—the war itself was the stupidity of prideful men at its finest.

Hewitt set his empty tankard back on the table. "You believe there are Mages behind the war?"

Rafferty rubbed his thumb along the side of his nose, eyes still shifting about the room. "How should I know? I'm just an entrepreneur." He swept his tankard up for a sip. "But from what I remember of *The Mages of Auld*, Ephria and Wauld had a falling out over Mages rather than land. It was one of the reasons Ephren banned the story, if you ask me. Seems to me that Wauld has as legitimate a reason to want us to be one country again as we have reason to remain separate."

Hewitt grinned, the smile large and calculating. "You're either the most idiotic man I've ever met, or you're too smart for your own good."

Rafferty returned the broad smile. "I'd venture to say they're the same thing."

"You may be right," Hewitt said, then turned to Thom. "I'd recommend you choose better friends, Lieutenant. He's a dangerous one."

Thom let out an amused scoff. "Oh, don't worry, Major. I never believe a word he says."

"Ah." Rafferty clucked his tongue on the roof of his mouth as he scanned the interior of his tankard. "Looks like I'm fresh out. Get me a refill, would you, Thommy?"

Thom raised his brows at him. "You've got legs, haven't you?"

"Yeah, but I'm on the inside of the booth."

"All you had to do was ask," he replied, slipping out of his seat and gesturing to the crowded bar.

Rafferty frowned. "It'll take forever to get any service."

"Better get going, then."

The weasel grumbled but headed off into the ever-increasing crowd of soldiers.

Thom dropped back into his seat, taking advantage of the open space. He took a swig of his ale as Hewitt and Evylin passed each other a shrewd glance.

Hewitt took the lead. "How do you like serving in the army, Lieutenant?"

Lowering his tankard, Thom scanned Hewitt first, then Evylin. "Ah, I see what this is." He scoffed. "I like it just fine. The draft wasn't a disappointment to me as it was to most men. I would've volunteered had they asked."

"Two volunteers in one family?" Evylin raised her brow. "How patriotic of you both."

"Patriotism had nothing to do with it," he said coldly. "For me or Deckard."

"Really? He claimed a quite different story when we first met."

"Shocking," he muttered but said no more.

"You said this is your first time working under your brother's command?" Hewitt asked.

Thom took his time answering as he lifted his ale for another sip. "It's our first time working together as soldiers."

"Do you like working with him?" Evylin asked.

There was another hesitation. "I guess. He's a good officer. Fair and reasonable, though he demands nothing but the best out of his troops."

Hewitt tugged on his beard, nodding in interested approval.

"But I think . . ." Thom stopped and shook his head. "No, never mind."

"Go on," Hewitt prompted.

"No, it isn't pertinent."

Evylin leaned against the table. "That's hardly fair. You can't start to say something interesting and then refuse us the details."

He passed her a sardonic grin. "It doesn't matter."

"Then there's no reason *not* to tell us."

Evidently seeing her determination, he sighed. "Fine. As I said, it's nothing. It's just . . . I don't think I'd want to serve under him again."

Surprised by his admission, Evylin looked at her uncle.

"Why not?" Hewitt asked, eyes narrowing in similar confusion.

Thom shrugged. "He's my brother. It's hard to respect your commanding officer when you know he was afraid of the dark until he was ten, never could figure out how to climb a tree, not to mention every other stupid flaw brothers know about each other."

A light "humph" escaped Hewitt as Evylin smiled. She tried to imagine Deckard as a child but struggled to conjure the image. He was too proper and reserved to be anything but a man. "What other flaws did he have?" she asked wryly. "Did he tease you mercilessly?"

"Deckard?" Thom scoffed. "Not a chance. He was too busy playing 'Mr. Perfect' to do anything wrong. It was bloody irritating."

"Oh, I see. A well-behaved child, was he? Sounds dreadfully boring."

Hewitt grunted.

"Yeah, well, you get used to it." Thom took another swig, set the tankard down with a *thunk*, and rolled his shoulders. "Don't get me wrong, Deckard was—*is* a great brother. He was always considerate and . . . caring. To both me and our sister. But he was also a prig."

Evylin pressed her lips together in amusement.

Thom let out a tense chuckle. "He still is," he muttered.

"Still?" Hewitt pressed.

Thom slouched in his seat. "It isn't—it isn't like he's a bad person. I don't even think he realizes what he does most of the time, but . . . well, everything he does—every choice he's ever made . . . They're all about being perfect, about being right. And when you grow up watching that . . . it's hard to see anything else."

Hewitt's bushy eyebrows rose on his wrinkled forehead. "Sounds like ambition to me."

A cynical smile came to Thom's lips. "You'd be right."

"Don't you have ambition?"

"Of course. But I don't pretend to make altruistic choices when, in truth, I'm choosing what will get me what I want."

Evylin's good humor cooled at Thom's report. Since she'd met Captain Deckard, she'd struggled to figure him out. No matter how pleasant, his charm didn't fool her. She saw past the genteel persona he offered those around him. He was far more cunning and sly than people gave him credit for. His good nature was as much a weapon as her sword. And he knew how to wield it with as unparalleled a skill as she.

He wasn't a bad man, but neither was he as noble as he presented himself.

Staring down into the amber ale before her, Evylin wondered what that would mean for her. She liked the captain well enough. She thought she might even enjoy being his wife. But she had to be careful. She couldn't let him control her the way he manipulated others to his whims, no matter how altruistic they seemed.

No, Evylin determined; it didn't matter how amiable and amusing Deckard was. He had his own agenda, just as she did. And if it came to it, she couldn't let him trick her into abandoning her and Ryen's dreams for his sense of the greater good.

CHAPTER NINETEEN

The sun hung low in the sky, the cold wind cutting through the streets as Deckard returned to town. He'd spent the afternoon working in the camp—noting the variation of exemplary and shoddy work in its rushed assembly the previous night—and meeting with the few officers on site. Only a handful of soldiers remained within the encampment.

Deckard counted his numbers—two hundred thirty-five recruits with Hewitt's addition—and did the calculations. There were fifteen settlements left in the Shires. Fifteen stops for him to collect another two hundred sixty-five volunteers. A daunting number. He was halfway through the assignment, halfway through the Shires, and fifteen men shy of halfway through his recruits. The odds weren't impossible, but they were improbable.

His gamble on Hewitt had to work.

The soldiers were still out and about, enjoying their day off, as he walked to the Loore home. He wondered if he should have kept the men in camp. More time training would make for more impressive recruits, and that might be the offset he needed.

But there was little Deckard hated more than an officer with no understanding of his troops. And ninety percent of his recruits were young. Having escaped the last draft, few were over the age of twenty-three. They wouldn't respond well to an iron fist, and he was not inclined to rule with one. He remembered being a soldier at their age; he'd joined up at twenty himself. And officers who ran their companies and squads through fear earned hate from their troops. Those who imparted responsibility and trust earned admiration. The latter gained respect and obedience, while the former only earned contempt and disregard.

As he passed small groups of soldiers who greeted him gratefully, Deckard was reassured he'd made the right decision.

Returning to the Loores' home, Deckard hesitated at the door before remembering Serene's charge. Forgoing a knock, he walked right in to receive a resounding welcome from the master and mistress of the house.

"Good to have you back," Jorge called. "Care for an ale?"

"Thank you, but no," Deckard replied, scanning the empty parlor. Jorge sat at the dining room table while Serene arranged the last trays of food in front of him. "Is Evylin still out?"

"I'm afraid so, dear," Serene confirmed. "As I said, she and Hewitt are always off somewhere."

Deckard couldn't stop his frown. "It's getting rather late."

"Oh, they'll be fine." Jorge tossed a hand through the air. "They're known to stay out all hours."

"All hours?"

"It's perfectly safe," Serene insisted. "Trollenston is as lawful as they come. And she's got Hewitt with her. No need to worry."

Of all women, he didn't need to worry about Evylin's safety, but that didn't negate his disappointment.

"If you want to find her, I can guess where she'll be," Serene offered, not waiting for a reply as she marched to the front window. "That is the way to the Shepherd's Rest. You go right down that road there, straight ahead for about five blocks, and then make a left. You can't miss it."

Deckard backed away from the window, committing the directions to memory. "Thank you," he replied. "I hate to abandon your hard work, but I'll try to be back with Evylin shortly."

"Nonsense." Her hands fluttered as she shooed him off. "Go find that girl. And when you do, tell her I said she's a ninny for spending all her time with that old cod when she could spend it with such a man as you."

Deckard tossed a wave toward Jorge, then bowed to Serene. "Thank you again, ma'am."

"Call me Aunt, would you?"

Deckard nodded and stepped out the door. The wind nipped at his ears, but he didn't mind. Late in autumn, he found the regular sunshine this far south a welcome novelty. And in the darkening sky, the rising cold reminded him of home.

Following Serene's directions, Deckard had no trouble finding the tavern. Soldiers poured in and out of its emerald green door, laughing and singing and having a splendid time. A pair of exiting young soldiers caught sight of him and cheered, "To the Captain!" lifting imaginary tankards.

Deckard dipped his chin in gratitude. "Evening, men. Having a good time, I see."

"Yes, sir," one private said, his dark hair falling into his eyes. "It's been a right scream in there."

"It has?" Deckard looked at the foggy windows.

"Yes, sir. Private Rafferty's got us all in stitches."

"Private Rafferty?" Deckard frowned, remembering the white-headed weasel who joined in Rasnaack. The magistrate had suggested to Deckard that the man might accept a role in the army in exchange for the pardon that came with a commission. And while he hated to take on criminals, his numbers demanded he not be over particular.

"Yes, sir," the soldier repeated once more. "He's been telling the most hilarious tales. Can't be real, any of 'em. But the stories he invents!"

The other private leaned forward, his lazy grin betraying he'd had one too many drinks. "*And* he's been showing off his magic."

Deckard furrowed his brow. "Magic?"

"Tricks, sir," the first private clarified, "with cards and such."

"Ah, I see." He took a deep breath, renewing his lighthearted mood. "Well, off with you both, men. Enjoy the rest of your evening."

"Yes, sir," they said in unison before ambling down the street.

Turning back to the noise bleeding through the tavern walls, Deckard scanned the building. He'd never been one to enjoy raucous crowds and revelry. Many of his fellow soldiers lamented his subdued nature early in his career. Those he considered friends now didn't mind his preference for a quiet night at home. But if Evylin preferred to spend her time in the tavern with her uncle, he worried she'd take exception to his more reserved nature.

Deckard bolstered his courage and slipped into the tavern, coming to a halt once over the threshold. The door clicked shut behind him, caging him in the disorienting chaos that packed the building, wall to wall. The warmth of the room hit him first. With so many bodies in one place, an immediate sweat rose at the base of his neck from the extreme juxtaposition to the chilly exterior.

Laughter, heckles, and applause rang through the tavern. Deckard shifted through the crowd, noting their gazes fixed on the center of the room. There, Private Rafferty stood on a large, circular table, hands raised in the air as he spoke, commanding the attention of his audience.

And seated around his platform, Deckard caught sight of his goal.

While Hewitt rested back in his chair, arms crossed, watching the private with a dry grin on his lips, Evylin held a hand to her mouth to hold in her mirth as Thom leaned in, one arm around the back of her chair, whispering in her ear.

Deckard's brow furrowed at the sight while Rafferty's voice rang out. "But that's nothing, gents," he said with a flick of his wrist. Light flashed against the gold piece that appeared like magic between his fingers. "A single coin is small potatoes. What if I make an entire sack of coins disappear all at once?"

The patrons threw calls of disbelief and excitement at him.

"I've done it before. I can do it again."

"Not a chance, you twit," one soldier called out. "Get down off that table."

Rafferty snickered, then squatted in front of Evylin. "They don't think I can do it, Eve. Can you believe that?"

Evylin propped her elbows on the table. "With ease."

The weasel tapped a finger on her nose. "You doubt me, too, eh?"

"Most definitely."

"I'll just have to prove it, then!" He popped back up, the table wobbling. Yet, he held his footing. "Who's gotta bag of coin they'd like to offer up?"

Deckard broke through the crush of soldiers then and crossed his arms. "I recommend you use your own, Private."

The entire tavern fell silent at the sound of his voice. The soldiers snapped to attention at the sight of their commanding officer. Rafferty wobbled on the table as Thom drew away from Evylin, his arm sliding off the back of her chair. Hewitt watched coldly, his humor gone.

Yet, Evylin's smirk didn't falter. "Come to join the party, Jonn?"

Deckard hesitated, unsure how to respond. Her invitation was friendly, but he was standing in front of forty or more of his men. He couldn't relax here. He might be a relatable officer, but he was also a respectable one. And he couldn't afford to come across as casual and unbridled.

In the spare second that Deckard worked to formulate his response, Thom leaned over to Evylin with his chin tucked down as he muttered under his breath. She let out a puff of laughter.

Deckard straightened, leveling an unamused glare at his brother. Whatever the comment, he knew it had been at his expense. And in this crowd, he wouldn't be a joke. "As you were, men," he ordered.

The soldiers turned around instantly, reengaging in conversations with one another. They kept their heads down and moved out of Deckard's way as he strode across to the table where his brother and wife sat, still chuckling together.

Private Rafferty leaped off the table, landing near Deckard. "Evening, there, Captain. Pleasure to have your company," he said with a mock salute.

Deckard spared the man a glance. "Thank you, Private, but I'm afraid I must ask you to leave us."

"Ah, come on, Deckard," Thom called. "He's a friend."

"He's a soldier," he corrected.

Evylin leaned back in her chair. "You're right, Thom," she said, a glimmer of amusement in her eyes. "He's not much for fun, is he?"

No matter how playful, the flippant remark hit Deckard in the gut, but he refused to let it show on his face. Here, he'd spent the day worried about proving himself to Evylin, and his brother had undermined him the whole time. And what was Thom doing befriending her anyway? The last Deckard knew, his brother was harboring a mountain-sized weight of resentment toward her. Now, here he was, joking away like they were old pals.

Hewitt stood and set a hand on Evylin's shoulder. Deckard couldn't tell if the action was possessive or intended as a message to his niece. "Are you here to join us, Captain?" he asked.

Deckard took a deep breath, containing his agitation. "No, I'm not," he said, then turned to Evylin. "I'm here because I was looking for you."

Evylin's sarcasm was less confident as she replied, "Congratulations, you found me."

Hewitt squeezed her shoulder, drawing her eyes to him as Rafferty snickered behind Deckard.

Now sure that Hewitt *was* sending his niece some message, Deckard studied the man an extra second before turning back to Evylin. "Your aunt has dinner on the table, and I'm here to bring you back."

Evylin opened her mouth, but Hewitt spoke before she could. "Our apologies," he said, his deep voice rumbling above the hubbub of the room. "Time got away from us. Let's go, Evie."

As Hewitt patted her shoulder once more, Evylin frowned. Her dark eyes flickered from Thom to Deckard and back with uncertainty. Then she pushed back from the table, her chair scraping against the wooden floorboards as she rose.

Thom hopped up beside her. "Uh, well, it, uh—this was fun, Evie." His hand rose as if to shake hers before he appeared to think better of it, curling his fingers into a fist that dropped back to his side. "Have a good evening."

"You, too, Thom," she said, edging around Deckard.

"Major Glaas," Thom said with a nod to the man.

"Lieutenant," Hewitt replied in kind.

As the pair started on their path toward the door, Deckard met his brother's gaze, making sure to infuse all his irritation and confusion into one look. He raised his brow in a silent question: *"What's going on here?"*

Dropping his head, Thom wilted. "Sorry," he muttered.

"We'll talk about it later," Deckard whispered back. Then, thinking better of leaving the air strained between them, he reached over to pat his brother's arm. "See you in the morning."

Hurrying to catch up with Hewitt and Evylin at the door, Deckard pushed through the crowd of soldiers just as Rafferty's sharp voice called out, "Wait!"

The three of them turned as Rafferty dashed straight for Evylin. With his slim, wiry frame, he quickly slipped through the throng of soldiers. He bounded out of the sea of patrons with a huge grin and stopped before Evylin. Short as he was for a man, they stood at the same height.

"I almost forgot," he said, and with a flick of his wrist, a small, folded piece of paper appeared between his fingers.

Evylin gasped, took the paper, and peeked inside its fold. Her jaw dropped as she instinctively checked the pockets of her skirt. "You little thief! How did you get this?"

He winked. "Tricks of the trade, Eve. Can't give away my secrets."

Tucking the paper into her pocket, Deckard caught a glimpse of a familiar script. *His* script. His tense shoulders relaxed at the realization that she'd kept his note with her all day. Was it mere happenstance? Or had she been thinking of him as he had thought of her?

"Till next time, Eve." Rafferty saluted first her, then Hewitt, and Deckard. "Major. Captain."

As the weasel disappeared into the crowd, Hewitt opened the door. Deckard followed Evylin, passing a nod to a few soldiers waiting to enter the tavern. He slowed his gait once on the street, but she pushed ahead, unaware of the distance she put between them. He was about to lengthen his stride to catch up with her when Hewitt pushed past him.

Deckard thought about joining them, then hesitated. When he caught up with her, Hewitt immediately began muttering to Evylin. Deckard furrowed his brow, watching as she tossed her uncle a bemused smile, chin tipping back to glance over her shoulder. Deckard eased his expression to be sure she didn't misinterpret his reaction.

But Evylin's smile faltered, and she turned back to whisper to her uncle.

The man grunted before speaking in her ear once more.

With little doubt they were discussing *him*, Deckard chose to leave them to their private conversation. He wouldn't deny that it irritated him. But he didn't feel right about pressing his way in either, not after Lawton's warning against trying to come between them. Hewitt wouldn't allow it. Evylin wouldn't want it.

As they walked, Deckard watched the unheard conversation unfold, confused by the rising animosity between them.

A long, hushed reply from Hewitt.

A sharp, hissed retort from Evylin.

A scowl from him.

A blank stare from her.

Hewitt began again, but Evylin cut him off before he snarled at her, ending whatever rebuttal she'd started. She turned away from her uncle, her head dipping down.

Suddenly, watching them walk side by side—Evylin turning away from her uncle as he strode down the street, his head held high—Deckard wondered if he'd already come between them without intending it at all.

He smoothed down the front of his coat. Was *he* the reason for their heated exchange? Serene had said just this afternoon that they had never exchanged a cross word. Yet now, they were arguing. Was it because he'd come to collect her? They were used to spending their time in town however they pleased. And now, no matter how unintentionally, he was interfering.

Rounding the final turn, Hewitt stopped at the street corner. The Loore residence was still three houses down, but he set a giant hand on Evylin's trim shoulder. "Give Serene and Jorge my excuses," he said.

"What?" Evylin's disappointment scrunched her nose. "You're not seriously leaving, are you?"

Hewitt didn't appear bothered by her distress. "I don't have any interest in sitting around while Serene flaps her gums about town gossip. Besides, you'll have him," he thrust his thumb at Deckard, "to keep you entertained. You don't need me."

Evylin frowned. "But I *want* you to be with me."

Though Deckard supposed it should hurt—her choosing her uncle over him—he didn't feel the weight of disappointment. Why should she choose him? They weren't a real couple, despite his intention to make the most of their situation. He couldn't even say they were friends. Why should she choose a stranger over the man she felt loved her more than her own father?

That was the crux of it, Deckard realized: She wanted the man she trusted at her side. Her rejection of Deckard had nothing to do with him; it was all due to the relationship neither she nor Hewitt was willing to release.

With a gentler expression than Deckard had yet to see on the man's face, Hewitt rapped his knuckles under Evylin's chin. "I know," he muttered. "Get inside. I'll see you tomorrow."

Evylin pressed her lips together as she looked down at the dirt street. Her hands curled into fists, but not before Deckard noticed her fingers trembling.

Startled to have observed her fear, Deckard hesitated. What did she have to be afraid of? Him? Surely not. If his promises to her last night hadn't alleviated her worries, he wasn't sure what could.

But that wasn't the problem.

Deckard glanced over at Hewitt, the truth blatant. Whatever confidence Evylin portrayed to the world outside, she was just as afraid of being without her uncle as he was of being without her.

Doubtful it would work even as he turned to the man, Deckard felt beholden to try. "You still have a few hours left on your day off, Major. You'd be a welcome addition."

Hewitt glowered. "Don't try to charm me, Captain. It won't work."

"I wouldn't expect it to."

The gruff man nodded, first to Deckard, then to Evylin. "Goodnight, Evie."

Shoulders drooping, Evylin returned the farewell. She began to turn, headed for the house, and Deckard moved to follow.

"Captain," Hewitt said, stopping them both in their tracks, "might I have a word with you before I go?"

Deckard shared a surprised look with Evylin before turning back to the man. "Of course."

Hewitt leveled his heavy gray stare on his niece, his bushy eyebrows raised as a signal to leave them. She narrowed her gaze and looked back to Deckard. He lifted his shoulders in a shrug as a promise that he was as much at a loss as she. She sighed and turned away.

Once the door to the Loore home shut behind her, Hewitt stepped closer, glaring down at Deckard. Though the man only stood an inch or so taller than himself, Deckard couldn't deny that he made an imposing figure. Broader than two men and with muscles that would make a bear look weak, the veteran general matched all the military lore that had turned him into legend.

"Your morning go as planned?" Hewitt asked, his tone accusing.

Attempting to gauge the man's agenda, Deckard scanned his fierce expression. A lesser man might have wilted under the imperious and violent glare of Hewitt Glaas. But Deckard had experienced enough aggressive and demanding officers that whatever immediate fear the bear-like man instilled faded quickly.

"I suppose it did," he replied, proud of how unaffected his voice sounded. "Magistrate Steevensun is more than happy to offer his assistance."

"Mm."

"What can I help you with, Major?"

Hewitt cracked a trio of knuckles on his left hand. "Would you care to explain why you abandoned your wife the morning after your wedding?"

Confusion was Deckard's first reaction. Disbelief, his second. "I'm sorry, but I'm not sure you heard me before," he said, glaring back at the man. "I had a meeting with the magistrate."

Hewitt scowled. "You should have scheduled it for a different time. You lived in the same house as Evylin for the past three days. You had to notice she was never awake as early as you."

"I don't see what this has to do with my job. If I had it my way, I would have stayed with her all day. But it isn't exactly like we're on our honeymoon here. I'm an officer with an assignment."

A sound far too much like a growl came from the beast of a man. "Evylin is your wife. *She* is your assignment now. Her happiness is your job, and you abandoned her."

"I don't see why you're concerned about her happiness," Deckard said, the image of Evylin laughing as Thom whispered in her ear vivid in his memory. "Seems you had no trouble cheering her right up without any help from me."

Hewitt scowled, but Deckard didn't relish being scolded by the protective old watchdog. "Do go back to camp, Major. You have your own assignments to worry about."

Deckard didn't give Hewitt the time to respond. He made a sharp about-face, marched up the steps, and pushed into the house, leaving the man on the street. Serene and Jorge greeted him as friendly as ever, but Evylin only smiled politely before returning to her meal.

Taking the open seat at her side, Deckard accepted the plate Serene set before him as she leaped back into whatever conversation she'd been carrying on before his entrance. He didn't mind the woman's nonsensical chatter. It offered him a distraction as he ate and ignored the discomfort between him and his wife.

The whole day, Deckard had worried about showing his intention to care for Evylin and make her happy. Now, he realized it was all for nothing. She didn't need him to take care of her. Nor did she want him to. She had her uncle at her side, and there was no place for any other man. Not while the two of them clung to their past with such ferocity.

Very well, Deckard decided. If Evylin didn't want him, he wouldn't force himself on her. If leaving her to her independent ways would make her happy, then so be it.

When there was a break in Serene's chatter, Evylin took the opportunity to excuse herself. Deckard rose with her and walked her to the stairs. She started up without a word and only paused when he called her name. When she turned back, her expression showing surprise at finding him at the bottom of the staircase, he kept his voice low to ensure the Loores wouldn't overhear.

"I wanted to let you know I'm returning to camp," he said courteously.

Evylin stepped back down. Her brow was furrowed with either pure confusion or a tinge of disappointment. He hoped it was the first, not intending to hurt her but rather to give her the space she desired.

"I'm sorry," he continued. "I hate to leave you, but I need to prepare for my speech tomorrow and complete a few tasks I left unfinished."

Evylin considered him briefly before whispering, "Tell me—" Her lips lifted wryly. "Do you always stay out late and get up early?"

Deckard returned the grin, thankful she wasn't angry with him. "More often than not."

"How do you survive on such little sleep?"

"I manage."

Evylin stared at him, evidently unsure what to say.

Hoping to make their parting easier for her, Deckard dipped his head in a bow. "I'll be back quite late. Please don't wait up."

Her eyes grew a fraction wider. "You're sure?"

"I am."

"Oh."

Deckard forced his smile to remain. "Have a good night, Evylin."

"You, too, Jonn."

Taking the initiative, Deckard turned his back to her and headed out the front door once more. The crisp night air stung after so long in such a cozy space. He rushed headlong toward the camp in an attempt to forget how nice it would have been to spend the evening in the warmth of the home and Evylin's charming presence. Even after the discomfort that had surfaced between them, she seemed ready and willing to spend the rest of the evening with him. But he'd chosen to abandon her once again.

Looking up at the two moons orbiting Terraeus, Deckard fought the guilt for doing precisely what Hewitt had accused. The brighter ivory moon glittered at him with a pearlescent shine, more than three-quarters full as it began its waning descent. The smaller, shadow moon hung suspended as a waxing deep gray, always a duller glow in the distance.

Deckard ran a hand along the fresh stubble that rose on his jaw. No matter the guilt he felt, he hadn't lied; he did have work to do. He was determined to spend at least two hours running through his speech, working out what recruits were possible from the upcoming settlements, and making plans to integrate Hewitt into the training regime.

But in the back of his mind, Deckard fought the urge to forget his duties and return to his wife. He felt the little velvet bag in his coat pocket pressing into his abdomen. He wanted to turn back and offer the gift as an apology for leaving her. He wanted to give her his heartfelt promise to be a dedicated husband.

Yet, after a long day of unwelcome revelations, Deckard felt certain the gift would do more harm than good. He feared she would see it as an attempt to usurp Hewitt's importance, taking the symbol of their future as an assertion of his will.

So Deckard shoved down his guilt with the assurance that if Evylin had spent the day perfectly happy without him, then she'd remain perfectly happy without him now.

CHAPTER TWENTY

15TH OF TERRAEN, 1573

On the second morning of their marriage, Evylin awoke to a note rather than her husband once more. This time, it awaited her on his empty pillow and was more letter-like in composition. Considering his impending speech in the town square, he had much to do to prepare, the note said, and while the task of recruiting soldiers would keep him from her the entirety of the day, he would be sure to keep an eye out for her in the crowd.

Torn between annoyance and guilt, Evylin stared at the sweeping flourish at the bottom of the note: *"Yours, Jonn."*

Such a lovely sentiment, yet if he was really *hers*, why wasn't he there with her? Why hadn't he chosen to stay last night?

Why did it matter?

Evylin dropped the note back on the pillow and scrambled out of bed. She shouldn't care if Deckard lived his life separate from her. He was treating their marriage as what it was: a convention of convenience. He wasn't beholden to her any more than she was to him. They'd married to secure his job and her freedom. It was wrong of her to harbor any expectation that he'd abandon his work to keep her company. It would be selfish of her to ask him to do so.

But as she looked over to Deckard's side of the room—tidy and barren, with only his trunk as a sign he'd ever been there at all—Evylin couldn't help her disappointment and worry.

The concern welled up, exacerbated by her conversation with Hewitt on the return from the tavern last night. Rather than his usual quiet companionship, he'd begun to berate her when he reached her side.

"You shouldn't have mocked him like that, Evie," Hewitt said, his voice a low growl.

Evylin gaped up at him. "It was only a joke," she insisted quietly. "He understands my sense of humor."

Hewitt's voice dipped deeper. "Whether you like it or not, he's your husband now. Make sure you act like it."

"What are you talking about?"

"This is your life, Evie," he replied roughly. "You're stuck with him. And he's the one who decides your future. If you ridicule and embarrass him, he won't be so likely to make your life easy."

Glancing over her shoulder, Evylin chanced a look at Deckard. He walked at a respectful distance from the pair of them, a pleasant expression on his face when he noticed her gaze. She turned back to Hewitt. "I don't understand," she whispered back. "I thought he might like to join us. How is that a problem?"

"He's your bloody husband," Hewitt spat. "The man you're supposed to be so in love with, you couldn't wait to marry him after only three days. And tonight, you treated him with the same regard you show his brother."

"So what? We *aren't* in love. He knows it as well as you, Thom, and I. Who cares if we don't act like it?"

"*He'll* care. You heard his brother. Appearance is everything to him. And rather than welcoming him with open arms, you made him look like a fool in front of dozens of his men."

Evylin stared up at her uncle, wondering if he was right. She hadn't thought about the way her teasing could come across. She was inexperienced in romance, and it never crossed her mind to treat Deckard differently than before their marriage.

"You tricked him into marriage, Evie—"

"That was your doing," she reminded firmly.

"I did it for *you*," he returned. "And he knows that. He's lost his future to you. And that sort of loss can quickly turn to resentment. A piece of advice from a man who very much enjoyed his marriage: You'll only be happy so long as you are *both* happy."

With his words still ringing in her ears with the morning light, Evylin clasped her hands, her metal wedding band biting into her finger. The admonishment caused her to question every interaction she'd had with the captain thus far. Had she really embarrassed him in the tavern? Did he not appreciate her sense of humor as she thought? Could she even make him happy? She'd yet to consider that, but now it seemed woefully self-absorbed of her not to.

Heeding her uncle's advice, Evylin had intended to apologize to Deckard last evening. She couldn't risk earning his resentment. No matter how strange their arrangement, they'd chosen to entwine their lives. And while she intended to pursue her and Ryen's dreams foremost, she found she also wanted to provide Deckard with happiness as he'd so generously promised it to her.

But then he'd left.

Evylin had waited for his return as long as she could without completely ignoring his directive. Finally, she'd set aside her novel, turned down the lamp, and drifted off in a matter of minutes. If not for his note, Evylin never would have known that Deckard had returned. She didn't wake in the night, and his side of the bed was still without a wrinkle. It was as though she had no husband at all.

Evylin stared at the room in the morning glow. There was no use questioning her choices now. They were married, and even if they *could* technically call it off, she wouldn't return to Whickam Village. She wouldn't give up on their dream—she wouldn't let it die too.

If making Deckard happy meant leaving him to the demands of his job and attending every speech in every settlement along the way, she supposed that was what she'd do. She'd accept it if their friendship stayed distant and mild. But if it eventually meant something more . . . something uncomfortably intimate . . . well, she'd chosen marriage. It was only fair that she accepted everything that came with it, no matter how much she feared it.

The morning wore on slowly for Evylin. With Hewitt settling into his new role as major at the camp, she was alone with Serene until Nelle and Nixon visited. Her cousin was like her mother—frizzy brown curls, toothy smiles, and abundant enthusiasm. While Evylin never cared much for their constant chatter, today, she found it a welcome distraction from her unsteady thoughts.

Deckard's speech meant a long break from the workday at a late morning hour, and Jorge swung by to escort the four of them to the town square. As the only area within Trollenston large enough for a crowd to gather, the citizens packed into its building-cramped center.

Though used to the crowded market, it was unlike any gathering she'd ever attended. More and more townspeople arrived, forcing the stragglers to remain on the outskirts of the square, drifting down the dirt streets in search of a view. People pressed in on all sides as they stood near the makeshift stage, which was just large enough to hold the magistrate and captain.

From a distance, Evylin watched Deckard speak with Magistrate Steevensun. Or rather, the verbose magistrate was speaking while Deckard listened. Smiling encouragingly at the old man, Deckard was undoubtedly playing him like a fiddle with his impeccable manners and charisma.

Serene and Nelle giggled at Deckard's fine appearance, and Evylin couldn't help her prideful grin. The elegance of his formal uniform and the confident lift of his imperious stature would sweep every woman in Trollenston off her feet—unattached or otherwise. While he wasn't excessively or strikingly handsome, his velvet coat made him even more noble and charming than usual. And once he spoke in that refined manner of his, it would be all over.

Playing with the button of her coat, Evylin chuckled silently to herself. Of all the men who'd come and gone from Trollenston, she was pleased to know her captain surpassed them all.

Magistrate Steevensun stepped forward to hush the crowd. He gave a meandering introduction that rambled on for far too long before finally getting to the point. "I urge you all," he said, wispy white hair blowing in the breeze, "mark the captain's words. The king sent him to us, and it is our duty to listen."

With that, Magistrate Steevensun stepped back and bowed to Deckard.

Taking two long strides, Deckard reached the edge of the stage to look out over the crowd. Their numbers—while still mostly female—greatly outnumbered the populace of Whickam Village. Though there were still only a few men, the odds were higher, and Evylin hoped it would make up for what he'd lost in her village.

As Deckard scanned the people, Evylin stood straighter, wondering if he could see her. But his gaze never turned in her direction.

"Ladies and gentlemen," Deckard began, his warm, rich voice filling the square, "it is my privilege and duty to extend the gratitude of our sovereign King Ephren for your diligence and fortitude. Our king knows that you are the backbone of this country. The very lifeblood that keeps it running. Without you . . ." He paused for effect. "Our kingdom would fall."

While Jorge and Serene exchanged an approving glance, Evylin's brow drew low. He'd used the same introduction with the exact same inflection in Whickam Village. She supposed it made sense. Why alter something so simple as an introduction to a speech? But it didn't strike her as impactful upon hearing it a second time.

However, she shifted in the press of the crowd and listened on.

"My speech will be short, I assure you," Deckard said with a smile. "Our king sent me to you for one important purpose: to *ask* for your help once more."

The same tension she'd felt in the village crept in amongst the townspeople as Deckard continued, "Our king feels your hesitation and concern. He has not sent me here to *take* from you. Not again. Why has he sent us, then?" He rested a hand on the pommel of his sword, and she remembered the repeated action from last time.

"Because he needs you," he said emphatically. "You know our war and our cause; I won't waste your time with the age-old story. We've fought for almost two centuries—that is not a fact any one of us can forget."

Pressing her lips together in a disenchanted smirk, Evylin crossed her arms. It was the same speech. No less eloquent or well-spoken. But somehow less impressive, knowing he'd run the lines so many times that they were now rote, like a bard performing a play.

Evylin let her mind wander for the rest of the speech, ignoring the crowd's favorable reaction. The people around her muttered with approval and humor at his mention of the old legends and "The King's Knight." And while she kept her eyes on the well-trimmed and dashing form of Captain Deckard, she didn't hear another word.

Working a button in and out of its loop, Evylin tipped her head to the side as she inspected Deckard. *Who is he,* she wondered. There were three opposing versions of the man from her experience: the charming gentleman, the legend seeker, and the ambitious captain.

Hewitt insisted that Deckard was striving for the worth of a legend; his desire to impress meant he would settle for nothing less than greatness. A theory that Thom's appraisal supported. However, the lieutenant's opinion wasn't quite as favorable. He presented this ambition as far less magnanimous and servant-hearted than it came across, implying that the captain was an actor—a manipulator who could play anyone to his ends.

And Evylin didn't know who was right.

"Help us be the generation who ends it." Deckard's voice rang through the silent town square, drawing Evylin back to the present. Her gaze returned to his face, seeing the genuine smile softening his expression. "Help us make the difference."

Evylin sucked on her lip, teeth tugging on the edge. He spoke with such sincerity. And yet, the repetitious refrain didn't sound as sincere the second time. Or was that just the voice of Thom in the back of her head?

Deckard's bright eyes drifted from person to person in the crowd. He opened his mouth to continue his speech but paused when his eyes flickered back—back to Evylin.

Surprised he'd found her in a crowd of so many, Evylin fumbled with her button as Deckard's mouth turned up in delight, eliciting a shy smile of her own. His eyes crinkled at the edges, and it felt, for all the world, like he was genuinely thrilled to see her there. As though she were more than just a strange woman tied to him because of a lost bet but was, instead, the woman whose company he prized over all others.

Someone in the crowd coughed, and Deckard blinked, breaking their connection.

Evylin continued to play with the button on her coat as Deckard concluded his speech. "I will be here until sundown," he said, attention going back to the general populace. "I'd love nothing more than to speak with any of you and answer whatever questions you may have." Then he bowed and turned to Magistrate Steevensun, letting the old man take charge once more.

As the magistrate took his merry time dismissing the crowd, Evylin watched Deckard descend the stage's short steps. Since he stood over normal height, she could see him above the Shire men and women. He moved to stand at Lieutenant Peery's side, the top of his dark hair all she could see of the officer.

Back to chewing on her lip, Evylin frowned, the question repeating: Who was this captain? She had no fear that he was a *bad* man. He would not be cruel, harsh, or even unkind; of that, she was confident. But what would he require of her as a wife?

A man with ambition—with a desire to present himself as perfect—would certainly have high standards for every area of his life. And what would that mean for her? If he wanted perfection, could she meet his wifely expectations? And what if she didn't? She'd married him to fulfill her promise to Ryen, to see their dreams come to life. What if Deckard didn't approve of all that would entail?

The wooden button slipped again through Evylin's fingers, undone in its loop. She couldn't let go of that promise. No matter what.

Therefore, she had to ensure he didn't ask it of her.

Hewitt told her to secure Deckard's happiness. He was an ambitious man. How better to make him happy than to assure him of his freedom? She didn't need to rely on him. He could focus on his work as a captain unencumbered by her presence. There was no need to worry about lost futures or growing resentment. Life could be exactly what it was before.

Now, Evylin just needed to convince Deckard of that.

CHAPTER TWENTY-ONE

Stepping off the stage, Deckard fought to quell the lingering sense of distraction. As he'd concluded his speech, he made sure to meet the eyes of several young men within the town center, hoping to impress the weight of his message upon them. But as his gaze swept back to the front, he caught sight of a brunette woman standing next to a bald, middle-aged man and a frizzy-haired woman. An immediate jolt crashed through his chest, and his eyes flew back to her.

She was there.

Deckard held Evylin's gaze, smile growing. He knew it was foolish, the way his heart kicked up to patter like a schoolboy's at the sight of her. But after leaving her, all bundled and cozy in their bed that morning, he'd felt the deepest regret. And it thrilled him to see her again—even at a distance.

But as Peery gave his usual, "Excellent job, Deckard," he forced himself not to think about his wife. He had work to do and a promise to keep to himself.

After several minutes, the magistrate ended his discourse and released the crowd. They milled about, their chatter growing to a loud hum. Time ticked slowly after his speech. No one wanted to be the first to step forward, and sometimes, no one wanted to be there at all.

Deckard had to keep reminding himself as he scanned the crowd, not to look for Evylin. She wasn't his goal. She wasn't why he was here.

A young man approached Deckard and the three soldiers with him. The town man's shaggy brown hair hung low, sweeping over thick brows and dark eyes. He wore a leather vest and a stained tunic, and most of the townspeople watched him with notable disdain.

He held his chin dipped and his shoulders slumped, but his broad, muscular build displayed a solid wall of strength.

"I'd like to volunteer," the young man said, voice low, though it wasn't as deep as Deckard expected, betraying his youth.

Deckard kept his welcome subdued to match his manner. "It'd be our honor to have you. What's your name?"

Lieutenant Peery balanced the ledger in his arms as Sergeant Stewert handed him a freshly inked pen.

The young man's eyes darted between them before responding, "Ethenn Loxley."

Deckard offered his hand. "It's a pleasure to have you with us, Private Loxley. Lieutenant Peery will take your information, answer any questions you have, and give you an assignment as a member of the Third Volunteer Company in the Ephrian Army."

The young man let go of Deckard's hand and moved to speak with the other officers as three more men walked up behind him. This group seemed far more enthusiastic, so Deckard adjusted accordingly.

After hours of talking with men of all ages, the crowd was gone, and the night sky sparkled with stars. The magistrate was thoughtful enough to send them lunch, but Deckard had been too busy to eat. Thom stopped by at the end of the evening to report and look over the numbers. As the recruits were to report to camp first thing in the morning, the officers were alone in the square.

"Thirteen," Peery noted, looking up from the ledger. "That puts us at—"

"Two hundred forty-eight," Deckard calculated readily.

"Not bad," Thom commented.

"Mm." The Shires bred hearty men; they'd all make good soldiers. But thirteen wasn't enough to cover his losses.

Placing a hand on Deckard's shoulder, Thom pierced him with his sharp gaze. "It's a good number, Deckard."

"It's not enough."

"We'll make it up. We still have so far to go."

Deckard held back his concern. At the beginning of the day, fifteen seemed to be his magic number. Fifteen settlements left, fifteen men short, and an average of fifteen men needed to make the cut. With one settlement removed from the list, that number changed.

Fourteen settlements, seventeen men short, and an average of eighteen on each stop.

His odds were growing worse.

But then, Thom was right. Thirteen was only two short of his original need. He could make that up in one stop easily.

Thom, Peery, Fisher, and Stewert returned to camp, and Deckard went to the Loores'.

He put his hands in his pockets to avoid the cold wind. His fingers caught on the velvet bag. An anticipatory tremble shot through him. Then his gut went hollow with dread.

This was only their second day of marriage, and Deckard had yet to speak to his wife.

What a pitiful excuse for a husband he was. Hewitt was right. He was forsaking his duty in the name of his job. He was protecting his heart while excusing his avoidance of her.

No more.

Deckard entered the Loore residence, its warm hearth beating back the cold. The scent of tea and dinner mingled invitingly. The moment he rounded the corner, Serene leaped up to prepare a plate.

"Hurry, get your fill," she demanded. "We've already had our dinner. You poor man, you must be starving. Evie, get your husband an ale. After the long day he's had, he needs it, I'm sure."

At the table, Evylin rose, but Deckard held up a hand. "No, please," he assured her. "I'll just have tea."

Evylin hesitated, her eyes meeting his as he approached. He fought his rising heartbeat but offered her a smile anyway.

"Nonsense," Serene said, then waved at her niece. "Go on, Evie."

Though Deckard had no taste for ale, neither did he care to fight the woman's hospitality. Evylin backed away from the table as he moved for the seat beside hers. But when she rounded to pass him, he caught her hand, pulling her to a stop.

Evylin stared up at him, wide-eyed.

Having surprised himself by the gesture, Deckard's smile turned crooked. "Hello," he whispered.

"Hello," Evylin returned softly.

Standing so close to her, their arms pressed together as his fingers enclosed her hand, Deckard realized his heart had kicked back up. Knowing it was foolish to encourage his infatuation, he let her go and took his seat while she disappeared into the kitchen.

"Deckard, my friend," Jorge said, his voice booming as Serene handed Deckard an overfilled plate, "you gave the most rousing speech! You missed your calling as a magistrate, I think." The man lifted his tankard. "Evie, bring me another ale too."

"I thank you for the honor you pay me, sir," Deckard said politely. "But I feel Allore has not called me to that purpose."

Evylin returned, her wool skirt swishing gently. She wore a simple dark gray skirt and a white blouse under a brown cardigan that nearly matched the color of her hair. Gentle waves framed her face, pulling free of the well-worn, light blue ribbon. He liked how soft and feminine her hair was—a pleasant contrast to the fierce and powerful woman herself.

Immediately, Deckard admonished himself for those thoughts.

Evylin plunked a tankard down for her uncle. Then she joined Deckard, placing a matching tankard before him.

"Thank you," he said as she took her seat.

Evylin set her hand on his arm, and his breath caught as she leaned close. "It's not ale," she whispered.

Unnerved by her nearness, Deckard glanced at the Loores.

Jorge was busying himself with a swig of his . . . well, Deckard assumed his *was* ale. And Serene was pretending to absorb herself by refilling her cup of tea. Her wry smile betrayed her amusement at the presumed sweet affections of the couple.

Taking advantage of their polite distractions, Deckard angled toward Evylin. "What is it, then?" he whispered back.

She patted his forearm, then replied, "Water."

An amused scoff escaped Deckard. "Is there a particular reason you're keeping me sober?"

"You're the one who didn't want ale."

Recognizing her kindness through her sarcasm, Deckard gave himself permission to brush his knuckles against the back of her hand. "Thank you."

She nodded, pulling away to lift her half-empty teacup.

With their private conversation ended, Mr. Loore returned to his praises. "How you can speak in front of a crowd like that is baffling," he pronounced.

Serene beamed. "And how eloquently you speak."

"Steevensun should take note," Jorge added, wagging a finger at Deckard. "Listening to him after you was a chore."

"You're both too kind," Deckard said between bites. "And I can't thank you enough. For your compliments or your hospitality."

Serene began telling Evylin how lucky she was to have snagged Deckard. She went on to gossip about the young women in town who weren't so fortunate in obtaining husbands of good character. That led her to discuss the women who hadn't found husbands at all. Few of them got a word in from that point on, but Evylin did manage a handful of witty comments that made Deckard laugh.

In the prolonged chatter, Deckard noticed Evylin cover a yawn with the back of her hand. He took the excuse to bid the Loores goodnight. He moved to clear his things from the table, but Serene slapped his hands and insisted he leave it for her. Ready to be out of his uniform, Deckard thanked her again and moved on without argument.

Evylin followed him upstairs, and he held the bedroom door for her. She gave him a polite smile before crouching beside her trunk. Thanks to her attentions at dinner, Deckard teetered on the edge of hope and uncertainty as he shut the door behind him.

"Did you have a good day?" he asked, undoing his coat buttons.

Evylin tossed a look over her shoulder. "Yes, I did."

"What did you do?"

She continued digging through the slapdash items. "I spent the day with Serene and her family." She swiveled to look at him, and a dry tilt lifted her grin. "You missed meeting Nelle and her husband. Much to your dismay, I'm sure."

Deckard smiled. "I am quite sorry," he said, folding his coat before carefully packing it into his trunk for the next leg of their journey, "as it was a missed opportunity to learn more about you."

Evylin huffed. "If you want to learn about me, it's not them you should ask."

Though there was levity in her tone, Deckard paused. In every joke, there was a hidden truth. And he couldn't tell whether she was insinuating he should ask her or if she didn't want him asking in the first place.

Deckard loosened the knot of his cravat. "Well, I would ask Hewitt, but I'm not sure he'd answer me."

Evylin's laugh was restorative. "No, I don't think he would."

"Shall I ask you, then?" he prodded.

Dark eyes rising to meet his, Evylin smirked. "I can't promise you'll like the answers."

Deckard slipped the silk tie from around his neck, his next words tumbling out before he knew what he was saying. "Well, that's what I like best about you."

Evylin paused. "What is?"

The soft fabric of the cravat slipped through Deckard's fingers as he tried to formulate a response. He was venturing into dangerous territory. Conversations like these could lead to truths he wasn't ready to divulge. Truths that might make her uncomfortable with his presence.

He let out a nervous chuckle. "Your honesty," he concluded. "I like that you tell the truth, no matter what the person wants to hear. That's why I asked for your opinion about the town and the odds of finding volunteers. You're honest. And that's a rare commodity these days."

A lighthearted twinkle lit her eyes. "I'm flattered."

Sensing the danger had passed, Deckard relaxed. "I am curious," he continued, tucking the cravat into his box of ties, "to hear your opinion once more. If you're willing to give it."

"How might I help, Captain?"

Deckard grinned brighter at her teasing manner. "I wanted to ask you in Whickam Village," he explained, "but I didn't get the chance."

"It must be awfully important if you've been waiting so long."

"Not important, no. Just a valued opinion."

Rising from her trunk, Evylin dropped a bundle of clothes onto the bed before taking a seat next to it. The twinkle in her eyes reminded him that she was ever teasing, even in her honesty. She'd give him the truth, no matter what, and there would be an edge of humor woven through it as well. "And what opinion do you seek, Captain Deckard?"

The way her dark eyes latched onto him, so full of laughter and attention, made Deckard freeze. He liked her. Far too much.

Clearing his throat, Deckard hoped his expression didn't give away the truth. "It isn't often that I'm given the chance to ask," he began. "People often give their opinion unsolicited, and it's always in empty adulation. But I'm curious to know, from someone who won't perjure themselves to flatter me: What do you think of my speech?"

The instant dip in Evylin's smile was a kick to Deckard's gut he hadn't expected.

"Ah," he muttered, dropping her hesitant gaze.

"I didn't say anything," Evylin noted.

Deckard gave her an absolving nod. "That's all right, you . . . I understood."

"Understood what?" She crossed her arms. "You asked for my opinion, and I haven't given it to you yet."

Deckard shifted from foot to foot. "What do you think, then?"

Evylin tucked some of her dark waves behind her ear. "I liked it in Whickam Village. As my aunt said, you are quite eloquent. And I did feel it was inspiring."

Deckard opened his mouth to thank her. Then her words sank in. "You liked it in Whickam Village?" he asked.

"Yes," she confirmed.

"But you didn't like it here?"

She hesitated, then sighed. "No, I didn't."

"It's the same speech."

"Exactly."

Deckard frowned. "What's wrong with that?"

Evylin's nose scrunched in irritation. "You do remember asking for my *honest* opinion, don't you?"

"Yes, of course."

"Then don't get cross with me when I give it."

"I'm not . . ." Deckard sighed and started over. "I'm sorry, I just don't understand. You said you liked it in your village, but now you don't. Why not?"

"Do you mean it?" she asked flatly. "Your speech, your story. Do you mean it?"

Taken aback, Deckard tried to keep a cool head. "Of course, I mean it. Why would you think I didn't?"

"Because it's the *exact* same speech," Evylin concluded. "The same actions, the same pauses, the same everything. It doesn't ring as sincere the second time you hear it."

Deckard didn't know what to say. He'd worked on his speech for months. It was the only thing that made him confident he could convince men to join the army. Not because it would cajole, trick, or pressure anyone into service but because it *was* sincere. He'd taken a piece of his life and offered it to the public.

And she thought it insincere?

Deckard took a deep breath to quell his embarrassment and indignation. "I appreciate your criticism. And I'll take it under advisement."

Evylin smirked, her fallback to humor grating. "Is my honesty still what you like best about me?"

"Don't do that," he retorted unthinkingly.

"Do what?"

"Don't make a joke out of—" Deckard frowned, realizing the moment for what it was: their first fight.

Disheartened, he ran a hand over his face and looked up to see Evylin's confused expression. "I'm sorry," he hastened to say. "You're right. I asked for your honest opinion, and I can't be upset you gave just that."

Evylin eyed him as though she was unsure of his sincerity even now.

Taking a seat on the far side of the bed, Deckard leaned toward her. "Thank you," he said earnestly. "And yes. It is still what I like best about you."

Dipping her chin, Evylin's expression remained guarded.

With an internal sigh, Deckard worried he'd damaged their already tenuous relationship. He wasn't sure how to fix it. So he defaulted to her preferred fallback, gently nudging her elbow. "Perhaps I just like you a little less now."

Two seconds passed, during which Deckard thought he'd made a horrible mistake, before Evylin's laugh cut through the tension. Her eyes twinkled in the low lamplight. "What an ungentlemanly thing to say," she teased. "I do believe you're not the same man I met in Whickam Village."

"I'm most certainly not," he replied, smiling.

"Oh?"

"I'm married now."

Her laughter gave Deckard the most unsettling sense of joy—as though he was indulging himself in some secret vice. But her infectious good humor filled his chest like a heady wine, heating him from the inside out as the rest of his senses dulled.

Forcing himself back to sanity, Deckard gestured to the pile of clothes she'd dropped on the bed. "Would you like me to step out so you can change?" he asked.

A light flush colored her temples. "Oh, no, that's—that's fine. I'll just . . . it would be faster if you changed facing that way, and I changed this way."

Watching her hand flick from one side of the room to the other, Deckard found her embarrassment amusing. "That's very practical of you," he noted.

"That's what happens when you have a general for an uncle."

"That," Deckard said, sitting up straighter, "I can relate to."

"You have an uncle who's a general?"

"No. I've just been a soldier long enough that my officers ruthlessly hammered efficiency into me."

"I see," she said, gathering her bedclothes.

At the cue, Deckard turned away. The room was silent as they prepared for bed. He tried not to listen too closely to her movements—eliciting inappropriate imaginations—and focused on his own tasks. He took extra time, packing his trunk with care. The army would leave the following day, and he hoped to be out of the house early once more.

"I've changed," Evylin said, her trunk lid banging shut.

Deckard gave a mute nod, focused on removing the silver captain's insignia from his velvet coat.

"Are . . . are you mad at me?"

Caught off guard, Deckard pricked his finger on the insignia's pin and grimaced. He rushed to return it to its box and then turned. Evylin stood in her nightdress, the brown cardigan wrapped around her for modesty. He realized as she worried her bottom lip that she was genuinely concerned.

Deckard hurried to rise, but she continued before he could get a word out. "I didn't mean to offend you. You said you wanted my honesty, and I didn't think—"

"Evylin," he interrupted, shaking his head vehemently, "I'm not offended. I've forgotten it already."

"But I didn't realize how important it was to you, and now I feel like I've hurt your feelings or . . . or made you upset."

Deckard couldn't help his fond smile at her concern. "You haven't made me upset, I promise." He stepped closer to the bed, hoping to assure her with his candor. "I will admit, it is concerning. It makes me wonder if my officers have been lying to me." He held her gaze as reassuringly as he could. "But I'm glad you told me the truth. It means I can consider how I might improve."

Evylin continued to chew on her bottom lip. "Only if you're sure."

"I'm sure," he insisted.

She nodded, accepting his confirmation.

Deckard motioned to the bed between them. "Shall we go to sleep?"

He let her get into bed first, making sure she was comfortable and her modesty placated before he joined her. It was odd to him, sleeping next to a woman. He liked it, although it wasn't much like he'd imagined. His fellow soldiers often mocked him for his propriety—even Thom teased him regularly—but he'd always held high expectations when it came to the world of romance. And he'd never felt that loneliness was a just reason to abandon his scruples.

Evylin carefully slipped her cardigan off under the blankets before dropping it to the floor. A bemused laugh escaped him, and she frowned. "What?" she demanded.

Deckard turned to stare up at the ceiling, the plaster swirls yellowing in the corners. "Nothing," he whispered. "Just marveling at how I got here."

The long beat of silence from Evylin's side of the bed drew his gaze back to her. She lay on her side, facing him, though near the mattress's edge so they weren't touching. Her dark eyes were locked on the sheet beneath her.

Realizing how his words may have sounded, Deckard shifted to face her. "Evylin?"

"Hm?" she murmured, eyes still cast down.

Deckard cautiously brushed a single strand of her soft brown hair off her cheek. "I've been thinking a lot these past two days," he said. "And I feel like I should apologize."

Her dark gaze lifted then.

"My job is . . . well, it's demanding, and it takes a lot of my time. But it isn't fair of me to leave you so often."

Evylin shook her head, almost in a panic. "It's all right," she insisted. "I understand you have work to do."

"Work or not, I'm still your husband."

She started chewing on her bottom lip.

He grinned at the nervous habit. "And I'm not blind to the fact that this is not part of your dream—that *I'm* not part of it."

Her eyes darted between both of his.

"But now that I'm here, I want you to know I intend to do whatever I can to make it everything you imagined."

Evylin frowned, and Deckard hoped he hadn't upset her. He didn't want to reveal too much or scare her with his feelings. Nor did he want to anger her by presuming he *could* help bring her dream to life.

But then she sighed. "I'm sorry too," she whispered.

"For what?" he asked, genuinely confused.

"For this whole mess. I didn't . . ." She turned to lie on her back. "I didn't think it would be this hard."

Uncertain, Deckard asked lightly, "Am I that difficult?"

"No," she said, looking over at him. "No, you're not. It's just . . . I didn't think about this part. About learning how to live together."

A sober smile tugged at Deckard's lips. "It *is* a bit strange, isn't it?"

Evylin's expression turned adamant. "But I don't want you feeling obligated to me, Jonn. Married or not, it doesn't have to change who we are."

Deckard wasn't sure he liked the sound of that.

"You can focus on your work and know I don't mind," she said. "There's no need to worry about making my dreams come true. You've already helped me get them. So don't worry—I won't make demands of you. Your life doesn't have to change. We'll live as we did before. The only difference is the fact we share a name now."

And a bed, Deckard thought bitterly but kept his mouth shut.

So that was it. That was all she wanted from him: a name that would grant her the chance to travel and be free.

"All right," Deckard said despite the disappointment that ripped through his stomach. "If that will make you happy. . . ."

"I've told you," she said in an encouraging tone, "I'm not like my sisters. I don't need a man always at my side to make me happy. And I won't stand in the way of your career."

Right, he thought. His career. That was why he'd agreed to this, wasn't it? The pursuit of making a difference in this world.

"All right," Deckard whispered again.

But it wasn't "all right."

Holding Evylin's dark gaze as the dimples appeared on each cheek, Deckard realized it wasn't "all right" at all.

He hadn't married her for his career; he'd married her because he liked her and saw the chance to become something important to her.

Thom had been right—Deckard wasn't foolish enough to believe that Hewitt would convince General Rand to excuse his lack of men. He knew there was little chance of his success at all. He'd agreed to marry Evylin because he wanted the chance to make her happy, to be the man who changed her life and gave her everything she ever wanted.

It was the most foolhardy thing he'd ever done.

Evylin didn't need him to change her life. She didn't even want him to be part of it. And he'd risked everything on the whim of a fleeting fancy.

Attraction—that was what had convinced him. The romantic notion that after thirty-two years of unrealistic expectations, he'd finally found the perfect woman: stunning, intelligent, and strong. A woman with ambition and wit, one who was as idealistic as he. She was impossible, a woman unlike any other. And she was practically handed to him.

The shadows of the dimly lit room taunted Deckard while he stared at the ceiling. Blinded by the allure of his own fantastic ideals, he'd let Hewitt dupe him into marriage with a woman who wanted nothing to do with him. It was pure idiocy.

Deckard doused the oil lamp, hoping the darkness would usher in sleep. But nothing could distract him from his rotating thoughts. Not when he'd realized what a witless mistake he'd made.

CHAPTER TWENTY-TWO

16TH OF TERRAEN, 1573

Rising the next morning felt like treading in the ocean, fighting to keep his head above the waves of sleep that threatened to hold him under. The mattress cushioned Deckard, and the blankets hugged him in their warmth. With the icy chill of the morning air, he knew he'd be riddled with gooseflesh and shivers the second he abandoned the bed—an altogether unwelcome sensation. And whether she knew it or not, Evylin had pressed against his back again, intensifying the temptation to stay.

Listening to her steady, deep breaths, he envied the weight of her sleep. Even when he was a child, he'd roused at the lightest sound or movement. He'd never experienced such a pleasure as her heavy rest.

But, while Deckard would have liked to linger in the comfort of their bed, he forced himself off the mattress and into action. After their conversation last night, he knew better than to languish in temptation. He had work to do, and his wife had given him full permission to ignore her in its favor.

Dressed in his gray and black travel uniform, Deckard ensured his things were prepared for the trip ahead, then wrote a hasty note to excuse his absence. Evylin's slow, tranquil breaths taunted him as he moved about the room as silently as he could manage. He took a final look at her sleeping form, hidden under the blankets. Only her dark brown hair peeked out, splayed over the pillow.

Deckard wanted to wake her and say goodbye. He knew what a travel day was like, constantly shifting and riding to check on the different platoons. It would take a day and a half to reach Berkley, the last settlement in Estshire. And in that time, he would have little choice but to ignore his wife in favor of his work, whether she'd approved of it or not.

Instead of giving into his guilty conscience, Deckard shut the door without a sound, descended the stairs to accept the waiting Serene's final bits of hospitality, and left the Loore home after offering his manifold gratitude.

The rest of the morning passed in a blur. Deckard ran through his exercises and trained with Thom, going out of their way to find a place to practice in private. After, they returned to camp to meet with their fellow officers. Hewitt was there for the meeting. For the first time, he didn't glare at Deckard. Instead, he stared attentively; he was a soldier waiting for his orders.

Knowing what Hewitt was capable of, Deckard set him as head over all the training, much to the chagrin of Major Moris, the original head officer. The pudgy man scowled at Deckard, insulted by the newcomer's sudden promotion. Deckard didn't care much about the man's squabbles. He'd done a poor job training the recruits. The only reason Deckard had chosen him for the assignment in the first place was due to his friendship with General Rand. Looking back now, he knew it was a mistake. And he was ready to rectify that, no matter what sort of trouble it got him in later.

After dismissing the officers, Hewitt requested a moment alone. Prepared for another diatribe, Deckard braced himself.

"Did I understand you correctly?" Hewitt asked, gaze hard as iron. "You're putting me in charge of *all* the training?"

"Yes," Deckard confirmed. "I want you to do whatever you think will teach these men how to be as good a fighter as you. As good a fighter as Evylin."

His eyes narrowed. "Do I have your permission to do *whatever* will achieve that goal?"

Deckard heard the unspoken suggestion within the question. "You have some idea I'll be uncomfortable with, don't you?"

"I have no way of knowing what sorts of things you're comfortable with, Captain."

"What is it you want to do?"

"I want Evylin to assist me."

Deckard lifted his brow. "You can't be serious."

"I am."

"No."

"Why not?" Hewitt asked, surprising Deckard with his docility. He expected the man to demand his way. Instead, Hewitt approached the subject with an abnormal calm. "You said you want the men to fight as well as her. I can best teach that by showing them what they need to do. And I can guarantee that she handles the sword better than anyone in this camp—after myself, of course."

Deckard held up his hand to halt the argument. "I'm aware of that. And I'm not denying that you're right. But it won't go well. The very thought will appall Major Moris, and Major Sheelds won't support it either. Whether you want to or not, you work with them now, and they will not approve of a woman training with the men."

"The law only states women can't be soldiers; it says nothing about them being skilled in the art of combat," he countered. "There is nothing standing in the way of her training with the soldiers as long as she isn't one of them."

"Nothing but propriety."

The glare returned with a vengeance. "Are you suggesting my niece isn't proper?"

"Not at all. I'm suggesting that every other soldier in this camp will not accept a woman as a trainer. To their loss, but that's the way of it."

"So you're refusing my plan?"

"Yes."

"You said you wanted these men to be as good a fighter as I. As good as her. Has that changed?"

"No."

"Then she'll assist me."

Deckard pinched the bridge of his nose. "Are you ignoring my orders?"

"No, Captain, I'm following your original orders," Hewitt said flatly. "You want the best? I'll give you the best damn soldiers you've ever seen. But I can't do that without *my* best asset beside me."

Deckard stared back at Hewitt, pondering the man's case. It was unheard of; it was improper by the standards of the world at large. And if it got back to his commanding officers, it could ruin him.

"You were a general," Deckard said. "You know what the highest-ranking officers will say if they hear I've let my *wife* train my *soldiers*."

"She's not the one doing the training."

"That's not how they'll see it."

Hewitt snarled. "I'll make them see it."

Coming from any other man, Deckard wouldn't have hesitated to disregard the threat. But this was Hewitt Glaas—the drafted soldier who'd risen from private to general in five short years. He'd done the impossible. He was the man who'd cut through an entire horde of Waulden soldiers defending the border village of Axbridge during a raid. The soldier who'd headed up a stealth mission to penetrate and take down the brutal Waulden Lieutenant General Iresen—a vile man who'd overtaken the port city of Norswich in northern Ephria. It was this ex-officer standing before him who was responsible for tearing through western Ephria and driving over twenty Waulden officers back across Allore's

Arm, the mountain range that separated the countries. According to the dozens of stories Deckard's officers had told him through the years, it was all thanks to *this man* that Ephria was still in the fight.

"You do realize," Deckard said cautiously, "that if this comes back to haunt me, it'll affect her too."

"I'm not an idiot," Hewitt growled. "I gave her to you; I know whatever the hell happens to you, happens to her. And, trust me, I won't let *anything* bad happen to her."

Though every logical impulse within him told him to say no, Deckard nodded. "All right. You have my permission to do *whatever* you think will make these recruits the best possible soldiers in the Ephrian Army."

Satisfied, Hewitt bowed to Deckard. "Thank you, Captain. You won't regret your decision."

Though doubt lingered, Deckard knew if anyone could make good on that promise, it was Hewitt Glaas.

The journey from Trollenston to Berkley was dull. But Deckard did his duty, keeping his attention on his job as an officer rather than his desire to visit Evylin.

He greeted her when she arrived at camp, of course. Taking note of her coat—split in the back to allow for riding—and the trousers beneath, Deckard didn't hesitate to provide her with a horse. Most men would find her apparel improper and unladylike. But growing up with an impetuous sister who refused to help on the farm unless she wore trousers like her older brothers, he held an understanding most men lacked. And he knew if Hewitt was going to have her train with the men, the trousers were the least of his concerns.

Deckard led her to the stablemaster, where the last few horses lay unclaimed. The man—Sergeant Norten—brought forth a brown mare with a docile temperament and steady gait that he assured her would prove a worthy steed for her journey. Evylin seemed caustic at the suggestion she needed a docile horse to manage, but Deckard noticed how she bit her tongue and accepted the mare with polite gratitude.

Despite her protestation the previous night, Deckard chose to ride at her side for the first half hour, knowing it would be impossible for him to break free of his work once it truly began. They shared pleasant conversation, their banter light and amusing as always. He had to remind himself often that her friendly disposition and quick remarks were the vernacular of the Shires. They weren't meant to be flirtatious, no matter how inviting her playful teases sounded.

Once he paid her his dues, Deckard excused himself and went to work. From then until dinner, he only saw her from a distance. And while he'd done his best not to mind, he frowned every time he noticed his brother riding at her side.

Deckard didn't understand it. The last he'd known, Thom was angry with Evylin. And suddenly, he was over it? It was so unlike his brother, so completely unexpected. And he couldn't figure out when they'd had time to become such good friends.

The rolling hills of Estshire grew smaller. Having grown up in the northern Shire, Deckard knew the flat expanses that awaited them, and he chose to enjoy the way the golden sun hugged the edges of the hilltops in its descent. The dying grass turned copper, and the distant grazing sheep glowed bronze as the sky burned like a fire, with one final burst of light before the night claimed its expanse above them.

Calling an end to the day's journey, Deckard and his officers led the soldiers half a mile off the road to set up their camp. With a company of their small size, construction didn't take as long as some of the past regiments he'd been a member of. And with Hewitt's presence, the men moved even faster.

Deckard's tent went up first, and he took the time to stable and brush down his horse before hurrying to its canvas walls. Despite the necessity of the special treatment, he still hadn't grown used to getting such priority. After an abnormally long stint as a lieutenant, he'd earned his captaincy less than two months prior, and this was his first assignment as *the* commanding officer. Being the head officer was a privilege and honor. One he hadn't expected to earn but would endeavor to deserve.

The captain's tent wasn't large by normal standards. But within the army, it was luxurious.

While the lieutenants each had one-man tents, they were only big enough for a cot. The rest of the soldiers shared equally small tents with cots so narrow the average soldier's feet would hang off the end, no matter the average short stature of the Ephrian man. Deckard knew the discomfort of those tiny cots better than most since he was unusually tall compared to most of his men.

Even with its meager offerings, the captain's tent was vastly superior to any others. The army bestowed a commanding officer with a semi-comfortable, though still narrow cot, a large table with two chairs for work and meals, a small mirror affixed to a narrow wooden divider for privacy and a cleaner shave, and two thick rugs that covered the terrae beneath their feet.

Despite those luxuries, it was otherwise barren and intended for work and sleep alone.

Pushing through the canvas flaps, Deckard moved to the large table that awaited him just inside the entry and set to work. His men had already delivered his things and Evylin's trunk. He stood at the table and began to spread maps, ledgers, and notes across the surface.

It always amazed him how much there was to do, even when they were traveling. He had correspondence to maintain to keep his commanding officers apprised of his movements and successes—or lack thereof. He had his numbers to calculate. He had new recruits to distribute among his lieutenants, their platoons growing quite large with all the volunteers. And yet, for him to complete his assignment, they'd need to double in size. Though he'd been quite intentional in choosing officers who would earn him favor with the various higher-ranking officers above him, he'd also been sure that each was competent in their command.

After splitting the recruits from Trollenston into the five platoons, Deckard reviewed the map of Nettershire. He marked the villages from the towns, noting their overall populations and assessing how many volunteers he might expect from each one. The odds were not in his favor. But there was still hope that the Shires would provide the five hundred men he needed.

A crisp puff of cold air greeted Deckard as the entry flaps lifted. Evylin stepped in, Thom trailing behind her. Their laughter filled the air as his brother gestured toward the interior of the tent. "See?" he said, his boyish smirk lighting up his face. "It's just that simple."

Evylin crossed her arms playfully. "Yes, of course. I don't know how I couldn't find it myself."

Deckard rested his pen on the center binding of his ledger. "What were you trying to find?" he asked.

Evylin and Thom looked over at him, eyes widening as though just realizing he was there.

Thom scratched the back of his head, ruffling some of his dark hair. "Oh, uh—Evie got lost in the camp."

"I wasn't lost," she objected.

"What do you call wandering around aimlessly, then?"

She returned his snide expression. "I think I was making an impressive go of my search, seeing as how I've never stayed in a camp."

Deckard stood up straighter. "No one told you where to go?"

Evylin shrugged carelessly. "No."

"I'm so sorry," he said, stomach tightening with guilt. "I should have found you the second we arrived."

Evylin raised a hand to halt his concerned approach. "Not to worry," she insisted. "I was with Hewitt most of the time. But the other officers needed him, so I had to find my own way."

Deckard leveled a glare at Thom. "Seems I need to teach our fellow officers some manners," he said bitterly, then turned back to Evylin. "They should have made sure you found your way here before going about their work."

"Cut them some slack," Thom interjected. "They're not used to a woman being in camp. There's never been a reason to lead someone to your tent."

"And," Evylin added, tapping Thom's arm fondly, "one of your officers was gallant enough to escort me to you. So no harm done."

Deckard struggled to determine whether she was genuine in her sloughing off of his inattentiveness. "Either way, I was careless," he said. "And so were they. I'll be sure it doesn't happen again."

"Jonn, it's fine." Her rich, husky voice cut through him with its lighthearted yet insistent timbre. She was somewhere between urging and teasing him, and he couldn't fully understand why. "Thom explained the layout of the camp to me, so there's no need to worry."

"All right, if you're sure."

"I am."

He nodded, then turned to Thom. "Thank you," he said.

"Of course," Thom replied.

Deckard looked at Evylin, unsure of what else there was to say.

Thom cleared his throat. "Well, I guess I'll be off. I've got men to take care of." He began backing out through the flaps. "Night, Evie. Deckard."

"Thom," Evylin returned with her signature wry grin.

The tent flaps fell back in place, and suddenly, Deckard was alone with Evylin for the first time that day. Their eyes met in the silence.

"So," Evylin said, motioning to the space behind him, "this is your tent?"

Deckard gave the small canvas room a once-over before turning back to her. "*Our* tent," he corrected. "But, yes, this is it."

The dimples in Evylin's cheeks grew. "Ours? How positively odd."

"Indeed."

She drifted farther into the tent, away from him.

"Would you like something to eat or drink?" Deckard offered, not sure what else to do now that she'd arrived. He really ought to get back to work, he knew. But it felt wrong to ignore her.

Evylin halted her inspection of the tent. "It is dinner time, isn't it?"

"About there," he confirmed. "Are you hungry?"

"I'm always hungry."

He laughed. "Really?"

"Mm." Her smirk deepened. "Something you may as well learn about me now: Food is of the utmost importance."

Deckard couldn't share the sentiment. "Well then, I'd better see that you're properly fed," he said, moving toward the door.

"Jonn," she called with a worried cadence, "you don't have to go. I saw that you were working. Thom told me how to get to the kitchen tent from here so I can get dinner for myself."

Appreciating her goodwill, Deckard chose not to be offended that she thought he'd callously leave her to fend for herself. "That's completely unnecessary," he said, crossing to the entrance. He lifted the flap and called to a pair of soldiers on patrol. After giving them his orders, one soldier trotted off while the other continued on his post.

Deckard stepped back into the tent to face Evylin. "There," he said, raising his brow. "Now, neither of us has to leave."

Evylin crossed her arms, laughter sparkling in her dark eyes. "The perks of being the captain?"

"Something like that." He gestured to a seat by the table. "Please."

While she sat, Deckard returned to the other side of the table. "You were right," he said, taking up his pen. "I am working. But that doesn't mean I can't enjoy company at the same time."

Evylin rested her elbows on the tabletop, propping her chin on closed fists. "You're sure I won't be too much of a distraction?"

"Not at all."

"Even if I ask you hundreds of questions?"

Deckard glanced up at her from his ledger. "Are you planning on asking me hundreds of questions?"

She raised her eyebrows. "Will I distract you if I do?"

"Probably."

Her nose scrunched up pleasantly. "Then how about I keep them to a dozen?"

Deckard chuckled, returning to his numbers. "A dozen will do."

"Good." Evylin shifted, arms now crossed before her. "Where are we going?"

Forcing himself not to glance at her every chance he got, Deckard tried to mete out his volunteers appropriately. "Immediately? Or long term?"

"Both."

"Immediately, we're going to Berkley," he explained, letting himself look up at her. "Have you ever visited?"

Evylin shook her head. "No. I've never gone any farther than Trollenston."

"Then we'll have to be sure you visit the village. Not that it's likely to be anything grand. My notes say that it's only a few hundred more than Whickam Village. I imagine it will be quite like your home. But you should see it anyway."

Evylin bit back her hopeful smile. "I'd like that."

Deckard forced his gaze back down. "As to our long-term destination, we're headed to Loclight."

"Loclight?" Evylin's voice was light with awe. "As in the province or the city?"

Her excitement amused him. "The city is in the province."

"Yes, but the province isn't the city."

"True enough." Deckard looked up at her. "The army's headquarters are in Ephria City, which is our ultimate destination. But we locals call it Loclight."

"Locals?" Her expression grew teasing. "I thought you were a Shireman."

"I *was* a Shireman," he returned. "But I consider the city my home now. No matter how little I'm there."

Evylin furrowed her brow. "How little *are* you there?"

"Oh, uh . . ." Deckard ran a hand over his jaw, trying to consider the last time he'd been home for longer than a handful of weeks at a time. "It depends on my assignment. Before we left a little over a month ago, I was there for about two weeks to prepare, and the time before that . . . I think it was six months prior that either Thom or I were home."

"Right. I'd forgotten that Thom lives with you."

Deckard couldn't help his frown. Somehow, he'd forgotten too. "Ah, yes. Well, I suppose he'll have to find his own place now."

"Why?"

Meeting her gaze, Deckard was amazed she'd have to ask. "Because we're married."

Evylin laughed nervously. "Yes, but why should that mean he has to leave?" she said. "If he's hardly ever there, what does it matter if he stays with us on occasion?"

Lips parting in an unspoken question, Deckard blinked. His mind conjured images from the past two days: Thom's friendly escort of her to the tent, the pair riding amiably together, and the two of them at the tavern in Trollenston, laughing and sitting far closer to one another than even Deckard would have attempted.

They were so close—so comfortable with one another after only two days. And he couldn't understand how.

Deckard took a deep breath. "Evylin," he began, cautious of his words, "I meant to ask before, but . . . I'm afraid I'm confused. Why are you spending time with Thom?"

Silence fell as Evylin's expression scrunched in bewilderment. "Do you—you don't want me to spend time with your brother?"

"No." He rushed to correct her. "No, it's—it's not that, I just . . . He was furious. He wouldn't even speak to you, and now . . . it surprises me, is all."

There was another hesitation. "I don't understand. You're the one who told him to apologize, weren't you?"

"What?"

"What?"

Deckard gaped at her, more confused than ever. "Thom apologized?"

Her expression matched the confusion he felt. "Yes. I'd assumed you told him to."

"No."

"Oh."

Wetting his bottom lip, Deckard tried puzzling through this bizarre occurrence. "When did he apologize?"

"At the camp," she explained, her words quick as though reassuring him. "Before we left Whickam Village."

"Before we left?"

She nodded, sober and unsure.

Deckard's brow pinched together. "That doesn't make sense."

"Why not?"

"Thom isn't a magnanimous sort. It takes him days—sometimes weeks to admit he was wrong."

"Well . . ." Evylin drew in a long, audible breath before she sighed. "He apologized. He told me he wasn't angry with me in the first place; he was just concerned about you. And he's been trying to be my friend, I think."

Deckard thought to warn her, to tell her about his relationship with Thom, to make her aware that his brother might not tell the full truth when asked, that he might distort the past to make himself look like the victim. But this revelation—this spark of maturity in such an immediate apology—caused Deckard to hesitate. Was Thom getting better? Could he genuinely care about Deckard's happiness, ready to let the past stay in the past? Could it be possible that Evylin might bridge the massive expanse of their relationship, helping them to become the brothers they had always been meant to be?

Suddenly, a voice called out from the other side of the canvas, causing them to startle. "Dinner for you and the missus, Captain."

"Come in," Deckard called back.

The private entered with two covered plates, instantly setting them on the table before moving to leave. "Anything else you need, sir?"

"No, Private, thank you."

"Yes, sir."

The soldier disappeared, and Deckard faced Evylin once more. "I'm glad Thom apologized," he concluded, choosing to believe in his brother's goodness.

Evylin didn't respond, eyes studying him as though trying to figure out what he truly felt.

Deckard forced a smile to his lips. "I'm also thankful he's befriending you. He . . . well, he's never been very good at friendship."

"He hasn't?"

"No, but it sounds as though he's improved. And that makes me hopeful."

Evylin's expression softened. "Well, I'm happy to be his friend. And I hope knowing that eases your mind."

"It does," he promised.

"After all," she added, a light, playful tilt to her words, "now you don't have to feel bad for leaving me each day. You can get your work done knowing Hewitt and Thom will take care of me."

If Evylin pulled that dagger from her boot to stab into his gut, Deckard thought it would have hurt less. "Yes," he forced out. "I suppose you're right. Shall we have our dinner?"

CHAPTER TWENTY-THREE

17TH OF TERRAEN, 1573

Evylin stared at the village of Berkley as the soldiers assembled the camp around her, disappointed. It looked far too much like home, with the same stone cottages crowding the streets and clustered ivy vines growing up their walls. But Berkley sat on a plain rather than nestled in a valley like Whickam Village. To the far left, a herd of sheep scattered across the landscape. A collie ran alongside as a shepherd whistled his commands.

Evylin wondered if the rest of the upper Shires would reflect this flat terrain. She hoped not. It was dreadfully dull.

"Evylin," Deckard called, walking over, Peery following behind him closely.

Evylin did her best not to blush. She felt inordinately nervous around him after their night on that narrow cot. Though she'd sat up reading for a while, Deckard had stayed up to work, leaving her to fall asleep alone. Somehow, she'd managed to sleep through him joining her in the bed. Yet, she'd woken in the night, finding herself unconsciously snuggling deeper under the blankets and away from the cold—pressing herself firmly against his back.

Deckard had been right: The cot was small, and there was no avoiding one another. She couldn't complain since the canvas tent did little to keep out the cold autumn night, and he provided an abundance of warmth. *Like standing next to a fire,* Evylin had thought as she drifted back to sleep.

Sleepy Evylin hadn't had the presence of mind to be embarrassed, snuggling against a man who was still very much a stranger. But in the daylight, her face heated in his presence, worrying over what he thought of her behavior.

At his approach, Evylin hoped her smile hid her mortification. "Good morning," she said. "I take it you're off to see the magistrate?"

"I am," Deckard confirmed. "There's a chance he'll offer to host us in his home, but given the small size of the village, I wouldn't expect him to have room to spare."

Evylin brushed her hand through the air. "I don't mind either way."

"You're a better woman than most," he said, his gentle smile warming in the chilly morning air. "I shouldn't be long."

As Evylin gave her farewell, Hewitt stepped through the tents. Deckard passed him a polite nod, then gave Evylin one last smile before heading into the village with Peery.

The weight of Hewitt's hand rested on her shoulder. "Come on," he said, voice a low rumble. "I need your help."

As they walked through the camp, Hewitt began to explain. "Today is my first day as head trainer, and I intend to show these men what they can expect in the coming month."

Used to Hewitt's long strides, Evylin doubled hers to keep up with him. "How can I help?"

"You're going to be my demonstration."

Evylin's heart expanded nervously. "You're sure that won't cause problems? A woman helping to train soldiers?"

"It'll ruffle a few feathers. But I'd rather get those sorts out of my way. Besides," he grinned down at her, "they're not likely to face anything more frightening than a woman with a sword in battle. Best to prepare them while we can."

Evylin eyed a few of the soldiers around them wryly. "I'll do my best to desensitize them."

"Good. We have all five platoons to work with today, so it'll be a long one."

Evylin tugged at the buttons of her coat, wishing she could draw it closer against the frigid wind that whipped through the plains. "How does that work? Training with each platoon?"

"It's on a rotation. Since I'm instituting new policies today, the main work will be informing the lieutenants and their troops on what's expected of them. We'll start with First Platoon and work our way down. But in the future, it will be more structured."

"Mm."

"Don't worry," Hewitt said dryly. "You'll enjoy it."

"Enjoy what, exactly?" Evylin asked.

"Training with the men."

"Oh. Yes, I imagine I will."

"But . . . ?"

"Nothing."

Hewitt's brows dipped lower. "You're hesitating. Why?"

"It's *nothing*."

"You're worried about your husband disapproving."

Evylin looked up at him. "Shouldn't I be?"

"There's no need. Now," he said as they broke through the tents and out onto the training grounds, "I need you to focus. No one in this camp can best you but me. Everything I've taught you, I need you to show it off."

Though his dismissal of her concerns about Deckard wasn't reassuring, she was excited by the prospect of training with the men. "You always tell me not to show off. You say it makes me sloppy."

"That's because it does," he returned. "And if you show off what *I* taught you, then there won't be any sloppy exhibitions, will there?"

She grinned. "No, there won't."

He patted her arm, then turned away. "Stay here. I need to speak with my fellow officers, and there's no need to ruffle any feathers quite yet."

Evylin watched as Hewitt approached the two majors across the field. The one on the right was short, bald, and carried more weight in his midsection than she thought a soldier ought to. The other was a much better representation of his office. His dark skin rippled with muscles even through his gray coat. His black hair was smartly cropped, and he was on the tall side of average for an Ephrian.

While the officers talked, soldiers began to arrive. They were dressed in their gray uniforms, and each man's coat bore the insignia of a private on their left breast—the Ephrian crook and sword alone. A few of them eyed her as they passed, wary of the captain's wife. She imagined that their caution of her would only grow after the training began.

As she assessed the troop, she knew Hewitt was right; none of them would be difficult to beat. Having glimpsed their training program in the past, she knew it wouldn't offer a challenge.

Twisting the silver band around her finger, Evylin wondered if she should take it off for the fight. The pressure would feel strange against the handle of a sword, but it was a sensation she'd have to grow used to. It wouldn't look right to remove it from her finger.

"Well, hello there, Eve," Rafferty said, the sunlight glinting off his white-blond hair. "Come to watch us train, have you?"

Evylin dropped the hold on her ring. "Morning, Raff. Yes, something like that."

"Well, don't laugh at us too much," he said, silver eyes flashing. "From what Thommy says, you'd put us all to shame."

"I'm sure I don't know what you're talking about."

"No need to pretend around me, Eve. I think it's incredible that you can fight. Thom does too." He tapped a finger to his chin thoughtfully. "I'm surprised your captain approved of it, though. He seems too prudish to think well of a lady picking up a sword."

With startling clarity, Evylin remembered how Deckard looked at her after she'd beat Thom, his lips twisting up in an awe-filled grin as he applauded her success. "Oh, I think you underestimate how easygoing Jonn can be."

Rafferty huffed. "The captain's about as flexible as a tree. Didn't he give you a proper scolding after finding us together?"

Evylin scrunched up her nose. "Why would he scold me for that?"

His silver eyes twinkled merrily. "Your noble captain isn't much for us free-enterprising sorts. Believe me, it tore him up to accept me into his company. But here I am," he tossed his arms grandly, "and your dear ol' captain doesn't have a choice but to put up with me."

"I'm sure you enjoy every opportunity to make him regret it."

"It's more fun that way." He held up a finger and tapped her on the nose. "In case you hadn't noticed, our captain is quite the Serious Sally."

She arched her brow, intrigued. "Is that so?"

He nodded furiously. "He's a decent man, the captain. But he has impossibly high standards. Which makes him an easy target."

"And how would you know his standards, Private, after knowing him for only a fortnight?"

Rafferty's grin grew wily. "I beg your pardon, Eve, but I believe you've only known him for a handful of days. Granted, in a more intimate manner."

While Evylin blushed at the innuendo, a hand clamped down on the weasel's shoulder, and Thom shoved him forward. "Get a move on, Private. You've got training to start."

Stumbling the first couple of steps, Rafferty regained his feet quickly. "Aye, aye, Lieutenant!"

"We're not in the navy, idiot."

"I get seasick, sir." Rafferty saluted as he backed up, then tossed Evylin another wink. "Enjoy the show, ma'am."

Evylin and Thom chuckled as the weasel bounded away. Around fifty men, mostly young, stood at the right side of the field. They mumbled among themselves, failing to look soldierly.

"You're here to watch, then?" Thom asked.

"Isn't that why you're here too?" Evylin replied.

Thom cocked his head wryly. "You do remember that I'm an officer, right? The First Platoon is under my charge."

"Ah, I see. So you're here to learn just as much as they do?"

"In a manner of speaking."

"Good luck to you then."

He dipped his head in thanks and took leave of her. He called out to his platoon to sharpen up, then approached Hewitt and the other majors. The recruits snapped to attention—arms at their sides, backs ramrod straight, and heads held high. Even Rafferty followed the command, though the posture of attention looked bizarre on the weasel-like man.

Hewitt greeted Thom with a handshake and a few words. Then he turned and faced the First Platoon, locked as they were in their stance. He surveyed the men with sharp eyes, stepping ahead of the majors and Thom.

"Now that we're all here, allow me to introduce myself," he began. "I'm Major Glaas, your new trainer. You've all heard about me by now. I'm the ex-general with lots of stories from the past. Let me make one thing clear: By the end of your time under my instruction, I will expect you to be no less capable of those same feats of strength and skill.

"I don't accept poor swordsmanship. Nor do I allow for sloppy technique or negligence. You *will* end your tenure with me as the finest soldiers Ephria has ever seen. Whether you want to or not."

A few soldiers shifted nervously, but they all endured Hewitt's inspection.

"Captain Deckard has charged me with exactly how, when, and where your training will take place," Hewitt continued. "Majors Moris and Sheelds will continue your training but as I prescribe. It will be different from any training you've experienced before. Today, we'll discuss my expectations of you and your fellow soldiers. I'll give you some guidelines on how you're to approach your time under the captain's command, and I'll even provide you with an example of the outcomes I expect."

Hewitt paced before the soldiers. "Some of you have only joined us in the past few days, while the rest of you joined a little over a month ago. But know this: I don't care what training you've had previously." He scanned the fifty-some soldiers in a slow arc. "Forget it all."

At this, the squat major's eyes went wide, fury alight within them, and the dark-skinned major crossed his arms irritably. Thom stood at ease. His hands were clasped behind his back, but he glanced at Evylin. Hewitt's charge was a slight to the previous majors' training program. And it wouldn't be taken lightly.

"We're starting over today," Hewitt said, hand on his pommel. "I'm not going to teach you how to fight. I'm going to teach you how to win."

The soldiers stared back at him, excitement and fear mingling in their faces. A few looked doubtful of his claims. Others furrowed their brows as if they didn't understand the difference. Only Rafferty wore an expression of true understanding—his eyes sharp, head tilted forward, and muscles tense in anticipation.

Hewitt turned to Thom. "Who would you consider the most promising fighter in your platoon?"

Thom considered his men. "Private Haalston," he replied, an indifferent quality to his voice.

The name sounded familiar to Evylin, and she looked over the men as she tried to place it.

Hewitt turned to the majors. "Would you agree with Lieutenant Deckard?"

While the squat major glowered, the other spoke professionally. "Private Haalston is a quick learner. And he's grown more comfortable with a blade than most."

Hewitt turned back to the platoon. "Private Haalston, come forward."

A young man stepped out of the crowd, his comrades patting him on the back and muttering encouragement. Evylin recognized his black mop of hair and bronzed Setshire tan. He was the private from the tavern. The one Hewitt forced to give up his table. He wore a shy but proud grin as he straightened to attention once again.

Evylin studied the young man. He didn't look particularly strong or even agile. There wasn't cunning in his eyes nor focus within his demeanor. No sign he held any traits that made a skilled swordsman. Yet, Thom and the majors considered him the best? As a Setshire man, he would have been one of the first to join the Third Volunteer Company. Perhaps the value of his recommendation was due less to true skill but simply the time he'd had to practice.

"Private," Hewitt said, approaching the soldier, "do you know how to duel?"

Haalston nodded. "Yes, sir, Major Glaas."

"Excellent." Hewitt's cat-like smile spread onto his lips. "You will demonstrate your skills as an example of the training you and your fellow soldiers have received thus far. And as an example of the training and results you will receive from me, Mrs. Deckard will be your opponent."

The soldiers stared in shock as Hewitt beckoned to Evylin. When she crossed to his side, the field grew silent. Though she kept her head high, her stomach rumbled like a rickety cart, and her fingers tingled at her sides. A rush of anticipation welled within her.

Expression impassive as usual, Hewitt nodded to her. "Are you ready?"

"Always," Evylin said.

Hewitt turned back to the officers behind him. "Major Moris, please retrieve training swords for Private Haalston and Mrs. Deckard."

The squat major spluttered in response. "Wha—what can you possibly mean by this—this ridiculous joke, Major Glaas?" Major Moris demanded. "Do you intend to shame our fine company?"

Private Haalston gaped at Evylin in equal confusion.

"This is no joke, Major," Hewitt said evenly. "It will be a good example for all the soldiers. It will help them understand what a real swordsman can do."

Haalston's mouth dropped open.

"I must object, Major Glaas," Major Sheelds said calmly. "It is against the law for a woman to fight."

Hewitt snorted his derision. "It absolutely is not. The law states that a woman can't be a soldier, and Evylin is not. There's no law against a woman fighting."

Sheelds tipped his head in concession. "Perhaps, but I can't imagine it will please Deckard to learn his wife is making a spectacle of herself," he argued with composure, whereas Moris was irate. "If he knew of your intent, surely he wouldn't have agreed to your program."

A tremor ran through Evylin's stomach.

"By all means," Hewitt said, sweeping a hand toward the village, "if you're concerned, go tell him of my ill-doing. In the meantime, I'll conduct my lesson."

A strangled growl escaped Major Moris. He turned to Thom. "Lieutenant Deckard, don't you have anything to say about this?"

Thom shrugged. "What would you like me to say?"

Moris blanched with anger. "Major Glaas is about to humiliate the captain and our whole company. Surely you won't stand for it."

"Major Moris," Thom said with a sigh, "you were there when Deckard gave Major Glaas authority, same as I. If I were to argue with the major, I'd be going against our captain's orders."

"Stupid boy," Moris snarled. "This man is attempting to bring shame to your brother. And you're going to stand by and watch it?"

A scoff escaped Evylin, which earned an ire-filled glare from Moris and a look of wide-eyed shock from Haalston.

Thom turned to Hewitt. "Major Glaas, continue with your training."

Moris scuttled forward. "Private Haalston, I forbid you to listen to this man. You will not fight a woman!"

Haalston looked from major to major to lieutenant in fear.

"Major Moris," Hewitt spoke with disdain, "as you are in direct opposition to Captain Deckard's orders, I'm afraid I'll have to report you for insubordination. I no longer require your assistance. Leave us."

The tubby man glowered at him.

"That's an order," he clarified.

With clenched fists and grumbling complaints, Moris turned his back and marched away.

Hewitt looked to Sheelds, who watched his old comrade bumble away. "Major Sheelds, am I to expect trouble from you, as well?"

Sheelds met Hewitt's steely gaze unflinchingly. "No, sir."

"Good." Hewitt turned to the young soldier at his side. "Private Haalston, you will forget Major Moris's ridiculous commands and do as I ordered."

Haalston swallowed the lump in his throat, eyes sailing from Hewitt to Evylin to Thom to Sheelds and back. A tiny nod came from the terrified soldier.

Major Sheelds retrieved the training swords without instruction, handing one to the private and the other to Evylin. "Be careful, ma'am," he said kindly.

Though he underestimated her, Evylin saw by the sincerity in his dark gaze that he didn't mean to belittle her. "Thank you, Major," she replied.

"Private Haalston, Evylin," Hewitt waved his hand toward the field before them, "prepare to duel."

Haalston stared at her, mouth ajar.

Knowing the soldier's courage was failing, Evylin walked onto the field. The dry grass tamped down underneath her feet. She rolled her shoulders to loosen up. Though she and Hewitt trained their first day in Trollenston, she hadn't gotten exercise or practice since, and her muscles were already tense from disuse and hours on horseback. She gave the sword a couple of swings to get a feel for its weight and flex, keeping the movement subtle and relaxed. She didn't want to scare the kid any more than he already was. Nor did she want to give away exactly how comfortable she was with a sword. She liked the idea of amazing the men with how impressive a female fighter could be.

The soldiers stepped back as she approached to create space on the field. They quietly exchanged words, gathering together to share their thoughts. Rafferty moved between the lines of men, and Evylin could have sworn she heard him handling bets.

Ready, Evylin waited for Haalston. He hadn't moved away from Hewitt, staring up at the major as though hoping he'd say it was all an elaborate prank.

When it became clear no such thing would happen, Haalston took a single step toward her. "I don't want to hurt you," he said anxiously.

"I appreciate your gallantry, truly." Evylin tightened her grip on the longsword. Right hand beneath the cruciform hilt, left at the pommel. She shifted her feet into position. "But I'm not that fragile."

Haalston stole a look at her grip, then fixed his own. He swallowed what looked to be a painfully large lump in his throat again.

Their stares met.

They waited on the other.

Nothing happened.

"Very well," Evylin whispered and charged.

Haalston panicked. He shuffled back from Evylin's lunge, pulling mostly out of her range. The tips of their swords met in a light *clink*. She landed with a firm stance, annoyed. It would have been a good start if not for his flight preservation. If the kid wasn't going to fight her properly, there would be no competition at all. That wouldn't do Hewitt any good, nor would she enjoy it.

Backing up, Evylin glared at Haalston. "Raise your sword and parry my attacks."

Haalston shook his head but lifted the blade as instructed. "I don't want to fight you."

"You don't have a choice. The only way to be a good swordsman is to train with those better than you."

The private's hooded eyes flared with indignation. "I'm the best in my platoon."

"So I heard. Congratulations."

"You think I'm not a good swordsman?" he asked sharply.

"Typically, good swordsmen don't run away from their opponents." She sank deeper into her stance. "Seems to me that you need to learn how not to be afraid of combat."

"I'm not afraid of combat. I just don't want to hurt a woman."

"Either way, you're still scared of me."

The volunteers chimed in with laughter and goading comments. They liked the bantering. So did Evylin.

Haalston glowered. "I'm not scared of you."

"Prove it."

Haalston charged this time.

Evylin was ready.

Either the private's training hadn't taught him how to charge, or it was a skill he'd yet to pick up. He swung his sword far back before thrusting it forward with all his might. Even with his mediocre strength, Evylin had no interest in taking the full brunt of the blow.

Slipping to the left, Evylin pressed her sword up to parry. The blades clashed as she knocked his back. Then she elbowed him in his exposed rib cage.

The breath blew out of his lungs.

Evylin backed away, smiling.

Haalston growled and charged. He swung straight at her, and she countered with ease. It hardly felt like a fight. He didn't have any clue how to handle a sword, relying only on his amateur strength as he chopped away at her blade. He even waited for her to complete her counters in full before trying again.

Though Evylin would have preferred a longer fight, after the third poor slash and easy counter, she decided there was no point in letting it go on.

On his next attack, Evylin didn't bother to block. She stepped to the left as the blade fell and let his momentum carry him to the right. She swung the flat of her blade down to slap him on the hands.

Haalston yelped and dropped his sword.

Evylin twirled her sword back into her natural grip and finished in the proper stance. She might not have anyone else to fight, but she would end the session correctly, showing off Hewitt's training as he'd asked.

The volunteers broke out in cheers and laughter again. Rafferty pumped a fist, grinning like a fool. A few of the men around him grumbled as they began to pull coins from their pockets and dumped them into his waiting hands.

Hewitt called for attention, and the men fell silent. Haalston rejoined the line of soldiers while Evylin stepped to her uncle's side.

"I hope you all see what I mean now," Hewitt called. "You may know how to swing a sword, but no one has taught you how to use one. I will teach you not only how to wield it well but also how to win every fight you enter. Do you want to learn that?"

The soldiers nodded, smiles brightening their faces.

"I said," Hewitt yelled. "*Do you want to learn that?*"

"Yes, sir!" they shouted back, their expressions not stoic but certainly more soldier-like.

The beat of horses' hooves pounded toward the field. Hewitt, Thom, Evylin, Sheelds, and the platoon turned to see the approach of three riders.

"You see?" Moris demanded with an accusing point. "She's got a sword in her hand. The major is an absolute disgrace. We can't have such a man training our recruits."

Evylin wanted to laugh, but her heart plummeted as she took in the other two riders. Deckard and Peery surveyed the officers and Evylin with serious expressions. Though Deckard looked at her with admiration after her fight with Thom, he regarded her with skepticism now. His prior approval appeared to have arisen from the private entertainment of the duel, a bet that no one was party to except the four of them. Now, they were dealing with his work.

The three officers dismounted—Moris with far less grace than the other two—and approached.

Hewitt bowed his head to Deckard. "Captain, I don't know on what basis Major Moris makes these claims, but I don't believe I've done anything disgraceful."

Deckard spared a single second to glance at Evylin before addressing Hewitt. "Major Glaas, it is Major Moris's claim that you have determined to train our recruits by having them go up against my wife in a duel. Is that correct?" he asked.

"Not quite," Hewitt said without any hesitation. "I've chosen to train our recruits with your wife as my assistant. The first step is showing them the proper skills a master swordsman carries. The most efficient means of achieving this is by having the proclaimed best fighter in the platoon test what he's learned against a true swordsman—Evylin."

Major Moris puffed out his chest, point proven.

"Then it's as we discussed," Deckard said casually. He turned to Thom before the words quite sank in. "How'd she do?"

"How do you think?" Thom smirked, and they both turned to Evylin. "I must say, it was far nicer being on this side of the fight."

Deckard's charming smile twinkled in his eyes. "I'd expect nothing less," he said, surprising her with not only his approval but also his flippancy toward Moris's complaints. He turned to Hewitt. "Keep up the good work, Major, and let me know if you need any other support."

Moris began spluttering again.

"Thank you, sir," Hewitt said with another bow.

"No, no, no!" Moris spat, glaring at Deckard now. "Have you lost your mind, Deckard? It's a disgrace! An absolute disgrace to the—"

Deckard held up a hand to silence the man. "Is it your intention to stand in defiance of my orders, Major Moris?"

The major scowled. "It's my intention to save the Ephrian Army from ridicule and mockery."

Deckard ignored his fury. "Major Glaas's plans will develop our recruits into the strongest soldiers the Ephrian Army has seen in years. Are you willing to assist him?"

"No, sir."

"Very well. If you are determined to stand in opposition to my orders, then I will have no choice but to write a formal censure to file upon our return to Loclight."

Moris's lips began to quiver around his snarl.

"Shall I write the censure?"

"General Rand will have your head, boy," Moris threatened.

"I'm your commanding officer, Major Moris," Deckard said without concern. "You'll address me with respect, whether you feel it or not. So shall I write that censure?"

There was a heartbeat of silence while Moris pulled his pudgy hands into fists. "No, sir."

"Then you'll assist Major Glaas in *all* his intended training without complaint?"

"Yes, sir," he snarled.

"Splendid," Deckard said, then his expression softened as he turned to Evylin. "Now, if you'll excuse me, officers, I haven't seen my wife all day."

Deckard held out his hand, and Evylin took it in astonishment. He turned back to Hewitt. "I know you're still in the middle of training, but I'd like to borrow her if I might?"

Hewitt considered the proposition longer than was natural for an officer, then gave a firm nod. "Have her back for the next platoon," he said, turning to his men.

Moris joined Sheelds again, his face red with barely restrained anger. But the other major watched Evylin and Deckard with a strange glint of respect in his eyes.

"Peery, would you take care of my horse?" Deckard asked, drawing Evylin closer to tuck her hand into the crook of his elbow. "I'll meet with you in an hour or so."

The lieutenant began leading the horses toward the stable tents.

Without another word, Deckard led Evylin from the training field and into the maze of tents. "I hope you don't mind me taking you away," he said, keeping his voice low as other soldiers milled about the camp. "I'm sure you were enjoying yourself."

Evylin glanced up at him uncertainly. "Yes, it was enjoyable."

Deckard's smile turned down with an apologetic tilt. "Then I am sorry to take you away. I thought it the best way to show my approval of you and your unusual skills."

Evylin shared his amused smile.

"And, of course," he added, "I did want to see you."

"Ah, yes," she teased. "We are newlyweds, after all."

"Precisely."

Evylin watched the ground as they walked through the camp. It was odd to see his shiny, black boots matching her strides. She did a short hop-step to align her muddy-booted steps with his—right foot, then left foot.

She smiled at the funny sight of their paired steps. "It was quite entertaining," she said merrily, "the way you put Major Moris in his place."

Deckard scoffed, the lines around his eyes softening. "I've never liked Moris much. He's known to be a self-seeking snob, but he's easy enough to control and is good friends with the general." He raised his brow at her. "I suppose he didn't make a good impression on you either."

"What do you mean?" Evylin asked with mock sincerity. "I thought he was absolutely charming."

A few soldiers saluted Deckard as they passed, and he nodded at each. Despite his smile, he said, "I hope he didn't offend you too much."

"Oh, don't worry," she said, brushing the apology away. "I've heard that same complaint my whole life. Most everyone in Whickam Village disapproved of my work with Hewitt, both at the smithy and in swordplay. Being here is nice. It's the first time people have regarded me with a sense of awe rather than disappointment."

"Except for Moris."

"Except for Moris," she confirmed. "Perhaps I can win him over."

Deckard grinned caustically. "Don't get your hopes up."

"What? You don't think I'm clever enough to coax him into friendship?"

"I think you'd have better luck charming a snake than charming Moris."

Evylin angled in front of Deckard, bringing him to a halt. "Is that a challenge, Captain Deckard?"

Narrowing his eyes, which were a light greenish blue in the sunshine, Deckard studied her. "Not in the slightest," he said gently.

Unsure why he was staring at her in such a way, Evylin's confidence slipped. "Pity," she said, refusing to blush. "I always jump at a chance to prove myself."

Deckard lifted a hand to cover the slow, amused smile coming to his face. The bright afternoon sun reflected off the thin metal band on his ring finger, and Evylin blinked in surprise. Simple but fine, she realized that it was a wedding band.

Deckard caught her gaze and dropped his hand.

"When did you get that?" Evylin asked, wondering how she'd missed it.

A pair of soldiers came around the bend, and Deckard resumed their walk. "In Trollenston," he explained as she fell in alongside him.

"Yes, I assumed it was then," she said. "But when?"

"After my meeting with the magistrate that first morning."

"Oh." She bit her bottom lip. "Why—I mean, I—have you worn it before today?"

Deckard hesitated. "No, I was going to show it to you first but never really found the chance. But I felt it best not to wait any longer."

Evylin nodded, understanding but bemused.

The turn toward their tent came into view, and Evylin edged toward it, but Deckard held her fast at his side. "We're not going that way," he said.

"No?" Evylin said, increasingly bewildered.

"No," he said but offered no more.

"Where are we going, then?"

"Maybe I wanted to take a simple walk with my wife."

Evylin gave him a snide look. "How romantic of you."

They broke free of the last tents, and Deckard drew them to a halt. He looked down at her, a teasing curve to his lips. "You're my wife," he said. "I'm supposed to be romantic with you, aren't I?"

Feeling safer out of the camp's prying eyes, Evylin countered, "Only if our marriage was sincere."

A wry smile made Deckard's expression playful. "Our marriage *is* sincere, Evylin," he replied. "Whether based on utility or not, it's as real as any other. And despite its unusual nature, I'm of the persuasion that we should make the most of it. Wouldn't you agree?"

The simple answer was yes. But Evylin couldn't shake the words of Thom echoing in her ears. *"Everything he does—every choice he's ever made—it's all about being perfect."*

Evylin considered Deckard's regard. He seemed genuine, his eyes fixed on hers, lips lifted kindly, posture relaxed. She could almost feel the anticipation of her response in the air around them. If he didn't mean it, he was a fantastic liar.

After days of minimal interactions with her husband, Evylin was at a loss. She thought his work alone motivated him. But then there were moments like these when he showed such an interest in getting to know her and developing their strange relationship. How was she supposed to make him happy if she couldn't puzzle him out?

With a shrug, Evylin returned his smile. "I agree."

His expression softened, and he held out his hand again. "Shall we go, then, Mrs. Deckard?"

"Go where?" Evylin asked, looking between his face and his hand.

Deckard practically beamed at her. "Into Berkley."

Evylin looked over to the village, mouth dropping open. Into Berkley? Into a brand-new place with brand-new people and brand-new sights? Was she ready for that?

Turning back to the captain, Evylin took hold of his hand. "Yes."

CHAPTER TWENTY-FOUR

Berkley was a disappointment. Small and populated mostly by women, it was indistinguishable from Evylin's home. If not for the flat plains, unknown people, and altered layout, she would be hard-pressed to say they hadn't traveled backward.

It only took an hour to inspect the village before Deckard returned her to Hewitt. She promised she'd enjoyed the trip, not wanting to disappoint him. But in all honesty, she didn't understand how two places so far apart could be so similar.

On their walk back, Deckard informed her about his meeting with the magistrate of Berkley. The man was obliging but did not offer them a place to stay. "I'm sorry," he said, his brows pinched together. "I was hoping to ease you into camp life."

"I did want an adventure," Evylin replied cheerfully. "What's more adventurous than sleeping in a tent?"

Deckard tipped his head in consideration. "Sleeping under the stars?"

"True, but I do think that'd be rather cold."

"I hate to remind you, but winter hasn't even begun yet. And we're headed north. It's about to get a lot colder."

"Best to stay in the tent, then."

Deckard chuckled. "Well, I hope to provide you with better sleeping arrangements in the future."

They parted once he'd escorted her to Hewitt. She fought another soldier in the Second Platoon who was even less skilled than Private Haalston. They followed the same routine with the final three platoons. It was a long but satisfying day, even with the disappointment of Berkley.

Evylin shared dinner with Deckard in their tent, and it almost felt like they were back in Whickam Village after their light conversation throughout the day. Deckard asked her more about her family and her childhood, and she enjoyed telling him stories of her training with Hewitt and terrorizing her younger sisters. She told him about all the books she'd read and the ones she liked best. It pleased her when he mentioned that he enjoyed reading as well. However, when she discovered his preferred reading was of historical or militaristic texts, she found their tastes were quite different.

She was careful to say nothing of Ryen.

Once again, the night compelled them to sleep back-to-back. At first, it felt awkward, but Evylin quickly drifted off, comforted by his warmth, which made up for the insufficient blankets. Reflecting on his earlier warning, she recognized that if the north was set to bring even colder winters, she was grateful for the snugness of the cot. All she could do now was hope the heat from his body would suffice.

18TH OF TERRAEN, 1573

Deckard was gone again when Evylin woke, but this time without leaving a note. She double-checked the entire tent twice to be sure she hadn't missed it, surprised to find herself disappointed at its absence. When she finally concluded there was no note to be found, she forced herself to go about her day as usual. She braided her hair in preparation for training, then headed out to find the kitchen tent for breakfast.

Soldiers milled about, eating and chattering. A few discussed their speculation of how many new recruits Berkley would bring. Some talked about their homes, some about the places they hoped to see, or the jobs they hoped to be assigned. They all ignored Evylin.

Once Evylin gathered her meal, she made her way to Hewitt's tent, nestled next to the training grounds. He sat at a modest table, readying himself for the day's first training session. He welcomed her company, and the morning passed effortlessly as he shared his intentions for training the soldiers.

"Nothing soft like that idiot Moris planned," Hewitt said with a grunt. "Sheelds said the fool never took any of his advice. But he doesn't get a say now." Hewitt scribbled his plans in a small notebook. "I'm giving these men daily routines to ensure they're in the best shape of the whole army. Even on our travel days, they'll be required to condition their bodies. The environment of war isn't kind, and it won't be here either."

He gestured to her with his pen. "You'll be helping with that," he said. "Sheelds will aid in whatever way he can, but I can't count on Moris. You'll be my right hand. You'll watch the men and ensure they follow my guidelines. You'll train with them sometimes, too; they'll need the challenge. But I need you at my side as we get these men into shape."

"I'm not a teacher, Uncle," she reminded him. "And I don't care to be."

"That's not what I'm asking. I need you to be my eyes, Evylin. You know my demands better than anyone else. You can watch them and tell me when you see mistakes."

"And what about *my* training?"

"Don't worry," he said with a casual wave. "I've got special plans for that."

Hewitt left the tent then. The first of five platoons had already begun to arrive. Hewitt started their morning with their new exercise routines, using Evylin as his demonstration for the movements. None of the soldiers moved with as much mobility or speed as her, given their low conditioning, but a few felt gratified knowing they could beat her in strength.

Soon enough, they completed their first and second training sessions and headed to lunch. Arriving at the kitchen tent once more, Evylin spotted Thom and Rafferty sitting off to the far side as the First Platoon ate their meal. The men waved for her and Hewitt to join.

"How worried should I be?" Rafferty asked as Evylin sat down across from him.

"About what?" she asked.

"About training today," he explained. "Don't get me wrong. I'd love to be as skilled as you, but I'm rather sure that requires more work than I'm willing to put in."

"You'll never be good if you don't practice," Thom said.

Hewitt grunted but kept his focus on his plate.

"I've said it before, and I'll say it again." Rafferty held a finger aloft to emphasize his incoming point. "Practice is boring."

"What if it wasn't?" Hewitt asked in his unaffected monotone.

"I don't believe that's possible."

Evylin smirked. "You believe in Mages but not that practicing swordplay can be enjoyable?"

"Yep," Rafferty said proudly.

"Mm." Hewitt shrugged. "Well, I'm sorry, Evie, it seems my special plan for your training may not work out after all."

Evylin looked up from her plate, brow raised. "What?"

Rafferty leaned forward. "What?"

"Is there an echo out here?" Thom mocked, looking up at the sky in wonder.

Hewitt continued to eat, unbothered.

"Uncle, elaborate, please."

Taking his time, Hewitt chewed, then swallowed. "It was my intention to invite a small number of soldiers to join a special training group, working one-on-one with you and me, Evie. That's all."

Evylin grinned, thrilled with the possibility.

"And why won't that work out?" Rafferty demanded.

Hewitt gathered another bite of food on his fork. "Because I only had two candidates at the moment, and as you seem to have no interest, Private, I don't see it doing Evylin much good."

"No, no," Rafferty said hurriedly. "I'm interested."

"You said you don't care to practice."

"Yes, but this doesn't sound like practice," he countered. "It sounds like fun."

Hewitt tugged on his beard. "Very well. How about you, Lieutenant? Does that sound like fun to you?"

A chunk of potato fell from Thom's spoon to splash back into his stew, splattering his coat front. "What?"

"Oh, I think you're right, Thommy," Rafferty said, whacking him in the chest. "I just heard your echo."

Thom shoved him away, turning back to Hewitt. "You want me to train with you and Evie?"

Evylin smiled as Hewitt nodded. "Yes," he said. "You show a good deal of promise."

"But I—I'm nowhere near as skilled as her."

"Which is why you need to train with us."

Thom sat back with an elated grin, pushing a hand through his dark hair. "Wow, yeah, I'd—I'd be honored."

"Good," Evylin said, tearing off a bite of her rye bread. "I'll enjoy winning again."

Thom scoffed good-naturedly. "You'll beat everyone in this camp, Evie."

"That's a good point. Which makes me think," Rafferty said, then turned to Hewitt. "I get why you want Thom, but why do you want me? You've never even seen me fight."

Hewitt was unworried by the question. "You were a smuggler—"

"An entrepreneur."

"And with that line of work comes high levels of risk and the demand for skills the average man doesn't possess. I have no doubt that even untrained in swordplay, you'll pick up the finer points with little difficulty," Hewitt explained, then added, "You're also a sneaky bastard. And that typically makes for a dangerous opponent."

"I'm flattered," the weasel replied.

"So you'll both join us, then?"

Thom and Rafferty nodded.

"Excellent." Hewitt turned to Evylin. "We'll have our first meeting after the rest of the training today."

The excitement within Evylin rose. She'd never had an opportunity to challenge her skills with anyone but Hewitt. And while she'd beat Thom easily before, she knew he'd learn quickly. She didn't doubt Hewitt's positive assessment of Rafferty's unknown skill either.

Thom stood and nudged Rafferty with his foot. "Hurry up, there," he ordered. "I've got to get you and the rest of the platoon to work before I check in on Deckard."

While Rafferty grumbled about needing to take time to savor his meal, Evylin felt the blood drain from her face. "I missed his speech," she realized.

"You've already heard it twice," Hewitt said. "He can't expect you to come every time he stands up from here to Loclight."

"I don't know," she said, chewing on her bottom lip. "It means a lot to him, and I don't want to make him upset."

Thom laughed. "Upset? Don't worry, Evie," he said, patting her arm. "My brother may be a boring prat, but he's not stupid. You've been working—doing the job he already approved. He'll be fine."

Evylin wasn't convinced. After her critique, she worried he'd take her absence as a slight. What if he'd changed something and expected she'd hear it? What if he asked her for her thoughts again? She'd have nothing to say.

But then, what of their agreement? Evylin and Deckard had agreed not to be a burden to one another. He would do his work, and she would enjoy her adventure—no need to change anything else.

"Our marriage is *sincere."*

His words drifted at the back of her mind, reminding her that he wanted to make the most of their marriage. But did that mean ignoring their days-old promise? Did he *want* his life to change to include her?

The sky went black well before Deckard returned. He entered their tent, still dressed in his ceremonial uniform and regalia. Evylin closed her book to greet him, realizing this was the first time they'd seen each other that day. A strange revelation, as both spouses and acquaintances. She rose from her chair in nervous anticipation. But there wasn't a trace of disappointment in Deckard's expression. In fact, he was smiling brightly enough to cause his eyes to crinkle at the edges.

"Good evening," he said, letting the tent flaps fall back behind him.

Evylin returned the greeting, watching as he moved to pour himself a cup of water. "How was your day?" he asked.

"It was nice," she said cautiously. "Hewitt started his training regimen with the soldiers today, and I helped."

"It went well, then?"

"It did."

"Moris and Sheelds didn't give him too much trouble, did they?"

"No. Major Sheelds is quite helpful, actually. And though Moris scowled the whole time, he did as Hewitt ordered."

"Good."

Running her thumb along the spine of her book, Evylin took a deep breath. "How did your speech go?"

Deckard met her eyes and smiled. "It was perfect."

"It was?"

"Nineteen volunteers," he exclaimed. He ran a hand over the side of his face. "Can you believe a small village like this would bring nineteen volunteers?"

Evylin shook her head, relieved at his jovial response. "That is amazing."

"I wasn't expecting it." He took a seat at the table. "There are hardly enough men here to warrant such a number. But it makes up for the few we didn't get in Trollenston."

As they prepared for bed, Evylin noted that it didn't compensate for the volunteers they lost in Whickam Village, but she supposed Hewitt would make up for that loss himself.

19TH OF TERRAEN, 1573

The Ephrian Army left Berkley that morning, heading for Leedbury in Nettershire. Hewitt drove the soldiers with threats of being the next to duel with Evylin, and they packed the whole camp within an hour.

Riding on the same brown mare as before—whom she decided to call Fransis—Evylin watched the countryside roll by. Leedbury was a thirteen-mile journey, less than half the distance it took to reach Berkley. Deckard assured her they would arrive before sunset. She would soon see her first Nettershire town.

The ride went as usual. Deckard rode with her for the first half hour, then rushed off to his tasks. Hewitt rode up front with Sheelds, discussing their plans for the troops. The two of them were beginning to see eye-to-eye; the major had already come to approve of Evylin's skills as well. While Evylin considered riding with them, she decided she would rather ride on her own than listen to them talk about strategies and detailed regimens.

After four hours on the winding road, Evylin pulled back on Fransis's reins. She guided the horse to the side of the road, allowing the men to pass. She stared at the path ahead, her eyes locked on the gray spot in the distance.

It was only a small boulder, but Evylin saw it coming from a mile away.

The gray stone jutted out from the terrae as though it had grown out of its very depths. She dismounted when she neared the rock and took hesitant steps toward it, leaving a yard's distance between her and the stone.

Moss covered the right side of the boulder, which stood at the height of her knees. It was nothing of consequence. And yet, it meant more to her than anything that came to her memory. The words carved into the side bore a weight she didn't expect.

"It's quite something, isn't it?"

Evylin tore her eyes from the stone and smiled over her shoulder at Rafferty's approach. "If you find rocks to be interesting," she said wryly.

Rafferty chuckled as he stepped up next to her. "I can't say I find all rocks interesting. But this one . . ." He shrugged. "This one is significant."

Staring at the stone once more, Evylin nodded. "It is."

Rows of soldiers passed them, crossing the line between Estshire and Nettershire. Carts rumbled across into the next province, one wholly new to Evylin.

"I've dreamed of leaving Estshire for as long as I can remember," Evylin whispered.

"Seems like your dream is about to come true," he said. "So why haven't you crossed?"

Evylin looked to all those who passed on before her. Then she looked back at the ones yet to come. Behind her, the faded hills and the memory of Whickam Village felt farther and farther away. The noontime sun beat down over them, but it didn't change the fact that the air was colder even in the few fifty-some miles they'd journeyed. The wind whispered across the plains and through the trees.

This was the moment they'd promised to one another. Ryen should have been here. He was the mastermind of all their plans. Of all people, *he* should have been the one to cross this border. Instead, his fate left him in Whickam Village forever.

Evylin turned back to the stone, heart cold like the wind. "I want to remember what I felt like before," she said, unsure why she was still whispering. "So I can compare how I feel once I cross."

"How do you feel?" Rafferty asked.

Evylin took a deep breath in . . . and then let it out. "Ready."

Rafferty grinned and proffered his arm. "Shall we go across together, then?" he asked.

Hesitating, Evylin stared at his arm. This wasn't right. She shouldn't cross with Rafferty. She should cross with Hewitt. If his son couldn't be here, then at least he could be by her side. Or perhaps she should cross with Deckard. After all, she wouldn't have this chance without him.

But he wasn't here. And neither was Hewitt.

Evylin slipped her hand into the crook of Rafferty's elbow, and he grabbed Fransis's reins. With one last smile at each other, they walked toward the stone.

Then they passed it.

Rafferty stopped them two paces into Nettershire. He pulled away and held his arms out wide as though offering her the whole of the province. "Well?" he said. "How do you feel now?"

Evylin shifted her gaze from him to the soft grass under her feet and then to the winding road stretching ahead of them. She blinked a few times, taking in the sight of the soldiers moving steadily past her.

"The same," she muttered.

"Mm." Rafferty nodded. "Me too."

"I guess you can't expect a rock to change your life."

Offering her the reins, Rafferty smirked. "Maybe we'll feel different in Leedbury."

Evylin swung up onto Fransis's back as Rafferty said his farewell and hurried to catch up with his platoon.

Perched on the molded leather saddle, Evylin gazed at the province marker, weighing her disappointment. First Berkley, and now this. Not even her wedding felt like a meaningful moment of change. At what moment would everything finally fall into place? When would she experience the realization of their dreams?

Nudging Fransis back on the road, Evylin decided that maybe Rafferty was right. Perhaps she would feel different in Leedbury.

Farther down the road, Deckard galloped over on his black mare. Ever since she'd seen him training in the paddock behind the smithy, she'd found herself comparing the captain to her uncle, looking for the marks of a soldier. And while she found his gravitas and muscular physique lacking, she had to admit he was a far superior rider to her uncle.

Deckard pulled alongside her with a gentle but apologetic expression. "I suppose you saw we crossed over into Nettershire back there?" he asked.

Hearing the caution in his voice, Evylin decided to tease him about it. "Is that what that stone was? I wondered at its size."

He let out a thin chuckle. "I'm sorry I wasn't there with you. I hadn't wanted you to cross it alone."

"Oh, I didn't cross alone," she hurried to reassure him. "Raff was with me."

Deckard's brow furrowed. "Private Rafferty?"

Unsure what caused the disapproving tilt in his tone, Evylin furrowed her brow. "Yes."

His brows dropped low over his eyes, a darker shade of blue under the cloudy skies, and his lips pressed together in a reluctant smile. "I'm glad you weren't alone."

"As am I," Evylin said, then asked, "Is there some reason Rafferty shouldn't have accompanied me?"

Deckard hesitated. "I just don't fully trust the man."

"Because he's a criminal?"

His eyes widened. "You know of his past?"

"I do."

"And yet, you're friends with him?"

Evylin smirked. "He was a smuggler. That's hardly dangerous."

After a long, tense pause, Deckard turned away from her. She could tell he wanted to argue that Rafferty's illicit history, whether dangerous or not, proved faulty character. As a devout Allorian, he likely thought theft a grave sin. As a less-than-devout Allorian, she didn't share his scruples and saw no reason to forever ridicule someone for a momentary, harmless crime.

Deckard continued scanning the soldiers. "We're only a couple of hours from Leedbury now," he said, changing the subject. "When we arrive, I'll visit the magistrate. After, if you'd like, we can see the town together?"

Excitement filled Evylin's chest just before it deflated once more. "That would be lovely," she said regretfully. "But I'm supposed to train with Hewitt tonight."

Deckard smiled kindly. "Well, perhaps we'll find time tomorrow."

"I'd like that."

"And I *am* sorry about before," he insisted. "I did intend to be with you."

Seeing the guilt etched into the lines creasing his forehead, Evylin worried he'd feel she expected him to abandon his work just to make her happy. "No, that's all right," she assured him. "I was perfectly fine."

"I should have been there."

"No."

"I *should* have."

The intensity in Deckard's gaze pierced Evylin. She wanted to fight his concern, to promise him it meant nothing to her, and to reassure him she hadn't wished he'd been by her side as she'd taken such a meaningful step. But she knew he wouldn't accept her words, no matter how convincing they were.

She gave him a soft smile and hoped he'd accept her forgiveness. "Next time, maybe," she replied.

Deckard nodded, but he knew as surely as Evylin there was no "next time." Stepping beyond the border of Estshire for the first time only happened once. And he'd missed it.

CHAPTER TWENTY-FIVE

20TH OF TERRAEN, 1573

Their arrival in Leedbury the previous evening was a lackluster affair. Deckard and Peery rushed off to meet with the magistrate, and Evylin took in the town from a distance. The stone and oaken buildings reminded her of Trollenston's architecture, revealing that Nettershire had little more to offer than Estshire.

Training with Hewitt, Thom, and Rafferty provided a pleasant distraction. Rafferty proved to be just as slippery an opponent as Hewitt suspected. He was fast, clever, and didn't play fair. Though his technique couldn't hold a candle to Evylin's, she was challenged to outmaneuver him from time to time.

Thom provided a different challenge. He still had a lot to learn, but his strength and attentive nature forced her to stay alert. Though she won each bout with both men—even when she fought them two-on-one—it was a welcome test of her skills.

Of course, Hewitt beat them all.

Peery interrupted their training session with a note from Deckard. The magistrate of Leedbury invited the captain and his wife to stay in his home. Evylin left camp to join Deckard and the magistrate for dinner. She washed up and changed in the tent while Peery summoned a couple of privates to deliver their trunks, after which he escorted her to the magistrate's house.

Magistrate Obermen was a dull old man who spoke very little while his cackling wife, Luella, chatted about nothing of consequence. Their three young boys—the youngest twelve and the eldest fifteen—whispered to each other the entire dinner, glancing at Evylin and sniggering on occasion. Deckard was as delightful as ever. Evylin was uncomfortable.

Once excused from the table, Deckard led Evylin to their room at the back of the magistrate's house. "You made quite an impression at dinner," he whispered teasingly.

Evylin glanced up at him, bemused. "Did I?"

His grin turned sly. "I do believe I'll need to watch those boys closely. Can't have any of them making overtures to my wife."

Evylin laughed as he opened the bedroom door. "Ah, I see." She pulled away from him to enter their room. "Yes, I do believe that would be wise. They're such dashing young men."

"Oh, don't say that," he returned, eyes twinkling. "You'll make me jealous."

Laughter intensifying, Evylin moved toward her trunk. But Deckard didn't move from the door.

Inexplicably, Evylin's heart fell. "You can't stay, can you?" she asked.

"I'm sorry, no," he said. "I have to check on the men and make sure the officers know my orders for the night."

"Right, of course." She forced herself to keep smiling. "Don't worry about me. I thought of reading for a while, anyway, so don't be surprised if I'm still awake when you get back."

Deckard's expression spoke of gentle doubt. "I'll do my best to return quickly."

"Please, don't hurry yourself on my behalf," she insisted, worried he'd feel obligated.

The moment the door closed behind Deckard, Evylin's loneliness struck her. She was alone in a stranger's home in an unknown town in a completely new province. And she wished more than anything that the captain would come back.

But he didn't.

Despite her attempt to wait up, Evylin finally fell asleep. And when she woke the next morning, she was alone again. She had either slept through Deckard's return, or he'd never come back at all.

Suppressing the odd disappointment in her chest, Evylin quickly dressed and snuck out of the house unnoticed. Determined not to forgo breakfast entirely, she visited the kitchen tent to quiet her growling stomach, eating as she walked to the training grounds.

Upon her arrival, the large field was sparsely populated, with only a few of the First Platoon's soldiers ready for the start of their day. Hewitt stood off the side, talking with Thom and Major Sheelds. Moris wasn't around, but she imagined that Hewitt had found some job to keep him busy elsewhere. The irritable man grumbled and complained so much that Hewitt liked finding ways to get rid of him.

Evylin popped the final bit of biscuit into her mouth as she neared the men. Sheelds saw her first, bowing to her in greeting. Hewitt glanced around as Thom followed his lead.

"Good morning, Evie," Hewitt said. "We were discussing the day's agenda."

Evylin gave Sheelds a polite nod, tossed Thom a smile, and then looked up at Hewitt. "Don't let me interrupt," she said.

"I want the men dueling today," Hewitt resumed. "They need to put these techniques into practice if they're going to stick."

"You'll get no arguments from them," Thom said, then added, "Unless you're making them fight Evie, of course."

Evylin dug her elbow into Thom's side. "It isn't my fault your men dislike me so much."

Hewitt scoffed. "Any man who can't accept defeat at the hand of a woman doesn't deserve to be a soldier."

Clearing his throat, Sheelds drew their attention back to him.

"What is it, Major?" Hewitt prompted.

"If I may interject, Mrs. Deckard," Sheelds began, his rich voice soothing in the cold morning air. "I don't believe the soldiers dislike you so much as they are avoiding you."

Evylin looked from Sheelds to the soldiers and back. "Why would they avoid me?"

"You're the captain's wife, ma'am. A soldier would be a fool to form a relationship with you. They will, of course, be courteous if you need them. But they will also keep their distance to assure the captain they have no interest in stealing his wife."

Evylin studied the young soldiers as they hurried to join ranks, each pointedly ignoring her, aside from Rafferty, who waved his hello. She supposed it made sense. An intelligent man didn't draw undue attention to himself. But the knowledge didn't make her feel any better.

Turning back to Sheelds, Evylin returned his smile. "Thank you for the clarification, Major," she said. "But I don't think my husband would mind my making a few friends."

"Perhaps, but I'm sure he would prefer being assured of your safety, ma'am," Sheelds said kindly.

Sure that she shouldn't tell the major she was more capable of ensuring her safety than Deckard, Evylin only nodded.

"Regardless," Hewitt said, reclaiming the conversation, "the men need to practice dueling other men. Evylin is more skilled than most, but she is a woman. And that is very different than the opponents they'll face outside of this camp. I intend to focus on introducing one technique at a time and having them duel the next day to practice it. End of the week, I'll see who comes out on top in each platoon."

"I think we know who'll win amongst your men," Evylin said to Thom.

He leaned down to respond. "Haalston will be devastated that you've overlooked him."

"He won't ever see Rafferty coming."

Hewitt opened his mouth to continue when a sudden yell tore out behind them. A loud *smack* and a cacophony of excited cries erupted. The four of them turned to see the soldiers of First Platoon forming a circle around two soldiers grappling one another in the center.

Thom cursed under his breath, then bolted forward. Hewitt, Sheelds, and Evylin rushed after him.

Of Shire heritage, the fighting soldiers bore similar appearances: dark hair and richly tanned skin, of middling height and broad build. But it was clear within an instant which of them was a better fighter. While the one moved with nothing but a flurry of fists, the other found holes in his defense and hit where it hurt. He landed a punch to the soldier's side, then decked him across the face as he doubled over.

As Thom, Hewitt, and Sheelds barreled on, Evylin stopped to stand at Rafferty's side.

"I'd ask if you'd like to bet," Rafferty said, grinning from ear to ear, "but it's pretty obvious who's gonna win."

Evylin spared him a disapproving glance. Thom pushed past a cluster of soldiers as the superior private swept the other's legs out from under him. The man hit the ground with a groan as the other prepared to dive on top of him. But Thom rammed into the man, dropping him to the terrae.

"What the hell is wrong with you?" Thom demanded, standing over the men. "This is unacceptable, Privates! Both of you, stand up now and explain yourselves."

The soldiers rose in slow, aching movements. Moaning and holding his jaw, the fighter on the left had blood pooling around his nose and mouth. The other private bore no apparent injuries beyond a single red mark on his cheek.

"Well?" Thom held out his hands. "I'm waiting."

Neither man spoke; instead, the bloody one glared at his opponent, who stared at the ground.

"Private Brewer?"

The soldier spat blood on the ground. "He attacked me, Lieutenant Deckard."

A huff came from the other private, gaze still averted.

"You disagree with that, Private Loxley?" Thom demanded.

Evylin raised her brow at the familiar name. She didn't recognize the young man, so she knew he wasn't the blacksmith's son, but he did share a resemblance. A nephew, perhaps?

There was a long pause before the private lifted his shoulder in a shrug.

"What sort of answer is that?" Thom yelled again. "Private Loxley, did you or did you not attack Private Brewer?"

"He did," Brewer said.

"I didn't ask you."

Brewer sank back, blood trickling out of his now-crooked nose.

"Private Loxley!"

"No," Loxley said flatly. His expression was closed off, his shaggy brown hair hanging onto his forehead, almost into his eyes. And a bright red blush bled up from his collar.

"You shit," Brewer spat. "Look what you did to me!"

Loxley ignored him.

"What happened?" Thom demanded a second time.

Neither soldier replied.

Rafferty stepped forward. "If I may, Lieutenant," he called, drawing Thom's gaze back. "I can tell you."

With a heavy sigh, Thom motioned for Rafferty to go on.

"Both Brewer and Loxley joined up in Trollenston," Rafferty said. "And it seems they know each other."

"Do I need this backstory, Raff?"

"Yes, sir, you do."

"Fine."

"As I was saying," Rafferty paced forward, eating up the platoon's attention, "these two were friends of a sort. Only Brewer is an ass, and Loxley's not."

A ripple of low laughter rose from a few soldiers, and Evylin set a hand to her lips to hide her smile.

"Brewer's been goading Loxley the last few days. Telling him he's a pitiful soldier, calling him a wuss, a pansy, and all other sorts of pathetic insults. He's not very bright."

Brewer scowled.

"Today, he told Loxley he was going to show him just how pathetic he was." Rafferty shrugged. "Loxley didn't appreciate it, but the kid's quiet. And he stayed quiet. Seems Brewer doesn't take well to being ignored."

"Shut up, you pissant," Brewer called, the sound garbled. He coughed and spat out a bloody clot. "You don't know what you're talking about!"

"Actually, I do."

Thom crossed his arms. "Get to the point, Rafferty."

"Gladly." The weasel motioned to Brewer. "Seems this behavior is normal—Loxley not taking to the dimwit's insults. Their old friend, Carmichael, in Third Platoon, told me about it. They have a go at each other on a regular basis. All because Brewer's girlfriend, Penny, has had a crush on Loxley since they were twelve."

Loxley let out a single amused snort.

"I'll beat the shit out of you, Loxley!" Brewer spat.

"You already tried," the private said dully.

"You little—"

Thom reached out and knocked Brewer back to the ground before he could leap at Loxley. "That's enough!" He turned to glare at the other private before looking back to Rafferty. "That it? Brewer's jealous, and he goaded Loxley into attacking him?"

"Not at all," Rafferty said dramatically. "That was just his motivation for goading Loxley. I thought the context would be beneficial."

"For Allore's sake, Raff, spit it out!"

"Brewer, idiot that he is, said he'd shame Loxley in the duels today, said his pitiful skills were why he couldn't get a girl. A lame attempt at an insult, I thought, but as we've already determined, he's a nitwit."

"Rafferty."

"I'm almost there, Lieutenant." Rafferty gestured toward the soldiers, happily sharing his tale. "So Brewer delivers his witless line, and Loxley says, 'That's weird, 'cause I could have sworn Penny liked me better. Guess that farewell kiss didn't mean much.'"

Loxley kept his gaze down as the red crept up from his collar to the tips of his ears. Brewer snarled, still on the ground. Several soldiers chuckled around them.

"I thought the kid was pretty clever," Rafferty admitted. "Then Brewer punched him, and that was the only hit he got. Loxley's a right dangerous blighter."

Several more laughs ran through the soldiers as Evylin grinned.

Thom drew his shoulders back. "It was you who started it, then?" he demanded of Brewer, who remained silent. "At least we've got that cleared up. Your punishment will be worse. Now, get off the ground."

Brewer scrambled up, glaring at Loxley and Rafferty in turn.

Thom looked over the whole of his platoon. "Attention, all of you!" he called, and the men snapped to attention. "It was my faulty assumption that I'd taught you half-wits well enough not to get into childish fights. Seems that's not the case. Thanks to Brewer and Loxley here, you've all got a price to pay. *Every one of you* will be on kitchen duty for the next week."

A few soldiers grimaced, but most wisely took the punishment in silence.

Thom approached Loxley first. "While you didn't start the fight, Private, you should have known better than to engage in it. Therefore, you'll be working with Major Glaas here for the next month, taking care of the weapons, cleaning up the training field, and otherwise assisting him with *whatever* he requires of you. Understood?"

Loxley's dark eyes cut toward Thom before he stared blankly forward. That fire-bright blush heated his cheeks now. "Yes, sir."

"And you." Thom turned on Brewer. "You're a poor excuse for a soldier and an even more miserable excuse for a friend. Perhaps you'll learn how not to be a shit while you're shoveling it for the next month in the stables."

Brewer scowled but didn't reply.

"Now, go find a medic and get yourself cleaned up," Thom ordered.

Brewer did as commanded, and the rest of the soldiers lined up.

Thom turned and marched away, grumbling, "What a bunch of idiots."

Hewitt and Sheelds fell in beside him. Evylin slipped through the soldiers to join them.

"My thanks for the personal idiot you've provided to me," Hewitt said.

"Ah, yeah, uh . . ." Thom rubbed the back of his neck. "Sorry about that."

"It's fine," Hewitt said gruffly.

Evylin doubled her pace to keep up. "I don't know who got the worst punishment, really."

"Brewer, by far," Hewitt said, tugging his beard. He looked back over his shoulder. "At least the idiot you gave me shows some promise."

"Promise?" Thom asked, an eyebrow cocked.

"Yes." Hewitt nodded, a glimmer in his steely eyes. "Yes, I think so."

Evylin turned back to scan the broad-shouldered youth, his dark hair tousled after the scuffle. "He knows how to fight. At least with his fists," she agreed.

"Maybe the kid's just scrappy?" Thom suggested.

"It was more than that," Hewitt said. "He doesn't just know how to beat someone up. He knew exactly where to hit to make it hurt most. He knew the weak points."

The three of them waited for Hewitt to continue, but he shook his head dismissively. "Let's start the training."

Within moments, Hewitt had Sheelds calling out the paces. The fifty men ran circles around camp ten times, then began their strength and endurance exercises. As Sheelds walked them through the basic drills, Hewitt pulled Evylin to the side.

"Evie," he spoke softly, his gaze fixed on the soldiers, "I want you to keep an eye on our new friend, Loxley."

"Really?" she gasped. "You're that impressed with him?"

"There's something about that kid," Hewitt said. "He's either got a natural talent, or he's had training already. I want to see how he does in the duel today, but he may be a good addition to our little group."

"*Really*?" She gaped up at him.

"You already said that."

"I know. I'm just surprised."

"Why?"

She smirked. "You never accept people this fast."

"I never see people fight so well."

"Fair point."

Loxley proved to be even better than Hewitt and Evylin expected. He wasn't as adept with a sword as he was with his fists, but he still beat every opponent he faced. The hour of training convinced Hewitt. "I want to see what I can make of that kid," he told her.

"Well, try not to replace me," Evylin teased. "I know I'm old news, but I'd still like to think I'm your favorite."

Hewitt rapped her on the chin with his knuckles. "Always."

After the long day of training platoon after platoon, Evylin rushed back to the magistrate's home to clean up for dinner. While she didn't care to spend another awkward dinner with the Obermens, she didn't have much choice. And though it was no fault of her own, she felt rather guilty for not having seen Deckard the entire day.

Upon her return to the magistrate's house, she snuck past the household's gaze, dashing up the stairs. Her boots pounded precariously on the wooden floors, announcing her presence as she hurried to the guest room. Hastily, she opened the door and plunged inside. The door clicked shut behind her as she turned, then promptly froze.

Evylin's entire face flared with heat, and her mouth dropped open.

Deckard stared back at her, eyes wide. Tense silence accosted the room until he let out a breathy laugh. "My apologies," he said nervously. "I didn't expect you."

Mouth still hanging ajar, Evylin supposed it could have been worse. At least the only clothing missing was his shirt, which he held in his hands. And at that moment, he slid his arms through the sleeves to lift it up over his head. The white tunic fell to cover his surprisingly muscular chest and abdomen. For a man with such a trim frame, he clearly didn't lack strength.

Yes, she thought, *it could have been* far *worse.*

Evylin's hand flew up to cover her laughter. She averted her eyes and hurried to the other side of the room. The farmers of Whickam Village often worked the fields shirtless in the blistering summer heat. Such a thing shouldn't shock her. Yet, she'd never stood so close to or in such an intimate setting with a bare-chested man. Certainly not when it was so unexpected.

After a moment's recovery, Evylin cautiously turned back to Deckard. She kept her eyes on the brown blankets of the bed between them. "I'm sorry," she said, the awkward humor making her words tremulous. "I didn't think you'd be . . . here."

Deckard shifted hesitantly. "I hope that isn't a problem."

She shook her head with too much force to be genuine. "Not at all."

They fell silent again.

"Evylin," Deckard said, his voice smooth.

She stared at the nightstand beside him.

"Would it help to pretend this never happened?"

She pressed her lips together, fighting too much laughter to respond.

"Why are you laughing?" he asked bemusedly.

"I don't know," she said weakly. "It's just awfully uncomfortable."

After a pause, Deckard chuckled. "It is, isn't it?"

Evylin nodded furiously.

"Shall we ignore it, then?" he asked so kindly that Evylin felt compelled to look up at him at last. He wore a small smile, his white tunic almost glowing in the sunset.

She took a deep breath, then murmured, "I think we might have to."

Deckard's smile grew. "Then ignore it, we shall. But you should turn around now. I have to tuck this shirt in, which might add to the problem if you watch."

The very idea spun Evylin around with another fit of laughter. It took little time for him to call the all clear. When she turned, he'd begun donning his dark green coat.

Graciously, Deckard changed the subject. "Did training go well?" he asked.

"It did," she said, the words coming more easily. "Hewitt's found a potential candidate to join us in our training."

"*Your* training?"

"Oh, I guess I didn't tell you." She watched as he tied a simple white linen cravat around his neck. "Hewitt wanted to be sure I was still getting some training in, so he created a small group to work with me."

He gave an approving nod.

"It's just Hewitt, Thom, Raff, and me right now, but he's thinking about asking this private to join us if he does as well as we expect."

Deckard didn't show much reaction to her words, his eyes—a light greenish blue in the light—studying her face. "Do you feel like it's helpful? Like you're improving?"

"I do."

"That's good," he said, fastening the last button on his coat. "I'll head down so you can change."

"Thank you," Evylin said, expecting him to walk out.

Instead, he stepped around the bed to stand before her. Deckard stared down at her gently. Though used to looking up at Hewitt, few men in Evylin's life were genuinely tall. Most of the Shiremen stood less than a hand taller than her. Even her father stood near her height.

But looking up at Deckard made her feel far smaller than usual. And the kindness of his gaze set a nervous flutter flying in her chest.

"It's good to see you today, Evie," he whispered.

Evylin's smile faltered at his tenderness. "You too," she replied.

Another second passed, and then Deckard bent to place a quick, sudden kiss on her temple. "I'll see you downstairs," he said, turning and leaving the room.

Evylin stared at the door, considering the warm spot on her forehead. What had that been about? Aside from the kiss at their wedding, Deckard had yet to attempt any physical affection. She wasn't exactly opposed to such attention, but it did make her nervous.

They might be married, but they were still strangers. And Evylin wasn't ready to be more to him.

Her fingers trembled, instinctively reaching toward the novel on her nightstand. She brushed the folded scrap of paper she used as a bookmark, thinking of the pressed everbloom flower within. Her marriage to Deckard was a means of upholding her promise to Ryen—that was all.

"For now."

Evylin's chest tightened. Could she handle that? She'd always wanted to marry, to have a husband. She'd even wanted children. But giving herself to a stranger . . .

She couldn't do it yet. Not even if he was a man as kind and honorable as Captain Deckard. Letting him touch her, giving him that much control over her, trusting him that way . . . She couldn't. And she prayed he wouldn't ask it of her any time soon.

CHAPTER TWENTY-SIX

12TH OF OBSCURA, 1573

The days bled on as they traveled from Leedbury and north through Nettershire. Life settled into a routine. Daily, Evylin would wake—alone—and go about her day helping Hewitt with the recruits. In the evening, they would train with Thom, Rafferty, and Loxley—who'd requested they call him Ethenn.

Rafferty and Ethenn marched with the platoon on travel days, but Hewitt and Thom would ride at her side whenever they could. The five of them became fast friends. Ethenn was as natural a fighter as Hewitt thought. He was young—even younger than Rafferty, who she'd come to learn was twenty-three—and his quiet nature joined the group with unassuming ease.

While journeying through Nettershire, the Ephrian Army explored seven additional villages and two towns. Each visit followed a consistent routine. Deckard and Peery would first meet with the magistrate. As they progressed northward, it became increasingly uncommon for the magistrates to invite the captain and his wife to stay. If they reached a village in the morning, the magistrate would typically spend the day informing the local citizens. If they arrived later, notifications were sent out the following day. Afterward, Deckard delivered his speech, successfully attracting more volunteers at every stop.

The troops expanded, and Hewitt and Evylin grew busier each day. The platoons overflowed with an increasing number of soldiers. There were so many men that Thom and the rest of the lieutenants worked constantly most days. And Deckard seemed to disappear altogether.

Almost daily, Evylin saw her husband from afar, riding or walking through the camp, giving orders, and overseeing his men. Sometimes, they'd share a meal in the evening, but that habit grew more infrequent. All fears she'd held about his impending physical advances dissipated. She almost felt as though she weren't married at all.

For the first time in her life, Evylin experienced the freedom to live according to her own desires. She engaged in training, ate the simple but abundant meals provided by the army, read regularly, and traveled constantly. She had Hewitt's companionship, enjoyed the company of her new friends, and possessed everything she had ever wished for.

And she was immeasurably bored.

Life on the road, Evylin realized, was dull.

They'd traveled and trained with the army for almost a month. Nearly forty days had passed, and she wondered if this was all adventure offered—a stop here and there but mostly riding or walking and sleeping in a tent.

Evylin pressed into the training with Hewitt, wishing for new challenges and excitement. Though Thom had grown stronger as a swordsman, so had she. He rarely presented her with a fight she couldn't win. Rafferty was sly and crafty as always, but with his lack of training, even his wily nature couldn't match her skill.

Ethenn was a different story—strong like Thom and keen like Rafferty, but with patience neither of them possessed. Unlike the other two, he could wait Evylin out and endure her stamina. His talents owed their thanks to his upbringing as a hunter, they'd learned. The long hours spent stalking prey, eyes primed for movement, developed fast reflexes and endurance even she didn't possess.

She recognized the name Loxley from Trollenston. It would be hard not to after she and Hewitt had regularly visited the smith, Vernon Loxley. But given Ethenn's reluctance toward personal conversation, she'd thought it best not to ask after the relation.

The quiet Ethenn Loxley was certainly a challenge. He was as analytic as he was brawny, making him a dangerous opponent. And for a while, it made Evylin's days more enjoyable.

But soon, even its novelty faded.

"What is it?" Hewitt asked, riding at Evylin's side. The frigid breeze pressed behind them as though driving them away from the small town of Cherlam, yet another settlement of no note.

Evylin fidgeted with Fransis's reins. "What are you talking about?" she said, unsure whether she was unwilling or unable to explain.

"Don't try to fool me. You've been sulking for over a week now. I've been patient, but I won't ignore it any longer. Has Deckard been cruel to you?"

Evylin wrinkled her nose. "I don't think Jonn is capable of cruelty."

"What's he done, then?" Hewitt pressed.

"He hasn't done anything," Evylin said, staring at the horizon, wishing for anything other than the dry, grassy plains that stretched on infinitely.

The previous week, they'd stopped in Hiwood, a village on the edge of Nettershire and the closest Evylin had ever come to the sea. She could smell it in the air their whole visit, her promise to Ryen lingering in her mind. However, the village was settled nearly three miles off the coast, and she'd only seen the water from a distance, a shimmering gray-blue line that beckoned faintly. The salt air called to her, whispering, *"Come see the sea."* A silly but compelling demand that caused her heart to ache.

Now, they were back in the landlocked countryside, and from what Evylin knew, her next chance to see the water wouldn't be until their arrival in Loclight. With another month of travel ahead, she resigned herself to more of the dull, flat plains and fields.

Hewitt's gray horse twitched its ears as a fly buzzed by. "If it isn't Deckard, what is it?" he asked.

"It's nothing," she maintained emptily.

He remained silent, his stare demanding.

Evylin looked over the Third Volunteer Company. Hundreds of men marched along, leaving their homes to serve their country. Dirt and grass flew out of the tamped terrae in chunks from the horses' hooves. The Ephrian Army was tilling the Shires for volunteers.

"The world isn't what I thought it'd be," Evylin muttered.

"You've hardly seen the world," Hewitt said. "You can't expect going from one settlement to the next to impress you. Give it time."

"But is it any different outside of the Shires?" Evylin asked, the freezing wind slicing through her coat. She shivered. "Or is it more of the same?"

He turned away, eyes searching the horizon. He lifted a hand to scratch his beard, now trimmed and maintained. Soldiers weren't supposed to have facial hair, but a trim was all he was willing to give. "What are you looking for in the world, Evie?" he asked.

She tugged her scarf higher. "I don't know," she admitted. "But I can't accept that life is as simple and . . . *boring* as this. There has to be something else out there. Some other reason to live."

"What would be reason enough to live?"

For her whole life, Evylin would have said, "Adventure." The life she and Ryen had planned for themselves—*that* would be enough. As young children unaware of laws and logic, they vowed to leave the village when they came of age at seventeen. Then they would explore Ephria and, perhaps, the world should they decide it agreeable. They'd grown wiser at thirteen and worked out a more mature plan. Ryen would join the army, rise through the ranks, and prepare for their future. Then he would find her a worthy husband, knowing Lawton Glaas would never allow his daughter to leave unattached.

After that, they'd go off on their adventure together, becoming like the legends and heroes they so admired from the tales of old.

Now that Ryen was gone, the answer hadn't exactly changed, but it wasn't the same either. Yes, adventure should be enough. Keeping her promise to Ryen—that *should* be reason enough to live.

So why did it feel so hollow?

"There must be more," Evylin whispered, adamant and pleading at the same time. "*Life* must be more."

Hewitt's typical stolid demeanor didn't falter. "What is more and what is less is subjective," he said. "It's up to you to determine what each means."

Evylin frowned at him. "How am I supposed to do that?"

"It's innate, Evie. You know. We all know. Whether you've sat down to listen to yourself or not doesn't change that."

A pair of officers rode past, signaling the guard change. The sun dipped lower in the sky, coloring the army in a wash of golden light. Evylin and Hewitt rode to the side of the marching troops. The creak of wheels, the stamp of boots, the chatter of men, and the nicker of horses filled the air. From their distance, her and her uncle's conversation was wholly private.

Evylin looked up at Hewitt. "Do you know what your 'more and less' are?" she asked.

His gaze remained on the soldiers. "Yes."

At his closed-off posture, Evylin didn't press for details.

She sighed, surveying the troops as well. "I guess I need to listen to myself then. I fear I'm running out of time."

Hewitt turned to her, brow furrowed. "How's that?"

Evylin shrugged casually. "I thought this would be so different," she said. "But here we are on this monotonous parade through towns and villages identical to one another, and I'm no closer to adventure than I was at home. I left to keep my promise, changing my life almost irrevocably, and I'm starting to question whether adventure even exists."

Hewitt said nothing as he stared at her, gray eyes gloomy in thought.

"What do I do?" she whispered.

Suddenly, Hewitt reached over and cupped her cheek, his calloused thumb tenderly stroking her skin. "My dear girl," he murmured, "this is my fault. I've traveled Ephria; I know what's out here, and I should have prepared you better."

Evylin had to disagree. He'd told her all his stories. She'd known what was out here too. She just didn't realize that her expectations—the dreams she and Ryen held—were unrealistic.

"It isn't your fault," she promised. "I thought this was what I wanted, but . . ."

"It isn't what you thought it would be," Hewitt concluded. A softness laced his words, a side of himself he kept hidden from all but her. "I'm sorry, all the same."

They shared sorrowful smiles and rode on in silence. The soldiers' discourse harmonized with the rhythmic cadence of the horses' hooves and the rumbling of the wagons, forming a symphony akin to music. This was the chorus of the road, the essence of life within the Ephrian Army.

Evylin listened with disappointment. What was more and what was less? For so long, she'd thought this would be her "more." The very idea of travel meant happiness only a month ago. But she found the constant movement draining, tedious, and impossibly lackluster. She'd thought life on the road was a life of adventure. Instead, she found rigidity and . . . less.

"Evylin," Hewitt said, drawing her gaze, "what did you mean when you said your life has changed almost irrevocably?"

Confused by the singling out of those words, Evylin furrowed her brow. "Well, I mean, it has. What else could I have meant?"

Hewitt shook his head. "You said, '*almost* irrevocably.'"

Their narrowed eyes met.

"That means you think there's a way you could go back."

Evylin didn't understand his confusion. "Obviously, I don't think it will come to it," she assured, "but an annulment is always possible."

Hewitt drew back on the reins of his horse, cutting into Evylin's path. Fransis snorted irritably at the sudden stop, but Evylin was struck by the fierceness of her uncle's gaze, its sharp gray like flashing lightning.

"What are you talking about?" he growled.

Faltering under his intensity, Evylin fought to find words. "I'm not saying it will happen. Or that I want it to. Only that it *could,* if needed."

"How?"

"The same way all other ones happen, I suppose."

"No!" His voice rumbled with the singular, furious word. "How is that a possibility?"

"I don't understand."

"Evylin." Hewitt spat her name in furious reprimand. "Have you not consummated your marriage?"

Evylin blanched. Then she averted her gaze. "I don't see how that's any of your business," she muttered, far too embarrassed to be angry.

"It is very much my business," Hewitt growled. "Don't you understand this gives Deckard the opportunity to send you home whenever he'd like?"

Somehow, her discomfort gave her the gumption to say, "He wouldn't do that."

"Why not?" he said flatly. "Not because of love. That's never been part of your relationship. Because of your friendship? You two hardly spend time together. So please, enlighten me on what grounds you're so secure in his loyalty to you?"

"It would be going back on his word," Evylin defended. "Jonn is too honorable for that."

"And if he falls in love with another woman? What, then?"

Evylin blinked as though he'd slapped her. No, there was no love between them. Yet, Evylin realized at that moment that she had assumed that if Jonn Deckard were going to fall in love with any woman, it would be her.

In her silence, Hewitt continued, "Would you hold him to the bonds of a loveless sham of a marriage if he found another who returned his affections? One who would be a true wife to him?"

A shiver went down Evylin's spine. Due to the wind or fear, she couldn't tell. If Deckard wanted to annul the marriage, he could. He could send her back to Whickam Village to live out her days alone. And her promise to Ryen would come to nothing. Could she face that brutal future?

No. Evylin wouldn't go back, no matter what Deckard desired. Not even if it meant his unhappiness. She would demand he be faithful to his vows, even if she never loved him.

Hewitt's next words cut even deeper. "That's assuming, of course, that he'd be gracious enough to give you the choice," he said coldly. "The truth is that he'd send you home with or without your consent. In fact, he could do that now if he got tired of you. And what would you do, then?"

Evylin looked up at him in fright.

"I can't return with you, Evie." She saw her fear reflected in his sharp stare. "I signed a contract with the army. I cannot return to Whickam Village until my commission is up. I have enough pull with my fellow officers to keep myself in Deckard's companies, regiments, or whatever else he's given. I can stay with you for as long as you stay with him. But if he sends you home, we will be without each other. We will be *alone*."

The thought terrified Evylin more than anything. Returning home would be devastating but ultimately bearable. After all, she'd be with Ryen and could return to the rote but mostly independent life she'd always had. But if Hewitt wasn't there . . .

Alone.

Evylin couldn't be alone again.

Tears burned her throat, making her vision hazy. "I've trapped us here," she whispered in dread.

"The blame lies with both of us," Hewitt said gently. "I supplied the plan, and you agreed to it. This is our life now. And if you don't seal your marriage with Deckard, you're leaving our fates up to him. Do you honestly trust him that much?"

No. Evylin didn't trust him. She didn't trust anyone but Hewitt.

But that was even more reason she couldn't face a consummation. How could she give herself body and soul to a man she didn't trust?

A shaky breath escaped Evylin, turning to fog in the cold air. Her chest grew brittle like cold steel, making each breath harder. "I can't do it," she admitted weakly. "Not yet."

Hewitt's expression softened, drooping with somber regard. He took her hand, so small in his giant palm, giving it a gentle squeeze. "I understand," he said compassionately. "But you may not have that choice much longer. It must be done. And if you don't initiate it, he will."

The thought made her stomach sink.

Hewitt's brow furrowed. "I'm surprised he hasn't already." He pressed his other hand on top of hers. "It will be easier for you if you're the one controlling when it happens," he advised.

Evylin couldn't speak. Her voice had disappeared as though tamped down with the grass under the Ephrian soldiers' boots.

Hewitt gently patted her hand. "Consider it," he urged, "but decide quickly." After releasing her, he inquired, "Are you all right?"

Frozen under the weight of his charge and the frosty evening air, Evylin's skin prickled with fear. She stared back at him, her voice barely a whisper as she said, "I hardly know."

CHAPTER TWENTY-SEVEN

13TH OF OBSCURA, 1573

One month. One full month of waking up next to Evylin and walking away. One month of being afraid of his wife.

Deckard rose from the cot on the fortieth morning of their marriage, determined to change that fact.

It was Thom's intervention that straightened him up. After the speech in Cherlam, Thom joined Deckard, staying with him until the end of the evening. The rest of the officers returned to camp, and Deckard closed the ledger. He looked up to find Thom staring at him warily.

Caught off guard, Deckard instinctively asked, "What?"

Thom hesitated, then asked, "Why don't you spend time with Evie?"

Deckard stared at his brother for too long, trying to decide what to say. "I'm a captain, Thom," he offered. "My work keeps me busy."

Thom scoffed derisively. "Why do you ever try to lie to me?"

"I'm not lying," he said, defending his lie.

"Have you lost your mind? I work with you. You're not *that* busy."

Neither brother spoke for a considerable duration. Thom waited for a response while Deckard felt too embarrassed to provide one. Ultimately, silence prevailed, giving Thom the victory.

Deckard ran a hand over his face. "I'm giving her space," he explained. "She's independent, and I don't want her to think I'm suffocating her."

Thom studied him blankly. Then he rolled his eyes. "Well, you don't have to worry about that. You've given her space the size of the Veridus Sea."

Deckard looked away.

"I don't suppose that will foster marital affection, though, will it?"

Deckard gave his brother a chagrined glare. "Affection?" he repeated coldly. "Am I to expect that from a wife who didn't want me—*doesn't* want me?"

Thom frowned, but Deckard continued, "I was a last resort. And only that by the whim of her uncle."

With a wry chuckle, Thom agreed. "I still can't figure out why he picked you."

"Me neither."

"Regardless," Thom muttered, releasing a tired sigh, "you should spend more time with her. I think . . . she'd like that."

"Maybe you're right," he said, careful to keep his tone from turning bitter. "You do know her better than I."

"And whose fault is that?" Thom said smugly.

"Mine, obviously. But I'm not exactly as lucky as you. Hewitt may have picked me to marry her, but he picked *you* to train with her."

"Well, you're a terrible swordsman."

"And you're a terrible teacher."

Thom laughed. "Don't insult me because you're irritated. It's not my fault you can't seem to pick it up." He grimaced, reluctance in the twitch of his lips. "I think she's lonely, Jonn."

Deckard paused at that. Since the draft had brought Thom into the army, he hadn't called his brother anything but "Deckard." At first, he didn't like the formality, but soon, he found the professional name brought a distance to their relationship. It was as though Thom stopped seeing him as a brother, seeing him instead as a soldier when he called him by his last name. Their arguments got fewer, and their reactions were less snappish.

Thom's use of Deckard's given name served as an indication that it would be prudent to remain attentive. Furthermore, it suggested that he should stay vigilant for any additional signals that Thom was beginning to regard him more as a brother rather than merely as a comrade in arms.

Freshly wary, Deckard addressed the subject at hand. "How could she be lonely?" he asked. "She has Hewitt. She has you. She even has Privates Rafferty and Loxley."

"It's not exactly the same," Thom argued.

"She's never alone."

"She is more than you think."

Deckard didn't have a response to that.

"And—well, I don't mean to be in your business, but . . ." Thom averted his gaze awkwardly, "you're married. Don't you think you should try to—I don't know, fall in love or something?"

Deckard winced. "What if she doesn't want my love?"

Thom's jaw tightened. "You two have to spend the rest of your lives together. She's too smart to think that living life as indifferent spouses is a good idea."

Deckard conceded with a nod.

Thom narrowed his eyes. "I'm surprised at you," he said bemusedly. "You've always been a romantic with those stupid dreams of yours—always pining after some impossible idea of a woman. This should be easy for you."

"Being a romantic and having experience in romance are two separate things," Deckard noted sourly.

"That's the dumbest excuse I've ever heard," Thom scoffed. "She's your bloody wife. She's *gorgeous*. Not to mention, she's the most impressive woman I've ever met. And she's sleeping in your bed, with full permission for you to do whatever you like with her."

"Thom—"

"You have to feel *something* for her," he insisted.

"I do," he admitted. "But she doesn't."

Thom pressed his lips together. A vein ticked in his jaw as he stared out into the shadow-filled streets. "Do you know that?" he asked tensely. "Or are you just guessing?"

"I . . ." Deckard paused to consider, then shrugged. "I don't know."

"Then what do you have to lose?" Thom asked. "I mean, what's ever the endgame of romance, anyway? Every choice is in pursuit of marrying—or bedding—the woman. Well, congratulations. She's yours. You don't have to be afraid of losing the game because you've already won it without even trying."

Deckard didn't appreciate the metaphor but understood the point well enough.

"You should *try* to be happy together," Thom said, the words coming out strained. "I think she deserves that, don't you?"

Listening to Thom speak, Deckard smiled. This was the first time he could recall Thom trying to help him, the first time his brother had shown actual concern for *him*. Perhaps Thom really had grown up.

"What?" Thom took a step back. "Why are you looking at me like that?"

Deckard shook his head, brushing away the question. "Thank you."

Thom's chin dipped down. "No problem."

Patting his sheepish brother's shoulder, Deckard returned to camp with renewed purpose. He had work to do. Letting his marriage stagnate was an error for which he would take full credit. He'd reacted poorly, afraid Evylin wanted nothing to do with him while his heart was rapidly attaching itself to her. When she asked him to let her live as before—unchanged in every way but in name—it scared him to think she might refuse his growing affections.

To complicate matters, Deckard couldn't forget the advice of Magistrate Glaas either: *"Don't fall in love with her before she falls in love with you."*

Every moment Deckard thought of Evylin, those words haunted him.

"Don't fall in love with her . . ."

How could he not? Her beauty aside, that quick wit and happy disposition made every moment with her a joy. Any time he saw her train, her skills impressed him and left him in awe. That bright smile with those adorable dimples, the way it lit up her amber-brown eyes when the light hit them. Every time she so much as smirked, Deckard knew he was looking at true beauty. Then he thought of how she moved when she trained and how those trousers hugged her frame as her muscular arms carried the weight of that sword. It was downright terrifying to Deckard how often he thought those things.

"Don't fall in love with her."

What a ridiculous, impossible piece of advice.

And he was already feeling the heartache of it.

But Thom was right. A marriage without love was no marriage at all. And even if she didn't love him yet, he knew he had to do everything in his power to fill their marriage with happiness.

The first step of his new challenge was to stop avoiding Evylin.

Deckard slipped from the bed on the frosty winter morning, careful not to disturb her. Evylin's sleeping frame adjusted to the newfound space on the cot. He shifted the blankets higher to keep her warm. In Obscura, the final month of eight, frost covered the ground each morning in Nettershire. And he knew Evylin was struggling with the ever-lowering temperatures as they marched farther north.

After dressing in his usual uniform, he decided to wear his green wool coat rather than the gray work one. As he completed his morning routine, Deckard pulled the velvet bag from the bottom of his trunk. He tucked it into his pocket and promised himself not to withhold the gift another day.

Deckard reached for a slip of paper amongst the maps and books on the table on his way out. He scribbled a note, folded it, and placed it on Evylin's trunk. With one last look at her peaceful face, he left.

His mornings were usually busy. But this morning, he had an even longer task list. In the cold predawn light, the camp was silent. He walked through the tents, drawing in an invigorating breath of frigid air. Per his routine, Deckard rose before everyone but the sentry soldiers to prepare for the day. In his teen years, he'd read a biography of General Theraan Lees, one of the greats who'd helped the first King Ephren rise to power. Lees insisted on an early morning of exercise and time alone to sort out his thoughts. Sure that this would make him a better soldier, Deckard adopted the habit for himself, maintaining it thus far throughout his career.

After completing his daily ritual, he informed his officers of his intentions for the day. Thom was gracious enough to take on the captain's duties. In fact, he wore a superior grin upon discovering that Deckard was taking his advice.

Typically, Deckard spent the day before his speech split between the magistrate and restocking supplies, amidst checking in on the camp and completing any other miscellaneous tasks. But with Peery's help, Thom promised they'd manage without him.

The sun peeked over the hillside, and the light violet-blue sky glowed gold at the edges. Deckard made his way to the training ground, where he found Hewitt with Major Sheelds.

"Good morning, Majors," Deckard called.

The two men bowed upon his approach, pausing their conversation. Despite their rocky start, the two worked well together, and the volunteers showed immediate improvement with their combined efforts. And though Moris still grumbled his complaints, the haughty major actually admitted to being impressed by the volunteer soldiers' rapid progress.

"Morning, Deckard," Sheelds said. "What can we do for you?"

"I've come to inform you both that Evylin and I will be taking the day off," he said, looking from Sheelds to Hewitt. "I hope that doesn't interfere too much with your plans for today."

Hewitt crossed his arms. "I suppose I could have Private Loxley take her place."

"I'm glad to hear it," Deckard said, taking note to ask after this private in the future. "Might I speak with you alone for a moment, Major? I have an idea I'd like to run by you."

Hewitt's brows tipped up, and Sheelds excused himself.

"What can I do for you, Captain?" Hewitt asked.

"I wish you'd call me 'Deckard' like the other officers."

"I'll refrain."

Deckard's lips lifted in a derisive grin before he forced his features back into professionalism. It wouldn't do for Hewitt to think his request was a joke. "I am quite impressed with the men's improvements," he said. "It's clear you're not only an expert swordsman but also an exceptional teacher."

"I'm rather sure you already knew that," Hewitt said stoically. "Now, what do you want?"

"I'd like you to train me," Deckard said steadily.

Hewitt hesitated, then let out a grunt. "Yes, Evie and I saw you training with Thom in Whickam Village."

Deckard wasn't sure whether to be embarrassed or thankful he didn't have to explain why he wanted help. "I didn't realize either of you knew."

The older man didn't bother to explain. "It'll take a good while to get you anywhere near decent."

"I expected that."

Hewitt's eyes narrowed. "How did you get to be a captain with no skills as a swordsman?"

Deckard wet his bottom lip, ashamed of the truth. "They wanted men who could recruit," he said flatly. "I'd proved to be well-liked and well-spoken, and if you aren't on the frontlines, they don't care if you can win a fight."

"But you care."

"I do."

Hewitt rested his hands on his hips, surveying Deckard. "I assume you want to keep it secret."

"Yes," Deckard confirmed. "It isn't good for morale when the captain can't fight."

"No. I'd say it's not," Hewitt agreed. "We can start in the morning. I'll tell Sheelds you've got a special project for me and have him handle the preparations. Evylin isn't exactly a morning person, but she'll get used to our meetings soon enough."

"No," Deckard insisted. "She's not to know about it."

Hewitt glowered. "She already knows you can't fight."

"I don't care about that," Deckard said, despite his disappointment in himself. "I don't want her to know about the training."

"Why?"

"I have my reasons."

Hewitt grunted. "Fine. You'll train with me then, though it's going to be twice the work for you."

Deckard held out his hand. "I look forward to it."

Hewitt stared at his proffered hand, then a sly smile stretched over his lips. He accepted the handshake with a vise-like grip, sending a jolt up Deckard's arm. "It'll be fun."

"I doubt that," Deckard noted. "But it'll be worth it anyway."

"Perhaps you're not quite the milksop I thought," Hewitt said, muscles stretching the arms of his coat as he crossed them once more. "You don't care that I'm going to beat you senseless each day?"

"If you're trying to frighten me," Deckard raised his brow, "it may be working, but I'm not going to change my mind."

Hewitt let out a deep laugh, and Deckard smiled. Perhaps he could win Hewitt's good opinion after all. Even if it did leave him with bruises that would never fade.

"What's so funny?" Evylin asked, appearing at their side.

Deckard drew in a sharp breath at her unexpected presence. For the past month, Evylin wore her training gear to near exclusivity, braiding her hair back and out of the way. But today, her hair hung free while the hem of a light blue skirt and the collar of her white blouse peeped out from under her thick, wool coat. She'd worn the outfit when magistrates hosted them, though such occasions were rare. Her appearance stunned Deckard each time with the contrast between the soft, feminine colors and her warm, tan skin.

Hewitt's rumbling laughter fell to a faint chuckle. "I was telling the captain here about the trainers back in my day," he lied smoothly. "How they'd send us back to our tents with welts so large we struggled to move for weeks. They beat every ounce of weakness out of us without hesitation."

Deckard accepted the implied threat. "I hope you never have to resort to such practices here. I do believe our volunteers would start interrupting my speeches to warn against joining us."

"But at least they'd become proper soldiers," Hewitt noted.

"Pity the men in your day weren't better students," he countered. "Perhaps if they'd been more attentive, their teachers wouldn't have had to resort to violence."

Deckard turned then, offering his arm to Evylin. "Are you ready for our day off?" he asked.

Evylin hesitated, taking his arm and glancing up at Hewitt. "I was actually coming to tell you about that, Uncle."

Hewitt shook his head. "The captain already informed me. Enjoy your day, and I'll see you later." He patted her cheek and walked away.

After watching her uncle go, Evylin bit her lip and turned to Deckard. He could sense her apprehension even without the tense way her fingers hovered rather than rested on his arm. Still, he smiled down at her.

"Shall we be off?" he asked.

Slowly, Evylin's expression softened, and she returned his smile. "Lead on, Captain."

CHAPTER TWENTY-EIGHT

The horse was ready when they arrived at the stable tent. Deckard had stopped by early in the morning with a bag of supplies to add to the saddle. The private on duty handed Deckard the reins of his black mare. It had been intentional, only taking the one horse. Though he hadn't known Evylin would wear a skirt when he left her a note this morning, he'd thought the proximity would foster marital bonding.

"I know it won't be the most comfortable journey," Deckard said, guiding the horse over to her. "But as I don't imagine that skirt will allow for riding astride, you'll have to sit in front of me."

Evylin hesitated, eyeing the pommel-less saddle. "I didn't realize we'd need to ride anywhere. Where are we going?"

"The countryside around Wayford is known to be the inspiration for many of the great Ephrian artists. And I thought we might enjoy a day away from camp," Deckard explained. "Do you mind?"

"I've never ridden a horse in a dress before," she said wryly. "But I guess it is a small adventure of its own."

Deckard held out his hand. "Then let me help you up."

Though thankful for the opportunity to hold her waist, he didn't linger before hopping up behind her. He had not experienced much physical contact with his wife beyond what their sleeping arrangements induced. And despite his Allorian virtues, he relished the necessity of their nearness now.

They rode north for half an hour before Deckard chose the spot. Though Wayford was most notable for its wildflowers and colorful springtime, the early winter didn't disappoint. It was all as beautiful as the paintings in Loclight depicted. Thin clouds floated through the sky, never fully concealing the sun's golden face. Little copses dotted the countryside, some surrounding a small lake to their right and others sprouting out of the terrae to create miniature havens across the plain. Dark green pines and shedding copper oaks mingled in the thickets. The grass looked like cream under the layer of frost. It was too early in the season for snow, but the crystalline edges of the water promised its arrival soon.

"Will this do?" Deckard asked, edging forward to see her reaction.

Evylin smiled brightly. "It's beautiful."

Glad of her approval, Deckard dismounted and helped her off the horse. Removing the saddlebag, he hobbled the horse and set her loose to graze, after which he enlisted Evylin's help to spread a blanket across the grass. When they sat, he showed her what else he'd brought: a small breakfast and plenty for lunch—knowing her appetite—along with a book for each of them and a map of Ephria.

"What's that for?" Evylin asked when he showed her the map.

"You said you wanted to travel the country," he replied. "I thought we'd look at the map, and I could tell you about all the places I've been. Then we can make plans to visit whichever sounds best to you."

Evylin blinked as though awed. "We can travel without the army?"

"It won't be often, but yes," he confirmed. "Hopefully, I'll earn leave soon, and then, we could go anywhere we wanted for a time."

Evylin played with a button on her coat, biting back a smile. "That would be wonderful."

"First," Deckard said, handing her the cloth-enclosed breakfast bundle. "Eat this. We have the entire day ahead of us, and I don't want you to starve."

"That would be a pity," Evylin said, popping a nettleberry into her mouth.

The food didn't take long to disappear, especially after she insisted he take some of the ham and fruit for himself. She showed serious contempt for his habit of skipping breakfast. He'd done his best to defend himself, but she'd rejected each excuse.

"It isn't healthy," she said, forcing more food on him.

Initially, he worried that their conversation might feel forced. Fortunately, it soon found its natural flow. And even during brief pauses, there was a comforting silence between them. He grew readily at ease as the morning wore on.

Once they had devoured the food, Deckard stood and held out his hand. "Shall we take a walk?"

"Why not?" Evylin said, accepting his help to rise.

Deckard could feel her grasp loosen once she stood, but he took the opportunity to slide his fingers through hers. She stared down at their entwined hands, but Deckard moved forward so she wouldn't have time to consider the action.

As he led her away from the blanket, the grass crunched under their feet. "I know traveling with the army isn't exactly filled with excitement," he began, "but have you enjoyed yourself so far?"

Evylin's cold fingers remained loose in his. "Yes, I suppose so. I like working with Hewitt and the soldiers. And training with Thom, Ethenn, and Raff has been fun as well."

Deckard expected those to be her favorite parts. And though he wished he'd made it onto that list somehow, he refused to be jealous. "I'm glad to hear that," he said, guiding them toward the lake.

Evylin stared at the glassy blue water. It could hardly be called a lake. There were many twice its size in Stocburrough. Deckard thought it more like a pond, though still beautiful.

"Do the lakes ever freeze over in Nettershire?" she asked.

"Yes, most of them do. I imagine it will only be another week before this has a thin layer of ice across the top."

Evylin stepped closer to the edge, pulling far enough away that Deckard had to let go of her. "I've always liked the water," she murmured almost unconsciously.

"Really?" Deckard asked in surprise. "I don't remember many lakes near Whickam Village."

Evylin shook her head, gaze locked on the water's surface. "We don't have any. Just streams and small rivers. But I've always liked them. And I've always wanted to learn how to swim."

"You can't swim?" Deckard couldn't imagine his childhood summers without the days at the lake, swimming until he turned into a prune.

She looked over her shoulder at him, smiling. "There was nowhere to learn."

"You missed out as a child," he said, putting his hands on his hips. "Something we'll have to remedy as soon as possible."

Evylin laughed. "Perhaps the sea in Loclight will do?"

Deckard grimaced. "It's a bit cold to swim there, even in summer. It would be better if I could take you to Stocburrough in Pyra. The lakes get warm, and the sun always keeps you from catching a chill when you get out of the water. It's the perfect way to spend a summer's day."

Evylin's smile grew. "I'd like that."

"Then we'll make it happen," he promised, stepping up to stand by her side. His hand itched to take hers again. The cold air had seeped away all the warmth her touch had provided, but he forced himself to be patient. The day was about getting to know her; holding her hand could wait.

Side by side, they watched the water in comfortable silence. The rocky edges rippled as fish swam lazily below. Sunlight reflected off the gently undulating water and into Deckard's eyes. He could almost feel the cold rising from its frosty surface.

"I've always wanted to see the ocean," Evylin whispered, startling him. "I had hoped to when we were in Hiwood, but . . ."

Deckard turned to her, brows pinching together. "I didn't know," he replied. "I would've made sure you saw it if I had."

Evylin shook her head as though coming out of some reverie. "It doesn't matter," she said, a hint too cheerily. "I'll see it in Loclight."

"You should have seen it in Hiwood." Deckard set a hand on her arm. "I'm sorry."

Evylin gave him a forced smile, then stepped away. "Shall we read for a while?"

Though her rejection of Deckard's apology worried him, he let her lead them back to the blanket. Evylin removed her novel from the saddlebag and took her seat. She propped the book open on her lap, then bent her head, effectively dismissing him.

Deckard joined her on the blanket and retrieved his book. After a few minutes of staring at the same sentence repeatedly, he looked at Evylin, hoping to find her as distracted as he was. Instead, he saw her turn a page, her eyes scanning the lines attentively. An amused smile lifted her lips.

Seeing her contentment, Deckard pushed himself to focus. While it took longer than usual, he was successful, engaging himself in the historical overview of Ephria's most notable officers and their accomplishments. After several minutes, he all but forgot the discomfort of the moment by the lake's edge.

The sun drifted overhead, and Evylin stretched across the blanket to lie on her stomach, continuing to read. The morning wind died down, allowing the sun to warm them, and they unbuttoned their coats to get more comfortable. Though Deckard always loved the summer most, there was something about the warmth of the sun on a winter's day that pleased him. Few things could compare, he found, and he soaked in its comfort.

Once the sun reached its zenith, Evylin sat up. She tucked a folded slip of paper into her book and closed it. "Are you as hungry as I am?" she asked.

Deckard put away his book. "I doubt I'm ever as hungry as you are," he replied. "But, yes, lunch sounds splendid."

They laid the meal out piece by piece. The spread was beautiful, brimming with cheeses, bread, cured meats, an abundance of berries, and crisp green beans. Deckard reached into the bag again to retrieve two wooden cups and the bottle of wine he had purchased in Cherlam the morning after his conversation with Thom two nights ago.

Evylin watched in surprise as he poured the wine. "What's the occasion?" she asked when he handed her the wooden cup.

Expecting she'd forgotten, Deckard was proud he hadn't. "Today marks one month of our marriage," he said, raising his cup to her. "I thought it was worth celebrating."

Her lips parted, but she hesitated. "Is that why you took the day off?" she asked gently. "To celebrate with me?"

"That was part of it, yes." Deckard held her gaze steadily. "But the real reason was to spend time with you. I know you said things don't have to change due to our marriage, but I'd like them to. I'd like to know you, Evylin, and to be there for you—to be your friend, if nothing else. We may not have chosen this marriage, but we did agree to it. And I intend to be a good husband to you."

Evylin's dark eyes searched his face. The frosty breeze tugged strands of her cool brown hair onto her cheek. Deckard reached across to brush them back. "If you'll let me," he concluded.

The silence lingered. Light pink flushed the corners of Evylin's richly tanned temples. Slowly, her surprise and confusion faded as her dimples returned. "What woman could say no to that?" she asked, then raised her cup to tap against his.

Enjoying the food and the sunlight on their backs, Deckard nodded to the red-bound novel beside her. "What is your book about?"

Evylin shook her head, mouth partially full. "You wouldn't like it," she said after swallowing. "It isn't about strategy or history or anything remotely boring."

"You think my books are boring?"

"I know they're boring," she said, gathering cheese and bread. "I tried reading the most interesting-looking one, and I nearly fell asleep after the first page."

He chuckled. "Tell me, then: What makes your novel so exciting?"

"That's the point of a novel, isn't it—to be exciting?" she noted. "They always have some adventure, danger, or romance to draw you in."

"And what does this one have? Adventure, danger, or romance?"

"A little bit of all three." She tossed him a playful grin. "Though this one is a bit heavy on the romance for me. It's about a knight who's in love with a woman from his village. She's kidnapped by an evil count who wants to marry her, and the knight travels to save her. But when he arrives to bring her home, he discovers the count is a Mage in disguise," she said dramatically, then took a sip of wine. "Now, he has to kill the count and reclaim his love."

An amused smile lifted Deckard's lips. It sounded like such a frivolous way to spend one's time. Yet, he couldn't help hoping the knight achieved his goal. "I suppose the knight succeeds and marries his love?"

"I don't know yet," Evylin said, reaching for another berry. "These stories don't always end the way you'd think. And Mages are awfully powerful. There's a chance the knight will die."

"But Mages are villains," Deckard objected. "The count can't win."

"I've read several books where the villains win," Evylin said. "And Mages aren't always villains either. Sometimes, they help the hero. Those aren't very popular, though. And if my father knew I'd read them, he'd be furious."

Deckard frowned. "I'm surprised they're still available. I thought the first King Ephren banned all books favoring magic."

Evylin gave him a sardonic expression. "Perhaps Nettershire is different, but the king forgets about us Shires down south. And we rarely abided by any but his most firm laws."

Deckard couldn't decide whether that was charming or off-putting. He was, for good or ill, a strict abider of their king's rules. And while he didn't agree with all the king's laws, he wasn't about to break them for his own personal comfort or pleasure.

He chose to keep those thoughts to himself. "Perhaps I'll read the book when you're done with it," he said.

Evylin laughed before realizing he'd meant it. "I didn't take you for someone who approved of novels. Or Mages, for that matter."

"Approval of Mages has nothing to do with it," he insisted, sure to make his expression quite serious. "I need to know if the knight wins back his love."

Her expression shifted into curiosity. "I didn't take you for a romantic either," she said.

Deckard cocked his head. "Why not?"

"Jonn," Evylin said, and his heart unnecessarily thrilled at how his name sounded in her voice, "you married me for your career. That's not exactly romantic."

Casually, he gathered a small handful of berries and offered one to her. "I shouldn't think there's anything more romantic than marrying a woman for mutual promotion, only to discover you never could have loved another."

Evylin paused, the accepted berry held between them. She took three slow breaths, eyeing him uncertainly. Then she drew back and averted her gaze. "You're quite the charmer, you know?"

"I don't care to charm you," he said honestly.

She breathed a nervous chuckle. "No? Why not?"

"Because you're my wife. And I want whatever you feel toward me to be genuine rather than cajoled."

She quirked an eyebrow at him. "Even if that feeling is indifference?"

"Even then," he swore.

"Hm." Evylin popped the berry into her mouth, motioning to the saddlebag. "Let's have a look at that map."

Obliging, Deckard unfurled the map and handed it to her. "Look it over while I clean up lunch," he instructed.

Evylin set the map on her lap, eyes roving over the rounded shape of Ephria as Deckard went about his task. On the right half of the island continent Allund, he once heard their nation compared to the head of a Giydan elephant. He'd only ever seen a sketch of the creature in an encyclopedia once but wasn't sure he agreed with the assessment.

With the last of lunch cleared away, Deckard shifted to sit beside Evylin. "What do you think?" he asked.

Evylin sighed, letting the map fall. "I don't know where to begin."

"I can help with that," Deckard said, then pointed toward the bottom right of the map. "That's Estshire, as labeled, and Whickam Village should be about there."

"I never realized how close it was to the shore," she said, her eyes wide. "It couldn't be more than a two-day journey to Olbury."

"Less than two days," Deckard confirmed, "when all is said and done."

Evylin grew silent, her fingers tracing the coastline.

"Here," Deckard said, pointing farther up the coast and into the center of Nettershire, "is Wayford. And here . . ." He drew his finger ever so slightly to the west, "is Stocburrough, where I grew up."

"It's so close."

"Yes. After Wayford, we go on to Stoclund and then onto Stocburrough. It will be our final stop in Nettershire."

She traced the uppermost corner of the province. "Does your family still live there?"

"All but Thom and me."

"Do they know you're coming?" Evylin asked quietly.

"They do. They know you're coming too."

Evylin's eyes shot to his.

Seeing the question in her gaze, he continued, "I posted a letter in Trollenston. They should have received it a few weeks ago."

"Have you heard back from them?"

"No, but I didn't expect to. They don't have any way to reach me but at home in Loclight."

Evylin didn't reply.

"Are you worried about meeting them?"

She frowned. "I guess I am. They can't be pleased with our arrangement."

"They don't know."

She looked up sharply. "What do you mean?"

"I didn't tell them the circumstances of our marriage," he said. "I simply wrote that I'd married a kind, intelligent, and beautiful young woman I'd met on my travels. That's all they ever need to know."

A slow, wry grin spread across her lips. "That's quite cunning of you."

"Which part?" he asked, smiling back. "Lying to my family about our relationship? Or complimenting you within my reply?"

"Why not both?" Evylin suggested, then turned back to the map. "You said you'd show me where all you've been."

Deckard accepted the map and complied with the request. He highlighted the various provinces he had explored during his military service, sharing stories from his time in the army. He specifically mentioned his favorite places: the vibrant capital city of Loclight and the bustling port city of Virwoud. To him, these locations exuded life and excitement, filled as they were with crowds and stunning architecture.

They talked about a few counties he hadn't visited yet, like the far west Ephrian Felbourne and Wesshire and the northernmost Helsford county. He avoided telling her about his time in Ostwatch, not wanting to relive the memories of the border town.

In the mountains bordering Wauld, Ostwatch and the settlements like it often received raids, and there was never enough support to keep the people safe. The entire border amassed the largest number of casualties in all Ephria since the Centurial War began. And Deckard had been lucky to make it out with his life.

Finally, Deckard asked where she'd like to go first.

"I don't know," she admitted, sounding overwhelmed. "I thought it would be easier than this. But there are so many places, and I feel like I'd miss out if I didn't see them all."

"I understand," Deckard said. "I remember when I first left Stocburrough. It felt as if there could never be enough time to see it all. But now that I've seen so much, I'd prefer to pick one and stay there."

"Pick one?" Evylin shook her head. "How would you choose? And why would you ever want to stop traveling?"

"It might be different if it weren't my job," he said, letting the map fall over the side of his knee. "But I've grown tired of always moving. Travel is only as good as the experiences you enjoy. And with the army, I don't get to experience much more than talking to magistrates and passing through each town and village. It hardly even feels like I've visited some of these places."

Evylin looked at the map once more. "Perhaps you need to visit them on your own," she suggested. "Without the army holding you back, you could see everything, explore the area, and really have an adventure. Surely, that would be reason enough to keep traveling."

Deckard smiled at her presumption. Travel didn't appeal to him like it did her. He hadn't joined the army for adventure. He joined to change the world.

But Deckard's life wasn't his alone anymore.

"Would that make you happy?" he asked. "Traveling the world forever?"

Evylin tilted her head thoughtfully. "Not the whole world," she said. "And maybe not forever. But at least until I've seen Ephria. I have to know I've seen it all and found one place that means more to me than any other."

Deckard set his hand on hers and leaned closer. "Then I'll help you do that," he promised. "In whatever way I can, I will help you find that place."

Evylin's expression shifted oddly when he touched her. Her eyes latched onto his, but he couldn't read the feeling within even as the sunlight warmed their dark brown to amber. She became strangely devoid of emotion. Or perhaps every emotion came on so strongly she couldn't choose what to feel.

"Will you?" Evylin asked quietly.

"It may take us time, but we'll find it," he vowed, wrapping his fingers around hers. "Together."

Evylin's breathing grew rapid. The sunlight glinted off the silver pendant of her necklace, drawing his gaze. Her golden skin glowed, the open collar revealing the slightest hint of her defined collarbone.

Deckard swallowed, cursing the distraction. He met her eyes, worried she'd take his downcast gaze incorrectly. But instead of finding reproach, she remained unexpectedly placid.

A moment later, Evylin turned her hand, interlacing her fingers with his.

Deckard glanced at their hands in shock.

She shifted closer, her side pressing into his.

Deckard's lungs contracted, and his gaze flew to hers. She held it steadily. "Evylin," he muttered, afraid to look away. Their faces were inches from the other's now. She stalled in her approach, but the suggestion was clear. "What are you doing?"

"Nothing," she whispered softly.

An eternity of seconds passed while Deckard tried to understand her intentions. His body thrummed with anticipation, the heat of the sun warming his skin. As much as he'd wished for a chance to kiss her again, he hadn't imagined it would come this soon. But if she was offering, he wouldn't reject the opportunity.

Cautiously, slowly to give her time to change her mind, Deckard leaned the rest of the way in. His lips met hers in a chaste, quick kiss, hardly any more romantic than the one on their wedding day. But it sparked something inside him, and the second he pulled away, somehow, he missed her.

Deckard opened his eyes, finding Evylin's had remained closed. Though he'd drawn back, she hadn't moved away at all.

She wouldn't let him kiss her again, would she?

He had to try.

With his free hand, Deckard cupped her cheek. Surprised by his touch, she gasped but remained motionless as he kissed her again. The wild strands of her hair tickled his fingers, and, miracle of all miracles, she kissed him back.

Deckard couldn't believe it. He *didn't* believe it. But he kissed her still.

Time slowed to oblivion. It was a new sensation for Deckard—this slow-building pressure in his chest as their lips tested each other. Her dark hair was warm, her cheeks even warmer. Or perhaps that was him growing warm. He felt as though the sun had soaked through his coat to pour liquid fire into his veins.

Deckard released Evylin's hand and wrapped his arm around her waist. He angled to draw her closer even as he feared it would end everything. She pressed her hand to his chest, and he thought for a moment she would push him away. But instead, she leaned in eagerly.

Sliding his hand from her cheek to the back of her neck, he deepened the kiss, and another gasp escaped her. Worried he'd gone too far, Deckard started to pull back, but she reached up to frame his face with her palms, keeping him near.

Between the sun's heat and the pounding of his heart, Deckard grew hot in his coat. If he hadn't been terrified that she'd come to her senses, he would have drawn away to take it off. Instead, he lost himself in her nearness. He wrapped his arms tightly around her, drawing as close to her as possible. She not only allowed this advance, but she seemed to relax into it.

The shock of her compliance drove Deckard to deepen the kiss again. He leaned in closer, his weight carrying them back, sending them off balance. After reaching out to steady them, he ever so slowly and cautiously eased her down until they lay on the blanket. Evylin's breath quickened, and once more, he worried he'd pushed too far, but she grasped the sides of his coat, holding him close.

Delirium carried away every remnant of Deckard's sanity. His veins practically boiled, and yet it was the most intoxicating feeling he'd ever experienced. He slid his hand to tangle in her hair, then trailed kisses across her cheek, sure he'd never enjoyed anything quite this much.

Suddenly, Evylin tensed. "I can't," she gasped.

Deckard pulled back reluctantly. "What?" he breathed, trying to think straight once more.

Breathing raggedly, Evylin pushed against his chest. He readily complied, sitting back as she scrambled away. "I can't do this yet," she said, a wild fear in her eyes. "I know we should—I know you can send me home, but I—I . . . I just can't."

Thoughts groggy from the sensation of kissing her, Deckard struggled to comprehend her words. "Evylin, I don't understand."

"I'm sorry," she said, panic tightening her expression as she drew farther away from him. "But I'm not ready."

"Ready for . . . ?" Deckard's brain caught up then. "Wait." He frowned. "Evylin, did you think I intended to . . ."

She stared at him, her breathing stilled.

Deckard sat back, ran his thumb along his damp lower lip, and sighed heavily. "Do you think I would force myself on you?" he asked. "Here of all places?"

Evylin held her breath, then muttered, "Yes."

Not sure whether to take offense at her presumption or be intrigued by her prolonged compliance, Deckard huffed. He pinched the bridge of his nose and submitted himself to the uncomfortable conversation. "I think it's clear that I'm not opposed to the idea," he said mildly. "However, I would rather our first intimate moment as man and wife not be out in the open."

Evylin wrapped her arms around her waist, staring uneasily at the lake.

"Did you think that was why I brought you here today?" Deckard asked worriedly. "To lure you out of camp and have my way with you?"

Evylin hesitated. "Yes."

Deckard dropped his face into his hand, disappointed in himself for unintentionally confirming her theory. All because he hadn't had the self-control to kiss her once and be grateful for it.

Taking a deep breath, Deckard bolstered his confidence. "That was not my intention," he promised. "I truly wanted to spend time with you, to get to know you. That's all, I swear."

She didn't face him, but she didn't reject his words either.

"I'm sorry that I . . ." Deckard grimaced, then continued, "that I kissed you. But it wasn't my intent when I brought you here."

She glanced at him at that, a cynical glint in her eyes.

"I thought you—" Deckard shook his head, abandoning the defense. "That doesn't matter. I only kissed you because I thought the moment was right."

She scanned him for a long moment before whispering, "I believe you."

"Thank you," he said, then asked the question to which he dreaded the answer. "Would you rather I not kiss you in the future?"

Evylin blinked, then scrunched her nose. "I don't know how to answer that."

"I'd prefer if you'd answer it truthfully."

"Would you?" Evylin asked, her deep amber eyes alight with frustration. "Because I'm not sure you'd appreciate it."

Deckard didn't hesitate. "Tell me, Evylin."

"I don't know," she said sharply. "That's my answer. We're married, so it isn't exactly like I rebuff your advances. But then you're so *courteous,* I think you'd respect it if I told you never to touch me again."

His throat went dry at the very thought, though he knew he'd do it if she asked.

Evylin scoffed, shaking her head. "But I don't know, all right? I don't know if I want you to kiss me again. Because it terrifies me. *You* terrify me. We hardly know one another, and you can kiss me like that? I don't understand it. And yet, somehow, I bloody enjoyed it."

Deckard wasn't sure whether to be proud or disappointed.

"So I don't know," Evylin repeated, wrapping her coat around herself. "Because I never want you to kiss me again while somehow wanting you to do it again right now."

They stared at each other in the wake of her vulnerable honesty. It was a confusing truth that Deckard didn't fully know how to handle. She didn't want him to kiss her, but she did. He terrified her—a strange thing. But she enjoyed his kisses—an equally strange but delightful thing.

Deckard sighed, releasing the last of his baffled frustration. He stood and held out his hand. "Come on," he said gently. "We should return."

Evylin stared at his hand, then looked up at him. "Are you mad at me?"

"No," Deckard promised, reaching lower with his hand. "Now, please, come back to camp with me."

After a brief moment of hesitation, Evylin took his hand, and he assisted her to her feet with a reassuring smile. Together, they packed the bag and retrieved the horse. The ride back to camp was quiet—an odd blend of comfortable and awkward as his arms wrapped around her and her back rested against his chest. Although nightfall was still a few hours away, both moons illuminated the sky as the winter sun dipped below the horizon, turning the sky a vibrant bronze and amethyst. The ivory moon appeared almost full while the shadow moon glowed as a softly faded orb.

"Jonn," Evylin said once they'd returned the horse to the stable tent. He looked over at her, expectant. "Thank you."

"For what?" he asked, confused.

She slipped her hand into the crook of his arm before he'd even offered it. "For today," she said, then gave a wry grin. "Even if I sort of ruined it."

Heart warming with hope, Deckard returned her smile. "On the contrary," he said, "it would only have been ruined without you."

She snorted derisively. "You are a bloody sap," she teased.

Deckard laughed. "As you say, my dear."

CHAPTER TWENTY-NINE

14TH OF OBSCURA, 1573

The first thing Deckard remembered when he woke was the velvet bag still waiting in his coat pocket. Lying in the cot with Evylin's back pressed against him, he held in his disappointed sigh. Her warmth and the rise and fall of her breath against his back urged him to turn and wrap his arms around her.

A smile crept onto his face, remembering their picnic in the countryside. Despite its awkward ending, they'd made a huge step forward in their relationship. And finally kissing her was a fantastic bonus.

For the first time since their marriage began, Deckard contemplated staying in bed until Evylin woke. It would be worth every consequence and missed opportunity to be at her side. He might even enjoy a leisurely breakfast with her, giving her the ring and his promise to go along with it.

But as he ran through the list of things he would have to cast off, Deckard remembered the one thing he couldn't ignore.

Should he arrive late for the meeting with Hewitt, he was concerned that the old bear would refuse to train him at all.

Deserting the cozy confines of the bed, Deckard went about his usual routine. He laid out his things for the speech, readying for the short transition he'd have between training and meeting with the magistrate. He pulled the velvet bag from his dark green coat's pocket and slipped it into the gray one he would wear that morning, determined not to let it off his person until he gave it to Evylin.

Taking the time to write a note, Deckard promised to see her that night if she'd wait up, then signed it with special care. She wouldn't know the effort it took, but he hoped she'd read his reluctance to leave her. He set the note on her trunk and left the tent.

The evening before, Hewitt sent a message to their tent to inform Deckard of their training location. Now, he rode to the specified field, a mile from the camp, and found Hewitt waiting for him.

"I hope I'm not late," Deckard said, leaping down from the horse.

The man grunted. "Depends on your definition of the term," he said, both hands resting on the handle of his training sword, the tip pointing down into the ground. "You arrived before I told you to, but later than I did. So which one of us is late, and which one is on time?"

Deckard stared at Hewitt, trying to deduce if the man was mocking him. Rather than answer the pointless question, he hobbled his horse before setting it loose next to Hewitt's on the large patch of frosted and dying grass. "Should we get started?" he asked.

Hewitt raised his sword, using it to point at another weapon a couple of feet away. "Pick it up," he ordered. "Then we'll see exactly how bad off you are."

The menacing way he held the sword made Deckard think Hewitt might block his attempts to retrieve the weapon as instructed. Though he would rather not play a game of cat and mouse this soon in their training—nor this early in the morning—he supposed it would be whatever Hewitt wanted. And he did expect some form of humiliation in their lessons, whether from Hewitt's design or Deckard's poor abilities.

"You saw me train with Thom," Deckard said, keeping one eye on his trainer as he approached the blade. "Shouldn't that have given you an idea?"

He picked up the sword, and Hewitt remained still, watching him indifferently. It gave him hope that games meant to embarrass him weren't on the agenda.

"An idea is not fact," Hewitt said, then set his left foot behind him and angled his sword forward. "I aim to see for myself."

Deckard copied the stance, though he felt far less impressive than Hewitt looked.

Hewitt attacked.

Raising his sword, Deckard attempted to parry the strike. It hit his blade with the force of a boulder. The impact numbed his fingers, making him lose his grip and sending the sword swinging away. Hewitt used his opportunity to strike again, and Deckard found himself more grateful than usual for the blunt edge of training swords. Though the bruise would hurt for days, at least there would be no cuts to treat.

Gasping and holding his left side, Deckard realized why Hewitt hadn't played games with him before. The whole of their training was a game—no need to add to his humiliation when his lack of skill already assured it.

"First lesson," Hewitt said. "Don't absorb the blow. Move with it. If you take the brunt of the hit, you'll never be able to defend yourself against a stronger swordsman. Given how lean you are, I'd expect you have some muscle, but up against someone twice your size, you'll get beaten around like a doll."

Deckard straightened. "How do I work on that?"

"You practice it," Hewitt said as though it were obvious. "Let's go again. Don't absorb it this time."

It took a total of thirteen rounds and thirteen bruise-inducing hits for Deckard to make a noticeable improvement. Hewitt took his time with each failed pass to show Deckard his mistakes and walk him through the correct motions. Slowly, the training began to click, and with each heavy swing of Hewitt's sword, Deckard managed to lock only his arms as he stepped back to ease the shock of the blow. He held his grip and blocked two more strikes before Hewitt broke his form again.

"Better," Hewitt grumbled. "But don't step back. Your opponent can drive you wherever he wants if you only move backward. Soon, they'll push you into a wall or over a cliff. Shift side to side, only going backward if you must."

This took fewer tries but just as many bruises. Somehow, Hewitt was finding ways to double down on his strikes even though Deckard began to learn how to move and deflect better. Yet, he felt certain he'd bear stripes of black and blue along his sides and arms for weeks.

After the seventh pass of struggling to sidestep Hewitt's attack, Deckard grunted as another full-force hit to his right arm caused a spike of agony.

"You've got to block those," Hewitt said, watching as Deckard rubbed his arm. "I'll keep hitting you otherwise."

Deckard forced himself to take a deep breath in and let it out in a slow, controlled stream before he replied, "Are you going to do anything but hit me?"

"I thought you wanted training."

"Yes, but I want you to train me how you've been training the recruits. Not beat me bloody."

Hewitt smirked, giving him a look too much like Evylin's for Deckard's tastes. "You've got twelve or more years of bad habits to break."

"Therefore, you intend to beat them out of me?"

"I intend for you to learn," he said, stabbing the sword into the ground before crossing his arms. "And the fact is, you already have faulty training ingrained into your head. I need to knock those bad habits out as I spot them."

"And it wouldn't make sense to start at the beginning?"

Hewitt raised his bushy brow, hefting the sword once more. "This is a sword." He pointed to the hilt. "This is the pommel, and this here is the grip. You wrap your fingers around it and under this bit here—the cross guard—so your hands don't slide up to this part—called the blade. Try not to touch that part. You might cut yourself."

Unamused by the man's sarcasm, Deckard shook his head. "You know what I mean. Train me like you're training the soldiers."

"Evylin is helping me with them, and you said you didn't want her to be part of your training."

"Then train me the way you trained her."

Hewitt frowned. "She was only a girl when we began. For the first while, we ran drills and worked on her strength. She could hardly keep the sword upright for the first month."

Deckard smiled at the picture forming in his head. A young girl with long brown hair trailing in the wind, charming dimples in her cheeks as she paced alongside her uncle. "Was she a quick learner?" he asked.

"Yes, but then most children are," Hewitt said. "She's only as good as she is because I made her master the basics for years before letting her fight. Every bit of Evylin's skill comes from having a knowledge of the blade and feeling it as an extension of herself. Anyone who spent as much time practicing as she has would be as impressive as her."

Deckard wasn't sure he agreed. Though he hoped to gain competence through training with Hewitt, there was no doubt in his mind that it would be impossible for him to match Evylin's skill, no matter how much he practiced.

Still, Deckard grasped the opportunity. "So do the same with me," he asked. "I've got the strength, but I lack the fundamental technique. Teach me that."

"I am."

"Without beating me senseless."

"Now you're taking the fun out of it." He grunted and gestured for Deckard to approach. For the next forty minutes, Hewitt walked him through the most essential fundamentals of swordplay. He taught him to fix his grip, some basic wrist movement and mobility exercises, the most effective stance and footwork, the best practices for fluid strikes, and the best way to block attacks.

"I've got to say," Hewitt grumbled as they packed their things. "I'm disappointed."

Wiping the sweat from his brow, Deckard frowned. Moments before, he'd been congratulating himself on the improvement he already felt from the training—minimal as it may have been. But it sounded like that was wishful thinking on his part.

Hewitt scowled, then added, "You're not as bad as I thought."

Deckard gaped at him.

"Don't get me wrong," Hewitt continued. "You're as bad as most of those recruits, but . . . you're not awful. And I was really hoping to beat you black and blue for the next month or so."

A nervous, surprised chuckle escaped Deckard. "I'm sorry to disappoint, but I'm afraid I'm not as much of a pushover as you seem to think."

"Good," Hewitt said, a hint of a genuine smile aimed at Deckard for the first time. "I needed to make sure."

Deckard stared at him. "Wait," he held up a hand as he sought clarification, "that was a test?"

"I had to be sure you were man enough for my Evie," he informed him. "After some of the things she's told me, I was starting to doubt it."

A spike of worry shot through Deckard. "What things?"

"Doesn't matter. You passed, and now I'm reassured I made the right choice."

In the confusion, curiosity, and conflicting thoughts that sped through his mind, Deckard couldn't form a response fast enough.

"Better get a move on, Captain," Hewitt said, pointing to the sky. "You don't want to miss your own speech."

Deckard gave the bright sun a furtive glance. There were so many questions on the edge of his tongue. What had Evylin said to her uncle? Did she not respect him? How was this an adequate test of his character? And the ever-remaining question: Why did Hewitt even choose him in the first place?

Swinging up into the saddle, Deckard pushed the questions aside. He had work to do, and answers could come later. "Thank you for your time, Major," he said. "I look forward to our next lesson."

CHAPTER THIRTY

Evylin had never been more confused in her life.

When she woke in the morning, her husband was gone as usual, leaving a note on her trunk. As she prepared for the day, everything in the tent seemed determined to remind her of him. His shaving kit and dress uniform awaited his return before his speech. His maps, books, and notes lay across the table in neat stacks.

Evylin frowned at the objects, her heart pattering uncomfortably. What had he done to her yesterday? Why couldn't she stop thinking about his damn kisses?

The conversation with Hewitt two days prior had convinced her of the necessity of sealing their marriage and emboldened her to allow Deckard's advances on their outing. She'd thought she'd be able to brave the whole ordeal, knowing it was the only way to ensure no one could separate her from Hewitt. She was ready to accept her fate, assured that in doing so, she could keep her promise to Ryen.

Evylin had been quite proud of herself for encouraging the first kiss and pleasantly surprised with her gumption to allow the second. But she'd been thoroughly amazed by how much she enjoyed the rest of the interaction. She'd forgotten what was happening for a while and let herself kiss him back.

It was more fun than she expected—kissing. It was almost a game of who could impress the other most with their affection. And she had a distinct feeling that Deckard had won.

The sensation had overwhelmed Evylin so much that it lingered in the back of her brain into the evening and through the night, coming to the forefront again that morning. It was like a phantom hovering around her, reminding her how lovely his touch had been.

Evylin could only compare the feeling to the exhilarating rush she felt during a fight. Her heart raced while her mind found calmness. A chill surged through her veins, tingling her skin with anticipation. Excitement heightened her senses, sharpening her perception of the world around her.

It was incredible.

And it was too much, too soon.

Evylin genuinely liked Deckard; he was kind, good, and handsome. However, he remained a stranger to her in numerous ways. While she dreaded the thought of him sending her home, she dreaded even more the idea of complete subjugation under him. And that rush brought on by his kisses . . . It made her feel bound to him in ways she wasn't ready for.

Thoroughly horrified by the thoughts plaguing her, Evylin hurriedly pulled on her coat and abandoned their tent. If she sat there much longer, surrounded by constant reminders of him, she thought she might lose her mind. But as she pushed through the camp to the kitchen tent, she found the reminders inundating her still. The soldiers wore the same uniform as her husband, and she couldn't help remembering the feeling of the embroidery of his captain's insignia under her fingertips. The breakfast of cured meat and crusty bread reminded her of the meal they'd shared. Worst of all, when she turned to find a place to sit, she caught sight of Thom. Though his hair was so much darker than Deckard's, his remarkable resemblance caused her heart to flutter.

Desperate to escape all thoughts of the captain, Evylin hurried from the kitchen tent, slipping between the tents nearest the breakfast line. Her gait was rapid, tearing away at the frosty grass toward the training grounds. She needed to find Hewitt. He'd give her something to think about that had nothing to do with her husband.

Breaking through the last line of the camp, Evylin marched straight for Hewitt's tent on the edge of the training field. Though it wasn't customary, Hewitt had demanded distance from the rest of the soldiers. He'd convinced Deckard he needed the space to think and plan properly. Evylin knew it was just his way of discouraging unnecessary interaction with the rest of the men. Her uncle liked his isolation as much as she disliked her own. And she was really the only person he cared to invite into his solitude.

When she neared Hewitt's tent, she heard movement within. Pushing back the flap, she stepped into the small interior, ready to greet her uncle. Instead, she found Ethenn sitting on a stool with a pile of training swords at his side.

"Oh," she gasped. "Good morning, Ethenn."

The young man looked up at her, hand frozen in midair over the blade that rested on his lap. After his appointment as Hewitt's assistant, the private had taken on all the small, tedious tasks Hewitt disliked most. Things like cleaning and polishing the hundreds of weapons used by the troops, which Ethenn was working on at that early hour.

Despite the young man's more volatile introduction, Evylin had found the private far more shy and reserved than she'd expected. He didn't speak unless spoken to, and he even kept his good-humored reactions tempered—smiling with pressed-together lips and laughing in a singular, short burst at each joke. And he blushed regularly.

Ethenn leaped up, knocking the sword on the ground as he rapidly shoved his rolled-up sleeves down. "Morning," he said nervously and retrieved the sword. "Is there something you need?"

Amused by the red flush creeping up his neck, Evylin pushed a step farther into the tent. "I just came to find my uncle," she said, then gave the tiny space a once-over. "I guess he's not here."

"No, uh—Major Glaas had a meeting this morning. He asked me to ensure the swords were ready for the first platoon of the day."

"I see." Evylin sighed, her plan of distraction thwarted.

Ethenn shifted his weight, training sword dangling from his hands. Though he'd improved enough to meet her gaze over the past month, Evylin could tell he still wasn't fully comfortable around her.

Rafferty—weasel that he was—had snuck around and gotten information about the young man behind his back. All the Trollenston volunteers knew about Ethenn Loxley, it seemed. Despite his apparent reserve, Ethenn was quite the back-alley brawler. In addition to his skills as a hunter, he'd begun getting into fights with the boys around town at a young age. Initially, due to an undercurrent of fire that few ever got to see, the then-thirteen-year-old town boy found a way to channel his anger issues into a money-making opportunity when a few of his friends convinced him to join the underground fighting ring of Trollenston. His youth made him an unpopular bet . . . until he started winning.

The story explained his fighting skills but not his quiet demeanor, which contrasted with the inner rage they'd only glimpsed once. However, under Hewitt's tutelage, Ethenn had already begun to thrive. His technique couldn't match Evylin's, but his skills were quickly catching up to hers, giving her the constant urge to improve.

"Was there something I could help you with, Evie?" Ethenn asked, bringing her back to the moment at hand.

Evylin shook her head. "No, I just . . ." She stopped, meeting the young man's dark brown eyes as an idea struck her. "Actually, Ethenn, there is something you could help me with."

His thick eyebrows rose under the edges of his shaggy mop of hair.

Setting her untouched breakfast on the edge of Hewitt's cot, Evylin turned back to him. "As it's morning, I still have to go through my paces," she explained. "You know, run a mile, then come back and knock out that whole exercise routine Hewitt made for us."

He nodded.

"But it's boring to do it alone. Would you care to join me?"

Ethenn glanced down at the pile of yet-to-be-cleaned swords.

To ensure she wouldn't have to be alone with her thoughts once more, Evylin jumped to remove the obstacle in his way. "I'll help you finish those when we're done if you come with me," she offered.

Narrowing his eyes in thought, Ethenn frowned at the pile. His fingers drummed on the hilt of the blade he still held. She knew he was debating Hewitt's anger if he failed in his task against the desire to join her. Ethenn was a hard, trustworthy worker but was far more interested in physical labor than tedious maintenance.

His gaze snapped back up to hers, that clever mind of his shining through his steady stare. "I've got a counteroffer for you," he replied, his voice low.

"What is it?"

"You help me get these finished up *first*," he explained. "Then we'll go."

Evylin couldn't help smirking at his finagling. Though she'd much prefer to exhaust herself before doing such mind-numbing work, she held out her hand at the chance to not be alone. "Deal."

CHAPTER THIRTY-ONE

When Deckard returned to camp, he moved with speed. He dropped his horse off at the stable tent, not allowing himself the usual time to brush her down and care for her. The mare was a perk of his captaincy; the high offices within the army supplied even more splendid pay, finer uniforms, a dress insignia of silver, a well-bred steed, and many other worthwhile offerings. To ensure he never let such luxuries go to his head as he'd seen so many others do, he made sure to take charge of his mare's care as often as he could.

But today, Deckard passed her over to the stablemaster, the urgency of preparing for his speech compelling him to get moving. As expected, he found their tent empty, the bed sloppily made. He hurried behind the changing screen to shave in the small mirror before changing into his formal uniform, gasping a couple of times at his already tender injuries and aching muscles. Once redressed, he switched the velvet bag from one pocket to the other, buckled his belt, and sheathed his sword.

"Deckard?" Thom called from outside the tent. "Are you in there?"

"Yes," he replied, straightening the cravat and his insignia before heading to the entrance. "I'm coming."

Once he stepped outside, Thom sighed. "I can't tell you how glad I am that you're the captain and not me," he exclaimed, bright eyes wide. "Seeing to a magistrate's ego is worse than mucking out the stalls in Loclight."

"I'm sorry you've had either experience. But I'll take over from here."

Thom glanced at him as they walked to the edge of camp. "How, uh—how was it yesterday?"

"It was good."

"The countryside as nice as everyone says?"

"Yes," Deckard said, thinking the company had been superior to the scenery. "Yes, it was quite remarkable."

"And you—you both had a good time?"

"We did."

"Good."

Setting a hand on Thom's shoulder, Deckard smiled at his brother. "Thank you," he said. "It was your advice that encouraged me."

"Really?"

"Really."

Thom pursed his lips. "Great, yeah, that's good. I'm glad to hear it." He scratched the back of his head. "I, uh—I'll come to see you this evening to check in."

With a final pat on his brother's shoulder, Deckard turned and headed into the village. Mentally, he ran through his speech, testing the feeling of every line. Since Evylin's critique in Trollenston, he'd considered making changes, but no adjustment felt right. So he settled for the fact that while it might not come across as sincere to those who heard it a second time, he felt its sincerity within himself. He meant every call to action because they were the very things that inspired his own choices.

The magistrate of Wayford carried an ego to match the title, and Deckard played along to bolster his cooperation. He found it the best way to ensure their compliance and aid if needed. One day, he hoped he wouldn't have to flatter anyone for the sake of the army, but for now, he'd do his job as best he could.

Deckard's speech went as usual, and a high number of men came forward. When Thom arrived, he had to help manage all the interest. Through the evening, forty-six men spoke with them. Deckard's hopes ran high. That number would have bridged the gap between the volunteers they'd collected and those they still needed. But then a few drifted away.

More followed.

In the end, Deckard only added twenty-four men to his company.

Peery recorded the total figures, presented them to Deckard, and returned to camp with the other officers, leaving Thom and Deckard alone to gaze at the ledger.

"That means we need another fifty-eight men," Thom concluded. "And we only have two more stops."

Staring up into the night sky, Deckard frowned at the glittering ivory moon that far outshone its shadow. "Stocburrough doesn't have the men," he said in resignation. "We can't count on more than five from there."

"Which leaves fifty-three to Stoclund."

Deckard met his brother's gaze. "They may qualify as a town by population standards," he noted, "but we both know that's by the skin of their teeth. The chances of obtaining fifty men there are impossible. The forty-nine from Wheylen was a miracle, and they have four thousand more citizens than Stoclund."

Thom didn't say a word.

The frigid night air cut through their coats, causing both men to shiver. Their journey through the southern provinces had drained their resistance to the chilly weather.

"How many men is Hewitt worth?" Deckard mused. "Ten? Can a legendary general's value be so little?"

"It depends on General Rand's mood," Thom offered. "He may be pleased by Hewitt's return. And perhaps he'll find the quality of our volunteers far outweighs that of any other numbers brought in."

"Knowing the general, he's likelier to complain we didn't bring back a thousand men of such high caliber." Deckard pressed his lips together. "I've lost, Thom."

"Stop that," Thom ordered. "We still have two stops; if we can get fifty more, you'll be fine. That's only twenty-five from each."

Defeat clung to Deckard. The numbers were impossible. Twenty-five men from Stoclund, he could imagine. But twenty-five from a village of five hundred? Their population only surpassed Whickam Village by one.

There was no chance.

Deckard would not reach his goal, and Rand would penalize him for his failure. Hewitt might save him from demotion, but for the rest of his current contract, he would not see any promotion or promise in his career.

He should warn Evylin. She deserved to know that their dream of travel was postponed indefinitely. But he feared her disappointment. Would she still think their marriage was worth it if he couldn't keep his promise to her? What adventure could he offer in an undesirable assignment?

"Deckard," Thom said, drawing his attention, "Wayford is hardly larger than Stocburrough, and we got twenty-four here. Don't give up."

Deckard gripped his brother's arm. "Thank you," he muttered, then took a deep breath, the winter air cutting into his lungs. "Let's go back."

With empty stomachs from the long night, they gathered food at the vacant kitchen tent. Thom kept trying to convince Deckard of the odds. Deckard was grateful but grew no more optimistic—not when he was so certain he would destroy the one chance of happiness for his and Evylin's future.

The brothers parted. Carrying the small plate in one hand, Deckard slipped his other hand back into his pocket. His fingers brushed the velvet bag, tracing the ring inside. He'd stayed out too late in hopes of more volunteers that never came. His breath fogged in front of him as he sighed, sure that Evylin would have abandoned the request in his note. There were many nights she went to bed well before his arrival, and he couldn't blame her. His late hours and early mornings wore on him. Undoubtedly, they wore on her as well.

When their tent appeared in the distance, Deckard caught the flicker of candlelight beyond the flaps. Suddenly, he worried she hadn't gone to bed. What would he say to her? Should he reveal his failure? Could it help for her to shoulder his worries too?

Deckard took one final breath in, then pushed inside the tent.

Evylin sat at the table next to the candle, her head bent low over a book. With her chin propped on a hand, her eyes darted up at his appearance. Immediately—stunningly— she smiled brightly. When she sat up straight, the blanket she'd bundled around her slipped from her shoulder. He could see her shiver even at a distance as she attempted to tug it back in place.

"Why are you still awake?" Deckard asked, crossing to the table.

"You asked me to wait for you, remember?" Evylin said, gesturing to the other chair. "Eat. I'll be fine."

"You're freezing," he objected.

Her grin grew sly. "Then you'd better eat quickly."

Deckard chuckled. "All right," he said and took a seat. "But if it gets too cold, I give you permission to run for another blanket."

"I have all the blankets already," she said, drawing the bundle closer around her. "How did it go in the village?"

Glad for the bite in his mouth, Deckard shrugged as he chewed. The pause gave him time to consider his response. "It went well, I think," he said. "Twenty-four volunteers, which is more than I expected from somewhere as small as Wayford."

"That's wonderful!" Evylin said, her excitement confirming the justice in his decision. If he failed, he'd tell her after Stocburrough. Until then, he would allow her to have hope. At least for the time being, one of them could be happy.

Nodding, Deckard took a sip of water. "And how was your day?" he asked, ready to move on. "I hope you didn't embarrass my men too much."

"They embarrass themselves. I merely supply them with the opportunity," she teased, tucking her hands into the blankets. "But no, I think they did well today. They paired up to duel each other, so Raff, Ethenn, and I spent the day training together."

A spark of jealousy flared for only a second. "And you won as usual, of course?"

"Actually, Raff won."

Deckard paused before taking another bite of his cold ham and cheese sandwich. "I didn't think he'd be much of a swordsman."

"He wasn't. But he's fast and clever, and Hewitt's been training him. He may not have the same skills as Ethenn and me, but he can outwit most people. And he's a risk-taker. Sometimes, those qualities paired are quite unsuccessful, but other times, they're impossible to beat. You just have to decide if the risk is worth the reward."

Taking what lessons he could from her words for his own journey to becoming a better swordsman, Deckard nodded. The way she talked about her friends amazed him. She didn't merely appreciate their presence. She respected who they were. Whenever she talked about Private Rafferty, she would mention his intelligence. Every time she brought up Ethenn, she'd talk about his keen observation and natural talent. Whenever she talked about Thom, she referenced his good humor and openness. And, of course, any suggestion of Hewitt placed him next to Allore, the Creator Divine, himself.

One day, Deckard hoped to be one of those men to her—one whom she admired and respected and couldn't help but compliment.

"Did you do anything else?" Deckard asked, nearly finished with the paltry meal. "Or am I to believe the only things you enjoy are training and waiting for me to reappear?"

Evylin smirked. "Well, those are my favorite things. Particularly the waiting around for you." Her eyes twinkled in the candlelight. "A good thing, too, as I have to do that an awful lot."

Despite knowing it was a joke, Deckard hesitated.

"I'm only teasing," she promised.

Choosing to accept her playful nature, Deckard raised his brow. "I'm not sure I believe that."

"Oh?" she said dryly. "And what if I'm not? Am I to expect some form of punishment? A lecture, maybe?"

"You could use a thorough reprimand for your flippancy," Deckard replied, then popped the remaining bite of the sandwich into his mouth.

"Surely not!" she laughed. "The honorable Captain Deckard could never be so cruel."

"Couldn't I?" he asked. "No, I think you're right. A lecture wouldn't do. It would need to be far more severe."

Evylin's smile creased her eyes. "And what severe punishment have I earned?"

Deckard held her gaze. "I won't give you your present."

Her expression faltered. "What present?"

"This one." He reached into his pocket and withdrew the velvet bag, holding it by its drawstring.

Evylin's eyes watched the little bag swing through the air, and her smile disappeared altogether. "You got me a gift?"

"It's rather late in the giving," Deckard said apologetically. "I meant it to be a wedding gift, but I could never find the right time to give it to you. Then I meant you to have it yesterday, but after . . . well, I forgot."

A slight pink flushed Evylin's temples.

"So I wanted to give it to you tonight," he said, shrugging. "Until you insulted me. Now, I suppose I'll keep it a little longer."

Evylin's good humor returned, and she crossed her arms. The blanket shifted off her shoulder to reveal her coat.

Deckard raised his brow, waiting for a reply.

After a moment, Evylin nodded. Her expression changed, lips turning down in a mockingly penitent frown. She reached out to put her hand on his. "How may I ever make amends?" she whispered, the words too sweet to be repentant.

Deckard stared into her eyes, fond of this version of their relationship. It reminded him of when they first met and his excitement whenever he spoke with her. This Evylin was the woman who drew his attention with her joyful disposition and witty comments. He liked that woman very much.

Taking hold of her hand, Deckard turned it over. He placed the bag in her palm and closed her fingers. "Wear it," he charged, releasing her. "That's all I ask."

Evylin paused before retracting her hand and opening the small bag. As she drew out the ring, she glanced back at him, her mouth falling open in surprise.

"I know you already have one," Deckard said before she could speak. "And I'm not asking you to stop wearing it. But I'd like you to wear this one as well."

"Why?" she asked, a breathless quality to her voice.

"Because I wanted you to have something from me," he said. "And the one Hewitt gave you represents your home, so I thought I'd give you something that might represent our future. Not to replace it, but to go alongside it."

Fingers trembling faintly, Evylin placed the ring on her palm. "But it's so . . ." She shook her head in awe. "How could anyone afford something like this?"

Deckard licked his lips, unsure whether her response meant she disapproved of the money he'd spent. "I am paid well, Evylin," he said, hoping to alleviate any worry about the cost. "And I've lived well beneath my means for many years. You needn't be concerned about that."

She stared at the ring as it refracted the dim light.

Her continued silence began to worry him. "Do you like it?"

Evylin's breath flew out of her in a scoff. "Like it? It's lovely! But I don't understand why you'd want to spend so much on me."

Deckard smiled. "May I?" he asked, reaching for the ring. "I'm glad you like it. Of all the rings I saw, this one . . . it felt right. I can't explain why, but I knew the minute I saw it."

Taking Evylin's left hand from where it sat on the table, Deckard lifted it. "This isn't just a ring, Evylin. It's a promise," he said, dropping his gaze to her hand. He slid the ring over her finger until it sat snugly against Hewitt's. "I intend to be a good husband to you. And even if jewelry is a paltry means of communicating that, I believe it can be a daily reminder. I don't care how we came to be married. I told you when I proposed: I will spend the rest of my life loving you if you'll let me. No matter what that looks like."

Evylin stared at her hand, then lifted her gaze to his, a soft warmth radiating in her amber eyes. "I don't know what to say," she muttered, taking his hand again. "Thank you."

Deckard squeezed her hand gently.

"I wish I had a gift for you," she continued weakly.

"I don't need a gift," he insisted. She began to protest, but he held up his hand. "If you must give me something, then promise you'll never doubt my intentions. Knowing that would be the best gift I could receive."

Though Evylin hesitated, she nodded. "I promise," she whispered.

Giving her hand one final squeeze, Deckard reached across to pull the blanket closer around her. "Thank you." He smiled and stood. "Now, let's go to bed. I'm exhausted."

CHAPTER THIRTY-TWO

Evylin couldn't sleep. The cold seeped through the tent walls and into her bones. The farther north they traveled, the colder it became, due to the climate and the season. And now, not quite halfway through the month of Obscura, she had never experienced a winter so cold. Every night, she worried she wouldn't be able to handle Loclight's weather.

The days weren't so bad. She wore her coat except during vigorous training, and the sun and her activity kept her warm. She often forgot the low temperature until she stood still for long periods.

But then night came, and with it, the sensation of ice pulsing through her veins.

Evylin tried to stop shaking. She'd even worn her coat to bed, though Deckard laughed at her. Somehow, the cold didn't bother him in the same way as her. But he remained silent even when she crawled under the blankets, bundled up with her scarf and two extra pairs of socks.

Now, she discovered, even that wasn't enough.

Squeezing her eyes shut, Evylin prayed for sleep. At least then, she'd be able to ignore the freezing air. She lost track of time, the seconds stretching into what felt like hours as she trembled.

The cot shifted as Deckard angled toward her. "Evylin," he whispered.

Afraid to open her mouth and hear chattering, Evylin hummed her reply.

"Are you still awake?"

"Yes," she murmured, rubbing her arms. It did nothing to help.

Sighing, Deckard turned over in the bed. The cot's small surface brought him closer than her comfort preferred, but she didn't try to move away, knowing she'd only end up on the ground. "We have to get you warm," he said as if to himself. "You can't lay here shivering all night."

"I'm afraid I don't see any way around it. We don't have any more blankets, and I'm not sure I could get a fourth pair of socks on my feet."

Deckard hesitated, then offered tentatively, "I can help get you warm."

Evylin's body tensed with immediate understanding. Another shiver racked through her. "Whatever you have to do," she said tightly, "do it."

Deckard shifted again, hovering over her as he adjusted the pillows. He told her to turn to face him. Doing as he ordered, Evylin felt him slide his arm underneath her pillow. She didn't allow herself to second-guess her decision but shifted under the covers once more. He enfolded her in his arms and pulled her close. Her cheek pressed against the nape of his neck, his chin resting on top of her head.

Deckard rubbed large circles up and down her arm and back with both hands. "Are you comfortable enough?" he whispered.

Evylin could hear his heartbeat, and her face heated at their nearness. Her arms were smashed between them, creating the semblance of a barrier. It wasn't exactly comfortable, but her skin began to tingle as his heat seeped into her. "I think so," she muttered, overly conscious of his legs touching hers. "I'm still cold, though."

"Yes, well, I'm not as good as a fire, so you'll have to give it a minute or two," he teased, still rubbing her arm. "Are you feeling at all warmer?"

"Mm-hm," she murmured, the distinction between the burning in her cheeks and the true heat she'd gained impossible to discern. She felt him nod.

"Try to sleep, then."

And she did try, but it seemed destined to be a sleepless night.

Lying in his arms, listening to his breathing, Evylin wondered what was happening to her. Her thoughts were muddled, and her heartbeat erratic. She didn't feel any more desire to be intimate with Deckard than she had the prior day, but . . . perhaps her fear was waning. After all, if a man could hold her this close and not make an advance, then surely, he was trustworthy.

No, she wasn't ready for consummation. But after a few more months of marriage, after really getting to know him, she might be. . . .

The heat from Deckard's body helped immensely. Her fingers and toes no longer felt like icicles, and the weight of his arms was comforting. His hand massaged her shoulder and upper back, soothing her tense muscles.

It all felt so nice, so reassuring. Her thoughts grew sleepy, and she found herself snuggling closer into him. A subtle tingle spread under her skin, a vibrant chill like the flavor of mint brightening her veins. And just before Evylin fell asleep, she wondered if everyone experienced such a feeling. Was the thrill of a fight always the same as the rush of affection? Or was Captain Jonn Deckard the closest thing to magic she could find?

15TH OF OBSCURA, 1573

Icy air woke Evylin. She peered sleepily across the bed to find Deckard missing as usual. But this time, something was different. His ever-pristine side of the bed held rumpled blankets, and she heard a hint of movement behind her. Turning, Evylin caught a glimpse of Deckard behind the changing screen. Her eyes fluttered open and closed, but she caught a flash of his bare arm.

Still half asleep, she waited for him to appear. The cold seeped into her again, and she wrapped herself deeper into the blankets. It helped, but it was nowhere near as warm as Deckard.

Her lids fell, darkness taking her back to sleep for seconds at a time before Deckard reappeared from behind the screen in his typical work uniform. He glanced at the bed, pausing when he saw her.

"Did I wake you?" he whispered, sounding worried.

Unable to manage words, Evylin shook her head.

Deckard hurried to slip his belt through the loop and came to kneel beside her. "I'm sorry," he said, ignoring her denial. "I tried to get up without disturbing you, but it wasn't easy."

"It wasn't your fault," she murmured. "It's cold."

Deckard grinned. "Yes, it is. Try to sleep more, though. It's not yet dawn, and we won't leave for a few hours. Can I get you anything before I go?"

Evylin's eyelids were heavy, so she shut them as she shook her head again.

Deckard ran his thumb over her cheek, warming the spot. She listened as he stood, then moved about the room. Eventually, she fell back to sleep, her head almost submerged under the blankets.

When she rose at last, he was gone. The winter morning remained icy, prompting her to hurry to her trunk for her warmest clothes. There, she discovered a note on the lid. She hadn't anticipated receiving a note after their goodbye that morning, yet even the brief message—*"I'll be back soon. Yours, Jonn"*—brought a smile to her face. She carefully folded it to place it at the bottom of her trunk alongside the others. Although she had never planned to keep all his notes, it felt wrong to discard them.

Once Lieutenant Peery received her approval, the men began to dismantle their tent. Within an hour of her rising, they had packed away the entire camp, and the Third Volunteer Company departed for Stoclund. They arrived in the early afternoon, and she spotted Deckard as he and Peery entered the town. With the camp rebuilt, she joined Rafferty and Ethenn for lunch while Thom was occupied organizing a hunting party, and Hewitt discussed the following day's itinerary with Sheelds.

"I've officially decided," Rafferty said after swallowing a bite of mutton, "I don't want to travel once we make it back to Loclight."

Evylin chuckled as she tore off a piece of biscuit. "Oh? Why not?"

"For one thing, this bloody routine of setting up camp just to take it down in the next few days is insanity. And it's about to get worse once we make it through Stocburrough." He shook his head. "A month-long hike to the city is enough to drive a man to madness."

"It's not that bad," Ethenn replied. "With the extra volunteers we've picked up, the improvement of the ones we already had, and the organization Captain Deckard's put in, it hardly takes us a couple of hours now."

Rafferty raised one of his white-blond brows at the kid. "You're a menace, Loxley."

While Ethenn frowned, Evylin smiled. "What are your other reasons?" she asked, taking another bite.

Rafferty thought for a moment as he chewed. "Well," he said around the bite, "I think it'd be far nicer to be in one spot. Maybe climb the ranks there. Get your commanding officer to like you so well that he gives you a puff job. Somethin' real easy. That way, I could serve out my time in peace. All this travel stuff is too much work for someone like me."

"You don't think that would get boring? Staying in one place all the time?"

"Well, sure," Rafferty said, then gestured to the camp around them. "But so does this. No offense to you, of course, but following your husband around while he tries to make new friends isn't exactly my idea of a thrilling adventure."

Evylin couldn't disagree. This journey had been dull—so far from the adventures she'd read that she'd begun to wonder if such a reality even existed outside of novels.

"At least we're seeing the country," Ethenn offered. "It's better than being stuck in one place forever."

"We're not seeing the country," Rafferty said. "We're seeing the Shires. And by the time we get out of Nettershire, it's going to be a sprint back to Loclight, believe me. All we'll get to see by then is the inside of our tents and wherever it is that Hewitt will conduct our training."

"It's still better than being stuck somewhere you don't want to be," Ethenn countered, and Evylin agreed.

Rafferty smirked. "That's 'cause you two didn't like where you were stuck. I, on the other hand, quite enjoyed where I was."

"If only we all could run our own smuggling syndicate," Ethenn told Evylin.

"It was a legitimate business venture, thank you very much."

Evylin nudged Ethenn. "We could run one together. What do you think we ought to smuggle?"

The kid gave her a sheepish grin. "I'm not sure the captain would approve."

"I'm not sure he'd get a say."

"That's a pity," Deckard said, causing Evylin and Ethenn to whirl around. "I'd hoped you valued my opinions."

Ethenn leaped to his feet while Rafferty sniggered, rising more languidly.

"Captain," Ethenn said, standing to attention.

Giving both the soldiers a glance, Deckard permitted their "at ease" before smiling down at Evylin. "If you're going to start smuggling, I'd ask that you plan it in a more private location," he teased. "I can't have my men thinking I'm party to criminal behavior."

"I haven't the faintest idea what you're talking about," Evylin replied merrily. "We were just discussing Rafferty's entrepreneurial exploits. Smuggling never came up."

"My mistake."

"Not to worry," she said, then tilted her head. "I'm surprised you're back so soon. Usually, the magistrates keep you for hours."

Deckard looked from Ethenn to Rafferty and back to Evylin. "Magistrate Lennen isn't the talkative sort, apparently," he said.

"You must be quite disappointed."

"Oh, terribly." He nodded to the soldiers. "Private Loxley, Private Rafferty, pardon the interruption, but I'm here to take my wife from you."

Rafferty's wiliest grin spread across his face. "Pardon me, Captain, but she may not want to go. I do think she and Loxley were amidst planning a heist. Could be quite profitable. Would you care to join in on the venture?"

"Afraid I'll have to pass," Deckard replied.

"Your loss."

Evylin stood, smacked Rafferty's chest, then elbowed Ethenn in the ribs. "I'll see you boys later. We can raid Stoclund to find that cask of Schonese wine you're always on about, Raff."

"That cask is worth quite a bit of gold, Eve."

"Too bad you don't have it, then."

"Maybe I do, and maybe I don't."

Evylin shook her head and accepted the arm Deckard offered her. "Keep an eye on him, Ethenn," she charged. "I think he's going senile."

"He already is," Ethenn replied.

Deckard escorted Evylin away from the men as Rafferty began to defend his claims. As they passed through the tents and clusters of soldiers, a cold wind cut through the pathways, and she leaned in closer to his side. "Where are we off to?" she asked.

"Into Stoclund," he said. "We've got some shopping to do."

"Shopping?"

"You need warmer clothing," he explained. "Not only for the nights but in general as well. I've noticed you've been struggling with the cold these past few weeks."

"You're quite observant."

He chuckled. "The winter wear you have is already failing you, and Loclight will be even colder when we arrive."

Evylin sucked in a frigid breath. "That sounds horrid," she muttered.

"Stoclund has some nice shops," Deckard continued through his laughter. "We should find everything we need here."

Though Evylin was hesitant, Deckard insisted on buying everything for her. He perused the shop, picking out several pieces she thought were unnecessary. He bought her two extra coats, a thick wool scarf, a secondary pair of gloves, several pairs of knitted socks, a heavy sweater, two nightdresses, and several skirts and blouses he felt were more suitable for the winter season. She made the mistake of liking a light green, satin gown, and though she urged him not to, Deckard made sure to place it with their order.

As Deckard paid for it all, Evylin took hold of her wedding rings. She didn't like the way he'd started buying her gifts. And such nice ones at that. It made her feel lacking, questioning how she could make him happy too.

After dropping off their purchases, they parted ways again. Deckard was off to his duties, and Evylin left for training. He made no special occasion at their farewell, and their day passed as normally as before he'd started paying more attention to her. That helped ease her worries. If he was free to go about his work, then perhaps these gifts and outings wouldn't be seen as demands on his time.

Still, Evylin began to wish she could find a better way to thank him for his kindness.

After a day of training, Evylin met Deckard at the tent in the evening. Though the magistrate didn't offer them a place to stay, he did invite them to dinner. Lennen's family was tolerable, making the dinner far less arduous than some dinners they'd endured with the magistrates of Nettershire.

However, after returning to camp and preparing for bed, Evylin discovered the wool nightclothes weren't warm enough. When she came around the corner in her coat, Deckard shook his head. "You shouldn't have to wear your coat to bed."

"Well, it's too cold," Evylin argued. "I won't be able to sleep without it."

Deckard sighed, wet his bottom lip, and met her gaze. "Would you be able to sleep all right with my help again?"

Evylin pressed her lips together. "I don't know," she murmured.

"Can we try?"

Evylin hesitated, not altogether opposed but fearing that she was demanding too much of him. Or worse, that she might lead him on before she was ready. "We tried it last night," she said.

"And it worked, did it not?"

"Yes, but I was wearing far more than even this."

"How about this, then?" Deckard set his hands on her arms. "Wear a sweater and an extra pair of socks if you think it necessary. But this coat . . . it can't be comfortable."

"It's better than being cold."

"You won't be cold," he promised.

Evylin tugged at the buttons of her coat. "You're sure?"

"You can always keep the coat by the bed if you feel the need," he suggested. "If you aren't warm enough, you can put it on later."

Pulling in a deep breath, Evylin eyed him. "You don't mind?"

"I don't mind."

"All right," she whispered, removing the coat and grabbing her new sweater.

Deckard was right; she hadn't needed the coat. He was warm enough on his own, and she drifted off to sleep faster than she expected as he held her in his arms.

CHAPTER THIRTY-THREE

17TH OF OBSCURA, 1573

Over the past few weeks, Hewitt had created a specialized training session for the soldiers. At each stop, while Deckard delivered his speech, he matched Evylin, Rafferty, and Ethenn against each platoon. They began with ten, then increased to twenty, then thirty, and continued sparring until they either lost or no more opponents remained to challenge.

"Ten on three," Hewitt called. "Remember, disarming or lethal hits disqualify. On my mark."

The trio stood together, facing the first set of ten from First Platoon. The ten prepared, their stances already improving in recent weeks. Evylin actually had to put in effort to fight several of them now. Though none quite matched Hewitt's standards, he'd done an excellent job training them.

"Ready . . . Go!"

As the ten charged, Evylin, Rafferty, and Ethenn staggered their steps. They'd come to work so well as a team that they hardly needed to communicate. They always knew the order of things.

Ethenn, the largest of them, could take a hit better than the other two, so he went first, knocking a few men back and carrying the weight of the onslaught. Then Rafferty ran in, using his speed to trick their opponents into chasing him. He'd started wielding dual short swords to help with his swift and crafty attacks. It helped him pull off riskier feints as he wove through the field. A hit from someone who wouldn't fall for his wily skills often wound up ending his run, but he'd take out several on his way.

Evylin followed at the back. She didn't have to defend herself as much, able to sneak in, removing the rest from the field in a matter of seconds. They relied on her skill and experience to act quickly and ensure victory. It didn't matter how many teams they faced; they won almost every bout.

"I wish I could join you," Thom said regretfully as training concluded and First Platoon dispersed to their respective tasks.

"The downfall of being a lieutenant, I suppose," Evylin teased, tugging out her fraying braid to retie it. "At least you get to train with us in the evening."

"It's different. You three get to work as a team while I watch on the sidelines."

"Don't be too jealous," she said, smirking. "It's the one time in my life I get to consider myself on a team with any of you. After we get to Loclight, my time as an honorary comrade is over."

Thom frowned. "I suppose you're right."

They walked between the tents toward the kitchen.

"It's idiotic, though," he continued. "You're better than every man here. If anyone should be a soldier, it's you."

Evylin chuckled. "That's sweet of you, but I don't want to be a soldier."

"Why not?"

"Because then I'd have a commanding officer and an assignment I had to follow. And quite frankly, I'm too happy with my independence to take someone's orders."

Thom scoffed. "And marriage to my brother is quite conducive to independence."

"Do I look constrained to you?" she asked, tossing her arms out to the side.

"You look married," he teased, then pointed to her hand. "Nice ring, by the way. When did he give you that?"

Evylin instinctively reached for the ring, ensuring it was in place. It was a nervous habit she'd adopted, checking on it every time it came to mind as though it might fly off her finger of its own volition. "The other night."

"A token of his affection?"

"He is my husband, isn't he?"

A muscle flexed in his jaw. "Seems like it."

"And tokens are signs of constraint?"

"Not if you're in love with the person."

Evylin stiffened at the sharpness of his words. "It's been a month," she said quietly. "I thought you were over this."

"Evie," he said, running a hand through his dark hair, "I'm not upset with you. I'm upset with him."

"Why?" she asked, furrowing her brow.

Thom hesitated, lips parting around unsaid words. He grimaced and averted his gaze. "Do you love my brother?" he asked so softly she almost didn't hear.

Evylin gaped at him. "What?"

"Do you love Deckard?"

Gaze darting around the tents to ensure they weren't overheard, Evylin took a step forward and lowered her voice. "You were there. Our marriage was Hewitt's idea, not mine."

"Then why did you marry him?" he demanded.

"Because it was my only chance."

"No, it wasn't," Thom argued. "You could have married any other man on Terraeus. Someone in Trollenston. One of the merchants at the market you visited. One of the bloody volunteers we brought with us."

Crossing her arms, Evylin frowned.

"Hell," Thom said with a caustic chuckle. "You could have married me."

"Thom—"

"But you didn't." He cut across her rebuttal, dark brows raised over those gray-blue eyes. "You married Deckard. Why?"

Evylin shook her head. "I . . ."

"Do you love him?"

"No."

"Then why did you marry him?"

"Why are you asking me this?" Evylin demanded. "After a month of traveling—of being my friend—why are you suddenly so concerned with *why*?"

Several seconds passed as Thom stared down at her, his sharp eyes flashing between hers. He took an unsteady breath, curled his hands into fists, and stepped back. "Our next stop is Stocburrough," he said.

Evylin nodded. "Jonn told me."

Thom mimicked the action. "That's good. You need to prepare for it."

At her confusion, he continued, "Our family lives there, Evie. And if you don't love Deckard . . . It's going to be difficult."

"Oh," she muttered, tugging on her rings.

"My family . . ." Thom ground his teeth. "They're going to ask you a lot of questions. And if you're not prepared to tell the truth—which I don't recommend—then you'll *need* to lie. They will not accept a false marriage between Deckard and you. They love him too much. And Deckard won't let them think he's married for anything but love."

Evylin set a hand to her mouth, understanding. Being with the Deckard family would mean acting like a newly wedded couple, deeply in love. "I didn't even consider that," she muttered. "I was so concerned they'd hate me for marrying him so suddenly that I didn't think . . ."

Thom wore a compassionate frown. "And, in case you didn't know, Deckard is good at acting."

Evylin looked up sharply. "Thom, what if they ask me questions to which I don't know the answers? Like how he takes his tea or about his work. Or how his friends in Loclight are or . . . or . . . or when we fell in love. How do I answer those?"

A tense chuckle escaped him. "They aren't going to interrogate you. Deckard is perfect in their eyes. I'm the only one smart enough to see through his act. So if he tells our parents and sister that you two met five years ago, and he didn't say anything because he was too nervous to screw it up—they'll believe him." He scoffed, then added, "If Jonn told them that you hung the moons, they'd bloody believe him."

Evylin didn't know how to take that. Their family thought Deckard was perfect. They would believe everything he'd say. Why fear, then? If she didn't have to convince them of her love, wouldn't they accept her just as she was?

But Deckard was their prized son. Somehow, she'd expected it to be the case, and *that* was the root of her fear. Could any woman be good enough for the beloved firstborn?

"Well," Evylin said softly, "I suppose I'll have to win them over, then."

18TH OF OBSCURA, 1573

Evylin was terrified. She woke with her nerves aflutter, jittery at the thought of meeting the Deckard family. She fumbled with the buttons on her coat, struggled to tie her hair back at a natural-looking angle, and couldn't sit still for longer than a few seconds. Deckard was, of course, gone at her rising, leaving only a note, so she had no one to keep her company and distract her from the anxious thoughts.

Their ride to Stocburrough would only take three hours, according to Deckard. As usual, he rode at Evylin's side for the first half hour before rushing off to check on his men. The flat lands of northwestern Nettershire wound out ahead of them for miles. She spotted a group of cattlemen in the distance as they neared Stocburrough, and farmlands appeared long before the village center. The fields showed splotches of menial underground crops growing in the winter season, their bursts of dull green bearing frosted tips.

When the square finally came into view—only five buildings in total—Deckard left to visit the magistrate with Peery. The moment the captain's tent went up, Evylin walked straight in and exchanged her trousers for a skirt and fresh blouse. Her mother's voice rang in her head as she dressed, warning her to brush out her hair and wear something modest but beautiful. With her wind-tossed waves, Evylin knew there'd be no taming it, so she settled for tying back the top layer with a blue satin ribbon. Finally, she slipped a sweater over her shoulders and walked around the screen just as Deckard entered. The tent flaps rustled behind him, bringing Thom in next. He chuckled under his breath.

Still jittery from the anticipation of meeting his family, Evylin struggled to get out a greeting. "I didn't expect you back so soon," she said.

Deckard approached to put a hand on her arm and kiss the top of her head, the affectionate gesture stunning her. "Magistrate Felds knew I'd want to get to my family, so he let me keep the meeting short."

"What he means," Thom said, glaring at the ledgers on the table, "is that Felds is terrified of Mother."

"He's just smart enough not to cross her," Deckard corrected, turning to look over Evylin's refreshed appearance. "You look nice. I suppose I ought to change as well, or else you'll put me to shame."

"She'll put you to shame either way," Thom sniped.

"There's no doubt of that," he agreed as he disappeared behind the changing screen.

"While I thank you both for the compliments," Evylin said, able to think again without Deckard touching her, "they're quite unsolicited. I'm not after either of your good opinions but only that of your mother's."

"Good luck," Thom said wryly. "She'll never forgive you for marrying her favorite son."

"I'm not her favorite," Deckard called.

"And the sky isn't blue. Evie, take my advice: Mother adores Deckard, and if you want her good opinion, make sure she thinks you do too."

"Hm." Evylin wrinkled her nose as Deckard walked out from around the screen, pulling his coat over a fresh tunic. She studied him as if trying to size him up. "No, I don't think I can manage that. At best, I can pretend he's tolerable."

Deckard buttoned his green coat. "He's lying to you."

"Shocking."

Thom shook his head. "You'll need to do more convincing than that, Evie. You could pretend that you find him funny. Sometimes, he says things that resemble humor."

Evylin considered the suggestion with mock seriousness. "No, I don't think so. I've never been good at false laughter." She regarded Deckard once more, then held a finger aloft as though coming to a grand idea. "Ah! I *could* claim a middling level of attraction to him and suggest I think he's of standard intellect."

"That's perfect!" Thom tossed his hands in the air dramatically. "She'll love you in an instant."

"Do you two mind?" Deckard groused, though he grinned at their antics. He offered Evylin his arm, brow raised. "I'd like to get to my family's home with a shred of dignity intact."

Evylin accepted the escort. "From what I hear, your ego will be only stroked for the next three days. If nothing else, I'm ensuring you don't lose sight of yourself."

"Your care is heartening, to be sure."

"Anything for you, dearest."

Thom grumbled, then turned and walked out of the tent.

A handful of soldiers helped them load their things onto a cart, and they headed off for the Deckard family farm. Located more than half a mile from the village square, Evylin sat between the brothers as Deckard guided the horses while Thom gave her a thorough tour. He pointed out landmarks of Stocburrough—though there weren't many—and of their youth—which were plentiful. The brothers knew all the farmers and could name the plants in the fields even when they'd barely sprouted above ground. Growing up in the tiny village sounded like it had been the most wholesome childhood.

"That there is the tree Deckard never could learn how to climb—actually, that's all the trees." Thom's hand swung in all directions as he recounted his stories. "Over there is the lake where he got bitten by a trout. That house there is where he fell off the roof."

"You fell off a roof?" Evylin gasped.

"He did," Thom confirmed without giving Deckard the time to reply. "And over there is where he tripped on a pumpkin vine and nearly broke his ankle. Thankfully, I was there to help."

"You made fun of me the entire time," Deckard argued.

"I was helping you learn to laugh at yourself. It's a vital skill to success in this world."

Deckard shook his head. "You make it sound as though I were a monumental oaf."

Evylin patted Deckard's arm. "It sounds like you were an adorable child."

"Thank you," he said.

"A clumsy child," she clarified. "But adorable all the same."

Deckard gave her a beleaguered glare, but she could see the amusement in his green-blue eyes.

"So," Evylin began, her anxiety settling into an odd blend of peace and anticipation as the brothers talked about their childhood, "what sort of produce does your family farm?"

"All the farmers tend to change their crops throughout the seasons," Deckard explained. "We rarely farm one product, though my father does like to grow wheat. He says you can never have too much wheat because everyone wants flour in their pantry and bread in their bellies."

"Your father sounds like a wise man," Evylin replied.

Deckard nodded, a contemplative, contented smile on his face. "He is," he confirmed. "He's also kind, generous, and caring. And he loves to tell stories."

"Which reminds me," Thom said with an elbow to Evylin's ribs. "He likes to embarrass his children, so he'll tell you all sorts of highly embellished stories you shouldn't believe."

"Oh, I do hope so!" Evylin exclaimed, intrigued by the thought. "You've told me Jonn's embarrassing stories; it's only fair I hear yours too."

Thom scowled playfully at her. "Jonn, we'd better keep her away from father," he warned.

Evylin smiled, tugging her scarf tighter. "Now, what about your mother? Is she likely to tell me your secrets too?"

An amused scoff escaped both brothers.

"No," Deckard replied. "Mother is not the sort to reveal others' secrets. I'd venture to say that even a wolf isn't as protective of its pups as our mother."

As the winter winds blew, Evylin reached up to brush her hair out of her eyes. Her stomach squirmed at the thought of their mother. What if the truth came out and Mrs. Deckard learned Evylin was using her son? Would she take it upon herself to convince Deckard to annul the marriage?

Reminding herself that no one else knew of the breakable condition of their marriage, she bolstered herself in that confidence. "She sounds like Hewitt."

Deckard and Thom shared a look around her, then let out twin snorts of humor.

"You know," Deckard said, tapping her knee with his knuckles, "I think you're onto something there."

Thom leaned over, arm pressing up against hers as he added conspiratorially, "I'd venture to say that she could bend the whole company of soldiers to her will as easily as him too."

Evylin tried not to feel even more frightened. Her attempt at laughter came out as more of a scoff, and she cleared her throat before continuing in hopes of better news. "So then, I know about your parents. And obviously, I know Thom."

"Obviously," Thom mumbled.

"But what about this sister of yours? What's she like?"

Deckard pursed his lips in thought, then chuckled. "What is there to say about Meria?"

Thom rolled his eyes. "What *isn't* there to say about Meria?"

Deckard's grin grew sly. "Meria is the baby of the family and the clear favorite of us all. She's impetuous, charming, smarter than is reasonable, good-humored, passionate, and headstrong."

"She's like you," Thom added.

Evylin couldn't help comparing herself to Deckard's description of their sister. "I'm flattered."

Deckard passed her a smile.

"She's also as protective as our mother," Thom added.

Evylin frowned, looking up at Deckard. "Will she be angry I stole you away?"

Deckard scoffed. "You hardly stole me. I've been away from home for more than a decade."

Evylin shrugged. "Euna was still suspicious of Albina's husband, Maac, even after their wedding. And I still don't think she approves of Dolia's fiancé."

"I imagine she hates Deckard, then," Thom suggested.

"Probably," she said with amusement.

"Hopefully," Deckard said, "I can earn her forgiveness one day."

"I'm not sure it will matter," Evylin replied. "Unless you expect to be stationed in Whickam Village any time soon."

Both brothers' lighthearted scoffs underscored the truth: The army did not assign soldiers to Whickam Village. Instead, troops were deployed along the border, engaged in combat against Wauld, rather than overseeing the shepherds and farmers of the Shires.

In the distance, two houses appeared, dark specks on the horizon. "That's the Cohpers' home," Thom said, pointing to the house farther down the road.

"The Cohpers?" Evylin asked.

"Vaan's family," he said as though that should explain.

She leveled her unenlightened glare at him. "Ah, yes."

Deckard tipped his head down. "Vaan and I were best friends growing up," he explained. "And now he's married to Meria."

"Oh," Evylin said with a light gasp. "I didn't realize she was married."

Thom huffed. "Quite. Somehow, the beanpole convinced our little sister to fall in love with him. Never could figure out how."

"Vaan is a good, honorable man," Deckard argued.

"He's boring."

"He's responsible."

"No wonder you two were such good friends," Evylin teased. "How long have they been married?"

Thom glanced Deckard's way. "Five years?" he asked.

Deckard shook his head. "Six," he corrected. "Liliette is four now."

"Liliette?" Evylin asked, head beginning to grapple with the names.

"Their little girl," Deckard said, then smiled at Thom. "Which reminds me: Meria should have had the baby by now."

"Ah, yeah, I'd forgotten about that. You still think it'll be another girl?"

"That was the bet I made, wasn't it?"

"And you won't back out if I win?"

"You should know by now that I never renege on a bet."

Evylin laughed at them. "You bet on your sister's second child?"

Thom shrugged. "It makes it more fun."

As they drew nearer to the first house, Deckard slowed the horse's pace. Smaller than the Glaas family home, the farmhouse's dark oak façade held a cottage-like appeal. A stone chimney jutted out on the front, smoke drifting from its stack. In the vast fields surrounding the house, a modest barn hovered in the background where a pair of horses grazed lazily. A forest lay behind the property, and Evylin imagined the young Deckard and Thom running about the trees and the winter fields, pretending they were not meant for crops but for battle. Her imagination twisted then, giving her an image of Ryen and herself fighting off Mages and monsters.

Heart stuttering, Evylin sucked in a sharp breath. "Jonn," she muttered, staring at the farmhouse warily, "I've just thought of a problem."

Deckard's brow pinched together with concern. "What is it?"

"I don't know what to call your parents," she said.

Deckard's expression turned bemused. "I've never thought about that," he said. Evylin waited as he pressed his lips together in thought. "Vaan grew up calling them 'Mr. and Mrs. Deckard,'" he continued. "But after he married Meria, they told him to call them by their given names. So I'd say that's your safest bet."

"What are their names?" she asked unsteadily.

"Our father's name is Mathes, and our mother's is Serah."

Evylin nodded, committing them to memory. Mathes and Serah.

A light scoff came from Deckard. "Strange," he muttered.

"What is?"

He eyed her. "You are."

Evylin smirked. "Excuse me?"

"Having a wife, I mean," he said, then shook his head. "Teaching my wife the names of my parents. *That's* strange."

Evylin sighed as Thom shifted beside her. "Yes," she said. "Yes, it is."

Deckard stopped the cart and gently tucked a strand of hair behind her shoulder. "But I like it," he whispered with a charming smile, nodding toward the house behind her. "Welcome to our home," he added warmly.

Evylin wondered at the wistful sound as she turned to the farm. The front door opened, and her heart raced as the Deckard family poured out. Thom leaped off the cart, Deckard following suit on her left. He took the time to turn back and help her down before leading her around the cart's bed to see Thom embracing a trim and young blonde woman. The pair laughed while an older woman stood close at their side, hands pressed together excitedly. The sun reflected off her light brown hair, revealing the faintest tinge of red that mimicked her eldest son's. On the stoop, an older, dark-haired gentleman waited, a little girl held in his arms. Even in that small glimpse, Evylin saw the immediate resemblance between Mathes Deckard and his sons.

When Deckard stepped into view, his mother, Serah, abandoned her other children, hurrying over to him. Deckard broke free of Evylin to meet his mother, pulling her in for a hug. A faint glimmer of tears shone in the woman's eyes, her chin hardly making the journey to peek over her son's shoulder.

Evylin set her hand on the end gate of the cart as she watched the family's heartfelt greetings. The blonde woman—Meria, she had to assume—tugged Thom toward their mother and brother. She tapped her mother's shoulder, drawing their embrace to an end. "Trade me," she insisted.

Serah turned to Thom, and Meria sailed into Deckard's arms. The force of her hug carried him a step back.

"Oh, Jonn, I missed you," she exclaimed. "Can't you tell the army you need more time off to visit?"

Locked tight in his sister's arms, Deckard laughed. "Perhaps you could attempt it for me."

"She'd do a damn fine job," Thom said, one arm still around his mother's shoulders. Serah slapped his rib cage. "Sorry—language, I know. Can we get inside? It's freezing out here."

Drawing back, Deckard dipped to kiss his sister's forehead as their father approached, the little girl in his arms watching with wide blue eyes. Deckard released his sister to greet Mathes, careful not to crush his niece in the process. They spoke to each other with hushed words before Thom moved up to take his turn, repeating the process. Thom resembled their father most with their shared broad build and stature—nearer the average Shireman in height than Deckard's tall frame. Seeing the family now, Evylin deduced that the height came from his mother's side.

Once the men had said their greetings, Deckard leaned down to his niece and said, "Hello, Liliette. Do you remember me?"

The little girl grinned but buried her face in her grandfather's broad chest.

Meria stepped up next to her daughter, tickling the girl's cheek. "She'll remember soon enough—won't you, Lili?" She brushed some blonde hair out of Liliette's eyes. "We talk about Uncle Jonn and Uncle Thom all the time and just how jealous we all are of the whole country for taking them away from us. Isn't that right?"

Liliette giggled, nodding bashfully.

Deckard chucked his sister under the chin, then turned, drawing the family's attention to Evylin. Under the instant inspection of the Deckard family, Evylin gripped the wooden gate tighter. From the road, she'd enjoyed watching the reunion at a distance. She felt more like a spectator and less like Deckard's wife.

Reaching out his hand, Deckard summoned Evylin to join them. She held her breath, released her hold on the end gate, and forced herself to traverse the gap. Serah, Mathes, Meria, Liliette, and even Thom watched her approach, a mixture of polite and curious smiles on their faces.

As Evylin's fingers met his, Deckard drew her next to him, his expression encouraging. Tucked into his side, she could feel his breathing grow rapidly. He opened his mouth to speak, then paused.

With a scoff, Deckard's brow pinched together. "I'm not exactly sure how one goes about this sort of thing," he admitted.

"Allow me," Meria said, stepping forward to stand before Evylin. "Welcome to our family, Evylin. I'm Jonn's one and only sister, Meria." She leaned back to brush her hand over her daughter's arm. "This little munchkin, here, is my girl, Liliette. She may seem shy now, but don't be surprised when she begs you to be her best friend by the end of the night.

"Of course, the handsome man holding her is our father," Meria said, and Mathes winked at his daughter before giving Evylin a charming smile that rivaled both of his sons.

"And the beauty to his right is our mother."

Serah Deckard's welcoming grin didn't falter as she took in the couple, but Evylin couldn't help the urge to hide behind her son as her sharp hazel eyes landed on her. Though Meria's friendly disposition should make her more at ease, her throat grew tight under their mother's gaze. She couldn't help but feel that the woman knew something was amiss.

Evylin took an instinctual step closer to Deckard. "It's wonderful to meet you all," she managed, though it came out weakly.

The Deckard family exchanged amused looks before Mathes handed Liliette to her mother. He walked over to the couple. His sons clearly resembled him with their deep-set eyes, elongated faces, prominent brows, and slender lips. His striking blue eyes also possessed a charming sparkle that could instantly put anyone at ease.

The lines on Mathes's face creased as his smile grew, and Evylin felt herself returning it. He rested one hand on Deckard's shoulder and the other on Evylin's. Warmth and comfort radiated from the weight of his palm, alleviating her worries.

"Welcome home, both of you," Mathes said, his deep voice steady and rich like Deckard's. He looked at Thom. "All of you."

CHAPTER THIRTY-FOUR

Evylin

The evening turned into a delightful reunion filled with lively conversation. Even though the Deckard home was small, it radiated a wonderfully cozy charm. The fireplace added a comforting warmth to the parlor while rows of books and amateur paintings graced the mantel. The room was beautifully filled with handmade furnishings: a few inviting chairs, a tea table perfect for sharing stories, and a rocking cradle tucked away on the far side. Soft knit blankets were lovingly draped against the back of the sofa, inviting everyone to feel at home.

Liliette played with a dollhouse by the cradle while Meria readily introduced them to the newest addition to the Cohper family: baby Jonn.

"That's ridiculous, Meria," Deckard protested when she made the announcement. Yet, an awed smile filled his face as he stared at the baby newly placed in his arms.

Watching Deckard whisper gentle greetings to his nephew, Evylin blanched. She'd never been good with children. She liked them just fine but never knew what to do with them. Perhaps it was because her nieces protested the idea of playing make-believe pirates.

Evylin desired to have a child one day . . . several years from now. A boy, she thought, with curly brown hair, a smattering of freckles, and stormy gray eyes. But only after she'd carried out her promise to Ryen.

She shunted the thoughts aside in favor of getting to know the Deckard family. Serah was a splendid hostess, providing tea and readily getting to know Evylin. Her brown and green-flecked eyes were attentive as she listened. Graciously, she didn't ask too personal of questions, but she did ask about the wedding, and Evylin struggled to make it sound less contrived than it was.

After completing his workday, Vaan joined the party. He was of average height and quite lean, with deep brown eyes and richly tanned skin—a true Shireman. He doted on Meria and his children, had a hearty laugh, and a gentle manner of speaking. Evylin could readily see why he and Deckard were close friends.

Throughout the evening, it became quickly evident that Thom had been right. The whole family treated Deckard as though his every action was divine. Yet, Evylin didn't see it with the same cynicism as his brother. Deckard acted with kindness and consideration at all times. He frequently assisted with household tasks, ensured the fire remained steady, proactively brewed a second pot of tea, and made an effort to engage personally with each family member.

In contrast, Thom showcased his usual banter, easily firing back snappy replies while reclining in his chair.

Mathes started to tell the promised stories of his children, humiliating each of them in turn. It pleased her to learn the full stories behind Thom's earlier tales. But aside from the original four, Deckard's childhood exploits remained rather tame. The stories of Thom and Meria's escapades often ended with Deckard stepping in to help them, cover for them, or even protect them. Several of the stories featured Vaan as well, revealing he'd been a good-natured if timid child.

Evylin quickly felt at home with the Deckard family. They welcomed her into every discussion and ensured she understood any references to their relatives or friends. They showed genuine interest in her childhood and family background. She shared details about Hewitt, mentioning his return to the army as if Deckard's speech had inspired his recommissioning. When Serah discovered that her uncle was in Stocburrough, she urged Deckard to retrieve Hewitt so he could join them at dinner.

"He's a soldier under my command, Mother," Deckard replied. "I can't show favoritism."

Serah raised her brow. "Your brother is also under your command, and he's here, isn't he?"

"Yes, but—"

"Evylin's uncle is no less family."

Though Hewitt would disagree, Evylin appreciated the sentiment.

"Take one of the horses and fetch her uncle while we prepare dinner," Serah ordered, then began instructing the rest of her children. Thom was to help Mathes get more wood for the fire while Vaan watched the children so that Meria could help in the kitchen. "And, Evylin, dear, you can join us as well if you like. Or, if you'd prefer, you may rest upstairs. I'm sure you could use a break after all your travel."

"No, I'd love to help," Evylin promised, happy to spend more time with the lively women.

They rose to do their work, but Deckard grabbed Evylin's hand, drawing her to his side. The rest of the family moved around them, pretending not to take an interest in the couple as they hurried to their tasks.

"I'll be back shortly," Deckard said, dropping her hand once the rest of his family had left the parlor. "Are you all right to stay here by yourself?"

Evylin smirked up at him. "Are you worried I'll reveal your secrets in your absence?"

Deckard let out an amused scoff. "I don't have any secrets you'd care to share," he said pointedly, then added slyly, "At least, none that you know."

"Is that so?" Evylin replied, amused.

Deckard lifted one shoulder in a noncommittal shrug. His expression grew serious once more. "Truly," his voice dropped low as he tipped his head, "are you comfortable being here alone? You could come with me if you'd prefer."

Appreciative of his thoughtfulness, Evylin softened her amusement. "I'm fine, Jonn," she promised. "Your family is lovely, and I'm happy to stay."

Joy flashed through Deckard's eyes. "Then I'll go get Hewitt."

Evylin caught his coat sleeve before he left her. "He won't want to come," she whispered.

"I'm his commanding officer," he replied. "I'll give him a direct order if I have to."

A twitch of humor pulled her lips up. "Because your own commanding officer ordered it herself?"

"My mother doesn't command me," he said, leaning down and pressing a kiss to her temple. "That's your job now."

Before she could calculate a witty response, Deckard bowed quickly and left the room. A surprised puff of laughter burst from her lungs. She shook her head and joined the women in the kitchen.

It felt like being home in many ways, working alongside Serah and Meria. Their conversation was light yet engaging. Evylin's heart pinched, remembering her mother and sisters. She wondered if Dolia had married yet. She and Devaan had talked of a winter wedding in Trollenston's chapel rather than the tiny village kirk. Had their blessed day passed yet?

And what of her other sisters? Had Euna ever heard from Druan? Was there any word on Albina's husband, Maac, earning leave soon? And what of dear Calyn? Had she found what she was looking for?

With thoughts of her family in mind, Evylin decided to write to them. She'd ask Deckard if she could use some of his writing supplies. They were army-provided, but surely, they wouldn't mind if a page or two was used for personal business.

A couple of hours later, the Deckard family sat down to dinner with Hewitt in their company. He stayed close to Evylin's side, though he was more cordial than usual.

Over the course of the meal, Hewitt and Mathes wound up discovering that they'd served in the same company for a time. Mathes was several years older than Hewitt, but the same draft had caught them. Though they'd never known each other, they'd trained under the same captain as privates before their paths diverged. And while Hewitt went on to a grand, twenty-two-year career, Mathes accepted his discharge after ten years of service.

As the conversation progressed, Evylin learned that Serah Deckard had raised her boys almost entirely alone. The five-year age gap between Jonn and Thom was due to Mathes's commission. Meria wasn't born until after her father's return. It was rather similar to the Glaas daughters' upbringing. Though the draft of 1538 should have taken Lawton along with his younger brother, he'd been recovering from a case of pneumonia and hadn't passed the health requirements. Over the next decade, Lawton married Laurisa, inherited his father's smithy—which eventually became Hewitt's—and produced three daughters: Euna, Albina, and Evylin.

When the '48 draft came, Lawton's luck ran out. He became a soldier, rose to captaincy, and only returned early due to a severe injury. Calyn and Dolia's births came after his return.

All the while, Hewitt and his wife, Irena, had only Ryen. His work as a general kept him from home for far too long. A choice Evylin knew he regretted.

The discussion shifted to the army, the training of the soldiers, and, surprisingly, Evylin's skills in swordplay.

"Ah," Mathes said with a twinkle in his eyes. He raised his wine glass to Evylin. "Now, I know how you did it."

Bemused, Evylin paused. "How I did what, sir?"

"How you convinced my son to give up his idealistic notions."

Evylin scrunched her nose, and Deckard cleared his throat. "Father," he lamented.

"What?" Mathes gestured toward him. "It's a perfectly reasonable line of thought. Thirty-two years is a long time for a man to remain single. Even Thom has had his sweethearts."

"Let's not discuss that," Thom grumbled.

Mathes brushed off the comment. "But you? Bah. No woman was 'enough,' wasn't that what you said?"

Deckard shifted uncomfortably, and Evylin didn't know whether to blush or laugh.

Then Mathes smiled brightly. "But our lovely Evylin..." He lifted a finger dramatically. "*She* is enough. Now, I understand why."

Seeing the humor in the man's eyes, Evylin returned his grin. "Swordplay was a requirement to secure Jonn's affections?" she teased. She patted Deckard's hand. "I had no idea you were so romantic."

Deckard gave her a disparaging look, but Mathes spoke for him. "It isn't the swordplay itself," he said. "It's the ambition, the drive. A woman who *chooses* the hard path? She could be enough."

Clearing his throat, Deckard set his wine glass back down. "Ambition had nothing to do with it," he said dryly. "It was because she could beat Thom."

Meria squealed in delight, demanding the story, and Thom lifted his eyes to the ceiling as if in prayer that Allore would smite him then and there.

Despite the laughter around the table, Evylin found herself staring at her plate. It didn't make sense. The way Mathes spoke, Deckard had never had a sweetheart. Or perhaps any courting he'd done had never been serious. All because he was too idealistic to entertain a woman who didn't match his standards.

So why had he married her? After thirty-two years, why give up your dream only to save your career? Because his career was his dream? That didn't sit right in Evylin's stomach. Deckard was an idealist, a perfectionist, and born to serve. Since the day she met him, those were the monikers she'd heard, given to him by his father, his brother, and his lieutenant.

Yes, Deckard was all those things, but he was also something more. Something she couldn't quite name. . . .

When dinner ended, Serah secured Hewitt's promise to return for tomorrow's dinner before he returned to camp. Meria and Vaan left to put their children to bed, and Mathes offered to help his wife in the kitchen. Watching the older couple was a precious sight. He hummed a light ballad as they cleared the table, and Serah swayed gently to the tune.

Sitting in the parlor, Thom shivered dramatically at the display. "I forgot how sappy they are," he sniped, but Deckard watched their parents with a fond smile.

Thom settled back into his chair. "Well, what's it to be?" he said. "Shall we induct Evylin into the family with a hand of Crooks and Crowns? Or are your old eyes too tired for such competition?"

"Ha," Deckard mocked, turning to Evylin, catching the moment she attempted to cover a yawn. "Might I take the excuse of a tired *wife* to escape the humiliation of losing at cards?"

"If you must," Thom muttered, sipping his wine.

Evylin chuckled at their banter. "I don't mind staying up," she offered.

"But I do," Deckard said, settling his hand on her lower back to usher her toward the staircase. He called his goodnight to his family, then guided her up to the second floor. A narrow hallway awaited them, and he led her to the second entrance on their left.

They entered a tidy bedroom that she immediately knew was his childhood room. A nice-sized bed sat against the left wall, and next to it, a singular nightstand with an oil lamp, a stack of dusty books, and a framed sketch of five people with the words *"Mama, Papa, Jonn, Thom, and Me"* written under each figure. Across the room was a short bookshelf, full to bursting yet organized, with carved animals displayed on top, along with a spare block and a whittling knife. A desk sat against the far wall, clean and neat. Their trunks rested beside each other on their right.

"So," Evylin muttered as she studied the room, "this is where Captain Jonn Deckard grew up, is it?"

Deckard shut the door behind them. "It is."

She tossed him a smirk. "This is a boring room, you know. I can't learn anything new about you from it."

"And what is it you already know about me?"

"You're a bloody neat freak."

He laughed.

"And you really love your family," she continued, gesturing to young Meria's drawing on his nightstand.

Deckard ran a hand along his jaw. "Yes, I believe you're right about both."

They shared a smile, and Evylin moved for the trunks. "I suppose I'll change first, shall I?" she asked.

"Yes, of course," he said, turning away.

They went through their usual routine of preparing for bed. She swiftly pulled on her nightdress and hurried to the bed to sit and stare at the wall as he changed. When they slid into bed, she was happy to discover warm sheets for the first time in weeks.

"Oh, this is lovely," she whispered.

Deckard chuckled. "The comforts of home are superior to those of camp, aren't they?"

"They really are," she concurred, laying her head on the cloud-like pillow. "I've never been so thankful for a bed warmer in my life."

"Trust me, after twelve years in the service, a bed warmer is a luxury you'll never take for granted again."

"After just a month, I think I've already learned that lesson."

His eyes twinkled with humor in the moonlight. "Goodnight, Evie," he said and, to her shock, turned away to sleep on his side.

Staring at his back, Evylin frowned. "Jonn," she whispered.

"Hm?" he replied.

Evylin hesitated. "Did I do something wrong?"

Deckard turned to look back at her, brows pinched together. "Why would you think that?"

Blanching, Evylin stared at the sheets. She lifted one shoulder in a shrug, the other pinned to the bed.

"Evylin, what is it?"

"You're not upset with me?" she asked uncertainly.

He turned onto his back. "Why would I be?"

"I don't know." That was part of the problem.

"Evylin," he pressed, "what's wrong?"

Mortified, Evylin kept her gaze averted. "I just . . . I—I didn't expect you to sleep like that."

A second ticked by before Deckard finally said, "Oh. I see." He sighed, dipping his chin to catch her eyes. "It isn't cold in here, Evylin, that's all. And when you mentioned how nice the bed was, I thought . . . I didn't think you'd want that."

"No! No, I know," she defended hastily. "I don't—it isn't that I *want* it. It's just . . ."

Deckard didn't wait for a better explanation. He lifted his arm, and she allowed him to slip it under her neck as he drew her close against his side. He wrapped his arm around her, settling his hand on her bicep.

"I've grown used to it too," he whispered, his words tickling the top of her head.

Allowing herself to relax, Evylin closed her eyes. Without the biting cold and in a larger bed, Deckard slept on his back rather than crushing her to his chest. But she felt no less cocooned within his embrace. She could hear his heartbeat as her head rested on his shoulder—slow and steady.

Evylin held her arms tightly against her chest, creating a sense of distance despite her legs pressing against him. His breath stirred the wisps of hair at the top of her head, occasionally tickling her ears, yet something about it felt comforting. Within their embrace, her mind began to drift into sleep, intertwining with a gentle surge of emotions.

It might be a mistake on her part—letting him hold her. Deckard might take it as an invitation for more, whether she was ready for such intimacy or not. Perhaps their closeness would encourage him to try to kiss her again.

But maybe, she thought as she drifted off, *that might not be such a bad thing.*

CHAPTER THIRTY-FIVE

19TH OF OBSCURA, 1573

Though Evylin found a note instead of her husband when she woke the next morning, she tamped down her disappointment. They might be in Deckard's home village, but that didn't mean he could shirk his responsibilities. Nor could she forget hers.

After the positive reception of her swordplay, Evylin didn't bother hiding her trousers when she went down for breakfast. Mathes, Serah, and Thom, already enjoying their meals, greeted her warmly.

"There's a plate ready for you," Serah said, spreading jam across a particularly fluffy-looking biscuit. "Jonn told us you appreciate a good breakfast."

Evylin sat next to Thom where the plate piled high with food waited. "Thank you. You didn't have to do that."

"Nonsense," Serah insisted. "We heard you stirring, and Thom says you're needed at camp early this morning."

"Training with your uncle?" Mathes asked.

Evylin nodded. "Exactly."

"I take it you're used to mornings without Jonn around," Serah said, giving her a conspiratorial smile. "He's always been an early riser. Never did have time for breakfast."

"Mm. I've told him my sentiments on his terrible habit," Evylin said, pulling together a mouthwatering bite of potato hash and ham.

Thom lifted a slice of toast. "Jonn misses out on everything good. He's too busy 'getting the important things done,'" he said, then elbowed her. "It's what makes him so boring."

Mathes shook his head with a humorous grin. "He's always been a hard worker," he said. "Always seeking ways to improve—both himself and others. Do you remember, Serah, him telling us at just thirteen that he wanted to reorganize the barn because he thought he could make it more efficient for my work?" The Deckard parents chuckled together, and Mathes shook his head. "That boy had a servant's heart from the start."

Evylin shoved a forkful of eggs into her mouth to avoid responding. She'd assumed Deckard's fixation on work was, as Thom had suggested, a mere striving toward perfection. It was why she'd suggested that their relationship remain amicably indifferent; he could focus on his work and not mind her needs. Now, she wondered if she'd made a mistake.

A servant, through and through. Had Deckard taken her suggestion as a slight? She'd imagined herself a burden and tried to make him happy by removing that weight from his shoulders. But what if he saw it as a rejection? What if Deckard would be happier caring for her than ignoring her?

Despite the distance between them, Evylin knew Deckard enough now to be sure he would. Caring for others was what he liked best—not soldiering.

Unease made her stomach swirl, but Evylin forced herself to finish her breakfast. Deckard had taken the army horse back to camp, leaving the cart for their return tomorrow, so she and Thom rode two of the farm horses. As neither of them was much for conversation in the morning, they made it more than halfway before Evylin grew bored with the silence.

"Did you enjoy being back in your old room?" she teased.

Thom shifted in his saddle. "Not particularly."

"You prefer your tiny tent?"

"It's better than some."

"It can't be better than a warm bed."

"It is when the alternative is somewhere you don't care to be."

Evylin scrunched her nose, eyeing him. The mornings always heightened Thom's cynicism, but she didn't expect such a sharp retort. "You're not happy to be home?"

"That came out wrong." Thom ran a hand down his face. "Of course, I'm happy to be home. It isn't like I don't love my family or that I don't want to be with them; it's just . . . I always feel out of place here. You can understand that, can't you?"

"Yes," she said compassionately. "Probably better than most."

"I know," he replied. "It's one of the reasons I like you so much."

"That's quite sweet of you," she replied, reaching over to poke his ribs. "I think being home has made you sappy."

They crossed the camp's boundary near the stable tent, where a private awaited to look after the horses. After exchanging brief farewells, Evylin headed to the training grounds while Thom went to reclaim First Platoon from Lieutenant Cormier.

The morning passed with its usual routine. Exercise and training with one of the platoons—Fourth Platoon, in this case—before she went off to find her friends while Hewitt spent his lunch break working with Sheelds and Moris on the newest program they'd designed.

The majors were finally behaving like a team. Whatever prejudice Moris held toward Hewitt and Evylin for their unorthodox style, he'd learned to manage alongside tolerating their presence. He no longer sneered whenever she came near or when Hewitt gave him an order. He held his tongue, keeping all sharp remarks to himself. And while he didn't speak to Evylin in general, he was far more pleasant now that he'd decided to ignore her.

Rafferty pestered Thom with questions about his childhood in Stocburrough during their lunch. It was amusing, but Evylin found herself regularly distracted from the conversation as she attempted to catch a glimpse of Deckard around the camp. She'd yet to see him. Usually, she at least saw him from a distance.

But even as they finished their meal and returned to their separate work, Evylin couldn't find him.

Her thoughts reverted to her earlier worries. Had she unknowingly rejected Deckard? It would explain why he'd been so distant in their first few weeks of marriage. But surely, she hadn't drawn his resentment. After all, in the last several days, he'd begun to pursue her company, giving her gifts and making her promises.

"I will spend the rest of my life loving you . . ."

Evylin frowned internally. Did Deckard love her? Or was it just a manner of speech?

No, of course, he didn't love her. He'd made that promise before their marriage to encourage her decision. And Deckard was an honorable man, just as she'd always known. He might not love her, but he would certainly behave as though he did. It was only right for a husband to seek his wife's happiness.

Was Evylin happy? She didn't know.

This whole risk had been in pursuit of the adventure she and Ryen dreamed of. That was her graveside promise the night before she left: She wouldn't let their dream die. Yet, the reality of adventure seemed less than all their childhood imaginations, and she hadn't done any more than explore the Shires.

It's only been a month, she reminded herself. *I have won dozens of duels, but there's no princess to rescue, and dragons aren't real. As to becoming a legend worth five hundred tales . . .* Evylin decided that was perhaps too frivolous to be practical.

But I will *see the sea in Loclight,* she thought. That would be enough, wouldn't it?

It might have to be. Evylin's life wasn't her own. As Hewitt had warned, her fate was tied to Deckard's. Wherever he went, she would go too. Whatever assignments the army gave, they would be her assignments as well, in their own way. Marriage to Deckard meant a chance at adventure. However, it also came with the chance of rote and confining military posts.

And what of the future? Deckard would retire one day, whether at the end of his current commission or a decade or two after that. What would he do at that point? It was clear he loved his family and that his childhood village held a special place in his heart. Perhaps he'd wish to return to Stocburrough and take over his father's farm.

Evylin tugged on her rings. *That* would be no adventure at all, and her promise to Ryen would slip through her fingers like a sword after a hand-numbing hit.

"What's this about?" Hewitt asked, tapping the bridge of her nose.

Waking from her worried reveries, Evylin unscrunched her nose. The soldiers were jogging away from the training ground. The day's practice had ended without her notice. She was meant to be Hewitt's second set of eyes, but instead of catching faulty feints and sloppy binds, she'd drifted into her worries.

"Sorry," she scoffed. "I grew distracted."

"I've told you," Hewitt said impassively, "distraction kills more than swords."

Evylin nodded at the repeated lesson. "'Focus is a swordsman's best weapon,'" she quoted his favorite line back to him. "I know."

"Mm," Hewitt grunted, then put away the last of his supplies before they headed for the stable tent. Forgoing their training with Rafferty and Ethenn, they met Thom there to return for family dinner.

As they rode, Thom told more stories of their childhood, though most were expounding on the same stories she'd heard the day before. Flat farmlands, with softly yellowed grasses and cold dirt fields, spread around them. Tuberous vegetables grew on some plots, but most were at rest for the winter.

Thom and Hewitt led the horses to the barn when they pulled up to the farmhouse. Evylin hurried for the door, ready to be out of the freezing winter air. The door opened as she neared, warm light beaming around Deckard's figure. Evylin paused, her heart stuttering at his appearance.

"Good evening," he said, shutting the door behind her. "How was your day?"

"Good," she replied, suddenly nervous as her earlier worries whispered at the back of her mind. "And yours?"

"Not much to report," he said, hanging her coat for her. "I spent the morning with Magistrate Felds, then spent the afternoon with my family."

"You took the day off?" Evylin asked, surprised and slightly disappointed.

"I did," he said. "I would have invited you to join me, but I didn't want to take you from training."

Right, Evylin thought. *Because I told him we should live separate lives.*

Draping her scarf over the coat hook, Evylin smiled at him. "That's probably wise. While I wouldn't have minded, I do think Hewitt would have."

"And I wouldn't dream of incurring his ire," Deckard said wryly. He gestured toward the dining room at the back of the house, where the chatter and laughter of his family awaited. "Dinner's ready, but if you'd like to change, we'll wait for you."

Grateful for the chance to be out of her sweaty clothes, Evylin stepped toward the stairs. "I'll be quick," she promised.

"Take your time," he called after her.

Not heeding his charge, Evylin changed in a flurry. The clean dress, cozy sweater, and newly tamed hair were refreshing, but the worry of holding up dinner forced her not to take longer than necessary, and she was back downstairs in a flash.

Everyone was seated, including Hewitt and Thom. Ever the gentleman, Deckard stood to hold her chair for her. The hospitality of her in-laws hadn't failed, and another prepared plate and glass of wine awaited her. Sitting between Hewitt and Deckard, she enjoyed the family's stories and easy camaraderie. Meria's laughter made her miss her sisters. Liliette's singsong voice reminded her of the nieces she'd left behind. And watching the happy Deckard family together, Evylin understood why Jonn liked his home so much. Being surrounded by love that pure was wonderful.

But it wasn't what she'd promised Ryen. It wasn't enough. It wasn't "more."

Ashamed of her thoughts, Evylin struggled to finish her meal for the second time that day. She stared at her perfectly boiled potatoes, dusted with salt and parsley and drowned in butter from the Deckard's dairy cow. What was "more"? Hewitt said she already knew, and yet her mind was absolutely blank. How was she to find the answers to a question that was so vague?

"Another glass, Jonn?" Mathes asked, raising the wine decanter. Though Evylin expected him to say no, Deckard raised his glass readily.

As he poured, Mathes glanced up the table's length. "Hewitt?"

Holding up a hand, Hewit shook his head. "I ought to be on my way," he said. "The dinner was splendid, Serah."

"You'll come again tomorrow," the woman insisted.

Hewitt wiped his hands as he accepted. When he stood, he motioned to his niece. "Evie, walk me out, would you?"

Rising, Evylin followed him out onto the stoop of the Deckard home. The winter wind cut over the flat farmlands around them, and she regretted not grabbing her coat before shutting the door behind her.

Hewitt gave the house a once-over as he stepped onto the brown grass. "Well, Evie," he said thoughtfully, "that's not such a bad family you've lucked into."

Evylin rubbed her hands over her arms to help keep from shivering. "Yes, they're very nice."

"And they like you."

"They like Deckard," she corrected self-derisively. "And I'm rather sure they're all too afraid to disappoint him by disliking his wife."

Hewitt shook his head, reaching out to rub his rough thumb across her cheek. "No, my girl, they like you for you. And that's good. If you're going to spend the rest of your life with that man, it's a blessing to know his family approves."

Evylin tightened her arms around her, unable to produce a reply.

His hand settled on her shoulder. "What's wrong?" he asked gently.

"Nothing," she deflected.

"Don't try to fool me. You were lost in thought at camp, and you picked at your food tonight more than you ate it." His gray eyes pierced into her. "That's not a good sign."

She scoffed, the air from her lungs puffing into a fog. "You're annoyingly observant."

"I know."

Looking up at the ivory and shadow moons, the gold and silver stars twinkling around them, Evylin whispered her confession. "I think I like him."

Hewitt was silent a moment, considering her. He cleared his throat. "That's usually beneficial in a marriage."

She hummed sourly, then met Hewitt's gaze again. "What if this is what he wants?"

"What are you talking about?"

"I did the math," she explained. "Deckard has eight years left on his army contract. What if he wants to retire to Stocburrough after his commission ends to run the farm and raise a family?"

Hewitt studied her blandly. "You're worried about what might happen *eight* years from now?"

"Shouldn't I be?" she asked, desperation seeping into her weak voice. "I made a promise, Hewitt. The night before we left, I made *him* a promise."

Hewitt's expression shuttered, growing cold, the way it always did when they spoke of Ryen.

Evylin shivered and tightened her grip on her arms. "We were supposed to do this together," she hissed brokenly. Her eyes burned with sudden tears. "But now, I have to do it alone because I will not let his dream die—no matter what it costs me."

Jaw tense, Hewitt stared past her.

"Even if it costs me *him*." She said the last word with a sweep of her hand toward the Deckard house.

Hard steel-gray eyes met hers. "That won't happen."

"You can't make that promise," she whispered.

"He doesn't want this," he said, the low rumble of his voice soothing to her heart. "He wants what you want, Evie—to be a legend worth five hundred tales. That's why you're enough, and all those other women weren't."

"How could you possibly know that?"

"Because he's said as much himself."

Evylin shook her head, a caustic scoff slipping out of her.

Hewitt stepped back to her then, their eyes almost level as he stood on the terrae before the stoop and tenderly took her face in his warm, rough, and comforting hands. "Even if I'm wrong," he whispered, "even if he desired this life, this farm, this mundane existence . . . If given the choice, he'd choose you."

Trapped under his bright, knowing gaze, Evylin wondered if Hewitt could possibly be right this time. Would Deckard give up his dreams for her? Wouldn't that just cause the resentment Hewitt had warned her of from the start? But what if Hewitt was right? What if Deckard *did* desire to be a legend . . . ?

"'The King's Knight,'" Evylin whispered, remembering Deckard's favored tale from *The Traveler and the Rook*, the children's book of fables and legends.

Hewitt tapped her chin with his knuckles, then stepped farther away into the night. "It's too cold out here. Get back inside, Evie. And don't be late for training tomorrow."

Evylin watched him go, chewing her lip. Deckard longed to be like Euon Sergus; that's what Hewitt claimed to know all from one speech.

The wind tore through Evylin's shirt, and her whole body trembled, pushing her back inside. The Deckard family's laughter met her the instant she opened the door. Deckard's deep, heart-tugging laugh thrummed most keenly in her ears. She held in a breath as her confession whispered back to her, *"I think I like him."*

That was a lie. Evylin *did* like Deckard—more than she liked any other man.

But that didn't change the greater truth: Ryen's dream was more important than anything else. Because if his dream died, then he died too. And Evylin couldn't take that.

So she'd rescue a princess, slay a dragon, and, *no matter the cost*, she would find adventure.

For Ryen.

CHAPTER THIRTY-SIX

20TH OF OBSCURA, 1573

Evylin stood in Stocburrough's tiny square under the cloudy but blue winter sky. She'd imagined nothing could be smaller than Whickam Village, yet the center only held a meeting hall, a tavern, a general store, a smithy, and the magistrate's home. There was no paving and nothing grand about the architecture. In fact, the entire square made her nervous it would all collapse, and no one would ever realize there'd ever been a village there at all.

"Ladies and gentlemen," Deckard said, beginning his speech, "it is my privilege and duty to extend the gratitude of our sovereign King Ephren for your diligence and fortitude. Our king knows that you are the backbone of this country. The very lifeblood that keeps it running. Without you . . ." He paused, and Evylin muttered the final line with him, "Our kingdom would fall."

At her side, Thom chuckled. "He's always had a flair for dramatics," he whispered.

The whole Deckard family had attended the speech, and she felt it was only right to join them. Mathes and Serah stood on the other side of Thom, their faces filled with pride, while Meria and Vaan held their little ones farther down the line.

Tipping her head up, Evylin whispered back, "It's one of his finest qualities."

Thom scoffed quietly. "I didn't take you for a woman of drama."

"Only when it suits."

Deckard's refined voice filled the square, compelling men to heed its call. When he spoke of Euon Sergus, Evylin twisted her rings, thinking of Hewitt's promise the night before. Thom shifted uncomfortably, but Evylin kept her eyes on Deckard. How many times had he given this speech now? While her mother had taught her mathematics, language, history, and the basic sciences, geography had little use for village children. She wasn't sure how many settlements were in the Shires, and she'd lost count of the stops they'd made along the way.

The crowd grew silent as Deckard continued to speak. "Sergus's story, legend or not, taught me a valuable lesson: One man can make the difference. Sergus knew he was nothing without the men who stood by his side. And while I can never be Sergus, I can be one of those men who made the difference."

Thom shook his head. "You know," he murmured sourly, "after thirty-two years, you'd think he'd grow up."

Evylin frowned. "What are you talking about?"

"Why did the king send us?" Deckard's voice easily filled the small center. "Because we need the men who can make the difference. This war has been raging far before any of us were born. Help us be the generation who ends it. Help us make the difference."

"Here, here!" someone in the audience called.

Deckard smiled in the direction of the man, concluding his speech. But Thom didn't answer Evylin's question. And when the magistrate stepped forward to dismiss the gathering, Thom shifted away. Mathes set a hand on Evylin's shoulder, drawing her attention. "It's no wonder your uncle decided to join the army once more," he remarked. "I'm inspired to join myself."

"I'll be right there with you, sir," Vaan said, holding Liliette snugly in his arms.

Despite his enthusiasm, Evylin knew the army wouldn't accept him. Deckard had confided in her that his brother-in-law suffered from a falling sickness that gripped his body in seizures if he grew too stimulated or overworked, a result of a bad fall from a barn loft as a teen. It was the only reason he'd been passed over for the draft that conscripted Thom five years prior. But as Vaan was sensitive about his condition, the family was careful not to speak of it.

"You most certainly would not," Meria objected, swaying baby Jonn as he napped. "I've lost both my brothers to the blasted army. I won't be losing any more of the men I love."

"I'm afraid I must agree," Serah said, brushing a hand over Evylin's arm. "It's bad enough having both boys taken from us. But now, we have a wonderful new daughter stolen away as well."

The woman's kindness evoked memories of Laurisa Glaas's ready affection, and Evylin smiled. "It has been a pleasure getting to know each of you. I will regret saying goodbye."

Suddenly, Thom grabbed her arm. "Come on, Evie," he said, pulling her away as his family prepared to leave.

"Where are we going?" she asked.

"We leave tomorrow," he said, gesturing toward the tree line. "Deckard's gonna be caught up all day with work, so I'm gonna show you some of our favorite spots before it's too late."

Though trousers would have made the trek easier, Evylin lifted the hem of her skirt and followed Thom into the woods. The giant, gnarled trees spread across the dying grass and decaying leaves. Moss, it appeared, was all that survived the winter frosts of Nettershire, covering the trees in vibrant green. Though most of Nettershire was covered in flat plains, Stocburrough held small caverns and steep, rocky drop-offs.

They made several stops along the way as Thom guided her on a tour of Stocburrough's finest areas. He told her story after story about them as kids at each glen, stream, and outcropping. Many of the tales reminded her of her childhood with Ryen, fishing in the stream and sword fighting in the woods. They walked across the hard terrain for what felt like miles before Thom brought her through the edge of the trees to a craggy overlook.

"And this," he said, surveying the landscape, "is the grand finale."

Evylin's lips parted in awe. She stepped up to the rocky edge, looking over toward the frozen lake below; it was far larger than the one in Wayford. Ice weighed down the pines and bare bushes while mist clung to the edges of the trees, blending the countryside into the cloudy sky above.

"This is beautiful," Evylin gasped. "We have nothing like this in Whickam Village."

"Yeah, but you have ivy," he said slyly. "And that's just as good, right?"

She rolled her eyes. "Right."

Thom sat on a nearby rock as she continued looking out over the lake. The overcast sky hid the sun, a chill permeating the air. Evylin pulled her scarf tighter about her neck. None of the Deckard family bundled up the way she did. Thom and Deckard were the least concerned of them all, relying on their coats alone for warmth, making her worry about the weather so far north.

"Do you like Loclight, Thom?" she asked.

"Sure," he said casually. "It's a hell of a lot better than most places."

"And you get used to the cold?"

He eyed her. "You're worried about the cold?"

"Estshire rarely gets like this."

"I suppose it wouldn't." He rubbed his bare hands together. "Yeah, I mean, you get used to it. It's still cold, but it doesn't bother you so much after a while. You learn to live with it. Like Deckard."

Evylin smirked. "Is that right?"

"It takes a while, though."

"It's strange," she said, watching as the wind rustled the trees around the iced-over lake, "being around your family."

"Because you have to pretend you love him?"

Evylin's throat tightened, but she managed to say, "Because you all know him so well. And it makes me feel like I know nothing at all."

Thom stared at her. His eyes were so like Deckard's, shifting to and from that bright blue. But instead of turning green, his perceptive gaze shifted gray. "What do you want to know?" he asked.

Despite the gloves on her hands, Evylin went for her rings. "Everything."

He scoffed dryly. "Pick one question, and we'll see where we get."

Evylin moved to a boulder near him, leaning against its cold surface. Her eyes studied the misty horizon. "Why did he join the army?"

Thom ran his hands through his dark hair. "Yeah, great, start with an easy one," he muttered flatly. "It's simple, really. Jonn wanted to be Euon Sergus. Always. I suppose that translated into being a soldier, as we don't have knights these days."

Evylin felt an amused tinge of bitterness at Hewitt's being right. "Is that still what he wants?"

"Probably."

"Probably?"

Thom shrugged. "We don't really talk much, Jonn and me. But if the last twelve years haven't changed anything, his goal has always been to become the reincarnation of Sergus." He flicked an invisible piece of lint off his trousers and added, "Best of luck to him."

Confused by the bitterness in his tone, Evylin considered his answer. Deckard's desire was to be like Sergus, the most notable hero of legend to walk their island continent, Allund. Since the six-hundreds, Euon Sergus had been a famed knight to a king whose name was long forgotten. *The Traveler and the Rook* taught of his manifold goodness, a man whose life was dedicated to service—just like Deckard's. And though the idea of serving their country didn't appeal to Evylin on its own, she did think it was far superior to being a farmer's wife.

If Deckard's ambition strove to be like the legendary knight, then adventure was inevitable. She could see her and Ryen's dream come to pass while remaining with the captain for whom she was coming to feel deeply. It made her smile with hope.

"I hate it here," Thom muttered, the words hopeless as they disrupted her thoughts. "I always have."

Evylin hesitated, shocked by Thom's blank stare, as cold as the frozen lake before them. His hands were fists on his thighs, his jaw rigid like forged metal.

"It was supposed to be me, you know?" he continued tightly. He didn't look at her but kept his gaze on the slow-rolling fog. "I was supposed to be the soldier."

Uneasy, Evylin said, "You are a soldier."

"I'm a *drafted* soldier," Thom corrected. "I was lucky."

She gasped at the shocking statement. Every man in Whickam Village from the ages of seventeen to forty-five had been drafted. Her brothers-in-law, Druan and Maac, had been taken from their wives and daughters because of it. For the past one hundred eighty-six years, there had been a draft a decade, tearing apart families and livelihoods, raping the country of its men. And Thom called himself lucky?

"I know what you're thinking," Thom said, looking at her, fury in his sharp gray-blue eyes. "The drafts are cruel. But it wasn't cruel to me. It was my only chance."

"I don't understand," Evylin said.

Thom set a hand to his chest, expression growing adamant. "I was stuck here," he said, "because *he* broke our deal."

Evylin blinked, lips parting in shock.

"You want to know why Deckard left?" Thom said angrily. "Because he's a bloody selfish coward."

Thom rose, pacing to the edge of the overlook. "We had a deal," he spat bitterly. "Jonn and I—we both wanted to be soldiers. It was everything to us." He turned to her. "But there was the farm to consider. There were our father's wishes to consider. And Jonn was the oldest, so really, it was up to him what happened.

"We made a deal when we were kids," he continued. "Deckard was fourteen, and I was nine. He said it was his job as the firstborn to take on the farm and to ensure his family was cared for. He said making my dreams come true was part of that. So he promised he'd inherit and let me be the soldier."

A snide grin twisted his expression. "He lied."

The cold cut through Evylin's coat, seeping into her bones. "I don't understand," she whispered again.

"Deckard promised he would forget his impossible dream of becoming a bloody legend," Thom said. "For six years, I thanked him, over and over. I told him how glad I was to have a big brother like him, who would give up his dream to let me have mine. For six years, I saved to buy myself a sword and trained myself, dedicating every free moment to the future ahead of me.

"Then," he scowled, "the army came to Stocburrough. I was fifteen, and I was so bloody pissed that I couldn't volunteer yet. I was ready to join, but I was two years shy. And lo and behold, Jonn volunteers out of bloody nowhere."

Thom's eyes were like ice as he held her gaze. "Six years of dedication and, in one moment, it was all for nothing."

Setting a hand to her cheek, Evylin tried to process the story. There had to be more, some better explanation . . . Deckard wasn't flippant with his promises. Everything he did was for the care of others; that's what she'd come to understand in the past month of life with him.

But the fact remained: Deckard had made a promise to his brother—a promise that sounded a lot like the one he'd made to her—and he'd broken it.

"You want to know why he left?" Thom asked, his smile twisted with true pain. "It's because he's a bloody idealist who thinks he's better than everyone else."

Unsure whether it was the cold wind or the sharpness of his voice, Evylin blinked back the tears that came to her eyes. "I'm sorry," she whispered.

Thom turned his back to her, his shoulders drooping. The dull gray light threw shadows across his face, emphasizing the hollows of his sharp features. Although he had a muscular build, he appeared almost gaunt, as if the steeliness of his voice wounded him just as deeply as it did her.

"I'm sorry too," he muttered. "I didn't mean to—I know that you're stuck with him. And he is a good man; it's just hard for me to see it."

It was one side of the story, Evylin knew. She only had Thom's perspective. But it was hard to understand what could be on the other side. And it was frightening—the idea that Deckard would abandon his promise for the ideals he carried. That he would go back on his word in pursuit of his own promotion.

Would he do that with her? If he had the chance to become like Sergus, would he forget his promise to show her Ephria and give her the adventure she desired?

Evylin sucked in a frozen breath of air. "You're my friend, Thom," she said gently. "And I'm sorry that you feel he betrayed you, but Jonn is my husband. I can give you sympathy, but I don't know what else I can offer."

Thom stared at the dirt, a hollow scoff slipping out of him. "Nothing," he said sadly. "You can't offer me anything." He looked up then, giving her a pitying stare. "But there's something I can offer you."

Evylin frowned, but he continued, "The bargain you struck . . . It's going to fail."

"What are you talking about?"

"The *bet*," he said, emphasizing the word. "Deckard marrying you in exchange for Hewitt's volunteering. It's not going to do any good."

Evylin's knees weakened, but she held her feet steady. "Why not?"

"There are not enough men."

"I thought Hewitt was to make up for that."

"No, Evie," he countered. "There are *not* enough men. No matter how many Deckard gets today."

She could only stare at him.

"Your marriage only bought you a trip through the Shires, I'm afraid," Thom said. "General Rand—the officer in charge of Deckard's assignment—doesn't like Deckard. He wants to ruin his career."

"Why?" Evylin demanded in shock.

"Because he can't control Deckard the way he does the other men. He's a threat, so he wants him gone." Thom took a step toward her. "A failed assignment like this would merit a menial punishment from most commanding officers, but with Rand—" He grimaced. "It'll likely mean an undesirable assignment. Demotion, maybe." He hesitated, his chin dipping. "Possibly, discharge."

"For bringing back a handful less men than assigned?"

Thom shrugged caustically. "Rand *hates* Deckard. He hates how much everyone else likes him. His popularity and good nature make Rand furious because he can't earn the same amount of respect with the iron fist by which he rules. Should Deckard rise far enough in the ranks, he could undermine Rand at every turn."

"Therefore, we're at the mercy of selfish ambition?"

"Unfortunately."

Evylin held her face in her hands, trying to rummage through the possible consequences.

An undesirable assignment. Not ideal, but it was manageable. At worst, they'd be stuck in some small village or a crime-riddled city for a few years. Knowing how hard-working and well-liked Deckard was, she had no doubt he could work his way out quickly.

A demotion would be handled similarly. Again, correcting it would take a while, but there was little reason that Deckard couldn't fix it in time.

A discharge . . .

What would Deckard do if the army let him go? If his dreams of being a soldier were lost, if his chance to become Sergus-reincarnate was gone . . .

Her promise to Ryen would dissolve like the mist skating across the iced-over lake.

"I'm sorry, Evie," Thom said, genuinely apologetic.

Touching her rings through her gloves, Evylin met his stare. "Jonn knows this too?" she asked.

He nodded.

Evylin returned the gesture. He knew, and he'd chosen not to tell her. Why? Did he have hope that he could change it? Or did he fear that she'd leave him when she discovered his failure?

With a sigh, Evylin stood up straight, her body numb from the cold and the truth. "I'd like to go back, Thom," she said.

He wrung his hands but joined her. "Please don't think ill of me," he almost begged. "I love my brother, but I—I also hate him for what he's done. And it makes it hard . . . It makes everything hard."

Hesitantly, Evylin patted Thom's arm. "You're kind to be honest with me," she said. "As for your relationship with Jonn . . . I can be of little assistance. But I meant it; you're my friend. So if I can help in any way, please tell me."

Thom's smile was anything but joyous. He averted his gaze and gestured toward the woods. They walked back, the afternoon growing colder as the sun rapidly descended behind the clouds. Evylin watched the terrae beneath her boots. A trip through the Shires—was that *really* all her marriage had bought her? Undesirable post, demotion, or discharge. None were pleasant, but all were survivable.

"I won't let our dream die," Evylin's whispered words rang back to her in the frigid woods. *"That I promise you."*

Her hands curled in the folds of her skirt. If any of the possibilities they faced ended her chance to keep her promise to Ryen, she would have to separate from Deckard. That was her only choice. The marriage could be annulled, but it wouldn't be wise. If her father found out, he'd be able to recall her home. Yet, if she played on Deckard's sense of service, she could keep their marriage intact. She and Hewitt could travel together, perhaps—exploring Ephria, having adventures together.

Maybe her "more" was seeing Ryen's dream come to life. And once they'd done all she'd promised Ryen, perhaps she could return to her husband, ready to settle for a life less than she'd imagined before. Maybe that would be enough, and life would be worth living at that point.

Or maybe life had ended when Ryen left her.

Maybe there was no such thing as "more."

CHAPTER THIRTY-SEVEN

Deckard stared at the door from the dirt road, darkness cloaking his approach. Yet, his feet refused to finish the walk. The first snow of winter began just an hour ago. It came down in a thick sheet, dusting his head and shoulders like specks of starlight. The lawn of dried grass was already covered in a layer of white.

He couldn't remain in the cold, he knew. But he couldn't enter the house either. Not when he'd have to face his whole family and Evylin, knowing he'd failed.

Two recruits. Only two recruits from his own home village.

After gaining less than twenty in Stoclund, his odds were insurmountable. He should have given up all hope when they left the town. Now, he was just hollow, aching with fear of the future.

Taking in an icy breath, Deckard straightened his shoulders. No matter how despondent he felt, he would not ruin their final night at home. He couldn't make it about him and his embarrassment. His family deserved his best in their final hours together.

Deckard entered the house to the sound of laughter. His heart wrenched.

Gently, he stomped his boots, freeing them of snow on the mat. Affixing a smile to his face, he moved into the parlor. Continuing to the back of the house, his family sat around the dining table, cards in hand. They were in the midst of a heated round of Crooks and Crowns (once known as Clubs and Spades), popularized when the Shepherd King came to power. The king purportedly played every night with his men during their campaign to end the tyrannical Auldan polity. It was a simple game to rid yourself of cards faster than the rest of your opponents by playing on communal and personal piles.

Deckard had never been good at it, but his smile grew as he saw his family uproariously enjoying themselves with Evylin and Hewitt at their sides. Evylin's dimpled smile lit up her face as Vaan good-naturedly accused her of cheating. Thom and Hewitt sat on either side of her while Liliette sat on her lap, helping to hold Evylin's cards.

Focused on the game, none of Deckard's family noticed his arrival. Instead, it was Hewitt who caught his gaze. The men exchanged polite nods. Mathes caught the gesture and turned.

"Ah, Jonn," his father exclaimed. "I take it your delay means you did well. Lots of volunteers?"

The whole table turned then, their hopeful and joyous stares causing his heart to pinch. "I wouldn't say lots, but there were a couple," Deckard replied, proud of how confident his voice sounded. "Don't let me interrupt your game."

"Here," Serah said, rising from her seat. "You take my cards, and I'll get you dinner."

"No, no." He hurried forward, setting a hand on her arm. "Keep playing. I'll go get it myself."

"There's no need, dear. I'm happy to help."

Deckard started to object, but Thom cut across him. "Let him get it, Mother," he said. He smirked at Evylin. "Jonn doesn't like to play games anyway."

Evylin's eyes twinkled with humor. "Is that so?" she asked.

"It depends on the game," Deckard replied.

"You've always struck me as a gambler," Hewitt said, thumbing the ridges of his cards.

Deckard raised his chin, realizing it was the first time Hewitt had ever joked with him. "I do enjoy a good bet on occasion," he returned. "But only if the stakes are high enough to make it interesting." He turned his gaze from the older man to Evylin as he spoke.

Her lips pursed in dry amusement, and Deckard set his hand on his mother's shoulder. "Sit back down," he ordered. "I'll get my meal and join you all in a moment."

She began to acquiesce but frowned instead, catching sight of the dampness of his hair and coat. "Is it snowing outside?"

"It is."

On Evylin's lap, Liliette let out a squeal and immediately begged her parents to let her go out. Evylin sounded scarcely less eager as she smiled at Hewitt and announced, "I've only seen snow once."

And with that, the whole table rose to head out into the cold.

Deckard watched the group abstractedly, letting them all funnel to the entryway where they bundled their coats. However, his mother stayed at his side. "Here," she said, grabbing his arm and tugging him toward the kitchen. "Take off that wet coat and sit by the stove. I'll get your dinner."

Following her instructions, Deckard removed his coat and hung it over the back of his chair before warming his hands by the softly glowing stove. Soon, Serah joined him with a plate full of stewed venison, pickled peppers, and seared tubers. She pulled up a stool to sit at his side.

"Now, tell me," she said after he muttered his grace, "was it a mistake?"

Deckard paused, thinking she meant his marriage to Evylin.

Then she added, "Choosing Thom for your mission."

Relieved, Deckard returned to his meal. He'd always gone to his mother for advice, even after leaving home. Whenever he faced hard decisions, he wrote to her, asking for guidance. When Rand assigned him the mission to gather volunteers in the Shires, giving him the opportunity to build his own team, Deckard immediately thought of his brother. While they technically lived together in Loclight, they were so seldom there during the same time that they really only shared a house. Yet, they'd fallen into a sense of understanding over the last five years after Thom was drafted. Deckard's thought had been that perhaps bringing Thom onto his team would be an opportunity for reconciliation and to build the relationship he'd always wished to have with his brother.

Upon his letter asking for advice, Serah discouraged him but left the final choice to his judgment.

"Not a mistake, no," Deckard replied. "It's not been easy, but . . . It was the right choice. This assignment has provided us with a chance to become friends. We've worked well together, and he's advised me well too."

Serah smiled softly, though her eyes held doubt. "I'm glad to hear that."

"I'm very proud of him," Deckard said, hoping to reassure her. "He's become an excellent soldier and officer."

"It's good of you to be so forgiving, Jonn." Serah placed a hand on his arm. "But has he forgiven you?"

Deckard chewed slowly, still under his mother's touch. His baser instinct bristled at the question. He needed no forgiveness; he'd done nothing wrong. But Thom didn't see it that way.

"I don't know," he admitted quietly.

Serah nodded knowingly.

Wanting to prove her motherly wisdom wrong, Deckard said, "I think so. After all, he's encouraged me in my relationship with Evylin. I don't think I would have had the opportunity to marry her if it wasn't for him."

Her brow furrowed. "How so?"

Knowing he couldn't reveal the full truth, Deckard said what he could. "You could say he convinced her to give me a chance, I suppose."

Serah sat back, pulling her knitted wrap closer around her shoulders. Her hazel eyes glinted in the light from the stove, the left corner of her mouth lifting shrewdly.

Deckard stopped chewing. He knew that look of his mother's. It was an expression all three of her children feared. The one that told them they were about to be in big trouble.

At thirty-two, it still made Deckard squirm uncomfortably.

"Why do you lie to me?" she asked pleasantly.

Deckard blinked, unsure what lie he'd been caught in this time.

His mother tapped her fingers on her skirt, waiting.

Swallowing, Deckard cleared his throat. "I'm not sure what you're referring to, Mother."

"Your marriage."

Deckard's stomach dropped. He tugged at the cravat still tight around his collar. "Why would I lie about my marriage?"

"You tell me."

"I wouldn't."

"Yet, you are."

Unable to formulate a believable lie in response, Deckard sipped his wine.

Serah had mercy on him. "I can see the affection you share for one another," she said kindly. "But I can also see the discomfort between you. Your marriage is not what it seems. The abruptness of it—if you were any other man, Jonn, I would believe you'd been caught in a compromising position with that young woman."

He choked on the wine. "Mother—"

"But you're *you*," she pressed. "Philandering has never been your vice. You're too scrupulous and righteous to sully yourself that way."

"You say that like it's a bad thing."

"It isn't bad, Jonn. But it does make you rather pompous when regarding the follies of others."

"If you're talking about Thom—"

She held up a hand to silence him. "What your brother has or has not done isn't part of this conversation." Her reddish-brown eyebrows rose, impressing her next words upon him. "Why did you marry her?"

The emptiness of the house echoed in Deckard's ears. The wood in the stove popped, and the clock from the living room chimed the late hour. While the others played in the snow, he sat contending with his mother. Yet, he felt as cold as if he'd been left in the snow to freeze.

Deckard set his plate aside, unable to stomach more. "Would you believe me if I said I don't know?"

Serah's expression softened with triumph. "I would."

He sighed.

"But only because I believe you haven't been honest with yourself." Serah sat forward again. "My dear boy, you have never been good at honesty. You live for others, meaning oftentimes, you play a role. You're so seldom yourself that I don't believe you truly know who you are anymore."

Deckard tensed under the charge though he had no means by which to refute it.

Serah took his hand. "I love you, Jonn. I know you. And while I can see your marriage is another role you're playing, I can also see your feelings for Evylin are genuine, as are hers for you."

His throat grew dry. "We aren't in love," he confessed. "We're strangers."

She listened calmly, encouraging him to bare his soul at last.

Deckard gripped his mother's hand tightly. "We married for mutual advancement. She needed a husband, and I needed soldiers. Our marriage was the cost of her uncle's recommission." He ground his teeth at the admission. "I waited thirty-two years to find a woman who was enough, and in my weakness, in my loneliness, in my *desperation* to become a success, I chose to marry a stranger because I thought—" His breath caught, the words sticking in his throat.

Deckard dropped his head back to stare at the ceiling. The wooden beams were cast in deep purple shadows, the faint glow of the stove flickering orange against their edges. Rows of dried herbs and illus flowers hung from the rafters. There, in his childhood kitchen, he faced the devastating truth he'd ignored for the last month.

"I chose to marry her because I thought she was different," he whispered, lowering his gaze to their hands. "Because I dreamed that she was enough, even though I knew nothing of her. And I've spent the last month trying to prove to myself and to her that it was worth it, that it wasn't a mistake. But now, I know I was wrong.

"I've lost, Mother," he murmured coldly. "I've failed my assignment, and I will see severe punishment. Worse, I will be forced to break my promises to my wife. And I fear she will leave me for it."

Deckard's heart seared with regret, like a wound left to fester. He should have admitted his failure in Wayford before he ever gave her that ring or his empty promises. Now, he could only sound like a liar. As though he'd intended to manipulate her when he'd known he couldn't provide for her happiness.

Would Evylin be angry at his failure? She had a right to be, of course. His life wasn't his alone anymore. Their marriage had changed that. And while he'd meant every promise he made, his inability to complete his mission marked his absolute impotence to carry out his vows either.

She'd won the bet. Their marriage was meant to secure her happiness. And yet, she'd be the one to suffer most.

Whatever punishment Rand assigned, it would take years for Deckard to earn leave. There would be no traveling Ephria, no venturing out together, no opportunity to show her what the world had to offer. And this deal they'd struck to give her the life of her dreams would be for nothing.

The gentle touch of Serah's hand on his cheek broke Deckard from his sullen thoughts. She lifted his gaze to hers, a mother's compassion shining in her eyes. "My darling Jonn," she said softly, "whatever the circumstances of your marriage, you feel for her, don't you?"

Weakly, Deckard nodded.

Serah smiled. "You believed she was enough," she whispered. "So, my child, be enough for her."

His eyes, welling with tears, flashed up to his mother's.

Her thumb brushed his cheek. "Tell her the truth. Not just about your failure," her hand dropped to his chest, "but about your heart. She will not deny you."

"She doesn't want me," he murmured brokenly. "She never has."

Serah's lips lifted wryly. "Why do you lie to me?" she repeated the question.

Bemused, Deckard's lips parted, but nothing came out. He wasn't lying. Evylin never wanted their marriage. He was a consequence, a price to be paid. If she could have left without him, she would have. And whatever he felt for her, whatever he hoped to give her, she would see it as a paltry substitute in the wake of his failures.

A sudden burst of sound erupted from the front of the house. The others came in from the cold, their laughter and chatter brimming with wintry joy, disrupting his despondency.

Serah stood, placed a kiss on the top of his head, and whispered, "Trust her, Jonn. She loves you, even if neither of you knows it yet."

And then she left him.

Deckard sat in the dark kitchen, the stove's warmth almost too hot now. Did Evylin have feelings for him? It was too good to be true, but his mother was never wrong. Her keen sight and wisdom were famed in Stocburrough. She'd seen past his lies. Surely, Evylin wasn't a good enough actress to be the singular person who duped his mother.

But instead of relief, Deckard felt the sharp pressure of pain slice his heart. If he was forced to forsake all other promises, there was one he could keep: He would ensure her happiness. No matter how much it hurt, he would let her go. He would maintain their marriage should she desire it but allow her to travel without him. Hewitt had friends left in the army; he could pull strings and get an assignment that would give Evylin the adventure she desired. Deckard would allow them to ride away together, even if it meant his perpetual loneliness.

Because now that he'd found her, he knew no other woman could be enough.

21ST OF OBSCURA, 1573

Saying goodbye to his family was far more painful than usual. Over the past decade, Deckard had grown used to leaving his family after the occasional visit. Yet, this time was as difficult as the first day he left Stocburrough twelve years ago, knowing it would be years before he saw them again. Sweet Liliette and baby Jonn weren't likely to remember him. His parents would age, and Meria and Vaan would change. He'd be kept separate, only knowing of their lives through letters.

Deckard held his head high despite the numbness carving a pit in his stomach. His future might hold disappointment and loss, but he wouldn't let that taint his final memories with his family.

The cart ride back to camp was torturous. Neither Thom nor Evylin spoke, both conscientious objectors to mornings. The silence left Deckard with nothing but time to think about his troubles, and the gentle press of Evylin's side against his was a constant reminder of the heartbreak awaiting him in Loclight.

When they reached the edge of Stocburrough, the Third Volunteer Company, a total of four hundred sixty-one men, were prepared to move out. Deckard helped Evylin off the cart, his hands tingling traitorously as they touched her, then excused himself. He pressed into his work, desperate for distraction. Without the time to train with Hewitt, Deckard's muscles were tense, wishing for action. Despite his trim frame that refused to broaden with muscle, growing up on a farm had built strength, endurance, and an appreciation for the centering physical exertion could bring.

When the ride lacked physical demand, Deckard kept occupied by checking in with his officers, catching up on everything he had missed in the last three days. He inquired about each platoon, eager to discover if any soldiers had distinguished themselves. Each officer highlighted a few men, but none were as remarkable as Private Loxley, although Private Rafferty was frequently mentioned as well.

When Deckard checked in with Thom—the final officer on his list—he mentioned this favorable regard for Loxley. "It seems your young friend has impressed the other officers," he said. "Do you think he has the desire to rise through the ranks?"

Thom furrowed his brow. "Ethenn?" he scoffed. "Doubtful. The kid is impressive, but he's not what I'd call a leader. He's too . . . quiet."

"Quiet doesn't always mean soft-spoken. He could prove to be authoritative."

"You clearly don't know Ethenn," Thom said dryly. "He *is* a good soldier but shows no interest in taking charge. Plus, he has anger issues."

Deckard frowned. "That's worrisome, I suppose."

Thom nodded. "The kid's like a long match. Trust me, when it finally burns up, you don't want to be on the receiving end of his fire."

"Sounds like he needs some guidance," Deckard surmised.

Thom glared at him. "What? Do you want to be his mentor? Not sure the world could bear another you."

Stung, Deckard didn't respond. Biting comments from Thom were expected, but ones with this potent a dose of venom . . .

They'd gone almost ten years without a resurgence of their childhood arguments. Now, Deckard eyed his brother warily. This was why his mother had warned against bringing Thom on the mission. Separate, the brothers had managed to grow into indifferent companionship. Together, the resentment and bitterness resurfaced.

"Thom," he began gently. They'd ridden far enough from the troops that he didn't fear the men overhearing them, but he had no desire to depart from civility. "Is everything all right?"

Thom's dark brows hung low over his eyes. "Of course, everything is all right. Why the hell wouldn't it be?"

"I know being home is hard for you. As nice as it is to be with family, it can be a bit much."

"Don't do that."

Deckard frowned. "Do what?"

Thom snarled. "Don't pretend like you care."

Deckard's heart collapsed like a tent with its support split in two. "I *do* care," he insisted. "I always have."

"About your lofty ideals," he countered. "And damn anyone who gets in the way."

Anger flared, heating Deckard's face. "I'm not trying to argue with you, Thom. I'm trying to be here for you. I don't understand why you can't see that."

"Look, I get it. You've just had a thrilling time being back home with Mother, Father, Meria, and Vaan to fawn over you. I'm sure you feel like you can take on the world now."

"You think I feel good about myself?" Deckard's brow pinched with so much tension it hurt. "What world are you living in? You are the one person who knows what I know:

It's over. I failed. I'm headed back to Loclight and to disciplinary action. How could I possibly feel good about myself?"

That knocked a fraction of sense into Thom. "Yeah," he muttered dejectedly. "I know."

Deckard tightened his grip on his reins. "Then maybe you could give me some grace and recognize we've both had a rough few days."

"Don't compare our time, Jonn." He scowled. "You go home and get treated like a king while I'm shown nothing but indifference."

"That is absolutely untrue," Deckard protested. "Mother and Father have *always* shown you just as much love and care as they've shown me."

"Now, who's living in another world?"

Deckard glared back at his brother. "This is going nowhere. I asked because I was genuinely concerned about you. If you'd prefer that I didn't take an interest in your happiness in the future, that's fine. I'll keep my concerns to myself."

"That's probably best," Thom spat, eyes straight ahead in dismissal.

The brothers avoided each other for the remainder of the journey. They had a brief interaction when setting up camp, but it ended as soon as Deckard issued his command. It was a small mercy for both men. Although Thom might bear a grudge, his duty as a soldier was clear. He would fulfill his responsibilities, even if he despised his superior officer.

Deckard's mood was foul the rest of the day, though he kept his ire inside. He let himself get lost in the overabundance of work. There was much to do after his time off in Stocburrough, the final stop on his recruitment circuit. He had to prepare for their return to Loclight, perfecting their route home. With their increased numbers, they'd move slowly up through the gentry lands of Ephria. The Shepherd King had prized his homeland of the Shires, keeping them out of his feudal states. From the southernmost Setshire to the northernmost Nettershire, the land belonged to the farmers and herdsmen to work and tend. But outside the Shires, Ephren placed his most loyal friends as nobility to safeguard in his name.

Because of this, Deckard would have to move his men carefully through the gentries' fiefs. They wouldn't stop him, but he couldn't go too near the noblemen's estates. Instead, he'd skirt them, visiting the towns and cities under their holdings. After all, it wouldn't do to tramp through a lord paramount's sacred hunting grounds.

With his mind arrested by the heavy burdens of his work, Deckard stayed out late discussing supplies and logistics with Peery and Cormier. His thoughts regularly drifted to Evylin, wishing to see her, but he told himself the distance was for the best. She had requested they remain what they were before; now, it was necessary—no need to foster affection that could never be satisfied.

It wasn't until he returned to the tent in the blisteringly frigid night that he remembered one vital fact: Evylin couldn't sleep without him in the cold. She was bundled deeply under the blankets of the cot on his arrival, shivering mercilessly.

"Oh, Evie," he whispered, kneeling next to the bed, "I'm sorry for taking so long."

Her head peeked out of the blankets just enough to look up at him. "It's fine," she said with a wan smile. "You took a lot of time off. I'm sure there's much to catch up on."

Hands fisted at his sides, Deckard allowed himself one more lie and nodded. There had been catching up to do, but none of it so pressing as to stop him from going to bed at a reasonable time.

He hurried to complete his nightly preparations and climbed under the blankets beside her. There wasn't a second's hesitation on Evylin's part as she turned over and into his chest. His arm slipped underneath her pillow to support her neck, as was their new habit, and wrapped his arms around her. Evylin kept her arms crossed between them, still protecting her timidity at their embrace. Her head fit beneath his chin, her hot breath seeping through his tunic and onto his skin. Deckard squeezed his eyes shut, reminding himself that this meant nothing more than their marriage to her—a utility.

As her breathing grew steady in sleep, Deckard lay awake for long after. He wished to go back and change everything. He would have recruited more men in Setshire and Estshire. Or if that proved impossible, he could at the least have warned her before their marriage: She would not enjoy life as his wife. They had no future together.

Evylin relaxed in his arms, and Deckard drew her closer. It hurt, and it would only grow more painful, but he would treasure every last second he got to hold her in his arms. Even if his failure took this wonderful woman from him, he would savor each moment because she was the one he'd waited for. He was sure of that now. On the brink of disaster, he'd finally found the woman who was enough. And now he'd have to give her up.

CHAPTER THIRTY-EIGHT

25TH OF OBSCURA, 1573

Hewitt hit Deckard with another stinging slap.

Blowing out a long breath, Deckard struggled to hold in his frustration. As his discomfort increased around Evylin and the argument with Thom felt more and more irreparable, a slow-burning anger seethed in his chest. While he accepted the possibility of separation from Evylin in pursuit of her best interest, he'd tried to fix the damage done to his relationship with Thom.

But upon his attempt at reconciliation, Thom only said, "I don't want your apology. It's just one more way for you to prove you're the better man. And, quite frankly, I've no interest in thinking well of you anymore."

The weight of disappointment and guilt accumulated heavily in his chest over the last four days. Although he attempted to separate those feelings from his work, they inevitably began to interfere, resulting in a lackluster training performance. Despite showing significant progress over the previous week and a half, he found himself backsliding in his sessions with Hewitt.

"You're moving too slowly," Hewitt critiqued. "Stay active as you parry. Focus on the task at hand."

Deckard paced the secluded field, his entire body sore. In their first few sessions, they'd only sparred enough to discover Deckard's overall skills. They'd spent the rest of the time refining them. After their first week, Hewitt changed up his instructions, wanting to test Deckard's capabilities to learn and adapt. Since then, bruises mottled Deckard's pale skin, and each hit Hewitt landed seemed to smack a previous mark, causing a sharp spike of pain.

Lifting his sword again, Deckard set his jaw. Hewitt gave him a few seconds to prepare, then charged.

Two blocks, one attempted parry, and another hit to his leg ensued.

This time, Deckard grunted, the sore limb forcing the sound out of him.

Hewitt stared, his bushy brows low over his eyes. "Focus," he repeated.

Releasing a slow, uneven breath, Deckard nodded. He ran a hand over his sweating brow, then motioned for Hewitt to continue. Skeptical gray eyes scanned him before Hewitt returned the nod.

They went through three more passes.

Four blocks, a failed parry, and a hit to the left hip.

Two blocks, a good parry, a failed block, and a hit to his chest.

One block, a failed block, and a hit to his left leg again.

Deckard yelled against the pain this time.

Hewitt backed away, eyes narrowed.

Letting his sword hang at his side, Deckard worked to control his rapid breathing. He stared up at the overcast sky, attempting to open his lungs and suck in oxygen. He was usually good at containing his pain, gritting his teeth and pressing it down. He never cried out and was embarrassed that he had now.

When Deckard regained enough control, he turned around to find Hewitt standing by the horses.

"Where are you going?" Deckard asked.

"We're done," Hewitt said.

He gaped at him. "We've only been at it for half an hour."

Strapping his training sword to the horse, Hewitt didn't respond.

"I can keep going," Deckard insisted, walking over to the horses. "It's only an old bruise that's inflamed or something."

Hewitt whirled on him fiercely. "What happened?"

They stared at each other, Hewitt waiting while Deckard floundered. The question didn't make sense. What happened to his leg? Nothing. Hewitt had just hit it too many times. He shouldn't have lost control, though. Another man, maybe. But not *Deckard.*

Without warning, Hewitt's hand swiped out and gripped Deckard's collar, the bear-man's knuckles grazing the base of his throat. Deckard went rigid, and the instinct to jerk free brought his hands up to knock Hewitt's hand away. But he froze instead, seeing the urgency in Hewitt's eyes.

"What *happened*, Deckard?" he demanded.

Realizing the man thought his distress was about Evylin, Deckard broke Hewitt's grip (easily enough to know Hewitt let him) and stepped back. "Nothing has happened," he said coldly.

"Nothing?" he repeated in a deep growl. "*Nothing? Are you fool enough to try and convince me *nothing* has happened?" Hewitt's hand rammed into Deckard's chest, shoving him back. "*Me?* The one who watches your every move. The only person my niece trusts. You think you can trick *me* with your lies?" He snatched Deckard's collar with both hands and roared the question into his face. "*What happened?*"

In a flash, Deckard struck Hewitt's hands away before crashing into his chest, pushing the man backward. He flipped the sword in his hand and swung it down onto Hewitt's leg, hitting the same place as his bruise. "*Nothing happened!*"

The reaction was over before Deckard could process his intentions. He knew it'd only worked due to the surprise it caused them both.

Drawing in a ragged breath, Deckard dropped the sword to the snowy ground. "Nothing happened," he repeated hollowly. "That's the problem."

The cold winter wind cut across the countryside. Their horses searched the layer of white covering the terrae for patches of grass. Dislike and distrust bound the men in silence. Aside from their training sessions, they avoided unnecessary interactions or conversations with one another at camp. And, until now, they'd been successful.

But standing in the frigid morning, Deckard realized the time for avoidance was over. "Why did you do this?" he whispered.

Hewitt's face was impassive. "Give you a chance at success? Or a better wife than you deserve?"

"Yes," Deckard confirmed. "Why give me either of those things?"

The man raised a shoulder in a flippant shrug. "To make her happy."

"Why would this make her happy?" A mirthless chuckle slipped out. "*How* could this make her happy?"

Hewitt stepped toward him. "I didn't just watch that girl grow up, Deckard. She may not have been mine, but I raised her. From the moment I returned, she followed me everywhere, begging me to teach her, to mold her into something greater than this world has ever seen. And I did.

"Whickam Village couldn't contain such a creature. She wanted more than it could ever give. She would have left the village years ago if she were a man. She would have changed the entire country—even toppled the monarchy if she wanted. When she wants something, she will never give up on it; damn the person who gets in her way.

"But she's not a man," he concluded. "And she couldn't leave."

Hewitt's words rang in Deckard's head with a hallowed cadence. The way he spoke of Evylin was astounding. Hewitt didn't just admire his niece; he revered her. It was nearly heretical. And Deckard finally thought he understood why the man left the village he'd sworn never to leave.

Hewitt had deified his niece.

Deckard wondered if Evylin felt the same about her uncle.

Hewitt stuck a massive finger in Deckard's face, emphasizing each word as he continued, "I watched as she went from a girl to a young woman and then to a woman in full, all the while letting little pieces of herself die as her hope faded. That village was crushing her—killing her. I wouldn't allow it any longer."

Somehow, Deckard found the strength to challenge the man. "Why not leave with her on your own, then? Take her away without an attachment to a man she doesn't love and an army she can't serve."

Hewitt shook his head. "Lawton would never have allowed it. My brother never supported her, and he was jealous of her love for me."

Though Deckard had only had one open conversation with Magistrate Glaas, he knew Hewitt was right. The way Lawton spoke of his brother made it clear that the bad blood between them was far too thick and his pride far too grand to consider his fatherly duty to his daughter's happiness. It reminded him too much of the relationship between him and Thom. Brothers at unmanageable odds with one another.

But all that still didn't explain one thing.

"Why let *me* marry her?" Deckard asked. "How could you let a man you don't respect marry the woman this world doesn't deserve?"

Hewitt stared at him blandly. "Whoever said I don't respect you?"

"You've made it perfectly clear that you'd like nothing to do with me."

"I don't like you," Hewitt admitted. "That doesn't mean I don't respect you."

Deckard frowned, baffled.

"I fully respect you, Deckard. I think you're an unmitigated fraud, but I respect you."

Not sure that anyone had ever insulted him so strangely, Deckard gaped at him. "How could you respect someone you dislike so much?"

"The way we present ourselves doesn't define who we are. At the end of the day, we can't change our core selves," Hewitt said, giving him a pointed stare. "You told me who you were when you gave your speech. I may not like the man you choose to present to the world, but the man you truly are at heart? I could never disrespect a man like you."

Now, Deckard really didn't know what to say.

"You want more from this world than most," Hewitt continued. "I'd yet to meet a man whose dreams for his life outdid Evylin's. But when you came along? You want more—more than any man can achieve. If anyone can give Evie the future she deserves, it's you. And I wasn't about to let that chance slip past her."

Deckard struggled to regain his voice. "I want to serve my country," he said weakly. "How is that . . . *more*?"

Hewitt scoffed. "You may choose to be blind to it, but service means nothing to you. Ambition like yours isn't containable. It's the same thing that drives Evylin. Accept it or not, you don't care about serving Ephria. You care about it remembering you."

Deckard stared up at him, utterly confused as to how anyone could deduce that as his motivation. Such a selfish desire didn't propel Deckard's motivations and actions. Did it?

He shook his head. It wasn't the battle he needed to fight today. Hewitt thought Deckard could give Evylin the life she deserved, fulfilling her dreams. And he couldn't.

"I've failed," Deckard muttered, holding Hewitt's steely gaze. "I was sent to the Shires for five hundred men, and I fell short."

Hewitt's gray eyes narrowed. "You're expecting a censure?"

"I'm expecting a demotion," Deckard corrected, then let out a scoff. "Or worse."

The veteran's confusion was clear. "You failed," he said. "That deserves punishment, yes, but not one so severe. Why would this earn you a demotion?"

"General Rand has it out for me."

"Rand?" Hewitt huffed. "Is that snake a general now? Why does he have it out for you?"

"Thom thinks it's because the other officers like me."

Hewitt frowned in doubt.

"I think it's because I'm not afraid of him," Deckard admitted. "At least, I wasn't. Now, I'm not so sure."

"Mm. Rand always was a prick," Hewitt said, tugging on his beard. "Never liked him much. He bought his rank and expected the respect those titles typically *earned*. Still, he ran a fastidious and effective company during my time. But I can't imagine he's won any more *friends* in the army now than in those days."

"No," Deckard confirmed. "He's not well-liked. But he prefers it that way."

Hewitt nodded thoughtfully. "So you failed his assignment, and now he'll punish you more severely because you don't bow to his heavy hand?"

"More or less."

"Hm." Hewitt stared off into the distance, scanning the low-rolling hills of the Cotaasis Province. They'd left the Shires behind, exchanging the valleys and fields of shepherds and farmers for the thick forests of the central Ephrian civilization. In the middle of their country stretched dense woods teeming with wild beasts.

Long-corrupted legends claimed the woods were once inhabited by The Living Land, a nature spirit safeguarding the creatures of its glens and forests. This spirit was thought to be benevolent, except when angered by man. In such cases, it would emerge from the terrae itself to avenge those who disturbed the balance of its realm.

The folk tale was clearly false. And with the spread of the Ephrian civilization, most of the animals—bears, wolves, and deer alike—had retreated deep into the forests. They were growing harder to hunt, hiding in their dens. Now, not even the legendary forest of Ephria offered the adventure he'd promised to Evylin.

The thought of her caused Deckard to dip his chin. "I can't fulfill my vows to her," he whispered.

Hewitt's gaze fell on him with a low-burning fury. "I beg your pardon?"

"I can't give her the future I promised."

"Like hell, you can't."

Deckard's brows pinched together. "Did you not hear me before?" he said tersely. "Rand is going to make the rest of my contract absolute misery. You think that's the life Evylin deserves?"

"Why do you think I'm here?" Hewitt demanded. "I'll protect my girl, Captain, and you needn't worry about your general's grudge."

Deckard had spent far too much time under General Rand's command to trust the word of Hewitt Glaas. It didn't matter how much pull the old legend carried with his name; he didn't hold the same rank. He was a major going up against the second most powerful man in the Ephrian Army. He couldn't change anything.

"It doesn't matter," Deckard said.

Hewitt scowled. "What are you talking about?"

Releasing the dejection and dissatisfaction of the last week, Deckard sighed. "She doesn't want me," he said. "Even if you were Allore himself, miraculously shielding me from Rand's wrath, it wouldn't matter. Because Evylin doesn't want me."

Hewitt's laugh was mocking. "Say you're right, you dolt—for one moment, pretend she holds no desire for you; why should it matter? You're her husband."

"And you'd force her to live a life with a man she doesn't love?" Deckard snarled. "What good does that do her?"

Hewitt opened his mouth to respond, but Deckard wasn't finished. "Tell me, Major, do you think she'll be happy with me? Do you think following me around while I comply with the whims of the army will satisfy her? Is that the future she deserves?"

The glare he earned from Hewitt was answer enough.

"*She doesn't want me,*" Deckard concluded. "She doesn't want this life. And I'm not selfish enough to ask her to stay in it."

A dangerous flicker sparked in Hewitt's eyes. "Are you planning to send her home?"

Deckard sighed emptily. "Only if she wants me to."

The spark of fury turned into a flame, and Hewitt slammed Deckard in the chest. He stumbled, barely keeping his footing, the bear-like man yelling, "No! She is not to leave you, do you understand that? I don't care if she says that's what she wants. You do not send her back!"

"Why?" Deckard yelled back. "Because you don't want to be without her?"

Hewitt growled.

"You'd force her to be unhappy, all so you can keep her around like a pet?"

"She's *mine*," Hewitt bellowed, his voice rumbling through the clearing. His giant fist captured Deckard's coat again, twisting the wool in his grip. "I will *not* lose her too!"

Flecks of angry spittle hit Deckard's cheek with the same ferocity as the man's words. But it was the confession that struck Deckard hardest.

"Like Ryen, you mean?" Deckard prodded, hoping to get some answers for once. "You won't lose her like you lost your—" He didn't get the rest of the words out. He hit the frozen terrae with a *thump*, Hewitt standing over him, thrusting a finger into his face before Deckard could rise.

"*Never*," Hewitt hissed, "*never* speak my son's name again."

Heart hammering from adrenaline, Deckard refused to recoil under the man's aggression. He wouldn't back down from him even if it meant he lost what little respect he'd earned. "You want me to care for Evylin, right?" he demanded. "You want me to make her happy? Then you need to tell me what the hell happened thirteen years ago."

A snarl curled Hewitt's lips back, and for a split second, Deckard imagined the man might tear into him like the beast he resembled.

Instead, Hewitt stepped away, leaving Deckard prone on the ground. "I've given you my trust, Captain," he charged, stomping toward the horses. He removed the hobble from his horse, then turned to pierce Deckard with a glare. "I've given you my girl. Don't disappoint me."

Hewitt swung up on the gray stallion without another word.

Deckard sat in the snow long after Hewitt's horse carried him away. He stared at the training sword left behind, unsure if he was unable or unwilling to rise. The snow enveloped the sword's edge, frosting the metal.

Deckard reached over and pulled the weapon to his side. He forced himself to his feet, staring at the melting snow dripping down the blade like tears. Hewitt's voice kept ringing in his head like the *clang* of a hammer on steel. *"Don't disappoint me."*

Too late, Deckard thought.

He let out a deep sigh, then walked back to his horse. Hewitt feared having his niece taken from him. That was understandable. But Deckard wasn't trying to take them from each other. Whatever the uncle and niece's futures held, they would be together. It was Deckard who might not be with them.

In the saddle, Deckard guided his mare toward the camp. They still had fifteen days until their arrival in Loclight. Whatever would come, he couldn't keep the truth from Evylin any longer. She needed to know what was coming, that he wasn't the man he wished he could be for her.

There was a chance—a fraction of a chance—that she would respect his honesty. And if she did, a sliver of hope might remain. There might be a tiny thread of happiness they could grab onto together.

Though if Deckard was honest with himself, any chance of happiness had slipped through his fingers weeks ago.

CHAPTER THIRTY-NINE

26TH OF OBSCURA, 1573

The days wore on strangely for Evylin. Training grew more stimulating as the soldiers improved, her friends growing in skill along with them. Ethenn managed to challenge her with increasing difficulty. And even though she enjoyed how it pushed her, the additional stimulation couldn't quite distract her.

After their departure from Stocburrough, Deckard had pulled away. He distanced himself further than ever before. It didn't bother her at first; it helped her work through some of the concerns she held after her talk with Thom, giving her a true perspective. She liked Deckard—she might even grow to love him—but she'd made her vows to Ryen long before the captain had come to Whickam Village. She wouldn't break them now, even if it broke her heart.

Evylin also saw how Thom's bitterness tainted his every thought. She looked back on their past conversations with a fresh insight. She couldn't trust Thom's opinions, and she couldn't take his word at face value. He was predisposed to complain about Deckard. And after the fight between them, Thom's complaints never ran dry.

"If it bothers you so much," Evylin said to him yesterday, tired of his brooding, "you could make up with him. Then I wouldn't have to listen to you whine constantly."

Thom frowned at her sharp words. "I'm sorry my confidence irritates you so much. Had I realized, I wouldn't have trusted you with it."

Rolling her eyes at his melodramatic reply, Evylin refused to accept the insult. "There is a difference between listening to a friend who needs compassion and being held captive while someone complains about something they have total control over."

"It isn't my fault!" he insisted. "Deckard was the one who picked a fight."

"And you said he apologized for it."

"Oh, Jonn always apologizes. It's part of what makes him such a *perfect* person. But the problem is when he admits his faults, all of a sudden, it's *you* who's in the wrong if you don't forgive him."

"Why shouldn't you forgive him?"

"Because this is what he does, Evie," he replied sourly. "He lives his life with absolutely no understanding of how his choices affect those around him. He pretends to care when it's only an act to get what he wants. I have watched my entire life as everyone—*everyone*—admires him. I've been the only one smart enough to see through him since we were boys. Until I met you and Hewitt, that is.

"That's why I'm telling you these things," he concluded. "That's why I trust you. I'm confiding in you because you're the person who needs to see through his act the most."

Evylin couldn't disagree with Thom, not completely. There was a layer of deception to Deckard's persona. A false bravado he presented from time to time. But she'd shared his company long enough to know when he was putting it on and when his charm was just his natural personality coming through.

Or, at least, she'd thought she knew him well enough to tell the difference.

Over the past five days, Evylin had begun to question the friendship she'd built with Deckard. As he drew away, staying out longer and longer, she began to worry more and more. Though he was always kind and considerate toward her—keeping up a pleasant conversation and holding her through the night—he spent no more than a handful of minutes a day with her. He said it was due to the nature of their fast-paced travel, and though she didn't quite believe him, she couldn't deny the evidence of his claim.

Every day involved a hasty construction of the camp, followed by its dismantling each morning as they rushed to Loclight. He stated that the men required double the supervision, which resulted in twice the time needed before he could attend to his other responsibilities. Daily, he expressed regret for his absence, and she consistently forgave him. However, after speaking with Thom, she began to question whether he truly meant it.

She liked Deckard, but she still didn't fully trust him. They had only been married a little beyond a month, after all. And while their relationship had been polite and friendly, it had been primarily distant. She wanted to see the best in her husband, yet she feared what their future held.

Through training and time with her friends, Evylin learned to manage her loneliness. Hewitt was often busy, and Thom was a miserable grouch, but Rafferty and Ethenn remained fun and delightful. Rafferty made her laugh with ease, and Ethenn was showing marked improvement in his sociability. He spoke up more often now, and she found his stories and thoughts entertaining.

Her friendships helped make the journey enjoyable. She trained, laughed, and shared meals with them. With the rare exception of when they were on assignments she couldn't join, she was usually accompanied by at least one friend. This companionship kept her distracted enough during the day that she didn't miss Deckard and his once-pleasant company.

But then there were those moments when the sunlight would hit Thom just right, and her breath would catch. His eyes would turn the same blue as Deckard's, and his dark brown hair would take on a certain bronze quality—glowing a similar reddish-brown. In those moments, his laugh and smile—however cynical—were no longer his own but a reflection of his brother's.

When these thoughts refused to leave, her chest tightening with an overpowering twist of pain, Evylin would seek out Hewitt. Every time, he'd remind her that this was only the beginning of her journey. "Trust me," he promised. "I won't let you have anything but the life you deserve."

With Hewitt's reassurances, Evylin managed to bolster a fraction more confidence.

Yet, it dissipated each night when Deckard returned to their tent—his cool demeanor and the awkwardness between them resurfacing. And Evylin knew this was her fault. From the start, she'd pushed him away by attempting to give him independence from her. She'd meant to secure his happiness, and she'd hurt him instead. Now, he was hiding from her, likely fearful of her further rejection when he came clean at last.

A rejection she regrettably thought she'd have to give.

At last, the morning came that put an end to the strain between them. Evylin rose to find Deckard's customary note on her trunk again. But this one held more than his usual excuses. It said that he would be back soon to spend the day with her, followed by his elegant signature, the same as always, written with care and intention.

Evylin dressed in a hurry, not knowing how long he'd been gone; she might have slept through his intended absence. She ended up waiting for him at the table, worrying. He was taking the day off. He'd only done that twice on their trip: once to spend the day with his family and once to celebrate one month of marriage with her. What was the occasion today? Would he tell her about the lack of recruits to fulfill his assignment? If so, should she tell him she already knew and was prepared for the worst case? What if he asked her intentions should the worst come to pass?

Finding herself playing with her rings, Evylin forced herself to sit on her hands just as Deckard entered, with his clothing mussed and a hint of sweat on his brow. When he looked up to see her, he paused, expression softening.

"Good morning," Deckard said, a small smile on his lips.

"Good morning," Evylin muttered, unable to say anything else.

Walking farther into the tent, Deckard unbuttoned his coat. "I need to change, then I'll be ready," he said, disappearing behind the divider.

Neither spoke at first, but the sounds of his rustling clothes became too much, and she broke the silence. "Ready for what exactly?" she asked, aware of how unsteady she sounded.

"I have something to show you," Deckard said, his arms appearing as he lifted the shirt over his head.

The image of his bare chest popped into Evylin's mind, and she turned away. "Oh? What is it?"

"It's supposed to be a surprise."

A surprise? Like another gift?

"Why?" Evylin asked before she realized it.

There was a pause before he replied, "Because I thought it'd be more fun that way."

Evylin had no response to that.

Deckard appeared again, pulling on a fresh gray coat. "Is that all right?" he asked, brows pinched together. He wore that expression so often recently that Evylin wanted to go over and rub it right off.

Instead, she pressed her hands against her sides. "Of course," she said with a smile that she feared fell woefully short of sincerity.

Though he hesitated, Deckard suggested she bundle up before leading her into the cold winter air. The army had camped in the wilderness on their way to Banbury, a large town on an earl's fief. Trees surrounded the road, branching overhead like a tunnel of brambles with their leafless limbs. The camp was alive, with soldiers tearing down tents. Deckard led her to the stables, where two horses awaited them: his black mare and a young palomino. She was surprised not to be riding the brown mare, Fransis, but accepted the spry gelding.

The path out of camp led past Hewitt's tent, which was already packed away. A few privates were loading the training supplies under his watchful gaze. He spotted her and Deckard and lifted his head, catching her eye and giving a pointed nod.

Evylin's chin tipped up, realizing he knew—or presumed—the purpose of this outing. She wished she could ask him and better prepare herself. But she followed Deckard onto the road, accepting her ignorance.

Deckard tightened his grip on the reins. "We aren't far," he said. "If you don't mind riding fast, we can make it in an hour."

Evylin looked at the muscular horse beneath her. "Is that why I'm not riding Fransis?"

Deckard furrowed his brow. "Is that what you called the old mare you've been riding?"

"Mm-hm."

An amused grin pulled at his mouth. "Well, yes, you are correct. I thought you could use a horse with more speed today. However, the mare's real name is Maragold. And this gelding is Regon." He indicated the palomino she rode.

Evylin scrunched her nose. "I like the name Fransis better."

Deckard's chuckle drew her gaze. He rode so well, at ease like he'd been born to be an officer. "What's your horse's name?" she asked.

A smirk lifted his lips. "I didn't name her," he said. "When I became a captain, they gave her to me, and the hostler who trained her picked the name."

"Quit stalling and tell me her name."

Deckard glanced at her, hesitating. "Calyn."

"It is not!"

"It most certainly is," he insisted. "They tell me it means 'pure,' and the hostler swore she was the purest-bred horse he ever saw."

"You're a terrible liar," Evylin said, her cheeks tingling in the crisp air.

Deckard laughed. "I'm not lying, I swear."

Shaking her head, Evylin refused to believe him.

Adjusting the reins, Deckard urged the mare to move faster. "Are we going to ride, or would you prefer to get there at sunset?"

Not as comfortable on the gelding, Evylin gave him a cautious nudge forward. He responded well with a steady and sure gait. "All right," she said, happy to be smiling at Deckard again, "we can go. But when we get back to Loclight, we're finding the hostler, and I'm demanding her real name."

The journey was swift, and soon Banbury appeared on the horizon. They eased the pace of their horses when still about a mile away from the town that seemed to float in the distance. While smaller than Cherlam in Nettershire, Banbury was fortified by walls, with numerous buildings towering within it like dark gray clouds. Deckard guided them off the road toward a small hillside path.

"We aren't going to Banbury?" Evylin asked, confused.

"Not yet," he said, glancing over his shoulder at her. "We've got plenty of time before the company catches up."

The ride had helped her forget her worries, but now they seeped back in. "Don't you have to be there to meet with the magistrate?" she asked.

"I took the day off, Evylin," he reminded her. "Peery will take care of that."

He led her down the sloping path, through the thick trees. Despite the bare and snow-laden branches, the overcast sky kept the forest shrouded in shadow. She studied Deckard as they rode, his back straight and his head held high. His hair looked more brown than red in the faint afternoon light. She wondered at their destination, thinking of their last excursion and the beautiful countryside of Wayford. Thinking of that day reminded her of the kiss they shared there.

Evylin tensed, and Regon snorted beneath her. What if Deckard tried to kiss her again? Her heart beat faster, half from panic, half from hope.

Her distracted thoughts fluttered away when they broke through the trees. Evylin gasped. She stared out across a rippling, glassy span of water. For miles, it was all she could see. An expanse larger than she'd ever beheld.

"It's not an ocean," Deckard said, voice apologetic. "But it's as close as I can get you to it for now."

Evylin turned to him for a second, then back to the incredible sight.

"I know it doesn't make up for Hiwood," he continued gently. "It doesn't make up for anything. But I had to make sure you saw this."

Pressure built in Evylin's chest, the pain and anxiety from the last month and a half weighing on her. Tears welled, burning as they fought to escape. *Damn conscientious man.* She forced them back with a deep breath, which melded with the rising tension in her chest.

Deckard nudged his horse down the path, and Evylin followed. At the edge of the snowy woods, he hobbled their horses, helped her down, and removed one of the saddlebags. They walked onto a pebbled beach, rocks of all shapes and sizes littering their path. Some were as small as her fingernail, others massive enough to climb. The tree-studded hillside rose high above them, white capping the pines and outcroppings. All around the lake, the craggy hills jutted out strangely. Far across the water, a grand, spired building sat on top of one of the plateaus.

"What is that?" she asked, pointing at the looming edifice.

Deckard narrowed his eyes at the spot. "The Earl of Cotaasis lives near Banbury, so I'd imagine that's his home. I've always heard it was beautiful."

Pursing her lips, Evylin surveyed the tall, many-spired building. "It looks depressing to me."

Deckard chuckled as he continued down the beach. "I imagine it's not so dour when you're closer."

Evylin followed, watching his movements carefully. Usually, he'd have offered his arm or even held her hand. But so far, he'd made no move to touch her aside from helping her on and off the horse. She didn't like it.

He stopped at a large rock, its broad top flattened and just the right height for them to sit atop. He helped her up, then took a seat at the far end. He began unloading the saddlebag, pulling out a small picnic. A smorgasbord of hard cheese, cured meats, dried fruit, and bread—a barrier between her side and his.

They ate in mostly contented silence, though she wished he would just get on with it. If he'd brought her here to admit his failure, he didn't have to make her wait in silence for so long. Even if he had provided a splendid lunch.

At last, Deckard spoke. "I have to admit something, Evylin," he said softly. "I didn't bring you here to show you the lake alone."

Keeping her eyes averted, Evylin tore a piece of bread. "What for, then?"

"I need to tell you some things."

Her heart jolted with the urge to run back to their horses and ride until she reached Hewitt. She didn't want Deckard to tell her anything. Not when the result might mean parting from him. Not when it might end her adventure before it even began.

But Evylin nodded for him to go on.

"I should have told you days—no, I should have told you a week ago." Deckard ran a hand over his face. "But I was afraid to worry you, and I convinced myself that was a good enough reason to withhold the truth."

He fell silent, and they sat staring at the water.

"I failed, Evylin," Deckard confessed brokenly.

The sorrow in his voice pulled her eyes from the water to him, his shoulders hunching and his expression cast downward as he spoke. "General Rand gave me a directive to obtain five hundred volunteers from the Shires. I knew it would be difficult. *He* knew it would be difficult. But we need the men, and I thought I could do it. I failed."

"But you recruited so many men," Evylin said, hoping it would change the facts. "And you have Hewitt. Surely, that's enough."

"It isn't," he said. "I'm thirty-nine men short."

Thirty-nine. It didn't sound like so many. "Will Hewitt not make up for that?"

"No," he told her, his word absolute. "It's a failure to not complete my assignment, and there will be consequences. Which I expect will be an undesirable position and little prospect of future promotion . . . in the best-case scenario."

Evylin pulled away to slide off the rock. She paced toward the shore, the pebbles grinding beneath her feet until she stood only a few feet away from the water rippling at the rocky edge. Though Thom had prepared her for this, she fought to believe it could be that bad. Considering how well Hewitt had trained the men, could the army be truly angry with four hundred sixty-one soldiers who could fight better than anyone else they'd recruited? Likely better than anyone else in the whole Ephrian Army.

But it wasn't the army they were fighting. It was Rand and his jealousies—his hatred.

Staring into the deep gray water, the implications of Deckard's honesty hit her fully. This wasn't just a confession of his failure; it was an admission of lost hope. He didn't expect the best-case outcome. He believed a happy future was impossible.

And he intended to let her go.

Evylin's hands curled into fists. He might have given up, but she wasn't done with him yet. She would have her adventure, and she'd keep him.

"So what?" she muttered, then turned back to him.

Deckard stared at her in surprise.

"So an undesirable position awaits you?" She shrugged. "So what? It might be disappointing, it might be difficult, but *so what*?"

"We'll be stuck somewhere, Evie."

"It doesn't matter."

"I won't get leave," he objected. "Not for years. I can't keep my promise to you. I can't travel with you."

His eyes were cold, shifting back to their bright, crisp blue as he whispered, "I can't help you find your dream."

There it was, the brutal truth of the matter. Her hopes floated away like fallen leaves in the wind. Deckard had promised to travel Ephria with her to find the place she loved most *together*, and now he was turning away from that promise.

The pressure of tears threatened, but she held them back. "So what?" she whispered again. "I was stuck in Whickam Village, and by some miracle, I made it out of there. We'll make it out of this too."

"You don't know that. Rand could send me anywhere. It could be far worse than an isolated village."

"And it could be far better."

Deckard grimaced doubtfully.

"Either way," she pressed, "I'll take my chances."

"You know my luck," he said with a rueful grin. "I'm not good at winning when I gamble. We took a risk, and it's not going to pay off. For either of us this time."

Evylin's lungs tightened. "You regret it, then?" she asked weakly. "Taking the bet?"

Eyes flashing to hers, Deckard leaped off the rock, hurrying across the pebbles to stand before her. "No," he insisted, taking hold of her arms. He paused, drawing in a long breath for a moment and finally releasing her with a dejected nod. "Yes," he said. "Yes, I do. Because I gave you hope that this could turn out differently. I made you a promise I could never fulfill."

Unable to speak at the sight of his sorrow, Evylin stepped closer. She looked up into his eyes, desperate for some sign he hadn't completely given up on them. She studied the rigid cut of his jaw, sprinkled with soft brownish-red stubble, and noticed the heavy set of his brow. How long had he carried this weight alone? How long had he felt the shadow of his failure looming?

No wonder he consented to their marriage. He was as desperate as she. And in all the time they'd been together, he hadn't said a word.

Evylin tugged on her rings, eyes locked with his, their hue a soft blue in the cloudy light—gentle as ever but tinged with fear. His appearance and demeanor were so different from what they had been in Stocburrough. There, he'd been happy. So confident and sure. Even knowing his fate already, he'd been at such peace at home with his family.

"Why did you leave?" Evylin wondered aloud, not content with his brother's answer to the question.

Deckard's brows pinched together in confusion. "What do you mean?"

"In your speech, you said you became a soldier to make a difference," she replied. "When I asked you after the duel, you said you wanted the chance to be more. But in Stocburrough, you were happy. Why did you leave?"

Deckard was silent, his eyes flashing between hers nervously. He took a step back, and she could see him swallow visibly. "It wasn't about me or what I wanted," he deflected. "To be a soldier is a life dedicated to sacrifice and taking care of others. That's more important than anything."

Evylin quirked her brow disbelievingly. "Either you're a martyr, or that isn't the truth," she challenged.

When he said nothing, she demanded, "Why did you leave?"

His jaw tightened, his gaze averting to the pebbles beneath them. In his prolonged silence, she worried she'd have to press him again, but then he muttered, "I didn't have a choice."

Evylin sucked in a sharp breath at the brutality of his words.

He turned back to her, blue eyes turning so dark they looked almost black. "You don't understand," he said flatly. "I had to leave."

Evylin stepped back instinctively. "Why?"

Shoulders tight, Deckard closed his eyes. He took a deep breath, then leaned against a large boulder, his demeanor hollow and void of feeling. "I was five when Thom was born," he began. "Not a large age gap, but enough to cause trouble. The first few years, it wasn't a problem. We would play together, and I adored him. I was so happy to have a little brother. But Thom was competitive, and as I was so much older, I could do things he couldn't. My success earned praise from family and friends, and Thom would want to repeat my actions too."

He paused, jaw clenching. "And he'd always fail or get scolded for trying."

Deckard frowned at the lake. "It didn't seem like a problem at first. He just wanted to be like his older brother. But I kept winning, and he kept losing. And it became a point of contention between us. Thom felt insecure about his failings, taking it to mean he wasn't good enough."

Deckard fixed her with a firm stare. "I want to make it clear that this was a conclusion *he* came to on his own. No one told him he wasn't good enough. Our mother and father, Meria, even Vaan—none of them ever told him he was lacking in any area. *I* never told him he was lacking. But he wanted to prove himself, and he took every failure as a mark of his inferiority."

He sighed, dropping her gaze. "Eventually, it caused him to resent me, watching me succeed where he couldn't. When Thom was about . . . four or five—that's when it started. He lashed out whenever he felt I was showing off or if I got the attention he wanted. I was young and didn't understand, and Father wasn't there, so Mother tried to explain it to me. 'You have to be strong for him,' she'd tell me. 'You have to be kind when he can't be.' And I did try, but it got worse, and he . . . he started getting violent.

"I was so much bigger than him at first that it wasn't a problem," he said with a shrug. "I could push him off or hold him back if need be. But as he got older, he got stronger and angrier. And in my frustration . . . I retaliated. I'm not proud of it. I never was. But I'd hit him back or shove him harder than I needed. And it became a cycle.

"As we grew older, we grew better at fighting too." He grimaced again. "Our parents did what they could to tame our arguments, and it *would* get better for a while. But eventually, it would become too much for him, and Thom would lash out again."

Evylin's heart constricted with pain for both brothers.

Deckard stared at the water, his gaze vacant. "One summer, the tension became worse than ever." His voice was soft, as though giving it strength would cause too much pain. "We got into some petty fight about something I don't remember. Thom was so angry that he ran off into the woods to hide. Once I'd cooled off, I went after him to apologize. But . . . the time hadn't cooled *his* anger.

"He'd climbed a tree and was waiting for me." Deckard shook his head with a self-mocking smirk. "Said he knew I'd come looking for him. So he waited, and when I appeared, he jumped from the tree and knocked me to the ground. We fought, as we usually did, but for me, it was more about getting free rather than hurting him.

"But I grew so angry." His hands fisted as though fighting his brother in the present. "There I was, trying to be a good brother, and he couldn't let it go. I used every bit of strength I had to shove him off, but I didn't realize how near we were to the lake or how close our scuffle had brought us to the edge. I kicked him off . . . and he rolled over the side of the drop-off."

Evylin's hand rose to her lips, stifling the gasp that threatened to slip from her lungs.

He fell silent, eyes glassy. "He was there one second and then, just . . . *gone*. I rushed to the side, but I wasn't fast enough. I couldn't catch him.

"I didn't see him land, but I heard it," he whispered, and Evylin shivered. "It was the worst sound I've ever heard. He reached out to break his fall, but it broke his arm instead. He was so torn up, so bloody and cut to bits, lying at the bottom of the ravine. I thought I'd killed him."

Evylin's heart pounded as she watched Deckard. There was horror on his face, a fear that made him tremble even now. She remembered the lake Thom had taken her to and wondered if it was the same one. The drop-off was only twenty to thirty feet, but sharp rocks and jagged roots had jutted out from the hillside. A fall like that might not kill someone, but it would cause serious injury.

"I knew," Deckard murmured. "I knew then that it was too dangerous for us to be together. I knew one day we *would* kill each other. Even if by accident. And I knew I had to leave."

With a steadying intake of breath, Deckard raised his head. "The army came through not two weeks later," he explained, voice strong and even. "And I had my answer."

Evylin closed her eyes, the truth clear. Broken promise or not, Thom had it all wrong. Deckard didn't leave for any selfish reasons; he left to save his brother's life.

"I knew it would hurt him," Deckard said sadly. "He'd always wanted to be a soldier, but he wasn't old enough. And I couldn't stay any longer. I spoke with my father and explained. He supported my decision, and so I volunteered. I hoped that in my absence, Thom would find happiness in Stocburrough, caring for the family and running the farm in peace without me there to compare himself to. But he took it as an affront, and he's hated me ever since."

His words stopped, but they kept sinking deeper and deeper into Evylin's heart.

Voice trapped somewhere inside, Evylin stood with uncertainty by the water's edge. Thom was wrong about his brother. Every choice and act might be in pursuit of perfection, but it wasn't for himself. It was in service of those he loved. He chose to leave his family and his home so his brother could be free of him, in the hope that Thom might find happiness without him.

It was too heartbreaking to fathom.

And she realized it was what he intended to do to her.

Evylin crossed the gap between them without worrying about the implications and wrapped her arms around Deckard's waist. She pressed her cheek into his chest, hoping he could feel how sorry she was. How much she wished she could change what had happened.

His arms folded around her, and he rested his head against hers.

"I didn't know," she muttered into his coat.

Deckard ran one hand down the length of her hair. "I know," he whispered back.

"If I had known. . . ." She didn't finish that statement. Had she known, would she have behaved any differently? She still cared for Thom; she still valued his friendship. She simply possessed a clearer understanding of his faults now.

Deckard's hands came up to frame her face. "It's good he has you," he whispered, eyes suddenly a deep green.

How did they change so often? she wondered.

"I'm not sure he's ever had a better friend." With another deep breath, Deckard rested his forehead against hers and closed his eyes. "I should have told you," he continued. "I should have warned you when I saw how close you were getting."

Evylin wasn't sure he was right. What good would it have done to warn her of Thom's envious and embittered feelings? She'd always known Thom to be cynical and sarcastic. The past lent context, but it didn't change the present. And Evylin had been a stranger to Deckard. Yes, they married, but why should he have trusted her with this painful truth? She didn't trust him with the pain of her past either.

In their closeness, Evylin noted each line and freckle on Deckard's skin. Most times, she forgot the six years separating them. But this close, she saw it. Each wrinkle seemed amplified in this intimate inspection.

Brushing her fingers along the crinkles beside his right eye, Evylin wished she could smooth them, removing whatever weight had etched them there.

At her touch, Deckard opened his eyes. His gaze floated over her face. It flickered to her lips, and Evylin's heart fluttered.

So he did want to kiss her again.

Well, she wouldn't stop him.

"Deckard!" a voice yelled from a distance.

Deckard and Evylin swiftly distanced themselves, gazing down the beach as Thom approached, arms waving. Deckard took Evylin's hand, and they jogged down the beach to Thom, who stopped short to catch his breath. He eyed them upon their approach, noting their intertwined fingers before drawing up. "Sorry to interrupt," he said tensely. "But it couldn't wait."

Deckard let go of Evylin and stepped closer. "What is it?"

"Peery just returned from the magistrate's," Thom said, expression uneasy. "And, Deckard, the prince was there."

"What?" Deckard gasped.

"Prince Ephren?" Evylin asked in awe.

"Yes," Thom confirmed, then frowned. "And he's asked to meet with you."

CHAPTER FORTY

Evylin

Evylin and Deckard glanced at one another as they entered Magistrate Prokter's home. One servant took their coats as another requested that they follow him. Deckard wore his ceremonial uniform, and Evylin, the navy satin dress from their wedding. But though they might look the part, she didn't believe for a second either of them felt ready to meet the Crown Prince of Ephria.

Thom had filled them in as they rushed back to the camp. "Peery returned twenty minutes ago," he explained. "Said he asked for the magistrate, and they ushered him into a drawing room. Then they announced the magistrate *and* the prince. Peery was—well, he still looked shaken when he got back. I can only imagine a surprise meeting with the prince wasn't on his list of expectations when you asked him to cover for you."

"Nor on mine," Deckard replied.

"Peery said the prince asked after his commanding officer upon introduction, and he told him you were enjoying the day with your wife." Thom paused there to glance at Evylin. "That particularly intrigued the prince. He couldn't believe we had a woman traveling with us and immediately requested both you and Evie join him for dinner."

Evylin heard it once said a request from the royal family was never actually a "request." To deny them anything was to declare your opposition to the throne. They would be joining Prince Ephren for dinner whether they wanted to or not.

At first, the worried expression on Deckard's face concerned Evylin. Then she realized this unexpected meeting might not be such a bad thing. In what novel did meeting a prince not start an adventure? And though saving a princess might be too lofty a goal, she thought dining with a prince might satisfy that particular item on her and Ryen's list.

With her hand tucked into the curve of Deckard's arm, they walked into the large foyer of the magistrate's home. *Really,* she thought, *the house must be a mansion.* Twice the size of any home in Whickam Village, its ceilings stretched high above them. The décor and furnishings were the finest she'd ever seen. Granite floors, golden stair rails, and jacquard curtains adorned the home. *This* was the way Evylin imagined the world would be: grand, beautiful, and filled with excitement.

Deckard appeared less enthusiastic, his jaw clenched and posture rigid, a tension tangible in the muscles beneath his velvet coat. Their footsteps reverberated in the tiled corridor. Two servants opened a grand double door at the end. Their escort stepped inside and bowed deeply as they entered the dining room. "Your hosts will arrive shortly," he announced.

An eight-foot table stood ready, adorned with exquisite porcelain, gleaming flatware, and a luxurious tablecloth. Candlesticks ran along its length, causing the crystal and silver to glimmer. Surrounding the table were ten cherry wood chairs—four on each side and one at each end.

However, the table was the least striking feature in the room. A luxurious curtain of dark green velvet draped along the back wall, framing three large windows. The setting sun bathed the room in an enchanting glow. Walls adorned with silver and emerald damask displayed large paintings of landscapes and portraits. The flooring was rich wood, with a massive rug positioned beneath the table.

"I've never seen anything like this," Evylin whispered as the servants shut the doors behind them.

"It may surprise you," Deckard said quietly, "but the magistrates of the Shires are rather humble compared to the rest of the country. This is about what I expected."

"It's stunning," she marveled, wondering if the rest of the house could be this lavish. She didn't imagine anyone in the world held such wealth as she saw before her.

Deckard didn't respond, and she looked up at him. His brow had furrowed again, his hands at his sides as he tightened and loosened them into fists.

Evylin didn't bother to contain her chuckle. "Relax," she said, patting his arm. "This will be fun."

His jaw remained tight. "I doubt it."

Before Evylin could reply, the doors swung open behind them. Laughter echoed down the hall, prompting them to turn. A group of men and women approached, adorned in elegant attire. Two men wore formal soldiers' uniforms, while the rest wore dashing suits. The two women in attendance made Evylin feel drab in her simple satin dress. The party presented a spectacle of extravagant beauty in rich silks and velvets, elaborate epaulets and embroidery, dazzling jewels and precious metals.

The servant entered the room, bowed once more, and announced the party's arrival. "His Royal Highness, Prince Caspar Ephren; His Honor, Magistrate Theodore Prokter, along with his wife, Lady Selia Prokter, and their children, Mistress Elisa and Master Theodore II." The servant paused before proceeding. "Lieutenant Colonel Aldan Haart and Lieutenant Benedict Lilifoot, guests of the prince, accompanied by Lord Vincente Carlile, advisor to the king."

Identifying the oncoming arrivals required little effort. The soldiers' uniforms identified them; the darker-complexioned man wore the silver braid of a lieutenant colonel, and the curly-haired one bore a lieutenant's insignia. The ages of the Prokter family clarified their identities, and the prince looked nothing like his father's advisor. Nevertheless, Evylin wondered how she would manage to remember their names.

The party laughed and chatted loudly, overlooking the introductions. They strode into the room, completely disregarding the servant, except for one individual. Lord Carlile, she presumed, nodded to the servant and expressed his thanks. The doors shut behind them, and the servant vanished through a side door at the back of the room.

"Well, now," said the newly identified Prince Ephren. He clasped his hands together and stepped over to the waiting couple. He fit right into the room, dressed in an overly embellished emerald coat. His dark brown hair was well-groomed, and his wide smile was a tad too friendly to be genuine. "You must be Captain Deckard. How are my new soldiers?"

Deckard bowed, and Evylin curtsied. "I am, Your Highness," Deckard said, head still dipped in respect. "Your men are ready to serve."

Prince Ephren didn't bother to respond before turning his attention to Evylin. "And you're his precious new wife?" He ran a thumb and forefinger along his jaw as he studied her. "I can see why you needed the day off, Captain."

The two soldiers snickered behind him.

With an appropriately polite smile, Evylin studied the heir to Ephria. He was a near-perfect image of her imagination of the Shepherd King: handsome with dark features and warmly tanned skin, as though he'd spent the day in the pasture with his flock. Yet, he carried himself with a marked arrogance that didn't match the first King Ephren's purported humble heroism. But his boyish smile and light turn of phrase gave Evylin the courage to return his jest.

"On the contrary, Your Highness," Evylin said lightly. "It was I who needed the day with my husband. He's so dedicated to his work, you see, that I must demand his attention from time to time."

Feeling Deckard tense, Evylin slid her hand farther up his arm.

The prince watched the movement with a keen eye. "How remarkable," he said, grin turning sly. "My own wife doesn't ask to spend the day with me."

"What a shame," Evylin said, smiling up at Deckard. "I can't seem to get enough of my Jonn."

While Deckard gave her a sidelong glance, the prince laughed heartily.

The side door opened, and servants appeared, carrying trays of food. "Ah," Prince Ephren cried. "Splendid! Captain, you must meet our magnificent host. He's very intrigued by all the men you've brought."

The magistrate stepped over, then, and introduced himself. "Tell me," he said, setting a hand on Deckard's shoulder to lead him to the table. Evylin followed, hand still hooked to Deckard's arm. The magistrate sat at the end of the table and gestured to the seat on his left. "How did you convince all those bumpkins to leave their homes? I never thought I'd see so many Shiremen before my walls."

"I must attribute my success to the sense of duty and loyalty in the Shires, Your Honor," Deckard said, pulling out the chair for Evylin next to his.

"Captain, please," the prince called from his seat of honor at the far end. "If you'd give me the pleasure, I'd very much enjoy the presence of Mrs. Deckard at my side."

The dinner party froze, turning to stare at the couple. Evylin blanched under their gazes. Lady Prokter sat to her husband's right, eyeing her, while the young boy sat next to her, smirking over at his sister. The lieutenant colonel had already taken the seat at the prince's right hand while the other soldier waited, and the daughter glared at Evylin with fury.

Deckard's fingers were white on the back of the chair. He glanced at Evylin, then fitted a smile on his face and turned to the prince. "Of course, Your Highness," he said respectfully. "It's an honor."

Though Evylin had no more desired their separation than Deckard, she had little choice. She didn't understand why the prince wished for her company, but one did not deny royalty.

Deckard slipped Evylin's hand from the crook of his arm, meeting her gaze with something tense in his own, eyes a fiercer blue than normal. She couldn't tell whether it was frustration or worry in his expression. He lifted his chin before she could figure out his pointed stare, telling her to go.

Evylin walked around the table, her discomfort growing under their dinner companions' unwavering stares. The magistrate's daughter, seated between the lieutenant colonel and lieutenant, frowned while Lord Carlile held out the chair for Evylin.

Once they were seated, the servants began to serve the meal. Evylin's eyes met Deckard's across the table, finding that same serious look in his eyes. However, he turned away as Magistrate Prokter resumed his diatribe against the Shires, and Lady Prokter critiqued her son's table manners.

"I'm terribly sorry to take you from your husband, my dear," Prince Ephren said, voice pitched low. "But I can't bear to be in the presence of beauty when it isn't right at my side."

Evylin gave the prince a cautious smile. "You're too kind, Your Highness."

"Oh, come now," he said as a servant filled his wine glass. "You had a wit before; don't let it disappear now. Do tell me, where in my whole kingdom could a man find such a magnificent creature as you?"

Bemused, Evylin hesitated. She supposed his appreciation for her wit wasn't surprising. Men and women bantered as a matter of conversation in the Shires. As the royal family originated from the region, though nearly two centuries past, it made sense they'd share the same appreciation for friendly witticisms.

Evylin relaxed, deciding to enjoy herself. When else would she get to converse with a prince?

She smiled slyly as she replied, "A small village in Estshire. I'm sure you've never heard of it, Your Highness, as it's really rather insignificant."

"Truly?" His voice was casual and hearty despite its posh accent, filling each word with joviality. "Well then, what do you think of Banbury? Is it as dull as your tiny village?"

A plate was set before Evylin, and she took the opportunity to glance at Deckard. He was distracted by the endless blathering of the magistrate, so she turned back. "I don't believe there's much in the whole of Terraeus as dull as the village I grew up in."

Prince Ephren ignored his plate and sipped on his wine instead. "Is that so?" he asked, chuckling. It was a warm and welcoming sound. "Do go on. I love hearing of those miserable old places," he said to the lieutenant colonel, smirking at his side.

Evylin cut some of the venison on her plate. "To remind you of all the wonderful things that fill your life?" she teased habitually.

Laughing loudly, Prince Ephren leaned back in his chair. "Precisely! I have never been to the Shires, but I hear they're absolutely disgusting. Livestock everywhere, with the people so uncultured. How it managed to produce a flower such as yourself is a wonder."

"I hear," Miss Prokter said, the youth clear in her soft voice, "it takes manure to grow things well, and that's why the Shires are so disgusting."

Prince Ephren's brown eyes darted to Elisa Prokter in amusement before turning back to Evylin. "Do you have any correction for our Miss Prokter, my dear?" he asked.

Regarding the girl's silly jealousy in the same way that she might Calyn's—misguided and innocently ignorant—Evylin tipped her head. "Not at all. You've heard right, Miss Prokter."

The prince laughed, and the girl's cheeks burned red.

"So the shit-infested Shires manage to produce more than just crops?" The prince nudged the lieutenant colonel with his arm. "Can you believe it, Aldan?"

"No, Your Highness," the soldier replied.

After a sip of wine, Evylin set her glass back on the table. "Didn't the first King Ephren hail from Estshire?"

A flicker of annoyance passed through Ephren's eyes. "A mark on my heritage I try to forget. What a disappointment, being the lineage of the Shepherd King and his muck-riddled past."

Evylin raised her brow. "Though I'd venture to say it's better to be a descendant of a Shepherd King than no king at all."

The prince and the officer laughed. "You *are* a quick one," Ephren said, angling toward her. "Is that why your captain noticed you? It's easy to see how lovely you are, but capturing a man for good takes more than looks. How did you entrap him? With your wit?"

Evylin's eyes flickered to Deckard. He was watching her this time, drawn by either the laughter or a natural glance. Though he gave her a gentle smile, his eyes remained intense, as though cautioning her. Then the magistrate drew his attention away once more.

Turning back to the prince, Evylin kept her words light. "What woman knows what drew her husband to her? What was it that drew you to your wife?"

Ephren huffed, dropping deeper into his chair. "A dowry and the approval of my father," he said, taking a long sip of his wine.

A glimmer of understanding came to Evylin. Before her wasn't a man who enjoyed lighthearted teasing for entertainment's sake alone, but a man locked in a loveless marriage seeking companionship. It wouldn't do to encourage him, but, as he was the prince, it wouldn't do to ignore him either.

"Please, my dear," Ephren pressed. "Tell me how you charmed your husband. I'm interested to hear your cunning plan."

Evylin pulled together a forkful of carrots and potatoes. She saw no reason not to play along; as a married woman, she was safe from the prince's wiles. Which was the probable reason he sought her attention; he could tease without any risk of breaking a heart.

"Well," she said, hovering the fork above her plate, "he lost a bet to me."

Evylin took her bite, and Ephren raised his brow. "A gamble for a marriage? I've never heard of a woman so conniving."

"Nor have I, Your Highness," the lieutenant colonel said, grinning brightly.

"Tell us, then," Ephren goaded. "What induced your captain to take this bet? He must have thought the odds were too far in his favor to lose."

"I dare say he did," Evylin agreed. "I don't think he believed I could win at all."

"What was your game, then? Cards?"

"No, no." She chuckled. "I'm miserable at cards."

"Dice?"

"You really want to know?" Evylin asked, meeting the prince's dark gaze.

Ephren nodded, resting his arms on the table's edge. "I really do."

"I challenged his brother to a duel. And I won."

The whole table fell silent, and Prince Ephren narrowed his eyes. A blush spread over Evylin's neck, all the way up to her cheeks under the party's inspection. She chanced a look at Deckard to see his lips pressed together. With one subtle shake of his head, she finally read the message in his gaze: Be careful. The Shires were traditional and religious but not like the rest of Ephria. They were laid-back, tolerating occasional impropriety as amusing quirks. But they weren't in the Shires anymore, and Evylin's unique hobbies were no longer an acceptable curiosity.

A thin, nervous laugh seeped out of her as she turned back to the prince. "That was a joke," she offered. "Though poorly executed, I admit."

Ephren's expression remained impassive while the rest of the table watched in a blend of horror and curiosity.

"Obviously," she continued, twisting her rings, "I wouldn't know the first thing about swordplay. I find it quite frightening."

"One of the few things that frightens her," Deckard interjected brightly. "Pardon my wife's sense of humor. She grew up quite close to her uncle—a veteran with a rough tongue. It can be charming, but it's known to get her into trouble."

Evylin held her breath, but the prince leaned back in his seat with a light chuckle. The rest of the table relaxed with him. "I see," Ephren said, his gaze scanning her thoughtfully. "I imagine that's part of the allure."

Though tension remained evident on his jaw, Deckard smiled and replied, "Indeed."

"I do apologize," Evylin said demurely. "I'm afraid I'm quite lost without Jonn at my side. He always manages to keep me in check. One of the things I love most about him."

Though she spoke to the prince, Evylin's eyes darted to Deckard and found his grin partially obscured as he took a sip of wine.

Ephren let out a good-natured huff. "Well, I'm glad I've taken you from him, then. I like a woman with a loose tongue. It's always so much more entertaining."

With the impropriety solved, Lady Prokter resumed her conversation with the lieutenant. "As I was saying," she started, "the price was too good to pass up, so we had the whole house done. I never knew how reasonable damask was."

"What was it, then?" Ephren asked Evylin again. "If not a sword fight."

Knowing better now, Evylin checked her unbridled tongue, giving a more palatable lie. "I bet him that he wouldn't marry me," she said. "And Jonn's not one to lose a bet."

The lieutenant colonel's smirk grew wicked, whispering to the prince, "Not when the prize is as fine as this one."

Evylin didn't think she was meant to hear the comment, but the prince was more discreet with his whispered reply, and the two men sniggered together.

On her left, Lord Carlile leaned near to whisper, causing her to startle in her chair. "You should be careful how much you tease him," he said in a tone only she could hear. "I would have warned you sooner, madam, but the lady on my left is almost as demanding as our prince."

"Lord Carlile, don't pester our beautiful friend with your senile remarks," Ephren commanded. He couldn't have known what the advisor was saying, but evidently, he gathered the sentiments.

"I beg your pardon, Your Highness," Lord Carlile replied good-humoredly.

Ephren patted Evylin's hand in a comforting gesture. His skin was soft—softer than even hers. Like his hands had never seen a day of work in all his life.

"No need to worry yourself about the old codger, my dear," he said, his eyes roving over Evylin more brazenly than before. They trailed from her face, down her throat, and to the modest neckline of her dress. "He's only along because my father thinks I need a babysitter. But the doddering fool can't stop me from having fun."

The prince slipped his boot beneath Evylin's skirt and ran the toe along the side of her slipper-clad foot. "Do you like to have fun, my dear?"

Suddenly, Evylin realized how wrong she'd been. The prince wasn't looking for friendly banter. He was a shameless flirt who intended to seduce her in front of her own husband.

Managing to smile bashfully, though she would've rather spit in his face, Evylin dipped her head. "I must admit, Your Highness, I'm as dull as my village in the Shire."

His fingers trailed along the back of her hand, then curled around her wrist. "You're sure?" he whispered. "It sounds as though you like a man who gambles. And I quite enjoy thrilling risks."

Disgusted, Evylin crossed her legs to draw her foot from his. She feigned pursuit of her wine to slip from his grasp as well. She couldn't outright deny him, but she would *not* accept him either. "As I said, Your Highness, my husband does quite a good job keeping me in line. And he's all the risk I need."

The civility in Prince Ephren's sly grin disappeared. "Very well," he said, then leaned toward the other side of the table. "Miss Elisa, do tell me, darling, how is it you always look so lovely in candlelight?"

The young Elisa Prokter beamed, and Evylin fought not to choke on her wine. She'd always heard the king was a good and noble man, that Ephria's cause was righteous, and they were defending their nation's honor. But if this prince was a byproduct of such a king, then Evylin had to question if anything she'd heard about the royal family was true.

As the prince went on to flirt with poor, gullible Elisa, Lord Carlile whispered to Evylin again. "My apologies, madam," he murmured. "I'm afraid some men never learned to be gentlemen."

Though the lord's candor surprised her, Evylin gave him an appreciative smile. His eyes were a rich brown that garnered trust, and his crooked grin lent his wrinkled face a youthful quality.

"Not at all, sir," she replied quietly. "I'm grateful to say I'm immune to such barbaric behavior as my husband is gentleman enough for the whole of Ephria."

"That's high praise," he said, giving Deckard a glance. "I imagine he runs a fine company of soldiers, then?"

"He does," Evylin confirmed, following Carlile's gaze.

Deckard nodded while Magistrate Prokter continued to ramble, but his eyes darted to her, meeting her gaze. Their eyes locked for a brief moment, and a slight smile appeared on his lips.

"Do you like traveling with the army?" Carlile asked her.

Evylin turned to the lord. "Yes, it's nice to see the country. Though I will admit, it's less exciting than I expected."

"You miss your home, then?"

"Oh, no, uh—not so much," she said, tucking a stray strand of hair behind her ear. "I miss my sisters and my mother but not the village itself."

"Ah, yes. You did say it was dull, didn't you?"

"As most villages are, I presume."

"Hm, I think you're right. Though I'll confess I'm not one for travel myself. Never was, even as a lad. Always preferred books and studies to time outdoors."

The books caught her attention, but the studies completely lost it. Nevertheless, Laurisa Glaas instilled in all her daughters the importance of engaging in polite conversation, regardless of their interests. "What do you study?" she inquired.

"Mostly the sciences and economics. But I've always had a special interest in the histories. It's part of what qualifies me to be the king's advisor, you see. I know a bit about everything, so I can keep him apprised of it all."

"Yes, I can see how that would be helpful."

He dipped his head humbly, and then his expression grew playful. "Of course, the king also keeps me around because I'm a silly old man with an interest in the mystical. And he likes to laugh at me."

"The mystical?" Evylin said with her interest sparked anew.

"As I said, I'm interested in the histories. And I have always been most fascinated with the Mages of erstwhile."

Evylin smiled widely. "The king's advisor approves of Mages? Isn't that a conflict of interest?"

Some of Carlile's wispy white hair danced as he shook his head. "I wouldn't say I approve so much as I am fascinated by their stories. And I've always been of the mind you should understand the enemy you plan to fight."

"But Mages aren't real."

"Perhaps not," Carlile conceded. "But Wauld believes they are. And it is my opinion that studying the beliefs of our opponent could be quite useful in the pursuit of victory."

While there was little Evylin knew—or cared to know—about the history of their island continent, there was one fact no Ephrian escaped: At Ephren's uprising, the country once known as Auld broke into two factions, forming Ephria and Wauld. Since then, the eastern half pretended the Westerners didn't exist. They didn't teach their children about them, they didn't discuss them aside from in relation to the war, and they didn't consider them of consequence beyond when times grew tough. Ephria thrust all their problems onto Wauld's shoulders rather than the Ephren monarchy. The whole of Ephria believed their struggles would disappear if Wauld would leave them alone.

But that was the extent of Evylin's knowledge of the West. Even Hewitt couldn't tell her much more, and he'd been to the border. Wauld was a mystery that most Ephrians didn't care to solve.

"Does Wauld really believe in Mages?" she asked.

"Yes," Carlile confirmed. "It's part of their religion. However, from my research, the Faith of Eight is not the origin of Mages but rather a result of them. Like astrology. Allore made the stars, but some choose to worship the creation rather than the Creator."

"Except in this case, the creation they're worshiping is pure fiction."

Carlile chuckled, a hearty, rumbling sound that made her think of a roaring fire. "So it would seem."

They both gave attention to their meals, noting the young Prokter boy going for seconds. Evylin decided she liked Carlile quite well. He was a good man and had proven such from recognizing the servants at his entrance to his apology to her. She was sure such a clever and intelligent advisor could only suggest good things for their monarch.

As their plates neared emptying, Evylin spared one glance at the prince. Once assured his focus was on the lieutenant colonel and Elisa, she turned back to Carlile. "Can I ask you something?" she whispered.

Lord Carlile's thin face angled her way. "Please," he said, gesturing for her to go on.

"Why are you in Banbury?"

His left brow arched up as his dark eyes twinkled at her. "The official reason is that we're passing through on our way to Virwoud to inspect the port and our shipments."

"And what's the unofficial reason?" Evylin asked, keeping her voice soft enough not to draw anyone's attention.

"Let no one claim I could spread such a rumor, but it's suggested the prince has a mistress at the port."

Evylin let out a silent scoff, lifting her glass of wine. "I pity the woman."

"I pity *any* woman who catches his eye. Thankfully, most are intelligent enough to stay away." He frowned as Elisa Prokter giggled at the prince's latest flirtation. "However, there are the unfortunate few who aren't."

Rolling the wine around her tongue, Evylin let the dry tannins seep into her palate.

"Might I ask *you* a question?" Carlile whispered.

Swallowing the wine, Evylin nodded.

"You weren't joking before, were you?"

Evylin furrowed her brow.

"When you said you won a duel for your husband's hand."

Evylin's throat constricted. "I don't think I should discuss it."

"Because you think I disapprove?"

"Because I don't want to get my husband in trouble."

Carlile gave her a sympathetic smile. "There's no fear of that, madam," he promised. "And I don't disapprove. I think it's bloody fantastic."

Evylin tugged on her rings, trying to gauge his sincerity.

"Rather like Mages," he added with a bright smile.

Evylin relaxed at his goodness. "A work of fiction?"

"Or perhaps better said, the inspiration of legends."

A thrill worked through Evylin's chest. *The inspiration of legends.* One worth five hundred tales? "You're too kind," she whispered, her grin threatening to take over her face.

"I'm honest," he said with a wink. "If that makes me overly admiring, I do apologize."

The sudden clatter of Prince Ephren rising interrupted the dinner, and the rest of the group stood rapidly as propriety dictated. "All this conversation has made me thirsty," the prince declared. "Aldan, Benedict, let's go to that tavern you found. It'll do me good to be among the people."

While the prince and his friends moved from the table, Magistrate Prokter thanked them for joining the dinner. Lord Carlile whispered to Evylin, "Don't mistake his magnanimous statement for a fact. He's going to have Haart and Lilifoot clear the tavern of all but those he deems worthy before he even enters the building."

Pressing her lips together, Evylin remained silent as the prince departed. The Prokter children went their separate ways, and Deckard came to reclaim Evylin, exchanging pleasantries with Carlile.

"It was a pleasure, Mrs. Deckard," Lord Carlile said, bowing. "I hope we'll meet again one day."

Evylin smiled at him. "I hope so too."

"Captain." Carlile gave him his own respectful bow. "Your wife is a wonder. And you are a lucky man."

"Thank you, my lord," Deckard said. "My good fortune is not lost on me."

"Goodnight to both of you."

After passing through the granite-tiled halls, the servants handed them their belongings, and Deckard helped Evylin into her coat. A boy hurried off to retrieve their horses, and they stepped into the frigid air. Deckard pulled on his gloves, the falling snow dusting his reddish-brown hair with flecks of white.

There was an odd tension in his movements. Instinctively, Evylin knew he was trying to figure out how to address her faux pas during dinner. She decided to ease his struggle.

"I'm sorry," she said.

He looked over sharply, and Evylin held his surprised stare. "I've never been so humiliated in my days," she admitted. "Banter is a way of life in Estshire, and I didn't know . . . No man has ever taken my teasing as an invitation."

Deckard sighed, looking up at the twin moons. "The world is different outside the Shires," he said, then gave her an apologetic frown. "And *I'm* sorry. I should have prepared you better. But from here on, know that northern men tend to take banter as flirtation."

Evylin paused in stunning revelation. "Is that how you took it?"

The stable boy appeared, the silky black mare and flax-colored gelding's hooves clomping on the cobbled drive. Deckard helped her onto her horse before leaping up onto his and leading them through the gates of the magistrate's estate.

A surprisingly shy grin came to his lips. "Yes," he admitted, "that's how I took it."

Evylin gaped at the night, shocked. All the way back in Whickam Village, Deckard thought she was flirting with him. And yet, he hadn't discouraged her, even after admitting he actively worked *not* to encourage the feelings he knew he couldn't return. It made one thing startlingly clear: Deckard liked her from the start.

Riding through the small city, snow gathering on the roofs and sprinkling their heads and shoulders, Deckard looked over at Evylin. "Was that how you meant it?" he asked.

Evylin's heart pattered strangely. That gentle, embarrassed grin on his face was somehow endearing, and his ever-changing eyes held hers with a tenderness and devotion that made her breath catch. Deckard liked her. And she realized suddenly that she very much liked him.

Turning to face the road, Evylin smirked wryly and said, "Only some of the time." Then she nudged her palomino to a rapid trot.

CHAPTER FORTY-ONE

27TH OF OBSCURA, 1573

Evylin walked to the edge of the camp as the soldiers demolished tents around her. The air remained frigid in the morning, a fresh dusting of snow blanketing the terrae. She shaded her eyes, looking toward the stone walls of Banbury. She was glad to be leaving the city. Dining with a prince wasn't nearly as wonderful an experience as one might think. But she allowed herself to mark the task of rubbing elbows with a royal off her mental list. After all, turning down a prince was its own sort of adventure.

In the distance, Evylin caught sight of the object she was searching for. Coming out of Banbury's gate, a horseman and a cart headed toward the camp. She smiled, seeing Deckard riding proudly next to his men on the cart. He'd left a note saying he'd gone into the city for supplies but would return shortly. A cloud of dust rose behind them, and she waited patiently.

Ever since their return to camp last night, an odd sense of confidence filled Evylin. It was as though knowing of Deckard's true feelings for her—whether or not he'd said them aloud—gave her a newfound clarity. When they'd reached the stable tent late at night, he'd helped her dismount, but she didn't let him pull away as quickly as usual.

"We'd better get you inside," she teased, brushing the snow from his shoulders playfully. "I don't care to play nursemaid if you catch a cold."

Deckard's bashful smile returned. "I don't get sick," he said.

"Never?"

He considered it. "Very infrequently."

"Let's not mar your reputation, then, shall we?"

"Agreed." He offered his arm, and they made their way to their tent.

Evylin snuggled closer to his strong frame in the cold night, relishing his warmth and proximity. The dried grass was mostly hidden beneath a delicate layer of snow. It felt enchanting, white specks swirling through the air around them. Even as she shivered, she appreciated the cold's assistance as Deckard took her hand from the crook of his elbow and slid his arm around her. Her skin prickled with anticipation, senses buzzing lightly. Suddenly, she wanted him to kiss her, to experience that brilliant, overwhelming rush again. And surprisingly, she found herself wanting *him*.

When Deckard pulled away to hold the tent flap open for her, she quickly ducked inside, a blush heating her cheeks at her inner thoughts. Unsettled, she quickly gathered her nightclothes and disappeared behind the changing screen. She stood without moving for a full minute, staring at herself in the small looking glass, clothes held to her chest. Did she *really* want Deckard? Did she trust him enough to give herself to him?

No. No, it was still too soon for that. But . . .

Evylin bit her lip. It *wasn't* too soon to kiss him again. That she could endure quite easily.

A sly grin came to her lips, now determined to bait her husband into a kiss.

Peeking around the divider, Evylin called to Deckard, who was reviewing a ledger on the table. He looked up as she said, "I have a problem."

His brow pinched worriedly. "What is it?"

Fighting off a smile, Evylin stepped into view. "I can't get my dress off," she said, turning so he could see the buttons that lined the back. More for decoration than function, she never undid them, sliding the dress over her head easily. But he didn't need to know that. "I can't reach them on my own."

Deckard's lips parted, but no words came out.

"Could you . . . ?" She paused and bit her lip demurely. "Could you undo them for me?"

Deckard blinked at least half a dozen times before clearing his throat and crossing the tent. "Do you need them all undone?" he asked tightly.

Evylin pulled her hair over her shoulder, giving him a clear view of her neck and back. "Yes, if you don't mind."

Slowly, carefully, Deckard's fingers fumbled with the tiny buttons, slipping to brush her thin chemise underneath as he worked. Each small touch sent tiny, thrilling tingles down her spine. Then he stepped back and murmured, "They're undone."

Evylin pressed a hand to her chest to hold the dress in place, though she kept it loose enough that one sleeve slid off her shoulder, tugging the chemise with it. The winter wind nipped her bare skin. "Thank you," she said, smiling up at him.

Deckard's eyes remained fastened on hers rather than her bare shoulder. He gave a tense nod and walked away.

Evylin's lips twitched with a frown. Had she not been obvious enough? Bemused, she stepped behind the divider again. Shouldn't any man see such a request as an opportunity?

But then, Captain Jonn Deckard wasn't just any man. And her hopes had a fatal flaw. He'd asked her in Wayford if she would prefer that he not kiss her, and she'd said yes. No matter that she'd immediately contradicted that statement, his honor would require a more direct invitation.

It felt like a challenge, and Evylin was determined to try harder. She slipped on her nightdress and tugged the tie strings free so the neckline hung loose around her collarbone—a blatant invitation when she'd so purposefully kept it tight since their first night together. Brushing her fingers through her hair, she hoped the waves fell with an alluring quality. She adjusted the collar to drape off her shoulder, assured of her success. Then a chill slipped under her nightdress, and she shivered, her whole body covered in gooseflesh.

Evylin scowled at the cold night air, grabbed her sweater, pulled on wool socks, and abandoned all hope. When she rounded the corner, she headed straight for the bed, irritated at her failure. Deckard didn't notice her ill mood, taking his turn behind the divider.

Crawling under the blankets, Evylin crossed her arms and glared at the tent wall. A single oil lantern on the table lit the space, shadows clinging to the corners. She grumbled internally, but in the silence, she heard the soft rustle of Deckard's changing, and her lips turned up.

She'd give it one more try.

When Deckard joined her in the bed and held her close, Evylin tilted her face toward his. "Thank you," she whispered, "for today."

Deckard's eyes had grown dark green in the dim light. "It was the least I could do," he said softly.

Sure that she'd done it, Evylin let her smile grow affectionate, tipping her chin up.

But instead of kissing her, Deckard closed his eyes and whispered, "Goodnight."

Evylin's jaw almost dropped open in shock.

Snuggled in Deckard's warm embrace, Evylin brooded. The bloody man was blind. How could he not have perceived her designs? The blasted incorruptible paragon of chastity. *Well,* Evylin decided, *I'll just have to find more direct ways to corrupt him.*

Once the bright morning came again, Evylin scoffed at her silly thoughts. No, she wasn't ready to take Deckard to her bed in a marital fashion; her mistrusting sensibilities wouldn't quite allow for that. But she did like him, and she thought the time might come sooner than she'd once expected.

Watching as her husband and the soldiers drew nearer, Evylin smiled and stepped closer to the roadside. Deckard raised a hand in greeting, and he split off from the cart to join her.

"Good morning," Deckard said upon his approach. "What are you doing over here?"

Evylin set a hand on the black mare's shoulder, looking up at him seated regally on the horse. "Last night, I realized I made a mistake," she said lightly. "I can't live without Prince Ephren. I must go to him."

"Ah, I see." Deckard feigned a frown. "Yes, well, I will miss you, but I suppose I can't blame you for seeing the value in a prince."

"Far more valuable than a captain."

"Indeed," Deckard agreed, running a hand along his jaw. "Unfortunately, I must inform you that you've lost your chance. The prince and his companions left for Virwoud this morning."

Evylin sighed dramatically. "Then I guess I'll have to stay with you."

"A shame, if there ever was one," Deckard replied, dismounting. He landed before her with a pleasant smile, just before looking past her and frowning. Evylin turned to follow his gaze as the distant call broke through the air.

"Captain!" a rider yelled, barreling up the road on a frothing mount. "Captain Deckard!"

Deckard hurried around Evylin, raising his hand to draw the man's attention. "Here!"

The rider neared, pulling the horse to a skidding stop. The soldier sat uneasily in the saddle, panting as hard as the horse beneath him. Evylin recognized him but couldn't place the face until Deckard said, "Lieutenant Lilifoot?"

Evylin's eyes widened. The man was the prince's friend, the curly-headed lieutenant from dinner.

At Deckard's prompting, the lieutenant explained his panicked arrival. "We were ambushed," he said, pressing his hand into his side. His tan fingers shone with blood between them, a wet patch growing larger on his coat. "They've taken the prince and Lord Carlile. I'm the only one who made it out alive."

Evylin turned to Deckard in shock. Ambushed? What kidnappers attacked in the brightness of the day? Whoever orchestrated the attack must have known the prince's intended route and planned accordingly.

Deckard motioned to two of the soldiers who'd gathered in a crowd around them. "You won't be alive for much longer if we don't take care of that," he said, ordering his men to get the lieutenant to the surgeon.

"You have to save him, Captain," Lilifoot insisted.

Deckard nodded, expression steady. "Of course, Lieutenant," he said, turning to

Evylin as the soldiers carried the man away. She gaped after the wounded soldier, watching the small group disappear. She'd never seen so much blood. She thought she should have been bothered by it. Instead, she found herself vaguely curious about what had caused the wound.

Setting a hand on her shoulder, Deckard drew her gaze. "Go get Hewitt," he instructed. "Bring him to our tent. I'll need his help planning."

"Our tent is already torn down," Evylin muttered.

Deckard released her and turned to another soldier in the crowd. "Find Lieutenant Deckard," he ordered. "Tell him to have the men rebuild the camp. We aren't going anywhere today. Tell him I need my tent up now!"

The soldier nodded and rushed off into the camp.

Turning back to Evylin, Deckard pulled her away from the road. "Get me Hewitt," he ordered again. "We have to make a plan."

"Jonn," Evylin said, pulling him to a stop. "What are we going to do?"

"We're going to save the prince."

Evylin couldn't stop bouncing on her heels. Not when she went to find Hewitt and lead him to their tent, nor as she stood across the table from Deckard, listening to him speak. She couldn't help it. She was just so excited.

This was it. This was the very thing she and Ryen had hoped for. Well, not the *very* thing. But saving the crown prince was even better.

With Hewitt, Thom, and Evylin there, Deckard recounted his meeting with Lilifoot in the medical tent while the surgeon stitched up his side. According to the wounded man, their attackers came out of nowhere. There were twenty men in the prince's guard, an elite force of the army's best men. But the kidnappers had surprise on their side. They'd used bows, leaped from trees, and thrown knives from the brush. Lilifoot didn't know where they'd taken the prince but did see a few on horseback riding southwest as he escaped.

"He said the road was muddy," Deckard added. "I think we should head there and look for tracks. I've told Peery to alert the magistrate once we've left to have the city guard come to take care of the bodies when we're done."

Hewitt crossed his arms. "And the rest of your plan? We can't very well take all these men gallivanting across the countryside."

"They'll stay here and wait for us to return while we find and rescue the prince,"

Deckard said, then spread the map of the Cotaasis Province flat on the table. He pointed to Banbury. "First, we need to figure out where they were going. Lieutenant Lilifoot said they went southwest."

Thom looked over his shoulder. "They could have headed to Shaafen."

"That's at least a day's journey," Hewitt said, shaking his head. "There's no way they'd be waiting to ambush him so far from home. Besides, Shaafen's a village. They wouldn't have enough skilled men there to attack a squad of the crown's best soldiers."

Deckard ran a hand along his jaw. "They must have been mercenaries. There's no one in this area with enough trained men to take down the prince's guard."

"But who would hire mercenaries?" Evylin asked. "And why would they want to kidnap the prince? Is there a rebellion in Ephria?"

"Not that I've heard of," Deckard said. "But you're right. There must be some unrest. No Waulden operatives could have made it this far past the border without alerting the army somehow."

"So it's an Ephrian?" Thom said, frowning. "After a ransom?"

"No ransom is worth risking the king's justice." Hewitt scoffed. "And no man who can afford so many mercenaries is that foolish."

"What, then?" Evylin asked.

Deckard stared at the map. "Who and why doesn't matter. We just have to save him."

"If not for Lord Carlile, I'd question even that," Evylin remarked.

Deckard scoffed amusedly but shook his head. "If anyone discovered we did nothing, we would all face charges of treason. Self-preservation compels us as much as duty. We must save the prince."

"How do you plan to do that?" Hewitt asked roughly.

Deckard tapped the map. "First, we'll go to the site of the ambush. If we can, we'll track the men until we find them. If we can't track them, we'll pay the Earl of Cotaasis a visit. He might have seen something."

"That's a fine start," Hewitt said, bushy brow raised high. "But if you think the four of us will be enough, you're mistaken. This band took down twenty of the crown's best men. Even we don't stand much of a chance."

Deckard paused, his eyes darting to Evylin. "I wouldn't suggest we go with such a small number. I thought to bring your most promising fighters along with us."

"That would be Rafferty and Loxley."

"Just two?"

"And then us four."

"Six is hardly better than four." Deckard paused once again, taking a deep breath. "And I'd like to make it clear now that Evylin won't be coming with us."

It took a moment for his words to sink in. Then Evylin gasped. "What?"

"I'm sorry," Deckard said quickly as though to stave off a fight. "But I'm not going to risk my wife's life."

Hewitt glared at Deckard. "If you want my best, you want Evylin."

"Not if it puts her in danger."

"Jonn," Evylin said his name like a plea. He couldn't leave her behind, not when this was everything she wanted, the very reason for their marriage. "This is what I've trained for. This is who I am. I want to go."

Deckard's sympathetic frown only upset her more. How could he do this? She was a better swordsman than him. If anyone should stay behind to keep out of danger—

But Evylin didn't have to fight this battle alone.

Hewitt's huge hands thumped when they hit the table. He leaned forward, eyes like iron as he addressed Deckard. "She is worth five men," he argued. "And she'll have *me* to protect her. As if that wasn't enough, if you're so concerned about her safety, I'd imagine you'd kill any bastard who got near her yourself. So would Rafferty, Ethenn, and your brother."

Thom nodded without a moment of hesitation. "Damn right."

"If you want a team that can get this done, you need Evylin on it," Hewitt said, then shoved a thick finger into the map's center. "We can search the entirety of this county, but once we find the prince, we'll have to fight to save him. And the only way you'll be sure to get him out alive is if you have your best fighters with you. Aside from me, Evylin is your best."

"And you think six is enough?" Deckard countered. "You and Evylin may be worth ten together, but the rest of us? The prince had twenty men at his side. Soldiers trained to protect royalty. And all but one of them is dead. You think six of us are going to be enough?"

"I didn't train any of those men," Hewitt said flatly. "And I'm not suggesting you take only us six, though we would likely do just fine. We'll bring another dozen as backup."

Deckard shook his head, and Evylin knew the number of men wasn't the problem. He was too afraid of putting her in danger to risk it. He wouldn't let her come, not even if she hated him for it.

Hewitt's gaze grew cunning, and Evylin knew he saw the truth too. "Do you want to die out there, Deckard?" he growled.

"Of course not—"

"Then you'll bring Evylin. Because if you don't," he raised his brow, "I won't go with you either."

Evylin's heart lurched. She wanted to go, but if it came down to it, she didn't want

Deckard to go alone. Without Hewitt, Deckard *would* die. And while she might not be in love with her husband, she certainly had no interest in becoming a widow. She couldn't lose Deckard, not now that she was beginning to feel something for him.

Quietly, Deckard glared back at her uncle, and she could see he wouldn't budge, not when he thought he was protecting her. "She can't come," he said, sealing his fate.

"Then you'll die, and your brother will die with you," Hewitt threatened.

No. Evylin took a step forward, determined not to let it go that far. She'd forfeit this adventure to protect him if it were between Deckard's life and death.

Her heart snagged on the promise she'd made. *"I won't let our dream die."* She closed her eyes, knowing the truth. This was her moment, her very reason for leaving the village. If she abandoned this rescue mission, she would abandon her promise to Ryen. Something she'd never do.

Decision made, Evylin reached out and grabbed Deckard's wrist. He turned to her, eyes wide. "You made me a promise, Jonn," she accused, voice low. "This is why we married—for me to have an adventure. You said you'd give me that." She stepped closer, speaking so only he could hear. "And that you'd love me, no matter what it looked like."

He tensed but didn't pull away.

"*This* is what it looks like," she charged.

Deckard held her gaze worriedly, his reply as adamant and hushed as hers. "I don't want to lose you."

"Trust me," she whispered. "I can do this."

He sucked in a breath to speak, then grimaced, turning away from her. "All right," he relented.

Relief washed through Evylin, and she released him.

"Excellent," Hewitt said. "Now, where was the prince's ultimate destination?"

Sighing, Deckard pointed to the road that led to Virwoud.

"Visiting his mistress, eh?" Hewitt muttered. "Let's hope this teaches him to let one woman be enough."

While Deckard, Hewitt, and Thom began to plan, Evylin listened distractedly. It was really happening. *Our adventure is finally beginning,* she thought. *I've won the duels. I'll save the prince, and the sea awaits me.* If only she could find a dragon, then her legendary status would surely follow.

I won't let our dream die.

CHAPTER FORTY-TWO

After refining their plan, Deckard sent Hewitt to gather a dozen soldiers to accompany them while he and Thom gathered their gear, and Evylin went to get Rafferty and Loxley. They left the camp within half an hour. Fast, but not fast enough in Deckard's mind. Every minute spent at camp was a minute more for the abductors to move farther away.

In the chaos, Deckard didn't have a chance to explain himself to Evylin. Despite his yielding, he could feel a distance between them, an irritation affecting their movements around each other. But perhaps the mood shift was simply on his side, knowing she'd manipulated him so easily.

The trees grew thickly along the road, boughs hanging above their heads. Only a little snow had made it through the dense branches, even as bare as they were, and small piles of white dotted the terrae. Without the sun to warm the ground, the dirt was muddy, and the air was colder still as they approached the scene of the abduction. Up ahead, bodies lay in the muck, their blood discoloring the puddles around them.

Deckard hated death. It was his least favorite part of his job. Though he hadn't been in many battles, his time as a corporal sent him to Ostwatch in Harmouth Province. Beside the Allmar Mountain range, known more colloquially as Allore's Arm, the town was on the edge of the border between Ephria and Wauld. Through the narrow passage between the countries lay another town—a Waulden town—and every couple of weeks, there was a raid, either by their enemy's designs or their commanding officer's.

Two years into his service, Ostwatch revealed to Deckard the true brutality of war. That experience erased any lingering childhood fantasies of fun and adventure. Ostwatch marked his first kill and the ever-present danger of death. It also brought him a circle of friends who made the tough days easier, many of whom tragically did not survive their time in the town. The few who made it through moved on to new positions and even more successful careers than his own.

Deckard often questioned how he hadn't died in Ostwatch. As a young man, he'd been an even worse swordsman, and luck wasn't that reliable a companion. But he never failed to send a silent prayer of thanks to the Heavens when he remembered those days.

Coming upon the dead bodies, Deckard glanced at Evylin. He wondered if she'd ever seen something so incomprehensible as dozens of slain men. She'd never killed a man, he knew that. And it was part of what worried him about bringing her on this mission. She still had innocence; her fantasies remained uncorrupted.

Yet, Evylin didn't betray any sign of emotion beyond curiosity as she stared at the lifeless forms. She tipped her head, studying the scene as though the soldiers were a puzzle rather than men who'd had their lives stolen away.

The volunteers didn't share her composure. Hewitt had hand-selected eight privates to accompany them, along with Lieutenant Cormier, Major Sheelds, Sergeant Stewert, and Corporal Smyth. While the more experienced officers held their own, the privates held hands to their noses and grimaced, struggling to look at the bodies.

"Ethenn," Hewitt called, motioning to the young soldier.

The private dismounted and moved around the edge of the muddy tracks and bodies, eyes taking in the details. "Captain?" he asked hesitantly.

"Yes, Private?"

He scanned the surrounding area before turning back to Deckard. "The lieutenant said they were on horseback, correct? The prince's squad?"

"He did," Deckard confirmed.

Ethenn squinted around the forest, then shook his head. "Where are they?"

Deckard dismounted as well and approached. "What do you mean?"

"Twenty horses wouldn't wander off on their own," he explained. "They must have taken them. The attackers, I mean."

Deckard walked carefully around the edge of the scene. "Good. That means we won't have to figure out which were theirs and which were the attackers'. Southwest is that way, so we'd best search for their trail."

Ethenn nodded, his dark eyes roving over the dead men and their broken bodies. "I don't think they were professionals."

"What makes you say that?" Deckard asked.

"Not all the attackers got away," he said, pointing to a few of the dead men who weren't wearing a uniform.

Thom scoffed, standing at Deckard's side. "They killed twenty of the king's best men, kid. One or two dead doesn't make them amateurs."

"That doesn't make them professionals either. They had the element of surprise and numbers on their side. Look." Ethenn pointed up at the trees and then to the men on the road. "There are clearly broken branches where the men hid. The lieutenant said they had archers and men who jumped down upon them, right? That means they had at least ten to twelve men out of these six spots. He also mentioned there were others on horseback. He didn't give a number, but I'd guess it to be another six at least. And he didn't mention being able to kill any of them. That means the number of their dead was so small that those left alive made it seem inconsequential. We have four men dead here, aside from the prince's squadron. I'd guess that means there were at least twenty-five men for these to go unnoticed. Either way, I'd call them smart, not professional. At least, not in kidnapping."

"Wow," Rafferty said, silver eyes wide, "I've never heard him talk so much."

Ethenn's ears turned bright red.

Deckard forced himself to stare at the empty faces of the attackers. They looked like any other Ephrian men. But he supposed Waulden men weren't so different in appearance. It could have been that they'd slipped in slowly, building up a garrison behind enemy lines. But the emblem on one of the men's coats caught Deckard's eye: two crossed spears.

Deckard beckoned to Thom, pointing to the coat. "Does that symbol look familiar to you?"

Thom blew out a puff of air. "I've never been good with the marks of nobility. But I'd bet my life it belongs to the earl."

Though he'd had the same thoughts, Deckard shook his head. "We can't accuse him without further evidence. We'll follow their tracks, and if it leads us to the earl, then we'll have information worthy of passing off to General Rand." It might give him a bargaining chip in the outcome of his fate.

Upon Deckard's order, Ethenn led the way, following the horses' tracks to the point they diverged from the road. After taking time to study the nature around him, the private returned. "We'll need to walk to be sure I don't miss anything. Horses are easier to track, but if these men are as smart as I'm guessing, they'll try to throw us off their course. And that'll make it harder to follow on horseback."

Their small band dismounted and guided their horses into the trees. It was slow going, especially given their party's size and the thickness of the trees. The private went ahead, taking each step with care and stopping to examine larger areas. As time progressed, Private Rafferty struck up a quiet conversation with Evylin, Thom, and the rest of the privates. Though Deckard assumed there was an open invitation, he chose to speak with Hewitt instead.

"How does Private Loxley know how to track so well?" he asked.

"Ethenn was a hunter," Hewitt explained, tugging at his beard. "Began at an early age with his father. They went out for a week or more at a time. They dressed the animals themselves, cured them, and sold them. The kid's an expert archer, a butcher with a knife, and he's not half bad with a hatchet either."

"Sounds like he's well-rounded. There isn't much need for anything but archery and swordsmanship in our job, though."

"There isn't much need for any skill in your job," Hewitt said slyly.

Their search lasted for hours. Longer than it should have, in Deckard's opinion. The sun reached its tipping point by the time they broke through the trees and faced the looming mansion of the Earl of Cotaasis. A dark blue banner with two crossed silver spears hung from the walls.

Thom turned to Deckard, dark brows raised. "Looks like I was right."

Frowning, Deckard stared at the stone building. Its five spires stretched into the sky. He could see the lake below the cliffside from their vantage on the hill. Banbury was to the north at their back. The earl would have known the prince was coming through. Even if the king hadn't announced it to him directly, he would have heard from his friends in town. But why would he want to kidnap Prince Ephren? The first King Ephren granted the Tybaalt family their earldom at the founding of Ephria as a reward for their loyalty and strength in battle. Why would a dedicated Ephrian noble family turn against their benefactors now?

"We can't assume anything," Deckard said, addressing the entire troop behind him. "There's a chance these men took the earl's home by force. They could be using it as a hideout to keep their cover. To accuse a nobleman of treason without proof is sedition. We must think the best of the earl until we have proof to the contrary."

Rafferty snorted. "I've met enough noblemen to have all the proof I need."

Deckard highly doubted that. The Shires didn't have nobles. Where would the weasel have met one?

"We're certain the tracks lead there?" Hewitt asked, stepping to Ethenn's side.

"Not *certain*," Ethenn admitted. "I haven't followed the tracks fully yet. But if they didn't go there, they're skirting far closer to a nobleman's house than I would."

"Maybe they're not smart enough for that," Thom offered.

"They tripled back on their tracks in the forest," Ethenn said. "That's why it took us so long. They're smart. And we shouldn't be standing out here. They could see us from this distance."

Deckard nodded. "He's right. Get back into the cover of the woods. Private Loxley, I want you to follow the trail, but I don't want you going alone."

Hewitt pointed to Rafferty. "You go with him," he said, then turned to Ethenn. "If you need to scout something or sneak into anyplace, have Raff do it. You're both quiet and alert, but he's faster than you. You'll be safest with him."

Though Deckard didn't like the idea of sending a criminal with the young soldier, he nodded for Ethenn to follow the command. Ethenn and Rafferty left their horses behind and snuck out to follow the tracks. The soldiers secured their horses to the low-hanging branches of the trees, and Thom spoke up.

"I've got a feeling this is going to take a while. Should we practice to pass the time?" he suggested.

Standing with Sheelds by the horses, Hewitt removed two practice swords from his saddle—coincidentally, the swords he kept there for his practice with Deckard—and tossed one to Thom. "Use these," he said. "We don't need you dulling your real weapons."

"Evie," Thom called. "You want the first go?"

Quickly, Deckard set his hand on Evylin's arm and dropped his voice so only she could hear. "May I speak with you a moment?"

Evylin hesitated but nodded. She turned to Thom. "Why don't you warm up with Private Haalston? I'll take the winner when I get back."

They walked to the far side of the clearing, stepping past the trees to ensure their privacy. Surrounded by pine and oak trees, the forest floor held more decaying leaves, needles, and grass than snow. The few birds still on their journey south twittered while a light snowfall drifted through the branches overhead.

Coming to a stop, Deckard faced her. "I want to explain myself," he began. "What I said before—the reason I wanted you to stay behind—"

"I know," she interrupted.

Deckard took an involuntary step back at the sharpness in her gaze.

"Jonn, I'm not the one you should be worried about," she continued. "I've trained for this moment since I was a little girl. I can fight better than most men. I won't get hurt."

He shook his head. "I trust in your abilities, but—Evylin," he ran a hand through his hair in exasperation, "you've never been in a fight like this. You've never had to kill anyone."

That caused her to pause. Her eyes narrowed, scanning him curiously. "Have you?"

Deckard's jaw tensed as the blood, the screams, the crying, and the horror of Ostwatch flashed through his mind. "I have," he muttered. "And it takes a toll."

She was silent, gaze thoughtful. Then she stepped forward and set a hand on his arm. "I'm not you," she whispered gently. "I'm not afraid to kill someone if I have to."

Letting out a weak scoff, Deckard held her pitying gaze. "You should be."

Evylin shifted from foot to foot, expression softening with compassion. "Do you know how many?"

"Twenty-one," he answered immediately.

"All soldiers?"

"Yes."

"You were doing your job."

Deckard grimaced. "That's not the kind of job I want."

The glove on her hand blocked its warmth, but not the way it felt as she rubbed his arm. Deckard stared down into her beautiful face, which was soft with sympathy, if not understanding. She didn't say anything, and there couldn't be anything to say. He'd sealed his fate long ago. It didn't matter that his commission would expire one day. That was eight years away. By then, the war could have killed him and everyone he knew as well. The way things were going, Wauld would've won, at the very least.

Evylin's lips lifted in a smirk. "You're a terrible soldier."

That pulled a soft laugh out of Deckard. "I *am* a terrible soldier," he agreed, then sighed. "And a terrible captain."

Evylin shook her head. "No, you're not a terrible captain," she said, tugging playfully on a button of his coat. "You're good at leading. You make people want to follow you by being loyal to them and taking care of them."

Deckard set his hand on hers, giving it an appreciative squeeze. He hoped she meant that *she* wanted to follow him, that his care and promises were winning her heart. But then, if he really were the man she described, his goodness would cost him. If the consequences of his failure were too great, he'd have to let her go. And that eventuality was getting harder and harder to accept.

Her hand, held against his chest by his own, tugged on the button again. "Even if you are irritatingly protective at times," she said.

Deckard smiled and let her hand fall away. "Will you forgive me for trying to make you stay?"

Her expression grew teasing. "Just don't let it happen again."

"No promises," he replied. "Let's head back. You've got some practicing to do."

As they walked through the trees, Evylin headed directly to the center of the clearing. A cluster of soldiers stood watching two of the fighters duel. It seemed Thom had already defeated Haalston, as he was now engaged with another private whom he dispatched with surprising ease. Deckard noticed that his training with Hewitt and Evylin had significantly enhanced his skills.

With the bout ended, the defeated private offered his sword to Evylin. Thom smirked with dry humor, twirling his sword lazily. "Go easy, will you?" he said. "I've got some of my own platoon out here."

Evylin shrugged casually, sinking into her fighting stance. "Don't worry. I haven't even warmed up."

Evylin and Thom didn't bother with practice paces. They went straight into a duel, the soldiers around them falling silent as they watched. They were in for a short show. Evylin disarmed Thom in thirty seconds, her movements so fast that Deckard couldn't track them. One second, their swords were tangled in a flurry of blocks and parries, and the next, she landed two hits on Thom and kicked the sword from his hands.

Thom shook his hands out. "You don't fight fair," he grumbled.

She smiled brightly. "I learned that from Rafferty."

Though the other soldiers sniggered, they all vehemently declined in the face of Evylin when offered the opportunity to spar. She and Thom went through four more bouts—all victories for Evylin—before Thom raised his hands in surrender. "I'm done."

"Oh, please," Evylin said, striking the ground with the tip of her blade. "We've only gotten started."

"I've had enough humiliation today. Major, why don't you teach her a lesson?"

Hewitt and Evylin grinned at one another knowingly.

"I've had that lesson so many times, I've lost count," Evylin said, playing with the grip on her sword.

"You might learn it this time," Hewitt offered.

"I doubt it, but I'm happy to try."

Taking the sword Thom offered him, Hewitt's smile grew wide. "It's been too long. You won't be ready."

Evylin dipped her head in a bow. "I have no hope of it."

Deckard and his soldiers watched with rapt attention as uncle and niece matched up. Hewitt's massive frame made Evylin seem unusually small. They held their swords at the ready, their stances set. Then they began.

The fight stunned Deckard. Ever since he started working with Hewitt, he'd been curious to see them fight. Her skills were magnificent, but he couldn't imagine her trim frame defending well against the great man's forceful blows. She didn't even try. Instead, she moved with the blows. Evylin let the sword carry her, adjusting her offensive attacks as necessary. Not once did she ever commit to defending. She flowed around the attacks, twisting and ducking. She was like the wind, flowing gracefully around Hewitt as he attacked with finesse and strength.

The strain was clear on Evylin's face. No matter how skillful she was, Hewitt was wearing her down. Sword fights didn't last long because the endurance required to defend and attack wore the body down quickly. Your only hope of survival in a real fight was to be fast. But this fight continued for more than five minutes. And Evylin's strength was failing.

In a desperate effort to outwit her opponent, Evylin slid between Hewitt's legs, hopped up, and whacked him in the back. While it wouldn't have been a fatal blow, it would have been more damaging than any Deckard had ever managed to get on the man.

However, Hewitt whirled faster than he should have been able to, knocking her sword wide. She couldn't recover quickly enough to parry, and the tip of his blade hung inches from her chest as she drew up short.

"Don't get fancy," Hewitt said, sword primed for the kill.

Evylin laughed. "I had to try."

Dropping his sword, Hewitt patted her shoulder. "Showing off opens you up to more technical attacks."

Evylin gave him a nod.

"Someone's coming," Sheelds called, voice low as he scanned the trees in the direction of the earl's mansion.

The clearing grew tense as the troop listened.

Rafferty and Ethenn broke through the trees, and a collective sigh fell.

"You're a skittish lot," Rafferty said, his light eyes shining. "You worried the earl's going to come get you himself?"

Deckard frowned at the sight of them. "Why are you both wet?" he asked, noting their dripping hair and splotchy clothes.

"We fancied a swim," Rafferty said, shivering.

Ethenn explained. "We found a draining pool at the back of the wall, sir. Aside from the front gate, it's the only way in, so Raff went under and confirmed we could fit through. Once inside, we snuck around, but it was too open for us to learn much. The guard is heavy around the stables, though."

"The stables?" Evylin asked. "Why would they keep them there?"

"Earls have no need for prisons in their homes," Deckard offered. "I'd imagine it's the only cell they can create."

Hewitt nodded in agreement. "All the better for us. We don't need to be searching through a house that size to find him."

Given the priority of getting the men warm to avoid hypothermia, Deckard forced them into the trees to change. They didn't have full outfits for them, but they were able to get out of the soaked clothing.

"How many guards were there?" Deckard asked when they emerged.

"At the time, ten or so," Ethenn said, drying his hair with a blanket they'd removed from one of the horses' backs. "They were moving around, so we didn't get a good look."

"To be safe, we could count on twenty," Hewitt suggested.

"Do you think we can take that many?" Deckard asked.

"Our eighteen against their twenty?" Hewitt's grin took on a dangerous quality. "No problem."

Of course, he had reason to be sure of himself; the man's time in the service left legend-like stories the soldiers still told thirteen years later. The problem wasn't the skills of their men but trying to fit eighteen soldiers through a drainage grate and into the back of the earl's property undetected.

"I don't think that will work," Deckard concluded. "Our group is too large for such a surreptitious attack."

Hewitt scanned the troop, his gray eyes taking on a dubious light. "We need speed, not brawn, to get out of there fast enough," he agreed.

"Then the plan is moot?"

"No. We'll just change it slightly."

"How?"

"We take a smaller team inside to save the prince and his advisor. The rest of the troop will be waiting out here to help us make a quick escape."

Deckard furrowed his brow, not liking where the suggestion was going. "How small of a team?"

CHAPTER FORTY-THREE

The hours inched by as they waited for nightfall. Their only entertainment was limited to conversation or training, so their group did both. Deckard did little of either. However, he did watch, gaining confirmation of Ethenn and Rafferty's skills. Both were impressive, but Ethenn was, in fact, an abnormal talent.

Unwilling to start a fire and risk attracting attention, they ate a cold lunch and supper. About an hour before sunset, Hewitt forced the team he'd selected to rest. "There's no use in wasting your energy now," he said. "The focus and training will kick in when it's time."

Their small band of six—Hewitt, Evylin, Deckard, Thom, Rafferty, and Ethenn— huddled among the trees. Hewitt had developed the plan perfectly. Their six would go in and save the prince. Lieutenant Cormier and Major Sheelds would split the remaining soldiers between themselves. Cormier and his men would create a distraction while Sheelds and his team waited to aid in their escape.

As they waited for the sun to set, Deckard wondered at the kidnapping. Why would an Ephrian earl have taken the prince? It didn't make sense. Not unless there was a rebellion among the people. But why would they rebel? The present King Ephren wasn't the most effective ruler they'd had, but neither was he a tyrant. Their people were safe, and their country was cared for. Who would want to overthrow the monarchy that had protected them for so long?

And why take Lord Carlile too? That was a puzzle he couldn't solve. Why kill the prince's guard but leave an old man alive? Why *take* a mere advisor captive alongside the prince? Unless there was more to the king's advisor than met the eye. . . .

The air grew colder, and Deckard shivered. He sat at the edge of the camp, watching the earl's mansion. Snow coated the grand lawn, capping the slate-shingled roof and stone wall.

When the final rays of golden light slipped away, leaving the sky a violet shroud of night, Cormier left with his men. The band of six prepared, tightening their belts, checking weapons, and bundling up. When they left, Sheelds and the rest waited with the horses on the hilltop.

Drifting down the snowy slope, their small group moved like shadows. Ethenn guided them toward the drainage grate at the back of the mansion. It was a small, rounded indentation at the base, almost entirely hidden by the large pool of water, frost lining its edge. A gentle stream flowed over the cliff, cascading down toward the distant lake below.

Evylin pushed past Deckard and grabbed Rafferty's arm. "You said this was a pool," she hissed. "This is *not* a pool."

Rafferty scrunched up his nose. "What else would you call it?" he whispered back.

Suddenly, Deckard realized her concern. The pool was larger than he'd expected as well, but it wasn't a problem for him—because he could swim.

"Evie," Deckard set a hand on her shoulder, "it'll be all right. It can't be very deep, and I'll be right with you."

Shaking her head, Evylin stared up at him wide-eyed. "I'll drown."

"I'll get you through," Deckard promised.

Though she didn't look convinced, Evylin followed him to the water's rocky edge. They stood huddled together, eyes on the black, icy pond that awaited them.

"Listen to me," Hewitt whispered. "This isn't training anymore. If you have the opportunity, kill your opponent. Do not hesitate, and do not think about it. Your life is at risk the moment we enter this water. When we get to the other side, let any fear you feel go. Focus."

They all nodded, and Deckard worried again that he should have stayed behind with Sheelds. He wasn't ready; his skills as a swordsman were still not up to par. He might cause them more harm than good on this rescue mission. But Hewitt had pulled him aside, charging him with the task of escorting the prince, staying away from the fight—and Evylin would go with him. So here he was, knowing Hewitt had trusted him to keep Evylin out of the greatest danger.

They entered the frigid pool, stifling their urge to cry out. Descending carefully, they took slow, silent steps. Ethenn signaled for them to follow, then submerged beneath the water. Thom went next, and then Deckard put his hand on Evylin's shoulder.

"Your turn," he whispered. "I'll get you to the other side, trust me."

A couple of sharp breaths later, Evylin sucked in as much air as she could and went under. Deckard followed. Submerged in the pitch black, the water felt like knives across his skin. He kept a hand on Evylin's back, pushing her forward as he swam. Holding their hands out to guide their way wasn't easy, but the pool was narrow, and they found the grate quickly. Once on the other side, Evylin flailed, grabbing at him.

Aware she'd run out of air, Deckard tugged her closer and made for the surface. Her frantic movements made the ascent more difficult, causing them to break through the water with an audible splash. She gasped in a lungful of air, shivering against him. "You're all right," he promised in a low tone, swimming them to the shore.

Shaking in his arms, Evylin let him carry her out of the water. Once her feet touched the ground, she stretched herself across the snow, her chest pumping wildly. She closed her eyes, a grimace on her face.

Deckard knelt next to her, brushing the wet hair from her cheeks and forehead. "You're all right," he said again, a shiver running down his own spine as the wind threatened to freeze him as well.

Hewitt got out of the water and forced Evylin up. "We've got to move."

Evylin stumbled as they ran, but they made it to the back of a shed where Ethenn was already hiding. Huddled behind the small building, they peered around, weapons at the ready. Deckard assessed their odds, counting the guards patrolling.

"Fifteen at the stable," Hewitt reported.

"And ten more patrolling the front," Deckard added.

They exchanged a look of worry, both men trembling visibly in the cold.

"This is going to be more difficult than I thought," Hewitt admitted.

Ethenn pointed toward the front gates. "The fire's started," he said as a small trail of smoke rose in the distance. That was Cormier's job, starting a fire in the copse of trees by the front gate, drawing the men away.

They watched as the fire grew, shivering silently. When it blazed a ruby red, the flames catching the dry winter trees, the guards cried out. Several rushed for the gate while two others headed inside the house, perhaps for backup.

"We'd better be quick," Hewitt said, turning to Ethenn. "Can you thin them out?"

"My arrows are wet," he said, though his smile was sly. "They'll be harder to aim at fast-moving targets. But I've got a better idea."

Ethenn pulled an arrow from the quiver on his back, then reached into the waterproofed leather pouch on his hip. In seconds, he wrapped the arrowhead in a cloth.

"Whatcha got there, Loxley?" Rafferty whispered.

"Oil-soaked cloth."

"Yes," Thom mocked, "that's a normal thing to carry around."

"I'm a hunter," Ethenn said flatly as though that explained it. The young man pulled out a flint and steel from the same pouch. "I can light up that bale of hay," he said, pointing to the stack next to the stable. "It'll drive them back, but you'll need to be quick."

Hewitt's grin carried a dangerous edge. "Do it."

Ethenn lit the arrow and drew back on the bowstring, holding the tension as he aimed. He took a deep breath, and Deckard felt a prickle of frigid air rush over his skin. Then the arrow flew.

It hit low, almost missing the bale. But it was enough.

The straw sparked, a vibrant flare of flame searing across the bale.

"Go!" Hewitt ordered as the hunter drew another arrow. While his aim might be hampered, he could distract the guards with his ranged attacks.

Hewitt, Thom, and Rafferty ran to the right side of the shed, charging the guards. Hewitt took three men down in thirty seconds. Thom fell behind as he grappled with his own assailants while the old veteran mowed through the men. Rafferty's dual blades shone in the light as he slipped around the guards, circumventing their head-on attack to assassinate a few from the back.

Deckard and Evylin rushed out from the left. They ran around the battle toward the stable, doing their best to avoid the guards. But they were spotted, and two men ran their way.

"Keep going," Evylin said, pulling up short.

Deckard hesitated, reluctant to leave her. Yet, she quickly proved she didn't need his protection. The firelight glinted off her blade as she disarmed one man and swept the legs out from the other. She plunged her sword into the first man's gut, and he crumpled into a heap. She yanked her sword free, then sliced the second man's chest with a flourish.

Mouth agape, Deckard gasped as she slashed through her first two kills indifferently.

Evylin spun around, finding him there. "What are you doing?" she yelled, running over to him. "Go!"

Heart pounding, Deckard followed her order. How was she so calm? He'd seen men crumble into sorrow after their first kill. Yet, she showed no more emotion than when she sparred.

He set his jaw, sure the shock would hit her later, but they had a job to do now.

Rounding the stable, they entered through the back. The hay bale spark had caught the far side on fire. Wood crackled, and horses trumpeted in fear from their stalls.

Deckard grimaced as the smoke blew across their path. "We'd better hurry."

They glanced into the first empty stall. Nothing there. Running along both sides of the stable, they searched the empty stalls, taking only seconds at each to seek the prince's location. The fire was spreading, the heat rising, and Deckard felt sweat bead on his forehead.

"Here," Evylin called at her fourth stall.

Deckard ran over. It wasn't the prince but Lord Carlile. The old man stared up at them, a streak of red dried on his cheek, a split wound on his brow.

"Where's Prince Ephren?" Deckard asked.

"I'm here!" a panicked voice called farther down the line.

Deckard cast an apologetic look at Carlile before rushing across the stable to the stall where Prince Ephren was bound.

"Help!" the prince shouted upon sight of him.

Using the hilt of his sword, Deckard broke the stall's lock.

"Get Carlile," Evylin ordered, rushing into the stall with a knife in hand. "I'll untie him."

Deckard rushed back to the lord's stall. He beat the lock free and pushed his way in. He didn't have a knife, so he fumbled to untie the ropes.

When they finally fell to the hay-strewn floor, the advisor rubbed his wrists. "Thank you," Carlile said.

As Deckard helped him up, Evylin cried out. Bolting from the stall, Deckard saw her wriggling in a guard's grasp. The man had his arm around her shoulders, but he hadn't expected her agility. She kicked down and to the right, connecting with his knee. The joint cracked as the leg bent wide. The guard screamed, releasing her.

Spinning, Evylin's knife jammed into the man's neck, and he slumped to the ground. She straightened, jaw set, her demeanor placid. A third kill and no sign of anything but unwavering concentration.

Deckard watched, baffled, as Evylin scooped her sword from the ground and turned to the prince, who still cowered in his stall. "Let's go," she ordered.

Prince Ephren stared at her like she was an angel of salvation, then followed her out. The fire crackled right above their heads, billowing smoke causing the group to cough into their sleeves. Lord Carlile waited at the back of the stable, but Deckard had an idea.

"Free the horses," he said.

"We don't have time—"

"It's a distraction," he interrupted.

Evylin nodded, a smirk coming to her lips. "You're not as dull as Thom says."

"Tell him that if we live."

They sent Ephren to wait with Carlile, then Deckard and Evylin opened the stalls, setting the horses loose and sending them out the front of the stable. It wasn't just a distraction; Deckard couldn't stand the idea of leaving the animals there to burn. But it would aid their retreat.

Escaping the blistering heat, they led the prince and his advisor into the snowy night.

They turned the corner just in time to see Hewitt take down another man. The horses wound through the fight, the threat of their thundering hooves scattering the earl's guards. Ethenn had joined the fray with his sword, Rafferty at his side. Thom jerked his blade from the chest of one assailant only to turn and face another.

Reinforcements spilled out of the mansion, fresh guards running toward them.

Evylin pointed to the shed. "Get them out," she commanded, dashing off before Deckard could stop her.

"Evylin!" Deckard's feet shuffled forward to follow. Only his duty to the men beside him kept him still.

"She's incredible!" Prince Ephren gasped in awe. "I've never seen a woman like her before."

"If we don't get you out of here, you'll never see a woman again," Deckard grumbled, pushing them around the shed.

Hidden but not yet safe, Deckard surveyed the courtyard quickly. The stable was ablaze, and guards littered the ground. Hewitt and Evylin fought, side by side, a near magical force of deadly strength, unstoppable and almost unbelievable in their unified teamwork. Beside them, Ethenn fought with unparalleled skill, Rafferty with blinding speed and dexterity, and Thom with control and finesse that Deckard had never before witnessed from his brother.

Slowly, the five drew back toward the shed in a steady retreat.

Though he wanted to stay and ensure their safety, Deckard turned back to the prince and his advisor. "Hurry." They sprinted to the drainage grate. "Under you go," he ordered, pointing to the water.

"I can't swim," Ephren said.

Deckard gaped at him, incredulous. He didn't mind helping Evylin, but pushing the prince through was an honor he didn't care to receive. "I'll get you through," he said, nevertheless, guiding him into the water. "But don't struggle, or it'll make it more difficult."

Ephren made it more difficult.

Getting through the grate took twice as long as it did with Evylin. When they finally emerged, the prince panicked and shot up, gasping for air. Deckard yanked the screaming prince from the water before reaching back to assist Carlile. The old man trembled on the bank while the prince whimpered softly.

Deckard rolled his eyes, sighing with relief as the thunder of hooves met his ears. Sheelds and his men were there, helping the prince and advisor mount up quickly. The fire roared behind the walls, the muffled yells of the guards reverberating through the stone.

Deckard stared at the still, black surface of the pool, waiting. The infrequent clang of swords grated on his nerves. *Where are they? They should be here by now.* He stepped to the edge, hand on his hilt, preparing to return to help. Before he could dive back in, the water broke with a splash. Ethenn came through, Thom following just behind.

"Go!" Thom yelled, both he and Ethenn running to the horses. "They're right behind."

Rafferty made it through next, bolting out of the frigid water.

But Deckard didn't move until he saw Evylin appear, gasping for air with Hewitt at her side. Deckard grabbed her hand and pulled her from the water. Without enough horses for them all, Hewitt would ride with Carlile. Deckard hoisted Evylin onto his horse, then slid into the saddle behind her.

The first guards broke through, but Ethenn released an arrow, making the shot despite the wet fletching. With Sheelds and his men guarding behind, they bolted away from the earl's estate. Cormier's men met them in the forest, riding hard through the dark trees.

Evylin shook on the horse in front of Deckard, her hands gripping the saddle. Pulling her closer, Deckard felt her heart pounding through her back. Absently, he wondered how high the number of her kills had gone. Then he wondered if she even knew.

CHAPTER FORTY-FOUR

It was exhilarating. The night air caressed Evylin's cheeks like starlight kissing her skin. Each of her senses felt sharply heightened, her whole body alight with a chill radiating from the base of her neck and down her spine. She could feel everything with such intense clarity: the way the horse moved, its muscles flexing with each stride, how her clothing clung to her icy skin, the pressure of Deckard's arm around her waist, his chest against her back.

In the wake of her first battle, Evylin felt fully alive for the first time in her life. The world was brighter, the sounds sharper, the energy purer. And as her heart hammered to the beat of the horse's gallop through the trees, she knew *this* was the adventure she sought.

This was their dream.

Their rescue party rode back through the thicket—now clear of the bodies—and finally brought their tired horses to a walk. A collective sigh passed through the group when they were a half mile from camp with no sign of the enemy's chase. The horses huffed in exhaustion, each breath a cloud as it hit the winter air.

Deckard's arm loosened as he leaned forward. "Are you all right?" he whispered, his words tickling her neck and sending more chills down her spine.

Resting against his chest, Evylin smiled. "Yes, I'm perfect."

"I'm sorry I left you back there."

Evylin laid her hand on his arm, pulling it tightly around her again. "You have nothing to be sorry for. You did exactly as you should have."

Deckard didn't respond, but she could feel his breathing ease as his chest pressed against her back.

The camp came into view, and the glow of the ivory moon dimmed in its first quarter, allowing the almost full shadow moon to project its silvery light. It mixed with the flames of the copper sentry fires to lend the camp its own day in the middle of the night. Deckard gave orders when they arrived at the stable tent, leaving his officers and recruits to care for the horses. Their small team remained with the prince and Carlile. Stiff from the cold and the hard ride, they dismounted in slow, stilted movements. A few of them nursed superficial injuries, but all in all, they were whole and well.

"You're all most assuredly owed a debt by me now," Prince Ephren said when they'd gathered around. "By me *and* Carlile."

The lord nodded, a bloody nick etched on his brow. Evylin surveyed the men, both bearing cuts and scrapes from their captivity. The prince cradled one arm while Lord Carlile favored his right leg. But otherwise, they looked no worse for wear.

"It was our honor, Your Highness," Deckard said with a bow.

Prince Ephren's wet curls sprinkled them as he shook his head. "No, no. I would be dead if it weren't for you and your team, Captain. I heard the earl's men; Tybaalt's got it out for me and my father. But now, the treasonous earl will rue his betrayal."

"It *was* the earl, then?" Deckard asked warily.

"Yes," Prince Ephren said. "I heard them mention him by name. He orchestrated the whole thing."

Lord Carlile stepped closer. "When we arrived, the prince was unconscious, but I saw the earl myself. He gave the men who ambushed us orders to put us in the stables. I believe they were hired ruffians from the town. Thieves and other scum."

Rafferty grumbled something under his breath while Ethenn sent Thom a knowing look at the advisor's unintentional offense.

"If you hadn't shown up when you did," Carlile concluded, "I'd be dead and the prince under extensive questioning."

"Why would they question him?" Hewitt asked.

"I'm not sure. The earl said something about wanting answers. As they never asked me anything, I assumed they were after something from His Highness."

"I can't fathom what they'd want," Ephren exclaimed. "They had to know I'd never betray national secrets."

Evylin wondered if anyone was stupid enough to give him national secrets.

The prince trembled in the cold. "Would it be possible to obtain a change of clothing?" he asked.

Deckard nodded immediately. "Of course. We should all change at once. Your Highness, my lord, if you'll follow me, I'll lead you to our supplies."

"Excellent," Prince Ephren said merrily. "Your efforts will not go unrewarded." He angled to leave, and then his eyes landed on Evylin. A roguish grin spread across his face. "Especially you, my dear. You have my most dedicated regard."

Evylin dipped her head and ducked behind Deckard. "Thank you, Your Highness," she said meekly.

Deckard gestured for Ephren and Carlile to follow and led them away.

Once they rounded the corner, Rafferty grabbed Evylin's arm, eyes flashing brightly. "We have to celebrate," he demanded. "This is a momentous occasion. We saved the bloody prince of Ephria! If we don't stay up half the night reveling, we've no right to call this a victory."

"I'm for it," Evylin laughed, turning to the other three.

Thom and Ethenn were nodding, but Hewitt glowered. "If we're going to 'revel,'" he muttered, "we'd better do it by my tent. Everywhere else will be too close to the men, and I'd rather not invite them to join."

With their plans in place, Hewitt remained to help Sheelds, Cormier, and the rest of the men. Rafferty tore off in a random direction while Ethenn and Thom walked through the tents with Evylin, exchanging their sides of the story as they went.

When Evylin slipped inside the captain's tent, her cheeks were sore from smiling. She threw her soaked coat onto the back of a chair. Her numb fingers struggled to unbutton her blouse, and she forced herself to slow down. But the tingling, finally alive sensation was dwindling, and she feared the thrill she felt would wear off any moment.

Pushing herself faster, Evylin dried herself thoroughly, rubbing life back into her skin. She pulled on one of her new coats over a wool skirt and thick blouse, along with her spare gloves. Shivering from the cold, she let her hair out of its braid and ran her fingers through its soaked ends, drying it with a towel. She'd never been so happy in the cold.

Assured she'd staved off any frostbite, Evylin returned to the snowy night. "I've done it," she whispered to the boy she'd left in Whickam Village. "I saved a prince. It isn't *exactly* what we said, but it's close enough."

She smiled at the night sky, the stars twinkling at her as though proud of her accomplishment. "We've finally begun our adventure."

Lost in her thoughts, Evylin nearly ran into Deckard, and he caught her arms to keep her from stumbling on the slick terrae. "Oh," she gasped, then began to laugh. "You startled me."

Deckard released her once she was stable. "My apologies," he said, his brow furrowing. "Were you talking to yourself?"

"No," she lied.

"Oh." He looked over his shoulder at a group of riders headed toward Banbury in the distance.

"Is that the prince?" she asked.

Still in his wet clothes, Deckard sighed. "Yes. He's going back to Magistrate Prokter's for the night. He'll rejoin us in the morning. They'll continue to Yarmouth without us since we can't move with the same speed."

"Who were those men with him?"

"Fifteen of my recruits."

She looked up at him, confused.

"He's taken them for his personal escort back to Loclight."

Evylin frowned. "That won't count against you, will it?"

"I have no idea," Deckard said worriedly. "I'm beginning to fear they may demote me."

Evylin grabbed his hand and ordered, "Stop it. You just saved the prince, for whom you're getting these bloody volunteers. They can't punish you for giving him what he demanded."

Deckard didn't respond, his gaze still on the town. He shivered in the cold, and she squeezed his hand. "You need to change," she reminded him, but he didn't act as though he'd heard her.

Evylin reached up to turn his face toward her. "Jonn, you need to change."

Deckard stared down at her, brows pinched together.

She couldn't help smiling at his expression. "Stop being so sad," she said. "We did it! We're alive, and we saved the prince of Ephria. Now, I'd rather you not perish of hypothermia, so go change out of these soaked clothes, then come to Hewitt's tent. We're celebrating."

"Celebrating?" Deckard said the word as though it were foreign to him.

Evylin squeezed his hand once more before turning to walk away. "Hurry up. You're already late."

She left him in the snow, knowing he'd follow eventually. Thom and Ethenn were sitting around a campfire when she arrived. They'd set out benches and stools from the kitchen tent, and Evylin took the empty seat near Thom.

"Do you think Prince Ephren will actually reward us?" Ethenn asked.

Hewitt scoffed as he walked out of his tent. "Not likely," he grumbled, sitting next to Evylin. "I'd imagine he's already forgotten us."

Ethenn frowned. "He did seem rather careless."

Thom laughed. "Congratulations, kid. You've figured out the royal family. The whole lot of them are self-absorbed narcissists who don't care about us 'little' people. No matter what Deckard says in his speech."

"But they're our rulers. Shouldn't we respect them?" Ethenn asked.

"It doesn't matter if we respect them or not. Yes, they're our rulers, and we're their soldiers. So long as we do what they say, we can hate them and everything for which they stand."

"What do they stand for?" When no one answered Ethenn's question, the young man shrugged. "That's something I've always wondered."

"Quit wondering about anything," Rafferty said, appearing at the edge of the firelight. He held a small barrel in his arms and a sack tossed over his shoulder. "I've got wine!"

"Are you angling for a promotion?" Thom smirked. "'Cause you're on the right track with that."

"Where did you get wine?" Evylin asked, smiling along with the men.

Rafferty set the cask down on a bench and pulled wooden mugs from the sack. "I brought it with me."

"It has the captain's name on it," Ethenn said, pointing to the paint at the top.

"That's because I didn't want anyone else drinking it," Rafferty replied, draping his arm across it like a prized pet. "I've been saving this for a special occasion."

Evylin stared at the writing underneath Deckard's name. "Wait a minute," she said, working out the foreign script. "That's not from Ephria."

"It most certainly is not," Rafferty confirmed proudly.

Evylin smiled in disbelief. "That's the wine—the one you got caught stealing."

Rafferty winked at her. "Indeed, it is."

"You've carried it all this way with you?"

"It's Schonese!" Rafferty exclaimed. "What's more, it put me in prison and landed me here. You'd better believe I wasn't about to leave this behind in Rasnaack."

Tapping the cask, Rafferty reached for Evylin's mug. "Ladies first."

Once they all had a glass of the deep crimson wine, Rafferty raised his high above his head. "To that moronic prince and our brilliant rescue!"

"Here, here!" Thom called, clinking his mug against Evylin's.

"To plans that work and princes who don't."

He got Ethenn to laugh at that one.

"To victory and doing our ruddy jobs!" he yelled the last words, and they all cheered, lifting their wooden mugs to tap them together.

Evylin paused and looked around the fire. The scene was how they'd always pictured it. Reading all those novels, dreaming all those years. She and Ryen knew that adventure looked exactly like this. A daring fight with impossible odds, then victory, and celebration with your friends.

Her smile faltered as she glanced at Thom. The shadows fell across his face, the fire tingeing him red, and for a second, he looked so like Jonn . . . Where was her husband?

He should be part of this moment. Yet, she worried he was sulking, mourning the loss of his volunteers. Or perhaps the cold had made him ill. She ought to have stayed with him to make sure he was all right. . . .

"Captain!" Rafferty called, tossing his hands into the air in welcome.

Evylin's eyes soared over to see Deckard walking through the snow. Warmth spread through her chest at the sight of his tall, noble form approaching steadily. His black boots and trousers contrasted with the white of winter, and his snug gray coat hugged his trim frame. The fire cast a glow of copper over him, his hair shining far more red than usual.

When he approached, Rafferty placed a mug in his hand. "Drink, Captain!" he ordered. "We're all way ahead of you."

Deckard looked over their group. "It seems that you are. Are we drinking to anything in particular?"

Thom raised his mug. "The blasted nincompoop who got himself kidnapped!"

They all roared with laughter, the wine in their bellies relaxing their finer taste in humor.

Deckard eyed his brother, then raised his cup. "I'll drink to that," he said and took a long swig. The rest of them cheered, but he stared down into his wine. "What the bloody hell is this?"

"Your refined taste doesn't take to it, sir?" Rafferty asked mockingly.

"On the contrary. It's the best wine I've ever tasted."

Rafferty jumped onto his bench and raised his mug. "To the captain and his exemplary palate!"

"To the captain!" the rest of them roared.

"And to the Schonese Empire who made it!" Rafferty added.

"Schonese?" Deckard gasped, nearly choking on his last sip. "Where did you get Schonese wine?"

"Don't tell him," Thom said, frowning. "With his scruples, he'll tell you we shouldn't be drinking it."

"And then try to send it back," Evylin teased. The two tipped their cups together.

Deckard turned to Rafferty. "You stole it, didn't you?"

"Not at all, Captain," Rafferty lied. "I was in the middle of transporting it when I was otherwise indisposed. The previous owner had no hope of getting it back and so wrote it off. For all intents and purposes, this wine had no owner, so I felt I ought to give it a proper home."

"As I suspected," Deckard muttered, his hand lifting to toss the rest of his wine back. "Give me another, will you?"

"Immediately, sir!" Rafferty said, taking the mug from him.

Deckard took the empty seat by Ethenn, catching Evylin's eye across the fire. They shared a smile as he accepted the refilled mug from Rafferty.

"Now," Rafferty said, holding his hand out to Evylin, "no celebration is complete without a dance."

"What are we to dance to?" she asked even as she accepted his hand.

Rafferty pulled her out of her seat, gesturing to the men with a sweep of his free arm. "You're telling me in this crowd of talented soldiers, you think none of them can sing?" He tutted at her. "Come now, Eve, you must think better of them than that. Which of you will sing for us?"

The men remained silent as the fire crackled.

"And you call yourself soldiers," Rafferty said, then cleared his throat. In his light tenor, he began a drinking tune about a bawdy girl named Lilamae and swept Evylin into a dance. She held on tight and allowed him to spin her around as he sang. Thom shook his head, began clapping to give them a beat, then joined the song. Soon, it seemed every one of them started to sing, and Evylin wondered how much time they'd all spent in taverns to know the lyrics so well. Deckard looked particularly bashful, skipping some more choice words.

When the song ended, Rafferty handed Evylin her mug, and she emptied it. He started another song and whisked around the fire to drag Ethenn up and shove him toward Evylin. While the other men continued to sing, Rafferty yelled, "You've got to learn to talk to women eventually, kid!"

Though Ethenn's neck warmed with red, he smiled and offered his hand to Evylin. She happily shared a dance with him, too, and while he wasn't as light on his feet as Rafferty, they'd both drunk enough to compensate for his ill-training. Evylin danced with Hewitt next, then Rafferty handed her another drink and made sure she polished it off before pushing her into Thom's waiting arms.

When that dance was over, he proffered the wine again, but Deckard took the drink before she could grab it. "I think she's had enough," he said.

"Don't be a spoilsport, Captain," Rafferty said and gestured to Evylin. "Look, she's absolutely fine."

Evylin laughed, feeling flushed from all the dancing. Holding one hand to her mouth, she stared up at Deckard. His eyes were twinkling deep green in the firelight.

"I'm not here to ruin anyone's celebration, Private Rafferty," Deckard said, then downed the wine himself. "I'm here to dance with my wife."

Following a cheer, Rafferty began another joyful tavern tune while Deckard twirled Evylin across the snowy terrain. He sang along, his voice light and unsteady as they danced. The other men clapped and sang loudly, creating an almost magical haze in the atmosphere. It felt reminiscent of the journey back to camp—wind in her hair, a smile on her lips, her heartbeat racing. Evylin longed to experience every moment like this—fully and completely alive.

As the song concluded, Deckard began to let Evylin go, but she stumbled, falling toward him. The men gasped in surprise as Deckard caught her just in time. Evylin burst into laughter, leaning against his chest with his arms securely around her.

"I tripped," she muttered through her laughter, trying to pull herself upright. "I never trip."

Deckard held her steady, watching her worriedly. "Are you all right?"

Evylin nodded but stopped as the action made her dizzy. "I'm fine," she insisted, taking a step back, knees buckling.

Wisely, Deckard hadn't let her go, saving her from falling. "I think you've had enough celebration for one night," he said, supporting all her weight. Then suddenly, he swept her legs out from under her.

Evylin sucked in a sharp breath of frigid air and wrapped her arms around his neck. She looked into his handsome face, rather bemused by how they'd gotten so close.

"Thank you all for everything," Deckard said, hefting her higher into his arms. "But I'm afraid we'll be off."

The men said goodnight, and Deckard carried her away.

In her daze, Evylin didn't process their departure until they were back among the rows of tents. "Jonn," she said, tightening her grip on him, "why are we leaving?"

Deckard's arms were steady and his gait sure as they passed through the canvas halls of the camp. "Because you're drunk, and I need to get you sober before you fall asleep."

"I've never been drunk before," she admitted.

"That's good," he said as they crunched through the snow. "It isn't the wisest way to spend your time. Though I will admit, it can be enjoyable every now and then."

"The incorruptible Captain Deckard has been drunk?"

"Once or twice, though never intentionally."

Evylin hummed. "I'm a little dizzy."

"We need to get you some water," he said, then set her down in front of their tent. "Can you walk?" he asked, hands hovering at her sides.

Letting her head settle, Evylin stared at the tent's entrance. "I think so," she said and tried to take a step. It worked, though she wobbled, and very slowly, she walked inside as he held her arm.

Once within their tent walls, he led her to the table. "Sit down," he said, pulling out a chair. "I'll get you water."

Evylin plopped onto the chair. The darkness and quiet pressed in on her after the firelight and songs. Clumsily, she tugged off her gloves as Deckard set a mug in front of her.

"Drink that," he ordered.

Evylin took a sip, then set it down.

Deckard pushed it closer. "Drink the whole thing."

"I'm not thirsty," she objected.

"That doesn't matter." He nodded to the mug. "Drink it all."

Evylin pursed her lips but did as he said. When she set the empty mug down, he picked it back up and disappeared again.

"It's dark in here," she noted, staring at the oil lamp's flame flickering on the table before her.

Deckard chuckled on the other side of the tent. "We're normally asleep at this time."

Unbuttoning her coat, Evylin nodded and grimaced as her vision swam. "I'm getting tired."

Deckard set another mug in front of her. "Then we should get you to bed," he said, pointing to the cup as she raised it. "Drink the whole thing."

"Are you trying to drown me?" she asked, beginning to get annoyed with his pleasant smile.

"Never," Deckard promised.

Evylin didn't drink the whole mug but set it down halfway through. "You're being very annoying," she accused.

"You're being very stubborn," he replied and pushed it back to her.

"So are you," she grumbled.

Once she'd emptied the mug, Deckard took it away again. But this time, he returned empty-handed. "Are you ready to go to sleep?" he asked.

Evylin pulled at her coat. "I'm still dressed."

"Are you stable enough to change?" Deckard asked, helping her stand.

Evylin's head didn't spin as much as it had a few moments before, so she nodded. "I think so."

Deckard led her to the divider and helped her take her coat off. "I'll be on the other side," he said, his words cautious, "if you need me."

"I always need you," she muttered, finding that she meant it.

A light laugh breathed out of him, and he stepped back. "Get changed."

Smirking at his clear embarrassment, Evylin got to work. It seemed a never-ending chore as she fumbled with the ties and buttons, wrestled with the many layers of her skirts, and even tripped a couple of times. Deckard checked in regularly throughout the process, questioning her from the other side. Every time, she would assure him that she was fine and continue to fumble her way through. Finally, she rounded the divider in her nightdress, fiddling with the tie at the collar.

Deckard stared at her, his eyes drifting to her fingers, then right back to her face. "Are you done?" he asked.

Evylin abandoned the tie and let it hang loosely around her collarbone. "I'm still dizzy," she said.

"That's probably because you were just moving around," he said, reaching out to steady her. "Once you're in bed, you won't have to worry about that anymore."

Evylin tugged at the buttons on his coat. "You're not ready for bed."

"No, I'm not. It'll be my turn after you've lain down."

Realizing he'd guided her over to the cot already, Evylin looked up at Deckard, hands still on his coat. "I can't sleep without you. It's too cold."

"I'll be right back," Deckard assured her. "I just have to change."

Evylin ran her hands along the wool fabric, stretched tight against his chest, still damp from the freshly fallen snow. She could feel the strength of him even through the thick fabric. "Why haven't you kissed me again?" she wondered aloud.

Deckard froze under her touch.

A flash of worry caused her momentary uncertainty if she'd said the words or thought them. To be sure, she repeated, "Why haven't you kissed me again?"

Deckard blinked in shock. His mouth opened, but no words came out. He held her steady, eyes darting between hers. "I didn't think you wanted me to," he said at last.

"I told you I did."

"You said it terrified you," Deckard countered, each word measured. "I didn't want to assume you'd become comfortable with it."

Evylin shrugged, and his hands, still gripping her arms, accompanied the movement. "I am," she whispered.

Deckard didn't respond.

Thinking he didn't believe her, Evylin slid her hands farther up his chest. "I want you to," she said, her words little more than a whisper.

Deckard started to back away, though he didn't release his grip on her arms, keeping her steady. Or possibly to keep her at arm's length. "You're drunk, Evylin. I won't take anything you say to heart right now because I know you might regret it later."

"Jonn, I've wanted you to kiss me again for days." She grabbed the open collar of his coat. "For weeks. It isn't because I've been drinking or because we won today. I just liked kissing you. And I want to do it again."

"I don't think that's the best idea."

"Why not?" Evylin asked, gripping his coat tightly. "I want you to kiss me, Jonn. I'm asking you to kiss me."

Shaking his head, Deckard grabbed her wrists. "Evylin, I won't."

"You said you kissed me because you wanted to. Why won't you kiss me when *I* want you to?"

Prying her hands from his coat, Deckard glared at her. "Because I won't."

Evylin stepped closer. "Didn't you like kissing me?"

"Of course, I did," he admitted, brows low over his magically shifting green-blue eyes.

"Then why won't you do it now?"

Deckard stared down at her, his heavy breathing audible. His jaw grew rigid, and the pinch between his brows returned. Once more, he opened his mouth to speak but then shut it and shook his head.

"Jonn," Evylin whispered, and she didn't get out another word.

Deckard's hands rose to frame Evylin's face, and he bent, his lips meeting hers. He kissed her softly at first, then a bit deeper.

The same surge she'd experienced during the rescue kicked in, and Evylin's heart started to race. It swirled along her skin like the snow dancing in the wind. It urged her on, and she wrapped her arms around his neck, pressing herself against him. His arm slipped around her waist. The intake of his breath hissed in the air between their lips as he angled her chin up, his thumb brushing her jawline.

This kiss was different from the one in Wayford. That kiss had been tentative and exploratory, as if they were discovering the very act of kissing itself. This one . . . This kiss felt urgent and passionate. It made the world come alive—vivid, sharp, and enchanting—and she could hear the steady thrum of his heartbeat coming into time with hers.

Without warning, Deckard pushed her away, his chest heaving at the same pace as hers.

Body buzzing with the lingering sensation, Evylin watched as his tongue darted out to wet his bottom lip. She took a step forward, hoping to draw him back in, but he shook his head as he withdrew farther away.

"It's time to sleep, Evylin," he said sharply.

She stared at him—mind and senses still humming—unsure if he meant it. Then Deckard abandoned her to the cold, stepping behind the divider to change.

Evylin stood next to the bed, the frigid air seeping through her nightdress. Her heart and breath refused to return to their regular rhythm. Her skin still tingled where he'd touched her, her lips desperate for more. It was unbelievable—this reaction she had to him.

After the rescue, after the thrilling rush she'd experienced just hours ago, she was able to compare the sensations directly. And she found it was the same. What she'd thought was a symptom of adrenaline lit up her entire being now. The whole room glowed radiantly, even though only a single lamp's tiny flame flickered on the table. The sound of Deckard's movement behind the divider practically roared in her ears. The lingering scent of campfire and wine surrounded her. The knit of her socks pressed into her skin, her body tingling in the cold.

Life was in startling and sharp focus.

Evylin covered her mouth with both hands at the revelation. The intense response of her body frightened her. The demand for that alertness and passion was new and strange. It urged her to follow him behind the divider and kiss him without end.

A shiver ran through her, and she couldn't bear the cold any longer. She climbed under the blankets, trying to understand the impulses raging within her, studying the coolness that seeped through her mind and into her muscles, stilling everything but the urge for more.

More action.

More exploration.

More adventure.

More of Deckard.

What is this?

Deckard reappeared but kept his gaze averted as he walked to the table and turned out the lamp. Then he got into the bed and slid in close. Neither of them said a word as she turned into him, and he held her.

Evylin squeezed her eyes shut and tried to calm her pounding heart. But every sense she owned was picking up the world around her, causing an overwhelming feeling of information and emotion. She buried her head into Deckard's neck, and her senses focused on him: the heat of his body, the sound of his breathing, the smell of his tunic, the memory of his kiss.

Deckard sighed, the sound forlorn and wanting, and his chin pressed against her forehead as he drew her closer.

Evylin wrapped her arm around him, not caring if he misread her intentions. She wasn't trying to seduce him; she just needed his touch. Whatever was causing this explosion of sensation within her was frightening. What did it mean? Surely, it wasn't normal. No one had ever mentioned this strange tie between the feelings in a fight and the feelings of a kiss. How could the two have any connection?

"I'm sorry," Evylin whispered against his chest.

Deckard drew in a long breath before sighing heavily again. His thumb traced circles on her back, but he didn't speak. He held her, and Evylin trembled as her senses dulled once again. His heartbeat no longer pounded loudly in her ears like a marching platoon but thumped softly, muted in his chest. His touch didn't send the same current of energy across her skin but soothed her instead, easing her into sleep despite her churning thoughts.

What is happening between us? Evylin didn't know, but she was determined to find out. Because if it came down to choosing to fulfill her promise to Ryen or life with Deckard, she feared what that choice would cost her. She feared what it would do to her heart.

CHAPTER FORTY-FIVE

35TH OF OBSCURA, 1573

With little means to search for answers, Evylin sought the best source of knowledge known to man: Hewitt.

However, approaching him on the subject was problematic. Not only did the idea of discussing her intimate life make her uncomfortable, but she also couldn't let her uncle find out she'd yet to consummate her marriage. After their last discussion, she wouldn't be surprised if he locked her and Deckard in a room until the deed was done, and she had no interest in facing such humiliation.

So the week crept by as she struggled to think of a way to broach the subject with Hewitt. They returned to the tedium of military travel, and worse, Deckard went back to avoiding her. Each night, he held her, and each morning, he left her a note. Yet, that was their only form of contact the whole week.

He was distancing himself from her, she knew, preparing to give her up. And while she considered confronting him, she couldn't bring herself to do it. Not when she worried that she'd have to give him up too.

Worse still, training no longer seemed enough for Evylin. Not after she'd felt such a rush in the heat of battle. She began to attack her opponents with more intensity, hoping to recapture the feeling. It never came, and she often felt disjointed during the work. She'd run herself into a slump where all three of her friends won with little effort.

A fact they each noticed.

And at last, Hewitt approached her about it. "Have you and Deckard had a fight again?" he asked as they ate dinner together in his tent.

"No," Evylin said truthfully. They hadn't had a fight. They'd simply stopped talking to one another.

Hewitt drew his hand along his beard, expression doubtful. "Well, whatever the problem is, I suggest you fix it. You're losing your edge. If it's Deckard, tell me, and I'll set him straight."

"It's not Jonn."

"Then what is it?"

Seeing her opportunity, Evylin still wasn't sure how much to confide in her uncle. What could she say? That she hadn't done as he'd told her to, and now Deckard was pulling away, and she worried he would end their marriage?

Evylin stared at her bowl of cured sausage and rice. "It's just . . . everything is empty now," she murmured. "That night we saved the prince—it was the first time I ever felt like I was finally living. It was the first time I ever experienced anything so—so . . ."

Hewitt watched her as she struggled to find the word. "Complete?"

"Yes!"

He nodded. "It's the same for me. Fighting . . . it's the only thing at which I've ever been good. The only thing that has ever made me feel alive."

The shared experience comforted Evylin. Then she furrowed her brow. "Only when you're fighting?"

"Only then," he confirmed.

"Never any other time?"

He gave her an apologetic grin. "I'm afraid not."

Evylin focused on her meal, unsure of what to do. Yes, Hewitt had the same experience as her when fighting, but why did she feel that way when Deckard kissed her too? She'd already considered that the effect had lingered from the battle, but she'd felt the same when Deckard kissed her at Wayford. The feeling was almost identical, if on a smaller scale.

But if Hewitt never experienced the same feeling any time other than in a fight, how was she experiencing it with Deckard?

Evylin knew it wasn't love. Hewitt had loved his wife, Irena, more than anything. If anyone had been in love, it was her uncle. And he'd said nothing of having that experience with her.

Each day, her distance from Deckard grew, creating a disconnect in their once-budding relationship and distracting her with rising questions. She found little joy in daily activities. It was as if a part of her had broken.

Everyone noticed—the soldiers and her friends. Even Major Moris, of all people, asked after her one afternoon. (She later learned he presumed her to be in the family way, and she couldn't meet his gaze for days after.) She assured them all she was only tired from their travels. As soon as they were in Loclight and she could get a decent night's rest, she'd be right as rain.

Most of them seemed to believe her.

Thom didn't.

While they rode to their next stop, he prodded for answers. "You've been different ever since we saved the prince," he said, his gaze light blue in the afternoon light. "It can't be a coincidence. Are you feeling remorseful over killing those guards? Because if so, you only did what you had to do."

Evylin shook her head; she'd already discussed the topic with Hewitt. Though there was a lingering question of morality, he'd assured her that Allore didn't judge men for deaths dealt in battle. Her soul was safe, and her conscience was clean.

"Then what is it?" Thom pressed.

She gave him an apprehensive glance. "You're not the best person to talk to about it."

His chin lifted. "Did you and Deckard fight or something?"

Why does everyone assume we're fighting? she wondered.

Instead of voicing her thoughts, she reluctantly said, "The 'something' part."

"So . . . what? You think you can't talk to me about it because I'm his brother?"

"I think you won't want to hear about it because you're his brother."

He hummed warily. Their horses plodded along at a distance from the rest of the Third Volunteer Company. At the front of the line, Deckard gave a gentle tug to the reins of his mare and dropped back to speak with Hewitt.

Furrowing her brow, Evylin watched. They'd started doing that over the past several weeks—having conversations. It was disconcerting.

Hewitt patted Deckard on the shoulder like a friend, and the captain rode away.

Bemused, Evylin huffed and turned back to Thom. "Can I ask you something?"

"Sure."

"It's a bit odd," she warned.

"Now, I'm intrigued."

Evylin took a deep breath, biding her time before she asked the question that had eaten away at her for days. "What is it like," she started, the words hardly above a whisper, "kissing other people?"

Thom gaped at her for a full thirty seconds. "What?" he said at last.

"You *have* kissed more than one woman, haven't you?" she asked.

Thom rubbed his neck and turned away from her. "Yes."

"What is it like?"

"Almighty, I don't know! Why are you asking?"

Now that she'd breached the subject, Evylin found a renewed sense of confidence. "I'm just curious," she said. "Is it all the same? Or is it different?"

Thom fumbled in a search for words. "What—well, I mean . . ." He refused to look at her. "Different, how?"

"The way it feels," she explained. "Is it different with each person? Or does it always feel the same?"

He kept fidgeting, running a hand through his hair time and time again. "You really know how to make a man uncomfortable, Evie," he grumbled, then shook his head. "I mean, yeah, sure, it's different. But mostly because it's a different person. Otherwise, it's more or less the same."

"What do you mean?"

"Well, it's kissing." He let out a wry scoff. "Some people are better at it than others, but all in all, the feeling is the same."

"Really?" she asked, unsure how to feel about that.

"Yeah."

"With everyone?"

"With everyone I've kissed," Thom confirmed, pulling at some loose leather on his saddle.

Evylin pursed her lips, disappointed. Was it the same with everyone? It wouldn't matter if she kissed Deckard, or Ethenn, or Rafferty, or any other soldier in the army. She'd have that same rush to her senses each time.

Evylin couldn't fathom that. "So it's always exciting?"

Thom pinched the bridge of his nose. "Yeah, I'd say so."

"And it always feels like a fight?"

"What?" His hand dropped away, and he stared at her in shock.

Evylin rolled her eyes. "Like the feeling you get in a fight, I mean. That rush. Like the world is suddenly so clear, and everything comes into focus."

He didn't speak.

"What?" Evylin drew back, uneasy in his inspection.

Thom turned back to the road, brow low. "I can't say I've *ever* experienced that," he muttered, "in a kiss or in a fight."

"Oh."

Awkward silence clung to the air as they rode on, neither willing to face the other. It was uncomfortable enough to discuss the subject in general. But to do so with Deckard's brother when he knew exactly whom her experience was with. . . .

"Really?" Thom exclaimed, causing her to jump. "Deckard makes you feel that way? Really?"

Embarrassed, Evylin nodded as she rubbed her hand along her horse's mane.

He swore under his breath. "He's the prude of all prudes, and yet he can do that?"

Evylin rolled her eyes at his dramatics. "It was just a kiss, you idiot."

He glared at the marching soldiers, then frowned. "Wait—" He looked at her in surprise. "Just a kiss?"

Evylin blanched. "Uh—"

"Have you not . . . ?" He didn't bother finishing the question, and her blatant discomfort clearly gave the answer away. "Bloody hell," he murmured. "He really is a prude."

Reaching out, Evylin caught his arm. "You can't tell anyone," she whispered desperately. "They can't know."

Thom nodded, scanning her with renewed understanding.

The uncomfortable silence returned, and they continued down the road. Evylin tugged on her rings, staring at the horizon. There wasn't much harm in Thom knowing, she supposed. It wasn't as though he'd want her sent home. If anything, he'd help her keep the secret so she could stay.

Thom cleared his throat, drawing her attention. "Does this have anything to do with why you've been different the last week?" he asked.

At her silent nod, he continued. "Would you like to talk about it?"

With a sigh, Evylin saw no reason to hold back any longer. "We kissed," she confessed. "And now he won't talk to me."

Thom's face scrunched in bewilderment and disgust. "Why the hell would he do that?"

"I did ask him to."

"No, Evie—wait." He glared at her. "You *asked* him to kiss you?"

"Yes."

He grumbled under his breath, then said, "Why?"

She shrugged, blushing uncomfortably. "Because it's fun."

His eyes widened. "This wasn't the first time," he surmised.

She shook her head.

"Mm," he grunted irritably. Then he blew a raspberry. "Well, fine. Whatever. Why would asking for a kiss make him stop talking to you?"

"That's what I can't figure out," she admitted. "It's like he's upset with me, but I can't understand why. I think he enjoyed it as much as I did."

"Ugh—Evie, please."

"You asked!"

"At least *pretend* that this makes you uncomfortable," he complained.

"It's not my fault he's good at it."

His sharp glare stopped any further explanations.

Evylin held his gaze earnestly. "What do I do, Thom?"

Thom studied her, then turned to the road. "Why do anything?"

She tossed her arms in the air, exasperated. "Some help you are."

"Look," Thom gave her one of his more cynical smirks, "I don't understand why you're trying to make it work with Jonn in the first place. You don't love him. He doesn't love you. Now that I'm aware you don't legally have to remain married, I can honestly ask: *Why* stay together?"

The thought rankled in Evylin's chest. "Whether we love one another or not, if we weren't married, I'd have to go back home."

"You wouldn't *have* to," he noted.

"Oh? Could you convince my father to let me travel without a husband?"

He leveled her with a flat stare. "You could get a different husband."

Evylin's heart lurched at the very suggestion. She didn't want another husband. She liked Deckard, and she *wanted* to be with him. She was just afraid it would interfere with her promise to Ryen.

But Thom wasn't aware of her growing feelings.

His expression softened, compassionate but misinformed. "You could find someone else, Evie," he said gently. "Someone who understands you better. Someone you love, who loves you in return, out of passion rather than obligation."

The cold wind tore at Evylin's hair, stinging her eyes. He was wrong, of course. She knew perfectly well that what was between her and Deckard had nothing to do with obligation. They might not be in love, but their hearts were tied in a way she hadn't expected when they made their vows in Whickam Village.

But she wasn't ready to admit that.

With a forced smile, Evylin patted Thom's hand. "Thank you," she said. "You're a good friend, Thom."

He returned the smile but averted his gaze. "I'd give anything to see you happy, Evie."

The afternoon faded into evening, and Evylin pondered their conversation. She couldn't marry someone else. Not now that she'd begun to feel for Deckard, not when he stirred that strange sensation inside her. Even if she left him, it wouldn't be for another man. It would be for a promise. He would respect that. And it wouldn't be forever either. She would return to him if he'd take her back.

"I will spend the rest of my life loving you if you'll let me."

Well, she'd let him.

The question was, would he let her?

CHAPTER FORTY-SIX

36TH OF OBSCURA, 1573

"Good," Hewitt coached as Deckard managed to parry another of his attacks. "You're getting wise now."

Deckard dodged another swing from the man, then slipped in a feint and a hit to Hewitt's shoulder. "After all this time," he replied, "I ought to have learned your tricks."

Over the past week, their sparring time grew longer. Deckard was finally capable of enough endurance and technique to hold his own with Hewitt. He still never won, but he could feel his skills improving as his control of the blade increased.

For the first time in his life, Deckard felt like a swordsman. Like a true soldier.

It did nothing to improve his mood.

Deckard knew he was acting like a child, sulking about as he awaited the coming catastrophe. But he couldn't help it. Why allow himself or Evylin to get their feelings entwined when they'd just have to part in a handful of days?

Thankfully, no one confronted him about his behavior. Whether he'd done a good enough job keeping his feelings a secret or they were too afraid or disinterested to say anything didn't matter. They'd allowed him to live without interference, and he was thankful for that.

After their training ended, Deckard and Hewitt returned to their horses. While the bear-like man hardly showed any signs of fatigue, Deckard felt a bead of sweat drip down his back, even in the snow-laden hollow they'd found. He was worn—from the training and from how hard he'd been working each day. His muscles were taut, and his body ached; he longed for a rest that would never come.

"Tell me something, Deckard," Hewitt said as he returned the swords to their scabbards. "Where did you learn my son's name?"

Taken off guard by the impromptu conversation, Deckard turned from his horse.

"Was it my brother?"

A long beat of silence stretched as Deckard tried to remember. "I believe it was your sister-in-law's sister."

"Serene? She would, the old nag." He snorted derisively. "I'll take a risk and assume that means Evie hasn't said a thing about it."

"No," Deckard confirmed.

"Don't take it to heart," he said casually. "She doesn't trust anyone but me."

The truth, though not unexpected, was no less hurtful. Deckard refused himself the bitterness. Why should Evylin trust him? Especially now that their futures were inevitably about to diverge.

Hewitt held Deckard's gaze, expression determined. "That needs to change," he said.

"What does?" Deckard asked, bemused.

The man hesitated, then grimaced. "As much as I hate to admit it, I was wrong the other day."

The admission caused Deckard to raise his brow in shock.

"Evylin's not mine anymore," the major said. "And we both need to stop thinking of her that way. She needs to learn to trust you. And . . . you were right. If you're going to care for her, you need to know what happened."

Hope flared in Deckard's gut, realizing the man was about to explain the mystery that shrouded the heart of Evylin Glaas since he'd met her. He was going to learn the secrets she refused to speak aloud.

Hewitt's gray stare grew cold. "But believe me, if you *ever* mention Ryen to her—if you *ever* ask her about him before she speaks of him to you, you will lose whatever amount of trust you've managed to garner so far."

The thought snapped Deckard back to his senses.

"No," he said. The explanation would do him no good. Evylin was lost to him already, and this would only reveal her secrets unnecessarily.

Hewitt's bushy eyebrows dropped low. "What?"

"Don't tell me."

"Don't be an idiot," Hewitt spat. "You aren't protecting her sensibilities. If you're to be a good husband to her, you were right—you *need* to know."

Deckard shook his head, the disappointment and anger that had seethed within him over the last several weeks bursting out. "It doesn't matter anymore. Don't you understand that?" he demanded. "My future is forfeit. I can't give her anything."

"You can still make her happy."

"How?" Deckard laughed bitterly. "Rand can send me anywhere he likes. He could send me into Wauld itself, should he find that amusing."

"Stop pitying yourself."

"I'm being practical. Evylin is already unsure about our future. That much is clear. And I will not force her to stay by my side should Rand send me on some miserable assignment that will crush her just like Whickam Village did."

Hewitt paced along the trees, hands fisting. "How many times do I have to tell you?" he snarled. "I won't let that happen."

"And if it does?" Deckard returned. "What if there's nothing you can do to stop it?"

"I won't let it!"

"You can't promise that!"

They stared each other down, neither willing to let go of their stubborn resolve. Two officers, dedicated to the same charge they were willing to die to protect: Evylin.

A strange expression came over Hewitt's face then. Often, his mouth was turned down. But this was different. His gray eyes softened, and an inescapable look of sorrow dropped his shoulders. "You need to know," he said quietly. "Whatever comes, you need to know how to care for her."

Deckard would have fought him. But the surprise of Hewitt's dejected and broken demeanor kept him from uttering a word.

"My boy," Hewitt began, voice deep and rough, "was the most wonderful person you'd ever meet. From the moment he was born, he was smiling. Happy, kind, and smart as a whip." A wistful tilt overtook his lips, turning them up as he stared into the trees. "He was born one month before Evie, and they never knew a day without the other.

"You never saw two more perfectly suited people," he continued. "Both of them were so similar in disposition and yet complementary in all the right ways. He was gentle where she was strong. He was a leader, and she was a follower. He was intentional, whereas she was bold. They worked so well together. She idolized him, and he adored her. If he had . . ."

Hewitt swallowed roughly. "If he had lived, they would have taken over this world, side by side." He met Deckard's questioning stare. "He would have liked you, I think, and he would have asked you to join them for her sake."

"For her sake?" The words were out before Deckard realized he'd spoken.

"She liked you the minute she saw you. It's the only reason I considered it."

Deckard refused to let his vanity dissuade the truth of the moment. "But there was the fire?" he prompted.

"Yes," Hewitt said, raising his hand to his beard. "I was away on assignment, and some idiot left a candle burning in the village hall. Never did find out who it was. Everyone kept pointing a finger at someone else. However it happened—a gust of wind, a mouse scurrying around, a stray spark—the fire started in the middle of the night. There is no guard in Whickam Village, no night watch, and before anyone noticed, it had already caught on the neighboring buildings.

"In the rush of putting out the flames, no one noticed the houses burning behind the hall." He ground his teeth. "No one noticed *my* home engulfed in flames of its own. No one heard my son or my wife crying out for help. The doctor tried to convince me they'd both died in their sleep due to the smoke. But I never believed him. The flames had burned their bodies beyond recognition."

Deckard drew in a labored breath. He covered his eyes as his mind conjured the image of a young boy who looked far too much like Evylin, burning in his room, alone and afraid.

"I should have been there," Hewitt muttered. "I could have saved them."

"You don't know that," Deckard forced out weakly.

His steely eyes narrowed. "I *could* have saved them. I would have died before letting them down that way."

Deckard nodded, accepting the answer. He had no doubt of its veracity.

"It took a couple of weeks for me to get the letter, receive an honorable discharge, and return home," Hewitt explained. "I was a broken man when I rode back into the village. But I wasn't alone in my grief."

He pressed his lips together, a haunted look coming into his eyes. "Evylin was inconsolable. They said she hadn't left her bed from the moment she found out. They couldn't get her to eat, and they had to force her to drink. She was . . . a frail, tiny speck of a thing when I returned."

Hewitt paused, staring ahead as though seeing that girl before him. A glistening ring of tears lined his eyes. "I went to her the minute I arrived," he said. "Found her curled up in her quilts, strands of hair plastered to her cheeks, wet with tears. I still remember . . . She was wearing a nightdress with tiny pink flowers on the collar. I don't know why I remember that, but I always see it. Maybe because it's the last time I ever saw her wear something so soft and childlike, so sweet and innocent."

Deckard fought down the urge to cry, his heart breaking for the woman he'd come to care for.

"I scooped her up the second I saw her, and I held her close, and we both cried for . . . hours, probably." Hewitt ran a hand over his mouth and down his beard. "It was then I promised myself—I would never leave her. I'd failed my son, but I would never fail her. I would be at her side for the rest of my days, and I would find a way to give her the life she deserved."

He stopped and met Deckard's gaze again. "Then you showed up," he said like it was an accusation, "and I realized my time as her protector was at an end."

Hewitt stepped forward, pointing a finger at Deckard. "It's your job now," he charged. "You want to know why I chose you? Because *she* chose you."

Deckard shook his head, but Hewitt smiled sadly, surprising him into silence.

"We grieved together—her and I," he said. "We found some semblance of peace together and made our lives somehow happy. Or as happy as they could be. But I never made the mistake of thinking either of us got over it. I'm bitter, and she's independent. We've both isolated ourselves in our grief, with only each other for company. I refuse to care, and she refuses to trust.

"I've watched that girl for thirteen years as she went about trying to find something worth living for," he said, steely gaze locked on Deckard's face. "And the first time I ever saw her give any man a second thought was when she met you. The first time she ever suggested leaving without me was with you."

Hewitt gave a firm nod. "I knew then: You were the one. Whether she understood that herself or not—whether she knows it now or not—you are the man she chose. And you are the man who can give her what I never could on my own. I got her this far. It's your job to take her the rest of the way."

In the fight between overwhelming despair and shock, Deckard somehow managed to steady his emotions. Could Hewitt be right? Had Evylin *chosen* him? And if so, did that mean she could come to love him?

"You want to know how to make her happy?" Hewitt said, bringing Deckard out of his thoughts. "You want to know how to earn her trust? She fears loss. Stay by her side and show her you'll be there no matter what. Only then will she give you her heart."

Deckard's brow pinched together. Stay by her side? How could he when she deserved so much more?

Taking a step back, Deckard dipped his head. Regardless of what choice he made—staying with Evylin or letting her go—he owed the man his gratitude. "Thank you," he said, "for telling me about your son."

"Don't mention it," Hewitt growled, his expression hard and gruff once more. "Ever."

Deckard grinned wryly at the return of the beast. "Wouldn't dream of it," he promised.

The major nodded and stepped toward his horse, but Deckard grabbed his arm. "Hewitt," he matched the man's steely gaze with a bold one of his own, "I promise you I'll do everything I can to make her happy and keep her safe." He paused, then added the same vow he'd made to Evylin, "No matter what that looks like."

The dangerous, cat-like grin lifted Hewitt's lips. A meaty hand landed on Deckard's arm and squeezed. "I know you will."

CHAPTER FORTY-SEVEN

1ST OF GALATAE, 1574 — ANNALTIDE DAY

During the remaining six days of their journey, Evylin came to a decision. No matter what consequence Deckard faced for his failure, she'd stay with him. Evylin knew she didn't love Deckard—not yet. They'd still only known each other for less than two months. But how could she leave him when her feelings were growing, and he made her feel that strange sense of being truly alive?

Why should staying with him mean going back on her word to Ryen either? Whether he faced an undesirable post or a demotion, it wouldn't matter. She'd weather the storm at his side, and that would be its own sort of adventure. If he earned a discharge—which she thought highly improbable—then she'd simply remind him of his promise to travel Ephria with her. Perhaps it'd be even better if they weren't tied to the army.

Somehow, the decision brought her peace in their last days of travel. Despite his distant behavior toward her, she knew Deckard had more on his mind than their relationship. The fear of facing his commanding officers must be all-encompassing. So she let him stay aloof, hoping to bring calm and comfort to him rather than friction. If he needed to think and worry alone, then she would grant him that. And when they arrived in Loclight, he'd find his fears were unfounded, and she'd be by his side.

Evylin found a fresh sense of purpose and enjoyed her days. She started winning at duels again—much to the men's disappointment. She celebrated Annaltide Eve with Hewitt and their little band. Usually, the celebration involved gifts, custard cakes, paper crowns, and a village-wide dance on the first day of the new year. Since they didn't have the opportunity to purchase gifts, make cakes, or provide crowns, they settled for scrounging together a feast from the kitchen tent.

Now, on Annaltide Day, they crested the rise to see Ephria City in the distance. The late morning sun shone brightly, and Evylin's breath caught at the sight.

The city was spread over several miles. Built within a valley, it dipped down toward the sea. The ocean sparkled as she surveyed the land. Hewitt had explained that the city had seven districts. Outside the walls and to the west, the snowy land held small farms called the Fielders District, while the eastern side was the Cattle District—though they raised far more than cattle alone.

Inside the city walls, buildings sprawled chaotically, intertwining like a complex knot. Nestled within were the five distinct areas: the Mercantile District, Cathedral District, Quarter District, Military District, and Loclight District. Since the palace lay in the last section and the province derived its name from it, many people commonly referred to the capital city as Loclight.

A river ran through the capital and toward the western farms. The castle loomed next to the rushing flow; the district of the king's residence called to Evylin. It would take them another hour to pass through the gates, but her heart beat faster at the realization of one more of their dreams: She was going to see the capital.

Hewitt drew his gray stallion alongside Evylin. "She's a big city," he said. "You sure you can handle it?"

Evylin turned to him, feeling somewhere between laughter and tears. She chose the first. "I'll take it by storm," she replied.

His large hand clasped her shoulder. "That's my girl."

They continued with the army, their horses trotting steadily. After their time in Banbury, Evylin continued to ride the palomino, Regon. Although she missed Fransis, she had to acknowledge that his strength and agility offered a superior ride.

As they neared the gates, Evylin gaped up at the stone walls. They towered into the vibrant blue sky, the pewter stone etched with depictions of Ephren and his great host of rebels. Deckard's recruits funneled past the gate, the men remarking on the design. Guards in emerald and gray uniforms stood on either side of the massive iron doors, a grand feat of engineering, scanning the crowd as they entered the city.

The thrumming gallop of a horse approached from behind Evylin and Hewitt. They turned to see Deckard threading through the troops. He nodded in greeting and pulled up beside Evylin, his green-blue gaze locked onto her. "I missed crossing the Nettershire border with you," he said. "But I won't miss this."

Evylin's lips parted to thank him, to tell him how much it meant to have him at her side. Yet, no words came.

Deckard brushed her arm lightly, and then they turned forward and entered Ephria City.

Evylin gazed in wonder. The bustling crowd moved around the towering buildings, unbothered by the soldiers passing by. The cobblestone streets caused the horse's hooves to clatter. A persistent murmur filled the air, emanating from the citizens who moved about everywhere. The noise felt as though it enveloped Evylin from all sides.

They progressed through the streets, drawn ever deeper into the heart of the city. Evylin's senses were captivated by the vibrant sights of unusual shops, the inviting aromas from a nearby bakery, and the lively calls of vendors selling their goods. Feeling overwhelmed, she glanced to her right to confirm that Deckard was still riding beside her.

At the sight of him, she instantly calmed. He held his head high, looking wholly at home in the bustling city. A soft, confident grin lifted his countenance, which had been so dour over the last week. *He may have been happy in Stocburrough,* Evylin thought, *but he belongs here.*

As they ventured farther in, the streets expanded, and Deckard leaned over to note that they had entered the heart of Loclight. In this district, the buildings appeared more magnificent, each façade adorned with intricate designs and large windows. Towering above them was the palace, a striking structure made of white stone.

Before long, the company veered left onto a side road leading into another gated area. Soldiers patrolled the entrance, and Deckard excused himself, heading away to oversee the men. At her side, Hewitt explained that they were approaching the barracks of Loclight, the head of all military operations in Ephria. Upon entering, Evylin was amazed to discover a spacious courtyard and a grand building. She couldn't comprehend how such a vast space could be nestled among such close buildings. The construction inside the barracks was comparable to the finest designs outside its walls.

Soldiers surrounded the courtyard and lined the walkways, observing as volunteers entered in small groups. The newcomers, dressed in gray, appeared quite solemn, their attire contrasting with the officers in their dark green uniforms. A few men stood at the top of the stairs in even more distinguished vestments adorned with braids, ribbons, and medals. The one in the center bore the double golden braids of a general. By his haughty expression, Evylin guessed the white-haired, hawk-nosed man was the infamous Rand.

Once the last volunteers arrived, the general spoke. "Welcome to the Ephrian Army," he said, his voice deep. "We applaud your service to the king. I am General Rand, head of the Loclight military base. As you begin your career with us, we hope you find satisfaction in your duty. Sergeants Rowlin, Naalston, and Eedes will help you acclimate to the barracks."

Guided by the officers, the recruits moved toward the three sergeants at the bottom of the stairs. They each spoke to the men for a handful of moments before disappearing into the massive building.

Following Hewitt's lead, Evylin dismounted and allowed some barracks corporals to take their horses. Soldiers pressed around them, the courtyard almost too small for their numbers. "This is rather overwhelming," Evylin observed.

"Indeed," Hewitt muttered, eyes on General Rand.

Rafferty, Thom, and Ethenn appeared beside them.

"Guess we're about to say our goodbyes," Rafferty said, arms crossed as he glared toward the sergeants. "Our lives are no longer our own."

"This is what we signed up for, Raff," Ethenn said, then turned to Evylin and held out his hand. "It was a pleasure training with you. I'm awfully thankful for everything I've learned."

Evylin ignored his hand and gave him a hug. When she pulled back, his eyes were wide, though he grinned bashfully. "We'll see each other soon," she said, turning to Rafferty and Thom. "It isn't as though this is the end."

"I'm afraid it is, Evie," Thom said, his dark brow pulled low over his eyes. "We're all about to get new assignments. If we're lucky, a few of us might stay together. If we aren't, there's a chance we'll never see each other again."

Hewitt put his hand on Evylin's shoulder. "Not if I have a say in it," he said fiercely. "I have friends here. I can get us all assigned to the same detail. It might not be as fun as if a few of us went separate ways, but at least we'd be able to stay together."

Evylin looked up at him. "I'd say it's worth it."

The three men nodded, hopeful smiles gracing their lips.

"Until later then, Eve," Rafferty said, holding his arms wide for a hug.

After saying goodbye to Rafferty, Evylin turned to Thom, and he wrapped an arm around her shoulders. "I'll see you tonight," he said. "We live together now, remember?"

Evylin grinned up at him. "I'd forgotten about that. How long will it take you in there?"

He gave the barracks an annoyed glance. "Several hours. I'll have to stay to make sure First Platoon settles in all right. Then they'll want me to debrief with some of the commanding officers before I get my next assignment."

"Sounds tedious."

"It is." He gave her a final squeeze, turning to Ethenn and Rafferty. "Come on. Time to make real soldiers out of you two."

They waved to Hewitt and Evylin and walked away to approach the sergeants. While the recruits spoke with the officers, Thom veered toward the barracks. Ethenn followed, darting glances at Rafferty, Evylin, and Hewitt before vanishing through the door. Finally, Rafferty slipped away to the left.

"It's strange to separate from them," Evylin said quietly. "They were like brothers." The thought sent a wave of sadness through her, making her question if she'd felt that way about anyone since Ryen.

Hewitt cleared his throat. "I have to leave you too," he said gently. "I may not be a new soldier, but I am returning. And they'll have things for me to do."

Evylin hadn't considered his having to leave her. "Will I see you again soon?" she asked, not sure she could take a negative reply.

"Deckard offered for me to stay with you two until I find my own place," he explained. "I'll be there once I'm done here."

Relief flooded Evylin, and she returned his nod. Hewitt's fingers grazed her cheek before he walked away and met with the sergeants. His massive frame and height towered over the soldiers. A sergeant pointed toward the left door, and Hewitt nodded. Then the barracks devoured another one of her men.

Alone in the courtyard, the volunteers thinning out around her, Evylin wondered what to do. She hadn't seen Deckard since they entered, and now she worried the barracks had already taken him too. What was she to do by herself in this cobbled courtyard?

A cold wind cut through, and she shivered, wrapping her arms around her chest. Her eyes darted around the barracks, wondering if there was anywhere she could go to get out of the cold.

In her scan, she caught sight of Deckard walking toward her through the crowd of soldiers. Her breathing eased as he approached.

"Are you all right?" he asked, setting a hand on her arm. "You look lost."

"I feel lost," she whispered. "Everyone has disappeared into that building, and I don't know what to do."

Deckard's expression turned down. "Evylin, I have to go in as well," he said apologetically. "I have to meet with General Rand and give an account of my mission."

Unsure which was more unsettling, his leaving or his worry, Evylin stepped closer to him. "It'll be all right," she promised. "Your men have had better training than any others, and you can't change who chose to volunteer and who didn't. This wasn't a draft. They can't hold you responsible for your numbers."

Deckard's appreciative smile held no joy. "But they will."

"Jonn," Evylin began, but he shook his head and cut her off.

"I'll be back soon," Deckard said, then motioned to a nearby wooden door. "There's a small library just there. Tell them you're my wife, and they'll let you wait for me there. It'll keep you out of the cold."

Evylin wanted to stop him, to grab his hands and pull him into a hug like she'd given the others. But he moved away too quickly.

Deckard walked across the courtyard, volunteers and officers mingling in their gray and green coats. He took the tall, stone staircase that led to General Rand, waiting at the top.

Evylin watched as the old general's expression tightened when Deckard greeted him with a bow. They exchanged some words before the general beckoned him to follow. Deckard glanced over his shoulder once, then hurried to match the general's long strides. Soon, they reached the door at the far right of the building, and then Deckard was gone too.

CHAPTER FORTY-EIGHT

General Rand's office was like most of the rooms in the barracks. A bubbled glass window filled the back wall, supplying dim light, which was added to by the fire in the hearth and the oil lamps on the desk. Small and tidy, the office held a distinct sense of order. With dark walls, built-in shelves, and a walnut mantel, Deckard found it warm and welcoming.

Its unpleasant owner marred the effect.

Shutting the door with a firm *click*, General Rand glared at Deckard. His long nose always gave the impression that he was looking down at the object of his scrutiny, which was also due in large part to his elevated opinion of himself. "Take a seat, Captain," the general said, walking around his desk.

Deckard did as ordered, resting on the edge of the leather chair.

"Lieutenant Peery gave me your ledger," General Rand said with a single tap to the book on his desk. "Let's have a look at it, shall we?"

Rand opened the leather cover and swiftly thumbed through the pages, flicking his wrist so each one snapped. Upon reaching the last page, he shot a bored glance at Deckard. "Are your records accurate?" he asked in a low rumble.

Deckard forced himself to keep his head high. "I'm afraid not, sir," he said. "While we were in Banbury, we met with Prince Ephren. On his departure, there was an ambush that left him without a guard. Some of my company and I were able to retrieve the prince, thank Allore, but he required fifteen of my volunteers to escort him back to Loclight."

"Hm." Rand arched his silvery-white brow. "So not only did you fail to bring back the five hundred I'd assigned to you, but you also brought back less than the number your records show."

While his accusation contained flaws, it reflected the unembellished facts. "Yes, sir," Deckard responded calmly.

"How disappointing." Rand lifted the cover of the ledger. It slammed shut. "As a captain, I expected you to be more diligent when given an order. But duty doesn't matter much to you, it appears. Five hundred men was not a suggestion, Captain Deckard. It was a minimum."

"I understand, sir."

"You've been in the service long enough to know failure is not acceptable. Why would you think yourself safe to leave the Shires without five hundred men?"

Deckard was ready for the question. He'd served under the general long enough to know he always gave his prey a chance to defend itself before the final blow. The question was one last attempt to deflect his strike.

"Forgive me, sir. I had no intention of neglecting my duties," Deckard replied, maintaining eye contact. "Quite the opposite. I knew I needed an average of no less than seventeen men per settlement in the Shires. But the villages didn't have the men to spare. What's more, no cities populate the Shires; thus, there was no chance to assemble large groups. I depended on the towns to make up for the shortfall. By the time we reached our halfway point, I'd managed to gather just under two hundred fifty men, and it appeared I would meet my goal. It wasn't until the final few stops that I recognized its impossibility."

"That's poor planning on your part," Rand said flatly. "You should have gathered more than half the men in the lower Shires to buffer any failures in the north."

Though Deckard saw no means by which he could have assured any more men from Setshire or Estshire, he nodded anyway. It was time to bring his final gambit into play. "I did think that the recommission of Hewitt Glaas would carry a bit more weight than one singular soldier," he offered.

General Rand scoffed. "You think one old man can replace thirty-nine others? Is a relic of a soldier turned a major to make up for men who can fight for our cause? Glaas is past his prime, and we don't need more trainers. We need more soldiers."

Deckard's head dipped. He'd failed to deflect the blow, and the strike would now fall.

"Now, the question is," the general leaned back in his chair, "what will the consequences be for your negligence?"

"Whatever you see fit, sir."

"At least you accept responsibility for your failure. You have my respect, but it won't make the punishment lax."

Rand stood, picked up Deckard's ledger, and stepped to the bookshelf. He slid the leather book into a line of identical replicas, a few gaps on the shelf indicating the other officers who were out recruiting.

"This is rather fortuitous timing, Captain Deckard," Rand said, then turned. "Only yesterday, I received a letter from one of my colonels requesting aid. Of his three captains, one recently earned a promotion and reassignment, while another died in an attack along with some of his other men. Now, he needs a new officer and a company of men. It seems the job lines up with your timing perfectly."

Deckard swallowed the lump in his throat. He wasn't being given a demotion, then. If he took this assignment, he would remain a captain and lead a company. "Yes, sir."

The general smiled cunningly and resumed his seat at the desk. "I will write to Colonel Forsythe and inform him that I'm sending you along with a company of a hundred men. I'll have Lieutenant General Lewes write up your orders, and you can pick them up in the morning. You'll have three days to get your affairs in order and depart for Ostwatch on the fourth."

Deckard's skin went cold with fear. "Ostwatch?" he repeated.

General Rand's piercing eyes glimmered. "Oh, yes, you spent time there before, didn't you? All the better. You'll be of more use to the colonel than I realized."

Hands clasped in a vise grip, Deckard couldn't move. Ostwatch once more? His luck held ten years ago, but no luck could ever hold out that long, not for anyone, and certainly not for a man aged a decade.

"I'll submit your reassignment today," General Rand continued. "And you have permission to be on leave until the fourth. Do you have any questions?"

An ache tore open the pit in Deckard's stomach. The consequences were worse than he'd feared. He could've handled being sent to a small village in the middle of nowhere with nothing to do. But going back to live in constant fear for his life? Even a discharge would have been preferable to this.

Ostwatch was a graveyard. Soldiers only made it through if they were lucky enough to earn a promotion, garnering a reassignment. The higher ranking the officer, the less likely he'd escape. Most of them died within a year.

It wasn't an unfortunate assignment; it was a gamble with fate. Not to decide *if* he would die but *when*.

Forcing his eyes back to the general, Deckard shook his head. There were no answers that could explain Rand's contempt; there was no reason or argument to justify it. The bitter old man had found his opportunity to ruin Deckard, and he was taking it.

"Then you're dismissed," General Rand said and pulled a stack of paper across the desk. He picked up the pen next to him, eyes cast down in total dismissal.

Rising, Deckard's heart pounded with such a fury that he could feel it in his throat. Everything inside him wanted to argue with Rand. He wanted to remind him that no other captain had brought back men half as well trained as he had. He wanted to tell him that five hundred was too much to ask of a small countryside ravaged by a draft only five years ago. But none of it would save him. He'd dug his own grave, and any attempt to fill it in would only bury him alive.

Deckard grasped the cold iron doorknob when Rand spoke again. "Oh, and Captain Deckard—" he turned to see the general's imperious smile, "I heard you were recently married. My congratulations to you and your lovely bride."

"Thank you, sir," he said coldly, then left the office.

Deckard marched through the barracks' corridors, making his way to the library. He passed numerous rooms filled with soldiers. His recruits mingled among their new comrades, wearing expressions of excitement, nervousness, and overwhelm. While these men were only beginning their journeys, Deckard was nearing the end of his own.

Starting down the stairs, Deckard paused when someone called his name. He turned to see Thom hurrying his way. After they'd saved Prince Ephren, an unspoken agreement developed between them. Though the lingering discomfort remained, there wasn't the same animosity from Thom. And same as ever, Deckard let the conflict go in favor of regaining his brother's trust.

"Done with the general already?" Thom asked with a hopeful tilt to his grin. "How'd it go?"

Deckard's stomach twisted. "Not well."

Thom frowned. "I'm sorry. Did he—how bad was it?"

A pair of soldiers barreled down the stairs past them, and they moved out of the way. Deckard gripped the rail tightly. "Quite bad," he deflected.

A vein pulsed in Thom's jaw. "Tell me."

"We can talk about it later."

"Jonn," he said, voice fierce with demand, "what happened?"

"I got my reassignment."

"And?"

"I'm replacing one of Colonel Forsythe's captains in Ostwatch."

All emotion left Thom's face. "Ostwatch?"

Deckard nodded hollowly.

"Why?"

"How should I know?"

"Well, it's bloody ridiculous," Thom said sharply. "You can't go there. Even Rand isn't enough of a bastard to send you to your death."

Deckard said nothing as a few soldiers glanced their way.

"No," Thom demanded. "You're not going."

"My orders will be ready in the morning," Deckard said.

Thom snarled at him. "Don't be an idiot. You're not going."

"I don't have a choice."

"Damn right, 'cause I won't let you."

He gave a half-hearted smirk. "If only you were the general and he the lieutenant."

Thom grabbed his arm. "Jonn, you are *not* going to Ostwatch. I will not stand by and let you die."

"There's nothing you can do."

"That's not true," he insisted. "I'll—I'll talk with Rand. He likes me. He might listen—"

"Don't," Deckard interrupted. "I won't have you getting in trouble for my sake."

Thom scowled. "Then Hewitt will talk with him. He's got connections all over this place. Already, I've seen him rubbing elbows with Lieutenant General Lewes and several of the colonels. If anyone can get you out of this, it's him."

Thom's fear worsened the terror cutting through Deckard's gut. Pressure built in his throat, tears of disappointment and dismay threatening. But he managed an appreciative smile to cover his rising panic. "I think you're right," he muttered, patting his brother's arm. "I've got to get Evylin home."

Thom's face fell again. "What are you going to tell her?"

Deckard began to back down the staircase. "The truth."

Though Thom looked ready to argue, he let Deckard go and turned, fingers raking through his hair. Despite the tension between them, despite the horror he faced, it was heartening to know his brother cared. Deckard could still remember when his mother told him he'd be a big brother for the first time. It was a vague memory but one of his most treasured. He'd been thrilled by the news, sure it was a little brother. And he'd been right.

From the moment he met his baby brother, Deckard adored Thom. He would beg his mother to let him hold the baby, asking to help at every turn. He spent hours talking to him even though he couldn't talk back. It was his greatest desire from the outset to be the best of friends with his brother. He imagined they'd cherish and trust one another more than anyone else in the world. And it was his greatest disappointment to discover that Thom regarded him with contempt rather than companionship.

But the concern Thom displayed at the announcement of his reassignment assured Deckard that his brother *did* care for him too. And should he be on his way to die, he could leave the world with a sense that even if he hadn't done everything right, at least he hadn't done everything wrong either.

As Deckard neared the library, he took deep, measured breaths in and out, releasing the fists his hands had created. He couldn't let Evylin see his trembling. His troubling news wasn't a conversation for public society.

Though his head pounded, Deckard tamed the rest of his body and pushed into the library. The long room was bright, with windows lining the far wall. Books lined numerous shelves, all relating to military strategy, historical reference, weaponry, and other important knowledge a soldier might need to know. Deckard found himself grinning, knowing that Evylin would despise these books. He forced the smile away, knowing he shouldn't give her false hope.

He spotted Evylin in the third row of books, perusing the titles. She held her scarf and gloves, her coat hanging open as she strolled down the aisle, examining the spines of the books. She bit her lip in thought, a habit that Deckard found both frustrating and endearing.

Walking to her side, Deckard kept his expression impassive. She looked up as he approached, her eyes wide and hopeful. "Did it go well?" she whispered.

Deckard offered his arm. "Let's get home first," he said gently.

She looked ready to protest, but a clerk walked into the aisle holding a stack of books in his arms. Evylin draped her scarf back around her neck and accepted his arm. When they stepped into the courtyard, a fierce winter wind assaulted them. They hurried through the gate door of the barracks and onto the bustling street. Leading her toward the back of the city, Deckard kept his eyes ahead rather than on her entertained face. Perpetual awe seemed etched across her expression as she took in the city.

The cobbled roads were hard on Deckard's feet after spending the past three months on dirt and grass. The journey down to the Shires with his eleven officers had been quick, but the trek home took its time. Now, he viewed Loclight as a changed man in many regards.

After passing three blocks, Deckard slowed, coming to a stop. The houses in the Military District were like most in the city, butting up against one another in three-story stacks. Only the wealthiest living nearest the palace owned unattached homes. Some of the narrowest houses had each floor divided into three separate units. The single or lesser-ranked soldiers lived in those apartments. Others were much larger, two widths of the smaller size, set aside for the high-ranking officials and the men with large families.

Evylin's brow furrowed as Deckard pulled her toward number thirty-two. "Is this your home?" she asked, eyes scanning the beige stone and paned windows.

Deckard kept his gaze on the dark wood door. "Yes, it is," he said, turning the key.

Evylin dropped back to stare at the exterior. "It's so large."

"It's the size of your family's home, all in all. This one is taller, but it's also narrower," Deckard said, then reached out for her hand. "Come on. People are staring."

Letting him pull her inside, Evylin smirked. "My family had five daughters. We needed a house this size," she argued, scanning the small entryway containing a coat rack and tiled floor. "It's just you and Thom here, right?"

"Yes, it's just us," he confirmed, unbuttoning his coat. "When I became a sergeant, the army stationed me here in Loclight, but it wasn't until lieutenancy that my orders became long-term—a minimum of three years. They offered me the choice of a house or a one-bedroom flat. As Thom often passed through the city, I offered for him to join me and . . ."

He cleared his throat, hanging her coat next to his. "I did intend to have a family someday, so. . . ."

Evylin handed him her scarf, eyeing him curiously. "I suppose with Hewitt and me here, you do have a strange sort of family now."

Refusing to meet her gaze, Deckard fussed with the coats a minute longer. He couldn't encourage her, but she wasn't entirely wrong. Regardless of the state of their marriage, she was his wife. And he would happily leave all he had to her.

Turning back, Deckard gestured to the entryway. "After you."

Crossing the open doorway, Evylin stepped into the house. Though the size made it seem grand, neither Deckard nor Thom had spent much time on the home's appearance, leaving it far from properly furnished. Deckard was seldom home during the day, and Thom's assignments often took him out of the city for months at a time. It was the only reason Deckard thought their living together worked. For the minuscule periods of time that Thom was in Loclight, Deckard was busy with work, and they hardly saw each other.

To the right of the entryway lay the parlor. Built-in shelves—sparsely filled—flanked the fireplace, with only a couch and a singular chair before its hearth. A small side table sat next to the chair with an oil lamp on its final dregs. Deckard was thankful to see that the only mess in the room was the dust collected over the past three months. The thick gray curtains still hung closed, and Deckard walked over to pull them back. They both coughed from the kickback of dust as light filled the room.

"I take it you don't entertain much?" she teased, the sun making her hair glow.

"Not at all," Deckard said, suddenly nervous. A fight raged inside him; his heart desired to show her the house and let her marvel at the potential of the empty space, but his head knew it was time to tell the truth.

Evylin rubbed her arms in the cool air, and Deckard moved to the fireplace. "If you can brave the dust, have a seat," he said, using the last remaining logs to start the fire. In a handful of moments, flames sprang up within the hearth, and he turned to see Evylin seated on the couch. His heart pinched with bitterness. When they married almost two months ago, he'd been so optimistic. After thirty-two years of singleness, he'd thought his dreams for a family and a career he loved were within his grasp.

One failure had shattered those hopes.

Deckard sat in the chair by the fireplace. "Evylin," he said, staring at his clasped hands, "we need to talk."

"Your meeting didn't go well, then?" she surmised.

"No, it didn't."

Evylin shifted to sit across from him. "What happened?"

After one deep breath in and a slow breath out, Deckard spoke. "As expected, General Rand was not gracious about my lack of men. He's reassigned me to Ostwatch in Harmouth Province. I leave in three days' time."

"Three days?" Evylin repeated uncertainly. "That's rather soon."

"It is."

"Are you taking any men with you?"

Realizing she was asking about her friends, Deckard hoped they wouldn't be doomed to join him. "I'll be leading a company there, yes. But I doubt anyone we know will be assigned to it."

Evylin sighed wistfully. "I suppose our little team couldn't have lasted forever. It's too bad. I thought we worked well together."

"We did," Deckard said, realizing it was true. They did work well together. Though he hadn't been enthusiastic about Rafferty, the man proved to follow orders and was quite an asset. And everyone else banded together to do their job impeccably. Even their little celebration created a sense of connection between them. He was unexpectedly saddened to know he'd never get to fight with those men again.

Evylin reached over and took his hand. "Hewitt will come," she said reassuringly. "He promised that whatever happens, he'll stay with me. And while you two aren't exactly friends, he'll be by your side."

Deckard stared dully at their hands, grasping onto her as though she might save him. "He won't come to Ostwatch, Evylin," he said, then met her amber gaze. "And neither will you."

Evylin blinked in surprise, pulling away as his words sank in. "I can't come with you?"

"No," Deckard said with finality.

"Is it usual for them to refuse wives accompanying their husbands? Or is this Rand's doing?"

"It has nothing to do with army regulations or Rand's orders," he explained, amazed he had the courage to hold her bewildered stare. "Ostwatch is a mile off the border of Wauld. It's one of the most dangerous assignments the army can give a soldier. There are raids and attacks every week—sometimes, every day. Much of the populace are soldiers now because most citizens who remain alive have left the village."

Evylin's lips parted in understanding. "You don't want me to come with you because you think it's too dangerous?"

"I don't want you to come with me because Ostwatch is a death sentence," he corrected. "The army stationed me there as a corporal. Living through it once was a miracle. A second time will be impossible."

The words fell heavily on the two of them at the same time. He'd thought them, but he'd yet to say them aloud. Now, he realized how true they were. And how very much he didn't want them to be.

Evylin stared back at him, unmoving. The fire snapped behind the screen, making her jump. "Jonn," she whispered, but no other words came.

Deckard shifted forward in his seat. "I'm going to die there," he said gently. "It's a matter of months, if not weeks. I don't want you to come because I don't want you to live in that terrible place, waiting for me to die."

Evylin sucked in a broken breath. "You're giving up?" she demanded. "Just like that, you're accepting death? It's an assignment. It's only temporary."

"The only escape from Ostwatch is promotion."

"So get promoted."

"It isn't that easy," he said. "It took me six years to become a sergeant, two more to become a lieutenant, and another four to become a captain. I'm not a good soldier. I failed my last assignment, and I won't qualify for a promotion for nearly a year. And not a single officer makes it through a year in Ostwatch."

A sharp, frightened exhale escaped her.

"I will die within the year," he confessed weakly.

"You don't know that," she insisted, then added furiously, "I'll come with you. I'll protect you."

A fond smile tugged at Deckard's lips. He reached over and set a hand on her cheek. "Evie," he whispered, "they wouldn't let you." She sat still under his touch, eyes darting between his. He brushed his thumb across her cheekbone. "And I don't want you to watch me die."

The truth hung between them in a curtain of silence.

Her breath came out in a stilted puff of air. There were no fixes for this, no salvation for him. He was going to Ostwatch, and she would be made a widow.

"What will I do?" Evylin asked in quiet acceptance.

Deckard took her hand once more, letting their joined fingers rest on her knees. The moment was the end he'd dreaded, the one he'd hoped would never come. "There are two options," he said. "First, you can stay in Loclight. As a soldier's widow, you'll earn my pension and inherit everything, including this house. I'm sure Hewitt will make sure he's assigned to stay in Loclight with you, and you'd be free to do as you please. You could even travel if you like when he gets leave."

Her fingers tightened on his, and he set his other hand over them. "The other option," he said, sure this would be the answer, "is returning to Whickam Village as my widow."

She flinched.

"You'd be with your family . . ." *With Ryen*, he didn't add. "And you could start over. I would have liked to keep my promise to you for longer, but . . . we did have one adventure. And that might be all I could have ever offered."

Evylin didn't speak. The only sign she hadn't turned to stone was the way her breath swept back the wisps of hair around her face.

"I don't care what you choose," he promised. "Either way, you'll inherit. You could sell this house, take the money, and live the rest of your life in comfort."

"I don't care about that." The words hissed out of her, sharp and hollow. She jerked back, pulling away from his touch. And for the first time since he'd met her, a well of tears pooled in her eyes.

Deckard's heart broke as she glared at him. "I don't want the money," she whispered fiercely. "I want you."

The breath caught in Deckard's throat, choking him. Joy and despair raged within him. She wanted *him*. Whether or not she loved him was another matter. She cared for him, and that was enough.

But he couldn't yield. Not when death awaited him in the mountain village of Ostwatch.

Rising, Deckard stepped toward her, desperate to comfort her. He stretched out his hand, ready to kneel before her in contrition, when a sudden *rap, rap, rap* startled them both.

A shaky gasp escaped Evylin, and Deckard turned toward the door. He furrowed his brow, then remembered that the barracks' soldiers always brought the officers their possessions after sorting the large wagon loads and supplies. "That's our things," he muttered, internally cursing the army's timing.

Evylin didn't respond, and her eyes turned to the floor.

"I'll be back in a moment," Deckard promised, then hurried to answer the door.

The irritation welled in his stomach. If he were a man of brusque temper, he would have yanked the door open and yelled at them to return later. Instead, he forced down the fiery tension in his throat and opened the door, prepared to instruct the soldiers on where to deliver their trunks.

But no soldier stood in his doorway.

"Afternoon, sir," a young page said, dressed in his black and green uniform. The teen gave a little bow and looked up at Deckard in a bored manner. "Would you be Captain Deckard?"

Confused, Deckard hesitated. "I am."

The page held out a letter. "For you, sir."

Deckard took the large envelope addressed to Captain and Mrs. Jonn Deckard. The paper was thick, the calligraphy fine. He turned it over, noting the heavy emerald green wax seal with a crook and sword, a crown above them both. "What's this?" he asked, incredulous.

"An invitation, sir, from King Ephren."

CHAPTER FORTY-NINE

Hands shaking, Evylin tried to calm her racing mind. Deckard had walked away, giving her time to pull herself together. And she *would* pull herself together.

The sound of the street muffled the words of whoever was at the door, but Evylin didn't care about the conversation. She rose to pace the room. He'd given up. She'd decided to stay with him, and he'd decided to abandon her.

Taking slow and measured breaths, Evylin refused her tears. She wouldn't let him leave her. No matter what he said, she would go with him to Ostwatch, as would Hewitt. They'd be there beside him. They'd protect him. It wasn't exactly the adventure she and Ryen sought, but keeping him alive in an unlivable place . . . That was worthy of legend, wasn't it?

And she wasn't done with him.

"Evylin," Deckard said uncertainly. She spun to find him back in the parlor, brow pinched in confusion. He held an open letter in his hand. "We've received an invitation . . . to the palace."

Certain she hadn't heard him correctly, Evylin blinked. "Pardon?"

He offered her the paper, and Evylin took it. She stared at the elegant script that read:

To Captain and Mrs. Deckard,
His Sovereign Majesty, King Ephren,
formally invites you to the Annaltide Ball
in celebration of another year blessed by Allore.
He requests the pleasure of your company

to christen the coming days in splendor.
Expect a carriage at seven this evening.
Kind regards from your king,
Willem Ephren, King of Ephria and Allore's Hand

Evylin gaped at the words. She turned the letter over, unsure what she expected to find on the blank backing, then read it again. When she was assured she'd read it correctly, she looked at Deckard in shock. "Have you ever attended a ball at the palace?" she asked.

"No," Deckard said, his eyes wide. "And I've never met anyone who has. Only Commander Estham, head of the army, ever sees the king. And that's because he's considered an advisor. No working soldier runs in high enough society to earn the king's invitation."

"Huh." Evylin stared at the letter. "Do you think this is the prince's reward?"

"I wouldn't give him enough credit to remember us," Deckard said with a scoff. "But then I can't fathom why else they would invite us."

Running her finger over the wax seal, Evylin shook her head. "Can he really believe this would be enough?"

"He's a man who has never lacked anything. A party invitation is probably the highest flattery he could think of."

"How noble of him," she grumbled and tossed the paper on the side table.

Deckard didn't respond.

"Is there a bath in this house?"

He looked up, surprised, then nodded. "Two, actually," he said.

While Deckard insisted on heating and filling the water for her bath himself, she explored the house. The downstairs contained a dining room and kitchen, sparsely furnished like the parlor. The second floor held the first bath, two bedrooms, and an office. One room appeared to be a spare with only a narrow cot, while the other belonged to Thom. Though she hesitated, the door hung ajar, and she peeked inside quickly. Like the rest of the home, it held menial furnishings—only a bed, a wardrobe, a desk, and a chair. But this room bore signs of living. The bed was in a haphazard state, while a coat hung on the back of the chair, a couple of tunics flung over it. A stack of books sat on the desk, and a small pile of plates and cups littered the rest of the surface.

Sneaking away, Evylin peeked into the office. Despite its own dark wooden desk and plush rug, it showed little more use than the rooms downstairs. Books lined the shelves, and the desk held no clutter or misaligned articles. Deckard either didn't use his office much, or he'd taken the time to put it right before he'd left.

The third-floor roof pitched at a steep angle, and she found another spare room and an attic across the hall. Deckard had filled the tub in the bath using the pipes and the small stove in the corner of the room. Evylin walked past the bathroom and into the master. A bed, larger than most they'd shared, sat on the far side of the room. Made with precision, the thick cream quilt reached up to the two plush pillows. An extra gray knit blanket lay across the end. A rug covered much of the wood floor, and a large, built-in wardrobe lay next to the door.

Evylin ran her fingers along the dark wood footboard of the bed as Deckard stepped into the room.

"The bath is ready," he said, walking to the wardrobe. He opened the left side, pulled open a drawer, and removed a tunic and a robe. "Hopefully, our things will come before you're done, but in case they don't. . . ."

Taking the items from his hands, Evylin thanked him and proceeded to the bathroom. During her travels, she had managed to bathe at various magistrates' residences and in Stocburrough, but none compared to this one. Cleansing the dirt and grime from her body in the comfort of her own home, with the promise of several hours to savor it, made the experience feel almost sacred. She submerged herself in the warm water, delighting in how it enveloped every part of her skin.

Evylin held her breath, letting the absence of air sear her lungs. The water's pressure caused a humming in her ears, while her muscles relaxed, drifting away from reality. She thought of promises and adventures, of more and of less. She asked herself questions but found no answers. Then she broke the surface and leaned forward, resting her head on her knees. Water cascaded from her chin, creating tiny ripples with each droplet's fall.

Evylin finished washing her hair and body quickly, but she let herself luxuriate in the tub. The slow, dissipating steam cleared her mind. Whatever came, she could not leave Deckard, not while there was still a chance of adventure with him. If there ever came a time that being with him diverged from keeping her promise to Ryen, she'd reconsider. But for now . . .

Finally, Evylin climbed out of the lukewarm water and dried herself. She shivered despite the stove's warmth and slipped on the tunic and robe. If nothing else, she couldn't live in Loclight alone. Not when she'd have to brave the cold nights without someone to hold her.

Resolved, Evylin exited the bathroom. She found Deckard in the bedroom, unpacking his trunk. He looked up at her arrival. "They brought our things at last," he said. "I only use this half of the wardrobe, so you're welcome to the other side if . . ."

Their eyes met, and he cleared his throat. "If you want to," he concluded.

Without responding, Evylin began to unpack as well. Though she wasn't much for organizing, she decided she would make a show of claiming her half of the space. Hanging each piece with care, she made sure they presented themselves as though they were permanent. "There," she said, then frowned. "Though I suppose it should all have a wash."

Deckard glanced over with a curious expression. She wondered if he, too, found it peculiarly charming, seeing their things hanging side by side.

"I'd better go clean up," he said. "I'll take care of the trunks later."

Knowing it would take time to empty the tub, heat fresh water, refill it, and bathe, Evylin leisurely unpacked the rest of her belongings. She walked the length of the master, running her hands along the walls, windowsills, and furnishings. A nightstand stood on either side of the bed, but only the right side held any belongings: an oil lamp, a book, and a small timepiece, all covered in dust. Smiling at his marked territory, Evylin decided she'd do the same.

With her few pieces, Evylin went throughout the house, leaving traces along the way. She put a few of her novels on the parlor shelves and left a shawl draped over the back of the sofa. Then she hung her nice wool coat on the rack with the others. In the office, she put the box of money she'd earned from Hewitt and a few other books. Upstairs, on the left nightstand, she put a watercolor from Dolia, her jewelry box, and the stack of Deckard's notes. Once the trunk was empty and her belongings distributed, she felt she'd made her point. Any time Deckard walked through the house, he'd see signs of her. And he would know she had no intentions of leaving him.

Evylin sat on the edge of the bed and stared into the wardrobe. She had no idea what to wear to a ball. She'd attended dances in Whickam Village and Trollenston, of course, but nothing so grand as this, and she doubted she owned anything fine enough. After scanning her options, she settled on the light green satin dress Deckard bought her in Stoclund. Whether it was fine enough for a palatial ball or not, it was clean.

The wardrobe had a long mirror on the inside of the door, and she used it to pin back her hair. Though she knew her mother wouldn't approve, it wouldn't do to appear before the king with a tangled mane. Twisting sections until she'd finally gotten it all piled and secured at the back of her head, Evylin thought she looked rather elegant—a statement she couldn't have said of herself for the last few months.

Taking the green dress off the hanger, Evylin let the glossy fabric glide through her fingers. She'd heard Deckard's emergence from the tub not long before, and she wondered if he'd return soon. With a glance at the closed door, Evylin blushed at the idea of him walking in on her. Then she smirked and decided that wouldn't be such a bad thing.

Removing her borrowed robe and tunic, Evylin pulled on a clean chemise and stockings. The bathroom door opened in the hall, and she paused. She resumed tying off her petticoat as Deckard's footsteps neared . . . and began descending the stairs.

Evylin pursed her lips in disappointment. Deckard always was too much of a gentleman.

After she'd finished dressing, Evylin ran her hands down the front of her gown. The squared-off neckline lay low but hugged her décolletage demurely. Deep green embroidery lined the neckline and cuffs, reminding her of Estshire ivy. She took one final look in the mirror, adjusting the pendant on her necklace so it lay flat.

Night had fallen, casting an amethyst haze over the world outside as the lamps tinged the room in an amber glow. She checked the clock on Deckard's nightstand. The carriage was due to arrive in half an hour. With one last check on her hair, Evylin was satisfied with her appearance.

Deckard knocked on the door, and Evylin invited him to enter. The latch clicked, and her husband froze when he saw her. A soft smile brightened his earlier somberness. "You look beautiful," he said.

Taking in his ordinary trousers and tunic, Evylin smirked. "You look ready to go back on the road."

Deckard glanced down and chuckled. "Yes, I was planning to change. It's customary for me to wear my ceremonial uniform."

Thinking of the emerald velvet coat, Evylin tugged at the skirt of her dress. "It seems we'll match, then."

"That we will," he said, stepping to the side and waiting.

Evylin waited, too, confused by his silence.

"I made some tea if you'd like it," Deckard said, hand on the doorknob. "I'll be down in a few moments to join you."

Realizing this was his subtle way of asking her to leave, Evylin pressed her lips together. She stepped toward the door, her gown swishing around her feet, and he shut the door behind her. She glanced back, wondering if she should have let him dismiss her so easily, but shook her head and went downstairs.

The house was quiet and dark, with only a few oil lamps lighting the halls. The tea waited on the dining table. She pulled a novel from the shelf, then sat at the table, careful not to spill any tea on her dress. When she slipped the bookmark free, she peeked inside at the pressed everbloom flower. Lifting it out, she folded the page again and slipped it into the hidden pocket of her skirt.

When Deckard arrived, he took the seat across from her and poured himself a cup. The white cravat at his collar stood out against the dark coat, drawing her eyes to his freshly shaven face. Though he appeared relaxed, his expression was impassive.

"You look younger, clean-shaven," she remarked to draw him out of his introspection.

Deckard's hand went to his jaw absentmindedly. "I do?"

"Yes, but I have to admit," Evylin raised her brow teasingly, "I prefer you with a bit of scruff. More captain-like that way."

He scoffed lightly. "I don't think the general would agree."

"The general doesn't have to look at you every day," Evylin said, adding after a pause, "nor does he have to kiss you."

Deckard choked on his tea, and Evylin grinned brightly. "My elder sister, Albina, always lamented her husband's beard," she continued. "Said it was prickly. But I rather liked the masculinity of your scruff both times we kissed."

Hesitantly, Deckard replied, "I'd shaved when we married, and I kissed you then."

"That hardly counts. As I remember, it lasted barely a second."

"As I remember," Deckard said, leaning on the table, "you didn't want to be kissed."

Their eyes held, and Evylin sat forward, mirroring his stance. "Times have changed," she whispered daringly.

Deckard's gaze shuttered immediately. "Evylin," he said with an air of warning, "don't."

"Why not?" she said, voice low and challenging.

He released a tense breath, staring at her. His grip was white on his teacup, and she thought to reach across the table and pull him toward her. Perhaps she could instigate the kiss, promising she wouldn't leave him, no matter what he said. She'd go with him to Ostwatch and keep him alive for years to come. He wasn't allowed to die. He'd made a promise to her, and she would make sure he kept it.

A knock interrupted their heated stare, and Deckard immediately jumped from his seat. He rushed for the door, and Evylin slumped back in her chair.

"Impeccable timing," she muttered sourly.

Evylin bit the inside of her lip, listening as Deckard spoke with a man. It was the carriage from the palace. She rose from the table to join him in the entryway, determined to enjoy the night. Her fingers brushed the paper-encased flower in her pocket. Let Deckard keep his sorrows. She would relish the chance to celebrate in King Ephren's court with Ryen in her thoughts. Death be damned.

CHAPTER FIFTY

Throughout the carriage ride, Evylin and Deckard sat in silence. While he was absorbed in his thoughts, she gazed out the window in wonder, taking in the sight of buildings adorned with lanterns strung from one to another in celebration of the new year. Despite the winter's chill, people wandered the streets, enjoying the festive atmosphere.

When the castle came into view, her eyes grew even wider. Lavish gardens filled the massive grounds. Rows and rows of lanterns lit the greenery. It could have been daylight with how bright those lanterns shone. Men and women dressed in richly colored clothing crowded every inch of the property. They perused the gardens, gathered on the lawn, and sauntered up the grand staircase to the palace's entry.

Deckard assisted Evylin as she carefully managed the train of her gown while descending from the carriage. She linked her arm with his, her gaze still roaming. A lengthy, dark green carpet stretched over the pebbled pathway, guiding them toward the grand steps. Towering as tall as three men, the massive doors were etched with detailed metalwork. At the entrance, servants awaited to greet the guests and collect their coats. Once inside, a gentleman announced them by name.

The interior of the palace was equally breathtaking. The elaborate designs echoed the meticulous craftsmanship of the exterior. If Evylin found Magistrate Prokter's residence impressive, she could only describe the palace as extraordinary. Gilded and shimmering, the Ephrian palace was adorned with silver and crystal. It was more luxurious than anything Evylin had ever encountered in her life.

Hewn marble formed the floors and columns of the walls. Ceilings soared to remarkable heights, featuring intricate paintings of lush glens and ivy-clad valleys.

Visitors wandered through the halls, creating a constant, vibrant buzz in the castle. Nothing could keep Evylin's attention for more than a few seconds. There always seemed to be something of even greater splendor around every corner. They moved through several adjoining rooms, following the faint sounds of music above the din of conversation.

They moved with the crowd, finding their way to a grand ballroom. Deckard pulled Evylin to a stop by the wall. They took in the opulent sight. An orchestra sat on a balcony far above while people danced across the marble floor. A large table filled with extravagant foods—some Evylin had never seen—stood near the back wall. A few men lingered there, picking off the plates as they spoke. Women clustered around the room in little groups, chatting and giggling. Everything was a flurry of motion and sound, and Evylin loved it all.

"I don't see anyone here," Evylin said, scanning the crowd.

Deckard quirked his brow. "I assume you're joking."

She poked his side. "I'm referring to our friends," she said. "I haven't seen one of them."

"Did you expect to?"

"We weren't the only ones who saved the prince's life."

"No," Deckard said, then gave her a pointed look. "But I'm rather certain the only reason the prince even remembered me was due to my marriage to you."

"Oh, shut up."

Smiling, Deckard took her hand from the crook of his arm, lacing his fingers through hers and pulling her through the crowd. "I need a drink."

While he retrieved two glasses of sparkling wine, Evylin continued to scan the room. Her fingers found the pressed everbloom flower in her pocket as she watched dozens of men and women spin across the floor. The women wore dazzling gowns in silks, satins, gossamer, chiffon, and velvet in the brightest, most terrific colors. In the light of the massive chandeliers overhead, the guests looked like a field of spring flowers under the noonday sun.

Deckard handed Evylin a wine glass, and she muttered "thank you" distractedly, too enraptured to look away. Then she spotted a familiar face. "Jonn, look! It's Lord Carlile."

Deckard followed her gaze toward the elderly man. Intermittently, large gatherings obstructed their view of him, interposing barriers between them and the advisor. His black and silver suit emphasized his slender physique, and the laceration on his brow had largely healed. He didn't notice them as he was deeply engaged in a discussion with a young man and woman.

Peering through the crowd, Evylin studied the pair curiously. Their features were strikingly similar, marking them as family if not siblings. The pair's fair complexions, strong brows, sharp cheekbones, and thin lips were notable in the sea of strangers. And most eye-catching of all, their fiery red hair burned brightly in the luminous hall. The woman wore a silky sky blue gown embroidered with ivory thread, while the man wore a white coat with gold piping. They carried themselves with an imperious air, but the woman laughed gaily with Carlile, her brother smiling kindly at her side.

"Who do you think they are?" Evylin asked Deckard.

He studied them a moment longer. "I don't know. Perhaps they're nobles visiting for the holiday."

"Hm. Her dress is beautiful."

"I like yours better."

"It's nowhere near as elegant."

He shook his head as though that didn't matter. "Yours is far more ladylike."

She looked up at him, incredulous. "Are you telling me that because her neckline dips a few inches lower than mine, it makes her less of a lady?"

"Not at all," he replied. "I'm saying I prefer a little mystery regarding a woman's dress."

Evylin rolled her eyes, sure he was being far too much of a prude. Though the woman's gown plunged lower than any she'd seen before, it didn't reveal much. If anything, it made the woman appear *more* mysterious in her mind.

As they watched, the young man's deep-set gaze fell on them.

"Oh," she gasped, grabbing Deckard's arm, "I think we got caught staring."

The red-haired man turned to Carlile and spoke. Then all three of their party turned to examine them. Carlile raised his hand in greeting, saying a few words to his friends as he dipped his head. They returned the farewell, and he took his leave. However, the man and woman continued to observe Deckard and Evylin as the lord departed.

Evylin watched as the man said something, and his companion grinned. The woman lifted a finger to rest under her chin. Though Evylin wasn't versed in reading lips, she could catch the sentiment of their conversation. The pair found them just as interesting as Evylin found the two of them. Why, she couldn't understand.

"Hello again," Lord Carlile said, stopping before them. "What a pleasure to see you both."

Deckard gave a short bow. "The pleasure is ours, my lord. We were quite honored to receive our invitation."

Carlile waved a hand through the air. "It's the least Prince Ephren could do."

The least, indeed, Evylin thought. "We rather expected him to forget us," she admitted, watching to gauge his reaction.

"The prince does surprise us all from time to time," Carlile said, the candlelight flickering in his dark eyes. "And it would be awfully hard to forget the people who saved your life so daringly."

"We were only doing our duty for king and country," Deckard said.

"As were our friends," Evylin added.

"Of course," Carlile said. "And they all deserve an equal reward."

"Are they here, then? I haven't seen them."

Deckard nudged her, but Carlile took no offense at her prying.

"No, I'm afraid only you and your husband received tonight's pleasure," the advisor said. "You see, it would be improper to invite a party of soldiers to a royal celebration. But a singular captain and his wife are more than acceptable, as they would know the proper behavior at such a gathering."

"Ah, yes, our friends are quite the blackguards."

"Precisely," Carlile said, smiling as brightly as the chandeliers.

"Is that how you convinced the prince?"

"Evie," Deckard warned, but Carlile waved a dismissive hand and said, "Whatever do you mean, Mrs. Deckard?"

"It seems rather unlikely the prince would be aware of our arrival in the city only this morning," she noted. "Even if we did save his life. So it begs the question: Who pays enough attention to the happenings in Loclight to discover the prince's saviors' arrival? And who could move quickly enough to alert the prince? And who was close enough to the prince to convince him we deserved an invitation?"

Carlile turned to Deckard. "Your wife has a sharp mind, Captain."

"Indeed, she does."

"Then I'm right?" Evylin prompted. "You are the reason we were invited."

"I'd never presume to have that much authority over the royal family, madam," he said as the music came to a stop. "Now, if you'd please, I believe it's time for your reward."

Evylin glanced at Deckard, their eyes wide and mouths agape. They rushed to keep up with Lord Carlile as he moved through the crowd.

"I thought the invitation was our reward," Deckard said.

Carlile laughed as he led them out of the ballroom. "A party as reward enough for saving the prince's life? Your invitation is merely an excuse, Captain. And while it is a pittance, the king thought it a worthwhile gesture to give you an evening of fun."

They turned down the halls, through a back entrance, and out onto the grounds. "Stay near the lanterns," Carlile called over his shoulder. "You'll be warm enough there."

The heat from the lanterns' continual flames warmed the pathways as they moved into the garden. Stones crunched under their feet as they followed the king's advisor, weaving through hedgerows and arbors. Up ahead, a large crowd raised a cacophony of sound while a musician plucked a mandolin. She could hardly hear his melodious voice above the noise as he sang.

Stone benches curved at the edge of the roundabout, men and women sitting and standing in clusters around them. On the far side, an old man sat laughing at the story told by a young woman seated by his side. He wore a green coat with ivory embroidery, and on top of his white hair sat a platinum crown, large emeralds embedded with diamonds surrounding them. He bore the same facial structure as his son but with more severe, age-worn features. His bushy white eyebrows hung over his dark eyes, and wrinkles etched his face.

Lord Carlile walked straight over to the king, bowing low. "Your Majesty," he said, eyes to the ground, "may I present Captain Jonn Deckard and his wife, Mrs. Evylin Deckard?"

Raising a hand to stop the young woman's story, King Ephren rose from his perch on the bench. "Rise, my friend," he said, patting Carlile on the shoulder as he approached Deckard and Evylin. They bowed to their monarch. "Do introduce me to our guests."

"Captain and Mrs. Deckard," Carlile said, "His Majesty, King Ephren, welcomes you to his home."

"Indeed, I do! Rise, both of you," the king said, his deep voice resonant. Though most of the guests continued to talk, their eyes turned to the new arrivals. King Ephren only spared a quick look at Deckard before turning to Evylin. "My son told me about the woman who saved him. Surely, it could not be this beauty standing before me now."

Keeping her head bowed, Evylin wondered if he expected her to respond.

"Walk with me, both of you," he commanded before she had to decide, moving toward the path. "Carlile, you follow."

They made their way over the pebbles and between the neatly trimmed bushes. As a couple of guests passed by, Evylin stepped into the shadows, shivering from the chilly night air. Deckard drew her closer to his side.

King Ephren smiled at the group of young women, then tossed a glance to Deckard and Evylin. "Caspar told me about your rescue. I thought he'd dramatized it, but Carlile backed him up. If another of my advisers had done so, I might have thought they were trying to make my son look good. But that's why I trust Carlile. He doesn't cater to my son's vanity. Nor mine some of the time, which is a damn irritant." The king chuckled. "Caspar said he'd promised to reward you and your team. I make that promise to you now as well."

"You're too gracious, Your Majesty," Deckard said, his chin dipping low.

Ephren lifted a shoulder in a shrug. "Don't thank me yet."

Turning down a new path, their small group neared another roundabout where a dozen men gathered. They were laughing, drinking, and smoking, and Evylin didn't have to wonder why no women had chosen to join them. The noise and smell caused her nose to wrinkle, even from a distance.

King Ephren came to a stop and turned to Carlile. "Tell the commander I need him," he ordered, and the lord left his side.

"Now," the king said, turning back to them, "your reward will take two forms: One which my son recommended and one which I chose myself. First, you will each receive a sizable purse as a thank you. Then I'd like you to consider an opportunity I have for you. Ah, here's the commander."

A large man with massive hands and a flat face joined them, Carlile at his side. The man's uniform matched Deckard's, though his coat burst with ribbons and patches above the insignia, and he bore a triple braid of gold on his right shoulder. After bowing to the king, the man looked at Deckard, appraising his uniform. "Captain," he said with a nod.

Deckard returned the greeting with a bow.

"Commander Estham, this is Captain Deckard and his wife, Evylin," King Ephren said, his smile amused when he said her name. "They helped save Prince Caspar from that traitor Tybaalt. And as such, I intend to repay them and their team. The other men were all soldiers as well, is that correct?"

Deckard hesitated before realizing he was the one expected to respond. "Yes, Your Majesty," he confirmed.

"Excellent," Ephren said, clasping his hands together. "You're the man I need, Commander. You see, I require Captain Deckard and his team for a personal job. As such, I need you to remove them from whatever assignments they're currently posted to and place them under my direct authority."

Evylin's mouth fell open, and Deckard's hand tightened on hers.

A personal job for the King of Ephria? Could that be any less dangerous than Ostwatch? Or it might be something far less exciting, like being on his personal guard. Either way, it would save Deckard, and working for the king would surely lead them on a grander adventure than either she or Ryen ever imagined—and they imagined quite a lot.

Commander Estham hesitated. "Your Majesty, I'm afraid their officers will be relying on them to fulfill their posts. It will be an awful lot of work for their reassignments. And I'm not even sure what those assignments are, not knowing of all the men involved."

"Carlile," King Ephren prompted.

Lord Carlile stepped forward, a letter in his hand. "Captain Deckard, would you confirm these names?" he asked, unfolding the paper.

Deckard and Evylin stared at the list:

> *By decree of King Willem Ephren, the below listed are the official*
> *members of his personal squadron, for the service of Ephria in the*
> *Order of the King, and are, therefore, excused from all other prior*
> *engagements or assignments forthwith:*
> *Captain Jonn Deckard, General Hewitt Glaas, Lieutenant Thom*
> *Deckard, Private Dunstin Rafferty, Private Ethenn Loxley, and Mrs.*
> *Evylin Deckard.*

Surprised to see her name listed alongside the men's, Evylin looked up at Deckard. "That's correct," he said, eyes wide.

Carlile handed the page to Commander Estham.

"Thank you, milord," the officer said begrudgingly. "I cannot guarantee how quickly their reassignments will take place, Your Majesty. It may be difficult to replace them."

"They start their work with me in the morning, Estham," the king said. "Be sure it's done by then."

"Of course, Your Majesty," Commander Estham said, bowing his head. "May I be of any further assistance?"

"Yes, actually," Ephren said as though an idea had struck him. "If they are all working for me now, they should have a promotion, don't you think? What would be your next advancement, Captain?"

Deckard's voice came out unsure. "Lieutenant colonel, Your Majesty."

Pursing his lips, the king frowned. "*Lieutenant* colonel?" He shook his head. "No, that won't do. Commander, make Deckard here a full-blown colonel. No need to modify his importance."

Commander Estham turned beet red, mute at the two-rank promotion.

"Oh, and furthermore," King Ephren said, giving Evylin a sly grin, "as the lovely Mrs. Deckard will be joining the team, let's make it official. I think Private Deckard sounds appropriate."

Evylin's heart stopped. He couldn't mean it, could he? Her, a soldier?

"Your Majesty?" Commander Estham gasped, fumbling with his words. "But—but, Majesty, she's a woman."

"Excellent eye," King Ephren said. "Was it the dress or the figure inside of it that gave it away?"

"I don't mean to contradict you, Your Majesty, but it's illegal for a woman to serve in the Ephrian Army."

"I'm aware of my own laws, thank you, Commander. But missus—my apologies, *Private* Deckard won't be serving in the Ephrian Army. She and the men on that page will be serving me directly as part of my—oh, what did I call it, Carlile? That bloody thing those Calders suggested?"

"The Order of the King, Your Majesty," Carlile supplied.

"Yes, yes, that's it." Ephren nodded, beaming again. "My Order. So you see, Commander, your concern has no bearing as Private Deckard won't be serving you or any of your men."

The commander's eyes flickered to Deckard and Evylin. "Yes, Your Majesty, as you say."

"Good!" Ephren waved his hand dismissively. "I'm done with you for now."

As Commander Estham retreated, King Ephren smiled at Evylin and Deckard. "I take it by your stunned silence that you're both pleased. You should be." He began to walk toward the palace, and they quickly followed after him. "I have a special task I need taken care of, and it requires a team of people I can trust. As you proved your worth to Caspar and Carlile, I believe your team contains the right people for the job. So long as you don't let me down, I'll be sure to keep you happy, healthy, and in all other ways successful. Does that sound like something you're willing to do?"

Not sure they had a choice, even should they want it, Evylin nodded while Deckard said, "It's an honor to serve, Your Majesty, regardless of our profits. That is why we joined the army in the first place."

King Ephren laughed. "Nonsense! No one joins for any such altruistic reason. For money? To run from something or someone? To live out some fantasy? All those are likely. But to serve? Never."

They moved back inside and away from the cold night air. "Carlile, be sure to have my men pick up the colonel and his team tomorrow morning," Ephren instructed, then grinned at them. "We'll discuss the job in more detail then. The important thing is that I'm placing Ephria's future in your hands. We may be able to end this war yet."

"Father!" Prince Ephren called, hurrying over to them. Dressed in a brilliant red frock coat with silver braiding, he looked dashing. He put a hand on his father's shoulder, eyeing Evylin. "Look, you found them. Isn't she magnificent?"

King Ephren pulled away from his son. "Of course, I found them. That's why they're here," he grumbled.

"My dear woman, it's a true pleasure to see you again," the prince said, a sly glint twinkling in his eyes. "Don't you look every bit the Ephrian rose too? That's a gorgeous dress. It does you justice."

Evylin backed closer to Deckard. "Thank you, Your Highness," she said meekly.

"Caspar, leave the woman alone," King Ephren commanded. "She works for me now, and I won't have you harassing her. Colonel, might I suggest you take your wife and enjoy the evening? I find women delight in a few dozen dances in the order of a party. I look forward to meeting with you and your team in the morning."

With that, the king dismissed them, and Carlile bid them farewell. Hand in hand, Deckard and Evylin shuffled through the buffeting crowd, which carried them back to the ballroom. They stood against the wall, watching the dancers, silent as they processed the king's words.

Evylin couldn't quite comprehend the day's events. Within twelve hours, she'd gone from entering the city filled with hope to the devastating impending loss of Deckard, to the excitement of the party, and now she felt utter confusion as everything shifted once more. She couldn't even say what it was that had happened. The king had chosen them for some manner of task—that she understood—but he'd given so little information, all she could seem to remember was that he'd made her into a private.

The first female soldier in Ephrian history.

"I don't know what just happened," Deckard whispered, his eyes on the dancers.

Evylin laughed in shock. "Me neither."

A heartbeat passed between them.

"Well . . ." He pulled away from the wall and offered his hand. "I suppose we ought to do as our king commanded and dance."

With a bright smile, Evylin took his hand. He led her to the dance floor, set his other hand on her waist, and guided her into the dance with the other couples. The up-tempo beat carried their feet across the floor in a waltz. Evylin's heart fluttered as she stared up at him. This was it, wasn't it? They were about to embark on a grand adventure. In a shocking turn of events, her promise to Ryen would be fulfilled, all while she remained at Deckard's side.

It was everything she'd ever wanted.

This was it.

Her "more."

The beat sped up with the next song, and Evylin's thoughts dissolved into movement. Deckard's hand held securely onto her waist as he whirled her around the room. It felt like their dance in the camp, but she had more control now, unencumbered by drink. Her senses weren't dull this time—they were alive and excited. Ready to feel every step, every spin, and every touch.

Just like when she fought.

Just like when he kissed her.

Deckard's grip on her tightened with the decrescendo. He drew her close as the orchestra's strings carried into the next dance with a slow, swaying rhythm. A ballad Evylin felt sure she'd heard before drew their steps closer and made their turns gentler.

Deckard's eyes turned a light blue in the brilliant atmosphere, and Evylin's hand slid onto his shoulder. "Is this a dream?" she whispered.

"It very well may be," he replied dazedly. "There's a good chance we'll wake up to discover it was all a hoax. But I can't see why the king would lie to us. We did save his son. And while I don't know that it merits appointing us to his personal Order—whatever that means—I certainly know this: If it keeps me from going to Ostwatch, I'll do whatever he asks."

"Well, then," she smiled, drawing closer, "I suppose I'll stay with you a little longer."

His soft laugh tickled her neck. "I'm glad to hear it."

Resting her temple against his cheek, Evylin reveled in his nearness. While the rush had been subdued, she could still feel the spike in her senses with him this close. His touch sent tingles along her spine with the same feeling as when she narrowly escaped a sword strike. A coolness settled over her mind as the heat from his skin melded into hers, the sensation much like the focus Hewitt taught her to harness when going into a fight. The world around her glowed with a steady pulse, every sound, sight, and smell blending in perfect harmony.

The music slowed to a halt, and their feet stopped along with it. The audience clapped as the musicians prepped for another song, but Evylin didn't want to draw away. She wanted to stay in Deckard's arms so she could experience this feeling a bit longer.

But he pulled back, and the moment broke.

"I know we haven't even reached half a dozen dances," he said. "But would you mind sitting this one out? I'm afraid dancing is a thirsty business."

Evylin chuckled lightly. "I will attempt to tame my disappointment."

Deckard led her back to the table of food and drinks, and Evylin felt her stomach grumble. Dancing was a fine way to heighten her sense of being alive, but the hundreds of delicious foods to sample were almost equal to the task. For the next half hour, they basked in the luxurious spread, eating rich cheeses, buttery bread, smoked meats, sundry pickled offerings, sweet fruits, sparkling wine, and all other manner of magnificent fare.

After having their fill, they took a seat to rest their feet and their heavy stomachs. However, it wasn't long before Evylin demanded he take her back to the dance floor. Never in all her years had she experienced a party so splendid, and she refused to waste a second. And though they didn't reach a dozen dances altogether, when she felt she'd enjoyed herself to the fullest, she tugged Deckard toward the door.

"Right away, milady," Deckard replied teasingly.

In short order, they were in their carriage and on the road home. Though bundled in her coat, scarf, and gloves, she pressed into Deckard's side on the bench. The cold night fogged the carriage windows. She slipped her fingers into her pocket, touching the edge of the everbloom's paper. "Did he really make me a private?" she asked.

"As impossible as it is to believe," he looked down at her, "he did."

Evylin smiled, taking his hand. "And you're a colonel."

"Nearly as impossible," he said with a scoff. "It hardly feels justifiable—skipping an entire rank to make me sound more special. That's as bad as finding a loophole in his own law to make you a soldier."

"You don't think he should have done it? Either of them?"

"He's the king," he replied matter-of-factly. "He can do as he pleases, but . . . the laws are there for a reason. Shouldn't they mean something?"

Evylin wasn't sure. Laws were strange to her. She didn't resent them, but neither did she heed them all. If she felt their control unnecessarily prohibitive, she simply ignored them. As Deckard would take exception to the morality of such behavior, she kept those thoughts to herself.

Tapping their clasped hands against his leg, she moved on to a more entertaining topic. "What do you think the job will be?" she asked.

Deckard's expression grew even more contemplative. "Originally, I wondered if it might be a role as a personal guard for the royal family. But then he said that thing about the war . . . It must be more involved than guard duty."

"Do you think he'll commission us to find others like Tybaalt? Members of the nobility who are traitors?"

"Perhaps."

"Or what if he asks us to sneak into Wauld and assassinate their highest-ranking officers and politicians? Or even the king," Evylin suggested, remembering the plot line to *Justice from the Nether*, an amusing but gratuitous novel she'd once read.

Deckard grimaced. "I certainly hope not. That would hardly be any less dangerous than Ostwatch."

"But you'd take it over Ostwatch, wouldn't you?"

"I would," he said, the faint glow from the lanterns outside the carriage lighting his face as he raised his brow. "Not that I'd feel comfortable rejecting the king's offer even should he ask us to kill ourselves on the spot."

Evylin considered his words. The king had to know they couldn't deny him. Would that mean they'd want to refuse?

"Are you worried?" she asked warily.

"No," he said and squeezed her hand. "Whatever our fate, I'm not going back to Ostwatch. And if I die, at least it will be in an effort to save our kingdom rather than due to some senseless raid."

The carriage rumbled to a stop, and the footman opened the door. Deckard helped Evylin to step down as the carriage rolled away down the cobblestones, leaving them by their front door.

Evylin watched as Deckard pulled out his key. "If nothing else, we know one thing for certain."

The lock clicked, and Deckard turned to her. "What's that?"

Coming to stand close to him, Evylin looked up into his green-blue eyes. "I won't be a widow after all," she said fondly.

Deckard hesitated, lips parting and breath turning to fog between them. "It seems you won't," he whispered.

The seconds ticked by as they waited in silence for the other to move or speak, gauging whether the other really meant it. Evylin couldn't form words to tell him her thoughts. She didn't want words anyway.

Reaching for the lapels of his coat, Evylin thought to pull him in and kiss him. He beat her to it, leaning toward her as she angled up to him. The kiss didn't last long, but when he pulled back, their breath mingled as their eyes searched each other's.

Deckard drew back a little more, an expectant expression on his face. "Evylin . . ." He whispered her name like a question, but she pressed her fingers to his lips. She didn't need him to clarify what he meant. She understood perfectly.

In that instant, with her newfound commitment to their marriage, Evylin decided it was high time they consummated the damn thing. She held his gaze unflinchingly and breathed back, "Yes."

Deckard's arm slipped around her waist, pulling her close for another kiss. His left hand cupped the back of her neck, fingers lacing into her hair. The kiss went on, slow and steady, both testing and hopeful.

Evylin returned his advances fervently, and Deckard backed her into the doorframe as they grew more passionate. His hand withdrew from her hair and searched blindly until he found the knob. The door flew wide, and they moved into the house, bumping into the frame.

Their lips only parted for seconds at a time, adjusting and improving the kisses. Once they'd made it across the threshold, Deckard reached around and swung the door shut with a *thud*. His hands framed her face, keeping her close as he deepened their kiss.

Evylin's heartbeat surged to an unbelievable rate, her body reacting with that familiar rush. Clarity enveloped her mind, sharpening everything around her: the soft glow of oil lamps in the entrance hall, the scent of aftershave balm on his jaw, the taste of wine on his lips, the fabric brushing between them, and the tingle of his fingertips on her skin.

They kissed with increasing desire, their mingled breath coming out short. He unhooked the buttons on her coat, and she yanked off her gloves, letting them fall to the floor. Next came her scarf. Deckard flung her coat toward the rack. The next moment, his was gone too. His hands were at her lower back again, pressing her against him, and Evylin let him pull her into the parlor, arms around his neck, still locked in a deep kiss.

"Good evening to you as well," said a voice suddenly.

Deckard pulled away from Evylin, practically shoving her out of his arms. She gasped for air, whirling to see who had interrupted them.

There, on the wingback chair, Hewitt sat, smirking. Thom sat on the couch, gaping in disgust.

"Uncle," Evylin exclaimed, pressing the back of her hand to wipe at her mouth.

Deckard cleared his throat, hands behind his back. "Thom," he muttered.

"I would apologize for my absence," Hewitt said dryly, "but it seems you two made the most of it."

They averted their gazes, inching farther from each other.

"As it is," he continued, "I've been keeping Thom company the past couple of hours. We got your note about being out, Deckard, and decided to wait up."

"Our apologies," Deckard said.

"For which part?" Thom asked irritably. "Making us wait to try and save your life or for barreling in here like that?"

"Both."

Thom scowled.

"Take it easy," Hewitt said casually. "They're losing more than you." He turned back to Deckard. "In case you're curious, I did what I could for you. I spent the entire day talking to my old pals and fellow officers. All the ones who *should* be on my side. They were perfectly happy to ensure any assignment I wanted. But once they learned I wanted *you* reassigned, they all backed out. Rand is a real piece of work. Unfortunately, you'll be going to Ostwatch, and there's nothing I can do about that."

Deckard overcame his discomfort, his shoulders drawing back as he met Hewitt's gaze. "I appreciate your attempt, genuinely," he assured him. "But it seems that it's all taken care of."

Hewitt narrowed his eyes, and Deckard explained their invitation and meeting with the king. When he was through, Thom sat with his chin propped in his hand while Hewitt began to pace before the fireplace. "That's all he said, eh? It'll end the war?" Hewitt asked.

"That was the insinuation," Deckard confirmed. "He said we'd get the rest of the information in the morning."

"That's . . ." Thom scoffed. "That's incredible. And they're promoting us all?"

"Apparently."

Hewitt started pulling on his beard. "The king is an ineffectual sort of ruler. I wouldn't take much stock in his version of ending the war. But it doesn't seem we have much of a choice. Whatever the job, we'll have to take it."

"Why wouldn't we want to?" Thom asked. "It'll save Jonn's life and make us all impossibly rich. What could be better?"

"I don't trust a monarch's benevolence," he replied. "They don't give *anything* away for nothing. And I worry that this 'something' will be more than we bargained for."

"You're right," Deckard agreed. "But this is the answer to a prayer, and I'm grateful for it no matter what we learn in the morning."

Hewitt and Thom eyed him, but neither had anything to add.

Evylin tugged on her rings. Normally, she would have been happy to discuss the new assignment. But disappointment welled in her chest, and all she wanted was to slip back into the rush she'd felt with Deckard moments ago. Yet, standing here in the presence of her uncle and his brother, it seemed as if a lake as large as the one in Banbury was back between them.

"It's been a long day," Evylin said quietly. "I think I'll be off now."

Deckard gave her one of his warmest smiles. "I'll get Hewitt settled and be right up."

"Thom already showed my room to me," Hewitt said, then nudged his chin in the direction of the stairs. "You two go."

They said their goodnights, and though they walked up the stairs hand in hand, Evylin felt the awkwardness settling too heavily between them. Heat spread along the back of her neck, thinking of how they must have looked in front of Hewitt and Thom. They couldn't continue now. Not when both men downstairs knew what could be happening.

They readied themselves for bed, backs turned to one another as usual. She pulled the paper from her pocket, hiding the everbloom flower under the stack of notes on her nightstand. Then she shimmied off her dress. She glanced over her shoulder once, catching a quick glimpse of his bare back. She smiled bashfully and pulled her nightdress over her head.

When they were both ready, they turned and slid under the blankets. The bed gave them more space than ever before, but Deckard pulled her close and kissed her forehead. "Goodnight, Evie," he whispered.

"Goodnight, Jonn." Evylin laid her head on his chest, knowing that even if the moment had ended, it wasn't for good. He wasn't going to Ostwatch, and she wouldn't need to break her promise. They would have their adventure and each other. No need to rush anything.

PART III: Order of the King

With his very essence, he graced us.
With element and existent; with wisdom and might.
Author unknown, from an ancient text found in the ruins of Aulton

How can we suffer these blasphemers to live? They claim equality with the Creator Divine. Heresy!
They are false gods with selfish ambition. And we shall bleed their evil from the soil of our land.
Tavish Ephren, the first king of Ephria, circa 1388

NORHELS
HELSFORD
Newfourd
Ephria City
LOCLIGHT
HARTFOLLEY
VERIA
TINDON
AARGE
COTASIS

CHAPTER FIFTY-ONE

2ND OF GALATAE, 1574

"Bloody hell," Thom muttered, stepping out of the carriage under the palace's shadow. "This place is frightening."

Deckard helped Evylin descend next. She stepped to Thom's side and scanned the grand building. The creamy stone looked somber in the overcast morning. Its hundreds of windows were like mirrors, reflecting the world around them. A servant waited at the top of the stairs while guards flanked the doors and walked the perimeter. On the lawn, gardeners trimmed hedges and cleared the last remains of the Annaltide decorations.

"Have you never seen it before?" Evylin asked.

"Never this close," Thom said, still staring.

"It's stone and mortar," Hewitt said flatly. He started up the stairs. "Like any other building."

Thom scoffed. "Ah, yes," he said dryly. "Just like our farmhouse back home."

At the palace doors, the servant guided them through the empty, echoing halls. Without the clutter of partygoers, it somehow felt even more imposing and regal. The rooms seemed larger with the festive decor removed, leaving them stiff in their courtly appearance. They passed down a corridor Evylin hadn't seen last night. Portraits of men lined one wall—almost two centuries of Ephrian kings.

At the end of the hall stood large and elaborate wooden doors. Two guards waited on either side, along with Ethenn and Rafferty. The weasel leaned against the wall, his fingers tapping madly on his thigh, while the young soldier paced across the plush rug. Upon their arrival, they hurried over to greet them.

"This is it, isn't it?" Rafferty said excitedly. "They came to the barracks this morning and said the king requested to see us. And I knew—I just bloody knew—we're about to get our reward."

Ethenn came up beside him, a hopeful expression on his boyish face. "I told him to calm down," he promised. "Even if he is right, I can't imagine the king would look kindly on him asking for a duchy."

"Why not?" Rafferty exclaimed. "We saved his son from a traitorous earl. Why wouldn't he want to replace the ungrateful sods in his nobility?"

Evylin laughed. "I think you're a little off the mark there. Though perhaps only a little."

The men exchanged glances.

"Only a *little*?" Ethenn repeated.

"Perhaps."

Rafferty's silver eyes glittered greedily as the guards opened the doors. Their troop turned as one, nerves bubbling in Evylin's stomach. Whatever awaited them on the other side of those doors would be a mystery no longer. They were about to embark on something wonderfully unknown.

Evylin brushed her fingers along her skirt, feeling the pressed everbloom paper in her pocket. Their escort walked through ahead of them to announce their arrival. "Colonel Deckard, General Glaas, Captain Deckard, Corporal Rafferty, Corporal Loxley, and Private Deckard to see King Ephren on his invitation."

Hewitt glared at the servant as they walked past. "I'm a trainer, son. My proper title is 'Major.'"

"I believe you'll have to take that up with the king," Deckard muttered as they continued into the room.

Laid out in a long, arcing rectangle, the splendorous room glowed in the light from a stained glass window. Vibrant green marble columns and floors led the way to the matching throne. Evylin glanced up, seeing a mural-painted ceiling featuring rolling hills and a powerful, noble-looking man standing in plate armor with a flowing emerald cloak, a shepherd's crook in one hand, and a sword in the other. A whole host of men stood on the hills around him, banners and flags raised in support.

"My friends, my servants." Ephren's deep voice echoed in the hall, drawing her attention back to the throne. "Welcome to my home. Come nearer, please."

At the end of the room, in a flood of pale light, King Ephren rose from his marble throne. He stood on a low dais, a gem-encrusted crown radiant on his white-haired head. On his right was Lord Carlile, smiling back at them. However, Evylin only spared him a momentary smile in greeting as the people on the king's left stole her attention.

The man and woman they'd noticed at the party stood placidly to the side. Young but imperious, they surveyed the oncoming troop with sharp eyes. Their bright red hair was ablaze in the morning light. Based on their youthful appearance yet regal bearing, Evylin guessed the man was older, perhaps by a year or two, though neither of them could have been aged past their twenties.

He wore a long, simply embroidered cream cotton coat with narrow golden closures. It reached his ankles, where dark boots peeped from under the hem. His coppery hair was brushed back behind his ears to hang bluntly beneath his smooth, fiercely cut jawline.

The woman's eye-catching ivory gown perfectly framed her torso, hugging her slim waistline. Its bell-like sleeves sat off the shoulder, and the soft green gemstones of her sparkling necklace drew attention to her low neckline. Deckard would call it improper, but Evylin found it tastefully alluring. Her long, red curls draped around her pale shoulders, the curls burning like fire.

Eyes shifting between the pair, Evylin held her breath as the woman's eyes locked with hers. There was a cunning, wily gleam within them that suggested she knew more about Evylin than Evylin knew about herself.

Tearing her gaze away, Evylin faced the king just as their troop came to a stop. They knelt before the dais, heads bowed respectfully. Evylin watched the king's feet as he paced closer.

"Thank you for coming," he said. "Please, rise."

They did as requested, keeping their gazes lowered.

"As you may have noticed, my court is empty today. That was intentional. I have invited you here to thank you for the service you gave me. On behalf of my son and myself, I hope you will heartily accept this gift."

While servants hurried over, carrying a large trunk, Rafferty elbowed Ethenn. "Told you," he whispered.

King Ephren gestured grandly toward the chest. "A hundred gold crowns each."

Rafferty nearly fell over, jaw-dropping low.

"Money is, of course, a vulgar repayment, but it's a start. However, as you all heard, I have granted a promotion to each of you. This reward is conditional, as I cannot promote you without the proper assignment. The way you saved my son proved that you are capable of far more than the average soldiers. Therefore, I have a job for your little band. If done well, there will be further rewards and promotions. Is that satisfactory to your team, Colonel Deckard?"

"I believe it is, Your Majesty," Deckard said, then paused. "Though I also believe there are questions among us if you'd allow."

King Ephren waved his hand in permission.

Deckard turned to Hewitt. The older man cleared his throat and stepped forward. "We appreciate your generosity, Your Majesty," he said, bowing his head uncharacteristically low. "But I'm afraid your men have the wrong title for me."

"I had Colonel Deckard double-check the list of names," King Ephren said, his eyes narrowing. "Did he get it wrong?"

"Not exactly," Hewitt said. "I was once a general; however, I am now a major."

Ephren glanced at Carlile. "Wasn't he introduced as a general?"

"Yes, Your Majesty."

"And we didn't give him a promotion because . . . ?"

"There is only one rank higher than general, Your Majesty, and that is Commander Estham's position," Lord Carlile replied. "As there can only be one commander in your army, I thought it best to keep General Glaas as a general."

"Pardon my interruption," Hewitt said sharply, "but I'd prefer to keep the rank of major." When Ephren and Carlile looked at him, he added, "Your Majesty."

"Hm." Ephren shrugged. "Well, if you insist. Carlile, make sure the clerks or whoever is in charge of such matters fix the Major General's rank."

Carlile nodded respectfully, and Hewitt gritted his teeth. Holding back her laughter, Evylin couldn't stop her smile. While Hewitt's attempt to deflect the promotion technically succeeded—after all, Major General was lower than General—the king effectively made him one of the three most powerfully ranked officers in the whole army.

Letting the misunderstanding pass, Hewitt said, "I do have a question, Your Majesty." At Ephren's nod, he continued, "What is the job you're offering?"

King Ephren's smile grew sly. "I like you, Major General. You're bold."

"Thank you, Your Majesty."

Ephren glanced at Carlile and the pair on his right with a bright smile. "Well, shall we tell them?" When the redheaded man nodded in deference, the king turned back to the soldiers. "Gentlemen—and lady," he winked at Evylin, then gestured to the siblings, "allow me to introduce you to my guests: Lord and Lady Calder, brother and sister from Wauld."

Evylin shifted uneasily, eyeing the pair with newfound understanding. From the sounds of their titles, Deckard had been correct in assuming their nobility. But they were *Waulden* nobles.

What were the gentry of their enemies doing as guests in King Ephren's palace?

"My friends here have defected from their country, ready to be free of King Blount's unjust tyranny." King Ephren raised his chin with pride. "They believe in our Ephrian cause, having watched the oppression of Blount's reign grow fouler and fouler. They've witnessed firsthand the greed and corruption of his nobility. The citizens of Wauld are starving as his taxes and demands have ravaged the countryside and towns. And they wish to aid us in ending his reign along with the Centurial War."

The troop hesitated, glancing back and forth among each other, the king, and the Calder siblings.

Evylin recognized their shared thoughts. While Ephrians weren't starving, King Ephren's taxes strained them. His demand for soldiers and supplies worsened the situation. The Shires were dwindling and showing no signs of recovery. The rest of the country could hardly be better off. However, King Blount's intentions seemed more sinister, and King Ephren did show concern for his people's suffering.

"Lord and Lady Calder brought news from their country," Ephren continued. "They have a great opportunity for us, one that will allow us to smite the Waulden assaults for good." He donned a self-congratulatory smile, scanning the soldiers. "And that's where you all come in. From this moment forward, I am hiring you six to be part of the Order of the King. You will be my personal squadron, tasked with only the most important work in the pursuit of keeping our kingdom safe. And your first assignment will be working with the Calders to end this war."

Evylin's hands trembled at her sides, and she gripped the pressed everbloom flower through her skirt. She couldn't believe it. The King of Ephria was tasking them as his personal Order, assigned with a mission to save their nation. It was more than she and Ryen had ever imagined.

Deckard stepped forward, head dipping humbly again. "Forgive me, Your Majesty, but what exactly does this mission entail?"

King Ephren turned to the Calders. "Would you like to explain it, or shall I?"

The siblings, caught in a whispered exchange, drew up to face the king. The woman patted her brother's arm, and he stepped forward, head dipped in a humble nod. He was quite tall, nearly towering over the monarch. "It'd be my pleasure, King Ephren," he said, his mellow voice accented strangely. It made his words round and melodic, like a countryside reel.

The Waulden man faced the group, clasping one of his wrists before him. "It might seem odd," he said kindly, "the idea that two people could topple the Waulden monarchy. People who are so seemingly young too. But it'd be a mistake to underestimate us because of our appearances. Our positions in Wauld have granted us the opportunity to learn things—vital things that can cause great damage to the monarchy and its supporters."

Behind him, his sister cleared her throat. He glanced back, and she muttered something softly. Then he nodded bashfully.

"My apologies," he said, turning back to them. "My sister tells me I'm being too mysterious. I'll try to be clearer. My sister and I are Mages."

Evylin's heart skipped a beat. A gasp of disbelieving laughter burst out of her, and Deckard took a reflective step closer to her side. Hewitt and Thom grew tense, ready for action. Rafferty gaped excitedly while Ethenn watched warily.

"I know," Lord Calder said amusedly. "That's quite a thing to say in front of the Ephrian king and some of his most loyal soldiers. But the fact remains, that's what we are."

"There is no such thing as Mages," Hewitt growled. "They're a legend."

The Waulden man was unconcerned. "Legends are born somewhere, Major General. It just so happens that while Ephria chose to forget about us, Wauld kept us alive." He looked to King Ephren. "Graciously, your king chose to listen to us, though the past generations of Ephrian kings would have killed us on sight. And now, we will help you bring King Blount to justice and end this war."

"Why would you want to do that?" Thom asked boldly. "You said it yourself: Ephria doesn't support Mages. If you bring down your homeland, you bring down yourself."

The Calder sister smirked, her silky hair flickering like flames in the sunlight. "Sacrifices are necessary when you want to see the world change, Captain," she said, her voice deeper than Evylin expected. "And once Ephria sees how useful we can be, perhaps they'll give us a second chance."

"What if we won't?" Thom ventured.

The Waulden woman turned to King Ephren.

"The Calders and I have spoken at length," Ephren said. "And I believe their intentions are honorable. In exchange for their aid, I promised them the safety of their people. So long as they stay within Wauld's half of the continent."

"Which we are more than happy to do," Lord Calder promised. "All we want is to keep our people—Mages or otherwise—safe."

Deckard looked back at Evylin questioningly.

She shrugged, unsure what answers she could provide. She hardly believed she was awake. All those years of novels and childhood stories, she'd believed that Mages were a myth: villains for the tales, threats to keep your children on best behavior, shadows of adventure that could never be.

"How do we know you're actually Mages?" Evylin asked, surprising herself and everyone else. "You could be spies from Wauld attempting to infiltrate."

The Calders met her stare, intrigued, but it was the king who spoke. "I have ascertained the verity of their powers," Ephren said. "And secured their promise that they would not practice their heresy while here in my palace."

Worried the king might have fallen for a parlor trick, Evylin looked to Lord Carlile. The advisor dipped his chin in affirmation. He believed the siblings too. Evylin turned back to Deckard with a bemused but approving look.

Releasing a deep breath, he faced King Ephren. "We are at your service, Your Majesty."

"Splendid!" King Ephren motioned to the Wauldeners. "The Calders have discovered ancient relics of great power. If we can collect these relics, we will have enough strength to defeat King Blount, undeniably, and Wauld will never be able to contest our right to be a separate nation again." He took a step toward the team. "You will join them. This is a dangerous task, and for all their magic, they cannot succeed on their own. Beyond that, we can't have two Mages running about the country unchecked. No offense."

"None taken, Your Majesty," Lord Calder assured.

King Ephren turned his attention back to the troop. "You will protect the Calders and keep an eye on them as they redeem these relics. Whatever it takes, I want them brought back and set in my hands. Then we can send our reserves home and return to life the way my forefathers intended."

"In league with Mages this time," Thom muttered accusatorily.

King Ephren didn't appear to hear. "What say, you all? Will you aid your king and country to end the Centurial War?"

The heavy-handed request could not be denied. To say no to saving your country might be acceptable to some—especially if you didn't believe in the path laid out before you. But Deckard was right; saying no to the king meant suicide. There was no refusal. And staring up at the Calders, Evylin worried they were getting themselves into something far more dangerous than Ostwatch could ever be.

Deckard bowed his head. "Your Majesty, it would be our honor to serve you."

The rest of the team followed Deckard's lead, dropping their heads, but Evylin continued to watch the Calders. The woman whispered to her brother, her eyes on Deckard. The man narrowed his gaze, then shook his head, whispering something back.

"Wonderful!" King Ephren exclaimed, oblivious to their mutterings. He motioned to his servants again. "In that case, here's a final gift."

The servants rushed forward, paper boxes in their arms. They handed one to each soldier and backed away.

"Open them, open them," Ephren insisted.

Evylin lifted the lid. Inside the box was a dark gray wool coat with a military cut featuring a high collar and double-breasted buttons. However, unlike the simple design of typical army coats, this one showcased fine, black braiding across the front and intricate silver buttons. The same braiding decorated the collars and cuffs of the sleeves. On the left breast was a small silver and emerald insignia displaying a crook and a sword—the mark of a private. Above the emblem, "Order of the King" was stitched into the patch.

Evylin ran her fingers along the textured design. She looked over to find Deckard watching her with a gentle smile on his face. She was officially the first female soldier in Ephria, whether a member of the greater army or not. A feat of legends.

"You all seem adequately pleased," King Ephren said cheerily. "Now, I believe you have much to discuss. Time is, of course, of the essence in saving our country. The more days that go by, the more men who go with it. Therefore, it would be wise for you to leave first thing tomorrow. Do you believe that is possible, Colonel Deckard?"

Deckard fought for words. "We will do our best, Your Majesty," he promised, his eyes flickering to the Calders. "But I'm afraid I can't make that decision until I know our destination."

King Ephren turned to the Mages. "Do you see any reason why tomorrow should be a difficulty?"

"No, Your Majesty," Lord Calder replied.

"Then you see to it, Colonel," Ephren said. He gestured to Carlile. "And you see that anything they need is provided. Keep me apprised of all their plans and update me as they progress. This is more vital than any other effort."

The king turned back to the soldiers. "You are our salvation, you know? My Order of the King." He chuckled and looked to the Calders. "I must say, that grows on you. Excellent idea, my lady."

"Anytime, Your Majesty," Lady Calder said dryly.

King Ephren didn't wait for any further responses. "We will win this war yet!" He gave them all a proud nod. "Enjoy your planning."

With that, the king disappeared through a door to the right of the throne, leaving the rest of them to stare at one another.

Lord Carlile cleared his throat, drawing the group's attention. "If you'd follow me," he said, his full lips turned up in a smile, "we can get started."

CHAPTER FIFTY-TWO

Fear claimed Deckard's stomach, twisting it into an unsettled knot. The very concept of Mages made him uneasy. Even their presence in books gave him the most disquieting sense of alarm. Now that he knew they were real, his gut and head seemed at perpetual odds.

Get out while you can, his instincts told him.

You don't have a choice in the matter, his logic argued.

His heart, resting somewhere in between, urged him to tread cautiously. They couldn't refuse the king's offer, but neither did they have to fall for the Calder siblings' villainy.

Lord Carlile led them through the palace's halls to a grand sitting room. Long and narrow, the room was filled with emerald velveteen chairs and couches. An elaborately carved fireplace roared with a cheery fire, beckoning them to its hearth. The walls were covered in intricate paneling, and a massive stained glass window let in a wash of colorful light.

"You'll find maps and parchment there," Carlile said, gesturing to the circular table near the fireplace. "And if you need anything else, I'll be happy to assist."

Deckard thanked the advisor while the team funneled in behind the Calders. The woman, a gaudy display of jewels and silks, took a seat on the couch nearest the fire. "Everything is so green in Ephria," she noted, smiling at her brother. "It makes me think of Vayden."

Standing behind her, the Waulden man scanned the verdant room. Then he gave the soldiers a reserved smile. "Our brother," he explained. "Green is his favorite color."

Deckard watched the siblings curiously. They didn't appear dangerous or wicked. But a wolf hid in sheep's clothing often in the children's tales. And the stories always depicted Mages as evil, selfish creatures. At least, all the books he'd read. Evylin said she'd read heroic retellings of Mages, which seemed an oxymoron.

Glancing at his wife, Deckard noticed a sparkle of interest in her eyes as she studied the Calders. She seemed excited rather than concerned. His stomach grew more unsettled.

While Carlile sat at the side of the room, the Calders watched the reticent soldiers. They stood near the door, uncertain and uncomfortable.

Lady Calder laughed. "You can all relax," she said, her accent musical. "My brother and I may be Mages, but we won't steal your souls."

Taking the initiative, Deckard moved to the couch opposite the siblings. Evylin sat beside him, a stark contrast to the Waulden woman across from her. Evylin was tan and brown, whereas the lady was pale and red. Evylin wore a simple blouse and skirt, while the lady wore an elegant, provocative gown. It seemed to Deckard that Lady Calder was all flash and Evylin was all substance.

Thom took the seat next to Evylin, and Hewitt stood behind them, Ethenn at his side. Rafferty lounged in a chair a few feet away, beaming enthusiastically.

The Calders glanced at one another.

"Well, this is cozy," Lady Calder said with sarcasm. "Shall we dispense with formalities? If we're to spend the next untold months of our lives together, it will do us little good to stand on ceremony or titles."

Deckard cocked his head. "I beg your pardon, my lady, but I do my best to treat nobility with the respect they're due."

She snorted. "Well, that's the first thing you'll need to learn, Jonn," she said and raised a ginger eyebrow. "Mages aren't noble. We're granted our titles because of our power, not our blood."

Deckard was so unaccustomed to being called by his given name that he gaped as she continued. "We aren't landed gentry, and we aren't appointed by the king. In fact, we aren't rightly lord and lady of anything."

"What she means," her brother interjected, "is that His Majesty, King Ephren, misunderstands our titles. We know your names and ranks, but allow us to properly introduce ourselves; that way, we'll be on equal footing, yes?"

As none of the Ephrians objected, the Waulden man set a hand to his chest. "I am Highlord Auden Calder, Magister in the Order of the Flame. This is my sister, Highlady Ilain Calder, ViceMage in the same Order."

"You make me sound mundane when you don't say the full thing," Ilain noted.

Auden sighed, tugging at his high collar. "ViceMage in the Order of the Flame and Pyra's bloody Heiress. Grand enough?"

"I'm gratified," she bantered.

Deckard and Evylin exchanged a bemused look as Auden returned to his introduction. "We left our home because no one there is willing to stand up to our king," he said passionately. "We abandoned our posts in the Order to change that."

The emotion in Auden Calder's eyes could not be denied. He meant his words more than most people meant anything. No matter their heresy, it appeared the Calders were genuine. But that didn't mean he trusted them.

"Order of the Flame?" Ethenn prompted quietly. His neck flushed red when they all turned to him.

"Yes," Ilain confirmed.

"That's an awful lot like the Order of the King," he noted.

"Indeed, it is. Clever catch."

Ethenn blushed some more, looking away.

Ilain folded her bejeweled hands in her lap. "It was, in fact, a fine little suggestion I made. And King Ephren liked using the term in mockery of our institutions."

"And you approve of that?" Deckard asked.

"He may see it as a mockery," Auden said. "We see it as an honor. We aren't part of Wauld's Orders anymore—we created our own."

Ilain's eyes glimmered. "That's where you all come in."

"I don't buy it," Thom said sharply. He leaned forward and glared at the siblings. "If you two are such powerful Mages, why do you need us?"

"Which do you believe less?" Auden asked. "That we want to help Ephria? Or that we're Mages at all?"

"Why not both?"

Deckard frowned at his brother. "King Ephren trusts them, and it's our job to do the same," he said, though he didn't intend to put his faith in them at all.

"Actually," Thom returned, "it's our job to keep an eye on them. That doesn't suggest deep, abiding trust."

"Trust us or not," Ilain cut in, "we are what we say. Defectors and Mages." She lifted a bare shoulder in a playful shrug. "And we'd be more than happy to appease your curiosities."

"Lain, don't," Auden said, his eyes flickering to Lord Carlile.

Ilain waved a hand. "Vincente won't tell on us, now, will you?"

"What would there be to tell, milady?" Carlile replied, grinning.

"See?" Ilain turned back to the team. "How might we prove ourselves to you? What example of power would ensure your belief?"

No one said anything. Whether it was because no one knew what to ask for or whether they were too scared to speak up, Deckard wasn't quite sure. He himself didn't know what abilities a Mage held. The tales spoke of their great power, but Ephren banned the literature detailing their magic.

"Order of the Flame," Evylin said. She raised her brow. "You're . . . a Fire Mage?"

A cunning smile filled Ilain's face. "I am," she said huskily.

Evylin's eyes widened in hopeful awe. "You can control fire?"

The woman lifted a finger. "Oh, I can do so much more, Evylin. I can manipulate it—" She gestured with her hand, and the flames in the fireplace leaped. "I can summon it—" She raised the other hand, and a singular plume blossomed on her upturned palm. "*And I can control it.*"

With her last words, the flame grew, twisting its way around her hand until it flickered over her skin like a glove, causing her rings to glitter and her eyes to shine.

Deckard's throat was dry, his eyes locked on the magic, equally intrigued and terrified. He blinked, worried for his sanity. It shouldn't be possible. . . .

Ilain dropped her hand to her lap, the flame extinguished. "Satisfactory?"

"That's incredible!" Evylin gasped.

Ilain pursed her lips dismissively. "It's menial, but I suppose it's nice if you've never seen it before." She turned to Thom. "We are powerful Mages, yes. But we are also unfamiliar with Ephria, and there are only two of us. To find and retrieve the Ateri Relics, we'll need help."

"Ateri?" Deckard asked.

"It means power in the ancient Allminian Gaelic," Auden explained.

"Allminian?"

The Calders frowned. "Hm," Ilain said. "We'll have to fix that. In the meantime, just know these Relics were sacred religious artifacts the ancient Mages locked away in magical Keeps to protect them from the would-be evildoers of the world."

The troop stared blankly at this odd influx of information.

Hewitt crossed his arms and asked, "Why are these Relics in Ephria?"

"Mages once lived in the East too," Auden said, then added, "But they're not *all* in Ephria. There are four here and three back in Wauld."

"We're not going to Wauld," Hewitt growled.

Lord Carlile cleared his throat, drawing their attention. "King Ephren does require all the Relics," he noted, "even those in Wauld."

Hewitt's knuckles grew white on the back of the couch. "That's a bloody suicide mission."

"Not if we have the first two Relics," Ilain said calmly. "With you by our side, we should be able to get both of those in short order. Then we'll go to Wauld and collect the next three there."

"If it's so easy," Thom mocked, "why didn't you just get them before coming here?"

Ilain eyed him haughtily. "Darling, don't speak about things you don't understand. It makes you sound dim-witted."

Thom snarled, and Rafferty sniggered.

"As I said," Ilain continued, "the Relics are held in magical Keeps, protected by magical constructs. While Auden and I are quite powerful, we are not invincible. And to enter the Keeps unaided—*that* is suicide."

"If these Relics are so powerful," Evylin said thoughtfully, "why hasn't anyone recovered them before now?"

"There are a myriad of reasons," Auden replied. "Mostly, it's because no one knew where they were. The ancient Mages hid their locations in riddles, ciphers, codes, and puzzles. You have to unlock the first clue to reach the second, and so on. It's detailed, exhaustive work, and no one has been able to unravel the truth until . . . Well, until me."

Deckard raised his brow. "You deciphered their locations?"

Auden shrugged bashfully. "I'm a magister. It's our job to be bound up in books and texts. I just used my time less practically than the others."

"Seems perfectly practical now," Deckard remarked, then sighed. "Where are these Relics, then?"

Auden gestured toward the table with the maps. "Let's start with the first one, shall we?"

They all rose to surround the table, though Carlile remained watchful from his chair. Auden pulled a map of Ephria to the top and pointed to the northeastern corner. "The first Relic is here, in Norhels, Helsford. Its Keep will be nearby or possibly in the city. Once we're there, Ilain and I can channel the Relic's magic, guiding us to the Keep, then through its halls and into the Relic's Chamber."

He met Deckard's gaze then, expression dark. "The journey through the Keep will not be easy," he warned. "The Keeps were designed as the ultimate protection. We will have to fight our way to the Chamber where the Relic is held."

"Fight?" Thom asked, frowning. "Fight what?"

"Monsters," Auden said.

Ilain scoffed. "I'd hardly call them monsters," she said with a dismissive flick of her wrist. "They're creatures made of magic designed to defend the Relics. That's not so monstrous."

Deckard's breath caught in his lungs, but he kept his head held high. "This *is* why the king assigned us to work with you," he noted. "We can handle it."

Auden smiled gratefully. "I believe you can."

"What exactly is the point of these Relics?" Hewitt asked tersely. "You said something about religion. Am I to assume they're tied to your heresy?"

Ilain gave him a disappointed frown. "You see," she said wryly, "this is why you Ephrians aren't getting anywhere in this war. You think everyone in Wauld is a lunatic."

She crossed her arms in a mockery of Hewitt's aggressive stance. "No, Major General, they are not tied to the blasphemous Eight. They are, in fact, holy talismans given to the first men by Allore himself, a fragment of his very self. And their purpose is to serve as his divine power here on Terraeus. They are blessings that nourish the terrae, keeping the land safe and thriving. But as they have been hidden for nearly a millennium, magic is decaying, and the planet is dying. So as you claim to be our fellow Allorian, I'd imagine you'll be thrilled to recover these Relics yourself."

In the ensuing silence, Deckard tapped the tabletop. Ilain sounded sincere, but he couldn't believe that Waulden Mages were Allorian. Not when the Centurial War itself began because of their people's heretical faith.

Hewitt's steely glare said he was of the same opinion. "If these Relics are a gift from Allore, why were they locked away?" he demanded.

"Because they were dangerous," Auden said diplomatically. "To hold a Relic is to hold the power of Allore in your hands. That became a temptation for the ancient Mages. And the wisest among them decided to lock them away, protecting the world from any that might do harm."

The Ephrians exchanged worried looks.

Deckard ran a hand over his jaw. "And if we recover them now, don't we face that same problem?" he asked worriedly. "What's to say we aren't ending this war only to unleash a more terrible one in the future?"

Auden and Ilain shared a reluctant glance. Then he said, "Tell me, Jonn: Do you know a better way to overthrow a monarchy? To save not one nation but two? Can you give us a better plan to end a one-hundred-eighty-year war?"

"I cannot," Deckard admitted tightly.

"Then this is a risk we'll have to take."

His statement was met with heavy silence. The Ephrians shifted uncomfortably as the Calders held their chins high, resolute. Deckard trusted them less and less by the second. They were too smart and too manipulative with their words. Even if they were correct, he couldn't help fearing their mission would cause greater harm than good.

But he was a soldier. He'd been given a command by the king himself. He would go with the Calders, recover these Relics, and serve his kingdom, all while keeping a wary eye on these Mages for any sign of treachery.

At the side, Rafferty bounced on his heels. "Soooo," he said, breaking the awkward silence, "what do these Relics look like anyway? Are they, I dunno, expensive-looking?"

"They are each unique," Auden said, tugging at his collar. "Each represents the power within. However, as they've been gone for a millennium, we can't be sure. There *are* sketches and descriptions in many books in the Mages' libraries, though. And most depict them as amulets of some sort."

He paused, holding up a finger, an excited gleam in his eyes. "There are some accounts that show the Relics in the form of weapons. The *Almanac of Elgur* illustrates each Relic in various weapon-like shapes."

"Elgur was an old sot, and you know it," Ilain combated.

"He was a genius."

"He thought Mages should live out their days in isolation to perfect their connection."

Auden sighed. "We all have challenges," he muttered.

Finding himself amused by the sibling interaction, Deckard forced down his smile. Despite being Mages, Auden had a pleasant personality, and Ilain was quick-witted. He'd have to be careful not to let their camaraderie get the best of his judgment.

Turning back to the map, Deckard tapped the first Relic's location. "Norhels is almost a week-long journey," he said. "We'll need to be thoroughly prepared. With eight of us, we can travel light, but going into danger, we don't want to be short on supplies. I'd say we'll need at least three extra horses."

Ilain pushed away from the table. "You deal with the boring stuff, Auden," she said, then set a hand on Evylin's shoulder. "Why don't you join me? I have some questions about Ephrian society."

Though Deckard hesitated, Evylin met his gaze with cautious anticipation. She might be excited, seeing her novels come to life, but she was still wise enough to stay on her guard. He dipped his chin in an encouraging nod, and Evylin went to join Ilain.

While the women conversed, the men began their planning at the table. Deckard, Hewitt, and Thom offered ideas about supplies, discussed strategies for their journey, and asked Auden for a few essential details. The Mage welcomed their input and contributed some suggestions of his own. Not long after, Rafferty wandered over to the women, having grown bored. Ethenn remained close by, listening but frequently casting not-so-subtle glances at the other three.

"Once we've gotten the first Relic," Auden said, sliding his finger from Norhels down the map to Cotaasis Province, "we'll go to the next, here in Virwoud."

Deckard's brow furrowed. He looked at Thom and Hewitt. Could there be a coincidence that the second Relic's location was the prince's destination last month?

Auden shifted the pages, retrieving a secondary map of the western half of the island continent. "From Virwoud, we'll need to go to Wauld." He traced the navy lines of the country. More populous and sizeable than Ephria, though neither by much, it tipped up in the far northwest. That's where Auden pointed next. "Here in Verlund Reach is the third Relic."

Hewitt tugged on his beard. "It'll take almost a month to get there."

"We won't be going that way," Auden said, gesturing back to the Ephrian map. "The Relic in Norhels is a sister to the one in Verlund. And we have a channel that will speed up the process."

"These Relics relate to one another?" Deckard asked.

"Some more than others," Auden confirmed. "They are living organisms, like magic itself. They don't breathe or move, but they do have a pulse and a will."

Deckard grimaced internally at the idea. It was too similar to the blasphemy of which the Allorian priests warned. "Are you sure this is the only way to end the war?"

"If there was another way, trust me, we would take it."

"And *how* will these Relics end a war?" Hewitt asked fiercely. "I want an exact answer, not some wishy-washy promise."

Auden straightened his shoulders and met his gaze. "By granting my sister and me power strong enough to enter the Waulden capital and kill King Blount. From there, we will enact a new ruler and then return the Relics to their homes."

Hewitt smirked mockingly. "And what's to stop you from doing the same to King Ephren?"

"Nothing," Auden admitted, "aside from our honor and integrity."

"What if I don't trust your honor and integrity?"

"Then you'll be with us the whole way to put a stop to it."

Hewitt raised his bushy brows. "I very much doubt that if the royal guard of Wauld couldn't stop you from killing their king, we wouldn't be able to stop you from killing ours."

"You couldn't," Auden said plainly. "Not once we have all the Relics. As we recover each one, my sister and I *will* become stronger. But that *is* why you're going with us. If you ever suspect our goals are out of line with your own, you will have the opportunity to overtake us and put a stop to it."

"And if you're clever enough to keep your agenda hidden from us the whole time? What, then?" Deckard asked.

Auden met his stare. "The very fact you ask that question, Jonn, tells me you wouldn't miss it. Whatever hidden agendas my sister and I have, you are too suspicious not to discover them eventually," he said, smiling warmly. "Just don't fall for it when we try to lull you into a false sense of security."

Aware that the jest likely held truth, Deckard found himself relaxing. Auden nearly admitted to having a hidden agenda. But these siblings were clever; they knew the suspicion of the troop wouldn't allow them to keep secrets, not forever. So they were admitting to them now.

Deckard ran a hand along his jaw. He'd have to be vigilant. Whatever the Calders intended, they weren't wholly altruistic. And when their true colors were revealed, he would be ready.

Once they organized a list of supplies for Lord Carlile, the advisor and the Mages departed, and a servant guided the soldiers back to their carriages. Rafferty immediately commented on Ilain Calder's beauty, noting that she'd be a worthy conquest for any man. Deckard frowned, and Thom protested that a Mage wasn't to be trusted—especially not in a man's bed. Ethenn was notably silent on the subject, even when Rafferty goaded him for an opinion on the woman's fine appearance.

Deckard slowed his pace to walk beside Evylin as Rafferty and Thom continued their debate. His hand brushed hers, sending a spike of warmth through his arm. He took the opportunity to weave his fingers into hers. "When we get outside, we won't be taking the carriage back," he whispered.

She looked up at him, confused. "No?"

"We have an important stop to make," he said.

Evylin narrowed her eyes suspiciously but allowed him to keep his secret.

Servants waited with their coats at the entrance. Once bundled up, they walked to the pebbled drive where two carriages waited: one for the Ethenn and Rafferty and another for the rest of them. While the young men said their farewells, Deckard pulled Hewitt aside to inform him they'd return home later.

Deckard expected questions, but Hewitt nodded approvingly. "Make sure she enjoys herself," he said, then shoved Thom toward the carriage.

As their friends rode away, Deckard offered his arm to Evylin. They began down the long path to the gates. It would be a far walk, but with all they'd learned over the past few hours, he welcomed the time to think and discover Evylin's thoughts.

"So," he said as they crossed the cobblestone street, "that was . . . unexpected."

Evylin laughed, leaning into his side. "I can't believe it," she admitted. "All this time—all my life, I thought they were stories. And here . . . magic is real."

"It appears so."

"I can't believe it," she repeated.

"Me neither."

Glancing up at him, Evylin furrowed her brow. "You sound disappointed."

"Do I? I suppose I am."

"Why?" she asked. "This is incredible! It's like every novel I've ever read."

"Yes, but those are novels. And this . . . This is real life. This is dangerous."

"This is adventure," she said.

Deckard paused, realizing with awe that she was right. A wry smile tugged at his lips. "It is, isn't it? This is what you'd hoped for when you agreed to marry me."

The edges of her mouth lifted. "Well, I can't say I hoped for this *exact* scenario," she teased, then nodded. "But yes, this is . . . this is *more* than I could have hoped for."

Despite his rising anxiety, Evylin's happiness soothed him like a balm. It didn't matter if they were about to step into the most dangerous experience of their lives. She was truly happy. And he'd managed to play some small role in giving that to her.

The salt air drifted to them as they continued down the street, and Evylin's eyes grew wide. "The ocean?" she whispered suddenly. She looked up at him hopefully. "Is that where we're going?"

"Yes," Deckard said, thrilled at the bright smile on her face. "That's where we're going."

Her steps quickened, and he let her carry them faster. "It'll only be to look at as we're in the dead of winter," he warned. "But I thought you should at least see it before we leave."

After several more minutes, they navigated around the last buildings and made their way to the shoreline. Evylin's expression beamed at the sight of the sea a few hundred feet ahead. Her gaze swept over the sand, rocks, and waves, and her lips parted in awe. Her hand brushed her skirt absentmindedly, and she stepped forward.

Deckard released her, letting her approach the shoreline alone. The dull blue waves splashed into white foam on the gray sand. Here by the sea, the winter winds blew harsher, causing her wispy hair to dance around her face—making her look wild. And Deckard thought it was the closest image of who she really was that he might ever see. She *was* wild, filled with the desire for excitement and never-ending opportunities.

Evylin crouched down, letting her fingers touch the water. She didn't stop her hem from getting wet or back away from the cold waves. She let it meet her as Deckard watched from the beach. His smile fell away as the winter wind swept over the ocean, its whisper carrying the words that had haunted him since they left Whickam Village.

"Don't fall in love with her before she falls in love with you."

Deckard's heart pinched. He'd been a fool last night. He wanted to believe her words meant more than they did, that her kisses meant more. In the rush of the moment, after the wine and the dancing, after the smiles and the relief, he'd let himself be carried away by her beauty and affection.

It'd been a blessing that Hewitt and Thom interrupted them. Had they not been there . . . Well, Deckard wouldn't have had the strength or intelligence to stop their desirous actions.

Even this morning, he'd tried to convince himself that it was acceptable. They had another night in Loclight; he could show her the ocean, take her to the theater, and then finish what they'd started. She was his wife. Why *shouldn't* he pursue their marital bed?

In the end, he knew the truth. No matter how much she liked him, no matter if she would accept his sexual advances, she didn't trust him. Not truly.

If she did, she would've told him about Ryen.

And Deckard would never forgive himself if he pushed her because he didn't have the patience to wait for her love.

"Don't fall in love with her before she falls in love with you."

Evylin turned back, smiling at him. Her amber eyes shone in the afternoon light, her brown hair turning almost golden around the edges.

Returning her smile, Deckard now knew the magistrate's advice had been useless.

And it was far too late.

He'd already fallen in love with Evylin; he just hadn't known it at the time.

3RD OF GALATAE, 1573

When they arrived, eleven horses were gathered in the barracks' courtyard. Evylin, Thom, and Hewitt approached to greet the young soldiers while Deckard set their travel packs next to the mounts. Although there were only a few soldiers present, General Rand stood at the top of the staircase, arms crossed and eyes narrowed, observing their team's preparations for departure.

Deckard lifted his chin higher as he shook hands with Auden Calder. The Mage was dressed similarly to the day before, his high-collared coat a deep brown this time. However, his sister's gown was much more modest in a brown and navy brocade, and the skirt was cut with extra fabric for riding.

"Good morning," he said, nodding to the horses. "Looks as though we're about ready."

A few servants from the king's household milled around the horses, tugging on the ties to ensure their security.

"Do you *feel* ready?" Auden asked in a pleasant tone.

Deckard chuckled uneasily. "I doubt I ever could, but I suppose I'd best give it a go."

Ilain clicked her tongue. "Don't be so modest, Jonn. You'll lead us splendidly."

Still uncomfortable with her familiar air, Deckard smiled politely. "I certainly hope so, ma'am."

"You're too formal," she said, green eyes twinkling. "We'll fix that."

Ilain walked away, and Auden sighed. "Forgive her," he said quietly. "Ilain feels the need to impress, but she's really very tenderhearted at her core. Once we all settle into life on the road, she'll be easier."

Thinking Auden could have been describing Thom, Deckard grinned knowingly. "I understand completely."

When everything was double and triple-checked, the team looked to Deckard. With a nod, he swung onto his black mare. "Let's go," he said.

The rest of the team mounted their own steeds, with the three supply horses tethered to Hewitt, Thom, and Ethenn. They could not travel as quickly this way, but the added security made him more confident.

The horses' hooves clattered against the cobblestones, and Deckard glanced up at General Rand. The old man glared down at him for only a moment before he turned and walked back inside.

"Seems as though someone's disappointed," Evylin said, arriving at his side.

Deckard smiled, guiding his horse through the gate. "I can't say I'm sorry for it."

"He deserves worse."

"Perhaps." The group stepped onto the main street, the buildings towering above them. "I'd rather focus on what you deserve."

"Oh?" She smirked dryly. "And what is it that I deserve, Colonel Deckard?"

Deckard was about to say, "Everything," when he saw a heavy shadow drift back into an alleyway. The figure was large and faintly shaped like a rider on horseback. He scanned the dark alleyway as he passed yet saw nothing but refuse and stone walls. Had he imagined it?

"Jonn?"

Deckard turned to Evylin. "Hm?"

She glanced at the alleyway, then raised her brow. "Did you see something?"

Shaking his head, Deckard attributed it to his newfound paranoia from the knowledge that Mages existed and his childhood nightmares were real. "No," he said. "I was just trying to distract you."

She scoffed playfully. "Well, it didn't work. What is it that I deserve?"

Deckard grinned and urged his horse onward. "A censure. You're far too familiar with your commanding officer, Private. Something must be done about it."

CHAPTER FIFTY-THREE

Leaving the city behind, a tinge of disappointment made Evylin look back at the stone walls. She'd forgotten how nice a comfortable bed, warm baths, four walls, and a roof could be. *But,* she reminded herself, *our adventure is finally beginning.*

With that restoring thought, she faced the road with anticipation. They took the main highways, keeping their horses at a steady trot. As they needed the animals to survive the extended journey, they couldn't push them hard now. After riding through the day and stopping only for lunch, the winter sun disappeared below the horizon, casting the sky in a wash of rosy pink. The king sent money for provisions and lodging along their journey, but the land to the east of Loclight was mostly unsettled, and Newford, the nearest city, was over forty miles away. So they headed into the woods to find a secluded spot to camp.

"We've made it roughly halfway," Deckard said as they dismounted among the trees and snow. "If we hold the same pace tomorrow, we'll reach Newford by dusk."

While Deckard, Thom, and Rafferty set up the shelter-halfs, canvas lean-tos that would act as tents around camp, Evylin dug out a pit for the fire. Ethenn and Hewitt went out to hunt for their dinner, disappearing deeper into the trees. While the rest of them started their work on the camp, Auden and Ilain stood watching by the horses.

Gathering wood for the fire, Evylin wondered if the Mages felt they were above helping around camp. While they weren't exactly nobility, they were something even more special. Perhaps they felt menial tasks were below them.

But then, after a whispered word to his sister, Auden moved to join the men. Moments later, Ilain was at Evylin's side by the firepit. Bright red hair gleaming in the fast-dimming light, the woman smiled down at her. "Do you need help with the fire?" she offered.

Evylin reached for another log. "That would be nice, thank you."

"You're quite welcome," Ilain said, kneeling on the damp terrae Evylin had cleared out of the snow. "What do we do?"

Evylin paused. "Have you never made a campfire before?"

"No."

Though curious about how the siblings had managed to make it all the way from Wauld without her learning to build a campfire, Evylin thought it best not to ask. "I can teach you," she said, then finished stacking the logs. "First, you place two logs on the bottom, leaving enough room in the center for the kindling and tinder. You'll stack two more logs an equal distance away, facing the opposite direction. You place two more logs on top of those in the same direction as the first two, creating a sort of house to hold the tinder and kindling. Of course, there are other methods, but this is best to keep out the wind."

Evylin put the tinder inside the little square of logs. "Then you light it and maintain it throughout the night."

"That's easy enough," Ilain replied, studying the pit. "Do you light it now?"

Reaching for the flint and steel, Evylin said, "Mm-hm."

Ilain tossed her hand toward the logs, and flames sprang to life. "There," she said, a little wrinkle appearing on the bridge of her nose as she smiled.

Shocked by the sudden flames, Evylin jumped back from the quickly rising heat.

Ilain folded her hands in her lap. "You'll find having Mages around is quite convenient. We don't often do things the hard way if we don't have to."

"How does it work?" Evylin asked in awe. "How can you make fire out of nowhere like that?"

Ilain shrugged as though it were mundane. "It's simple actually—magic. It's all focus and thought. But like anything else, I've had to learn it," she explained.

"Can anyone learn magic?" Evylin asked, somewhat hopeful.

Ilain's light laughter gave the answer before she even spoke. "I'm afraid not. You're either born a Mage, or our power is out of your reach. It's something innate within you, you see, and you'll never have access to it otherwise."

With an internal flicker of disappointment, Evylin accepted she would never wield flame as this woman could. "But you said you had to learn it? How?"

Ilain gestured to the flames again. "We Mages have a natural connection to the resources of life, and, with proper training, we can control them. We are more adept at some resources than others, but we can use them all if we train long enough. It comes down to the depth of the connection to the resource. That relationship grants us the ability to connect with it. Once we understand them, it only takes a thought."

Evylin couldn't comprehend Ilain's words. "Only a thought? That's it?"

"That's it," she confirmed, then tilted her head. "Though that *is* a bit simplified. Sometimes, it can be hard to concentrate, so we use gestures or actions to help us. And then that becomes a habit, so even when it's easy, you'll often see us use our hands or close our eyes or something like that."

Letting that sink in, Evylin stared at the snow-laden trees. Magic had always been story-bound to her, living in novels and legends. Even the whispers of the Mages of Auld or the magical creatures were seen as folktales. Now, she wondered how much of it was real.

"And what are the resources of life?" Evylin asked.

Ilain blinked, then snorted. "You don't know about the resources?"

"No."

"Huh," she said bemusedly. "And you Ephrians claim to be Allorians."

A small spark of indignation made Evylin frown, but Ilain continued, "The resources are the very world around us. Allore used them to create Terraeus itself. Then he gifted the Mages a connection with them, allowing us to draw on his power for ourselves."

Evylin knew Father Dover in Whickam Village would have a fit if anyone made such a blasphemous suggestion around him. As she didn't particularly care, she asked, "And you said you're born with magic. Does that mean you and your brother have always been able to use it?"

"I also said we had to train," Ilain reminded her, adding, "In Wauld, all children are tested for magic. The different Orders travel the country looking for new trainees. As we lived in the Highloft Moors, the Order of the Flame was nearest, which was pure luck for both of us.

"Every year, they travel through each settlement to test those aged ten to sixteen," she continued. "Any younger than that, and they haven't had enough time for the magic to develop. Any older, and the child will be too hard to train. Our elder brother, Vayden, failed the test every year, and Auden had yet to pass either. But when I was ten and Auden thirteen, the Mages returned, and we both passed. They took us to Doorstunds Reach to train, and we've lived there ever since."

"They took you from home at ten years old?" Evylin asked in shock.

Ilain brushed a hand through the air. "It's understood that Waulden children may leave home. And life as a Mage isn't exactly hard, so it's a desirable fate."

Evylin shook her head, unable to fathom being taken from her family at so young an age.

"Besides," Ilain continued, "I had Auden with me. Honestly, I felt more sorry for Vayden than either of us. Though he was fifteen at the time, we were his only friends, and our leaving wasn't easy on him."

"I can't imagine it was easy on your parents either."

"They were sad, of course. But in the end, they knew our lives as Mages would be better than anything a life at home could have offered."

"Is Waulden life so difficult?" Evylin asked gently.

Ilain turned to the flames and whispered, "It is."

Taking her continued silence as a sign that the conversation was over, Evylin pushed herself off the ground. "Thank you for explaining magic to me," she said.

Rising, too, Ilain smiled brightly. "You're very welcome, Evylin. Anytime you have questions, I'm more than happy to answer."

Evylin nodded in gratitude and walked to the supply horses. She began to untie the bedding for the night. When Thom and Rafferty joined her, having finished with their half of the tents, she handed them a blanket and bedroll each.

"What did she want?" Thom asked, frowning at Ilain, now sitting by the side of the firepit with a sketchbook in her lap and charcoal in hand.

Evylin smirked at his suspicion. "She asked if I wanted to help her kill King Ephren. I told her I'd think about it."

Rafferty sniggered, and Thom turned his frown to her. "Evie, it's not a joke," he whispered. "They're dangerous, and we have no idea what they really want."

"Stop being such a worrywart," Evylin said. "There are six of us and two of them. Between the reservations of Hewitt, Jonn, Ethenn, and you, I hardly think they'll be able to pull the wool over our eyes."

Rafferty bumped elbows with Evylin. "You and I were clearly missing from that list, Eve. I suppose that means we're both more excited about our little quest than everyone else."

"I'd say you're quite right about that," she agreed.

Rafferty waggled his white-blond brows. "Now that you've had a chat with our lovely highlady, do you think I have any shot with her?"

Thom sighed and walked away as Evylin laughed. "She hardly told me of her taste in men."

"Well, find out and let me know, eh?" he said with a wink, then hoisted his load and trekked after Thom.

Evylin gathered her own stack and carried it to Deckard. After tying off the final ropes, he dismissed Auden with thanks. Glancing between their work and the work of Rafferty and Thom, she noted that the extra time Deckard and Auden had taken resulted in more solid tent construction.

"Special delivery," Evylin said, setting her stack next to the tent. Staring at the structure, she frowned. Each tent provided them with only enough cover to keep them out of the wind and any snowfall in the night. Otherwise, they were open for all the camp to see.

Deckard chuckled as he saw her face. "You look horrified," he said, beginning to untie one of the bedrolls. "Thank you for these, by the way."

"Why are we sleeping in such open tents?" Evylin asked.

Deckard scanned the camp. "It's a lot less work to set up and carry around. And since we'll stay in an inn most of the time, having full-sized tents with us would be a waste of valuable space. It won't be the most comfortable night's rest, but it won't be often either."

Though it made plenty of sense, Evylin still thought one regular tent that they all shared would have been better than these four menial ones. The cold she'd experienced during their travels with the army would be nothing compared to sleeping in the snow.

Evylin shook out a blanket. "I hope we brought enough of these," she muttered.

Deckard shrugged. "We're soldiers. It's part of the job."

"Perhaps that's part of *your* job. But that's not what I signed up for."

"You're a soldier now, too, Private Deckard," he said, stepping over to her. "And I believe I remember the king putting you under my command."

Evylin crossed her arms playfully. "Is it ethical for you to be married to a soldier under your command?"

"Probably not." He brushed some hair off her cheek. "But that didn't seem to bother the king. And I can't say it bothers me either."

"Hey," Thom said from the other side of the camp, making Evylin jump, "if you two would stop flirting, we could finish setting up the camp."

Having forgotten how small the clearing was, Evylin's ears grew hot. She exchanged a shy smile with Deckard, and then they split apart. He headed for the horses while she went to check on the stack of firewood. Counting the logs, she considered going out for more. She'd only gathered what was on the outskirts of their camp, and she worried it wouldn't be enough for the frigid night ahead.

Hewitt and Ethenn walked back into camp, a string of rabbits and a couple of grouse in hand. "It isn't a feast," Hewitt said as they knelt next to the fire and laid out their game. "But it'll do for one night."

Sitting next to Ilain by the firepit, Auden glanced up from a book. "Would you like help with those?" he asked.

"What, you have some sort of magic that can prepare dinner?" Hewitt asked tersely.

"Not exactly," Auden replied, closing the book. "But I was the only child who enjoyed helping my mother in the kitchen. I can make sure it's skinned and cooked properly. I can even season it well."

"You brought spices with you?" Evylin asked, sure that anyone who carried seasonings on a quest to save the world couldn't harbor an evil agenda.

Auden's grin turned sheepish. "Not much, but enough to make things better for nights like this one," he said, looking back at Hewitt, waiting for approval.

Hewitt relinquished his job to go speak with Deckard, leaving Auden and Ethenn to work together.

While the men prepared the meal, Ilain leaned closer to Evylin. "I'd flirt with him too," she said, eyes down as she drew the charcoal across the page.

"What?" Evylin asked, embarrassed.

"Jonn," Ilain said, gesturing with her charcoal. "He's handsome. I'd flirt with him, too, if he were my husband."

Auden frowned at his sister, tugging at his collar. "Stop it, Lain."

"Don't be a spoilsport." She poked his hand with her charcoal. He tried to swat her away, but a black mark stained his hand anyway. "I didn't say I *will* flirt with him, only that I *would*. But he's married, so I won't." Ilain sat back, eyes narrowing in consideration. "However, I will need to flirt with someone."

Ethenn glanced up from his butchery work, brow furrowed, and Evylin chuckled. "Does magic make you prone to flirtation?" she asked dryly.

Ilain grinned. "Only if you're a Fire Mage. As I am one, I get bored easily, and I find coquetry sates my impetuosity. So," she clasped her hands and scanned the men in the camp, "I must choose one of these handsome Ephrians to torment."

Evylin laughed, amused by the prospect. "In that case, it'd be rather fun to see Jonn's response to your flirtations. I don't think he'd know what to do with them."

"Oh, no," Ilain insisted. "I would never flirt with a married man. He *is* the most handsome by Waulden standards, but he's yours. And I rather like the novelty of these dark, strapping Ephrian lads."

"I suppose that removes me from the list," Rafferty noted, seated nearby.

Ilain grinned slyly. "As you would have no qualms with my teasing attentions, it would sort of take the fun out of it."

"I'd find ways to make it worth your while, milady."

Her gaze grew serious, and one fiery brow raised. "That's what I'm worried about."

Rafferty shrugged and let the suggestion pass.

"Which leaves me with the captain and the young corporal." Ilain rested a hand under her chin thoughtfully. "While Thom does look enough like his brother to be handsome, Ethenn is the most Ephrian, and that's . . . Mm." Her eyes twinkled as Ethenn froze, clearly listening. "Beguiling, I'll say."

Ethenn resumed his work, a peculiar expression on his face.

"However," Ilain continued as though conducting an important investigation, "while Ethenn is reserved and would be quite uncomfortable with my advances, the way he stares at me makes it clear he finds me beautiful. And while I don't mind that, I'd hate to cause any hurt feelings."

Evylin watched curiously as Ethenn shifted nervously, eyes on his task.

"Besides," Ilain said with a sly grin, "the real entertainment would come through Thom. He doesn't like me, he doesn't trust me, and he doesn't find me particularly attractive. He'd be far more annoyed by my attention than pleased with it."

Nodding as though she'd solved a puzzle, Ilain turned back to Evylin. "Yes, I've made my choice. I'll flirt with your brother-in-law."

Noticing Thom's scowl from where he sat in a tent behind the woman, Evylin laughed. "I think that's an excellent idea if you want him to hate you," she said.

"He already hates me," she noted. "I'm Waulden, a Mage, and not pretty enough for him. It can't get any worse, can it?"

Keeping an eye on Thom, Evylin was surprised when he showed no reaction. Either he didn't care, or he was pleased with the outcome.

"You may as well have some fun, I suppose," Evylin said. Then she rose, dusting off her knees. "I'm going to gather some more wood," she announced.

Rafferty hopped up and jogged to her side. "Can't have you wandering off alone in the dark," he teased. "Any number of wild animals could attack."

Though she knew it was an excuse to get out of any tedious work Deckard might find to give him, Evylin didn't mind. His easy chatter helped distract her from the cold and impending night. He admitted momentary disappointment at Ilain's disinterest but concluded that the idea of her teasing Thom was far more entertaining anyway. From there on, they discussed their mutual interest in magic. She told him what she could remember of Ilain's lesson and the things she'd read in books. He made all sorts of wild guesses on what else the Mages might be able to do.

When they returned, dinner was ready. The eight of them sat around the fire to keep warm as they ate. The rabbit and grouse were both delicious and butchered with expert precision. They'd brought a few extra supplies to add variety to their meals, so Auden had chosen potatoes to go with the dinner as they'd be the first to spoil. No one's plate was full by any means, but Evylin found she preferred the small plate. She was able to devour the meal in half the time, then tucked her hands and arms around herself against the biting wind. Both moons were mere slivers in the sky, hardly producing even the dimmest light and somehow making it feel colder out in the forest.

As he finished his meal, Deckard slipped his arm over Evylin's shoulders to draw her closer as she shivered. "Are you really that cold?" he whispered while Rafferty kept everyone else's attention.

A gust of wind kicked up, causing her to shake. "It seems I am," she said, allowing herself to take a deeper refuge in his embrace.

Deckard fell silent as he rubbed her arm. They listened as Rafferty told Auden and Ilain the story of how he'd smuggled the Schonese wine from the merchants at Bridgewater. He'd taken it all the way back to Rasnaack, where the magistrate caught Rafferty and tossed him in prison. When Auden asked about how he'd come to join the army, he then went on to explain the last two months of their lives.

Evylin continued to freeze in the night air but did her best to laugh along as Rafferty explained their exploits. He made her sound quite heroic in her fight against Haalston, though she'd nearly forgotten about the event. In fact, he overplayed her skills every time he talked about their training and recounted their rescue of the prince.

Another gust of wind blew, and Evylin shook even more. Deckard cleared his throat as Rafferty's story ended. "We should all get some sleep," he suggested. "We have a long ride tomorrow."

Auden and Ethenn began to rise, but Thom huffed. "You can't be serious. It's only been dark for an hour."

"Stay awake, then," he replied, standing and holding out his hand to Evylin to help her up. Once she stood at his side, he nodded to the rest of the troop. "Goodnight, all. We leave at first light."

Auden continued along his path, but Rafferty called Ethenn back to the fire, telling him not to be a pansy. A smattering of "Goodnights" followed Deckard and Evylin to their tent. It felt more awkward than she expected—preparing to sleep next to Deckard in front of the others. They would sleep fully clothed to preserve heat, lessening the discomfort, but despite doing all she could to keep her eyes on the tent, she caught Thom's glance at them from across the fire, and her cheeks grew hot.

Forcing herself to lie down and forget their companions, Evylin pulled the blankets up to her chin. The weight made her feel warmer, even if her body didn't know it yet. As she shivered, Deckard removed his boots.

Evylin stared at him, wide-eyed. "Aren't your feet going to freeze?" she asked quietly.

"I have wool socks on," he said, then his foot prodded hers. "You should take off your boots too. You'll be more comfortable."

"I'll be far too cold," Evylin protested.

Deckard laughed lightly. "Evylin, you won't be able to sleep with them on."

"I'll sleep better with them on than if I turn into an icicle."

He raised his brow. "If you don't take them off, I'll do it for you."

Evylin stared into his eyes, deep green in the shadows and hinting at mischief. "You wouldn't," she challenged.

Without a response, Deckard leaned forward. Evylin reached up to grab his arm but only managed to grasp his sleeve. "Don't you dare!" she ordered, laughing.

Deckard tossed back the covers and grabbed at her now kicking feet. "Ow," he muttered, shaking out one hand when she made contact. Then he turned, set a hand on her leg, and bent close until their faces were inches from one another. "If you aren't quiet," he whispered playfully, "you'll attract the attention of our whole camp and cause us quite the embarrassment."

Suddenly, acutely aware that his hand had never before touched her thigh, even if it was through a blanket, Evylin swallowed her laughter. Her smile grew nervous, though her heart pattered excitedly.

"Are you going to comply?" he asked. "Or am I going to have to explain myself to your uncle when he asks why I'm attacking you?"

Evylin laughed quietly and nodded her approval.

Bending down, Deckard unlaced her boots. When he found the knife hidden in her right boot, he froze, lifting it with care after a moment. Holding the blade between his fingers, he smirked at her. "Were you expecting to have to fight me off?"

Evylin kicked at him playfully. "One can never be too prepared."

"Mm." His eyes twinkled fondly as he returned to his work. Once he'd set both boots at the end of their bedroll, he tucked the blankets back around her feet. "There, now you can be warm *and* comfortable."

He lay down, and Evylin scooted close, thankful he was on his side and blocking her view of the fire. As usual, he used his arm to prop up her neck under her pillow. The other arm draped over her waist to pull her closer. Yet tonight, he also slid his feet to be entwined with hers. "Is that all right?" he whispered, their faces inches apart.

Evylin smiled, wondering how many times he'd sacrificed his comfort to keep her warm. He'd never complained, but she was sure he must have yielded to discomfort on many occasions. "I'm fine," she whispered back. "Are you all right?"

"As long as you're warm enough, it doesn't matter," he replied, confirming her suspicions.

"Jonn," Evylin challenged, "are you comfortable?"

A smile tugged at his lips. His eyes scanned her face, dropping to her lips. He began to lean in, and Evylin gasped, backing her head away. "What are you doing?" she asked. "We're surrounded by people."

"None of them can see, nor will they care."

"You don't know that."

His hand slid up her back. "Evylin," he said, his voice a little deeper than usual. "I'm going to kiss you."

While she considered protesting further, Deckard acted swiftly. His lips captured hers in a tender, lingering kiss, instantly sending a spike of clarity to her senses. He drew back, his eyes soft and his demeanor relaxed. "Thank you for asking," he whispered. "Yes, I am comfortable."

Suddenly bashful, Evylin pressed her cheek into Deckard's chest to hide from his gaze and the cold. Under the canopy of the tent, the wind couldn't get to Evylin, but the frozen ground still seeped through the bedroll. His arms tightened around her, and she listened as his heart beat its steady rhythm.

The voices drifted over from the campfire as she lay staring up at the tent's canvas ceiling. Ilain was telling the story of their journey now. It had been a furious ride through Wauld's moors and mountains to get to Ephria after abandoning their post in their former Order. She told the men how they'd camped in a similar manner as this, worried the Waulden Army would capture them on their journey. When they snuck into Ephria, their travel grew even more precarious until they got well through Harmouth Province and into the mainland. She spoke of relying heavily on magic to keep themselves hidden.

Evylin pressed closer to Deckard as she shivered again. His hand began to rub circles on her back. "Can I ask you for something, Evylin?" he said so softly she barely heard the question.

"Depends on what it is, I suppose."

"Be careful, please," he asked, his cheek pressing into her hairline, "with the Mages. They seem genuine, but I worry that they're deceiving us. I know you can take care of yourself, but . . . I just need to know you'll take caution with them. I need to know you'll be safe."

Hewitt began speaking, his gravelly voice reaching her from the fire. The sound soothed her, and she relaxed into Deckard's chest. She drew one arm from between them and wrapped it around his waist. "I'll be careful," she whispered back. "I promise."

Deckard's warm breath caressed her temple and tickled her ear. "Thank you," he murmured, his hand sliding between her shoulders to pull her nearer. His lips brushed against her hairline in a gentle kiss, and then he relaxed his embrace, letting his hand return to making slow circles on her back.

The fire crackled softly as Evylin shut her eyes, enveloped in his warmth, and drifted into slumber.

CHAPTER FIFTY-FOUR

4TH OF GALATAE, 1574

They reached Newford an hour after sunset. Their travels with the Mages differed greatly from their time with the Third Volunteer Company. On horseback, they could move faster and for longer distances. When they arrived in Newford—a port city half the size of Loclight—they didn't visit the magistrate or worry about setting up camp. Instead, they sought out the best inn they could find. Evylin much preferred this, glad for a comfortable bed, a fresh meal, and no camp duties.

Now, seated in the dining hall, warmed by a blazing fire in the corner, they filled their stomachs with smoked pork, biscuits, and root vegetables, a sense of comfort slowly easing into their travel-worn bones. The sparse patrons lingered at the far side of the room, allowing them to converse openly, albeit in a semi-hushed tone, after the kitchen maid had served their meal.

"At this pace, we should make it to Norhels in four days," Deckard said. Like the rest of the soldiers, he'd shed his coat and rolled back his sleeves. "We'll have to ride all day to make it there from Whithill, so I'd suggest we not begin our search until the next day."

Auden looked to Ilain as though seeking her opinion. She tipped her head in an approving shrug, and he turned back to Deckard. "That sounds good to us. It will be smart to get an early run at the Keep. They're deep, and we'll need to be at our best if we hope to make it through."

"What's inside these Keeps?" Thom asked suspiciously. "You said monsters. What kind?"

"Are you frightened, Thom?" Ilain asked, tapping the side of her mug.

He glowered at her. "No, ma'am, I'm not. But I like to be prepared before entering a fight."

Auden ignored his sister's smirk. "As the Relics protect the continent," he said, "so the Keeps protect the Relics. There are two types of defenses within each of them. First are the Shades, representations of the Relic and its powers. Made of magic and clay, they will do what they can to fight us off before we can get to the Chamber.

"Once in the Chamber, we will face the Guardian. Each of them holds one beast, a Guardian, to defend the Relic. They're terrifying and almost impossible to defeat, directly tied to the Relic's powers." Auden let his fork rest against his plate as he pierced Thom with a serious glare. "If you aren't scared, you should be. These creatures are more dangerous than you could imagine."

The soldiers picked at their food mutely.

Ethenn set his fork next to his empty plate. "What are the Relics' powers?" he asked. "You said there are seven, right? And that each Order is particularly skilled in one of them. But you never said what they were."

"You're very keen-minded, aren't you?" Ilain replied, eyeing him with interest. "In all our conversations, I think you were the only one really listening. Yes, there are seven Relics and seven Orders, which means there are seven powers. But it's a complex explanation. Are you sure you'd like to hear it now?"

Tugging on his shirt sleeves, which were already covering his wrists, he nodded bashfully. "I would."

"All right, then." She sat up primly, ready to explain. "There are two types of powers: Elemental and Existential. There are four elements and three existents. As a Mage, we are versed in one or the other, marking our classification. Though we *can* connect with any resource, we only have true control over the elements or the existents. Never both. I—" she set a hand to her chest, "am an Elemental Mage. That means I have control over the four elemental resources of Fire, Water, Terrae, and Wind.

"Auden—" she gestured to her brother, rings flashing in the light, "is an Existential Mage. He controls Day, Night, and Time. Every Mage has a specific primary resource with which they have the strongest connection. I connect with Fire; Auden connects with Day. Those resources are like breathing for us. We can connect to them with hardly any effort. The others . . . well, they're not so easy, but they still have a hierarchy all their own."

Ilain leaned forward, eyes fixed on Ethenn as though her words were only for him. "In order to offset any difficulty that we may have in connecting to the other resources, we can share energy and help one another access the powers that are more difficult for us. That makes us stronger together. And it's true for all Mages. The stronger the Mage, the more energy they can share. But like a muscle, we must build that power." She paused and shrugged. "And while Elemental Mages are much more common than Existential ones, we don't hold the potential for as great of powers as they have.

"Granted," she smirked, drawing her shoulders back, "that doesn't mean we aren't damn impressive ourselves."

Ethenn, Rafferty, and Evylin all chuckled at her jest.

"Which Relic are we going after first?" Evylin asked.

Ilain tore a piece of bread into two. "The Day Relic," she replied.

"Why that one?" Thom asked, head tilting toward her brother. "'Cause it's his . . . whatever—his first connection thing."

"We didn't choose it," Auden said. "There's a sequence we must follow."

"Why?" Ethenn asked.

Auden lifted a hand to pull at his collar, but Ilain slapped his wrist. "If you don't quit that," she muttered, "I'm going to lose my mind."

Her brother shifted awkwardly, defending himself, "I'm not used to these Ephrian collars."

Ilain sighed, then explained, "The ancient Mages designed the Keeps in the order of creation. Should you like to retain your life while retrieving the Relics, you are highly advised to follow their intended sequence. And thus, Day is first."

"Are the Keeps that dangerous?" Deckard asked.

Both Auden and Ilain met his gaze. "Yes," they said together.

Then Auden added, "But it's more than that. The Relics are a heavy burden. Their power is great, but so is their influence. The more power you carry, the more difficult it is to retain your sanity."

"If you have any bloody sanity left," Ilain grumbled, swatting Auden's hand away from his collar again.

Thom crossed his arms. "What makes you two think you're powerful enough to carry them, then?"

"Are you concerned for me, dearest?" Ilain winked flirtatiously.

"Troubled *by* you is more accurate."

Ilain's smile was patronizing. "Tut, tut. That hurts my feelings," she teased. "But no matter, my brother and I are more than adequately trained to carry the blessed burden the Relics provide."

"Just so long as we get them in order," Auden added.

Hewitt leaned back in his chair. "And why are you two the first to try gathering these Relics? Seems that Mages should be clamoring for the opportunity to be all-powerful."

"They are," Auden admitted. "But it takes years of dedication to unlock the secrets of the Relics' locations. The ancient Mages hid fragments of information everywhere, leading you on a wild hunt for answers. And some of the information is intentionally misleading. Not only do you have to be obsessively focused, you have to devote years of study to the task."

"And yet, a young Mage such as yourself managed what hundreds of others could not?"

Auden and Ilain exchanged amused grins before he replied, "Appearances are deceiving, and I never said I did it alone." Before anyone could respond, Auden continued, "You're very right—Mages are often selfish and power-hungry, and they do desire the Relics. But they've been gone for a thousand years. Many relegate them to myth, as your people did to Mages themselves. Those who are convinced of their reality are either too narcissistic to work with others or too impatient to do the work required. Ilain and I were lucky to be in the same Order together. Without each other, we never would have determined the path to the Relics."

"He's being modest." Ilain patted her brother's arm. "I helped him collect information, but he's the one who studied it and put it all together."

Suddenly, Evylin realized the peculiarity of that statement. "But if you're an Existential Mage, why did the Order of the Flame take you?" she asked.

"There used to be an Order for each of the resources, but now . . ." Auden paused as though rewording his thoughts. "There are only four Orders left since the Centurial War began. You're correct. As a Day Mage, I should have been a member of the Order of the Day. But that Order was located near Norhels, here in Ephria, and when Ephren rose up, it was destroyed. So the Order of the Flame absorbed it. Just like the Order of the Night absorbed the Order of the Sea, and the Order of the Wind took on the Order of the Terrae."

"The Order of the Time didn't take anyone?" Ethenn asked.

Ilain grinned. "The Order of *the Age* doesn't exactly care to associate with anyone. Plus, they didn't need to. There weren't enough Orders for them to take on."

Auden nodded. "As I'm a Day Mage, the Order of the Flame was my only possibility. We Day Mages are rare enough that it isn't a burden for the Order. However, they can't train us as well, being mostly Elemental Mages, so it's not an even trade as far as power goes. That's one of the reasons I'm only a magister while Ilain is viceMage."

"The training is a bit lopsided," Ilain agreed.

"What does that mean?" Evylin asked. "Magister and viceMage?"

"It is part of the hierarchy of the Orders," Auden said. "We *could* go into that now, but it would take quite a while longer to explain. The politics can be somewhat convoluted."

"Oh, ah—" Evylin scrunched her nose. "No, that's fine. I'm not that interested in politics."

"Why are Day Mages so rare?" Deckard asked, changing the subject.

"All Existential Mages," Auden corrected. "And no one knows for sure. We assume it's because the existents are such abstract powers. Often, those of us who can connect with them don't even realize the powers are there. Mages are often hiding in plain sight. That's why we test children every year in Wauld. I failed three times before I discovered my magic."

"Does that mean there could be Mages here in Ephria?" Rafferty asked, his silver eyes wide.

Auden's expression turned dry, and Ilain twisted the ruby ring on her right index finger. "It isn't likely," she said. "Only those from the West have the power of Mages. A Wauldener would have to live here."

"They would have had to move here nearly two centuries ago," Deckard said. "The Centurial War put an end to the mixing of ancestral lines. So unless your people have been sneaking in, I'd say an Ephrian Mage is out of the question."

Ilain smiled slyly. "I think you're quite right, Jonn."

Ethenn's forehead wrinkled. "You said there were Mages in Ephria before the war, though," he noted.

"Yes," Auden confirmed. "Mages used to live all throughout the continent. It wasn't until Ephren pushed back the Mages of Auld that they were relegated to the west."

"But you said only Westerners could be Mages," Evylin commented.

"It didn't start that way."

"Oh, I see." Evylin nodded. "So Ephren drove all magic across the mountains, ridding it from the East because of its heresy?"

"Not exactly," Ilain said. "Magic isn't exclusive to Mages."

The soldiers frowned, confused.

"A thousand years ago, magic thrived in our land," Ilain said. "After the ancient Mages locked the Ateri Relics away, their yearning for peace was thwarted by the Mages of Auld. They set themselves up as gods, rising as a dictatorship and wiping out all who opposed them. Namely, their greatest threat: Warriors."

Hewitt scoffed. "I haven't heard whispers of Warriors since my childhood. Now, you're telling me they're real too?"

"Quite real," Ilain said with a nod. "And quite eradicated. When Ephren rebelled, creating Ephria and Western Auld, now known as Wauld, he also divided the magic. Now, Mages are from the West, and Warriors are from the East."

Evylin leaned forward in her seat, intrigued. "I've never heard of Warriors before," she said.

"Neither have I," Deckard agreed.

"I have," Rafferty interjected smugly. "A sailor from Schon told me he used to know a Warrior. Said they're terrifying."

"They can be," Ilain said, twirling her fork. "They're all strength, intelligence, and violence. Though there used to be as many as Mages, the Mages of Auld didn't want them around to threaten their rule. They wiped the continent clean. Of course, they couldn't stop them from being born, but by destroying all evidence of them, none would ever know they possessed magic to begin with. And those few who escaped now call other countries their homeland."

"But they still exist?" Evylin pressed.

"Theoretically."

Ethenn tapped the rim of his plate. "Do you think they'll return to Ephria?"

"They're already in Ephria," Ilain said. "They just don't realize they exist. And they likely won't unless your people accept that magic isn't evil."

Beside Evylin, Deckard shifted uncomfortably. She knew he was thinking of their country's faith. The church would never accept the idea of magic being good, and she was surprisingly disappointed by the thought.

"It won't happen," Ethenn said, eyes downcast. "Allore denounced magic, and our people are too tied to their faith."

"Don't be so morose," Ilain said, reaching across the table to pat his hand. "Two days ago, you thought the same of Mages. Now, you've discovered just how wonderful we can be."

"What's more shocking," Rafferty said, slapping Ethenn's chest, "is that an attractive woman just touched your hand, and you didn't even blush. It's a miracle!"

Ethenn shoved Rafferty off and stood, face beet red as he muttered, "I'm going to bed," and left the table. As he disappeared from the dining room, Thom punched Rafferty's shoulder despite the snicker he couldn't hold back.

Finished with their meal, Deckard and Auden exchanged a few final words about their morning departure. Turning away from the two men, Rafferty quickly told the others what the Schonese sailor had told him about Warriors, which was disappointingly little. The man was supposedly unbeatable in a fight and bore unexpected strength. That was all, and it didn't sound magical to Evylin.

While the rest of them rose and headed for the door, Hewitt grabbed Evylin's arm, slowing her stride to match his. "It isn't true," he said.

Evylin looked up at him, expectant.

"Warriors," he clarified, "they aren't real. When I was a child, some said Euon Sergus was one, but it's just a way to make life more mystical. If Warriors really existed, we would have seen signs by now."

"You said the same thing about Mages," she replied lightly.

Hewitt glowered. "Stop it. I know you're teasing me, but don't let it be a joke. That means you believe in its possibility, even if only a little."

"What's wrong with that?" Evylin tugged on his sleeve. "I *want* to believe it. I know it's ridiculous, but so is everything in our lives. We're traveling to retrieve magical objects in the company of *Mages*, Uncle. How much more impossible can it get?"

Hewitt's gray eyes bored into hers. "Let us hope very little."

8TH OF GALATAE, 1574

The city of Norhels glowed along the shoreline, amber flames flickering against the burgeoning purple sky. The air smelled of salt, the ocean calling to her as they crested the hill. The sun was setting at their backs, casting a warm haze on the city.

Deckard pulled up alongside Evylin, and his black mare whinnied softly. "We made it," he said.

"No mishaps, no excitement," Evylin said, turning to him.

The sunset turned his hair a burnished red. "How are we supposed to find a magical Keep under a city?" he asked, surveying the landscape with a troubled frown.

Ilain appeared beside them. "Don't worry," she said, her own fiery hair ablaze. "We can feel it, Auden and I. The closer we get, the easier it'll be to find."

Exchanging an amused glance with Deckard, Evylin followed Ilain and the rest of their team down the hill toward the city. Her heart pattered excitedly, and her veins tingled with the memory of their daring rescue of the prince. She was ready to feel the rush again, to experience the adrenaline filling her whole body with life.

They'd enter the Day Keep in the morning. They'd fight Shades and Guardians, the magical creatures formed to stop anyone from taking the very thing for which they came.

Their journey may have begun without trouble, but Evylin doubted it'd stay that way for long. And she couldn't stop smiling, knowing the adventure she and Ryen had so longed for was about to truly begin.

CHAPTER FIFTY-FIVE

9TH OF GALATAE, 1574

Most of the city still slept as their team patrolled the streets of Norhels. Only the early morning bakers and merchants passed, each eyeing the heavily armed group suspiciously. Evylin didn't blame them. The eight members of their team made for a strange assortment. While the soldiers—including Evylin—carried several weapons, the Calders insisted they didn't need any protection beyond their magic. In their simple yet high-quality attire, the group resembled a band of bodyguards protecting a pair of nobles.

Following the brother and sister through the streets, Evylin yawned. When they'd asked how they would find the Keep as they left the inn, Auden only replied, "We'll look for it." Now, they'd been marching down the cobbled roads for thirty minutes, looking for something none of them had any idea how to discover.

The inn sat near the southeastern side of the city limits, but instead of searching the surrounding area first, Auden led them around the perimeter toward the west. They passed the gates, a small market, several shops, homes, and what looked to be a smithy as they progressed. Though they'd claimed that time was of the essence, the Calders moved slowly. They stopped every so often, closing their eyes and trying to sense the Keep.

"Have you felt any sort of pull?" Ilain asked Auden after a short time had passed. They'd stopped for another attempt, but she'd given up after only a moment.

Auden's eyes remained closed, his head tilting to the right. "Yes," he muttered, voice hesitant. Then his eyes flew open, and he looked to the north. "Yes. It's this way."

As the siblings took off toward whatever it was that Auden felt, Evylin and Hewitt exchanged a look. "Either they're playing some ridiculous game," he grumbled, "or this world is about to get a whole lot stranger for us both."

Evylin grinned as they trailed behind the others. "I have a feeling that 'strange' is an understatement."

Quickening their pace, Auden guided them upward through the city to the back gate. They gathered there, passing the morning fishermen returning with their catches. The salt air enveloped them, and the rumble of the sea resonated from half a mile away.

"It's out there," Auden said, taking a step toward the gate.

Ilain moved up next to him, her dark dress swishing. "I feel it now too."

"How does that work?" Ethenn asked, near the back of the group. "Can any Mage feel it?"

Auden spared the young man a glance. "Technically, yes," he said. "But it's complicated."

Without any more explanation, the Calders pushed through the crowd of fishermen. A few city men cast sidelong glances, but the soldiers' weapons and uniforms deterred any interaction, even though many gave a second glance to Evylin. Outside the city, they walked down the rocky hill. The terrain grew rough as they moved farther from the main path. Quite thankful for her trousers, Evylin marveled at how Ilain moved so well in her voluminous skirt.

After an hour of traversing the rocky hillside, the siblings slowed their pace. The call of seabirds screamed down at them as Auden and Ilain scanned the cliffs with intent. He took a step forward, running one hand along the face of a particularly large rock butting up against the jagged hill. "This is it," he said, the team piling up behind him.

Staring at the boulder, Evylin questioned the sanity of the siblings. Its large gray surface stood twice the height and width of Auden. If he thought there was any getting past it, they were quite out of luck.

"You've led us to a rock?" Thom demanded, incredulous. "How stupid do you think we are?"

"It's not a rock. Look there," Deckard said, pointing at the far-left edge. "There's an opening to a cave."

Auden and Ilain turned to stare at Deckard. "Good eye," Auden said. "I didn't expect any of you to see it. The Keeps are quite well hidden—enough to be sure no one can stumble upon them."

Evylin thought the ancient Mages had done an impeccable job of hiding the entrance as she still struggled to see the opening even after having it pointed out to her.

Deckard gestured to the stone face. "Shall we go in?"

"We'll enter first," Auden said as he and Ilain stepped forward. "The Keep will only open to a Mage's touch."

Standing at the cave's entrance, Evylin could finally see the narrow opening with clarity. Darkness obscured her view inside; the hole was only wide enough for one person to enter at a time. Auden slipped through the crack, followed by Ilain.

"Thom," Deckard said quietly, "watch the back. I want to know we have a way out."

The brothers exchanged nods, and then Deckard followed after the Mages.

Hewitt nudged Evylin forward. "In you go," he said.

The blackness loomed as Evylin squeezed into the entrance. With one hand on the hunting knife on her belt, she used the other to guide her down the stone corridor. It was impossible to see in the darkness of the underground stairwell, so she took each step with caution. Then a flare of light filtered up to her, revealing the curve of the wall.

With ease, Evylin hurried down the rest of the steps to find the Calders and Deckard in a circular antechamber, a golden orb floating between Auden's hands. "The path should light itself," he said when she joined them. "But this will help us all gather before we continue."

"Before we risk our lives, you mean," Hewitt said, appearing at Evylin's side, his eyes narrowed on the orb. "Should we have our weapons ready?"

"Not yet," Auden said. "First, let us remind you: What lies within the Keep is more dangerous than anything you've ever seen. The Shades will come in waves, each more difficult than the last. As generations of the Relic's power, they are infinite in number. We can't waste time trying to kill them all because there is no 'all.' They will keep coming. And after we've retrieved the Relic, we'll have to fight them again on our way out."

Auden's fierce green gaze carried a thread of gold within it as he continued, "Once we get past them, there's the Chamber Guardian to deal with. And the only way to defeat it is through magic. Ilain and I will work to connect with the Relic's power and destroy the creature. Until then, you will have to keep it occupied. Do not think this trial will be easy. We may all leave this day with many injuries . . . or death."

Ilain spoke then, her fiery hair shining in the orb's soft yellow light. "We want to offer you one final chance to turn back," she said gently. "If any of you would like, you are welcome to leave us now."

The six Ephrians stared back at the Mages.

"We aren't here for us," Deckard said proudly. "We're here for our country. Whatever our fates, this is where it begins."

Deckard drew his sword, and the rest followed suit. Evylin, Hewitt, and Thom held their broadswords, Rafferty clutched two short swords in his hands, and Ethenn lifted his bow.

Auden and Ilain shared a look, then smiled at the soldiers. "So let it begin," Ilain said ominously. The Calders turned and stepped into the hall before them.

Golden light flooded the hall like a sunrise. Radiant, yellow beams filled the narrow path of pale stone. Arched windows surrounded the walkway, inlaid with patterns of suns and rays of light. The Ephrians moved in behind the Calders, weapons ready. The farther they went, the brighter the room grew. Soon, it was so bright that Evylin almost forgot they were underground.

At the end of the hall was an iron door etched with another sun and rays of light. Auden gave them one last look before he and Ilain stepped up to its threshold. He placed his hand on the door, and a booming *thunk* reverberated through the hall. Evylin took an unconscious step back, bumping into Hewitt. He set his hand on her shoulder, and she looked up at him. He gave her an encouraging nod. Evylin smiled, then turned to face the door, rolling clicks echoing as the door began to slide open.

"Into the fray," Auden whispered.

Ilain took his hand and squeezed it. "We'll be fine."

The Calders entered the Keep, which was filled with blinding light. Following closely behind the siblings, Evylin shielded her eyes from the overwhelming brightness. The stark white gradually softened into a cream, then into a gentle yellow reminiscent of fresh butter or a daffodil.

Once her eyes adjusted to the brilliant light, Evylin blinked at the beautiful garden around them. Pebbled paths wove through grass greener than any Evylin had ever seen. Lush trees and bushes with cream flowers clustered around the garden. At the bottom of the white stone staircase, the lawn spread out on the roof of a tower, halting at the sudden edge, which dropped into the vast nothingness of the sky beyond.

At the other end of the tower, about five hundred yards away, an ivory stone obelisk rose high above them. "I take it that's where we're headed?" she asked.

Ilain held up a hand. "Listen," she ordered.

Evylin heard nothing: no wind, no movement, only the sound of their breathing.

Deckard grasped Evylin's arm. She looked up to see his eyes widen. "What is that?" he asked.

"The Shades," Ilain said, stepping around them. "The first wave approaches."

Suddenly, Evylin became aware of a subtle, pulsating hum that filled the air. All at once, a group of Shades appeared. Glowing, yellow forms climbed over the edge of the tower. They were humanoid in shape but surging with light. They rose to their full height as they crested the tower's drop-off, slightly taller than Evylin, with wide forms and long arms. The creatures bore blank faces and no distinguishing marks anywhere on them.

"On your guard!" Deckard called.

Ilain brushed her hand through the air, a breeze rising around them. The Shades, somewhere around forty in number, charged. Evylin tightened her grip on her sword. Closer now, she could see the light of the creatures glowing through the cracks of their clay forms. They sprinted for the troop, unarmed but nonetheless unnerving. She settled her feet, ready to defend. But before she could raise her sword, Ilain circled her hands before her chest and threw them out to the sides.

A deafening scream of wind shot out, blasting all the Shades off the tower.

"Run!" Auden ordered, bolting down the path with Ilain at his heels.

Charging alongside the Calders, they raced over the tower.

"Don't stray too far off the path," Auden said as they ran. "We have to make it to the Chamber as fast as we can."

They bolted across the rooftop, the pebbles crunching and rolling under their feet. Evylin felt an odd blend of tension and boredom, with her sword clutched in her hand, yet nothing to run from.

The hum rose around them again.

"There will be too many in this next wave," Ilain called, holding her skirts as she ran. "I won't be able to do that again. We'll have to fight this time."

Twice as many Shades leaped over the sides. The troop slowed, preparing for battle. Evylin held her sword at the ready, Deckard on her left and Hewitt on her right.

"Don't show off," Hewitt growled. "Just kill the bastards."

Evylin didn't need him to remind her. What she needed was the thrill of a fight to kick back in and give her that rush, raising her senses and honing her focus.

Tightening her fingers on the leather grip, she took a deep breath.

An army of Shades raced nearer, Ilain's wind knocking some of them back, a column of fire intertwined in the blast. Evylin would have marveled at the magic, but the rest of the Shades demanded her attention.

Evylin released her breath and brought her sword down.

It connected with a Shade's shoulder, slicing through like swiping through the air. The light blinked as the creature split and shattered to the ground. Then light burst about them in an explosion of searing white.

The world was radiant as Evylin lifted her arms to shield herself from the intense glow. Sparkling dots danced in her vision—yellow, orange, brown, and black—as she attempted to regain focus. She heard the others gasping and grunting, battling their own blindness.

"Don't kill them!" Deckard ordered just as something took a swipe at her. It hit her arm and grabbed on, but she struck out with her foot and managed to clip the side of its leg.

The sound of frazzled fighting on every side pressed in on Evylin, but she didn't let it distract her. Following the direction of her kick, Evylin rolled into the Shade. She slammed her tricep against its head, and the grasp on her arm fell away. She followed through with another kick to knock the creature back.

Blinking rapidly, Evylin managed to duck as she sensed another Shade coming her way. A coolness crept over her mind, the creature's arms gliding over her head in a soft *whoosh.*

There it was.

The focus.

The rush.

Body lit with energy and excitement, Evylin closed her eyes against the searing world and struck out with her sword. She heard the shatter of clay and instinctively turned her head away from any increasing flares.

All around her, the battle raged. Somehow, her auditory sense filled in for her blindness, creating a clear picture of her team. Rafferty and Thom swung wildly, panting heavily as they struck at anything nearby. Deckard and Ethenn fared only a bit better; their breathing was more labored, but their fighting was less frantic. Up ahead, she sensed Auden and Ilain managing their fight calmly.

Hewitt sounded like a madman, growling deep in his throat as he moved around the battlefield. She could hear his sword swinging, slashing through the air with precision. She had little doubt he was cutting down dozens of these creatures.

A thrill of pride leaped into Evylin's chest as she returned to the fight. She would join her uncle in this glorious adventure, this impossible moment of magic and danger. She would fight with him, as Ryen would have done.

Adjusting to the bright light, Evylin opened her eyes. She caught glimpses of Shades around them now. The numbers were thinning even as most of their team struggled. Hewitt and she were doing enough damage to keep them safe while Auden and Ilain handled the rest with their magic.

A Shade's blaze blew past Evylin when Auden slammed his glowing fists into its chest. Bits of his red hair had fallen onto his forehead. He turned and tossed an open hand out toward another. It blew across the field in an arc of sunlight and flame.

With no time to appreciate the magnificence of his magic, Evylin turned back to the oncoming Shades around her.

Their team battled fiercely against the beings, but more kept emerging over the tower's edges. Light flickered around them as they attacked the creatures. Many of their teammates were still fumbling blindly, struggling to protect themselves. Yet, Evylin and Hewitt continued to dominate the field.

Somehow, the flares were getting easier to manage. Whether it was because she could better time when to avert her gaze when landing the killing strike or because of her heightened senses, she couldn't tell. How did the world change so much when she fought? Why did everything become clearer? Her control over her body was easier to manage, and her eyes handled the burning flashes of light readily. Hewitt once told her that adrenaline didn't help in a fight. It caused you to get sloppier and tired you out more quickly. She knew adrenaline wasn't what this sense was, yet she didn't know what else it could be.

When Hewitt tore apart the final Shade atop the tower, he grabbed the collar of Rafferty's coat and pulled the weasel back to his feet. "Open your eyes, soldier," he ordered. "You can't fight like that."

"I can't fight with them open either," Rafferty insisted, blinking unceasingly as his unseeing silver-gray eyes watered.

As the brightness faded, Evylin hurried to Deckard's side as he rubbed his own eyes. "Are you all right?" she asked.

"Yeah," he muttered, trying to clear his vision. "It's just—it's hard to see."

Evylin scanned the rest of them. While Ilain grimaced and blinked rapidly, she seemed far better off than expected. Auden rushed the rest of them forward, vision unaltered. Thom groped about as blind as Rafferty and Deckard while Ethenn managed a fraction better.

"I'll stay at the back," the hunter said, still squinting. "I can pick them off that way and not worry about being in the fray of . . . whatever it is that they're doing."

"Better be in the front," Auden suggested. "They'll try to surround us and separate us. We'd rather you be closer to the Chamber than farther away."

Ilain grabbed her brother's arm. "We don't have time to stand around. The third wave won't wait."

"You three," Hewitt said to Deckard, Thom, and Rafferty, "stay in the center. Evie and I will watch the perimeter. You get whatever we can't."

All of them hesitated, but the hum of the Shades returned, and they started rushing toward the obelisk in the distance.

In less than a minute, the third wave of Shades climbed over the edges, and the attack began anew. Columns of fire and light seared through the air, knocking the unsettling forms right back over the side. Hewitt took the left group, tearing five asunder with one sweep of his sword. Evylin took the right, taking down a handful of her own. Arrows arced around them as Ethenn paced ahead. Deckard, Thom, and Rafferty waited, swords raised and eyes down.

Flashes erupted everywhere.

Cutting through these creatures was so very unlike when they'd saved the prince.

Killing these magical generations held little similarity to killing real men. There was no bone or sinew to tear through. No blood seeping from the wounds. No life leaving their bodies.

Hewitt always told her that killing was difficult. *"It hurts,"* he'd admitted. *"Taking a man's life. But it's necessary at times. And when you know that it's them or you . . . that makes it an easier weight to carry."*

Though Evylin didn't regret the lives she'd had to take during their rescue, she did feel remorse deep within her.

But this—this felt nothing like that.

This was pure thrill.

Though a few Shades slipped by her, Evylin held the line with great success. She spun away from the flares as she turned to face her next opponent. Small piles of clay crumbled over the manicured grass beneath her boots. She was tearing them down without a second thought.

A Shade leaped past Evylin, headed for Rafferty, and she turned to catch it in the back. The explosion of light caused her to dip her head down. She started to turn when another Shade grabbed hold of her from behind. Its hum was so loud in her ear that she felt her body vibrate from the pulse. She tried to kick herself free of its grasp, but the creature was stronger than she expected.

Tearing at its arm, she felt chunks of clay rip under her nails. But it didn't give way. Instead, it began to drag her away from the group and toward the edge.

A whistle brushed past her ear as a knife embedded into the Shade's neck, and she closed her eyes against the subsequent burst of light.

"Come on," Deckard said, grabbing her hand and pulling her up. "We've got to run."

They tore down the path after the rest of the team, racing away from the oncoming waves of Shades. Hand still in his, Evylin stared at him in shock. "Did you throw that knife?" she asked.

He glanced at her. "I had to."

"I didn't know you were any good with knives," she said, pulling away and slicing down a Shade that got too close. They both turned away from the exploding flash.

Deckard kicked another Shade away. "I'm not," he said, ducking as one more grabbed at him.

"And you threw one at my head?" Evylin gasped, swinging to kill the Shade.

"I had to save you," Deckard insisted, taking her hand again.

The team raced across the path as more Shades rose over the sides of the tower. Auden and Ilain were right; they were trying to surround them. Evylin's heart stuttered, knowing there was no way to pass them without engaging in an all-out fight. Having never endured a battle of this length, she could feel herself growing tired. She couldn't imagine that they would last long without a break for breath.

Ilain stopped dead in her tracks. "Auden!" she yelled and held out her hand.

Her brother turned back, Shades pressing in around the team now.

The Calders clasped their hands together.

The rumble of thunder issued from their grasp, and then a beam of fire and light exploded forth, disintegrating all Shades around them in one fell swoop.

"Run," Auden said between heavy breaths. "The next wave won't be far behind."

Hewitt and Ethenn patrolled ahead, alert as the rest of them followed rapidly.

"What did you two do?" Thom demanded.

"I told you," Ilain said weakly. "We can share our energy and increase our power. It's highly effective but comes at a cost."

"What cost?" Evylin asked.

"Such an intense force of power saps a lot of energy from your body," she explained. "Magic is all about focus and connection. When you release such a charge, that focus becomes a lot harder to hold onto."

They were a mere hundred yards from the obelisk when Ethenn called out, "They're coming over!"

Another army of Shades charged, crawling up over both sides. Evylin braced herself, the sword's hilt sweaty under her palms.

"Just run," Auden insisted. "We can make it if we just run!"

Hesitating, Evylin caught Deckard's gaze as he sprinted up to her. He grabbed her hand and pulled her along. The obelisk rose into the yellow sky, hundreds of feet in the air. Evylin could now see the details at the base. There were arches carved into the side, mirroring the hallway. A single opening awaited them, the sign of a sun over its top. Whatever lay beyond that door, Evylin couldn't imagine it'd be much safer than outside, but still, she ran for it.

A Shade crashed into Deckard, ripping his hand from Evylin's. "Jonn!" she cried, ready to charge after with her sword. But to her surprise, she didn't need to.

Deckard and the Shade rolled across the ground, then Deckard kicked up and knocked his assailant off. The creature landed on its feet, and Deckard pushed himself off the ground. Then he spun around to face his attacker faster than the average man could move. His sword swung with practiced ease, severing the Shade's head.

Evylin gasped, unable to appreciate his surprising skill as two new Shades came at her. She slashed through the first and kicked in the knee of the second. When she drew her blade back to kill the other Shade, Deckard's sword drove into its chest. Successive flashes of yellow burst before them, their arms lifted to protect their eyes.

"Let's go," he said, pushing her onward.

Around them, Thom and Rafferty took on a few Shades, keeping their gazes averted, while Hewitt killed four or five alone. Ethenn, bow stashed, wielded his broadsword, the weapon more effective given the beings' increasing proximity. He sliced through the creatures as he chased the Calders.

Evylin pushed her legs to go faster, feeling a tightness pulling at her rib cage.

"Keep going," Deckard said, drawing back. Evylin glanced behind to see him drop back alongside Hewitt to help Rafferty and Thom catch up. She was about to go back and help when she heard Ilain call for her.

Three Shades had overtaken Ethenn and begun to pull him toward the edge. Auden and Ilain were busy fighting off five others.

Doubling her speed, Evylin charged after Ethenn. He put up enough of a fight, kicking and punching, that she managed to gain on them. Taking her knife from her belt, she slashed the first Shade's chest. It fell to the ground with a blink and then a flare. Closing her eyes, Evylin used her sense of sound and memory to place the location of the other Shades and Ethenn. With the butt of her sword, Evylin rammed it into the second Shade's head, then she sliced the throat of the third with the knife.

Ethenn jumped up and pulled Evylin back toward the obelisk, immediately breaking into a run. "Thanks," he gasped, blinking against the remnants of the overpowering light.

"Anytime," she replied, vision clearing.

They made it to the door within seconds of the others, Ilain and Auden reaching it first. Without hesitating, Ilain grabbed Ethenn's hand and plunged through the door.

"Get in," Auden ordered, shoving Evylin behind them.

Stumbling through the doorway, Evylin prepared to fight off more Shades or even the Guardian. Instead, Ethenn pulled her farther down a spiraled stone staircase and against a wall as the other men piled in.

With a final flash of Day magic and subsequent flares from the Shades, Auden slammed the door shut behind him. He turned and leaned against it with a heavy sigh.

Ilain scanned them, then slumped against the wall. "Thank Allore," she muttered. "We made it."

Auden set a hand on her shoulder, facing the soldiers. "Well done, everyone. We— well, we made it through the first half."

"Now, onto the Guardian," Ilain added tiredly.

"That was . . ." Thom's fingers tore through his hair, slick with sweat. "That was bloody *insane*! You didn't tell us about—about that!"

"We didn't know," Auden said with a rather nonchalant air.

Deckard held up a hand to stop his brother's rebuttal. "Should we be standing here?" he asked through heaving breaths. "Aren't we still in danger?"

Auden shook his head. "No, this is the one moment of peace within the Keeps. This is our chance to catch our breath before we face the Guardian."

Hewitt glared at the Mage, seemingly untaxed by the fight. "And why would we be so lucky as to have a break?" he asked.

"If you had a treasure of great power," Auden said, "wouldn't you make sure you had a chance to retrieve it, should you ever need to? The Mages who designed the Keeps were wise enough to make the Relics recoverable, should they have the need."

Hewitt's narrowed gaze didn't soften, but he said no more.

"How long do we have?" Deckard asked.

"As long as we want," Auden said with a shrug. "But the longer we wait, the more likely it is for Ilain and me to lose the firm connections we've established with our magic."

Taking a deep breath, Deckard nodded. "Two minutes. Everyone, catch your breath and check for injuries, then we move ahead."

The two minutes passed in the blink of an eye. Assured that everyone made it through the fight without anything more than a few scrapes and bruises, they readied their weapons again and let Auden and Ilain lead them down the staircase into the Chamber.

As they crossed the threshold of the arched doorway, Deckard walked past Evylin and into the hall before them. His green-blue eyes grew wide, and his mouth dropped ajar.

As Evylin followed him and skirted around their team, she squinted against the brilliant light flooding the grand room before her. Clearly, they had entered the tower. The Chamber matched the rooftop garden in width and length, and its height extended at least as far as the obelisk above. The walls and floors gleamed with creamy marble streaked with golden veins. Towering columns stood every few feet, crafted from the same stone, radiating the same warm yellow glow as the sunlight outside.

At the far end stood a dais with a single-columned pedestal.

"Where are we?" Deckard whispered. And still, his voice echoed in the vast openness of the room.

Auden stepped to his side and answered, "We've entered the Day Relic's Chamber."

"I thought you said there'd be a guard here," Rafferty said, stepping past them into the room. "This place is as dead as Thommy-boy's love life."

"Excuse me?" Thom retorted.

But before he could say more, a tremor shook the ground, and a violent roar echoed around them. They stepped back, struggling to maintain their balance. A colossal figure emerged from behind one of the columns, its body covered in scales that glimmered like golden sunlight. Fierce horns jutted from its head, and a menacing snarl rumbled in its throat.

At first, Evylin thought the creature was a lizard. Then she saw the wings on its back. "That's not possible," Hewitt gasped at her side.

Thom stepped up, gaping at the beast. "It's a dragon," he muttered.

Evylin's body trembled, her blood thrumming through her veins. Her hand instinctively brushed her coat pocket, where she kept the everbloom flower tucked against her heart. She could hear Ryen's youthful voice, excited as they ran down the streambed, making their fantastic plans. *"And then,"* he said, *"we'll fight a dragon!"*

The Guardian roared again, flares of light shimmering through the air.

The troop scattered to escape the flames, but Evylin remained, locked in a trance. *Dragons aren't real,* her mind told her. And yet, there one stood.

Hewitt yanked her to the side, the heat of the flares blistering her skin before he pulled her away.

"Distract it," Auden ordered. "Ilain and I have to focus."

"How are we supposed to distract a *dragon*?" Thom yelled.

He never got an answer.

With Hewitt in the lead, the soldiers charged the Chamber Guardian. Ethenn, bow back in hand, sent off a shot at the creature. The arrow merely splintered off its glowing scales, ineffective. Hewitt and Deckard led the charge, rushing the dragon's legs.

Evylin drew up short, thinking better of following them. "Thom, Raff!" she called.

The pair followed her around one of the columns. "What are we doing?" Thom asked. "We have to help."

"We can't all attack it head-on." Evylin pointed to the end of the Chamber. "If we go around, we can make it think we're going for the Relic. It'll chase us and give Auden and Ilain time."

Thom and Rafferty shared a look, then shrugged.

"Let's do it," Rafferty said, taking off down the side hall. He slid out from behind the column and yelled, "Oi, ugly! Over here! We're going for your precious Relic."

The Guardian's reptilian head whipped around; its massive face scrunched as it prepared to blow out more sun-fire. From beneath, Deckard and Hewitt chopped at its legs, only irritating it rather than damaging it. An arrow from Ethenn landed under one of the wings, the weapon shattering but drawing the dragon's attention. He barely had enough time to avoid the dragon's flare as he escaped behind one of the columns.

"Don't forget us, ugly!" Rafferty yelled again. "Still headed for your Relic."

Evylin and Thom dashed to the far side of the room, rushing past Rafferty while the dragon roared behind them. Its massive legs shook the ground, causing Thom to stumble and trip both of them. They collapsed to the floor just as the Guardian approached.

White hot sun-fire pooled in its mouth as it spread its wings.

Deckard slid under the dragon, his sword slicing at the bottom as he went. Sparks ricocheted off the blade but didn't cut through the thick hide. However, it did catch the dragon's attention.

Ginormous feet stomped around Deckard, and Evylin's heart lurched. She pushed herself to her feet just as her husband rolled out of the dragon's reach. But a streak of crimson-red liquid marred the golden marble floor where he'd been. Her throat went dry. She wanted to run to him, but Thom grabbed her and dragged her away as the dragon's attention turned back to them.

The sun-fire sparked in the Guardian's throat again.

They dashed for the nearest column. Heat rose through the air around them as they made it behind the pillar. Evylin's shirt stuck to her back, sweat gliding across her skin. When the dragon roared suddenly, the sound moving farther away, they peered out cautiously to see what had drawn its attention.

In a dead sprint, Rafferty neared the dais, the Guardian barreling straight for him. It flapped its wings, and the colossal body lifted off the ground. Bright flames spurted in its mouth, ready to fly at the soldier.

Without thought, Evylin rushed from her cover. When she was close enough, she jumped onto the dragon's tail, which was still dragging along the ground. Using the golden spikes protruding from its hide as leverage, she climbed up. She pulled the knife from her boot and plunged it toward the underside of the tail. It didn't pierce the hide, but she felt something crack, so she tried again. Another crack and another attempt. Then the blade sank into the monster's flesh.

Twisting the knife, she yanked back, tearing muscle as she went.

The dragon's ear-splitting screech shook the room. With a violent whip of its tail, it bucked Evylin off. She crashed onto the marble floor, landing on her side. She rolled to absorb the blow, but numbness spread across her body as she skidded away from the dragon.

More arrows flew, and Hewitt charged the beast again. A gust of wind from the dragon's wings knocked the man and the arrows back.

Their momentary distraction dealt with, talons scraped against the floor as the dragon turned back to his prey, now at the dais. His roar preceded a massive bolt of sun-fire that arced for Rafferty.

Evylin tried to push herself off the floor, but she wouldn't be able to reach him in time. Nothing could save him now.

Light brighter than the sun flashed, and Evylin covered her eyes.

The sound of the dragon's rattling breath and beating wings vanished. The Chamber was silent.

Blinking the dark spots away, the haziness faded, and Evylin saw that the Guardian was gone. She looked down the hall, seeing Auden and Ilain hurrying to the dais. Ethenn helped Deckard rise while Hewitt and Thom rushed to Evylin's side. "What happened?" she asked.

The men shrugged, but Ilain gestured for them to join. "Auden and I channeled the power of Day and destroyed the Guardian," she explained as though it were a daily occurrence.

They followed the Calders up to the dais where Rafferty stood waiting on them. "What now?" he asked.

Auden's eyes narrowed. "What do you mean?"

"I mean . . ." Rafferty gestured to the pedestal as they drew near the marble dais. "How do we summon the Relic?

Ilain froze, eyes on the empty pillar as Auden rushed forward and set a shaking hand on the flat top. "We don't," he said, his voice hollow.

Evylin frowned, heartbeat still erratic. "How do we get the Relic, then?"

Auden met her stare blankly. "We can't," he said. "It's already gone."

CHAPTER FIFTY-SIX

"What do you mean, it's gone?" Deckard demanded. His abdomen throbbed, and he pressed his hand to the wound. A sticky dampness seeped through his fingers, but his focus was on Auden's confounding statement.

Auden tugged at his coat's high collar, brows pulled together. "Someone must have taken it," he muttered, staring at the pedestal.

A cacophony of questions rippled through their team. Thom and Hewitt both glared at the Mages, demanding an explanation. Rafferty swore and backed off the dais. But Ilain gripped her brother's arm.

"You know that isn't possible, Auden," she said fiercely. "You would have felt it."

"How?" Evylin asked.

The siblings ignored her question, holding one another's gaze. He shook his head, hair a deep bronze from the sweat that dampened it. Some unspoken conversation passed between them, and he nodded.

Deckard took a step closer, his side lancing with the action, but before he could speak, Auden's eyes went wide, and his head whipped around toward the Chamber's entrance.

"No," he murmured, and Ilain gripped his arm. His face contorted with something like rage. "No, no. It was here!"

"What are you—?"

Auden cut off Thom's agitated question, trembling as he spoke. "It was *here*. And someone stole it out from under our noses."

Questions poured from the group, but Deckard had had enough of the Calders' cryptic behavior. "What is going on?" he demanded. "Where is the Relic?"

"We have to go," Auden said, taking his sister's hand. "We have to stop them."

Stepping in their path, Hewitt set a hand to the Mage's chest. "You're not going anywhere until you answer our bloody questions," he snarled.

Auden glared at him, then turned to Deckard. "The Relic was taken," he explained sharply. "Someone followed us in and took it while we were distracted fighting the Guardian."

"How is that possible?" Evylin asked. "We would have seen them."

"Not if they shrouded themselves," Ilain countered. "With Night magic, you can cover yourself in shadow, becoming invisible to the outside world."

They all gaped at her.

Deckard was growing lightheaded, and he struggled to comprehend their words. "Who could be powerful enough to do that and make it through the Keep unscathed?" he asked.

Auden drew in a shaky breath. "I don't know," he admitted. "To our knowledge, we're the only ones who've unlocked the secret to the ancient Mages' ciphers. No one else should have the locations to the Relics."

"Does that mean they've been following us?"

"Unless we're wrong and someone else learned the correct sequence. Though," Auden glanced at Ilain, "that would be strangely conspicuous timing, two separate parties solving a thousand-year-old puzzle at the same time."

"How do you know it's at the same time?" Ethenn asked suddenly. "What if they stole it a long time ago?"

"I felt it," Auden admitted.

"Felt what?" Hewitt demanded.

"When the Relics are taken . . ." Auden stopped, then pressed a hand to his chest. "When *our* Relics are taken from their Keeps, we feel it. It's a fail-safe. A protection should any Mage try to take them with the wrong intentions. We're alerted so we can reclaim them if need be."

Auden's eyes went back to the entrance. "I felt it," he repeated. "Just now. The Day Relic was here when we entered, and when it left only moments ago, I felt it in my chest like a second heartbeat."

The room fell silent, the Ephrians trying to fathom what this meant for their mission.

"We have to go," Auden insisted, his deep voice commanding. "Whoever this Mage is, and whatever they want, we have to catch them."

"I'm not so sure that's a good idea," Hewitt said, arms crossed. "Seems to me, this Mage is more dangerous than the both of you—sneaking in here, staying alive while we fought the battle, and then making their way out. While we're all exhausted, they've already made it through the fray unscathed. Even *if* we could catch up to them, our odds aren't looking good."

"We don't have a choice," Auden argued. "We can't let them get away with the Relic. No matter who this Mage is, I guarantee you, they aren't as well-intentioned as us."

Deckard looked over his team's faces. Each soldier seemed wary, exchanging uncertain looks. But Evylin's eyes were focused solely on him, waiting for his directive.

Setting his jaw, Deckard turned back to the Mages. "We need to leave," he said. "Whatever their purpose in taking it, we aren't in any state to fight them. But that doesn't mean we can't track them."

The troop nodded, and Deckard turned to go. Searing pain tore through his side, causing him to grimace. "But first," he muttered, the room growing spotty, "I think I need to sit down."

As Deckard's knees gave out, Hewitt caught him. Blood slipped through Deckard's fingers where his hand pressed to the wound, and he heard Evylin gasp. Thom and Ethenn were there, helping Hewitt lower Deckard to the dais. Auden pushed through, Evylin beside him.

The Day Mage motioned to Hewitt and Ethenn. "Hold him up," he instructed, kneeling before Deckard.

Thom hovered at the side, hooded brow drawn in concern. "What are you doing?" he demanded.

"He'll be fine," Ilain promised with a dismissive wave.

Evylin sat at Deckard's side, a comforting hand on his arm and a worried expression on her face. He tried to smile at her, but the room shifted precariously with the movement, and he closed his eyes against the sensation. "I'm not sure I'll be able to walk out of here," he muttered.

Ignoring the comment, Auden unbuttoned Deckard's coat. "Remove your hand from the wound," he ordered.

"I don't think that's a good idea."

"Evylin," Auden said calmly, "take his hand away."

Despite her hesitation, Evylin wrapped her fingers around his hand. "Don't," he whispered, attempting to hold it steady. He was convinced that the blood would flow freely without the pressure, but he was too weak to fight her.

"What are you doing?" Evylin asked Auden, her fingers entwined with Deckard's, slick with his blood.

Pushing back Deckard's coat, Auden pulled his tunic up to expose the wound. A long gash opened his abdomen, deep red blood leaking from it. Evylin grimaced, but Deckard couldn't look away, bemused to see his own sinew beneath the gaping cut.

Instantly, Auden set his hand on the wound, and Deckard gasped at the pain. Auden closed his eyes and whispered, "I'm healing him."

Warmth spread across Deckard's skin, tingling around the gash. Then the sensation seemed to burrow into him, fusing muscle and flesh, heating his veins. The buzz was pleasant at first, like the sunshine. But as it built, the temperature rose to a burn, searing white-hot under his skin.

Deckard tried to bite back the pain but heard himself grunt against it anyway.

But soon, the feeling abated completely, and Auden took his hand away, his clean palm clear of any sign he'd touched a wound. Looking down, Deckard saw a red streak of patched-up skin on his abdomen, blood dried around the area.

"I'm not strong enough to completely heal you at the moment," Auden said apologetically. He adjusted his collar, the glint of a gold chain beneath catching the light only for a second. "But I caused the blood to clot and cauterized the wound. You should see it heal faster than normal in the next few days from the Day magic infused into it. However, you'll still experience lightheadedness and fatigue due to the blood loss."

Evylin's fingers loosened around Deckard's, but she didn't let go. "Will he be able to make it out on his own?" she asked. "We'll have to run back across the tower, won't we?"

"What about those doors?" Rafferty asked, pointing to the wall behind the dais.

As Deckard turned his head, he noticed two metal doors suspended in an archway. They reminded him of the gates to the botanical gardens in Loclight, adorned with intricate swirls and crosshatching. Each door featured a halved medallion: the left side etched with a sun and the right with two moons, the one superimposed above the other.

Ilain stepped toward the Chamber's entrance. "I'm afraid those doors don't lead us where we need to go," she said. "At least, not yet."

"Then we'll have to fight Shades again?" Thom asked, still watching Deckard with concern.

Auden stood, brushing his coat free of wrinkles. "I don't believe so," he replied. "The Relic is what animates the Keeps—including the Guardians and Shades within them. If it's no longer here, there's nothing to create the creatures."

"We need to get moving regardless," Hewitt grumbled, helping Deckard to stand. "Can you walk on your own?"

Deckard tested a step, then nodded. "I think so."

Hewitt and Ethenn backed away, but Evylin remained by his side. "Are you sure?" she asked, hands still clasped with his. Her brow furrowed, and her lips pulled down in worry.

Seeing her concern for him, Deckard wanted to do nothing more than to kiss her. Instead, he squeezed her hand. "I'm quite sure," he promised.

"Then let's get out of here, shall we?" Rafferty said. "This place gives me the creeps."

Most of them moved at a slow jog toward the other end of the Chamber, their eyes darting to and fro for any signs of danger. Deckard and Evylin walked near the back, Hewitt guarding them as they moved at a slower pace. Though he realized he'd already begun to feel better. By the time they'd crossed half the room, he was able to pick up his speed too.

"Don't push yourself," Hewitt warned.

Deckard kept moving steadily faster. "Honestly, I feel fine."

Auden and Thom ascended the staircase first, with Ilain and Rafferty next. Hewitt followed behind Deckard and Evylin as Ethenn watched the back. They wound their way up the steps and cautiously opened the door. When Thom gave the all clear, they moved back into the bright sunlight of the tower's roof.

The green trees were still and untouched. Nothing moved, and no sound could be heard. Deckard listened for the hum of Shades to emerge, but the silence remained. "We're sure they're not coming?" he asked Auden.

"We're not sure of much anymore," Auden replied, his green eyes searching the entirety of the garden.

"Let's go," Ilain said, marching out ahead of them all.

As they took a hurried but steady pace across the tower, the glowing yellow light of the sky began to fade. They watched warily as it shifted from gold to amber to bronze.

"Can you run?" Auden asked, his voice wavering as the space turned dark.

Deckard assessed his condition. The pain from his injury had nearly faded, and he sensed a resurgence of energy. It appeared that Auden's magic was more effective than anticipated. "I can," he confirmed.

"All right, then we sprint across," Auden said, picking up the pace. "I don't want to know what happens when the magic completely fades from this place."

With that ominous remark, they quickened their stride, boots crunching on the pebbled paths. They arrived at the iron door just as the sky deepened to a dark brown hue, and Ilain rushed to place her hand on its face. There was a moment of stillness . . . then the *thunk* of the lock as it disengaged.

They hurried into the hall, the door shutting firmly behind them as they exhaled in relief. Moments later, they stepped back into the afternoon sunlight. Yet, the day felt dimmer now compared to the bright glow that once filled the Keep's interior.

Deckard walked away from the cave, looking out across the shore. He took a deep breath of the soothing salt air. Then his knees buckled, and he collapsed. Evylin tried to support him, but Hewitt took the weight she couldn't carry alone.

"Idiot," Hewitt grumbled, pulling Deckard back to his feet. "I told you not to push yourself."

Feeling all the pain and exhaustion from the strength he'd lost in the Chamber, Deckard grimaced as he set his hand back to his side. "I felt fine," he muttered through gritted teeth as Hewitt pulled his arm over his neck. "Obviously, I was wrong."

"You'll be all right once you've gotten some rest," Auden assured him. "Do you think you can ride?"

"Ride?" Evylin asked, sending him a scathing glare. "He can't walk!"

Ilain patted Evylin's arm. "Don't worry," she said, a curious grin on her face as she considered Deckard. "He'll patch up nicely. And he only needs to stay upright to ride a horse."

"We have to get to Virwoud," Auden continued. "There's no way for us to track the Day Relic now. So our only hope is to beat this other Mage to the Water Relic."

"What if they just follow us there too?" Thom countered.

"It doesn't matter," Auden insisted. "Now that we know, we can be more watchful. But we can't risk them getting the other Relics. Not when we don't know why they want them."

Evylin began to argue, but Deckard caught her hand, which was still coated in his blood. "Evie," he said, holding her gaze. "I'm fine. And he's right, we need to leave."

"You have to heal," she insisted adamantly.

"I will. As we ride to Virwoud." She opened her mouth, but Deckard tightened his grip. "We have to go."

The Calders led them back to the city, with Hewitt supporting Deckard's weight. Once they reached the inn, Rafferty struck up a conversation with the woman at the desk to distract her while they carried Deckard inside. Hewitt dropped him off in their room while the others prepared to leave. Though he'd assured her he could manage alone, Evylin remained at his side. He was grateful as each movement sent shooting pains through his lower torso. She helped him remove his torn and stained coat and tunic, swapping them out for his spares. He noticed she wasn't nearly as uncomfortable with his bared chest as before, treating the moment with a more clinical demeanor.

"We'll have to stitch this," Evylin said, looking at the hole in his specialized Order of the King coat. She grimaced at the still-damp blood on the gray wool. "And give it a thorough cleaning."

"They gave us two," Deckard noted, buttoning the coat as he sat on the bed.

She raised her brow. "And what happens if you try getting yourself killed again?"

He grinned dryly. "Then we'll stitch this one up."

Within an hour, they rode out of Norhels's gate to the south.

Thom pulled his horse alongside Deckard's while they trotted down the road. "You're sure this is a good idea?" he asked warily.

Despite having always felt comfortable atop a horse, Deckard disliked riding wounded. He lacked his usual control, each step jarring his side. "No," he admitted quietly so as not to worry Evylin, who rode with Hewitt just ahead of them. "But we don't have spare time to lose."

"We don't have a spare of you either," Thom replied.

The brotherly concern surprised Deckard, and he felt his mouth twitch up in a smile. "I'll be fine," he promised for what felt like the tenth time.

Thom didn't buy his reassurance, but he didn't press him either. He rode by or near his side the rest of the day. The troop pushed through the late afternoon and into the evening, only stopping once the night grew too precarious to continue. They'd chosen not to bother with finding settlements each night in favor of a more direct route to Virwoud. However, they refused to let Deckard help set up the camp. Deckard protested as Thom and Ethenn erected the tent and Evylin prepared the bedroll.

Hewitt even slapped Deckard's hand when he tried to untie the blanket from his saddle. "You'll reopen the wound," the burly man said, then forced him to lie down.

Deckard was sure he wouldn't be able to relax, let alone sleep, with them milling around the camp. Yet, in a matter of moments, his eyes grew heavy, and his body eased into the abyss of dreams. Sunlight streamed through Deckard's mind, and Shades ran toward him—bright beacons of light and clay. But instead of fighting, Deckard let them come. He stood and absorbed them, his body tingling with their light. The pain in his side disappeared. The army of Shades melded into a single ray and struck Deckard's heart. His body was alive with power, stronger than ever before.

When the radiant light died down, Deckard stood in the Relic's Chamber, the pedestal in front of him. But it wasn't empty.

On the creamy marble rested a glowing golden amulet. A yellow topaz was affixed in the gold setting. He reached out, fingers brushing its metal ridges, shaped like flares of light. The gemstone was warm to the touch, pulsing the same rhythm as the hum of the Shades—like a heartbeat.

Deckard's eyes drifted up to the metalwork on the door. The sun and moons glowed bright yellow and deep purple. The door began to open, and darkness flooded in.

10TH OF GALATAE, 1574

Deckard woke on his back, Evylin tucked next to his side. The soft violet shade of predawn filtered through the snowy treetops. The camp was still, and the embers of the fire smoked. Snow gathered on the banks all around them, the horses nickering softly as they rested.

Releasing a deep breath, Deckard gave himself five seconds in which to remember the Day Relic's Keep. One second to relive the fear of the Shades surrounding them. For another second, he permitted himself to consider the monstrous dragon they'd fought and another to remember the unthinkable pain as its talon ripped through him. Next, he considered the shock of the missing Relic. And for a final moment, he experienced the rush he'd felt in the chaos of it all.

It was odd, the heat that curled up his spine, filling his body like the Shades had in his dream. He'd felt stronger, more in control. He'd even fought better, saving Evylin with that otherwise impossible knife throw. He couldn't explain it; he just knew he could make it. Perhaps Hewitt's training was finally getting him somewhere.

Though, he'd almost died at the hands of a dragon, so continuing his training would probably be beneficial.

Gently, Deckard pressed at his wound, testing for pain. When he felt none, he pressed harder. Then he lifted his shirt to feel the wound. The skin was smooth.

Worried by the absence of his injury, Deckard shifted so he could see. All he found was his stomach, flat and solid as it had been before they'd entered the Keep, as though the talon had never struck him. He supposed Auden had been right—the Day magic had healed him quickly and perfectly.

Deckard slipped away from Evylin, lifting her hand from his chest and setting it gently on the ground. He pulled on his boots quietly and buttoned his coat. Then he grabbed his sword belt, buckling it as he walked over to Hewitt and Ethenn's tent. The men slept on either side of the ground, facing opposite directions. Hewitt snored softly, looking oddly peaceful.

Cautiously, Deckard kicked the bottom of Hewitt's foot. He jumped back in expectation as the man flew up, knife outstretched. His gray eyes scanned Deckard's face, then narrowed.

Deckard tipped his head toward the trees.

Letting out a deep breath, Hewitt rose. He gathered his things, and they walked into the woods. After several minutes, Hewitt spoke up. "You sure this is a good idea with your injury?" he asked.

"I'm not injured anymore," Deckard said, stepping over a large root. "Auden's magic healed it."

"What, completely?"

"Completely," he confirmed.

The man snorted, tugging at his thick beard. "I suppose having Mages around isn't such a bad thing after all." He stopped in the middle of a small open clearing. "Here's good enough."

Deckard stared at all the growth around the edges, knowing he'd have to be cautious of where he stepped. Instead of voicing his concern, he drew his sword. "What's our lesson for today?" he asked.

"No lesson today. After how well you did yesterday, I want to see you put that into action."

"How well I did?" Deckard scoffed. "I got injured. And I couldn't see worth anything."

"Yet, you managed to defend yourself, protect Evie, and even kill a good number of those bloody things. That giant beast only got you because you took an idiotic risk."

Though his instinct was to deflect the praise, Deckard accepted it. "I did feel more confident. For that, I owe you my gratitude."

Hewitt hefted his sword, ignoring the comment. "Let's get on with it."

18TH OF GALATAE, 1574

Deckard missed the block, and Hewitt's sword hit his shoulder again. Deckard had grown used to the bruises and repeated hits over the past months of training. But a week had passed since they'd left Norhels, and his anger resurfaced.

"I don't understand it," Deckard said irritably. They'd traveled outside the town of Lynnpoint to train in private as they did whenever they stayed at an inn the night before. Birds flew above them from tree to tree, chirping lightly. Nearing the south, the early signs of spring were all around them, though the snow remained on the ground.

"Don't understand what?" Hewitt asked with his sword at his side.

Deckard threw his hands wide. "Even you said I did well in the Keep. I thought I was learning, that I was getting better. But it's like I'm right back where I started."

"Sometimes, a man needs a real fight to reach his full potential."

"What do you mean?"

"You think too much, Deckard," Hewitt said, sheathing his sword. "You've got skill, but you can't access that when you're always thinking about it. In the Keep, it was either act or die. Your skills took over. In our training, you have too much time to think. You get in your own way."

Deckard frowned. "So I should stop thinking?"

Hewitt nodded.

"That seems counterintuitive. How do I act without knowing what I'm going to do?"

A knife flew at Deckard from Hewitt's hand. Lifting his sword, Deckard knocked it off its path just as it narrowly missed embedding itself in his shoulder.

"You just act, you idiot," Hewitt growled. "Like you did in there. You don't think about it. You do it. You have the skills to be a good swordsman. But you get in your way by thinking about it too much."

"I don't know how to fix that," Deckard said.

Hewitt redrew his sword. "First: Relax. Let your mind be at peace."

Deckard took a deep breath, rolled his shoulders, and let his feet settle into the snow. "What next?"

"Next, we fight," Hewitt said and immediately charged.

Their swords met. Deckard rolled with the blow, then pressed his sword up and over Hewitt's, tapping the man on the shoulder.

They broke apart, Hewitt with a hearty laugh. "Better," he said, charging again.

Deckard blocked the first two strikes, then Hewitt hit his arm with the flat of the sword.

"But not good enough," Hewitt revised.

That was what worried Deckard.

CHAPTER FIFTY-SEVEN

20TH OF GALATAE, 1574

"We should arrive in Virwoud tomorrow morning," Deckard told Auden, taking the seat nearest the Mage. "Do you think we'll be able to find the Keep easily enough?"

Auden's hair glowed in the firelight. "Well, it is the Water Relic, so I'd imagine it will be close to the ocean," he quipped.

"The Day Relic was close to the ocean too," Ethenn noted. "Is that common?"

"In a way," Ilain replied. "All the Orders are set near the ocean, as are the Keeps."

"Why?"

"There's something about the salt air," she said with a poetic lilt. "It clears your head and helps you to focus. The perfect atmosphere for magic."

Ethenn glanced up from the rabbit he was skinning. "So . . . it will be easy, then," he said, "to locate the Keep?"

"I wouldn't say easy," she replied. "Just not as difficult as one might think."

"Either way," Auden said, butchering another rabbit, "it will be Ilain who finds it first."

"Because the Water Relic is Elemental?" Ethenn stated more than asked.

"You're quite attentive, aren't you?" Ilain said, scanning him with interest.

Ethenn shrugged. "I'm a hunter. That's our job."

Approving more and more of the young man, Deckard smiled. He'd grown fond of their troop. Ethenn proved to be an asset, intelligent and strong. Thom had always had skill, but these days, he showed marked improvement in his attitude and willingness to follow orders. Even Rafferty had grown on Deckard, his ability to shift the mood more useful than he'd expected.

He'd even grown to be less jealous of their relationship with Evylin. He understood now why she enjoyed their time together. And he had to admit that he'd not allowed himself to have that sort of relationship with her. It was his own fault that she didn't come to him to have fun. He didn't often have fun himself.

Watching as Evylin chatted with Thom and Rafferty on the other side of the fire, Deckard wondered if he'd ever be able to be that relaxed with her. Thom sat beside Evylin, his shoulder bumping into hers from time to time as they laughed or turned to each other. Rafferty lay on the ground beside them, head propped up on a log while his left foot rested on his right knee. He and Thom started sniggering at something Evylin had muttered.

"What's so funny?" Deckard asked, allowing himself to join the fun.

Evylin's eyes flickered to his. "Oh, just discussing our beloved Prince Ephren and his wit."

Deckard raised his brow. "I thought I'd convinced you not to leave me for him."

"He's just so rich and handsome."

Thom elbowed Evylin. "Two things Jonn is not."

"And what a shame it is," Ilain said slyly. "For you're not half as handsome as your brother, Thom."

Rafferty's laughter bellowed through the night air while Evylin laughed demurely behind her hand.

"Shut up," Thom grumbled, kicking Rafferty's leg.

Hewitt huffed from his seat near Deckard, muttering, "I live with children."

Normally, Deckard would agree with the man's sentiments. It was his prerogative that one should live seriously. But he couldn't deny the camaraderie Evylin and the young men shared because of their lightheartedness. Even Ilain got to join their little circle, being quick-witted and lively herself.

Evylin sat up straight and announced, "I have a game for us as we wait for dinner."

"A game, eh?" Rafferty said, grinning madly.

"Yes," Evylin confirmed. "One you'll like quite well, Raff, as it involves gambling."

"Oh, I do enjoy a good bet!"

"So does Jonn," Evylin said, her eyes twinkling in the firelight.

Deckard returned her smirk. "My betting days are behind me," he said. "I learned my lesson well."

"But you must join us for our game," she insisted playfully.

"Jonn isn't much for fun, Evie," Thom said, tapping her knee. "You know that."

Deckard stared at his brother suspiciously. He often questioned Thom's relationship with Evylin, uneasy with how friendly he'd grown. He always excused it because of their Shire heritage, where banter and familiarity were commonplace. But then moments like these would occur; Thom would deride Deckard and touch Evylin more freely than even Hewitt or Rafferty. At first, Deckard thought he was irrationally jealous. But he was growing tired of his brother's liberal attitude toward his wife.

Deckard held his brother's gaze, brow lifted. "Oh, Evylin and I have had quite entertaining times together," he challenged. "I dare say, more fun than you'd expect."

Thom paused while Rafferty sniggered. "That's some bold innuendo, Colonel," the weasel sniped.

"That was the point, Corporal," Deckard returned.

Evylin blushed even as she grinned. "See," she said, turning to Thom. "Jonn is full of surprises."

"Evidently," Thom muttered, glancing at Deckard with uncertainty.

Deckard didn't flinch away from his questioning gaze. He wanted him to see the line he'd clearly drawn: Thom could be jealous of Deckard's job, his friendships, his respect, and his possessions. But Evylin . . . Jealousy of her was off-limits.

"What's your game, Evie?" Ethenn asked.

Evylin's gaze shifted between Deckard and Thom before turning to the hunter. "It's a little sport for you all. You see, I learned something recently." She set her hands on her crossed legs demurely. "Jonn's been training."

Hewitt grunted and slapped Deckard on the back. "Told you she'd find out."

Giving the man an annoyed frown, Deckard scoffed. "I'd say a month and a half isn't a bad run at keeping a secret."

"A month and a half?" Evylin repeated, her smile wide. "Well, now you have to play my game."

"I don't know what your game is," he said, "but I very much doubt I'll end up with a shred of dignity by the time it's through."

"It's quite an easy game," she promised. "You show us what you've learned in these sixty days of training by fighting Thom."

All the spectators' eyes grew wide, most of them chuckling under their breath. Only Hewitt remained stoic, waiting with narrowed eyes.

Deckard scratched the thickening beard along his jawline as he considered her words. "That hardly sounds like a game," he noted. After his conversation with Hewitt two days ago, he'd started improving again. But two days was a very short amount of time, and Thom had trained with both Hewitt and Evylin for two months. Deckard's odds weren't high.

"Well, I'll explain it. The game comes from the betting." She gestured around them. "Our friends here wager which one of you will win."

"We all know how that will go," Thom remarked.

Unable to disagree, Deckard gave Evylin a sarcastic smile. "I think I'll pass."

"Come on, Colonel," Rafferty chimed in. "Let us have a bit of fun!"

"It's hard to have fun when it's at my expense."

"That's the point," Thom said smugly.

"Now, Thommy-boy," Rafferty shook a mocking finger at him, "I'm sure Eve's not so cold-hearted as to embarrass her lover."

Evylin blanched at the term.

"Surely, she believes in her dear colonel more than she believes in you—her least important friend."

Thom took a failed swipe at the weasel.

Rafferty grinned. "However, I'd grant he does seem to be proving your earlier point: He's not much for fun."

Deckard met Evylin's steady gaze. He knew there was no winning for him. If he said no, they'd all call him a disappointment and a spoilsport. But if he said yes and made a fool of himself, there'd be no chance of impressing her. And hadn't that been the whole point of training with Hewitt in the first place? To prove himself worthy of her.

No matter which choice, he'd lost already.

"Fine," Deckard said. If he was going to lose, he might as well prove Thom's analysis false. And he might manage enough of a fight to prove himself not a totally incompetent swordsman.

"Really?" Evylin asked, surprise lightening her voice.

Realizing she hadn't expected him to go along with her game, Deckard felt his confidence rise. "Really," he assured her.

"Excellent!" Rafferty clasped his hands together. "Let's start the betting, shall we? Go on, Thommy-boy. We need to see our competitors side by side."

Thom rose at the goading, moving to stand near Deckard. "You're serious?" he asked. "You'll fight me?"

Deckard knew why Thom was surprised. Even though they'd trained together in the past, there had always been a clear understanding between them: They wouldn't take it seriously. It was never a duel but a means for Deckard to practice. This was serious. This was a fight.

Deckard stood up as well. "It's been fifteen years. May as well give it a shot."

"Fifteen years?" Ethenn asked, the surprise clear in his voice.

Thom smirked. "That's when I started winning."

"And what?" Rafferty prodded. "Our colonel's a sore loser?"

"Not at all," Deckard returned. "Thom's a sore winner."

Evylin laughed with Rafferty and Ethenn.

Ilain leaned forward, chin in hand. "Is he a better loser, then?"

"He's the grumpiest loser you've ever met," Rafferty huffed, and Ethenn and Evylin nodded in vehement agreement.

Thom scowled. "You lot are the worst friends a guy could have, you know?"

"You're a pretty terrible friend yourself," Rafferty replied, then rubbed his hands together as Hewitt retrieved the training swords. "All right, shall we start the bidding at one bronzer a pop? Or are we higher rollers than that?"

"I'll put five *silvers* on Jonn as the winner," Ilain said, digging into her coin purse.

Thom scoffed. "You're gonna lose it."

"I'll take my chances, darling."

"Excellent start, Highlady," Rafferty said, taking her coins and pulling out a scrap of paper to mark the accounts. "Who'll join our lovely Fire Mage? Highlord Day Mage?"

Auden scanned both men. "Three silvers on Jonn."

Rafferty raised his brow. "Two for the colonel already?"

"You've made the mistake of starting with the two who have the least information," Thom said, wearing one of his more overconfident grins. "They're both still in awe of his impeccable principles."

"And his dashing smile," Evylin added. "I'll take Auden's bet, even. Three on Thom."

"Aw, thank you, Evie," Thom replied with a bow.

Evylin met Deckard's eyes, a sparkle of mischief there. He took no offense at her betting against him. He felt like doing the same.

"Little Loxley?" Rafferty said, turning to the young man.

Ethenn's head pivoted as he stared back and forth between the brothers. "Sorry, Colonel Deckard," he muttered. "I've got to go with Thom."

Deckard gave him an approving nod.

"How much, kid?" Thom prompted.

"Oh—uh, three, I guess."

"And I'll put five in on Thommy-boy to match our sweet lady over there," Rafferty said, then turned to Hewitt. "How about you, Major General? You gonna bet?"

The man glared at Rafferty, left brow raised.

"I'll take that as a no," he muttered, turning back to his sheet. "All right, then. We've got ourselves a two-to-three ratio, with the Calders in favor of the colonel and our little band of misfits in favor of Thommy. The games can commence!"

Deckard turned to Thom and held out a hand. "Good luck," he said.

Thom's grip was aggressive. "Same to you."

The pair walked to an open space at the edge of camp where Hewitt awaited them. He handed a sword to each. "I've trained you both," he said. "I win either way."

"You lose either way too," Deckard added.

Hewitt shook his head. "Whoever loses, it's on their head. I taught you to be winners. If you fight as I taught, it'll be an impossible draw."

Thom angled toward Deckard, taking a single step back. "You sure you want to do this?" he whispered hesitantly.

Deckard tightened his grip and rolled his shoulders. "My wife bet on my brother over me. What have I got to lose?"

"Good point," Thom said, tossing Evylin a wink. "Guess she believes in me more than you."

"It seems so."

Thom drew farther away, adopting a different stance than in the past. He wasn't as rigid or technical, but he wasn't sloppy either—he was relaxed and confident. "Ready?" he asked.

Deckard settled into his own stance, a basic one where he angled his left leg forward—ready to lunge with the right—feet hips-width apart and arms close to the chest with the blade out over his right shoulder. He was ready, but he had no intention of showing his cards on the draw. "Whenever you are, little brother."

Thom sprang forward. His sword swung with a feint up and into an undercut, looking to trick Deckard on the first swing and knock him out with no effort.

Deckard managed the attack with an easy block. He shuffled back, unwilling to parry just yet. He'd watched Thom fight plenty, but there was much that had changed since they last sparred. The successive hits were as strong as he remembered but with a layer of finesse that hadn't been present when they were children. What remained, however, was the way Thom fought with too much confidence and bravado. There was something that pushed him to take risks in his attacks that would have shaken a less skilled swordsman.

Or at least one who hadn't had Hewitt as his trainer.

As Thom went for another fancy feint, Deckard parried at last.

He slipped his blade under, pushing his sword up and in as he shuffled forward into Thom's space. The pressure of their weapons kept his brother's sword high, angling his arms out of the way, and the tip of Deckard's blade slipped under his rib cage.

Thom saw the hit coming too late. He tried to maneuver away but only managed to stumble after the point of Deckard's sword found its mark.

It was over in less than fifteen seconds, and while it held no fantastic displays, for the first time in nearly two decades, he'd beaten his brother in a duel.

The camp was silent as Thom stared at Deckard with wide eyes.

Tossing the sword to his offhand, Deckard offered the other in a handshake. "Well done."

"Was that it?" Rafferty asked, incredulous.

"That was it, Raff." Thom scowled but took the handshake before skulking off to plop back down next to Evylin, who chewed on her bottom lip.

With a huff, Rafferty crossed his arms. "That was a monumental waste of entertainment."

"I thought it was perfectly entertaining," Ilain said, then held out her open palm. "I do believe you owe me seven silvers plus my original five."

"That took like five seconds," Rafferty grumbled. "You can hardly call that a duel."

"My apologies," Deckard said as he stepped back toward the camp and offered Hewitt the sword.

"Wait," Evylin said, popping up. A slow smirk tugged up the left side of her mouth. "It's my turn."

Everyone in the camp looked between the couple with near-synchronized rotations. From Evylin to Deckard. Deckard to Evylin. And right back again.

A nervous chuckle worked out of Deckard's chest. "No," he said. "I did *not* sign up for that."

"Oh, come on." Evylin stepped toward him. "You just beat Thom with ease. It's hardly a full display of your training."

"And a duel with you wouldn't be adequate either, as you'd beat me in one second flat."

"You aren't giving Hewitt's training much credit."

"I give him all the credit in the world," Deckard returned. "He trained you."

Evylin's smile grew. "Play along, Jonn. I want to see what you can do."

Though Deckard was about to refuse, he hesitated, seeing the look that sparked in her eyes. She was flirting with him, no doubt in his mind. But there was something else, an awe he wasn't sure she'd ever directed his way.

She was impressed.

Deckard looked at Hewitt.

The man tugged on his beard. "You lose either way," he advised.

"I'm aware of that," Deckard muttered, then turned back to Evylin. "All right, I'll play along."

"You will?" Evylin asked, beaming at him.

"I will."

Rafferty hopped up again, bright and wily. "Yes! We've got ourselves another challenge! Who'll start out our betting?" he asked, then pointed to Ilain. "Highlady Calder, you won a handful of extra coins there. Care to start us off?"

"Oh, no," Ilain said, tucking the coins away. "I'll keep my winnings, thank you."

"She knows a lost cause when she sees one," Deckard said and moved back toward the field.

Hewitt grabbed his arm, stopping him. "Let me see that." He gestured to his sword. "I want to be sure it's weighted correctly for you. If you're going to fight Evylin, you'll need all the help you can get."

Deckard handed it over, and Evylin grinned. "Are you trying to give him an advantage, Uncle?" she teased.

"Nothing will give him an advantage," Hewitt said, then tossed the sword to Evylin. "That's better suited to you anyway. Let's get you another, Deckard."

Certain it wouldn't matter what sword he used, Deckard followed Hewitt to the horses. While Rafferty continued trying to coax money out of the others, Hewitt slowed to walk at Deckard's side.

"She's not going to be easy on you," he whispered.

Deckard stretched his back, sure of his impending humiliation. "I didn't expect she would."

Untying a couple of swords from his horse, Hewitt glanced at Deckard. "Rely on your technique. She'll try to show off, so you can outmaneuver her if you're careful," he said, offering him one of the swords.

Deckard's brow furrowed as he took the weapon. "Do you want me to win?" he asked.

"I want you to earn her respect," Hewitt corrected. "You have no hope of winning. How's that one?"

Feeling the weight of the charge, Deckard lifted the sword, turning his wrist to test the feel and action. "It's fine."

Hewitt nodded. "They're all the same."

Deckard scoffed. "So you only brought me over here to warn me of my demise?"

"I brought you over here to ensure you don't make a fool of yourself."

"I suppose I should thank you."

"Don't." Hewitt stomped back to the fire.

A wry grin came to Deckard's lips, and he followed the man. When they arrived back, Evylin was swinging her sword in lazy figure eights while Rafferty made his final deals.

"How about this?" he said, pointing to Auden. "I'll give you ten to one?"

Both the Calders were grinning at the exchange. Auden shrugged, his hands falling back to his thighs with a light slap. "Why not?" he said, entertained. "I'll take Deckard as the winner, one in ten."

"You're going to lose everything you just won," Ilain warned.

"But I just won it, so it's not much of a loss, now, is it? And there's a chance you're wrong, and I'll win."

Deckard scoffed. "There's no chance of that at all."

"Don't be so hard on yourself," Evylin said, tossing him a crafty smile. "You never know what will happen."

"So we've got Thommy, Ethenn, and me for Evie on five to one odds," Rafferty said, scribbling his notes. "Then our Highlord Auden at ten to one in Deckard's favor. You sure you don't want in, milady?"

"It's no gamble if everyone bets on Evylin," Ilain said, straightening her skirts. "And I'm not betting on Jonn."

"Seems you're not as dumb as you look," Thom said snidely.

"That's ironic," she said. "Seems you're *exactly* as dumb as you look."

Deckard walked over to the small open clearing where Evylin waited. She held her sword to the side, shifting her weight between her feet. "Are you ready?" she asked, pushing her braid over her shoulder.

"I doubt it," he replied, lifting his sword to rest above his right shoulder, the hilt crossing his chest. His feet were firmly planted on the ground, and his knees were bent, poised for action.

Swiping her sword through the air in an intricate flurry, Evylin dropped her left foot back. The blade stopped as her hands stilled on the hilt. Her smirk confirmed Hewitt's early thoughts: She wanted to show off. "At your leisure, then," she said.

The woods around them went quiet, their friends all waiting to see what would happen. Deckard didn't think they needed to be quite so on the edge of their seats. They all knew what the outcome would be.

Though Hewitt often started their duels by charging him, there had been a few days during which they'd worked on Deckard's offensive attacks. Evylin had made it clear she would wait on him, so he let his breath slow down, calming his mind before he prepared his attack.

"Focus," Hewitt emphasized repeatedly during their training. It was the key to victory.

Letting his head cool to the point his instincts took over, Deckard lunged forward, propelling his movement with his back foot, sword angled to dip under Evylin's. She cut off the move with ease, swiping the weapon down to knock his away. He'd expected it and lifted the blade up this time. She blocked it again.

He backed away enough to reset, then tried a similar attack. Trying to follow Hewitt's advice, he stuck with the basics. But soon, Deckard realized this was the wrong approach as Evylin blocked each attempt with ease.

Their swords clashed together three times before he disengaged, backing away. "You're toying with me," he noted.

Evylin shrugged casually. "We are trying to have fun, aren't we?"

"You're trying to have fun," he corrected. "I'm trying to mitigate my embarrassment."

A little teasing was all the encouragement Evylin needed to go on the offensive. She swept forward, swinging up in a dramatic cut toward his blade.

Deckard defended it well, sidestepping while the blade took the brunt of the blow. She was stronger than most men would give her credit for. And by the glint in her eyes, she wasn't even trying.

Determined to do better than any of them expected, Deckard felt Hewitt's advice clicking in. While Evylin was busy attempting flashy moves, he would take the fight seriously. He didn't need to be better than her—he needed to be smarter.

So when Evylin drew her sword along her side to slash high, Deckard saw an opening. Since his height allowed, he met her sword with his and pressed up, too far for her arms to reach comfortably. Then he slammed into her, bumping her back.

As Evylin staggered away to recover, a gasp came from their spectators.

"Look at you," Evylin said excitedly as she steadied her grip again.

Deckard never relented in his stance. "It's a start."

Evylin charged again, still brandishing her sword like it was a plaything.

Letting his reflexes take over, Deckard defended each of her strikes well, better than he expected. Six straight hits between their swords clanged in the air. Without giving himself the luxury of thinking about it, Deckard pushed heavily against her sword, then went on the offensive. Evylin hadn't expected it, and his blows were much too strong for her. From his height and strength, his hits pressed her back, making it impossible for her to regroup and parry.

Evylin's smile dropped away, and Deckard thought for a shocking moment that he had her. His next slash hit hard, and she should have stumbled. Instead, her eyes narrowed, and her expression fell impassive.

Twisting their blades together, the tip of Evylin's sword drove Deckard's to the right, flinging his arm wide. With this opening, she swung her sword into his side with a hard slap, and then she spun around, carrying the sword to the other side. She drove her shoulder into his chest, knocking him back, then whacked the flat of her blade to the side of his head. Deckard let his sword drop to hold his ringing ears.

Instantly, Evylin gasped. "I am so sorry," she said, tossing her sword to the ground. She hurried to him, hands dropping to his arms. "I didn't mean to do that."

Deckard grimaced through the pain. "I'm all right," he promised. "My pride's a bit sore, though."

Evylin began to chew on her lower lip.

Deckard took her face in his hands. "I'm all right," he repeated.

"You're sure?" she asked worriedly.

"I'm sure," Deckard said, then released her and turned to the others, who sat watching open-mouthed. "We have our winner as expected."

Thom and Rafferty cheered while everyone else applauded.

"Damn, you got close there, Colonel," Rafferty said.

Hewitt patted Deckard's shoulder, then set a hand on Evylin's arm, drawing her aside.

"It wasn't *that* close," Deckard replied, taking a seat back at the fire. He pressed a hand to the side of his head, the spot already tender. He'd have a bruise in the morning.

Thom pursed his lips as he stared over at him. "You got closer than I'd anticipated," he said.

"High praise indeed," Deckard joked. He did feel he'd held his own in the fight. He hadn't done as well as he would have liked, but he'd had her on the run for a moment.

"All right, then," Rafferty said, rubbing his hands together. "Time to settle the debts."

"The singular debt, you mean," Auden said. "Enjoy your success."

While Rafferty divvied up the smattering of coins, Ilain raised her chin in the air. "Convinced yet?" she asked her brother.

Auden sighed. "I'll admit, it seems likely."

"Likely?" Ilain scoffed. "It couldn't be more obvious!"

"What are you two on about?" Hewitt demanded as he and Evylin returned to the group. She took the empty seat next to Deckard, giving him another apologetic look.

Auden held up a hand to silence Ilain before turning back to Hewitt. "My sister has a theory. Ow!" He clasped his side when Ilain jabbed him. "Fine, *we* have a theory."

"What theory?" Thom asked, crossing his arms.

Ilain's hair glimmered in the firelight as she drew her shoulders back. "I should think you'd all have guessed by now," she said.

"Guessed what?" Deckard asked.

Ilain shrugged. "Evylin is a Warrior."

Everyone around the firepit went still. The night seemed to freeze in place, all eyes turning to look at Evylin. She stared at Ilain, a look of pure confusion written across her face. The breeze brushed through the trees, lifting the wisps of hair around her cheeks.

A baffled gasp slipped out of Evylin. "That's . . . I'm not . . ." she stuttered.

But in her denial, something clicked deep inside of Deckard, as though the world finally made sense. It didn't matter that the word meant so little to Deckard. He might not understand what being a Warrior entailed or how Ilain Calder had come to that conclusion. But when he looked at his wife, somehow, he knew the truth of it: Evylin was magic embodied.

CHAPTER FIFTY-EIGHT

Evylin didn't know how to respond to Ilain's absurd claim. Everyone was staring at her in expectation, but she struggled to comprehend the idea. She, a Warrior? Was that possible? What did it even mean?

"That's ridiculous," Hewitt said without hesitation.

Deckard, however, seemed less certain. "Why would you think she's a Warrior?" he asked.

"I don't think it," Ilain said, twisting the sapphire ring on her right hand. "I know it."

"How?" Ethenn asked, staring at Evylin as though in awe.

Ilain shrugged flippantly. "If you're looking for proof, I have it."

"You'd better have some damn thorough proof," Hewitt demanded.

"I do."

"Then out with it," Thom spat. "If you're so sure about this, make us believe it too."

Ilain raised her copper brow. "Patience is a virtue, dear," she said, turning back to Evylin. "Do you need proof too? Or do you know it to be true yourself?"

Evylin opened her mouth to deny it, but no words came out. She looked to Hewitt for help, only to find his bushy brow knotted together in agitation.

"Hm." Ilain pursed her lips. "I see I have more convincing to do than I thought. Very well. We'll start with the most recent evidence. Don't tell me none of you noticed how little trouble Evylin had relying on her other senses while fighting blindly in the Keep. If that's not enough, we'll go further back. Have none of you realized she's impossible to beat? Her skills are superior to all of yours in this camp except for Hewitt."

"You're saying her skill has nothing to do with the work she's put into her training?" Hewitt demanded.

"Not at all," Auden said placatingly. "Warriors have a natural inclination for fighting and warcraft. But, as with Mages, they must refine it. It's no easy thing, and it takes focus."

"An untrained Warrior will look like any other human," Ilain clarified. "They take to the training faster than usual, but they must still put in the work. It's no slight against the effort either of you has put into her training. It's that she has what it takes to become better than the rest of the world entirely."

Evylin stared at the ground. Could she really possess magic that granted her abilities beyond the average human and not even know it? Was that why she felt such a rush in a fight? Could that be why she felt the desire for more?

"What else?" she asked, meeting Ilain's eyes again.

"You need more?"

"Yes."

Ilain tipped her head. "The surest proof, only you can give."

"What?"

"When you fight," Ilain leaned forward, "do you feel alive in a way you've never before felt?"

Evylin drew in a sharp breath.

"You do, don't you?" The Mage's expression grew bright with excitement. "Your whole body lights up with energy, and everything changes, doesn't it? Your senses are heightened, and you don't miss a thing. Fighting is easier, acting is easier, thinking is easier. You're more you than you've ever been in your life."

Evylin's stunned silence was confirmation enough, but she nodded anyway. No one but Hewitt understood that side of her. No one else knew what it was like to feel something so incredible and exhilarating.

The thought returned the ability for speech to Evylin. "That's not proof. Hewitt feels that too."

Ilain's expression brightened. Then she turned and slapped Auden's arm. "I bloody told you so!" she exclaimed. "You refused to listen—said it was impossible. But look." She tossed a hand toward Evylin and Hewitt. "They're standing right in front of you. Two fully-fledged Warriors."

Gaping at his sister and turning to uncle and niece, Auden shook his head. "It's not pos—well, it's just unheard of."

Hewitt growled. "I'm no magical creature, and neither is Evylin."

The three young men on the far side of the fire stared up at their mentor in wonder.

He noticed their expressions and snarled, pointing a threatening finger at them. "Stop it!"

Their chins dipped down.

But Deckard didn't share their fear. He eyed Hewitt for a moment, then Evylin. "You feel that?" he asked. "Both of you?"

Evylin twisted her braid around her finger, uncomfortable with all the attention. "Yes," she mumbled.

He turned to the three men. "Do any of you experience the same?"

Thom shook his head, Rafferty frowned in disappointment, and Ethenn shrugged, his ears pink.

"Yeah," Deckard muttered. "Me neither."

"You wouldn't," Ilain said. "Not even we Mages experience that. Don't get me wrong; we have something similar. Magic doesn't course through your veins without making itself known. But it's not like that."

"It doesn't change anything," Hewitt insisted, his words harsh and final. "What we feel is nothing but our skills and intuition combined. There's no magic to it."

"You can deny it all you like," Ilain retorted with a huff. "It doesn't change the fact that you're both Warriors."

"Why does it matter?" Evylin asked, conflicted. Half of her wanted to agree with Hewitt, standing by his side in solidarity against the highlady's claims. The other half wanted to cling to this fantastic claim that she was somehow more than she'd ever imagined. "Whether you're right or wrong, there's no point to it. We're soldiers, and fighting is what we do. Magic doesn't factor in."

"Of course, it does," Ilain argued. "It's who you are. To deny that is to deny Allore."

Hewitt scoffed bitterly. "You're going to bring piety into it now? Guilt us into your delusions?"

Deckard ignored him. "What does Allore have to do with it?" he asked.

Auden spoke before his sister could, keeping his tone calm and rational. "Warriors—*and* Mages—are vitally important to Terraeus," he explained. "And that's why it's so significant that by Allore's grand design, you've somehow become part of this team. You see, Warriors are the counterpart to Mages. They are both a support and a check for the powers a Mage possesses. They are the balance in the world. A depiction of how the Creator Divine creates. It was his original purpose that magic would be a protection and provision for his people. It's only the selfishness of man that caused this system to break down, as evidenced by the actions of the Mages of Auld."

The troop was silent. Evylin sat uncertainly, uncomfortable with the religious emphasis. Balance. Support. Protection. Thom crossed his arms, Rafferty yawned, and

Ethenn stared at the ground while Evylin turned to see Deckard's reaction. He stared at the Calders curiously, hand on his jaw and brow pinched in thought.

Chewing on her lip, Evylin glanced back at Hewitt. His dark eyes said more than any words could. He didn't want her to believe their claims. And he refused to accept it himself.

Evylin shook her head, letting out a breathy laugh. "This is ridiculous," she said, echoing his sentiment. "I don't possess any magic, and neither does Hewitt."

Deckard's hand landed on top of hers. He remained silent, but she could see the skepticism in his eyes.

"It doesn't matter if you believe it or not," Ilain said, the firelight flickering across her face. "You're filled with magic, and it will reveal itself. In fact, it's already begun."

Evylin shook her head. "If you're right, it'll prove itself later, and there's no use in debating it." She gestured to the pot of soup. "Now, can we tuck in? You two can regale us with whatever other impossible tales you like while we eat."

Auden shared a look with his sister, then nodded in acquiescence. Rafferty jumped up to get bowls and helped Evylin serve everyone. The conversation was slow to return as half the camp held onto their irritation even as they pretended everything was fine. But Deckard, Ethenn, and Rafferty all managed to get things back to a normal rhythm within a handful of minutes. They ate in bouts of chatting and laughter as everyone relaxed.

Everyone but Evylin.

By the time she'd finished her soup, Evylin was desperate to part from the crowd. Her heart felt mangled, torn between her love for Hewitt and her hope for magic. What if the Calders were right? If they were, Evylin would be a legend for sure. A life of adventure, of fulfilling her promise to Ryen, would be more than possible. It would be certain.

Evylin pushed the thoughts away. Hewitt was right. They'd both worked hard to earn their skills as fighters, and no one could take that away with such a simple mention of magic.

But she *wanted* to be magical, to have inherited something she could have only dreamed of, something that had remained hidden in her until necessity called it into being. If there was magic inside of her, her life would truly be "more." *She* would be "more."

Deckard rose, taking her bowl and his to wash in the pail on the other side of the fire. She watched him uneasily, thoughts of magic giving way to guilt. Though he'd shown no signs, she feared his anger. After all, she'd embarrassed him in front of their friends. It wasn't her intent, of course. After seeing how well he did against Thom—how quickly he'd bested his brother—she couldn't stop herself. He'd amazed her. And she needed to test his skills against her own.

She'd never thought the duel could end with any semblance of humiliation. And she really didn't know how she'd let herself hit him on the head like that. It'd been a reflex, an automatic response with the thrill surging through her veins.

Hewitt set his hand on Evylin's arm, drawing her back to the fire. "Remember what I told you," he whispered as he stood. Evylin could only nod as he faced the rest of the group. "I'm going to sleep. If that first Keep was any indication, tomorrow will be a brutal day."

A round of salutations echoed around the fire. Hewitt brushed Evylin's cheek tenderly, his steel-gray eyes softening. "Goodnight, Evie."

"Goodnight," she replied, then he walked to his tent.

Deckard returned to sit beside her. She tried not to tense, but Hewitt's earlier reprimand rang in her head. He'd taken her aside after the duel, speaking quietly. She'd expected a lecture about showing off, knowing it had almost made her lose the challenge. Instead, he'd dropped his voice to a growl and scolded her for a very different reason.

"Are you blind?" Hewitt had asked flatly, continuing before she'd been able to get a word in. "For two months, that man has worked to prove himself to you. And instead of trusting him, you've tormented him."

"I don't understand—" Evylin whispered, but Hewitt cut her off.

"He did this for you," he said sharply. "Everything he's done has been for you. And rather than thank him for it, you've embarrassed him, playing with his affection like a toy."

Evylin shook her head then, hurt and bemused. "I didn't mean anything by it," she insisted. "I thought it would be fun."

Hewitt's tension had eased. It was as though her genuine bewilderment snapped him out of his rage. He set a comforting hand on her shoulder, yet his next words did anything but soothe her. "You may not have meant it, but he will feel it."

She stared up at him, desperate for understanding.

"Do you not see it?" he asked gently. "Do you not know how he sacrifices for you?" Evylin did know.

"You have withheld your heart from him while he's given his to you freely. You've refused to trust him when all he wants is to care for you." He stepped back then, determination in his gaze. "Tell him, Evylin. For your own sake, trust the man and tell him the truth."

"What truth?" she whispered, heart twisted and confused.

"Ryen."

Blinking at the flames while her friends conversed around her, Evylin realized her uncle was right. She thought her affection for Deckard was enough to overcome her lack of trust. She would have gladly consummated their marriage in Loclight and many times since had he asked her to. One didn't have to be in love to be intimate with their spouse, she reasoned. It was a vulnerability of body, not of heart. And Evylin could endure that quite happily.

But now, she saw it *wasn't* enough.

Evylin tugged on her rings. Two months. They'd been married for two months, and while Deckard had promised his devotion to her as well as his love, even if it was born of convenience, she'd refused him at every turn. Because she didn't trust him. She *couldn't* trust him.

Why not? Evylin wondered. Deckard had proved himself; there was no denying that. He'd given up his entire life for her from the start. She *should* trust him . . . But she couldn't.

Because, she realized, *if I give up that part of myself, I'll be risking something much worse than a broken heart.*

When Ryen died, it wasn't just heartbreak; it was total devastation. Everything Evylin was had been tied up in her cousin. And when he died, her very soul went with him. Her dreams, her hopes, her love—it was all bound in Ryen. Losing him was losing herself. And she couldn't risk loving someone like that again.

The wind blew in, and Evylin shivered. Farther south, the cold winter had abated some of its frigidity, and while Deckard still sat close, their sides hardly touched. Had the duel at last given him reason to resent her? Had her lack of trust driven him away again? Should she tell him about Ryen? Could she . . . ?

During Evylin's worried reverie, Ethenn and Auden had both abandoned the fire for a night's rest, and Deckard rose to follow. "I think that's it for me," he said, then grinned wryly at Evylin. "For some reason, I've got a splitting headache."

The lightness of his joke relieved Evylin's anxiety enough to tease him back. "How strange," she replied in mock consideration. "I can't imagine why."

"Perhaps it'll come to you later." Deckard tapped her chin playfully, then stepped around her to walk to their tent.

Though he hadn't asked her to, Evylin stood to join him. Rafferty was quizzing Ilain on her time in the Order of the Flame while Thom made baiting remarks—to which Ilain rose to the challenge with her own biting retorts. With her rolling thoughts, she didn't care to listen to the banter.

Due to the rise in the temperature, slight as it was, they'd begun distancing the tents from the campfire. It gave everyone a semblance of privacy—as much as an open tent could offer. Though a normally toned conversation could easily be heard by the others, a hushed one would be perfectly private.

Deckard sat on the edge of their bedrolls, tugging off his boots. His gray coat hung open, revealing his road-worn tunic. He'd begun to sleep without the coat, claiming he got too hot. A sentiment Evylin couldn't understand but found welcomingly attractive. The subtracted layer of thick wool from between them left only the lightweight cotton as a barrier between his muscular form and the hand she'd subconsciously begun to rest on his chest.

Looking up as Evylin approached, Deckard's eyes crinkled at the sides. He spoke quietly, saying, "I didn't expect you to join me so soon."

Evylin hesitated. "Do you not want me to join you?"

Deckard propped his boots at the end of the mat and began removing his coat. "I want you to spend time with your friends if that would make you happy. But if I'm being selfish, then, yes, I would very much like your company."

"Ah." She smiled and stepped closer. "While I hate to give in to your selfish desires, I must admit my happiness coincides with them this time."

"How fortuitous," he replied playfully, then set his folded coat next to his boots.

Evylin sat on the bedroll next to him and began untying the laces of her shoes. While Deckard lay down, she considered Hewitt's advice once more. Why hadn't she told Deckard about Ryen? It wasn't as though he would deride her for her broken heart. Nor would he betray her confidence. Yet, something within her couldn't speak of her cousin.

Shoes removed, Evylin began to unbutton her coat absentmindedly. She didn't want to speak of Ryen. He was her heart, her deepest self. Talking about him was like unveiling her soul. And that felt altogether too personal.

But Hewitt was right. Deckard had done everything in his power to prove he cared for Evylin, and she'd toyed with his affection all along the way. Perhaps she couldn't trust him with Ryen yet, but she could apologize for her flippancy.

When she lay down, Deckard pulled the blankets high around her shoulders. "Won't you be too cold without your coat?" he whispered. He stretched on his side to face her rather than on his back as was customary on the warmer nights. And rather than wrapping his arms around her to pull her close, he remained at a distance.

Evylin struggled to settle in beside him. "I'll be fine," she murmured.

Deckard's eyes searched her face for a moment, and then he set his hand next to hers on the bedroll. "Can I ask you a question, Evie?"

Uncertainly, Evylin nodded.

His eyes looked deep green as they lay under the tent's canopy. "Why don't you believe you're a Warrior?"

Evylin hadn't expected that question. "Oh," she said, searching for words. "Well, I suppose I just think it's silly."

Deckard raised his brow doubtfully. "Do you?"

Did she?

"I don't know," she muttered. "It's just . . . everything has become so fantastic. Mages. Relics. Now, Warriors? What's next?"

His fingers brushed hers. "Yes, everything is fantastic. But it's everything you wanted, isn't it? You dreamed of adventure, and now you've got it."

Evylin smiled as his fingers slipped through hers. *Yes,* she thought, *I have got everything I wanted. First, I explored the Shires. Not exactly the shoreline, but I did see the sea. And while I considered piracy on the beach at Loclight, I found it didn't suit me. So now, I'm traveling the rest of Ephria. I've won dozens of duels, rescued a prince, fought a dragon, and found Mages . . . Now, I may be a legend of five hundred tales: a Warrior.*

The thought felt hollow.

Shaking her head, Evylin met Deckard's gaze again. "I just don't understand how I could be a magical being. I've been training with Hewitt since I was a girl. It doesn't make sense for that to be extraordinary."

"It makes all the sense in the world to me," Deckard whispered, his warm words tucking around her like their blankets. "Because I finally understand how you can be so magnificent."

Suddenly bashful, Evylin dropped her eyes to their hands. His thumb brushed across the back of her hand, sending gentle tingles along her skin.

"I've always known you were special, Evylin," Deckard continued. "More special than any other woman I've ever met. It doesn't surprise me to learn you have magic because . . . well, I think I always knew."

Happily embarrassed, Evylin scoffed. "You're just being nice to me."

Deckard's laugh was quiet yet full. "What purpose would I have in being nice to you ever again? You hit me in the head."

Evylin scooted closer under the blankets. "I swear it wasn't intentional," she promised.

He squeezed her hand. "I know. Trust me, I know."

Trust.

The word pushed her back to Hewitt's charge, and Evylin bit her bottom lip. "Jonn," she whispered, staring at their hands again. Somehow, the sight of their fingers entwined stopped any other words from coming.

"Hm?"

Closing her eyes, Evylin took a deep breath. "I'm sorry."

Deckard hesitated. "What are you sorry for?"

"I didn't mean to embarrass you earlier. I thought dueling would be fun. But I didn't consider . . . Well, I didn't consider anything."

Deckard sighed, and Evylin continued, meeting his gaze again. "I know it was foolish. I shouldn't have asked you to fight me. But I didn't realize . . ." She shook her head. "I never meant to hurt you."

"Evylin," Deckard said, pulling their hands to his chest. His gaze was gentle, absolving. "It's all right. I'll admit, I would have preferred not to make a fool out of myself." He grinned lightly. "But I've always wondered what it would be like to fight you."

"Really?"

He nodded.

She smiled, inching closer still. "You didn't look like a fool," she promised. "You fought well."

Deckard let out a huff.

"No, truly. You're better than I expected."

"I'm still not good," Deckard argued.

"You're *very* good," Evylin promised, then smirked. "Just not good enough to beat me."

Deckard laughed with her and unwound their fingers to rest his hand on her arm. The sounds of the night pressed in around them as they lay there. An owl hooted out in the distance as Hewitt snored softly across the way. The breeze rustled the newly budding leaves. Crickets chirped at a steady beat. A gentle crackle came from the firepit; the remaining embers grew cold as the others went to sleep at last.

"Why didn't you tell me you were training with Hewitt?" Evylin asked.

Deckard averted his gaze, rubbing her arm absentmindedly. "There are two reasons," he began. "First, I'm a prideful person, and it embarrassed me that I needed it. A captain should be a skilled officer. And there I was, unable to defend myself while my wife could beat any man in my company." His eyes came back to hers. "The second reason is even more inane."

Evylin slapped his chest playfully. "Tell me."

"You'll laugh at me."

"Probably," she agreed, already doing so. "Tell me anyway."

Deckard's eyes shifted to blue. "I'm a man, Evylin. And men like to impress their wives."

Evylin held his stare, anticipation blossoming in her chest.

"I wanted to impress you," he explained, voice thicker than usual. His hand ran up her arm. "That's why I asked Hewitt to train me. I wanted to surprise you with how strong I'd become. I wanted to prove that I was worthy of you."

Words failed Evylin. Beneath her palm on his chest, she felt his steady heartbeat. His warmth seeped through his shirt. Her eyes dropped to his open collar, catching a glimpse of the muscular definition of his chest. She wondered what his skin would feel like under her fingertips.

"Does that answer your question?" he whispered, his words falling heavily between them.

Meeting his gaze once more, Evylin nodded. It answered more than one question. After their near consummation in Loclight, she'd wondered why Deckard hadn't pursued the issue. He'd kissed her gently a few times since, and he held her each night, but he never pressed for anything remotely as passionate or physical. But the way he regarded her now, his eyes inspecting every inch of her face—starting at her brow and temple, down across her cheeks and nose to her chin, then back up to her lips where they stayed—she knew he hadn't withheld for lack of desire.

Without thought, Evylin leaned in to kiss him. She didn't know if he'd expected it, but his lips met hers with equal yearning, slow and tender. She closed her eyes to savor the moment. Her fingers glided up his chest to touch that small, warm patch of skin exposed by his collar. Deckard's hand tightened on her shoulder. He pulled away, beginning to whisper something, but Evylin didn't let him get a full word out.

Grabbing the collar of his shirt, Evylin kissed him again with even more fervor. His hand slid down her back to draw her closer, and she relaxed into his embrace. Her mind took on that cool, alert state of focus, and her skin buzzed with life.

Evylin's hand rose to rest on Deckard's neck, the veins there pulsing hot under her touch. The feeling of his mouth on hers caused her heartbeat to spike. It felt exactly like when they'd been in the Keep, running across the tower to stay alive. Here now, this kiss gave her that hammering rush in her veins.

Deepening the kiss, Evylin pressed as close as she could, unwilling to let an inch of space remain between them.

Deckard's hand drew down, lower on her back than he'd ever dared. Then it brushed across her hip, pressing to push her flat beneath him. His fingers gripped her side, thumb pressing against her abdomen. The weight of his body on hers warmed Evylin, their legs twisted up together under the blankets. Deckard's breathing grew more rapid as he moved on to kiss her jaw, trailing down to her neck. She could feel his lungs pounding behind his ribs, her right hand resting on his back.

Letting her eyes open as she gasped silently for breath, Evylin stared up at the canvas tent. They couldn't let this go too far. Not surrounded as they were in the camp. Not even with the added distance of their tent from the others.

Deckard's lips moved up her neck toward her cheek again. Evylin closed her eyes, enjoying the cascade of energy that coursed through her. The world was alight, every sense trilling and amplified. His hand brushed along her side, rising from her waist, leaving a spread of cool tingles in its wake.

Evylin slid her hands to the base of his neck. Weaving her fingers into his ruddy brown hair, grown out from their months of travel and curling at the edges. She pressed her fingers through the soft waves, moving up along the sides of his head. Deckard growled into her ear before pulling away, grimacing in pain.

Yanking her hands to her chest in panic, Evylin flushed. She'd completely forgotten about the injury she'd inflicted on him earlier. "Jonn," she gasped quietly, "I'm so sorry."

Deckard's hands framed her shoulders, hovering over her. He kept his eyes squeezed shut, and his breathing came out stuttered. With a slow shake of his head, he let out one final exhale and opened his eyes. They locked onto hers—their color a vibrant emerald—as his lips pulled up in a pleased smile. "Don't be," he whispered back, his voice slightly hoarse.

Unable to stop herself, Evylin began to laugh, pressing her hands to her mouth to muffle the sound.

Deckard shifted off her and rolled over onto his back. He released a long, heavy sigh, and then his soft laughter joined hers. "You did that on purpose," he muttered.

Evylin turned to him sharply. "I did not," she promised.

His dry smile told her he was only teasing. She tried to slap his chest, but he caught her wrist and kissed her palm. Then he tugged lightly on her arm, drawing her to roll over. She let him tuck her into his side, his arm going behind her neck as hers rested over his stomach.

Deckard set his hand on her cheek and kissed her once more—gentle and ardent. When he pulled away, he sighed again. "You're an awful tease," he whispered, his lips still close to hers.

Settling her head onto his shoulder, Evylin stared up at him. "It isn't my fault you're so good at kissing," she replied, enjoying the embarrassed way he smiled at the canopy. "Maybe you should try making it more boring next time."

"I'll do my best," Deckard whispered back.

Evylin watched him a few moments longer, his figure silhouetted in the dimming firelight several yards away. Deckard began to run his fingers over her braid, tugging at it ever so slightly, and she closed her eyes, content with their nearness. She felt her breathing steady as she dozed, her thoughts growing cloudy to dream about the time she'd get to kiss him again. She hoped it wouldn't be long. And she thought, *perhaps next time, it might not end.*

She was ready for such a possibility. Her heart still locked Ryen away, but she could trust Deckard with the rest of her, she believed. He was good; he was loving. She could trust him. She might even love him.

Amid her reveries, Deckard's steady and earnest voice whispered, "Goodnight, my Evie." Then he pressed his lips to the top of her head, and she faded into sleep.

CHAPTER FIFTY-NINE

A long, frenzied cry pierced through Evylin's slumber, jolting her awake.

Bolting upright at the same time as Deckard at her side, Evylin blinked in shock at the scene unfolding in front of her.

Two men were dragging Ilain from her tent, and another grappled with Auden. Hewitt was already rushing for Ilain's captors, his sword at the ready. Ethenn clambered from their tent with an arrow nocked in his bow. A man leaped on him from behind, and both tumbled to the dirt from the impact. A fire raged over Thom and Rafferty's tent as the two of them staggered from it as fast as they could.

"Evylin!" Deckard yelled, already standing with his feet shoved into his boots. "We have to help!"

Knocked from her daze, Evylin jumped up. Refusing to waste time on the laces of her boots, she grabbed her knife and sword, running across the dirt in her socks. Men surrounded the camp: several swordsmen, three archers, and six who bore no weapons that she could see.

Hewitt took down Ilain's captors and helped her stand.

Deckard rushed to Auden's aid.

Thom fought one of the swordsmen while Rafferty charged the unarmed men. As he bounded toward them, one of the men stretched out his hands and blasted Rafferty back with a gust of wind.

"They're Mages!" Evylin called to the rest of the team, slipping her knife into her belt.

Ethenn was still rolling on the ground with the man who'd jumped him, fiercely throwing punches. Arrows sailed into the camp as Evylin rushed over to help, ducking as she ran. One of the arrows sliced through her shirt, nicking her shoulder. Ignoring the pain, she dove onto the attacker's back, pulling him off Ethenn. The young soldier rose and struck out with a knife, taking him down.

More swordsmen charged into the campsite, assailing Hewitt and Ilain again. He defended against them with ease as Ilain lit one on fire. A fierce cry of pain cut into the night air.

More attackers surrounded Deckard and Auden, restraining them for a moment. Auden unleashed a surge of energy that sent the men sprawling. "We have to get out!" he shouted while Deckard dealt with new attackers.

Three swordsmen came for Evylin and Ethenn. She parried the first man's attack, knocking him back before slicing open his gut. He slumped with a gurgle. The second man learned from his friend's mistakes and took more caution, backing away as they circled one another.

Ethenn managed the other swordsman as Evylin charged the runaway. She drove him toward the firepit, its embers a dull red as the heat disintegrated. With one swift kick, she knocked the man into the coals. He tripped on the crumbling wood and fell back. Evylin plunged her sword into his stomach, then pulled away. With the threat dispatched, that left only a handful more swordsmen, their attackers' numbers dwindling fast.

The ambush would amount to nothing.

Just then, Thom flew across the camp, his back slamming against a tree and throwing him to the ground unconscious.

Spinning around, Evylin saw the Mages move in, their hands gesturing. A gust of unnatural wind swept Ethenn's feet out from under him, his original attacker taking the opportunity to pummel him with the hilt of his sword. Ethenn's head lolled against the ground, a blooming patch of crimson immediately slicking the side of his dark brown hair.

Two Mages went straight for Ilain, both lifting their hands as they charged her. Chunks of terrae rose around them, the pieces hovering in midair. When they threw their arms forward, the dirt and rocks sailed straight for the woman. Her own hands rose, a wall of wind and fire blocking most of the storm, but another barrage was right behind it.

Evylin didn't see Rafferty amongst the fray, and she prayed he was safe. But she didn't have much time to worry as a Mage charged toward her. Tightening her grip on the leather hilt, Evylin raised her sword, prepared to swing.

The Mage lifted his hand, and Evylin's body froze. She'd already begun the strike, her blade in mid-arc as her body simply . . . *stopped*. Her muscles weren't tense or relaxed, just still. No matter how furiously she willed her arms to follow through with the swing, she couldn't get her brain to connect to them. She struggled against the feeling, thoroughly confused as to why her body wouldn't respond.

The Mage neared, his green eyes scanning her. He had the same red hair and sharp features as the Calders, but that was where the similarity ended. Though distinctly Waulden in characteristics like them, there was cruelty in his eyes and a foulness to the tilt of his grin. The Mage reached out to take the sword from her.

Evylin tried to fight him, but her hands wouldn't listen. He took his time peeling back her fingers, loosening her grip with ease. The sound of Hewitt fighting madly reached her ears, but she couldn't see him. The Mage lifted her sword, placing it just below her rib cage. Her mind screamed for her to move. His fiendish eyes shone in the firelight as he placed a hand on her shoulder, ready to thrust the blade up into her heart.

Evylin willed herself to move. To cry out. To do *something*. *Anything at all.* She didn't want to die like this.

The Mage's shoulders tensed, ready to plunge the sword in.

A shadow rose behind him, and without warning, his neck spun, almost completely inverted, with a shattering crack. The Mage fell, and Evylin's body returned to her.

Hewitt stood behind the crumpled form, his gray eyes fierce. "Run!" he yelled.

After being locked out of the use of her body, it took a moment for her brain and muscles to reconnect. Evylin tested a few steps before she reached down to grab her sword from the Mage's dead grasp. A shattering *crack* rent the air, and Hewitt shoved her out of the way. Evylin rolled across the ground. She landed on her feet, knees bent in an easy recovery. Lifting her gaze as she rose, the coolness of focus tingled across her skin, slowing the world as she took it all in too late.

A Mage on the far side of the camp held his arms high. A massive tree branch sailed through the air straight to the spot Evylin had stood only a second before. But instead of hitting her as was its intent, the branch slammed into a different victim.

Hewitt staggered back as the sharp wood split through his gut.

A breath escaped Evylin, and she blinked.

It hadn't happened. It couldn't have.

Hewitt grunted, dropping to his knees. His face turned to Evylin, pain etched on his features. "Run," he muttered again, blood already filling his mouth. A single trickle slipped across his lip and down his chin.

Evylin couldn't run. She couldn't even feel her legs anymore.

In the camp around her, the yelling and attacks still reverberated off the trees, but she didn't hear or see any of the movements.

It hadn't happened.

It couldn't have.

Evylin watched, her whole being numb, as Hewitt slumped to the terrae in front of her.

"No," she whispered weakly.

A pool of blood seeped from Hewitt's body, mingling with the dirt and embers around him.

"No." She began to sway, her head moving back and forth in denial. Her vision grew hazy as she stared at his lifeless body. "No."

"I won't let our dream die. That I promise you."

A silent scream ripped through her chest. This wasn't how it was supposed to happen. This wasn't the adventure she'd wanted. This wasn't the price she was supposed to pay.

Thunder sounded around her, and a black shadow blocked her view of Hewitt. Hands took hold of her from above, pulling her up into the gloom.

She couldn't fight.

She couldn't do anything but shake as tears broke free.

"No," she murmured again.

An arm wrapped around her waist, holding her close as they began to move, riding away into darkness. Evylin didn't care where her captor was taking her. The world meant nothing to her now. She couldn't take in any sight or sound to track her location and didn't care to.

All she could see through her tears was the blood streaming down the side of her uncle's face as he lay dying in the dirt.

CHAPTER SIXTY

21ST OF GALATAE, 1574

Time cried out all of Evylin's tears, and now she sat on the shadow that stole her away, an empty shell of agony.

At first, she thought one of the Mages had taken her captive. But through the night, she'd come to her senses enough to recognize the man at her back. A second rider dashed alongside them, the moonlight catching flashes of red hair. Auden. He'd made it free, along with her and the man who held her on their mount.

Deckard's arm pressed against her stomach, keeping her bound to his chest as he whispered into her ear over and over, "I'm sorry. I'm so sorry."

The pain in Evylin's chest didn't allow her to respond. Instead, she gasped in horror, fresh tears coming to her eyes any time she thought of Hewitt's broken body.

The tears coated her face. Their intensity no longer made sense to her. Somehow, her eyes kept pouring out while she sat frozen and silent. Her body seemed stuck in a cycle of overwhelming sorrow and complete stillness.

Unable to fathom how she could hold so much misery within her being and not split right apart, Evylin sat astride the horse, paralyzed, only Deckard's strong grip holding her upright. She had no control over her body, muscles tense while her face contorted in pain one second, losing any hint of emotion the next.

The same two thoughts pounded through her mind as the horses rode on through the darkness.

Hewitt is gone.

You're alone.

As the light of dawn crept through the trees, the men slowed the horses. They'd charted a course deep in the woods. Deckard leaped down from behind Evylin as Auden dismounted and ran over. Both men reached up and pulled her shaking form from the horse.

Deckard held her close while Auden took her hands in his. She thought for a moment that the Mage was trying to comfort her, but then she discovered he was prying her hands open. She'd clung to her sword the whole trip. The muscles of her fingers ached as Auden pulled them apart, removing the weapon from her grip.

Once he'd tossed it to the ground, Auden stepped back, and Deckard drew Evylin closer, pressing her face into his chest as he apologized repeatedly. Another wave of anguish shook her body, and her knees buckled. Deckard dropped to the snow with her, holding her tighter still.

With no strength to pull away, Evylin's muscles tensed afresh.

She didn't want him to hold her.

She didn't want anyone but Hewitt.

For the first time, her cries became audible to her ears. The sobs made her entire body tremble. "No," she moaned into Deckard's chest. "No."

Eyes shut to the world, darkness absorbed her as she saw Hewitt's body again. She hated the image. Torn and weeping blood, his torso had melded with that branch. His gray eyes were still open, but his gaze was glassy and lifeless, his mouth hanging ajar as though trying to tell her to run once more. She couldn't stand that they'd left him there, that his body would slowly decay alone until nature reclaimed it.

It can't be happening again, her mind screamed. She'd already lost Ryen, her best friend and very soul. Now, she'd lost the man who had saved her from desolation. The one person who had made her whole after grief broke her into pieces.

For years, Hewitt had been everything to her. All she'd ever learned, she'd learned from him. He'd defined the woman she'd become. He'd woven the entire fabric of her world into the pages upon which she'd written her hopes. Without him, would she even exist anymore?

For the entirety of her life, Evylin had looked to Hewitt for her answers. She'd relied on him to teach her and show her the "more" of the world. She'd only reached for her and Ryen's dreams because Hewitt was so much *more* than everyone else himself. And all she'd ever wanted was to prove to him that she could excel and thrive, to give life back to his son too.

But she'd driven him from safety and out into adventure, all so that she could prove herself to him. All to carry on his son's legacy, to make him happy as he'd made her happy.

Now, Hewitt was dead, too, and she had nothing left.

Deckard's hand rubbed circles across her back, reminding her of his presence. Her whole being cringed at his touch, remembering the real cause of Hewitt's death. Nothing would have changed if Deckard hadn't come to Whickam Village. She'd still be working at Hewitt's side in the smithy. Or they'd be on their way to Trollenston for the market. They would have celebrated Dolia's wedding with her. They would've been present for every holiday and birthday. They would never have abandoned Ryen and Irena but visited them on each anniversary of their death. They would still train, laugh, and manage happiness together.

But instead of that modest existence, she lay in the arms of the man who'd taken her from her family, the man who brought her uncle to his death.

Pushing herself free of Deckard's arms, Evylin scooted back in the snow.

Deckard stared at her, arms still open where she'd been. Tears filled his green-blue eyes.

No, Evylin decided, *he doesn't get to be sad.* He hadn't lost anyone. He'd only taken Hewitt from her.

"Evylin," Deckard whispered, reaching out to her, "I'm so—"

"No!" she yelled at him, the word tearing through her throat as it pulled a sob along with it.

Somehow, Deckard's expression grew even more sorrowful. But this time, Evylin didn't find the pinch between his brows charming in the slightest. This time, it made her angry.

"You don't get to be sorry," she hissed.

His mouth moved, but nothing came out aside from his breath, fogging in the frigid air around them. He reached for her again, and she pulled away.

"Don't!" she cried, the tears back with a vengeance. "I don't want you! I want Hewitt, and you've taken him from me!"

The words hit Deckard, and he slumped. "I don't understand," Deckard said, emotion ripping all semblance of gentility away from his voice.

Evylin backed farther away from him, unable to bear his presence. The snow burned her palms. "All—all of this," she muttered, her heavy breathing creating gaps as she spoke. "All of . . . all of it . . . is *your* fault."

Tears still pooling in his eyes, Deckard swallowed as he stared at her.

"We wouldn't . . . wouldn't be here if . . . you hadn't agreed," Evylin accused. "He wouldn't be. . . ."

It all hit her with renewed force: Hewitt's emptying stare as he faded away, the slowing of his breath until his chest ceased to rise, the truth that she'd never see him again.

Agony tore through her.

Evylin would never see Hewitt again.

The impossibility of such an idea had never occurred to her. How could someone so important fail to exist?

Evylin lowered herself to the ground, the weight of his loss too heavy for her to carry. She didn't care that the snow cut through her shirt or that it soaked through her socks. *Let the cold take me,* she thought. No pain could be worse than this.

Deckard rose from the snow, his steps carrying him away from her. The farther he went, the larger the tear in her soul. It hurt to be near him—and it hurt to have him go away.

Black boots shuffled past her after Deckard. "Jonn," Auden said somewhere to the side, "she's just upset."

"No," Deckard gasped out. "She's right. It is my fault. I've failed every step of the way. I was a fool to think it'd be any different now."

The justification of her anger welled up. Evylin *was* right. It *was* all Deckard's fault. He'd agreed to Hewitt's proposition and their marriage. He'd failed to secure five hundred men. He'd made them save the prince. He'd brought them here. And now he'd let her uncle die because he couldn't protect her himself.

And yet . . .

Evylin's heart didn't feel justified by the conviction of his guilt. *She'd* agreed to it all herself. Didn't that condemn her to the same sentence?

The pain resurfaced, but for a whole new reason: It'd been her fault all along.

"I won't let our dream die. That I promise you."

Everything Hewitt had done, he'd done for her, for Ryen. They'd dreamed of adventure, so he'd created the opportunity. He'd left his family and his home to ensure that dream. He'd broken his vow so that Evylin could keep hers.

She'd blindly pursued her promise to Ryen, damning the cost.

A tear dropped off her lashes, streaking down her cheek. She hadn't known that the cost would be Hewitt. In attempting to keep his son's memory alive, she'd killed him.

Evylin stared at the whiteness of the snow. Patches began to melt in the rising sun, raising the temperature with it. She heard Auden and Deckard talking in hushed, argumentative tones, their words muffled.

I should go to Jonn, she thought. *I should tell him the truth. It isn't his fault. It's mine, and this world kills everyone I love.*

Yet, it hurt too much to move, and Evylin lay there, driven back to tears. The right side of her face was numb from the icy ground. She wondered if she might be able to melt into it along with the snow. Could she, too, fade away and let the world swallow her up?

"Stop, Auden," Deckard demanded, a scuffle sounding from their direction. "Leave her alone."

Evylin heard a thump and looked to see Auden push Deckard off him. "We don't have time for this," the Mage yelled furiously, his accent thicker than she'd ever heard it. "Those men took my *sister*! I won't lose her!"

The urgency in Auden's voice brought Evylin back to reality. Here in these woods, a brother feared for his sister's life. The pain that she felt now, Auden would feel, too, if Ilain died. He could only have one resolve: to save his sister.

Evylin pushed herself up from the snow, limbs shaky with grief. The men glared at each other, but Deckard caught her movement and watched as she stood. He looked as broken as she felt, darkness circling his eyes, his expression drawn down in sorrow. She'd never seen him look so defeated.

"How do we stop them?" Evylin asked, her voice still tight from crying.

Auden turned to her, his eyes wet at the edges. He seemed surprised to find her so calm, taking a step back to settle himself. "They'll be going for the Water Relic," he said, then sighed. "We should too."

Warily, Evylin met Deckard's eyes. They'd turned pure blue in the early morning light, reminding her of Thom. "You both have family they've taken," Evylin said, walking over to them. Her legs trembled as she took small steps. "We have to save them."

Running a hand through his flame-bright hair, Auden stared at the ground. "This is more than that," he muttered as though he was trying to convince himself. "If they get the Water Relic, we'll be too far behind. It won't matter that we've saved them if we can't keep the Relics out of their hands."

"We don't know why they want them," Deckard said hollowly.

"After this, do you doubt their intentions are selfish?" Auden shook his head. "We have to focus on the Relics."

The suggestion of abandoning their friends burned in Evylin's chest. But Auden had a clear, terrifying point: If they didn't stop whoever these people were from obtaining a second Relic, there was little chance they'd be able to prevent them from taking over the whole continent.

"Why can't we do both?" Deckard asked, grasping for hope.

Auden's eyes didn't leave the snow. "We don't know where they've taken them. And we have no way of pinpointing their location."

"But they took them," Deckard said, stepping closer to Auden. "Which tells us something. Why wouldn't they kill them if they simply wanted us out of the way?"

Auden raised his head. "They need us," he muttered in awe. "They *have* been following us. This whole time, they've been on our trail, and we weren't paying enough attention. They don't know where the Relics are, so they're using us to find them."

"Why attack, then?" Evylin asked, throat sore. "Why not just follow and steal the Relics out from under us like they did at the first Keep?"

"We would have caught on," Auden replied. "If they kept stealing them, we would have taken measures to stop them. They need us, but they can't risk our interference."

"You mean they need you and your sister," Deckard said tightly. "The rest of us are expendable."

Auden met his gaze, surely aware of the danger such a reality would put Thom and the others in. "I'm afraid so."

Deckard nodded bitterly. "We can assume they're taking them to the Water Relic's location, yes?"

"Possibly. They may have taken them somewhere else entirely to hold them as prisoners."

"But they don't know that we're headed for Virwoud," Evylin interjected. "If they think Ilain knows the location, they'll make her lead them there."

A slight grin tugged at the side of Auden's mouth. "And she'll give them hell for it, to be sure," he said, renewed confidence entering his tone. "Ilain knows we made it free and that we have the chance to stop them. She'll lead them to the Water Relic, but she'll take her time with it. She'll give us the chance to catch up."

"You're sure she knows we're out here?" Deckard asked.

"We made eye contact as they took her down. I was already on the horse when the rocks hit her. She fell unconscious, but she'll wake, and when I'm not there, she'll know I made it out with you two."

"We might be able to beat them there," Evylin said, clutching onto the promise of saving their friends. It might be a flawed hope, but it kept her mind from straying to the loss she'd already suffered. If she could prevent anyone else from dying, she would put her whole being into it. "If we leave now, we can get to Virwoud and wait for them to arrive. Then we can save our friends and get the Relic ourselves."

Auden began to pace. "There were too many Mages at the camp," he said, his accent thick. "We'll have no chance of getting through that many with the three of us alone. It will be a suicide mission to take them head-on."

"Then we take them by surprise," she answered. "If they can ambush us, we can ambush them. When Ilain takes them to the Relic, we wait for them to go inside. Then we follow, just like they did to us."

Narrowing his eyes, Auden began to nod. "I can't cover all three of us in Night magic. I don't have that much control over it. But they won't take Ilain and the others inside.

Instead, they'll go in and ensure she led them to the right location first. While some of them go in to obtain the Relic, the others will stay outside to watch their prisoners."

"Are we sure they won't have killed them already?" Deckard asked stoically. "As we established, they're expendable."

Auden shook his head. "Ilain won't let them."

"She's a hostage too."

"She's the strongest Mage in two centuries," he countered. "Even if they tried to torture the information out of her, it wouldn't work. She'd only give it willingly, and she'll only do that if they're alive."

A false hope filled Evylin's chest. "So we wait for them to enter the Keep, then save our friends and charge in behind them?" she suggested.

"No," Auden said. "We split up. It will be better to go in two waves. They aren't likely to leave many people behind with Ilain and the others, so Jonn should be able to take care of them. Evylin, you and I will follow them into the Keep. Though I can shroud us in Night magic, I'm not strong enough to maintain it once inside. It'll let us sneak up on them, at least for a while. Once you've freed everyone, Jonn, you and our team will come in behind and take them by surprise."

Deckard glanced at Evylin before he turned to Auden. "Why wouldn't we save our friends and then charge as one?"

Although Evylin had suggested it herself, she now understood. "Because if we all go together, we only have one shot," she said. "By splitting up, we increase our chances of getting the Relic. If Auden and I go in and end up dying, at the very least, we can take down some Mages with us. Then it will be easier for you and Ilain to retrieve the Relic. We're a diversion."

A flash of fear tore through Deckard's now-green eyes. "I'm not all right with that plan," he protested.

"It's the only way to ensure we get the Relic *and* save our friends," Auden said flatly.

"Then *I'll* go with you," Deckard demanded, taking a step toward the Mage. "Evylin can save them, and I'll be part of the diversion. If anyone should die, it should be me."

The statement cut into Evylin, and she blinked back a fresh wave of tears.

"No," Auden said firmly. "Evylin is a Warrior, and I need her skills. It is a fact of magic that a Warrior and a Mage paired together are stronger than either one alone. If I have her with me, our chances increase exponentially. With you, they are nonexistent."

"I'm not important," Deckard pressed. "She is! If the two of us go into that Keep and die to preserve the lives of the others, wouldn't it be better to ensure that Ilain and Evylin live? That way, there is a Mage and a Warrior left together. If she goes with you, we'll only have one Mage left."

Auden remained silent, scanning Deckard's face thoughtfully. At first, Evylin thought he was trying to figure out what to say. Then she realized that wasn't it at all. Auden was studying Deckard, looking for something in the depths of his expression. He took one step forward, head tilting.

Deckard's breath rose and fell as he waited for the response.

Finally, a sigh pulled free of Auden, and he set a hand on Deckard's shoulder. "I'm sorry, Jonn," he said softly. "It can't be you."

Deckard pulled away from the man, turning to Evylin. "You can't do it," he pleaded. "You can't go in there to die."

Though he hadn't moved toward her or even tried to reach out to touch her, Evylin felt the intimacy behind his words and the softness of his gaze. The tears at the edges of his eyes made his feelings clearer than ever before: He didn't want to lose her.

Releasing a shaky breath, Evylin fought her desire to crumble back to the ground. It was all too much, the fury inside of her, the pain tearing at her chest. She was so broken already. She couldn't lose him too.

"We don't have a choice," Evylin heard herself whisper. "If you believe I'm a Warrior, as Auden says, then you also must believe that he's right about this. For us to succeed, I *need* to go with him."

"No," Deckard breathed, stepping toward her at last.

"Jonn," she said his name like it was a curse, taking a step back, *"don't."*

He glared at her, his brows pressed painfully close together. He looked ready to fight her—to scream at her in rage—yet he remained silent.

Evylin turned back to Auden, her body shaking from the cold and pain. "We should go," she said.

The Mage's eyes shifted between Deckard and Evylin as though trying to decide if it was wise to leave things so unsettled. He nodded, then stepped away toward his horse. "Virwoud is about five miles away," he said. "Once we arrive, we'll scout the area to be sure we've beaten them there. Then we can find the Keep."

Evylin looked back at Deckard. He'd closed his eyes, his breathing shallow. When he opened them again, the feeling they once held had changed. Though still damp with tears, a dullness had settled in their depths. Walking past, he gestured for her to follow, though he didn't look at her. "Come with me," he muttered.

Reaching into his saddlebag, Deckard pulled out a coat and boots—Evylin's coat and boots. "I grabbed these before we left," he explained. "It's all I had time to get."

Evylin stared at the clothing. Part of her wanted to demand how he'd had time to gather her clothes while Hewitt died. Another part of her realized what it really was: Deckard taking care of her once again.

After slipping on the coat, Evylin sat in the snow and took the right boot in her hand. Reaching inside, she found the small knife Hewitt had given her. She turned it over, the silver flashing against the morning sun.

Evylin fought fresh tears and tugged the boots over her wet socks. None of this should matter, not when someone so important had disappeared from the world. Shouldn't life freeze over like these woods? Shouldn't it stop and observe the great loss that had taken place?

And yet, she knew the world would never stop. It would never quit needing and taking. Today, they would try to save their friends and gain the Water Relic. Whether it saved Ephria or not, it wouldn't matter. They might survive the day, but they would not survive life.

Evylin tightened the laces of her boots, then slipped the knife beside her ankle. Deckard and Auden were both on their horses, waiting for her. She bent down and took up her sword, still waiting in the snow. The cold bit into her hands through the leather wrap on the hilt. Melting snow wept off the blade, dripping down to the terrae as though crying for the man who had forged it.

Evylin sheathed the sword next to the knife at her hip. She reached up to grasp Deckard's hand and hopped onto the horse behind him. She settled in, wrapping her arms around his waist loosely. He nudged the mare into a light canter, and Evylin forged her heart into steel.

They would attempt to save their friends and stop the evil Mages who'd taken them, but death would certainly come. And no matter when it came, she'd bled internally one too many times. Everything she was had already died twice over. She wouldn't do it a third time.

CHAPTER SIXTY-ONE

The city of Virwoud looked like all the others. Though not as large as Ephria City itself, nothing about it was truly any different. A fact that Evylin decided defined the world in which they lived. No matter where she went, everything was the same. And nothing was worth the cost she'd paid to learn that lesson.

The late morning sun shone with a dim yellow in the haze of the thick fog that rolled off the sea as they rode into the city, keeping their eyes open for any signs of their attackers or their friends. Evylin, Deckard, and Auden all forced themselves to stop and eat, knowing they'd need the energy to get through the rest of the day. But Evylin's aching stomach, heavy with grief, wouldn't allow her to fill it with much more than a slice of bread.

"We should search outside the city," Auden suggested as they dined, "near the bay."

As neither Deckard nor Evylin had the gumption to disagree, they went back through the city gates in search of the Keep. Their investigation wound through the outskirts for twice as long as the search for the Day Keep, and Auden continually apologized for his inability to find it.

"I'm just not very good with Elemental magic," he said, though neither of them questioned him.

Once Auden finally got a blip of magical direction, he led them farther into the wooded hills surrounding Virwoud. They stuck to the cover of the trees as much as possible to keep from being spotted by prying eyes while they continued the ambling search. Near the road, they moved cautiously to stay out of its sightline. But as they went deeper and deeper into the woods and came nearer to the shoreline, the sounds of the city bled away.

There, in the trees, silence hung like the heavy fog that surrounded them. Evylin couldn't find words as they walked. She was in a constant struggle between weeping and anger. After walking for some time, she settled into a strange sense of focus—a bridge between sadness and rage, creating a solitude she'd never before experienced.

In stark contrast to the rush of a fight, Evylin felt empty. She didn't care what happened to her anymore. Their mission wasn't a thrill to seek; it was a job to do. Her eyes narrowed on every sight. Each sound grew amplified, and every smell was enhanced. The snow-laden branches, birds taking wing, small creatures burrowing in the bushes, the glittering ocean to their left—Evylin didn't miss a thing as they walked. A fox hid deeper in its burrow as they passed. A spider wove its iridescent web in the far tree, dew glittering on its threads.

Then she heard it: the thunder of horses.

Evylin stopped and turned toward the sound. Both men walked on a few more feet before realizing she'd halted.

"What is it?" Auden asked, hurrying over to her side.

Staring out toward the road, Evylin squinted. "You don't hear that?"

"No. What do you hear?" Auden pressed, following her gaze.

Evylin glanced at Deckard, but he scanned the trees as deaf to the sound as Auden. Unsure how they couldn't hear the clarity of the horses' heavy hoof-falls, she turned back to the road. "Riders are approaching. You're sure you don't hear them?"

Auden's verdant gaze pierced her. "Evylin, you're tapping into your magic," he explained. "A Warrior's connection to magic grants the gift of heightened senses. It's one of the many ways your powers manifest."

Evylin chewed on her bottom lip as the horses drew closer. Deckard's gaze shot to the road.

"I hear them now too," he said.

"As do I," Auden replied, then turned back to Evylin. "It's good that you're reaching this level of focus. Keep pressing into it, whatever it is you're doing. It will help us succeed."

Trying to combat Hewitt's voice in her head, telling her Warriors were a ridiculous notion, Evylin asked, "Should we see if it's them?"

"I'll go," Auden said, handing the reins of his horse to Evylin. "I can hide myself with magic." He didn't wait for either of them to agree and headed for the tree line. As he reached its edge, a shadow fell over him, and he disappeared.

Evylin took a step back at the shock. Deckard came to stand by her side, though not as close as normal.

Looking up at him, Evylin could see the raised bump on the side of his head where she'd hit him. Most of his hair hid the mark, the length curling over his ears, grown out from their time traveling. But at his hairline near the temple, she could see a deep red welt peeking through. Instinctively, she thought to apologize for the wound once more. Then she realized her earlier accusation required far greater amends.

As she looked at him, Deckard met her eyes. Little emotion showed in his expression, yet somehow Evylin could tell through his hesitation that he meant to apologize as well. They stared at each other, both silent and still. The wind picked up a reddish-brown curl and brushed it across his forehead. Evylin's hand itched to brush it back, but her grief wouldn't let her touch him.

Crunching footsteps alerted them to Auden's return before he reappeared from the magical shroud. "It's them," he gasped, rushing to their sides. "And we were right. They've got Ilain leading them. It looks like she's been bound, as well as Rafferty, Ethenn, and Thom."

"How many are there?" Deckard asked.

Taking his horse back from Evylin, Auden shook his head. "About thirty altogether," he said. "Only about ten of them looked like Mages."

"Thirty?" Evylin asked, her concern increasing. She'd thought their odds would be unlikely, but three against thirty would be more than difficult. It would be impossible.

Auden didn't bother to confirm the worrying numbers. He began to lead his horse away, saying, "We have to follow them."

Once they reached the edge of the woods, they waited to break through the trees, walking rapidly as they stalked their prey. They made their way up a steep hill where the trees still grew thickly. There, they watched the road from a safe distance, obscured from sight.

The dirt road peeked from between the hillocks of Virwoud's shoreline, winding in and out of sight. The first two horses appeared. Ilain rode at the front, her hands tied to the saddle. A man rode by her side, his face hidden by a hooded cloak. Ilain spoke with the stranger, her expression tense.

The rest of their party followed. Auden had been close in his count: thirty-seven total, including their friends. Twenty armed men rode at the back while twelve other hooded figures paired up behind Ilain and the leader.

"The one at the front is a Night Mage," Auden whispered bitterly.

"How can you tell?" Deckard asked, scanning the group.

Auden snarled. "Do you see that clasp on his cloak? Two golden moons. A symbol of the Order of the Night."

"We already suspected that, didn't we?" Evylin said. "Whoever stole the Relic shrouded themselves, and you said it would be difficult for anyone but a Night Mage."

Tugging at his high collar, Auden nodded. "We need to be careful. Night Mages are vile, power-hungry sorts. They don't always start that way, but Night . . . It's a cruel resource."

Evylin saw what he meant as the approach of the group's rear brought Thom, Rafferty, and Ethenn into view. All three men had gags bound tightly across their mouths, and the ropes tied around their wrists were affixed to the horses as they stumbled beside them. They were haggard and beaten, muddy and mussed. A deep cut marred Ethenn's forehead; dried blood coated his temple and cheek. Rafferty had a bruise peeking out of his coat, trailing up his neck as though he'd been choked. Several scrapes marred the left side of his face. Thom had a deep welt by his right eye, his coat showing a telltale sign of blood as he limped, favoring his left leg.

At the fork in the road, Ilain directed the group toward the sea. "Hurry," Auden ordered, turning back to the trees. "We should tie our horses here and follow on foot."

Deckard and Auden hobbled the horses while Evylin watched their adversaries vanish down the hillside. The trio moved silently through the trees and across the road to the hill. At the top, they saw the group riding down the path to the sandy beach.

Moving low and slow, they tracked the band of Mages, darting from rocky outcropping to rocky outcropping. After a long trek, the party turned onto a crooked path that led through the hilly dunes. Scrambling up a hidden rise, the trio in pursuit hunkered behind a jagged, lichen-covered ridge of boulders. They made it just in time to see the leader dismount. Their enemy's band holed up in a hollow between the hills. Patches of grass peeked through the snow, the late afternoon light casting long shadows over the landscape.

They watched as the Night Mage walked over to Ilain, pulling her off her horse. Ilain snarled at his touch and spoke what Evylin imagined was a cutting remark. The faintest thrum of the Night Mage's chuckle reached their ears on the rise. He made an imposing figure, standing nearly a foot taller than Ilain, though she was taller than the average Ephrian woman herself. The Night Mage's cloak threw most of his form into shadow, but he carried himself like a man of great strength. Or, Evylin reasoned, it might have been with great power.

While the rest of the party dismounted, the leader held fast to Ilain's arm, guiding her forward. They both walked with proud strides, shoulders back. Yet, while the man carried himself with confidence and finesse, Ilain's steps were punctuated with irritation and disdain.

They walked around the curving hillside until they reached a large patch of stones butting up against its face. "There," Auden whispered as the pair neared the rocks, "that's the entrance."

"Where?" Evylin asked, shivering as they knelt in the snow, the chilly dampness seeping into her trousers.

Deckard pointed, his eyes narrowed to slits. "It's there," he muttered. "It looks like it leads down."

Auden drew a hand along his coppery stubble. "They're all underground."

The Night Mage dragged Ilain back to the group. As he spoke to his men, another Mage took Ilain from him. He shoved her toward Thom, Ethenn, and Rafferty, who were huddled in the shadow of a rocky rise, which butted between two other hillocks. Five armed men stood guard, and the Mage joined their watch after he tossed Ilain toward Thom. Her bound arms flew out to steady herself.

"Why doesn't she burn the ropes and free them?" Deckard asked.

"Focus is required for magic," Auden explained, "and Mages are able to muddle other Mages' focus by inundating them with magic."

The Night Mage gave orders, and ten swordsmen hobbled the horses while the others began to patrol the area. The remaining Mages surrounded their leader as he spoke.

Auden turned to Evylin, dropping to crouch fully behind the boulder. "Listen," he said, his stare intense and pleading. "We must work together if we're going to do enough damage in there. The idea is to take down as many of those Mages as possible. If we can split their numbers in half, it'll barely be enough."

He took hold of her arms. "I need you to focus," he commanded. "Like you did back in those woods. I need you to access each part of your magic and join them with mine. If we're both concentrating deeply enough, we can do what's needed. I know that."

Evylin took a deep breath, worried he had too much faith in her. "I don't know how to do that," she confessed. "I don't know how to be a Warrior. This is so new, so impossible. I can't . . ."

"It's innate in you, Evylin," Auden insisted, tightening his grip. "Believe me, it's there. I've seen you access it before, and you can do it again. You told Ilain you felt the magic in a fight. Feel it now. Embrace it in full, and let it flow through you."

Fighting the surge of panic within her, Evylin peeked over the boulder. Thom sat against the hillside with his injured leg stretched out in front of him. He and Rafferty glared at their captors while Ethenn stood next to Ilain like a protective guard dog.

Seeing their plight, her resolve strengthened. Evylin turned back to Auden. "Whatever I can do," she whispered to him, "I will."

Auden's smile turned proud, and he squeezed her arms. "I know you will."

"They're moving," Deckard warned, and they looked over the rocks together. The Mages and men were preparing to move while the Night Mage spoke to Ilain once more.

Auden turned to Deckard. "Here's your task." He pointed to the Mage guarding their friends. "Kill him first. He's the only thing keeping Ilain from using her powers. Once he's down, she can help you. The sooner you set her free, the more aid she'll be in fighting the others. She's always relied on her gestures too much," he added derisively.

"Once she's free," Auden continued, "free our men. Arm yourselves and get down to the Keep as fast as possible. Now, here's the important part." Auden held Deckard's gaze firmly. "Do *not* attack until Evylin and I have descended into the Keep. You *must* wait. If any men sound the alarm and draw more up top, none of us will stand a chance. Wait. Then kill the Mage."

Deckard's eyes held Auden's right to the end; then they flashed to Evylin. "I understand," he said.

"Good." Auden pulled away, then said quietly, "We must do this perfectly. No mistakes."

Evylin couldn't tell whether he meant those words for them or himself.

The Night Mage had returned to the Keep's entrance, his men at his side. Only the singular Mage and five guards remained behind to watch their friends.

Fifteen guards and eleven Mages prepared to go down into the Keep.

Twenty-six men for Evylin and Auden to fight alone.

The Night Mage stepped into the rock's opening and disappeared into the terrae. His men followed.

"We should go," Auden said, pausing to set a hand on Deckard's arm. "Good luck, my friend. I appreciate everything you've done for my sister and me."

The Mage stepped away, leaving Evylin and Deckard alone. Their eyes locked, but they remained silent. Evylin's chest ached in a way she didn't think possible. She didn't know what to say. Any apology seemed trite. A goodbye, too painful. A touch, too intimate for the tension between them.

"Don't die," Deckard whispered across the narrow distance between them. "Please, don't die."

Evylin couldn't hold his frightened gaze, dropping hers to the snow. She couldn't make that promise, and she didn't know if she even wanted to. But if she was going to die, there was one thing she knew she needed to say to him.

Closing the gap, Evylin forced her arms around his waist. Instantly, he pulled her close. The hug was raw and painful, and her throat burned with tears. All the emotion between them, all the hurt and fear, trembled beneath her skin. She could hardly bear the embrace. And yet, she never wanted it to end.

"Thank you," she whispered into his coat. She wanted to tell him what she was thanking him for: That even if it had brought her here, she did appreciate his sacrifices for her. Though she'd been a poor wife to him, he'd been a good husband to her. And if things had only been different, she would have loved him as she should.

But she held the words back with her tears, unwilling to speak the truth at what might now be the end.

Ripping herself from his arms, Evylin pushed past him and hurried to follow Auden. She refused to look back, knowing her resolve would break if she did. Auden had waited ahead for her, just distant enough to give them privacy for their goodbye.

When she reached the Mage, she found compassion in his gaze. He didn't understand the lack of a true marriage between them. He couldn't know they weren't in love. Yet, somehow, his sympathy for their loss vindicated Evylin's tightening chest.

The sun lowered toward the horizon, casting deep russet shadows everywhere. Evylin and Auden crept around the hill of the Keep's entrance to stay out of sight. Then they backtracked along the opposite side.

Nearing the rock's opening, Auden took her hand cautiously. "I'm not good with Night magic," he whispered apologetically. "Touch will help strengthen the shroud, but we'll have to move slowly. I can't hold the shadows around us if we move too fast."

Evylin raised her brows sardonically. "I have a feeling it'll be difficult to fight slowly."

He met her sarcasm with a dry grin. "It won't work once we're inside," he agreed. "Just before we enter, I'll uncover us so Jonn can see us enter and know when to attack. Once we're inside, it won't matter anymore."

Auden closed his eyes then, and a tingle of what she could only describe as power swept up Evylin's arm. Her senses spiked, the world coming into sharp clarity for one moment before Auden's figure grew hazy as though a dense fog coated him. Evylin glanced down, noticing the same strange haze around her form.

"There," he murmured, opening his eyes, a subtle darkness in their vibrant green depths. "The shroud is placed."

"I can still see you," Evylin warned.

He nodded. "And I, you. But to the rest of the world, we are invisible."

Trusting him, Evylin let him lead her around the hill, her hand prickling oddly in his. They inched closer to the Keep's entrance, eyes keen for the Mage and guardsmen left behind. The terrain was uneven and rocky, but covered in a shroud as they were, Auden and Evylin didn't bother with a cautious approach as they scrambled to the entrance. Another spike of power shivered up Evylin's arm, and Auden's figure became clear again. He'd dropped the shroud, making them visible once more.

She glanced over her shoulder to be sure the Night Mage's men hadn't seen them. Auden began to descend, but Evylin paused, lifting her gaze to the hill where Deckard hid.

She saw nothing but the lichen-covered boulders. With a singular tug on her rings, Evylin followed Auden down into the darkness.

They wound down the stairs and into a similar antechamber as had been in the Day Relic's Keep. The arched hall leading to the iron door was already lit, noting the Night Mage's presence within. Blue light flooded the space, casting a sapphire hue over Auden's figure.

When she stepped up to his side, hand on her sword, Auden placed his hand on her shoulder. She met his adamant expression with uncertainty. "This is it, Evylin," he whispered. "For centuries, Warriors and Mages worked together. Allore meant them to be a united team, a force of balance and power. Sometimes, a Warrior and a Mage choose to work together as a united pair, joined in a sacred Bond in dedication to one another, making their magic stronger. We—well, that's not something you and I would choose to do together. But I am asking you for this moment, Evylin, to be my Warrior."

The vibrant blue light shone in his darkened eyes as he tightened his grip on her shoulder. "We are going up against odds that no one should be able to defeat. But together, we can be something all eleven of those Mages down there are not: a double-edged sword."

If nothing else, Evylin could understand that metaphor. She didn't know if she believed she was a Warrior as the Calders claimed. Her loyalty to Hewitt pushed her to deny the idea. But her need for hope forced her to say that, somehow, yes, she was indeed one of those legendary Warriors she'd only just learned existed. And if they could be such a team, able to defeat any opponent with their powers, she needed to become that person.

"Will you be my Warrior, Evylin?" Auden asked.

Grasping his arm, Evylin held his gaze steadily. "Yes."

Auden's smile grew hopeful. Then a *thunk* echoed throughout the hall. Their gazes flew to the far end of the antechamber. Under the cerulean light, the iron door rumbled open. Auden pulled Evylin into his side, a sharp spike of energy rushing up her arm as the shroud's haze covered his figure just before two men left the Keep, another standing on the threshold.

Stepping into the glowing hall, the swordsmen ran at a quick pace through the antechamber. Slowly, the Keep's door slid shut behind them, their comrade, presumably the Mage who had opened the door, rushing back into the fray. Evylin and Auden pressed against the rock wall, unseen as the men hurried past. Blood splattered one man's coat, though both appeared uninjured. They took the stairs at a run.

Once they'd disappeared, Auden released Evylin. "Why do you think they returned?" she whispered.

"I'm not sure," he replied, eyeing the stairs. "Relaying a message, maybe? Whatever the case, we'll have to thank the Water Shades."

Evylin furrowed her brow.

"Shades don't bleed," Auden reminded her. "Whoever's blood was on that man's uniform belonged to one of their own."

Evylin let out a morbid sigh of relief. If the Shades took down enough men, perhaps they could make it out alive after all.

But then Evylin remembered they'd have to fight the army of Shades themselves.

Auden led the way through the domed space, and Evylin scanned the arching windows. The iron frames displayed designs of massive, tentacled creatures and oceanic plants. The sapphire light pouring through the panes made it feel as though they were walking through the deepest sea. Ahead, the iron door bore the engravings of those same tentacled creatures across its expanse.

As Auden raised his hand, Evylin drew her sword.

"Into the fray," he whispered as he had at the Day Keep.

Evylin glanced at him but didn't understand the significance of the phrase.

His hand landed on the center of the door. The *thunk* reverberated around them once again, and slowly, the door slid open.

Beyond the entrance, water gently lapped. Together, they stepped across the threshold and onto a staircase of blue marble. "Oh," Evylin gasped as she took in the Water Keep.

A long hall stretched before them, columned, open arches spanning its length. Other columned halls jutted off into a maze of other hallways, obfuscating the view to the other side of the Keep. Slate blue water spanned like a chasm, undulating hungrily at the sides of the halls.

Evylin's throat closed. She took a cautious step down as Auden descended confidently. Peering over the edge at the ominous water, she tightened her grip on her sword. "I think I should warn you," she whispered. "I can't swim."

Pausing, Auden glanced back at her. "Really?" he asked in surprise, and she nodded. His brow rose in dry humor. "Then best not fall in."

With a rueful scoff, Evylin followed behind him. Far ahead on the paths, the shouts of men reached them, and then came the unmistakable splash of water.

"Sounds like our friends have some company," Auden remarked, picking up his pace. "Be on your guard. We're likely to get some too."

Hurrying at his side, Evylin listened to the combat. So far removed from the battle, she could only make out the strain of fighting. But she heard the distinct sound of a body hitting the water. Her mind assaulted her with the image of being pulled into the darkness of its depths and dragged down into a watery death. Her heart pounded, but she remained alert as they carefully jogged the long hall.

A soft hum filled her ears all at once. It rose and fell in a crescendo of sound as though crashing in on itself like a wave. Another sudden splash to their side drew her attention as the first Shades burst out of the water.

"Look out," she called to Auden.

But Evylin hadn't needed to warn him at all. The Mage already held his hands raised, light and flame springing from his open palms. Several Shades shattered while the rest crawled onto the stone pathway. Their deep brown clay bodies rippled with water. Evylin charged, slashing at the remaining creatures. One Shade toppled, his chest split on the diagonal. She spun and thrust her blade into the other. Both bodies burst with violent sprays of salt water, stinging her eyes.

As the water spread across the stone floor, Evylin's chest rose and fell in a steady beat. Every droplet of water tingled against her skin. Her senses expanded, and her pulse quickened. Calm overcame adrenaline. The sensation she'd felt in the wood—that strange feeling of focus—heightened all her senses. Her mind and body grew hyperaware, but this time, something else came with it. The aching pain of Hewitt's loss didn't abate, but the grief seemed to channel itself into her body. Her muscles tightened like a spring ready to release, primed for action.

Hearing the battle ahead of her, Evylin's body urged her to rush onward and join the fray. She turned back to Auden with an anticipatory smile. "Let's get them."

He stared at her for a moment, his green eyes wide. Then he grinned and gestured to the hall. "After you, Warrior," he replied.

They ran.

More Shades appeared along the path, but Evylin cut through them before Auden could even lift his hands. They made it onto the first bridge, five more Shades creeping up immediately. Evylin sliced three, and Auden incinerated the other two with flame. He fought furiously, in a manner so unlike his usually reserved demeanor. Fire and Day flashed through the halls as Evylin spun her sword with steady precision. Her whole being felt alight like his magic, and she wondered absently if this was what he'd meant: Warrior and Mage working together, strengthening one another's magic.

When the bridge split, one path continued straight while the other branched left. Auden paused. His hand fidgeted, jittery, while Evylin bounced with anticipation, ready to move. He veered left.

The stone grew slick, water pooling at their feet, forcing them to slow their pace. Now, Shades appeared in a nearly constant barrage of attacks. They were soaked through, their salty clothes and hair sticking to their skin. Ahead, they heard the Night Mage and his men fighting on. Magic trembled within Evylin, a chill sweeping through her veins. She slashed and fought, and yet, she could sense the Night Mage ahead as he neared the other side of the maze where the Chamber's entrance and the obelisk awaited.

At each split in the halls, Auden paused, figuring out their direction. Every stop earned the Night Mage and his men more of an advantage. The power pumping through Evylin made her want to run and never stop. It pushed her harder and farther, yet she had to constantly rein in the instinct. Auden seemed no less agitated.

Battling Shades filled her with exhilaration, and vitality surged through her veins. Every part of her body resonated harmoniously with theirs, a cycle of energy flowing back upon itself time and again. Her speed outmatched theirs, and she cut through them effortlessly as if they were liquid. With each new Shade that emerged, puddles filled the stone path, leaving her increasingly drenched, but she didn't care.

They were nearing the end now. A man's voice shouted ahead, giving orders. Her senses heightened, she heard the sharp yet melodic lilt of a Wauld accent around the words, "Kill them, then meet us below." A door slammed in the distance.

"They've made it to the Chamber," Evylin warned, but it hardly mattered. Her body had begun to vibrate with energy. She was alive and primed for battle. What were a few enemy Mages to this might surging through her?

The thought shifted her focus. These were the men who'd taken Hewitt from her. In their midst was his murderer. And she would see each of them suffer for it.

Evylin attacked every Shade with twice the speed she normally fought. Auden hardly had the chance to call out which direction to go before she'd already taken it. Their opponents were within reach now. She'd be more than able to split open their guts the way they'd done to Hewitt.

A bellow rumbled through the Keep from deep below, the sound guttural and violent. Five Mages waited on an island of stone, the obelisk stretching high above them.

Evylin didn't stop.

The Mages stepped forward, hands raised. Evylin dropped to the stone, rolling beneath a torrent of shadow, water, terrae, and wind. Charred dirt crashed on top of her as the magic met a burst of flame and light. She rolled to her feet, sword at the ready, and Auden stepped to her side, the glimmer of Day and Fire sparking in his palms.

"I'd advise you to stand down," he said to them coldly.

The Mages eyed them, hands primed with their own magic. "I'm afraid we can't do that, Highlord Calder," said the man on the right, an amethyst shadow beaming around his palm.

Auden didn't question how the men knew him. "Into the fight, then," he said, the golden glow of Day magic flaring bright.

Two against five, Evylin and Auden leaped forward to fight the Mages.

Flashes of light and dark sprang forward alongside Elemental magic. Auden caught the Night Mage in the magical grip of his raised hand, freezing the man in mid-action. She recognized the magic; she'd been locked in the same manner the night before. Time was one of the three Existential resources, she remembered, suddenly realizing Auden had paralyzed this Night Mage by locking him in Time. Auden raised his other hand, and a column of Fire consumed the Mage in a violent torrent of ruby flame.

Evylin dodged the other Mages' attacks, spinning and ducking with more speed than ever. She struggled to draw closer, their powers pressing her farther back like an invisible wall. But she dove forward as one sent a blast of water at her. The spray rained over her, but she rolled onto one knee and brought her sword down on the Mage's legs.

He screamed, falling back as both appendages were severed.

Evylin rose to her feet and plunged the sword into his gut. The Mage choked on his blood, and Evylin spun as another Mage lunged for her. She kicked him back just as a wall of wind slammed into her, sending her rolling across the stone hall to the edge of the island. She caught herself before plummeting into the water, immediately turning to dash back for the Mage.

Then it all changed.

Shades sprang from the water, their forms rushing the Mages and Warrior alike. Forced to abandon her pursuit, Evylin turned and chopped down two of the creatures. The wind rushed again, pushing her farther into the fray. She cut down the army of Shades, each one blasting into a jet of water that puddled on the ground.

Lungs heaving, Evylin checked on Auden. While the Wind Mage fought her, the remaining two Mages had focused on the Calder brother. Shades descended relentlessly on the group. Flashes of light and flame erupted around Auden as he deflected the attacks on all sides. She prepared to sprint to his side and defend against the rush of Shades so he could take down the Mages.

Yet, another wild and croaking bellow shook the Keep's floor, and Evylin's eyes flashed to the Chamber's door. The distraction was her undoing.

The wind hit again as the Mage let loose all his power. She tumbled back. Newly risen Shades gripped at her, knocking her to the floor. Rolling with the momentum, Evylin tucked her knees and pressed on the stone to rise to her feet. She'd done it so many times in the past—it was one of the first things Hewitt had taught her. *"You need to know how to rise when someone knocks you down,"* he'd said.

Landing on her feet, Evylin struck out at the figures of Shades surrounding her. But it was too late. Her left foot landed in one of the slick puddles, and it slipped.

Evylin tipped backward, the edge of the stone hall vanishing beneath her as she fell off the island. She plunged into the water with a body-shaking splash. With a rush, the water embraced her as if it had yearned to hold her. A dull, humming crescendo surged and ebbed around her. Reacting to the cold, she gasped and inhaled instinctively.

Evylin struggled to cough up the water but swallowed more instead. The salt stung her lungs as her body fought against the suffocation. She lost her focus; only adrenaline remained. She needed to escape—to reach the surface. Yet, her frantic thrashing only pulled her deeper underwater.

So this is it, she thought bitterly. *I'll die at the hands of the very thing I longed to see.*

Entwined in the water's grasp, Evylin would have cried. But she'd been drowning ever since watching Hewitt die. It only seemed fitting that the sea would claim her life now.

A crash sounded above her. Evylin's eyes flashed upward toward the surface on instinct. A pale hand reached out to her from beyond the surface.

Desperately, Evylin grabbed onto it, and it pulled her up.

As she broke through the water, Evylin choked, her eyes closing as her lungs contracted. Her savior dragged her onto the stone island, a hand on her back as she spat up the salt water. Sucking in deep breaths of air, she slumped to the floor, throat raw from the regurgitation.

When she finally recovered, Evylin spun to face her rescuer. She gasped and tried to pull away, but the Mage grabbed hold of her wrists. "No, you don't," he spat, then slapped her across the face.

Evylin choked again, the stinging of her cheek helping to bring her clarity back. She tried to lurch away, searching for her sword. But the man held on tight, and the weapon was nowhere to be found. She'd lost it in the water, another piece of Hewitt gone forever.

Fresh tears burned her eyes, but she forced herself to locate Auden. The onslaught of Shades had been defeated, leaving the island eerily quiet. The three Mages remained, and Auden was a captive with a knife to his throat.

The Wind Mage yanked Evylin to her feet. He practically dragged her to the obelisk. "Open it," he ordered an empty-handed Mage. He removed the hunting knife from Evylin's belt, holding its sharp point against her back. "He'll want to see them."

Evylin met Auden's eyes. "I'm sorry," she murmured brokenly.

"We did what we could," Auden replied, dark sorrow in his gaze.

The Mage opened the Chamber's door, and they pulled their captives into the spiral staircase. Sapphire light poured over them like water as they descended. Then they stepped into the grand hall. It mirrored the Day Chamber in Norhels—columned, marbled, and massive, with a dais and pedestal at the end. But this Chamber radiated pure cobalt, and two giant pools flanked the marble path.

The Mages forced them inside. "Sire," Evylin's captor called. "These two were attempting to stop us."

Only four Mages remained alive inside, one clutching a wound on his right leg while another helped a third stop the bleeding on his mutilated arm.

The Night Mage stood at the dais, about to ascend. He turned, his still-cloaked head twisting back to see them, though the rest of his figure remained still. "Bring them to me," he said, his lilting accent smoother than the Calders and other Mages. His voice was distinctively refined and regal.

Forced to walk the massive Chamber, Evylin looked at Auden. His eyes were locked onto the Night Mage, and his brow furrowed in confusion as the man turned fully to face them. Their captors forced them to their knees before the Night Mage.

"Welcome," the cloaked man said, taking a step closer. "And my greatest thanks to you both. I've quite enjoyed getting to know the Day Relic these last twelve days."

Auden and Evylin glared up at him. She wanted to say something, anything, to make him regret stealing the Relic—for taking Hewitt from her. But she knew it was hopeless. Here, on their knees before the Mage's towering form, *they* were hopeless.

The Night Mage reached up and took hold of his hood. "Now," he said, "let's get to the introductions, shall we?"

PART IV: The Night Mage

Into the fray, into the fight;
With goodness and honor, with Allore's might.
"Psalm of Sigrid, the Golden Knight," *circa 253*

Princes and thieves, they are the same.
One takes by force, the other by ingenuity.
Nikleby Draaw, from "The Tricks of Nikleby Draaw"
(collection: The Traveler and the Rook)

ACRE
VIRWOUD

CHAPTER SIXTY-TWO

Black hood folded onto his shoulders, the Night Mage surveyed Evylin and Auden. His narrow face and frame matched his height. Yet, there was a firmness to his limbs that suggested brawn. He moved with grace and control, his shoulders relaxed. His pale skin was smooth with mature features that placed him near Deckard's age. His hair looked like pure gold, cropped short and slicked back with precision. A heavy brow sat over impossibly blue eyes, clear like a summer sky.

The Night Mage crossed his arms, a grin tugging at the left side of his mouth. He might have been handsome had those crystalline eyes not displayed conceit and cruelty so clearly.

Auden gasped at first sight of the man's face. "It's you," he snarled viciously.

The Night Mage tilted his head. "I'm aware of you and your exploits, Highlord Calder. But I don't believe we've met, have we?"

"No," Auden replied, words clipped. "I don't believe we have."

"Interesting that you feel you know me so well, then," he remarked casually. "It seems courtesy would state you introduce yourselves to me; that way, we can all know one another."

Shifting under the weight of her captor's iron grip, Evylin tossed a mocking grin at the Night Mage. "I'm afraid you misunderstand," she said. "I don't have the slightest idea of who you are."

The man's gaze rested on her face, his smile curious. "Pity for us both," he returned, then looked back to Auden. "Since you seem to be familiar with all parties here, Highlord, perhaps you could do the introductions."

Auden glared at the Night Mage with fire in his eyes. "Evylin, this is Crown Prince Rouland Blount II, ViceMage in the Order of the Night and heir to the Waulden throne."

The Night Mage gave a miniature bow while Evylin took him in with fresh eyes. Everything about their quest had changed now. Knowing the Crown Prince of Wauld was a Mage in pursuit of the Relics was devastating. It put an end to all questions about the importance of their mission. If Wauld obtained the Relics with the Crown Prince wielding them, she knew it would secure the total annihilation of Ephria.

"Your Royal Highness, this is Evylin Deckard," Auden continued, "a friend of mine."

"A friend?" Prince Blount stepped toward Evylin. He reached out, and though she tried to pull away, he caught her chin in a firm grasp. Staring into her eyes, a thin tremble of magic pulsed across her skin at his aggressive touch. "No," he whispered knowingly. "Not only a friend, surely. Not with your power."

Evylin held his penetrating gaze, conveying her hatred for him through the shared look.

His smile grew as his eyes roved greedily over her face. "Ah, a Warrior," he said reverently. Then he lifted his other hand to gently brush back the wet hair stuck to her face. "So rare. So valuable. You are a treasure, my dear. Do you know that?"

Evylin's breath grew tense under his stare and his touch.

Drawing his fingers along her jawline, the Night Mage shook his head. "How unfortunate you chose to align yourself with the wrong people."

Blount released her, then rose to his full height. He faced the Mages who'd brought the captives to him. "There were three who escaped," he said sharply. "Where's the third?"

"It was only these two, sire."

"Then we must assume the other waits to come to their aid," Blount said. He motioned to the third Mage. "Guard the Chamber door."

"But, sire, the Shades—"

One look from Blount silenced the Mage. Instantly, he turned and hurried back to the stairs.

"Now," Blount clasped his hands and turned to Auden, "first things first." He smiled cruelly. "Where are the other Keeps located?"

Auden frowned mockingly. "I'm afraid I don't know what you're referring to, Your Highness."

A light but sharp chuckle escaped the Night Mage. "That's quite amusing, Highlord. But the fact is, I know that you know. You and your sister wouldn't have started all this if you didn't."

"We were only bored if I'm being honest," Auden said, grinning along with the prince. "You know what it's like in the Orders. Train in the morning, read books in the afternoon, and then listen to the old bags as they lecture you because you tried something new. We got tired of the monotony."

"Ah." Prince Blount nodded along with Auden's words. "And did you not think someone would notice when you took a Relic? Did you not realize going after the most powerful objects in this world was treason?"

"Treason?" Auden asked in faux shock. "My goodness, all for a little fun? No, no, Your Highness. We would never betray Wauld and our *fine* royal family."

The prince's smile dropped. "Tell me, Highlord Calder," he said tightly. "Where are the rest of the Relic Keeps? Tell me now, and you'll save yourself a world of pain."

Evylin watched as Auden swallowed, and a tiny tremor passed over his lips. But he held Blount's glare with his own. "Afraid I can't do that," he said calmly.

"Very well." Blount gestured to the Mage behind Auden. "Hold him steady."

The Mage locked one arm around Auden's shoulders, setting his other hand on the crown of his head to draw it back. Evylin jerked against her captor's grip more forcefully than he'd expected and broke free. She swept at his legs, muscles primed to dart for Auden. Then a foot connected with her face.

Auden called out, gasping in pain. Evylin dropped to the floor, the entire left side of her face searing in agony. Blood coated her tongue, spurting from where she'd bitten into her cheek. She felt herself yanked off the floor by her coat.

The Night Mage met her gaze, his face a haze from the tears welling in her eyes. He drew her close, his breath caressing her skin as he spoke. "Don't try that again, dear one," Blount said calmly. "You'll only make it worse for both of you. Understand?"

Fighting through the misery, Evylin glared at him.

Prince Blount raised his dark blond brows. "Answer me," he ordered.

Evylin remained silent.

A fierce eruption of pain flared across her other cheek as Blount backhanded her. Then he pulled her closer, their faces a mere inch away. "Do you understand me?" he asked again, emotionless.

Shaking, Evylin tried to nod. "Yes," she gasped out.

"Good," Prince Blount said, tossing her to the floor.

Her captor took hold of her once more, twisting her right arm behind her so that if she tried to pull away, it would snap out of its socket. He used his other hand to grab hold of her throat, causing her to choke.

Once she was under control, Blount brushed her smarting cheek tenderly. "I hate getting violent with any woman," the prince said in a gentle whisper. "And especially with one so special and beautiful as you. However, I can't have people disregarding my orders. I'm sure you understand. Those of us in authority can't have that."

Evylin tried to swallow, but the Mage's grip on her neck made it difficult. Her cheek ached as she smirked bitterly. "Of course," she mocked. "I understand perfectly."

"Wonderful," he said, drawing his fingers down to her chin before stepping away. "I'm glad to know I won't have any more trouble from you."

When he turned from her, Evylin dropped her proud smile.

Blount swung to Auden, whose eyes were wide in worry and fear. "I don't care what you do to me," he said, his back arched under his captor's hold. "I won't tell you what you want to know."

"It'd be a disappointment if you gave it over that easily," Blount replied, standing in front of him. "No, this will be much more fun. For me, at least. For you, not as much."

The prince reached out, and Auden tried to recoil. But the Mage behind him remained steady. Blount gripped Auden's face, his finger pressing into his temples, palm covering his eyes. In an instant, Auden began to shake.

"No," he muttered. "No, not that. Not that."

Evylin's heart squeezed with uncertainty.

"Do you know, Evylin," Prince Blount said, eyes locked on Auden's whimpering expression, "what Night magic is capable of?"

Knowing it would be a mistake to ignore him, Evylin forced out her response. "No."

Auden trembled as tears coursed down his cheeks.

"The Night can be many things," Blount explained, his voice seeming to cause Auden's shaking to worsen. "It can bring safety and renewal. Sometimes, the darkness is protection. It aids in intimacy, drawing two people together as the security and secrecy of Night envelop them. Night can be such a positive thing."

Auden screamed then, sobs wrenching from his throat.

The sounds tore at Evylin. Her own tears broke free, hot against her tingling cheeks. Hewitt's lifeless eyes flashed back to her. The gaping hole in his gut mirrored itself in her grief, and she knew she'd never be whole again.

Blount's melodic voice was like a haunting refrain in the air. "But the Night can also bring terrors."

His fingers pressed deeper into Auden's skull, and another cry echoed against the Chamber walls.

"The safety it affords you, it also provides to your enemies," Blount continued. "Fear lives in the darkness. Suspicion, anxiety, nightmares—they lurk in the shadows. Terror haunts the Night and makes it horrifying." The tone of his words was cruelly fond. "Where else can you experience such pleasure and panic in the same place?"

"No!" Auden screamed out once more. He shook with such violence that the Mage holding him struggled to stay upright. "No! Stop it, stop it!"

"Do you understand what's happening to him, Evylin?" Blount asked, looking at her. Pleasure radiated in the depths of his eyes. "Do you know what I'm doing to him?"

Evylin shook her head weakly. "No," she murmured, slumping in her captor's grip. The slightest movement brought pain to her shoulder. Blood coated her tongue from the bite inside her cheek. And she knew, no matter how hard she tried, she'd never be able to save either of them.

The Night Mage grinned gently. "I'm showing him his greatest fears," he said, nails cutting into Auden's temples. "He's living through them as though they're real and watching as he's incapable of doing anything to stop them.

"I don't know what his fears are. It's not part of the magic for me to know." Blount's smile turned wistful. "But I like to imagine what it may be," he said, scanning his victim like a rare jewel or piece of art. "For Highlord Calder here, I'd imagine it's something like seeing his beautiful sister in trouble. Maybe her splendid, fiery hair is ablaze as she burns. Or he might be watching as she's murdered, her lovely, porcelain parts all torn to pieces. It could be his mind has made him a voyeur as she's violated again and again by my men.

"Those may be his fears." Blount paused thoughtfully. "Or perhaps it's something much worse than even I can't construct."

Evylin gaped in outrage and pure fear. Such a fascination with pain and trembling could only reveal the man's madness. Her heart faltered at his utter fascination and delight with the thought of Auden's torture. How could anyone be so evil as to find such depravity alluring?

"Stop!" Auden's voice sounded as though it was ripping in two. "STOP! PLEASE!"

"Tell me where the Relics are, Highlord," Blount said kindly. "Tell me, and I'll take it all away."

Auden wept. "No," he whispered as though in total devastation. "I can't."

"Then it will not end."

Screams pierced through the Chamber, driving straight into Evylin's chest. "Stop!" she called, leaning over despite the pain in her arm. She choked, struggling to breathe as the Mage tightened his grip on her throat.

"NO!" Auden wailed. "STOP! JUST STOP! I'LL TELL YOU!"

Evylin wilted, and the Night Mage's smile grew triumphant. His fingers dug deeper, and Auden screamed again, his body straightening like a rail. Then Blount released him.

Auden's limp form nearly tumbled out of his captor's grasp.

Blount watched patiently, crouching down to meet Auden's gaze. "Tell me," he said softly. "Where are they?"

Deep ridges were embedded in Auden's temple where Blount's nails had cut into his flesh, small droplets of blood welling. Tears stained his cheeks, his gaze flat and empty as it stared at the blue marble. "Which ones don't you know?" he asked hollowly.

"I don't know any of them," Blount said. "I worked out a few bits here and there, but those damn ancient Mages were such laborious zealots. When you and your sweet sister decided to make a run for it, I thought I might as well capitalize on your studies. So, if you please, give me all the archaic details."

Auden closed his eyes, a remorseful sigh shaking his body. "The Keeps are located within the province lines of the Orders. The ones in Wauld as well as the ones here in Ephria."

"Mm, yes." Blount drew his fingers along his smooth jaw. "The Order of the Sea was in Port Barrow, wasn't it?"

"Burlbarrow, now," Auden murmured.

"The Ephrians ruin everything," he said, tossing Evylin an amused smirk. "So where to next?"

"Next is the Night Relic," the highlord muttered, the words slow and tight. "Luckily for you. It's off the shore, near Taulence. After that is the Wind Relic."

"In Sutterlund?" Blount clarified.

Auden tried to nod, but the Mage still held his head too tightly in his grasp. "In the 'U' between Nemaurs and Gisors. Then you'll go to Vaura Province, about fourteen miles southwest of Loches, for the Time Relic."

Blount's gaze narrowed suspiciously. "Three Waulden Relics in a row? Are you lying to me?"

"No, I swear," Auden promised in a panic. "It's the order of creation. After Time comes Terrae in Olbury, Estshire."

Estshire? Evylin nearly gasped, shocked that her home province could hold a Relic. How had she lived so close to one for her entire life?

"Then," Auden concluded, "up to Ephria City for the last." He ground his teeth in a sardonic manner. "The Shepherd King didn't know he'd built his kingdom upon magic's greatest power."

A snide smile pulled at Blount's lips. "Yes, that sounds like the ignorant Shepherd," he remarked, clasping his hands in derisive gratitude. "Excellent work, Highlord Calder. You did a fantastic job discovering all that. I can't thank you enough."

The Night Mage set one foot back on the cerulean dais, then froze. "Oh, yes." He snapped his fingers and tutted, turning back to Auden with a bright grin. "I almost forgot the most important service you did for me."

At the prince's signal, Auden's captor adjusted his hold. He placed his knee in his back, pressing a foot on his bent leg and tightening his grasp. As Blount neared, Auden tried to struggle.

"No," he shouted. "You can't!"

Sure that Blount was about to torture Auden again, Evylin panicked. "Don't! He gave you what you wanted!" she yelled through the stranglehold of her captor's grip.

Blount merely glanced at her. He reached down to Auden's neck. "Yes, my dear," he said, tugging open the collar of Auden's shirt. His fingers looped around a golden chain, working it up over Auden's head. "He really did."

Suspended from Blount's hand was a heavy necklace, a gold pendant with a vividly glowing ruby at its center. The gem flickered as if it were alive, showcasing an inner light that danced like rusty flames within its facets.

"You should have known better, Highlord," Blount said, looking at Auden. "Did you think taking a Relic wouldn't bring hell down upon you?"

Evylin blinked, staring at the necklace as it swayed gently. "What is that?" she muttered.

Auden's eyes closed again. "I'm sorry, Evylin," he said softly. "We couldn't tell you."

Blount stared between them. "You lied to her? You and your sister?" He *tsked.* "That's bad taste, lying to your Warrior. Shall I explain it?"

Without waiting for Auden to reply, Blount stepped to Evylin's side. "You see, dear, this is the Fire Relic. The *first* Relic." He let the pendant dangle before her face. "Your friends stole it and left Wauld with the intention of betraying their countrymen. They've been plotting against us for years, it seems. But the good news is, they did the work for me. See, I've been after the Relics myself for the past decade. But it's hard when you're the prince, and everything is at your fingertips. There's so much information on the Relics out there that it all gets confusing after a while. I couldn't puzzle it out myself."

His blue eyes leered at the Relic, which flickered with internal fire. "And then the Calders helped me by taking this beauty," he spoke reverently. "The Order of the Flame was irate, of course. We can feel it, you know? When someone takes our Relic, we feel it deep within our hearts. A fail-safe, some say."

Blount smiled at the Fire Relic. "I think it's an invitation. An alert to let us know that power is up for grabs."

The prince stood then, clasping the pendant in his palm. "As it is, the Order of the Flame all felt it when these arrogant fools took the Fire Relic." He gave Auden a scornful glance. "They alerted the other Orders to what two of their most prominent Mages had done. I took it as a sign that my chance had finally come to pursue my destiny. I would follow these foolish thieves and use their knowledge against them. Then I'd do what my ancestors never could." He met Evylin's gaze with a proud glint in his eyes. "Mages will once again rule. But this time under my leadership."

Evylin looked past him to Auden. "You already had a Relic?" she said, unsure whether she was angrier with him and his sister or herself for believing them. "Why tell us we still needed it? Why not say there were six Relics instead of seven?"

Blount scoffed. "Lie upon lie, I see. There aren't seven Relics, my lovely. There are eight."

Evylin gaped at him, the truth coming to her. Eight Relics. And one already in the Calders' grasp. They'd used the Ephrian soldiers. They planned to betray them all along.

But why, and to what end?

Blount believed the Calders were against him and Wauld. So how could they also be against Ephria? If neither country held their allegiance, who did? Or were they just pursuing this for selfish gain?

The Night Mage slipped the Fire Relic into his pocket and turned away. "You really are shocking, Highlord," he said, stepping onto the dais. He walked over to the pedestal. "You and your sister's arrogance undid you here. Thinking you could outsmart the entirety of the Mages? And then to deceive your own team?" He chuckled. "What did you think would happen?"

Blount lifted another golden necklace from the cerulean pedestal, this one inlaid with a rippling blue sapphire. "No matter," he said, settling the chain over his head. "I've three Relics now and the locations of the rest. So I don't need you."

Blount gestured to the Mage holding Auden. "Kill him."

CHAPTER SIXTY-THREE

Deckard watched Evylin disappear with Auden around the hillside. Fear and pain lanced through his chest at their goodbye. He knew she'd been right that morning—his failures had brought them to this place. He'd never succeeded at helping anyone: not her, not Hewitt, not Thom. He failed their team, his family, and their country.

But Deckard had one last chance at redemption.

Deckard would not fail Evylin again. She might willingly sacrifice herself in the Keep, but he would not let her die. If he did nothing else, he would save her life.

Watching and waiting, Deckard hid amongst the rocks on the top of the hill. An eternity passed as he looked between their captive friends and watched for Evylin and Auden to enter the Keep. Suddenly, he caught sight of them at the rocks leading down into the terrae.

Heart hammering, Deckard whispered, "Be safe."

Auden descended, but Evylin paused. She turned back, looking up at the hill. He doubted that she could see him, but he smiled, knowing she'd looked back. Then she disappeared into the darkness.

Deckard forced his gaze back to their friends. The enemy Mage stood there, talking to the bound and gagged team. Only Ilain could respond, though she didn't seem inclined to. Left leg stretched out before him, Thom glared at their enemy.

Deckard's stomach tightened at the sight of his captive brother. He scanned the hillside to determine the safest route. The alcove in which his friends were restrained was tucked between other rocky hillocks. If he backtracked, he could sneak around them and slip through on the other side nearest the Mage. Once Ilain could use her powers, Deckard would be able to free the rest of their team. The other five guards would go down with little difficulty.

Slowly, Deckard began his trek down the hill with broadsword and knife at the ready. Killing made him uncomfortable, but today, he wouldn't hesitate, knowing it would save the people who mattered most to him.

As Deckard neared the bottom of the hill, he checked to be sure no one would see as he ran across the road to the other side. Once he made it, he slipped around the back, climbing over the craggy hillside. Then he snuck through the narrow abutment of the hills to peer at the enemy camp.

The guards talked distractedly, and the Mage was focused on the team. The four in Deckard's group clustered against the back wall. Rafferty and Ethenn stood together while Ilain sat next to Thom, cautiously examining his leg.

That worried Deckard. An injury was bad enough, but if Thom fought and ran on the leg, it could cause even greater damage.

Something caught the guards' attention on the far side of the clearing. The rustle of jostling weapons and the heavy footfalls of approaching men made him draw back. He kept his view just enough to see two swordsmen appear in the clearing. One had blood splattered across the front of his uniform.

Deckard blanched, instantly worried for Evylin and Auden.

"What is it?" the Mage asked the newcomers.

The swordsmen smiled. "It's the Keep, all right," the one on the left said, his Waulden accent thick. "He sent us back to tell you we don't need the prisoners anymore. The highlady stays, but he said to kill the rest."

"I told him," Ilain's voice spat, "if they die, I won't give him anything."

Deckard tightened his grip on his weapons as he listened.

"You think you can withstand Night magic's thrall, *former* ViceMage?" the Mage said with disdain.

Since he was unable to see her from his position, Deckard could only hear the caustic grin in her tone. "Oh, Highlord, you know who I am," she said mockingly. Her voice grew tense. "I'm Pyra's Heiress, the goddess embodied, and the most powerful, bloody Mage alive."

"Then why are you my prisoner?" the Mage retorted.

"Because I was waiting for him."

Somehow, Deckard knew she was referring to him, and however it was that she knew he was there, he couldn't hesitate. His fingers grew white with tension on his blades. He sprang from his hiding place, causing the guards to jump in alarm. But he was too fast for them to react.

Despite Auden's instructions, Deckard entered the fray closest to the newly arrived swordsmen. He drove his knife into one man's neck, then slashed the other man across the chest. His leather armor deflected most of the blow, but Deckard was already swinging again by the time the swordsman gripped his sheathed blade. Another strike, and the man fell to the terrae.

Before anyone else could react, Deckard tossed the knife to Ilain, then rushed for the Mage.

Without warning, the ground began to rumble dangerously. Deckard stumbled to the dirt, and the Mage tossed his arms toward him. Rocks rained down, pelting his sides and back as he rolled to dodge them. A large one connected with his knee, causing him to grunt in pain.

A scuffle came from the direction of his team, but he kept his eyes fixed on the Mage, who raised his hands once more. Twin boulders ripped from the hillsides above them, hovering in the air. Deckard's gut twisted, knowing those would be incredibly difficult to dodge.

Suddenly, a flame erupted at the Mage's feet, sweeping up to consume him whole. He didn't even have time to scream as the fire turned him to ash. He crumbled to the terrae before Deckard's eyes.

"I really need to stop relying on gestures," Ilain said casually.

Deckard turned wide-eyed to find only two guards remaining, one with Ethenn's still bound arms choking him while Rafferty beat the other across the face. Thom stood over the others, Deckard's knife in his unbound hand.

Ilain smiled, brushing the last remnants of rope free from her wrists. "Nice of you to come by, Jonn."

Deckard nodded distractedly. "How did you know I was here?"

"I didn't," she admitted.

He blinked, but it was Thom who spoke. "That was a bluff?" he demanded.

"No," Ilain said calmly. "It was a gambit. I'd been building up my focus for the last hour. While it wouldn't have been as effective, should they have been distracted, I was going to burn us free of our ropes, and that would have given us the chance to attack."

"You could have told us that," Ethenn noted as Thom sawed off his bonds.

Ilain smirked. "Now, where would be the fun in that, love?"

Deckard sighed, staring at the carnage of bodies around them. They'd done it. They were reunited. Now, they had to save Evylin and Auden.

As though reading his mind, Ilain turned to Deckard. "Where's Auden?" she asked.

"In the Keep," Deckard said, "with Evylin."

Her eyes darkened. "And the prince and his men."

"The prince?" Deckard gaped. "Prince Ephren?"

Ilain shook her head, the evening sun making her hair shine like fire. "No," she said, fear coming into her eyes. "Prince Blount of Wauld. He's a Night Mage, and he's after the Relics. He's incredibly powerful, and if we don't get down there, he will kill them both."

"Then we'd better get going," Rafferty said, coming to their side. He held a knife in each hand now, not as efficient as his preferred short swords but equally as deadly.

Though Deckard was scarcely less eager, he turned to Thom. "Can you make it?" he asked, gesturing to his leg.

Thom nodded, though he grimaced. "It's not broken," he assured him. "Just sprained."

"We'll have to run the whole way."

"I can make it, Jonn."

Ethenn walked back from the horses with a bow and quiver full of arrows slung across his back. He carried two swords, tossing one to Thom. "We'll have to deal with Shades down there, too, right?" he asked.

"Yes," Ilain said with a dangerous glimmer in her eyes. "But I'm an Elemental Mage, remember? This fight will be nothing with me by your side."

They moved toward the Keep's entrance. Thom matched Deckard's stride. "Why didn't all of you come to save us?" he demanded. "Why would you let Evylin go down there with Auden alone?"

Deckard clenched his jaw. "Believe me," he said, his voice a growl almost as good as Hewitt's, "I didn't approve of it either."

"They're thinning out the pack, aren't they?" Ilain asked but didn't wait for an answer. "Auden always was a martyr. He'd better hope he's dead by the time I get down there because if he isn't, I'll kill him myself."

"I'll help," Thom said, moving up to walk alongside her. It might have been the first time the two of them had agreed on anything.

When they marched down the staircase, Ilain was right at Deckard's side. "Stay with me the whole way," she ordered. "I can lead us straight to the Chamber, but I'll need protection."

"Then you'd better take Thom or Ethenn with you up front," Deckard said, ready to step back.

"No." Ilain grabbed his sleeve and forced him to face her. "It *must* be you."

When he frowned in confusion, she continued, "You and I are the ones with the most to lose. We are the ones who will do whatever it takes to succeed."

Deckard stared into her jade green eyes, noting how full of passion they were. "All right," he agreed.

Ilain released his coat. "All right," she repeated, then gestured onward. "Shall we?"

They descended into the antechamber with Deckard at the front, followed by Ilain, then Thom and Rafferty next, and Ethenn taking up the rear. Darkness covered them as they entered the narrow alcove. But all at once, everything turned the richest blue.

Resetting his grip on the hilt of his sword, Deckard felt his shoulders relax as he walked through the sapphire beams of light. His pulse steadied as his focus centered. Ilain was right; whatever it took, he'd get to Evylin. If only to be sure she survived.

"Let your instincts guide you once we're inside," Ilain charged as they neared the door. "Don't hesitate, and don't let fear overtake you."

"Don't worry," he said. "I won't let anything stop me."

Ilain's smile was as sharp as a knife. "Into the fray, then," she said, setting her hand on the door. "Into the fight."

They entered the Keep, descending the staircase into a hall adorned with intricate stone archways. Water puddled across the path, requiring them to be cautious with each step. Deckard, Thom, and Rafferty held their blades at the ready while Ethenn nocked an arrow. Together, they gazed into the labyrinth of corridors extending over the shimmering lake of blue.

"Guess we're in the right place," Rafferty said brightly. "Seems watery and challenging enough to me."

"Be careful not to fall into the pools," Ilain warned. "I'd imagine Shades will be waiting to drag you down. And we won't have time to save you."

Though his heart protested, Deckard knew the truth of her words. They couldn't wait while Auden and Evylin might be in danger for their lives. If they hesitated for even a moment, they might lose them both. And he wouldn't let that happen.

"It's awfully quiet," Thom said as they jogged forward. "Shouldn't we hear them fighting?"

"They're likely already in the Chamber," Ilain replied. "If they didn't get there on their own, then Prince Blount has them."

A *bang* echoed over the pools. Deckard and Ilain exchanged a look. "Or they just went in now," he said.

"We'd better—" Ilain began, then froze.

"I hear it too," Deckard said, a hum rising in the air.

While the two of them stared at the water, the rest of the men raised their weapons.

"What do you hear?" Thom asked.

"Shades," Ilain murmured, breaking into a sprint down the hall. "We have to move!"

Running through the passageways, Deckard caught up to her and followed at her side. A horde of Shades sprang up from the deep, splashing the edges of their hall. They jumped onto the stone, splitting and surrounding the group. Deckard, Thom, and Rafferty cut away at the creatures, and Ethenn dropped a few with his arrows. Ilain set a couple ablaze, then swept the rest off the platform with Wind magic. The burst of vanquished Shades soaked them to the bone.

"Keep going!" Ilain yelled to Deckard, who was now at the front of the line.

Deckard ran through the halls, slicing each Shade that arose. He kept slipping on the water filling the pathways but managed to retain his footing as he sprinted through the maze. He came to a fork, halls branching off the one they were already on. "Ilain?" he called, edging toward the left.

"Yes!" she called, appearing at his side. "Yes, go left."

They continued. Each Shade caused more and more water to puddle on the paths. Whenever they came to a split in the course, Deckard would call out his guess, and Ilain would respond. He got all but one correct when he began to go straight, and her voice rang out behind him, "Right, Jonn, go right!"

Halfway through, after he'd brought down another few Shades, Deckard looked across at the other end. He grabbed Ilain's arm. "There's a Mage over there," he warned.

She followed his gaze, hair plastered to her cheeks in dark red clumps. She nodded but didn't say what they were both thinking. If an enemy Mage remained outside the Chamber, then Evylin and Auden had been either captured or killed. His heart rebelled against the very thought of losing his wife, sure that if she was truly gone, he would know—he would have felt it in his soul.

"If he hasn't noticed us already," Ilain said, her fingers flexing, "then he will soon enough. Be on your guard. He'll try to use Water magic against us."

Resuming their progress, Deckard glanced at her. "You think he's an Elemental Mage?" he asked.

"You'd better hope he is," Ilain replied. "I'm not great with Water magic, but I'm a hell of a lot more powerful than the average Elemental. It's the Existentials who give me trouble."

More Shades reared up, and with them, so did a massive wave.

"Look out!" Ilain called.

"Keep to the pillars!" Deckard ordered.

As they hugged the columns, the wave soaked them anew and knocked the Shades back into the pool.

They continued to make progress across the stone paths, fighting against the slick puddles, the recurring Shades, and the onslaught of waves every few seconds. As another wave was about to hit, a Shade knocked Ilain back, and Deckard dove to grab her hand before she toppled over the side. But Rafferty had not been so lucky.

He'd fallen halfway into the pool when Thom caught his arms. Ethenn shot the creatures, which pulled at Rafferty, trying to drag him under. The arrows drove them back, and Thom yanked the weasel back up onto the stone.

They scrambled up and hurried on. Drenched head to toe from the constant waves and increasing spray from the dying Shades, Deckard felt as though he were trying to run through the pool itself. The number of times they had to halt to fight the creatures and hide from the Mage's attacks felt like the relentless drag of water.

Finally, they neared the last turn and entered the hall leading to the obelisk's stone island. Ilain sailed in front of Deckard, a fiery look on her face. "I'll handle this," she said.

While the men worked to keep up with her, Ilain sprinted down the pathway, drawing her arms into her chest. The enemy Mage stood near the Chamber door with his arms raised as he called forth another wave. But he wasn't fast enough.

As Ilain crossed the threshold, she planted her feet, then thrust her arms forward.

A cloud of fire burst from her hands. It built on itself, growing larger and larger as it flew across the island. The flame consumed the Mage in an instant, and the wave under his control shattered without his command.

The flame continued its roll across the room and crashed against the Chamber door, blasting it off its hinges. Deckard, Thom, Rafferty, and Ethenn ran behind Ilain as the charred door banged against the stone wall of the stairwell. Their weapons were ready and their eyes alert as they pounded down the stairs and into the Chamber deep below.

Pure blue surrounded them as they barreled into the room, Ilain still leading the charge. She raised her arms, wind ripping forward in a wall of force, knocking down everyone in its path. Nearest them, three Mages fell to the ground, already wounded by stirring pools of cerulean blue. At the far end, almost five hundred feet away, two other Mages worked to rise again near Evylin and Auden.

Deckard watched, his pulse pounding with hope, as Evylin rose, the knife from her boot in her hand. She leaped and sliced open the neck of the Mage nearest her. But instead of going to help Auden, she ran at the singular Mage rising in the center of the Chamber.

Even from the distance between them, Deckard could see that the man's eyes, blue as the marble of the room, were filled with rage as he watched their team rush into the space. He raised his hands, and the pools of water around them rose in jets. He sent the streams sailing toward Deckard and the team.

Diving out of the way, Deckard rolled toward one of the other Mages at the columns. The Mage tried to defend himself by sending a wave of water at him, but he appeared too weak to put much strength into it. Deckard stabbed him, a twinge of guilt unsettling his stomach at killing someone so unfit for battle. But one less Mage could make the difference in a fight like this.

"He's got the Relics!" Auden yelled, still grappling with his captor. "Blount has got the Relics!"

Another cloud of fire roiled around Ilain, ready to fly at the prince.

But the Night Mage lifted his hands, the pendant around his neck glowing brighter. The pools lurched, sending a wave crashing through the room. Ilain rolled forward in its grip, and Ethenn stumbled a few steps just as he let loose his arrow, the swell taking him down. The arrow sailed true, but the Night Mage disintegrated it with a curl of purple shadow. Thom managed to dispatch the other two Mages on the far side of the room before the Night Mage's wave caught him as well.

Evylin neared the Night Mage and leaped toward him with her small blade ready to strike. But he turned before she could reach him, blasting her away from him with a gushing stream of water from his hands. She crashed against one of the columns, a sharp gasp bursting from her as she crumpled to the floor.

Deckard's pulse pounded in his head. He wanted to run to her, but his eyes turned back to the fight, prepared to charge. He paused, watching as Ilain rose from the rushing swell around her, sending another boiling flame toward the Night Mage, and Auden sent his Mage reeling back with a burst of Day magic. For fear of catching their cross fire, Deckard watched for an opening.

Blount lifted a hand, another jet of water dissipating Ilain's attack into vapor. His other hand thrust forward, sending a deep purple shadow toward her.

Moving with furious speed, Ilain threw both hands into the air, a wall of fire arcing up to absorb the column of shadow.

Auden attacked from the other side, a flare of light streaking toward the Night Mage. But another shadow rose to fend it off.

Watching the chaotic flares of magic between the Calders and the prince, Deckard caught Rafferty's eyes on the far side of the Chamber. Hidden behind a column, the weasel nodded in the direction of the Night Mage, his eyes flickering back to Deckard as he flipped the shining knives end-over-end in his hands.

If Deckard could help distract the Mage, then Rafferty could sneak up behind and take him down.

Deckard nodded in return. Then he charged.

The Night Mage took the bait. Turning straight to Deckard, he exposed his back completely to Rafferty. He raised his hands. A jet caught Deckard from below, sweeping him up into the air. Its force knocked the air from Deckard's lungs, and his mouth filled with water upon his instinctual gasp. The Night Mage twisted his wrist, and the jet followed the movement up around Deckard to crash down on top of him like a fist.

Deckard's body slammed against the marble, and he felt something pop in his right shoulder, an intense fire immediately burning within. He bit back a fierce cry of agony, knowing his shoulder had popped out of its socket.

An angry growl rang out from the center of the room, drawing Deckard's spotting vision. Rafferty had jumped on the Night Mage's back, one dagger protruding from the top of his left pectoralis and the other from his right side.

It wasn't enough.

Rafferty's appearance had halted the Calders' attacks, giving the Night Mage the chance he needed. He blasted Rafferty off his back with a furious burst of amethyst shadow. Rafferty smacked into the ground and rolled across the marble.

Ilain and Auden flexed their hands, Fire and Day magic flying at Blount. But it was too late.

With one final gesture, the Night Mage vanished.

Deckard grunted as he tried to rise. A sharp ache shot through his shoulder at the attempt. The overflowing pool rippled across the room, lapping at his side. He looked around, eyes working to focus through the pain.

While the other Mages all lay dead on the floor, Blount was gone. "Where is he?" Deckard called.

With a heavy sigh, Auden closed his eyes and slumped forward. "Gone," he muttered.

Ilain ran to her brother and wrapped him in a firm embrace. Ethenn hurried to check on Rafferty as Thom rose near Deckard. "You don't look so good," his brother said, nodding to the dislocated shoulder.

"Yeah, well, neither do you," Deckard replied, turning to look for Evylin. Across the room, she stumbled up, grabbing at her rib cage.

The brothers hurried to her side. Deckard grimaced with the effort, and Thom's limp had grown more severe. Evylin looked up at them, worry etching her features. "Are you two all right?" she asked as they neared.

Deckard scoffed, looking over her own injury and then back into her amber eyes. Her cheeks were red and puffy, and most of her soaked hair had fallen free of its braid. He didn't know if he'd ever been so relieved in his life. He wanted to reach out and touch her face, but the pain of his unsupported arm made him gasp. He chuckled as her eyes widened. "I'm right as rain," he muttered.

The tiny smile Evylin offered back didn't match the one he'd hoped to receive. Instead, she leaned against the marble column and glared at the Calders as they approached, accompanied by Ethenn and Rafferty.

Auden met her gaze for a moment, then turned to Deckard. "Thank you, Jonn," he said, then glanced at his dislocated shoulder. "You seem to like getting hurt in the Keeps, don't you?"

"It does seem that way."

"I can heal it, but. . . ." He paused, glancing at Evylin again. His jaw twitched. "But I'm afraid I'll have to recover myself first."

Ilain set her hand on her brother's arm. "We'd better get out of here."

"Yes, we should," Evylin said flatly, the blunt words almost an accusation.

Deckard looked from Evylin to the Calders and back, recognizing the new tension. She didn't trust the siblings anymore, and he worried over what had caused such suspicions. Moreover, it bothered him that aside from Rafferty and Ethenn, who bore merely superficial wounds, the Calders were the only ones without physical injuries.

"What happened?" Thom asked, sword still at the ready, looking around as if their enemy was going to suddenly materialize in their midst. "How did Blount disappear like that?"

"Night Magic," Ilain explained. "He used a shroud to turn to shadow. He can move unseen and unhindered in that form. It's how he got the Day Relic."

The team slumped collectively in defeat.

"Let's go," Evylin commanded, nodding to the exit. "We should get somewhere safe to recover. Then we can figure out what we're going to do next."

"Sounds like a good plan," Auden replied, then he and Ilain turned to lead them out of the Chamber.

Deckard met Evylin's stare. "Watch them," she whispered. "They may try to escape."

The soldiers were all near enough to hear, and they each gave her a confirming nod. Rafferty and Ethenn tightened their grip on their weapons and quickened their pace to reach the Mages' sides.

Thom walked next to Evylin, hand on her arm in case either of them needed support. As they passed back through the receding pool, Deckard took one final look into the Water Relic's Chamber. It represented another failure they were leaving behind. But at least he'd saved Evylin.

Now, they faced another challenge.

Whatever the Mages had done to warrant Evylin's distrust, Deckard wouldn't disregard it. Nor would he take it lightly. They'd not only risked their lives for the Calders, but they'd also lost Hewitt because of them.

Turning around, Deckard held his right arm tight against his torso. He watched Evylin as she and Thom began to lean against one another as they worked their way out of the Keep at a halting pace. Every cell of Deckard's body tingled with the fury building inside him. The water tugged at his feet as he trod through the halls, the liquid acting as though it were following him toward the exit. His brain pulsated with heat, the welt on the side of his head thumping. With every step, the feeling grew. A sensation unlike adrenaline, but also unlike calm, washed over him. It left him with a strange balance between rage and peace, all while his body felt charged with energy.

At first, he'd thought it came from the pain in his arm. But as he stepped out into the dusky hillside of Virwoud, it left him. The searing pain in his shoulder doubled, causing him to begin trembling. He fought his way to the horses, knowing he'd be unable to mount one in his state.

Once they'd agreed to meet in the city, Auden took Ethenn to get their horses from the woods while the rest of them walked back. Each step weakened Deckard, and he broke out in a cold sweat. When they entered the inn nearest to the gates, Rafferty attempted his greatest charms to ease the worried innkeeper's mind at the group's frightening state. In the end, Thom showed the Order of the King insignia, and that granted them two free rooms for the night.

They walked into the first room, agreeing to stay together until Ethenn and Auden arrived. Deckard's vision grew more and more cloudy as he stumbled toward the closest of the two beds.

"Jonn," he heard Thom call from the doorway.

But Deckard couldn't respond. His knees buckled, and he blacked out.

CHAPTER SIXTY-FOUR

Evylin pulled away from Thom as Deckard stumbled. "Help him!" she ordered.

Both Thom and Rafferty hurried forward, but only Rafferty was fast enough to keep him from landing flat on the floor. "Ugh!" he gasped under Deckard's weight. "The colonel's heavier than he looks."

"Put him on the bed," Ilain instructed, hurrying over as Thom lifted Deckard's legs, staggering himself in the process.

Evylin stepped to the foot of the bed as the men got him settled. Her ribs hurt every time she took a breath, and a knife-sharp headache seared across her temples, but her worry for Deckard helped lessen that pain. "What's happened to him?" she asked, eyes locked on his unconscious form.

"He's gone into shock," Thom said tensely. "We have to wake him up immediately."

Pushing Rafferty and Thom out of the way, Ilain perched beside Deckard on the bed and placed her hands on either side of his face. Evylin cringed, no longer trusting the woman. "What are you doing?" she demanded.

Ilain didn't respond, and a flare of orange light burst beneath her palms. Deckard gasped awake. His eyes, shaded more green than blue, stared up at the ceiling as his chest heaved at a frantic pace. Evylin hurried to his side as Ilain stood and backed away. Kneeling next to him, her pulse quickened. Yet, his breathing steadied, the blackout having little effect.

Deckard's eyes fell on her, and he sighed just as the door opened, signaling Ethenn and Auden's arrival. Shutting the door behind them, Ethenn nodded to Deckard and Evylin while the Mage moved farther into the room.

Turning back to her, Deckard began to smile just before his brow pinched together in that way of his. "What happened to your face?" he asked, using his left hand to reach out to her. But his weakened strength and her distance didn't permit the touch.

"I'm fine," she promised, despite the increasing thrumming in her head. It felt as though her brain had gained its own pulse, attempting to pound its way out.

Auden stepped up to the bed. "Courtesy of Prince Blount," he explained distractedly, leaning to examine Deckard's shoulder. "He's the sort who sees a swift kick to the face as appropriate discipline."

"I'll kill him," Deckard and Thom said in unison, their outraged expressions almost identical.

Evylin shook her head. "Not if I kill him first."

Auden gestured to Thom. "Help me lift him," he instructed. "I need to reset the joint."

Evylin moved to the end of the bed to stand by Ethenn while Thom helped Auden lift Deckard into a seated position.

"Don't worry about me," Deckard said as they leaned him against the headboard. "I can keep. Take care of everyone else first."

"Stop being such a martyr," Thom said, scowling. "Let us be the ones who take care of you for once."

Frowning, Deckard fell silent and let Auden check on his arm. The Mage helped him draw it out, leaving a slight bend in the elbow. Deckard grimaced with the movement but made no sound. Auden took Deckard's hand and rested his free hand on his shoulder. "Now," the Mage said, his brow raised, "this is going to hurt."

"It already hurts," Deckard muttered.

"Ready?"

Deckard's eyes locked onto Evylin's at the end of the bed, and he took one deep breath. Then he nodded.

A golden glow radiated from the hand on Deckard's shoulder while Auden lifted their clasped hands. The joint rolled back into place with a snap, and Deckard cried out from the pain. Evylin flinched at the sound.

Deckard's eyes squeezed shut, and his head fell back against the headboard.

"The magic helped," Auden observed, prodding gently at the reset shoulder. "I imagine it'll be like the other wound. You'll experience some tenderness and pain for a few days, but the healing process will be quick."

"If it's like the last one," Deckard murmured, "it'll be gone tomorrow."

Ilain and Auden shared a look. Then the brother turned to Evylin and Thom. "You two are next," he said. "I'll take care of Thom first if that's all right. I'm worried about how long he's been on that leg."

Evylin nodded, her vision swimming, and Auden had Thom sit by the table along the far wall. After only a few moments of inspection, he diagnosed it as a sprain and mended it in full. "You shouldn't even experience soreness," he assured Thom, helping him stand.

Though Thom hesitated as he tested his leg, he gave Auden an appreciative nod. "Thanks," he replied warily.

Auden turned back to Evylin, his head dipping. "May I?" he asked, gesturing to her rib cage.

Evylin watched him suspiciously but allowed him to test her ribs. She fought sharp gasps of pain as he prodded her. After appraising the wound, he set his hand on it, and the location began to glow hotly.

"It's only a bit of bruising," he said, drawing his hand away. "You shouldn't feel any more pain there. However, I'm afraid your face will be a different story."

Forcing herself not to touch her cheek, Evylin swallowed. She didn't know if she wanted to see how bad it was, but she imagined it had swollen up and begun to bruise already.

Auden held her gaze now. "I need to check to be sure," he said, his words slow and cautious. "But I'm worried there will be internal trauma. If that's the case, then I'll only be able to heal the interior wound. I won't be able to heal the superficiality of it. At least, not until tomorrow."

"I don't care about that," Evylin lied.

Ever so gently, Auden set his hand on the side of her face and closed his eyes. "Mm, your brain has swollen," he said with disappointment. "I can feel the pressure of it building in your skull. While your magic as a Warrior is likely protecting you from the worst of the harm, we must stop it immediately, or it could cause you far more trouble."

After her approval, his touch grew hot again. It started slowly and built into a near-burning sensation. Evylin squeezed her eyes shut against the feeling. She could feel something changing, a tension releasing throughout her entire body. Then Auden removed his hand, and the heat went with it.

"There," he said, backing away from her. "That will help for the time being. Now, I recommend we all take a seat. Ilain and I have some things to explain, and it may take some time."

Auden joined his sister on the other side of the room to sit on the empty bed. The Ephrians watched the siblings with suspicion.

"First," Auden said, "I hope you will consider that Ilain and I have not abandoned you and that I did just heal you all. Whatever worries you have, let those things remind you that we are not your enemies."

"If that's true," Deckard said, adjusting his arm, "what caused Evylin to think that wasn't the case?" Instead of directing the words to Auden, Deckard turned to Evylin.

She drew her shoulders back. "They've been lying to us," she said.

Neither Auden nor Ilain reacted.

"This entire journey, they've had possession of the Fire Relic. Prince Blount took it from Auden. Then he told me that there aren't seven Relics but eight. Auden didn't deny any of it."

"There's no reason to deny it," Ilain said calmly. "It's all true."

The room fell into complete silence.

Evylin glared at the pair. Her heart was too fragile, too raw from the pain of the last twenty-four hours, to believe their sincerity.

"Well, I'm intrigued," Rafferty said, walking over to take the seat next to Thom. "Care to explain?"

"We'd be happy to," Ilain replied.

"We only lied to you because we didn't trust you," Auden said. "Just as you didn't trust us. We didn't steal the Relic for ourselves or keep it hidden because we *wanted* to hide it from you. We did it because we want to help save our country."

Thom scoffed knowingly. "So you *are* trying to take down Ephria."

"What did I tell you about discussing things you don't understand?" Ilain retorted, then enunciated each word precisely as she continued, "We don't give a damn about Wauld *or* Ephria, you dimwit."

"What?" Deckard, Evylin, and Thom said together.

"What Ilain means to say," Auden said with long-suffering patience, "is that we aren't working for either country. We're working for a collective of Waulden and Ephrian people who form what's called the Alliance. Our main intention is to end the Centurial War and restore the countries to Allund."

The floor creaked as Ethenn shifted from foot to foot, but the room was otherwise silent.

"What?" Deckard said again, this time in bewilderment.

"Nothing we've done has been for ourselves," Ilain insisted. "Our whole purpose is to bring our country back together and see Mages and Warriors keep the peace. As Allore intended all along."

"I was right!" Rafferty proclaimed excitedly. "I was right from the beginning! None of this has ever been about land rights and feuds long forgotten. It's about magic!"

Although Ilain grinned at the weasel, Auden's expression grew serious. "The war *was* about land rights and feuds. Ephren rose against the Mages of Auld, who were oppressive and tyrannical. But the Shepherd King was a radical who believed magic was evil, and he caused nearly two hundred years of war and death because of it."

"King Ephren was a man of Allore," Deckard said coldly. "He drove out the Mages righteously."

"Ephren was a fool," Ilain said sharply. "He hated Mages because he feared them. But the fact is, he drove them out and began a new rule of oppression. Yes, the Mages of Auld were tyrants. But centuries ago, there were Warriors *and* Mages who fought them. Ephren didn't see that, and he didn't care to. Why do you think you didn't even know Mages existed until we came here? Ephren didn't care about making the world a better place. He just wanted to control it."

"Why should we believe you?" Evylin demanded.

"It's history, Evylin," she said. "The only reason you don't know it is because your Shepherd King wiped the books of it. He turned Mages into myths. He changed the fundamental truths of the Allorian faith, all to fit his rhetoric."

Ilain's bright green gaze grew impassioned. "But we have books," she continued. "In the Alliance, we have sought and safeguarded ancient texts. This is how we know these things. This is our proof."

"Do you have one of these books?" Ethenn asked quietly.

Ilain turned to him, but it was Auden who spoke. "No," he said. "We couldn't risk bringing them with us into Ephria. They're kept in Wauld, protected by the Alliance members there."

"Then how are we to believe you?" Thom demanded.

The Calders were silent.

Evylin scoffed. "This whole time," she murmured. "This whole time, you were using us."

"You already knew that," Ilain said. "It's why none of you trusted us from the start. And yet . . ." She smiled sadly. "You came to trust us anyway."

"I never trusted you," Thom retorted.

"That's because you're stupid."

Thom scowled, and Ilain grinned pleasantly.

Auden sat forward, holding out his hands in a pleading gesture. "The Alliance desires to change this world," he insisted. "We want to see the Allund of old return, where Men, Mages, and Warriors work together to defend one another. We want to create together as the Creator Divine charged us."

He met each Ephrian's gaze as he spoke. "We are not after these Relics for personal gain," he vowed. "We don't desire to model this world after ourselves. We hope to model it after our god, in perfect balance.

"With the Alliance, we would govern justly. One Mage and one Warrior to guide each Order and defend the people of their province. They would be required to be active in the environments around them and learn the ways of the people who live there to help them rule effectively. Having an ultimate rule of one is fundamentally flawed. Men cannot be so subject to one almighty ruler who sits in his ivory tower and dictates their worth."

Auden took a deep breath and concluded his impassioned spiel with simplicity. "Allund would be a wise republic that kept its government small and personal."

Evylin didn't know what to think of his claims. Their arguments made sense, but how could they trust them?

Evylin glanced at Deckard. His head was bent down, deep in reflection.

She turned back to the Calders. "Why did you have the Fire Relic?" she asked.

"It was our first task," Auden explained. "Our job is to gather the Relics and return them to the Alliance to use to end the Centurial War. The Alliance has been studying the Relics for years, working to discover how to find them all. What we've told you is true—they are incredibly difficult to uncover. However, the Alliance has been working to find them since before we were born. It just happened to be the two of us who figured it out."

"You said the Fire Relic was last," Ethenn said.

Auden nodded somberly. "A lie," he admitted. "The Relics' order is a symbol of creation. Based on Ephren's hatred of magic, I suppose you don't know the 'Poem of Life'?"

All the Ephrians glanced at one another, only Rafferty showing any glimmer of recognition. "That's that old ditty about creation, right?" he asked.

"Yes," Auden confirmed. "You know it?"

"Nah," Rafferty replied with a shrug. "I just heard some sailors from Schon mention it in passing back in Bridgewater."

Auden lifted his head to recite: "First came Fire, the burst of Day. A tidal of Water doused the flame, Terraeus cast into the shadow of Night. Wind rolled in, a churning vortex of Time, to cool the molten Terrae. The Creator's grandest design, forever suspended in Space."

A long pause passed through the room. Evylin had never heard the poem, not once.

Auden scanned them. "Allore made our world, then granted the power of each resource to the Mages—to aid mankind. He then imbued Warriors with great strength, intelligence, and wisdom to support the Mages because he knew that carrying the power of a god could drive any human mad. Then he gave them the Relics, to create as he created."

"I thought Wauld was polytheistic," Rafferty said, tugging at his sleeve. "You know, Mages were reincarnations of the gods and all that." He waggled his brow at Ilain. "I believe you said something about being Pyra incarnate."

Ilain smirked. "We are quite impressive," she teased. "But we are *not* deities. However, the Mages of Auld wanted people to believe they were. With their totalitarian power, they changed the religion to the Faith of Eight. One 'god' per resource: Pyra, Radia, Hydrae, Obscura, Cyclae, Chronos, Terraen, and Galatae."

Ethenn frowned. "The months?"

Ilain nodded. "That's where they got their names."

"Which means there are eight resources."

"Yes," Auden said. "Four Elemental, which we told you about, and four Existential: Day, Night, Time, and Space. We kept the truth from you because it was the opinion of the Alliance's Administration that it was best if we'd let you and King Ephren believe there were only seven Relics, as we'd only be going to retrieve seven. That way, if anything went wrong and Ephren still tried to pursue the Relics, he'd always be missing one."

"Besides," Ilain added, "Space is almost impossible to connect with."

Deckard frowned. "Why's that?"

"It's the essence of the Heavens," Auden said, as though that explained it all. "The power to control Space is a dangerous and unfathomable thing. It's an easy one to hide because I almost never attempt it myself."

Evylin dropped onto the bed, sitting at Deckard's feet. She struggled to believe the siblings in her heart, but the information was too complex to be another lie.

"I don't understand," Deckard said, rubbing his temple. "Do you expect us to continue helping to collect these Relics so you can overthrow our king? He's the very one who sent us on this mission."

"And do you know why he selected you?" Ilain asked.

The team met each other's gazes.

"Because we saved Prince Ephren," Deckard said uncertainly.

Ilain shook her head. "I'm afraid that's not *quite* the truth, Jonn. No, your selection was because you were in the wrong place at the wrong time," she said, then cocked her head. "Or the right place at the right time. Depends on how you look at it."

"Tell us what you mean," Deckard commanded.

"King Ephren didn't choose you," Ilain said. "Carlile did. When you met him in Banbury, he noticed Evylin and saw the Warrior in her. Then he realized you were going to ruin everything. Your timing was terrible, you know. The Alliance had it all planned out, and then you showed up.

"Prince Ephren's kidnapping wasn't because Earl Tybaalt had defected to Wauld. It was because he's a member of the Alliance. They'd been planning the kidnapping for months. It was a way to trick King Ephren into taking Wauld more seriously by holding his son captive until we recovered all the Relics. Then your lot showed up, and Carlile knew you wouldn't let the kidnapping of a prince stand."

"The kidnapping was fake?" Evylin asked, disappointed.

"Technically, it was a real kidnapping," Auden said. "Just not as malicious as it seemed."

"They weren't going to hurt him or cause him any real trouble," Ilain promised. "They were only after the appearance of it all. While the prince was unconscious, Carlile warned Tybaalt that the noble captain he'd met the previous night would be coming to save them. They planned out a way to make it seem as though you'd succeeded and, furthermore, designed an excuse to bring you into the Alliance now that we were aware of Evylin's status as a Warrior. We are dreadfully short on our supply of them."

Evylin's heart thrummed uneasily.

"It all worked out rather well," Auden said, picking up where his sister left off. "We knew the king wouldn't want us going on our journey alone, and we needed his protection to ensure we could move about the country freely. When Carlile came back and told the Alliance he had a Warrior who could work with us in securing the Relics, they were thrilled. Carlile made sure that when you arrived in Loclight, Prince Ephren told his father about you all. Then Carlile talked him into making you our personal guard."

Evylin's stomach fell. "This whole time, we've been pawns? The Alliance has been pulling our strings without us even knowing it?"

"They are rather good at hiding," Auden said.

"But the important thing to know," Ilain continued, "is they didn't choose you because they wanted to use you and have done with it. They genuinely believe you are vital to the restoration of Allund. We want your help because we know that you—all of you—can be the difference we need to turn the tide and change this world. The question is: Will you forgive our duplicity and help us?"

Silence met her speech.

Thom's foot tapped as he stared down at it, arms crossed tightly over his chest. Ethenn ran a hand along the back of his neck as he chewed on the inside of his cheek. Rafferty's eyes never stopped moving from one face to the next as he leaned back in his chair. Deckard kept his gaze on the bed, his left hand still supporting his right arm.

Evylin dropped her eyes to her hands as she tugged on her rings. This was wrong. The Calders were asking them to defect. They wanted them to rebel against their kingdom, usurping the king's rights. All to raise up a government of magic. . . .

Suddenly, Deckard spoke. "Count me in."

Evylin's eyes flew to his face. Of all the people in the room, she couldn't believe he'd agreed. How could he betray Ephria? The servant, the man who sacrificed everything for king and country.

Deckard met her stare with confidence in his green-blue gaze.

A second ticked by before Ethenn spoke. "I'm in as well," he declared.

"Fine," Thom said from his place along the wall, "I'll come too."

"I suppose you can't bear parting with me?" Ilain asked, smirking at him.

Thom scowled. "I'm not getting left behind while everyone else gets to save the world."

Evylin stared at the three men. How had they come to this conclusion so quickly? How could they, after everything they'd experienced, after Hewitt?

The room grew quiet again, only Rafferty and Evylin's allegiance unannounced. Pushing back some of his white-blond hair, Rafferty turned to her. "Well, Eve? You gonna join up too?" he asked.

Evylin didn't know. If Hewitt were with them, she could only imagine what he'd say. Would the idea outrage him? Or would he see the potential good in the Alliance's desires?

Evylin looked at Deckard once more. There was no pinch in his brow, no tension in his expression at all. A small, encouraging smile lifted his lips. Why had he agreed?

"I don't see that I have much of a choice, Raff," Evylin said weakly. "How about you?"

Rafferty tugged at his coat sleeve again. "Wherever you go, Eve, I'll follow."

The Calders relaxed. "Thank you," Auden said, accent thick and filled with feeling. "We truly believe we can make our countries a better place. And with you, we stand a chance."

His copper hair hung low over his brow as he dipped his head. "But we face impossible odds," he continued. "Blount has the first three Relics, and that gives him a great advantage. The Night Keep will be perilous. Without any Relics to assist us in the fight, we'll be lucky to live through it."

"I've got one last question," Rafferty interrupted.

"Go ahead," Auden said with a nod.

"If Blount's got three Relics," Rafferty raised his arm, "what are these?" Two golden chains hung from his pale hand: One bore a glittering ruby, and the other a yellow topaz.

Auden leaped from the mattress, stepping toward Rafferty. "Where did you get those?" he demanded.

"Took 'em out of Blount's pocket when I stabbed him," Rafferty explained, the chains swinging lazily in his grip. "I knew I couldn't kill him that easily, so I thought I ought to get as many of these away from him as I could. Think they might be helpful?"

Ilain laughed with glee and bounded forward to kiss Rafferty's cheek. "You are the cleverest man I've ever met!" she exclaimed, taking the Relics he offered. As they settled into her palms, the gems began to glow. The ruby's flames flickered, and the topaz pulsed with light. Ilain's eyes met her brother's. "We have hope now."

Smiling as brightly as the Day Relic, Auden nodded. "Don't get too excited," he said, taking the flickering ruby from her hands. "You can't carry the Fire Relic this time either."

"I'm not an idiot," Ilain returned. "Neither of us will carry them, avoiding any unwanted side effects."

She turned to Rafferty, readily proffering the golden chain. "As our resident smuggler," she intoned, "we'll entrust you to keep these hidden until such a time as we need them."

The glow of the amulets dimmed the instant they dropped into Rafferty's hands, a wily grin on his lips. "Oh, I'll keep them safe," he promised with a wink. "Don't you worry."

As the Calders returned to their side of the room, Deckard relaxed back against the headboard. "Now, what is our plan to get to the next Relic before Blount?"

Auden and Ilain shared a look. "This is our best and only opportunity to get ahead of him," Auden said. "The Night Relic is next, and if Blount obtains it, it will be nearly impossible to take it from him later. He may have managed to get the locations out of me, but I was able to withhold the most important secret.

"The Night Relic is in Verlund Province, the most northwestern corner of Wauld," Auden said, lips lifting. "And Blount will have to travel through the entirety of Ephria and Wauld to get there. But there's a faster way. We will travel back to Norhels and reenter the Day Keep. Once we make it back to its Chamber, we can use the doors behind the dais to enter the Night Keep."

"How?" Evylin asked, bewildered.

"Space and Time magic," Auden offered. "The Mages who created the Keeps linked the two with a bridge between them. As the magic of Day and Night are two sides of the same coin, so are their Keeps. We should be able to cut our travel time in half and beat Blount to the Relic by a week or so."

"What's more," Ilain added, "Blount lost his entire team while he was here. He'll have to find more men to help him if he wants to get the Relics himself."

"In that case, back to Norhels," Deckard agreed. "First thing in the morning, we'll restock the supplies we lost. Then we'll head out."

With their fate decided, the troop parted. Deckard insisted on the Calders splitting up for the night. "We may be working with you, but you'll have to regain our trust," he told them.

Ethenn, Rafferty, and Thom took Auden to their room while Ilain stayed with Deckard and Evylin. As the men left and Ilain turned down the oil lamps, Evylin decided she'd share the second bed with Ilain under a twofold pretense: First, so she could keep a better eye on her; second, to ensure that Deckard was able to recover better.

At first, she thought she'd gotten away with her lies, but when she helped Deckard settle himself onto the bed, ever cautious of his shoulder, he pulled her close. "I know everything is wrong," he whispered. "And I know it won't be right again. But . . . please, believe me when I say that if I could, I would change everything."

Evylin wanted to yank her hand from his and run. Her chest constricted with unending tears, and her palm tingled at his touch. She couldn't do this again. She'd already broken one too many times. But what could she say? How did she respond to something so caring when it could only hurt her?

"Goodnight, Jonn," she said quietly.

As Evylin tried to leave, Deckard tightened his grip. "Evylin," he murmured. She met his gaze reluctantly, and his lips tilted up in a soft smile. "Thank you."

"For what?"

"For not dying."

Evylin's heart stuttered as he released her. She drew away to the other side of the room, fighting the tears that threatened her. The day had been too long and too hard, and she couldn't take the pain anymore.

But as she lay in the bed next to Ilain, the everbloom flower tucked into the coat pocket by her heart, Evylin feared her pain had only begun.

CHAPTER SIXTY-FIVE

22ND OF GALATAE, 1574

Deckard's head swam with disappointment and expectations. Fear and hope. Sorrow and possibility. Fortunately, his shoulder felt as good as new.

The following morning, he set out with Ethenn and Auden through Virwoud to gather supplies for their trip. Focusing on their checklist helped calm his worried thoughts. They navigated the streets lined with shops, smiths, and merchants, replenishing the supplies they'd lost during the ambush. Finally, they visited the Riders Services, where Auden sent off two letters: one to King Ephren containing fabricated details about their travels and another addressed to the Alliance revealing the truth.

"It doesn't feel right, does it?" Ethenn muttered to Deckard as Auden spoke with the clerk. "Lying to our king."

Deckard did his best to ignore the inner voice that told him how disloyal and irresponsible he was. Only two days ago, Deckard would have agreed with the young man. Even last night, he was on the verge of holding fast to his old loyalties. But now, he listened to the other voice that had begun to whisper in his ear.

"You can make the difference," Ilain had said the night before.

An echo of his own words. *"Help us be the generation who ends it. Help us make the difference."*

For more than two months, Deckard had stood before the men and women of the Shires, proclaiming the war had gone on too long. And now, here he was with the opportunity to end it, to be one of the people who made that difference.

Meeting Ethenn's eyes, Deckard shook his head. "He isn't our king anymore," he said. "We serve the Alliance now."

Once Auden returned, they hurried back to the inn. With Deckard and Auden's horses saved from the ambush, they'd recovered five others from the Night Mage's men. They led the freshly saddled horses from the stables to the inn. The others were ready, most of their things packed away. Deckard took the gray horse he'd reclaimed straight to Evylin. Hewitt's stallion. Ethenn had discovered it among the others, still saddled with Hewitt's things.

Seeing the horse, Evylin's expression fell blank. She muttered her thanks before filling the saddlebags with her things, keeping her gaze averted. Her left temple and cheek had turned a deep bluish-purple from Blount's kick. Deckard's stomach twisted with anger at the sight, but he moved away to his own horse.

Deckard knew grief must be crushing Evylin. And more than anything, he wanted to be the one to comfort her through it, to hold her close as she wept and mourned her loss. But the truth he'd always known remained: She didn't trust him. She wouldn't accept his comfort or his help. And she might never forgive him for his part in Hewitt's death.

"Ready?" Thom asked.

Deckard tied off the shovel he'd bought. He checked with the rest, then nodded. "Ready."

They all mounted their horses and departed from Virwoud, the hills quickly obscuring the city from sight as they retraced the road they'd traveled just a day before. Despite Auden's hesitation about the idea that morning, Deckard was adamant that they return via their original route.

Though the air was frosty, snow was rare this far south, and even now, the atmosphere began to thicken with the promise of impending spring. Most trees were starting to shed their heavy white coats, with little buds of leaves peeking out from their branches. They left later in the morning than Deckard had hoped, and the sun had climbed a third of the way into the sky already, bringing warmth as they moved through the countryside. The snow melted, and the roads grew muddy. They didn't slow down until midday when they approached the forest. Most of their team didn't recognize the area. But Deckard knew it instantly.

Pulling off to the side of the road, Deckard turned to the others. "We're going to make a stop here," he said. Evylin stared at the trees, her expression shifting to understanding. "This is where we camped the night of the ambush. I'm going in to ensure that Hewitt gets the burial he deserves. You don't need to come with me, but—"

"Of course, we're coming," Thom said, hopping down from his horse.

Deckard nodded appreciatively as they all joined without hesitation.

Everyone except Evylin.

Her amber-brown eyes were frozen on the tree line, and her face was completely void of emotion.

While Rafferty, Ethenn, and the Calders watched her warily, Thom and Deckard both stepped toward her. Giving his brother a fierce look, Deckard shook his head. It didn't matter that Thom felt close to Evylin; she wasn't his wife. And it was Jonn who needed to be by her side, if for no other reason than his part in Hewitt's death.

Setting a hand on her stallion's neck, Deckard looked up at Evylin. "You don't have to come," he promised, keeping his voice gentle. There was more he might say, but he thought it best to keep it simple.

Evylin finally moved, preparing to dismount. "I do," she said emptily.

Stepping back, Deckard gave her space. He made sure to remain close but did not touch her as they led their horses into the woods. They hadn't camped deep within the trees, having no reason to suspect an impending attack, so it took little time to come upon their camp. Three tents remained erect, the fourth burnt to ash. Bits of camping supplies were still strewn about the snow and mud. The bodies of the dead littered the dirt.

Two Mages.

Seven guards.

One ally.

Next to the cold firepit, Hewitt's body lay split open by the branch. His blood had frozen in the dirt after the cold nights. With his sword next to him, he looked like a fallen hero of old.

The hollow of the forest remained silent as though mourning the man. No bird chirped, and no woodland creatures rustled in the bushes.

Ilain stayed by the horses while the rest of them moved toward Hewitt. One by one, they broke away. Auden and Ethenn moved to stack the dead of their enemies on a pile to the side to burn, as was the custom to send pagans to the depths. Rafferty paused next, grabbing Thom's sleeve to halt him as well. Deckard brought his own feet to a stop, letting Evylin cross the final stretch of distance on her own. If she needed him, he'd only be a couple of steps away.

Shoulders beginning to shake, Evylin knelt beside her uncle. Her trembling hand reached out and shut his empty, gray eyes. Deckard heard her whispering but couldn't make out the words. He didn't think he should try.

Rafferty stepped to Deckard's side, shovel in hand. "Would you like us to start digging?" he whispered, eyes darting to Evylin as though frightened she would overhear.

"Not yet," Deckard replied. "She needs to decide where."

As Rafferty backed away, Deckard took a deep breath. He didn't want to rush her, but they needed to continue moving if they didn't want to spend the night in the open air. Slowly, so as not to startle her, he knelt beside Evylin.

As he bent down, he could hear her whispering brokenly, "I don't want to do it without you. Please, don't leave me too."

Evylin acknowledged him only with a fleeting glance before going quiet. She pushed Hewitt's thick brown hair back at the temples and arranged his scruffy beard. Her hand lingered on his sunken cheek, which was faintly blue from the cold and beginning to show signs of decay.

"Where do you want me to dig?" Deckard asked gently.

Evylin shook her head, tears beginning to drop off her lashes. "I don't know," she replied so quietly that he strained to hear.

Waiting by her side, Deckard kept his silence and let her take her time.

Lips pressed together around her emotion, Evylin began to shake again. "I don't know," she whispered when the sobs would let her.

Deckard couldn't stop himself from reaching out to her. He drew her into his arms carefully, making sure her unbruised cheek pressed against his chest. He brushed his hand over her hair as she cried. Though she didn't wrap her arms around him, neither did she pull away. He could feel the tension in her muscles, and yet, she stayed. As she trembled in his arms, Deckard laid his head on hers, feeling his own eyes filling with tears.

Squeezing his eyes shut, Deckard rebuked himself. It wasn't his time to feel this hurt. He had to be strong. Of all the people here, he had to hold it together for Evylin.

After some time, Evylin went still in his arms. Her breathing grew steady, and the tears fell silently before she drew back. "Wherever you think is best," she murmured.

Deckard nodded, then rose as she turned back to Hewitt. Taking one step away, he gestured to Rafferty. "Stay with her," he told the man, knowing he would be conscious of the balance between comfort and smothering.

"Always, sir," Rafferty said, handing the shovel to Deckard, then kneeling next to Evylin. He didn't touch her or speak a word. He didn't even look at her. But he sat near enough to be present, staring at his lost mentor.

Deckard walked over to Thom. Setting a hand on his brother's shoulder, Deckard waited for him to stop staring at Rafferty, Evylin, and Hewitt's body before giving him his own charge. "I need your help," he said, keeping his voice low. "We need to clear this area. Help Auden and Ethenn with the bodies, then get Hewitt ready for burial."

"What are you going to do?" Thom asked.

He tipped his head toward the woods, lifting the shovel. "I'll be just beyond those trees."

Thom's eyes darted to Rafferty and Evylin once more, but then he gave him a decisive nod.

Deckard walked into the woods. He knew he could have had any of the men do this work. Though it was a backbreaking task, they'd all carry the burden as an honor. But it hadn't been any of them who'd brought Hewitt to this place. And it wasn't one of them whom Evylin blamed.

Walking through the trees, Deckard searched for the right burial spot. One with enough flat space to move. Far enough from the campsite that no one could hear it when two swords clanged together. The place Hewitt should have chosen for their training yesterday morning.

Deckard stepped into a small clearing. There were too many trees, too many roots. It wouldn't do well for a sparring ground. But it was the most open option he'd found yet.

Deckard chose the spot near a tree on the far left. His shovel hit the cold ground with a shoulder-aching *thud*. As he dug, he imagined what Hewitt would say to him at that moment.

"You're an idiot," he'd begin. "Your shoulder was dislocated yesterday, and you're digging a grave today?"

"I have to," he murmured to himself, ignoring what little pain remained.

"Wearing your coat, too, I see. It's a miracle how stupid you are. You're restricting yourself."

Taking off his coat, Deckard smiled at the voice of the ghost in his head. "I know."

"Good," it said. "Now, put your back into it. This is my grave, and I want the best you've got."

Giving in to whatever form of madness this was, Deckard listened as Hewitt's ghost berated him. Sweat dripped off his forehead as he picked up his pace. Soon, his eyes watered, and tears began to mix in with the perspiration.

"Crying now?" he heard in his head. "Do you miss me beating you up that much?"

Silently, Deckard took the abuse of Hewitt's remarks.

"Or are you whimpering because I died out here, and you think it's your fault?"

Deckard knew it was his fault.

"You're taking credit for my death, aren't you?"

The shovel hit a rock and bounced back to whack Deckard in the shin. He grimaced but didn't make a sound.

"Taking the blame makes you an absolute saint, doesn't it? But you know," the ghost growled, "you're a damn fool."

"I know," Deckard muttered to himself.

Hewitt's ghost laughed at him. "You're good at that." The vision landed in the pit next to Deckard. He looked whole, exactly like Hewitt the moment before he'd died. "Playing the martyr. That's what you always do. Take the blame and let everyone else live free of the consequences. What's the point?"

Deckard didn't answer. His grief was getting the better of him, and he wouldn't indulge it any longer.

"Do you think it'll lower their expectations of you? Save you from their disappointment?"

"They're already disappointed in me!" Deckard yelled back at the apparition. "I'm disappointed in myself! It was my job to take care of us. It was my job to make Evylin happy, and instead, I got you killed!"

The ghost glared back at him. "Don't be so selfish," it said calmly. "Don't take my choices from me so you can be some virtuous paragon. I left Whickam Village of my own volition. It was my choice. This isn't your fault, and it isn't hers. And when you take away my responsibility for my death, you take away how much I loved Evie. I died *for* her happiness. And that makes me happier than you'll ever understand."

Deckard swallowed. The words hit him hard. The vision was too knowing, too realistic for his comfort.

"You're not real," he muttered, forcing himself to resume digging. "You're not real."

"Stop blaming yourself for other people's choices, Deckard," the ghost said. "You'll kill yourself trying to fix everyone."

Striking the terrae beneath the ghost's foot, Deckard saw it go straight into the dirt.

"You're not real," he whispered to the air.

The sun sank lower in the sky as Deckard kept digging. He had soaked his shirt with sweat by the time he heard the crunching of someone's approach. Turning around, he saw Thom standing over the grave.

"You know," he said, observing him, "you dislocated your shoulder last night. You shouldn't be digging a grave at all, let alone doing it by yourself."

"Auden healed it, remember?" Deckard wiped his forehead. "And I *have* to do this alone."

"Why?"

Deckard stared at the ground.

Hewitt's voice growled in his ears. "Don't take my choices from me, Deckard."

Releasing a long sigh, Deckard threw his head up to the darkening sky. "Because I'm selfish," he muttered.

Thom's brow furrowed. "Yeah, I know." He hopped down into the pit next to him. "Now, give me that shovel, and let me help."

It took another hour for them to prepare the grave. When they climbed out and walked back to the campsite, they found the rest of the group waiting. They'd placed Hewitt on a makeshift pallet, the branch removed from his stomach and a blanket resting over his body. Auden and Ilain stood to the side, chins tucked down. Ethenn stood by the pallet as Rafferty sat next to Evylin, his hand on her shoulder as she stared at her uncle.

Deckard stopped next to them. "We're ready," he said.

Evylin stood without a word, and Deckard took that as his cue. He reached down to grab hold of one of the pallet's arms. Thom, Ethenn, and Auden followed his lead. Rafferty stayed beside Evylin as they followed, Ilain trailing the team. They hoisted the pallet, and he led them on the long, difficult walk.

The night sky was a vibrant amethyst, the setting sun casting its last golden hue over the treetops as they arrived at the graveside. Rafferty handed Deckard lengths of rope to tie to the pallet to lower the body down. He pulled the knots as hard as he could, the rope burning his palms.

They lowered Hewitt down, and then Deckard turned back to the shovel.

"Jonn, wait," Ilain said, stepping forward. She set a hand on Evylin's arm. "May I?"

Evylin looked from the woman to Deckard and back. She nodded, and the Mage gave her a gracious smile. Coming to stand at the head of the grave, Ilain raised her hands, moving them in a small circle. The dirt rose and cascaded, soft and slow, into the grave. Terrae covered Hewitt's body like tea poured into a cup.

"By your grace," Deckard said reverently, "we submit the soul of Major General Hewitt Glaas to your care, Allore, the Creator Divine. May he find rest in the Heavens."

Magic filled the grave faster than manual labor ever could. Ilain stepped back to her brother's side. They were all silent, each staring and afraid to speak.

Evylin turned back to Deckard, fresh tears in her eyes. "I don't know what to do," she whispered. "What do I do?"

Dropping the shovel, Deckard wrapped her up in his embrace. He didn't bother answering. He didn't have an answer. But he held her as she clung to him.

Rafferty slapped Ethenn's chest and gestured back toward the camp. The men turned, the Calders moving with them. Thom remained, his heavy brow low over his sharp eyes. Rafferty hurried back and grabbed his arm.

"Come on, you idiot," he whispered, pulling Thom away.

While they all disappeared, Deckard and Evylin held fast to one another. Her body shook as she cried, and his resolve against shedding his own tears thinned. The sky faded into darkness, the gold and silver stars vibrant above them. The ivory moon was gone, restarting its cycle, leaving the full shadow moon to glow a bright silver.

Evylin pulled away at last, and Deckard let her put distance between them. She took a step toward the grave, tugging at her rings. "Every time I close my eyes," she whispered, "I see him."

He remained silent.

"He was everything."

"I know," he whispered back. "And you were everything to him."

She looked over her shoulder, tears glistening in the moonlight. "I don't know who I am without him."

Deckard's heart tore. He shook his head and took a step forward, opening his mouth to apologize. But he heard the ghost's whisper in his mind once more, *"Don't take my choices from me."*

Deckard dropped his gaze. "If I could bring him back to you, I would."

Evylin didn't reply but turned back to the grave.

Though he wanted to assure her of his sincerity, Deckard remained quiet, allowing her to take the time she needed to grieve.

"But you can't," she whispered at last. "And he's gone."

Deckard let out a shaky breath. "He would have chosen this," he offered. "Had he known it would come to this, he still would have chosen it."

Evylin looked at him then, eyes narrowed.

"He wanted to make you happy, Evylin," Deckard said. "I don't think he'd trade giving you this experience for anything."

"That's just it, Jonn," Evylin said bitterly, hands flying out to her sides. "I'm not happy. I haven't been happy this entire time. I thought I wanted a life of adventure and . . . and 'more.' But it turns out that adventure isn't that exciting, and I don't even know what 'more' means!"

Deckard stared back at her, feeling the truth of her words. He'd experienced a similar revelation in his first few months as a soldier. All the expectations of what the world offered rarely measured up to the ideas behind them.

Shaking her head, Evylin's gaze fell to the dirt. "Hewitt died for nothing."

Deckard reached out and took her shoulders in his hands. "No," he said firmly. "Never think that! He left Whickam Village because he loved you, Evylin. Because he wanted you to experience every dream you've ever had. His death *will* mean nothing if you let this all go."

"Then what am I supposed to do?" Evylin pleaded, eyes filling up again. "I don't know what I want anymore."

Deckard looked into her amber eyes. This was it—the moment she finally asked *him* to help her, to give her a purpose. And so he would.

"We have a job to do, Evie," he told her. "You are a Warrior, and the people of Ephria and Wauld need *you*. You're supposed to save them."

"And what happens after?" she whispered fearfully.

Shaking his head, Deckard brushed the hair from her wet and bruised cheek. "Don't think about that now. Only think about finding the Relics and saving our people. After that, we'll figure it out. Together."

Evylin's gaze dropped from his, and Deckard worried she wouldn't want to do it together. From the start, she hadn't wanted him, and there was a chance she never would.

Refusing to follow those thoughts, Deckard whispered her name tenderly.

She met his eyes again, chewing on her bottom lip.

Deckard couldn't stop his grin at the familiar action. "Focus on now," he whispered. "You can figure out the future later."

A heartbeat passed before Evylin let her head drop in a nod.

Pulling back, Deckard glanced at the grave. "We should leave soon," he said. "It's getting dark."

Evylin stepped over to the mound of dirt. Reaching into her coat, she pulled out a folded slip of paper. In the darkness, Deckard struggled to see what was inside of it until she lifted a single, dried, everbloom flower.

Eyes on the grave, Evylin dropped the flower. It fell softly, landing on the fresh soil, its creamy petals curving upward toward the sky.

"It's already dark," she murmured.

Then she stepped away.

With one last glance at the flower, Deckard followed her back through the woods to their old camp. The rest of the team had gathered what supplies they needed or didn't want to leave behind. The campground looked haunted. And Deckard supposed it was.

Knowing they wouldn't make it much farther through the night, Deckard wouldn't let them stay there. He guided Evylin straight to her horse. Once she mounted, he leaped onto his own steed. They rode out of the woods and back to the road, the Heavens above sparkling with stars.

Deckard heard Hewitt's oldest charge ringing in his head. *I've given you my trust. Don't disappoint me.*

The horses flew through the winter night, the cold air burning Deckard's skin.

"Don't disappoint me."

Deckard worried it might be too late. But he swore to himself he'd do all he could to see Hewitt's charge through to the end. Whatever it took—whatever he had to sacrifice— he would give Evylin the future she deserved. No matter the cost.

Also Available from V.K. Dixon

WARRIORS & MAGES
Fire & Night
Sword & Shadow
Relics & Thrones

ARCHIVES OF THE WARDEN
Lake of Glass
Vault of Stone
The Raven's Cry
Veil of Mist
The Wolf's Howl
Of Spirit & Ether (Coming Spring 2026)
Book Seven (Coming Fall 2026)

Acknowledgments

Five years ago, I began this story as a challenge to prove to myself that I *could* be an author. Now, I'm immeasurably blessed to be publishing the full trilogy.

This story wasn't easy. It took me on a journey I never expected, challenging me as a writer and as an individual. I have grown so much from the earliest inception of Evylin and Deckard's story up to this date. And I will forever think of *Fire & Night* as my first book (even though it is not my debut).

My greatest thanks to you, the reader. When I began this journey, it was only the faintest dream to have people like you experience the story too. I hope that your heart is full (if a little broken), and that you feel you've found a home with these characters as I have.

The deepest thank you to my husband, Josh. Without you, this story wouldn't exist. You are forever my JD—the inspiration of Terraeus's greatest hero.

Thank you to my family and friends, and especially to my little Sam, who gives me fresh reason to succeed.

To my editor, Brittany: I can never say enough thanks to you! God truly knew what I needed when He sent you to me. All my books would be nowhere near as good as this one.

A huge thank you to all those who read the serial version of this story and believed in it enough to become paid subscribers. Plus, a special thank you to Serenity for being *Warriors & Mages's* first and biggest fan.

And finally, thank you to God. You placed this desire to write in my heart twenty-five years ago. I pray my work honors you and your call on my life.

About the Author

V.K. Dixon writes fantasy and romance novels filled with found family, lasting love, and unique magic. She believes that the extraordinary gives us a deeper desire for the things beyond us—the things of God.